MAXIM JAKUBOWSKI was born in England but educated in France. Following a career in publishing, he opened London's famous MURDER ONE bookshop. He has published over 60 books, won the Anthony and Karel Awards, and is a connoisseur of genre fiction in all its forms. His recent books include seven volumes in the *Mammoth Book of Erotica* series, as well as *The Mammoth Book of Pulp Fiction* and more recently *The Mammoth Book of Pulp Action*. Other well-received anthologies include: *London Noir*, three volumes of *Fresh Blood*, *Past Poisons*, *Chronicles of Crime* and *Murder Through the Ages*. A regular broadcaster, he is the crime columnist for the *Guardian*. His fiction includes *Life in the World of Women*, *It's You that I want to Kiss*, *Because She Thought She Loved Me*, *The State of Montana* and *On Tenderness Express*. He lives in London.

THE MAMMOTH BOOK OF

Best
New Erotica

Volume Two

Edited by Maxim Jakubowski

CARROLL & GRAF PUBLISHERS
New York

Carroll & Graf Publishers
An imprint of Avalon Publishing Group, Inc.
161 William Street
NY10038–2607
www.carrollandgraf.com

First Carroll & Graf edition, 2002

First published in the UK by Robinson,
an imprint of Constable & Robinson Ltd 2002

ISBN 0-7867-1166-3

Printed and bound in the EU

10 9 8 7 6 5 4 3 2 1

Contents

Acknowledgments

PAYING MY FRIENDS FOR SEX by Matt Thorne, © 2001 by Matt Thorne. First appeared in PIECE OF FLESH, edited by Zadie Smith. Reproduced by permission of the author.

FULFILLMENT by Daniel James Cabrillo, © 2001 by Daniel James Cabrillo. First appeared in CLEAN SHEETS, 2001. Reproduced by permission of the author.

SITTING UNCOMFORTABLY by Sarah Veitch, © 2001 by Sarah Veitch. First appeared in CORRECTIVE MEASURES. Reproduced by permission of the author.

GREEK FEVER by Anne Tourney, © 2001 by Anne Tourney. First appeared in SCARLET LETTERS, 2001. Reproduced by permission of the author.

DIRTY POOL by Thomas S. Roche, © 2001 by Thomas S. Roche. First appeared in FLESH AND BLOOD, edited by Max Allan Collins and Jeff Gelb. Reproduced by permission of the author.

NIGHT ON TWELFTH STREET by Marilyn Jaye Lewis, © 2001 by Marilyn Jaye-Lewis. First appeared in AROUSED, edited by Karen Finley. Reproduced by permission of the author.

THE HILL by J. D. Sampson, © 2001 by J. D. Sampson. First appeared in VENUSORVIXEN, 2001. Author's permission sought.

PORNOGRAPHIC STORY by Rebecca Ray, © 2001 by Rebecca Ray. First appeared in PIECE OF FLESH, edited by Zadie Smith. Reproduced by permission of the author.

WHEN HE WAS GOOD by Marc Levy, © 2001 by Marc Levy. First appeared in SUSPECT THOUGHTS, 2001. Reproduced by permission of the author.

69 LOVE SONGS by Maxim Jakubowski, © 2001 by Maxim Jakubowski. First appeared in HANDHELD CRIME, 2001 and CRIME TIME 25, 2001. Reproduced by permission of the author.

SURRENDER DOROTHY by Lisa Montanarelli, © 2001 by Lisa Montanarelli. First appeared in BEST BISEXUAL WOMEN'S EROTICA, edited by Cara Bruce, as by "Lisa Archer". Reproduced by permission of the author.

AMONG THE BEKS by A. J. Horlick, © 2001 by A. J. Horlick. First appeared in SUSPECT THOUGHTS, 2001. Reproduced by permission of the author.

BOB & CAROL & TED (BUT NO ALICE) by M. Christian, © 2001 by M. Christian. First appeared in SWEET LIFE, edited by Violet Blue. Reproduced by permission of the author.

THE BACK OF THE STORE by Nola Summers, © 2001 by Nola Summers. First appeared in CLEAN SHEETS, 2001. Reproduced by permission of the author.

FIRST LOVE by Hubert Selby, Jr., © 2001 by Hubert Selby, Jr. First appeared in AROUSED, edited by Karen Finley. Reproduced by permission of the author.

TRIPTYCH by Helena Settimana, © 2001 by Helena Settimana. First appeared in BEST BISEXUAL WOMEN'S EROTICA, edited by Cara Bruce. Reproduced by permission of the author.

PINKLAND by Graham Joyce, © 1998, 2001 by Graham Joyce. First appeared in CROSSING THE BORDER, edited by Lisa Tuttle. Reproduced by permission of the author.

THE BOSS by Jazz Lloyd, © 2002 by Jazz Lloyd. Reproduced by permission of the author.

THE DEVIL AND MRS FAUST by Ian Philips, © 2001 by Ian Philips. First appeared in SEE DICK DECONSTRUCT. Reproduced by permission of the author.

MELINDA by Mitzi Szereto, © 2001 by Mitzi Szereto. First appeared in WICKED WORDS 4, edited by Kerri Sharp. Reproduced by permission of the author.

THE LINDY SHARK by Alison Tyler, © 2001 by Alison Tyler. First appeared in BEST WOMEN'S EROTICA, edited by Marcy Sheiner. Reproduced by permission of the author.

RAYBAN by M. Nason, © 2001 by M. Nason. First appeared in SUSPECT THOUGHTS, 2001. Reproduced by permission of the author.

THE MERMAID'S SACRIFICE by Christopher Hart, © 2001 by Christopher Hart. First appeared in EROTIC TRAVEL TALES, edited by Mitzi Szereto. Reproduced by permission of the author.

GATORS by Vicki Hendricks, © 2001 by Vicki Hendricks. First appeared in FLESH AND BLOOD, edited by Max Allan Collins and Jeff Gelb. Reproduced by permission of the author.

Introduction

With every new year that passes, erotic writing becomes more varied and exciting. A veritable explosion of talent and imagination has become a sheer torrent over the past decade since I began compiling erotic stories in the Mammoth series to a most gratifying response.

While some of the best writers in our curious field continue to sustain high levels of fascinating readability, confirming the fact that an erotic story is not just a succession of pointless sex scenes or pretentious mood pieces evoking past couplings or emotions, new magazine pieces and anthologies continue to unveil great new talents and a dazzling repertory of sexual and psychological variations that talk to us most intimately and connect with our complicated psyche in ways that surprise and delight.

Yet again this past year, erotic writing in web magazines has proven a great, fertile area of discovery, much of it progressing into print in collections here and elsewhere. Sadly, this is very much due to the scarcity of print magazines that might offer a showcase for erotic writing as opposed to an incredible flowering of themed anthologies. As in other popular culture genres, such as crime and mystery or science fiction and fantasy, it's in the magazines that new talent can find its feet, experiment and establish itself, and one can only regret the fact that innovative projects like NERVE or LIBIDO have moved off the news-stands and returned to the sheltering harbour of the worldwide web.

With every further volume in our series, I have effortlessly managed to uncover new voices in England, America, Australia, Canada and beyond. The present collection is no exception and unveils a handful of writers, all precious new voices who walk the delicate tightrope between the excesses of sheer titillation and the delights of sensuality with precocious assurance. I am confident we will see many more stories from most of them. My only regret, as ever, is the fact that I am unable to bring you voices from other languages in translation, due to financial imperatives; there is a goldmine of erotic writing in contemporary France right now which deserves a larger audience, and no doubt too in other countries (*The Mammoth Book of International Erotica* offered many such writers some years back but has since been overtaken by new generations of compelling foreign writers).

At any rate, I hope you enjoy the 2001 vintage of erotic writing collected in these hefty pages. As vintages go, it's a guaranteed classic. As ever, the combinations, characters, relationships and ideas defy taboos and the normal sexual smorgasbord with pleasure and elegance, as over 40 writers balance lust and sensibility with wonderfully innovative tales which leave little to the imagination and tease and please in exquisite ways. However sexually knowledgable the reader might think he or she is, I am convinced there will be some surprises and gentle shocks along the road, and maybe some of what you read here will change your life in subtle ways, leaving a germ in your heart or loins to linger and grow insidiously and improve your quality of life in curious ways.

Here's to the sexual imagination!

Maxim Jakubowski

Paying My Friends for Sex

Matt Thorne

Not having money was hard. But sometimes having money seems harder. It's not as if I'm rich or anything, but having enough cash to get yourself in trouble, well, you'd be surprised how quickly that becomes a burden.

I've never been an avaricious individual. Ever since I was a kid, my cash has gone on three things, and three things only: CDs, books, and the cinema. Most of my clothes were given to me; the rest come from second-hand shops. And although I spend more money on food than I used to, all this really means is these days I eat in expensive restaurants instead of McDonald's. I always eat out, and will do so until the day I die.

So when I unexpectedly started having more money, the only real evidence of my new-found wealth was in the increase of my book and CD collections. My cinema habits remained unchanged: there are, after all, only so many films you can see in a day. But although it was fun to fill out my literature and music libraries, after a while I realized there was little pleasure in buying music or books by bands or authors you didn't like. After that, I confined myself to only buying new books or CDs, or the back catalogues of bands I knew I loved. Even that got tiresome after a while (as much as I love Neil Young and Lou Reed, there's really no reason to own copies of *Landing on Water* or *Minstrel*). This meant I needed to find some new way of enjoying my money. At first I considered developing an interest in pornography. There seemed to be hundreds of adult videos, and it seemed likely that collecting these sorts of films would give me pleasure. But after I had ten or so, I realized I didn't really enjoy pornography, and was also embarrassed about having the tapes around the house.

The same morning I chucked the cassettes away, I got a letter from an ex-girlfriend. When we'd broken up I'd been quite stern with her, telling her not to try to get in contact with me. It was over two years since we'd last seen each other, and she was writing to ask whether I would now be prepared to meet her for dinner. She made no mention of her own romantic situation, although she did say in one line that she just knew I would have a girlfriend and if I wanted I could bring her along. I hadn't thought about this ex-girlfriend that much, mainly because I had been so upset when she'd broken up with me that I'd experienced a mini-breakdown that I didn't want anyone to know about. The main reason why I had told her not to get in contact with me was because I knew she had a habit of falling back in love with her boyfriends after she'd broken up with them and I thought it was probably safer to stay away from her until I'd made a fresh start. Once I'd got back on my feet, I'd always intended to contact her, but for one reason or another I didn't get round to it, and as I've never been one for nostalgia, not having her in my life didn't really worry me.

I wrote back to her a few hours later, telling her that I didn't have a girlfriend and hadn't been involved with anyone since we split up. As I wrote this I remembered reading somewhere about how when writing love-letters you should always forget about yourself and concentrate only on arousing pleasure in the person you're addressing. I couldn't remember if the passage came from Freud or Barthes (it sounded like something from *A Lover's Discourse*, but when I checked my library this volume was missing) or someone else entirely, but I realized that this was what I was doing now, and wondered whether it was such a good idea for me to meet up with Tracey again. I had always composed my letters to please her, and felt wounded every time a reply arrived. Not because they were deliberately hurtful, but because they seemed written with no awareness of the emotions they would arouse in me, which was fine when we saw each other all the time, but more difficult during the year we spent a continent apart. The address on the top of her letter was from somewhere in Chalk Farm, so I suggested we go for dinner at the Lavender in Primrose Hill. Three days later, her reply arrived. She would be happy to meet me in the location I'd suggested.

The reason why I had been single for so long was because of a random act of kindness I had committed two years earlier. A friend of a friend had died of a heart attack at an unexpectedly early age. His girlfriend, Marianne, needed someone to look after her and, having the space and the time, I invited her to move in with me. I had expected her mourning period to last three or four months, but it showed no sign of coming to an end. Over the previous two years she had become increasingly dependent on me and, although there had been nothing sexual between us, I felt too guilty to indulge in anything other than the odd one-night stand.

I arrived at the restaurant just before eight. Tracey was already waiting. She was wearing a short black dress. Smiling warmly as I entered the restaurant, she got up to embrace me.

"Tracey," I said as she hugged me, "it's so good to see you."

"You too." She looked down. "I wasn't sure if you'd come."

"So," I said, "tell me everything. Do you have a job?"

She laughed. "You're not going to believe what I do."

"Should I guess?"

"Not just yet. I have to give you some background details first."

"OK, start from the beginning. The last time I saw you, you were about to start drama school."

Tracey smiled with her head slightly tilted to one side and leaned back in her chair. It was more exciting to see her than I'd anticipated, and I was already trying to calculate how I would feel if we ended up going to bed together. The candle-light in the Lavender was doing an incredible job of bringing out all of my ex-girlfriend's most alluring features, from the small, springy, brown mole just above her soft upper lip to the exact colour of her curly brown hair. As always I was drawn in by her guilty-looking blue eyes, getting a sudden flashback of how her expression would harden when I trapped her into an argument.

"Drama school was great for the first term," she told me, "because there were so many new people and you can remember how lonely I was before we split up."

"Yeah," I replied, "I'm sorry about that."

"Sorry, why?" she asked, sounding as if her question was genuine.

"Gosh, I don't know if I'm ready to get into this."

"Get into what?"

"I had a breakdown just after you left me. And although initially when it happened I wasn't able to do anything or see anyone, eventually I managed to get myself together enough to start having therapy. And through the sessions I worked out why I treated you the way I did."

I noticed from the direction Tracey's eyes were pointing that a waitress had come across to our table. I felt glad of the interruption, amazed that I'd started talking about this stuff so quickly. Then I remembered how my therapist had spent our final session trying to convince me that I wouldn't feel properly healed until I'd seen Tracey again, and how adamant I'd been that that wasn't a good idea.

The waitress told us the specials and we looked up to the blackboard to decide what we wanted. I guessed from Tracey's small order that she was having money problems. While not wanting to embarrass her, I attempted to persuade her to have more than just a starter by letting her know that I'd pay.

"It's OK," she told me, "I'm really not that hungry. But if you order a nice bottle of wine I'd be happy to drink it."

I ordered the wine and my food, then said, "I feel terrible now, isolating you like that. But it wasn't jealousy. I always thought it was jealousy, but my therapist made me realize it wasn't that at all. I just needed to get something from you, something secret, something from inside, something you probably couldn't give. That's why I took us away from everyone else."

She nodded. "I do understand, and that's kind of why I

wanted to see you. You see, like I said, drama school was great
for the first term, but then I started missing you. And I looked
back on our time together with a fondness you'd never believe.
Every day I thanked God that we'd had those two whole years
together so I had something from every season to remind me
of you. Like, pick a day . . ."

"Hallowe'en."

"Scary badger."

"What?"

"You remember."

I thought about it and realized that I did. We'd gone to the
cinema together and on the way back we'd seen two liberal-
type parents trick-or-treating with a small child wearing a
cardboard badger mask. And we'd joked with each other
about how the parents would've convinced their child he
didn't want to be anything as horrible as a hobgoblin or
Freddy Krueger. "No," we imagined the two well-meaning
parents saying to their child, "what you want to be is a scary
. . . badger."

I smiled. "I find it hard to remember stuff."

"I know. When we broke up you said you'd never think of
me again."

"I didn't say that."

"You did."

"Well, it wasn't true. So, are you going to tell me what your
job is?"

"Phone-sex."

"Huh?"

"I knew you'd like that. Can I tell you about my audition?"

"For the job?"

"Yeah."

"Well, I'd been working for TicketMaster for a while and it
just wasn't working out. The rest of the people in the office
didn't like me because every now and again I'd have an audition for an advert and they'd all get really upset because I had
a life outside work. So, anyway, there was one woman there
who I became work-friends with, and one day she told me she
was leaving. She'd got a job working for a sex-line and it was
five times as much money for nowhere near as much work. I

was a bit sceptical, but she told me that, although there were a few dodgy men at the company, the main people in charge were all women, and by that time the little pound signs were dancing in front of my eyes and I'd agreed to go in for an interview."

The waitress reappeared at my elbow with the wine and the squid salad I'd ordered for a starter. I asked her what had happened to Tracey's food and she said she'd thought it would be better to bring it at the same time as my main course. Tracey nodded and said that was fine. I still felt guilty about ordering so much food when she was having hardly anything and tried to make up for it by overfilling her glass with wine.

Tracey continued. "So I went in for my interview and found myself in this windowless room with two women and one man. Although the man did most of the talking, it was obvious from the outset that the women were in charge. Anyway, my audition consisted of three exercises. The first two exercises were pieces I had to read from a script. This is quite a long anecdote, but the punchline's in the middle instead of the end so get ready to laugh. The script I was reading from was supposed to be as if I was talking from the perspective of a woman who had been led into sexual ruin. I had to go through this catalogue of things that my boyfriend had made me do and the twist at the end was that I had to tell the caller that I was now completely cock-crazy and even just knowing there was a man on the other end listening to my past exploits got me off. The script was kind of torturous and confused and I was trying to understand it as well as read it so I kept stumbling over my words, and I got to this bit where I said my boyfriend introduced me to swimming and just as I was thinking that was odd and waiting for some sub-aqua exploits, the man stood up and shouted at me, 'It's swinging, not swimming. My boyfriend introduced me to *swinging.*'"

It wasn't that great a line – she knew that – but the delivery was so perfectly Tracey that it made me laugh, identify with her and feel horny all at the same time. I knew one day lots of men would share this feeling, and it was this knowledge that

made me certain that, in spite of Tracey's considerable
fragility, she would one day achieve success as an actress.

She went on. "The second script was less interesting.
Standard sexy housewife, naughty knickers stuff. But then the
final exercise was an improvization. It'd been a while since I'd
been to a proper audition and you know how much I like that
sort of thing anyway so I got all overexcited and started acting
as if I was auditioning for a movie instead of a job on a sex-line.
You would have liked the scenario though. It was a bit close to
home and I could tell they'd come up with this idea for an
audition piece deliberately to make me feel uncomfortable so
I decided to take it to a real extreme. I was supposed to be an
actress who'd come for an audition for a part in a film and then
when I'd arrived I'd found out it was actually a porno instead
of a normal movie."

I popped a large piece of squid into my mouth and started
chewing. Tracey brushed a strand of stray hair out of her face
and carefully lifted her overfilled wine glass to her lips. As she
did so, I noticed her lipstick was completely the wrong shade
for her, making it look as if she'd been sucking gob-stoppers all
day long.

"The weird thing about this last exercise was that they
wanted me to do it over the phone. I suppose it wasn't that
weird, given that I was meant to be proving I could do a sex-
line job, but the way they handled it was odd. First off the
women came across and hooked me up to a headset, then the
guy went off into another room on his own.

"Like I said, from the moment I was told what the exercise
was I felt really irritated and wanted to embarrass them, so I
tried to make what I was saying as disturbing as possible,
telling him that I was only taking this job to support my baby,
and that I came from a really religious background, and had
wanted to be an actress my whole life, grown up on *The Kids
From Fame*, stuff like that . . ."

"How did he respond?"

"Well, that was it, after I'd been talking a couple of minutes
or so he stopped asking me questions and just kept saying 'go
on, go on,' and I could hear the clink of his belt and, y'know,
I knew what he was doing."

"What did you do?"

"What could I do? I kept talking, but I tried to make it sound as unsexy as possible, just praying he would stop. But he kept going and I kept going until he came.

"Ugh."

"I know. And the worst thing was he didn't even try to hide it. I think I probably could've handled the situation if he was just some pervert doing this job as a sneaky way of getting his rocks off, but he came back into the main room with his fly undone, shirt-tail still sticking out, and the two women looked at him and made another mark on their clipboards as if this was just another test I'd passed."

"Tracey," I said gently.

"Yes?"

"How long have you had this job?"

"Only a couple of months. It's all right once you get used to it. And I make it fun, playing little games with myself like working out which words will make them . . ." She looked at me. "Oh, dear. When I imagined telling you about this I thought it would make me sound glamorous and sexy."

Not wanting her to worry, I smiled at Tracey and let my fork drop back on my plate.

We stayed in the restaurant until eleven. By that time we were both a little drunk and I was reluctant for the evening to end. I felt more aroused than I had in months and didn't want to go back to the sexless friendship waiting for me at home. So I persuaded Tracey to walk down to a nearby pub for one final drink. The front of the pub was crowded so we went through to the back bar, which was empty except for an old man and a fruit machine. I bought us both Stellas and sat opposite Tracey. Her legs were crossed at the ankles and I found myself staring at the line where the hem of her dress pulled tightly around her toned thighs. She was telling me about a friend's play but I had long stopped listening to her words. Taking a large gulp from my drink, I swooped in on her, sliding my hand up under her skirt.

My fingers stopped as they reached the soft crotch of her knickers. My lips stopped as I realized they were pressing against a resistant mouth.

"I'm sorry," she said, with tears in her eyes, "I don't want to do this."

When I was sixteen I went on a school-organized trip to Keele University. The trip was designed to introduce potential students to college life and, given the excesses of this weekend away, I think the organizers managed an accurate distillation of most people's three-year experience. I was the only one my school expected to make it to university, so I went alone, although by the end of the coach journey up I had befriended a sizeable number of sixth-formers sent by other schools in the city. As my school was ridiculously suburban, a haven of bubble perms and teenage pregnancies, I had always been an outsider, so much so that the first years started a rumour that I slept in a coffin. I didn't go into school that much, spending most of my time in my bedroom listening to the Pixies and those first three Ride EPs. This was considered so outré in my neighbourhood that I was amazed to find that my tastes were shared not only by the sixthformers I'd befriended on the bus, but also the students who organized the last night's disco.

Those two days at Keele were, to that point, the best of my life. But as I returned to my isolation, I saw no likelihood of them ever being repeated. My parents were both intensely anti-social people, ashamed of their marriage and quick to discourage me from forming friendships with others. But my new-found comrades were reluctant to let me disappear back to my previous existence, bombarding me with calls until I agreed to come with them to a Primal Scream concert. I went with them and, over the next few weeks, found myself with my first ever social circle.

And after friendship came the inevitable romantic infatuation. Among my new gang was a beautiful redhead with goth tendencies and a tart sense of humour. The rest of my friends were dubious about some of her more extreme tastes, and I was the only one willing to accompany her to a Cranes concert at a local polytechnic. The show was terrible but the night was transcendental, and in the taxi home I tried to kiss her. She stiffened, pushed me away, and said she wasn't interested. As far as I could remember, I'd never told Tracey about this, but it was definitely a formative moment, making me overcautious in the opening stages of any subsequent relationship. If I got any sense that the woman I wanted didn't want me, I immediately backed off, even if their reluctance was only part of an elaborate flirtation. In some ways, I'd never really got over that first rejection, and now the same thing was happening to me again, I felt a fresh desperation. But that doesn't explain what I said next.

"Tracey?"

"Yes?"

"I'll give you five hundred pounds to fuck me."

During the taxi ride home, I wondered whether I regretted making my offer. There was no question that Tracey had been horrified, turning me down immediately and remaining upset until we said goodbye, but when I thought back to my sessions with my therapist, I realized the fact that Tracey would never want to see me again was probably a positive thing. My therapist had never accepted my excuse that I couldn't start another relationship because I was giving house-space to Marianne, trying to make me believe it was really because I held out hope that Tracey and I would get back together. Now that definitely wouldn't happen, I was free to get on with my new life.

Marianne was waiting for me when I got home, sitting in front of our television drinking a mug of mulled wine and watching a film featuring Veronica Lake. She moved her legs down so I could sit next to her. As usual, her eyes were rimmed with red and she'd dressed with the bare minimum of effort. I squeezed her hand and she flashed me a brief smile.

The following morning I went out with three female friends of mine. Hazel, Ivy and Elizabeth were all young, recently married mothers. I had met them through Marianne. Initially, they had been her friends, calling me up for news about how she was coping. But as she hadn't seen them in two years and they had stopped asking about her, I now considered them my friends, meeting with them once a week for a few hours of coffee and chat in a cafe in St John's Wood.

Every now and again, we were joined by the unofficial fifth member of our party. Her name was Anita and she was by far the most glamorous member of our quintet. Marianne would've been furious if she'd known Anita occasionally accompanied us, as Anita had supplied Marianne's boyfriend Donald with the drugs she believed had precipitated his premature heart attack. Anita had been having a low-key affair with Donald for several years, and Marianne blamed herself for being so understanding about her infidelity, knowing that if she'd been more possessive she might've saved his life. Donald was one of many men Anita had spent years seeing on the side, although she usually went for men of more considerable means. Between affairs, she was always short of money, lost without someone to pay for her.

Hazel, Ivy and Elizabeth were all fascinated by the fact that I had been single for so long. Ivy was the only one who flirted with me, although I knew this didn't count for anything, as she was as certain in her marriage as the others. But they couldn't understand why I didn't make a move on Anita. Every time the subject came up, I used the same excuse,

"Marianne would kill me."

"But how would she know?" This was Elizabeth, the most persistent of my three friends.

"She'd know. She'd smell it on me."

"I don't see why you're worried about that," said Ivy, sucking her lip. "You've let Marianne live with you rent-free for two years. She's in no position to tell you who you can sleep with."

"There's too many demons."

"Between you and Anita?" Elizabeth asked. "Why? You hardly knew Donald. Besides, you two have an incredible chemistry. I bet the sex would be amazing."

"I don't think so."

"Why not?"

"I get the impression that Anita can keep people at a distance even when she's fucking them. I hate having sex with someone who's got their barriers up."

"You only say that because you've heard how she talks about her businessmen blokes. It'd be different for you. You'd be able to break her down." The other two chuckled darkly at this, encouraging Ivy to add, "If I had your body I could do it."

I sipped my coffee and took a bite from my Russian cake, feeling unsettled. I still wasn't really over last night and felt less comfortable bantering than I usually did. I knew myself well enough to know what I really needed was sexual reassurance and although, in a strange sort of way, that was what my friends were trying to offer me, thinking about Anita made me uneasy.

"Let's talk about something else."

That evening, I went to a party with my bank manager. She was one of the normal girls who'd made my life so difficult at school. We'd become friends by chance when I went into my hometown bank to open a third account. She'd been impressed by the amount of money I'd been depositing and asked me out on a date. We'd quickly discovered that there were the same differences between us now that there'd been at school, and we'd gone home separately. This had been a big blow to me as she'd been one of the most unobtainable girls in my school and, having spent a large part of my adolescence masturbating with her in my head, I was keen to see whether the real deal rivalled the fantasy.

After our unsuccessful date, we had concentrated on forming a workable business relationship. I needed more from my bank manager than most people, and was on the phone to her several times a week. And once long enough had elapsed for us not to be embarrassed in each other's company, we started going out together as friends. I became her walker, accompanying Vicki to social events once or twice a month. These events were not grand affairs, consisting mainly of nights in the pub or dinner-parties organised by her friends.

Tonight's party was in Jamie's Bar in Charlotte Street. One of Vicki's friends had just returned from two years in Australia and a gathering had been organised to welcome him back. Vicki didn't seem that excited about the party, and unusually for her, wasn't even worried about changing for the evening, meeting me straight from work. Seeing her in a conservative suit reminded me of how great she used to look in her school uniform, and I wondered again about my impotent reaction to the women in my life. It was odd: I was excellent with strangers, no matter how attractive, able to go into a club or bar, find someone single, and persuade them to take me home with them. But as soon as it came to anyone with whom I had the slightest emotional connection, I became a complete drip.

Feeling depressed, I drank too much and found myself telling Vicki what had happened with Tracey. I made a joke out of it, saying that it was probably not a good idea for me to tell my bank manager I'd been offering ex-girlfriends extravagant amounts of money for them to sleep with me.

She downed her glass, winked at me, and said, "I could do with some money."

We went to her place. In the taxi we bartered about the price: Vicki saying she wanted twice the amount I'd offered my girlfriend; me saying for that much money I expected something special.

I wasn't that surprised by the way she reacted. Vicki had spent the whole of her adult life working with money, and no doubt saw this as a neat way of mocking its black magic. The idea of being paid for sex clearly appealed to her, as did taking a human transaction so lightly. I paid the driver and we went into her house.

"So," she asked, "how do you want me?"

I thought back to all those adolescent afternoons. My fantasy had always been that while I was masturbating about Vicki she was somewhere masturbating about me. I told her this, thinking that was maybe how we'd start.

She chuckled. "You know, I never did. Not about you. I must've done it about almost every boy in the class, but never about you."

I couldn't reply. She noticed my sadness and said hurriedly, "I would've done, though, you know, if I'd known you were doing it about me."

"You must've known."

"Why?"

"Every boy in the year used to masturbate about you. We used to compare experiences."

She looked at me. "Really? I honestly had no idea. Can I tell you about a fantasy of mine?"

"Of course."

"I used to fantasize about groups of boys in the class masturbating over me. You know, with all that AIDS talk in assemblies sperm was seen as such an evil substance. But it didn't seem that way to me. I wanted to be totally coated in it."

She must've noticed my horrified expression, as she immediately eased back from our sexual conversation and asked me instead if I wanted a coffee. I nodded and she went out into the kitchen to make me one. I took advantage of the spare moment to assess my surroundings. Houses always look strange when there's only one person living in them, but Vicki had done a good job of making her place look comfortable. Before Marianne moved in with me, there had always been something defiant about my decoration, as if I was trying to create a home that would be the envy of anyone who visited it. But nothing I could buy from a shop could add the warmth created by another person's belongings.

Vicki was clearly less troubled by being alone, and although she couldn't quite disguise the fact that she had too much space to herself, the lounge looked like somewhere she'd be equally happy entertaining friends or watching television alone. I liked the fact that she'd left stuff out (a hairdryer lying on its side next to a rectangular white extension-plug; a box-set of *Friends* episodes by the television; three cotton-wool balls dyed scarlet with nail-varnish on a copy of the *Express* next to the electric fire), and began to relax as I settled down into her settee.

She returned with my cup of coffee. After her revelations about her childhood come-fantasies, I didn't feel like watching her masturbate any more, and anyway, that was far too passive. It was time for me to become masterful.

"Take your trousers off," I told her.

"Let's see the money first."

"What?"

"Cash up front. I don't want you changing your mind after you've had me and pretending the payment thing was just a joke."

"OK. How much did we agree on?"

"A thousand. Do you carry that kind of money with you?"

"No. Will you take a cheque? You know I'm good for it."

"Do you have your cheque-book on you?"

"No, but come on, Vicki, you're my bank manager. You can easily debit my account whenever you want."

"Write me an IOU."

"I don't have a pen."

"There's one on the table."

I got up and wrote out an IOU, wondering what was behind this banter. Although a thousand pounds wasn't bad for one night's work, I couldn't believe that Vicki was genuinely only doing this for the money. The way I looked at it, the play with potential prostitution was just spice to stoke up enough excitement to get us through a one-night stand. If she was taking it seriously . . . well, fuck it, if she was taking it seriously, I'd just make sure I got my money's worth.

"Right. Now get those trousers off."

She stood up, walked across to the table and checked the IOU. Seemingly satisfied, Vicki came across to me and put one foot up between my legs.

"Unbuckle my shoes first."

I felt pleased she was bossing me back, thinking that this proved she was getting into what we were doing. I gripped her ankle before following her instruction, a motion that seemed to please her. Shoes removed, she turned her back to me. I sank down slightly so her bottom was directly in front of my face, then waited as she undid the buckle on her belt and slowly lowered her trousers over her buttocks. She was wearing a flimsy pair of white translucent knickers: the kind that pulled tight between her legs so that the material covering her bum formed a triangle. I gripped her hips. She let her trousers fall to the floor and stepped out of them.

"I bet you're a man who likes bottoms."

I giggled. "What?"

"Let's see, shall we? What happens when I do this?"

She slid her fingers under the elastic of her knickers and pulled them down. Using a foot to flip them onto a pile with her trousers, she leaned forwards and pushed her bum up in my face, using her fingers to pull open her cheeks. The light was good in Vicki's apartment and I had a full view of the soft creases of her anus. She was right: I did like this sight, although few of the girls I'd been out with had shown it to me so readily, and it was a hard thing to request of a one-night stand. I could see why Vicki was so willing to reveal hers to me. I know this sounds strange, but it was absolutely beautiful, the skin moving so perfectly to the small hole in the centre with each tuck in exactly the right place. From this angle I could also see a rear view of her vagina, which was equally well defined, the flesh of her outer labia almost spookily symmetrical. Vicki seemed to revel in my slow appraisal and after my nice, long look I pushed my tongue onto her welcoming folds. I held Vicki's hips and managed to get deep into her, curious whether she liked having this done to her as much as I liked having it done to me. I licked for a while and then asked her, "Can you touch yourself while I do this to you?"

"Well, I can, but you'll have to hold me open."

"That's OK."

She released her buttocks and I took over, opening her even wider. The muscles in my tongue felt pleasurably strained as I buried my mouth into her bottom, wanting her to feel totally loose. She fingered herself slowly at first, but when I showed no sign of wearying she speeded up. I wondered if she would be prepared to come with me and felt scared about how much I wanted that to happen. But I also wanted to come too, and as her moans grew shallower I stopped sucking her asshole.

"What's wrong?" she asked.

"Nothing. I realise it's not very romantic to interrupt the sex like this but, seeing as I'm paying . . ."

"Yes?" she asked, impatient.

"What are you like with orgasms? Do you come? Can you come? Do you always need fingers, or can you come just from fucking? Can you come lots of times or is it one-time-only, lights out?"

"I'm weird. Back to front. When I masturbate it takes for ever, but I guarantee if you fuck me for more than three minutes that'll hit the spot."

"That's not back to front, that's perfect. And can you still fuck after you've come?"

"Yeah, but if we're gonna do that can we use lubricant? You don't have to wear a condom."

"Of course. Have you got some?"

"I'll fetch it."

She moved away from me and went out into the hallway. I watched her go, finding it sexy to see her bare legs beneath the jacket of the work-suit she was still wearing. I waited while she went upstairs, rubbing my cock through the pocket of my trousers. When Vicki returned she could tell I was looking at her cunt and stopped beneath the main light, letting me see her. As I'd expected, she had a neat bikini line, an unnecessary precaution for one so fair, but nice to look at all the same. Although this was definitely an incredibly sexy moment for me, I couldn't help feeling slightly disappointed. *Seeing Vicki Wade's cunt . . .* this was a childhood dream come true, but how could it hold the same magic for me now that it had done back then? I remembered one time when a boy from our school had told us that he'd seen Vicki doing stretches in the gym, and her leotard had ridden up so high that, as he'd put it, "he even saw her pin". For months afterward I'd dreamt about being in his place, even (if you'd caught me in a weak moment) prepared to give up my life to share the sight.

Maybe I should've offered her money back then. She probably wouldn't have accepted it, but who knows? Of course, in those days I couldn't even get near her, let alone start a conversation that would lead up to me offering her money to show me her cunt. It's odd, but even now, the thought of Vicki's adolescent vagina tucked inside that unfaithful leotard seemed sexier than the reality in front of me. I'm not a pervert, and have no interest in schoolgirls (even women my age dressed up in school uniform), but the power of that missed moment was so strong that the fantasy almost managed to obliterate what was happening now.

Vicki seemed to notice my distraction and brushed her fingers down over herself. She pretended that she too was distracted, but then quickly looked back at me and smiled when she saw me grip myself through my trousers again.

"What do you want me to do?"

"I want to come inside you."

"I've already said that's fine."

"I know, but I need to be sucked first."

"Oh, OK." She walked back to me, knelt down and unzipped my fly. Pulling open my trousers, she slid my cock out through the slit in my boxer shorts and took it into her mouth. I don't really need to describe the experience other than to tell you she was good at it, although to be honest I've never been with a woman who wasn't. Remembering her promise of how little sex she needed to orgasm, I let her suck me longer than I normally would, eventually stopping her with a gentle pat on both shoulders.

She looked up at me, and her expression seemed so open that I snapped out of porno mode and stroked the side of her face. She bent down, unlaced my shoes, and stripped me from the waist downwards. Picking up her blue tube of lubricant, she squeezed a blob onto her palm, spread it over my cock then rubbed the rest inside her. Pulling my cock forwards, she slid herself gently on top of me. I kissed her, realizing as I did so that it was the first time our lips had touched. It's embarrassing and inappropriate, but the first time I fuck someone I always want to tell them I love them. Thankfully, tonight I conquered that urge and mouthed it softly to myself instead. Our fucking was surprisingly (for me, anyway) forceful: a proper, deep, heterosexual shag that carried us both to orgasm and left us woozily clinging to each other. We stayed like that until Vicki climbed off of me and asked,

"Did you get your money's worth?"

Marianne was asleep in front of the television when I got back. She often nodded out in the lounge, waking up again about three or four and going to bed. Feeling bolder than usual, I decided to carry her upstairs. When we reached the landing she awoke and, after taking a few seconds to adjust to the situation, sniffed my neck.

"You smell of sex."

I didn't say anything. She smiled, and let me carry her to her room and drop her on her bed. As I turned out her light she said, "Someone called for you. There's a message on the machine."

I went downstairs and played the message. It was Tracey, apologizing for the other night and saying she wanted to see me again. Tomorrow. Although it was after one, I called her straight back. She reminded me of her address and told me to come over at seven o'clock. I replaced the receiver and went to bed.

The following morning Marianne and I both awoke earlier than usual and decided to have breakfast together. This was quite an unusual occurrence for both of us and, as we lacked even the most basic supplies, I headed off to the deli. When I came back Marianne had made me a coffee and was sitting at the end of the table sipping hers, wrapped in a dark-blue silk dressing-gown.

"So," she said, as I hunted for a grapefruit-knife, "who was the lucky girl?"

"On the phone?"

"No . . . last night."

"Oh. My bank manager."

"Really?" She laughed. "I thought you were too rich to have to sleep with someone for a raised overdraft."

"I was. Until someone started eating me out of house and home."

She looked at me, clearly shocked. I'd never referred to money before, and she'd stopped bringing it up after her third straight week of thanking me for my generosity

"I do feel ready to start looking for a job," she said in a small voice, "although if it's all right with you I'd rather stay here and pay you rent than move out. I'm just so comfortable here."

I didn't answer, preparing her grapefruit in silence and placing it in a bowl in front of her.

I arrived at Tracey's house an hour and a half late. This was a deliberate tactic, my childish way of getting revenge for her knocking me back after our previous date. She pretended she wasn't aware of the time, greeting me with a hug. Feeling optimistic, I'd stopped off at an ATM on the way and taken cash out of each of my three main accounts, now having nearly a thousand pounds on me. It was good to feel my ex-girlfriend's body against mine and I clung on to her until she broke away.

"Would you like a drink?" she asked. "I have beer. Or whisky."

"Beer, please."

She fetched a bottle from the kitchen and handed it to me. Tracey had already strategically placed an opener on the coffee table and I used it to uncap the drink.

"Aren't you having anything?"

"I will in a minute. I already had a little too much this afternoon."

I could tell she was nervous. Tracey was not a casual drinker, and when we'd been going out together she had only drunk at home at moments of extreme emotion.

"Are you OK, Tracey?"

"I'm fine," she replied, sitting on her sofa.

She was wearing a cream cardigan, a white halter-neck and a short grey skirt. Tracey had always had a thing for flesh-coloured stockings, and was wearing a pair this evening, with no shoes. I sipped my beer, waiting to hear why she had summoned me here.

"The offer you made the other night."

"Yes?"

"Does it still stand?"

"Of course."

"What if I don't want to have sex with you?"

I wasn't in the mood for this sort of game playing, and wasn't about to beg. I put down my beer and stood up. "Then I don't think you should."

"No," she said, looking up at me, "I don't mean that. Oh, God . . ." She rubbed her forehead. "What if I want to do other things?"

I sat back down. "What sort of other things?"

"Safer things."

"I can wear a condom."

"I don't mean that sort of safe. I mean, emotionally safe."

"I'm not sure I follow."

"Well," she said, "would you want to see me?"

I smiled. "Of course. But let's not make this so clinical. Why don't you come over here with me?"

"But how will we work out the money?"

"The money doesn't matter to me. How about if I give you five hundred pounds anyway, and then you can decide how far you want to go?"

"And you won't get angry with me?"

"Of course not. Don't be stupid."

"Or tell anyone? Or hold it against me?"

"I don't know anyone you know. And it's my idea. How can I hold it against you?"

She still didn't seem satisfied. I was beginning to wonder if this was such a good idea, but was feeling too turned-on to leave.

"And you accept that this will be a one-off? You won't force me to do it again later because I agreed to it now?"

I couldn't understand why she was being like this. Throughout our relationship I had almost always been the submissive one, never forcing her to do anything. I might have been a little more forthcoming than her about my desires, but that'd only been because she rarely talked about what she wanted, preferring to go unhappy than verbalize her discontent.

"Tracey, I'm not about to cast judgement on you. I offered you money the other night because I was desperate to sleep with you and couldn't cope with being rejected. I can understand why you were offended . . ."

"I wasn't offended, just scared. I'm frightened by you wanting me."

"Why? You work on a sex-line. You have men wanting you all the time."

I realized the moment I said this that it was a mistake. Suddenly, everything became clear to me and I saw my way out of this. But first I had to listen to her response.

"Jesse, this is why I got so upset the other night. I told you about the sex-line because I thought you'd find it sexy and funny, but I didn't think it would change the way you thought about me. After I said it I remembered how afraid I was about telling you about my sexuality. This is something I've been wanting to tell you for ages, in fact, that's the whole reason why I got in touch with you again. But then at dinner you told me you'd had a breakdown and I couldn't tell you the truth . . . well, I mean, I told you part of the truth, about how I missed you and was glad we had all that time together, but I couldn't get to the heart of it. I couldn't tell you . . . Look, you know what you said about your therapist telling you that what you were feeling with me, when you isolated us, wasn't jealousy but you wanting something from me, something I couldn't give?"

"Of course."

"Well, you and your therapist got it completely round the wrong way. What you wanted was to know the truth about me, but because you were so jealous you didn't want to hear it."

What she was saying made sense. I thought back to my bank manager telling me about her come-fantasy and how that hadn't turned me on at all. I had often told Tracey I wanted to know what she masturbated about – and in my head I thought I did – but the truth was, if she wasn't doing it about me I didn't want to know.

"The truth is, the reason I freaked out the other night was because it felt like you were making the offer out of anger. And it reminded me of how you always used to view sex as something you had to take from me, as if I was deliberately withholding it. That 'something I couldn't give' was an honest sexual response, because I always felt you were judging me.

"But the thing is, I do want to do something with you. Something that'll get rid of all the hurt and make you think well of me. And, although it sounds strange, and it did upset me at first, I think you paying me for sex is a good idea. Only you have to be doing it for pure motives. You have to do it because you want me."

"I do want you."

"Good." She came across and sat next to me. Taking control, she straddled me and pushed me back on the sofa. She'd washed her hair recently and I could smell her shampoo as her long brunette curls fell over her face. As she started kissing me, I considered how this evening's experience was already so different from my previous night with Vicki. I had completely forgotten how Tracey kissed, the soft pulling that felt so reassuring after her resistance in the bar after the restaurant, and as I let her take charge, I found myself thinking back to when I first got my money and was trying to develop an interest in pornography. Although it had quickly stopped working for me, it was only now that I realized why. It was my lack of imagination, and my inability to bring details from my own life into my appreciation of the films. My one-night stands were few and far between and, to be honest, they weren't fantasy-occasions, instead usually arising from desperation and mutual need. And although I've always had lots of women in my life, it's been hard to eroticize them, as I've known them as friends rather than sex-objects (I realize the two are by no means mutually exclusive, but until last night with Vicki, it'd always seemed that way to me). So when I watched pornography, I found it hard to enjoy the variety, which I guess is the whole point in the first place. It was difficult to identify with the well-built men, and unless the women looked like Tracey, or other ex-girlfriends, they didn't seem sexy either. I'm not a natural voyeur, and watching other people having sex always makes me feel like I'm the one being exploited, not them, as if I'm stuck in someone's house and still having to be the polite guest even when my hosts start going down on each other.

Now that I was having sex with Tracey so soon after I'd had sex with Vicki, and was rediscovering myself as a sexual person (albeit in quite an unconventional way), I felt like I might like to watch pornography again, using the woman on screen as a point of connection between Tracey and Vicki and whomever I ended up having sex with next.

I was amazed at how much the money was adding an extra energy. When I'd been going out with Tracey, our intercourse had always been extremely fraught, a cycle of tears, excitement, pain, pleasure and tears. The first few times had been terrifying, a form of lovemaking I was completely unused to, having previously only been with women who saw sex as a friendly adult kinship. Now I was paying Tracey she seemed to be trying to fit her need around working out how to make me happy. The way she was kissing me showed she wanted me, which is something I've always needed to know in order to enjoy sex with anyone. These last two statements sounds antithetical. Let me explain. What I mean is, nothing is as big a turn-off for me as a woman saying, 'I want to make you happy.' But a woman who wants me (even if she's only pretending) is all I need for the sex to work. This is why I always aimed low when picking people up, and why paying my friends for sex was turning out to be so successful. I'm not vain enough to imagine I could sexually excite a professional prostitute, but I also knew that it would be imposssible for a friend (or an ex) to have sex with me without feeling something. And with Tracey I thought it went much farther than that, as I saw now that she'd always needed this sort of excuse to really enjoy sex, and may even previously have had this sort of fantasy herself.

She stopped kissing me and pushed herself up. "How much would you pay to pull down my top?"

"I told you. I'll give you five hundred pounds whatever we end up doing."

She shook her head. "No," she said, "I want to negotiate."

"OK." I smiled. "I guess that could be fun. Are you wearing a bra?"

Tracey got up and pulled her curtains. Then she turned on a table lamp and switched off the main light. Before taking her position on top of me, she pulled off her cardigan and hung it over the back of a chair.

"Yes, I'm wearing a bra."

"So you're only talking about me seeing your bra, not your breasts?"

"For the moment, yes."

"And, let me get this straight, am I paying you to pull down your top yourself or for me to do it?"

"Either."

"So there's no price difference between those two options?"

"No. Come on, how much?"

"Well, it seems quite minor, so let's say ten pounds."

"Twenty. I take it you have the money with you?"

I felt surprised that Tracey was being as serious about the money as Vicki had been yesterday, especially as I'd assumed I'd have to persuade her to take the cash. But I enjoyed my role in the fantasy, taking a twenty-pound note from my inside pocket and laying it out on the table.

"OK," she said, fingers going to the thin cord around her neck.

I reached up and stopped her, saying, "No, I want to do it."

I untied her and pulled the top down over her breasts. She was wearing a white strapless bra and her nipples were visible through the material. I attempted to stroke them.

"No, no," she told me, "you haven't paid for that yet. How much to see my knickers?"

"What type are you wearing?"

"Does that affect the price?"

"No, I'm just curious.

"Mmm," she said, "you just reminded me of something."

"Dinner in the oven?"

"No. A memory. From when we were together."

"Dangerous territory."

"Doesn't have to be. Anyway, this is a nice memory. It was about the third or fourth time we slept together, and we met unexpectedly, or maybe I hadn't been planning to go to bed with you but it ended up happening anyway, and you were surprised because I wasn't wearing matching underwear and I felt really weird because I didn't even have that many niatching sets and you'd already seen most of them."

"So you're not wearing matching underwear today?"

"I am, actually, although I didn't think about that this morning. Well, kind of matching, they're white string-knickers, with a small red design in one corner."

"Let me see."

"How much?"

"Forty."

"Cash on the table."

I unfolded another two notes. "Are you sure you don't want me to give you the whole five hundred right now?"

"And spoil the fun? I'm enjoying myself, aren't you?"

"Of course."

"Good." She smiled at me and pulled her skirt up. She tried to make the material stay as high up her thighs as possible so I could get a proper look at her knickers. Shortly after we'd started going out, I'd discovered Tracey's diary. Just before we'd started going out she'd had a lonely night with some unsatisfactory ex-partner and come home and detailed all the things she liked and didn't like. Eventually I was forced to admit my betrayal of her trust, but prior to my confession it provided a useful shorthand on how to please her. She liked having her breasts caressed rather than kissed, preferred having her knickers gently slipped down her thighs rather than taking them off herself, sometimes enjoyed being fingered to orgasm with her knickers still on, although that was never quite as nice as being eaten out. She liked sucking cock; sometimes more than being fucked. Her favourite fantasy was imaginary incest (something only ever exciting to those who hadn't suffered the irritation of real-life siblings) and except for very, very rare occasions, hated being on top.

She laughed. "I bet you're just dying to touch me, aren't you?"

Tracey never used to be this confident. I knew it had something to do with the money, but I also thought it was probably connected to her new job. I'd always known Tracey had the perfect voice for sex-line work, but felt surprised that she'd actually gone through with it. I wanted to ask her more about what the job was like, but after her previous outburst, felt scared about spoiling the mood.

"Can I touch your cunt and breasts at the same time?"

"If you're prepared to pay for it."

"I'll give you fifty pounds. But you also have to rub my cock."

"For fifty, I'll only do it through your trousers."

"That's all I want, for the minute." I counted out the cash and put it on the table. "Although let me touch you for a bit first."

"OK. Can I lie back more?"

"Of course. It'll make things easier."

She shuffled backwards, reclining against the arm of the sofa. I moved round between her legs, leaning in to kiss her as

I began to gently stroke and squeeze her breasts. Her kisses were more open now, her mouth more relaxed. I quickly embraced her and then began to rub the heel of my hand over her cunt. I touched her breasts at the same time, kissing her again. After a few minutes, she pushed me back up and began stroking the tight crotch of my trousers. She stroked her hand around my shape, the heel of her hand rubbing my cock while her fingers softly dug against the underside of my balls. I let her do this for a short while, then pushed her back.

"Another fifty to see your tits."

She laughed. "Shall I undo it?"

"No, let me."

I put a fifty-pound note on the table, and Tracey leaned forward to let me unhook her bra. I was amazed at how unfamiliar her breasts looked, and wondered how I could've forgotten something so important. Why are visual memories the hardest to preserve? Especially sexual memories. I couldn't believe that in my fantasy-world I had robbed Tracey of her real body and replaced it with an anonymous alternative. I had forgotten how easily she flushed; that her shoulders were lightly freckled. Her breasts had become bigger in my memory, her nipples smaller, and the real-life combination was much sexier. But strangest of all, I had forgotten how Tracey looked at me differently when I started to undress her.

She kissed me. "Knickers too?"

"Let me do it. You know what you said earlier about not wanting to have sex with me, do you still feel like that?"

"I don't want to have penetrative sex. But everything else is OK."

I considered this. "All right then, I'll give you a hundred and fifty pounds to pull your knickers off and go down on you."

"OK."

Placing the cash on the table, I gently lifted Tracey from the sofa and brought her down onto the floor. She raised her knees and I slipped my fingers under the waistband of her knickers and gently tugged them down. Her cunt was already wet and slightly open, the pink bright beneath the spring of her light brown pubic hair. I pulled her legs slightly more open and gave her cunt a first kiss. She murmured something and I moved up to hear what she said.

"What was that?"

"I said I've fantasized so much about you doing this. Especially since the other night."

Remembering Vicki, I asked, "What did you do when you fantasized?"

"Touched myself, of course," she said, sounding surprised.

I couldn't stop myself asking, "When was the last time?"

She sounded slightly irritated as she replied, "In the shower at the gym this morning," and, not wanting to push my luck, I went back down on her.

It was incredible to be between Tracey's legs again, and I felt disappointed when she came quickly. I wanted to carry on and see if I could bring her to a second orgasm, but she stopped me and made me come up alongside her for a hug. We lay like that for a while and then I asked her,

"Would you like to see my cock?"

"Do I have to pay you?"

"No." I laughed. "It's a freebie."

I pulled open my fly. She looked at me, surprised.

"You wear underwear now?"

"Since Michael Hutchence died."

"Show me then."

I pulled out my cock. She stared at it for a minute and then looked up at me.

"I remember it."

"Do you?" I asked, surprised. "Exactly?"

"Exactly."

I looked at her, wondering if women's memories worked differently to men's, or whether the fault lay solely with me.

"So," I said, "two hundred quid for a blow-job."

"It's extra to come in my mouth."

"Two fifty, then."

I counted out the cash and she went down on me.

Marianne was already in bed when I got home. I knew she was probably still upset about what I'd said that morning, but found I didn't really regret it. Since I'd started paying people for sex, my generosity to her had started to seem unfathomable, and I couldn't understand why I'd been kind to her for so long. No one else seemed interested in her (in the whole time she'd lived with me she'd never mentioned her parents once) and she hardly contributed anything around the home. Besides, if it wasn't for her living here I could have my sexual adventures without venturing outside the front door. I wasn't quite ready to kick her out, but from now on I felt she should start doing something to justify her board.

I didn't have much to do the next day. I arose late, masturbated, then went out for lunch alone. When I got back Marianne was sitting in the garden, reading a book. I went through to my study and called Vicki.

"Hi, Jesse, how are you?"

"Good."

There was a moment of silence. I hadn't imagined that it'd be hard to talk to her, assuming that we'd quickly fall back into a friendly intimacy, maybe with a pleasant new sexual undercurrent to our conversation. But suddenly I was experiencing the same sort of shyness I usually only felt when I was talking to someone I really fancied.

"Is this a money conversation?"

"Kind of," I laughed.

"Oh," she said, "I'm glad you've brought that up. The thing is, Jesse, the other night and everything I did enjoy it, but I don't think it should happen again."

"Really?" I replied, wondering if she was serious, or just wanted to be persuaded.

"Yeah," she said, "I'm sorry. I can't really explain. It's not you, or the money. It's just that I'm not very good at the stage between casual sex and a proper relationship, and I know you're not looking for that right now . . ."

"Well . . ."

"I mean, I'm not either, and I want you to carry on being my walker, and well, if I'm going to be absolutely honest the next day I was a bit freaked out by the fact that I'd taken money from you and if you'll let me I'd like to give it back."

"No, Vicki, don't be silly, it was worth it."

"I don't have to give you the actual money. If you want I can just credit your account."

"No," I said, "I'm glad I paid you. But I understand why you don't want to do it again, and don't worry, this won't damage our friendship."

"Oh, good," she replied, "thanks, Jesse."

I finished the call, found my address book and flipped through until I found Anita's number. I dialled, and got her answerphone. So I tried her mobile.

"Hello?" she said, the background noise of a lively pub behind her voice.

"Hi, Anita, it's Jesse."

"Hi, Jesse, how are you?"

"Good. Where are you?"

"In Soho. Why?"

"Are you alone?"

"Yeah. Why?"

"I wondered whether I could meet up with you."

"Now?"

"Is that OK?"

"Of course. I'm in Waxy's Little Sister. Do you know where that is?"

"No."

"Opposite the Metro."

"The cinema?"

"Yeah. How long are you going to be?"

"About forty-five minutes."

"OK. I'll see you then."

I told Marianne I was going out and took a taxi into Soho. Part of me wanted to reveal that I was meeting Anita, just to see how she'd react. But I worried that giving Marianne clues as to what I had planned might inhibit me, so I kept quiet.

During the drive, I thought about Anita and wondered whether she would go for my suggestion. The fact that she was drinking alone in the afternoon seemed a good sign, as she only lapsed back into alcoholism between affairs, focusing more heavily on drugs when she was involved with someone.

I remembered talking about Anita with Hazel, Ivy and Elizabeth, and how they were convinced I'd be able to seduce her. It was almost worth not using the money as a motivation, but I realized when I thought about having sex with Anita the financial transaction was the part I was looking forward to most. It was knowing that I was going to offer Anita money that stopped me feeling intimidated by her, as it seemed more adult, honest and decadent than her booze, coke and affairs.

Waxy's Little Sister was a ghastly Irish theme-pub, and I couldn't understand what Anita was doing there. She was sitting alone with a pint and a small glass of whisky. I walked across and joined her.

"Hi, Jesse. So what's wrong? Is this to do with Marianne?"

"No, nothing like that. I was just at a loose end and wanting someone to have a drink with. You were the first person who came to mind. Well, second, after my bank manager."

She chuckled. "Isn't he working?"

"She. And yes, she is. But I thought I could persuade her to knock off early. Anyway, I'm glad you were free. Are you all right for drinks?"

She nodded. I got myself a pint and pulled up a chair beside her. Even when she was getting wasted alone Anita looked incredible. She looked posh and innocent, a fatal combination even without the added spice of her exciting private life. I'd always wanted her, but had been held back by fear. Her red hair (always a warning sign to me, since that first experience of adolescent rejection) made her look a little like Nicole Kidman at her most elegant, although with a slightly more inviting, open face.

"How are you then?" I asked, still nervous.

"All right. Starting to get a little bit wobbly. How about you?"

"OK . . . a little drained."

"Ennui?" She smiled.

"Something like that. Too much money and too much free time."

"I wish I had that worry."

I sipped my beer, sensing an opening. "You're all right for money, aren't you?"

"Are you kidding? I'm broke. I've never had this little money in my life."

"Really?" I said, and after enough large swallows, began my pitch.

The following evening I was feeling lonely again. I couldn't get hold of Anita, or Tracey, and knew it would be undignified to have another go at persuading Vicki to change her mind. Frustrated, I went downstairs to the lounge.

Marianne was lying on the floor, watching television. She was wearing a short skirt and a black top and when I sat on the sofa behind her I could see her knickers. She paid no attention to me, concentrating on the television. I stayed there for fifteen minutes, but finally couldn't take it any longer and asked, "How much money would you want to suck my cock?"

Marianne moved out the following morning. I would've been happy if she'd left the night before, but she clearly wanted to drag out her departure. I wasn't sad to see her go and, although I had said some seriously mean things to her in our argument the night before, none of my comments had been unfair. Two years of frustration had come out too fast, that's all. I wasn't a bad person.

"I think it's good that you kicked Marianne out," Elizabeth told me. "She's been sponging off of you for far too long."

"What was the argument about?" asked Hazel.

"Never mind that," Ivy interrupted, "what I want to know is, what is Anita like in bed?"

I answered both their questions, at length, by telling them the story of my past week. This time I definitely wasn't trying to reel anyone in, knowing that all three of my friends were happily married mothers who weren't short of money and liked to think of themselves as decent, moral individuals.

Ivy was the first to start turning the conversation. Her approach was obvious, getting me to repeat the concept over and over again ("So, let me get this straight. You've been paying your friends for sex?" "Yes, Ivy, that's right, I've been paying my friends for sex.") until it no longer sounded outrageous and they'd all accepted it as an acceptable thing to do. But Hazel was the one who made it personal.

"Would you pay me for sex?" she asked.

"Would you like to have sex with me?"

"Maybe. How much money are we talking about?"

"Well, I paid Vicki a thousand, Tracey somewhere around five hundred and Anita two-fifty."

"You paid Anita the least amount of money?" Ivy exclaimed, shocked.

I smiled, amused by her indignation. "I asked all three of them to name their price. Anita wanted two-fifty."

"That's terrible," said Elizabeth. "She must have such low self-esteem."

"How much would you want to sleep with Jesse?" Ivy asked Elizabeth.

"Definitely a thousand," she said, "at the very least."

It was fun checking into a hotel with three women. We went to The Tenderloin, a tacky rock-themed hotel that Ivy claimed was the only place for an afternoon assignation. I was shocked by her knowledge and wondered whether I'd been right to think of these women as being so innocent after all.

We took the lift up to the third floor and found our room. I could tell the three women were enjoying themselves, although I thought it probably had less to do with the sex than the fact that we were all doing something secretive together. They always got like this whenever we left the café, even on the most innocent of missions. I think it was because we were moving outside the expected limits of our friendship, and none of us had the emotional maturity to cope with that.

Ivy took off her shoes and jumped backwards onto the bed. She was the shortest of my prospective partners, although none of them was tall.

"So how are we going to do this?" asked Hazel. "Are you up to having sex with all three of us?"

"Not in a straight way."

Elizabeth looked worried. "I'm not doing any lesbian stuff."
I laughed.

"I mean, not that I don't like you both and everything," she said to Ivy and Hazel, "I just don't think I could bear it."

"I'm not sure about the masturbation part either," Ivy admitted. "I don't even do that in front of my husband."

"What is it that embarrasses you?" I asked. "Doing it in front of me or doing it in front of each other?"

"Each other," they agreed.

"'Cause I could call down to reception for three blindfolds. They do do that sort of thing here, don't they?"

"They do," Ivy admitted. "There's an S&M bag they give to favoured customers."

"What do you think?" I asked them.

"I'd still be embarrassed," said Elizabeth, "even with only you watching."

"I don't mind doing it," Hazel told me, "as long as you do get the blindfolds."

"Ivy?"

"Oh, God, honestly, Jesse, I don't think I'd even enjoy it. Can't you just fuck me?"

"Well, I will, but I wanted us all to do something together."

"OK, how about if I strip down to my underwear and watch you having sex with Elizabeth while Hazel masturbates?"

"But Hazel doesn't want you to see her masturbating."

"And I don't want you to watch Jesse having sex with me," added Elizabeth.

Sighing, I decided to cut my losses. Ivy would wait in the bathroom, Hazel would masturbate, I would fuck Elizabeth. The women would all wear blindfolds. I worried that this would turn the afternoon into a slapstick comedy, but they were adamant. We moved everything they might bump into and called reception, who sent up a boy with three blindfolds on a silver tray.

I asked if anyone wanted to undress before I blindfolded them, but they all wanted to stay fully clothed to begin with. Their anxieties had made me feel uncomfortable and I began to wonder whether this was such a good idea. But even if we stopped now our friendship would still be changed forever, and in spite of everything, this was still a sexual experience I wanted to have.

"You are going to wear a condom, aren't you?" asked Ivy.

"And not the same one," Hazel added. "A different one for each of us."

"I don't have any," I said.

We called reception and they sent the boy back with a packet of extra-safe Mates. Ivy went out into the bathroom and closed the door. Hazel took off her shoes. Elizabeth lay on the bed. She whispered to me that she wanted me to undress her, so I took her shoes off and unbuttoned her jeans. I felt most worried about having sex with Elizabeth and was trying to make sure the experience didn't feel inappropriately intimate. I pulled off her jeans. She was wearing simple, pale cream knickers. I removed them quickly and looked up at her face, watching her breathing as I went down on her, again trying to make the sex feel as straightforward and competent as possible.

I was paying so much attention to Elizabeth that I hadn't even had a chance to look at Hazel, who was probably the one of the three I was most excited about going to bed with. I gently nuzzled and kissed Elizabeth's clit, reaching up under her jumper and pulling the cups of her bra down from her large breasts. Behind me I had heard Hazel getting out of her dress, but she was managing to masturbate without making almost any sound at all.

I continued sucking Elizabeth, realizing my only real opportunity to look back at Hazel without Elizabeth sensing it was during the few moments it would take me to move from licking her cunt to fucking her. After that I could probably get another couple of glimpses but would have to really strain my neck. I would've sucked Elizabeth for longer, but I was so eager to see Hazel that the moment I thought Elizabeth was wet enough to fuck, I stopped and turned round. Hazel was wearing a long stripy top that, together with her hand, almost entirely obscured my view of her cunt, but her facial expression and the quick movement of her finger suggested that she had got over her embarrassment of masturbating in front of me.

I turned back from her, fixed my condom and slid my hard cock into Elizabeth's cunt. She was wet, but it did take a couple of thrusts before I was moving smoothly inside her. Seeing Hazel like that made me excited again, and I worried I wouldn't be able to last long enough to satisfy all three women. Elizabeth had been avoiding kissing me, so I didn't force it, gratified when I felt her hands holding my hips.

I didn't want to get Elizabeth too close and then stop, as I knew that would prove frustrating to her. I also didn't know where she was going to go when I swapped over to Hazel. In the bathroom with Ivy, I guess. I slowed down, and Elizabeth nodded, seemingly happy for me to stop. I pulled out of her, and helped her get dressed and go into the bathroom. The moment the bathroom door closed, I walked over and snogged Hazel. She seemed perfectly happy to kiss me, wrapping her arms around me and reaching for my cock.

"Hang on," I said, "I've just got to get rid of the condom."

"Forget the condom. Just get rid of it and fuck me."

She reached up and untied the blindfold. I snapped off the condom and lifted her off the chair, pushing my cock into her as I pressed her against the wall. She grabbed my hair and we started fucking furiously, finding a satisfactory position somewhere between standing and a crouch. We continued like that until I said, "I'm sorry, I'm getting close. And I've got to stay hard for Ivy"

"Can't you come twice?"

"Not usually."

"OK. Go down on me then. I'm pretty close too."

She lay back on the bed and I gave her head until she came. Afterwards, she squirmed and reached for my hand. I kissed her and we stayed on the bed until Hazel called out to Ivy,

"He's all yours."

"Come in here then," she called back.

"No, don't worry, I'm going down to the bar."

Hazel dressed and left the room. Ivy walked in, still blindfolded. I let her come towards me. She gave a short, dirty laugh as her fingers reached my chest.

"Come on, then, what have you got left for me?"

I felt vaguely irritated at Ivy for stopping me from properly satisfying Hazel, and for the way she had always previously been so flirtatious with me, but then joined in with Elizabeth's squeamishness when it actually came down to us all getting together. So I went down on her until her fingers were digging into my head, then fingered her as I fucked her from behind, making her come just before I emptied myself into her.

That was the last I saw of Elizabeth, Hazel and Ivy. They never contacted me again, and didn't return my calls or e-mails. Anita and I met once more for sex, but then she got involved with someone else and said she couldn't see me any more. Tracey, too, seemed to have decided against further meetings with me, and although Vicki was happy to talk to me about money, there was no chance of anything sexual happening between us. At first I was glad to be free of Marianne, happy to have the house to myself, but it didn't take me long to become lonely. And with no friends left, there was no possibility of pursuing my previous path. I lasted two weeks before I started buying pornographic videos again, watching them with a hunger I had never had previously. And when they stopped working I found myself in a phone-box, intending to try Tracey again, but after getting halfway through her number, stopping and dialling the digits on a small colour card in front of me, finally ready to begin the next stage of my existence.

Fulfillment

Daniel James Cabrillo

In 1978, before we got married, Joseph and I moved to Los Angeles from New York and rented a little house in the hills. A couple of months later, Joseph's friend Sid came out for a visit. He was in the dumps, his wife Barbara having recently left him.

After dinner one night Joseph got out some grass for Sid and him. I made a pitcher of martinis for myself, and we sat around the small swimming pool sharing Sid's morose mood. Sid and Barbara had married young, but hadn't missed the hippie years; our reminiscences brought the talk around to sex, including the time Sid and Barbara and Joseph and his girlfriend of the time – Katie, I think – made it together.

I had a question: had Sid and Joseph ever done Barbara alone without Katie, or Katie without Barbara? They hadn't, but they wanted to know why I asked.

My tongue loosened by martinis, I told them about how, in college, my boyfriend Billy and I had shared an apartment with another couple, Scott and Lisa, and we'd all gotten it on. I'd told Joseph about that, but Sid was interested, and anyway there was more. When summer came, Lisa went home to wherever she was from, but I stayed in the apartment with the two guys. Until then, we'd had this . . . protocol, I guess you'd call it. Our group sex was symmetrical – whatever one swapped couple was doing, the other did – and we never mixed partners unless all four were present. So when Lisa went home the group sex stopped.

After a couple of nights, I rebelled. Why should I go without just because Lisa was gone? Since nobody had a good answer, the three of us went back to fooling around.

The trouble was, being the girl with two guys was more exciting to think about than do. Whatever configurations we started with, we always seemed to wind up with me on my hands and knees, sucking one boy's cock while the other boy fucked me. And that gets old: you want to give a great blowjob you ought to concentrate on the blowjob; when you're fucking you like to be into the fuck.

What I'd really wanted, I told Joseph and Sid, was for Billy and Scott to fuck me at once, front and back. I'd tried to make it happen. I'd get us into the right position, I'd put the two cocks in the right places, but without the guys' co-operation it couldn't happen – and it never did.

"Wait a minute, Lorna," Joseph and Sid asked, "why wouldn't they co-operate?"

"They just wouldn't," I said.

"What did they say?"

"Nothing."

"Like, when you said, fuck me here and there, they just didn't do it?"

"I didn't say it."

"What do you mean, you didn't say it? You never told them what you wanted?"

"No."

"Why not?"

"Too shy, I guess."

Sid and Joseph looked at each other, trying to understand.

"Let's see if we've got this straight. You're one girl with two guys, night after night, all three of you naked, one guy fucking you while you suck the other's cock, and you're . . . too shy . . . to tell them what you want?"

"Yes."

Sorry, but that's how I was. And it never happened. I'd never been fucked in my pussy and ass at the same time, though I still thought about it.

OK, I didn't tell this story to Joseph and Sid for nothing. I knew that after I told it, we'd all be thinking about it. I certainly was. I knew that Sid was thinking about it, but he couldn't suggest it: he was a guest, and we had to extend the invitation. I knew that Joseph was thinking about it but wasn't sure he could handle it. Joseph and I had both had active sex lives in the 70s, but maybe because I was ten years younger than Joseph and grew up in the era of casual sex, my experiences and experiments had been broader-ranging than his. But Joseph had always liked that. Here I was, this little shy chick who'd gone to bed with him no more than ninety minutes after we met at a party, who was ready for just about anything, anywhere, and who'd done almost everything you could think of that didn't involve pain, animals, piss or shit. He always wanted me to tell him stories from my hedonistic past. They turned him on. I turned him on.

Still, things were different now. We were going to be married. I was his and he was mine. No matter how wild we'd been, we were monogamous.

Was it infidelity for Joseph to share me with Sid, his oldest and closest friend, to make my dream come true? I didn't think so, but it was up to Joseph.

We went on to other topics but my fantasy hung over us. About an hour later, during a lull, Joseph said to me, "So what do you think, Lorna? Should we try it?"

All I did was extend my hand to him; he took it and pulled me to my feet. He gestured to Sid and the three of us went into the house.

In our bedroom I grabbed a short nightie from my dresser and went into the bathroom to put it on. I listened at the door: though I could hear Sid and Joseph moving about, I heard no whispers: they weren't talking at all. I guess they were nervous. I was, too, but not that nervous. What I was mostly was excited – very.

When I joined the guys I found them undressed down to their boxers. I smiled and got right into bed.

Joseph and Sid got in on either side of me. I kissed Joseph, then I kissed Sid, then I lay flat on my back and let them take over. They each kissed me, then moved down: two pairs of lips kissed my ears, my neck, my shoulders at the same time; two pairs of hands lowered the straps from my shoulders, uncovering my boobs; each guy licked a nipple. It was perfectly symmetrical – what is it with group sex and symmetry – and funny, in a way. I couldn't help it; I giggled, and that momentarily stopped them, but I touched both their faces and caressed their cheeks to tell them to go on. They sucked my breasts and their fingertips moved down.

They were extremely polite. Whenever Sid's hand encountered Joseph's on my boob or belly, they'd both say, "Oh, excuse me, pardon me, no, you go." And they were cooperative: when their fingers reached the bottom of my nightie they lifted it up together and slid it off me. I still thought it was more silly than sexy, but I suppressed the giggle.

Which was a good thing, because as soon as I felt fingers – whose ever they were – moving through my pubic hair and touching the flesh between my legs, I got hot – really hot, really fast. Enough consideration, I wanted to get on with it. Up, up, I whispered, turning towards Joseph and pulling his face up to mine so I could kiss him. Sid slid up behind me; I yanked the elastic on their shorts, and the guys removed them. Now, all of us naked, I took hold of both cocks and stroked. Actually, I would like to have seen the two cocks, to study and compare them, but we were past that by now, all of us eager and squirming. Both pricks were leaking – I spread the liquid at the tips over their cockheads with my thumbs – and I was tingling from Joseph's fingers at my pussy. I'd never gotten this wet so fast, so wet that when I pushed onto Joseph's fingers they slid all the way into me. As I wiggled around I felt Sid slide a finger under me and join Joseph in my squishy pussy, then slip out wet and press on my asshole, pushing until the entry gave way and let it in.

I grunted, let go of their cocks and took their hands away, gripped their cocks again. "Come on, come on," I said. I put Sid's cock at my asshole and pushed myself back against him; I slid my heel up on the bed to raise one leg, put Joseph's cock at my slit, and clamped my arms around him.

"Fuck me," I said.

Joseph pushed; the head of his cock spread my lips and

entered. Sid pushed; the top of his cock began to squeeze into my asshole.

"Good!" I said, ready for invasion.

Then, nothing.

Joseph's cock stopped. "Push!" I cried and, though I felt his pushing, it wouldn't go any deeper. "Push!" I repeated and felt Sid trying but his cock wouldn't go any farther.

"Come on," I insisted.

I could feel the strength of their bodies as they squeezed me tighter between them, but their pricks wouldn't go.

"Oh, God, no!" I said, desperate.

"Wait-wait-wait!" I heard Joseph say. "Turn around!"

They turned me around and I got a glimpse of what Joseph thought was the problem. Sid's prick was bigger than his. I've always thought that Joseph's prick was the prettiest prick I'd ever seen, with its gentle upward curve and soft-domed head, but Sid's – straighter and more cylindrical – was longer and thicker. Joseph was thinking that the bigger prick shouldn't be the one trying to get into my asshole.

So now I was facing Sid and the guys changed ports of entry and pushed. Sid's prickhead entered my pussy, and Joseph's prickhead squeezed into my asshole and . . .

. . . went nowhere. Nothing. No difference.

By now I was going crazy. With the head of Sid's prick pushing against my clit and Joseph's prick creating all this pressure from behind and me wiggling against them both, I writhed with want.

"Do something!" I shouted with a sob cracking my voice, and when he heard that, sweet Joseph rolled out of the way, making room for me to flop onto my back and pull Sid on top.

Sid fucked me – slid his prick in all the way and went to town. God, I was hot. I thrashed, I bounced, I gripped Sid's skin, I lifted my ass up to welcome every thrust of his fat prick as it pounded my pussy.

"Goddamn it, fuck me!" I commanded, and Sid did.

But Sid didn't forget about Joseph, and why we'd gotten into bed. After a minute or two of mad, almost combative fucking, he grabbed me by my ass-cheeks and turned over onto his back, pulling me on top of him. Fine; this was just as good, I was just as happy being the principal fucker, staked on Sid and pumping like a piston, lifting my hips and plunging downwards to swallow him up – but as I did, Sid, still mindful of our purpose and still holding my ass, spread my cheeks apart. I felt Joseph get behind me, straddling Sid's knees, and try to place his cock between my buttocks. I could tell this was not going to work, the angle was all wrong, so I lay down flat on Sid and spread my legs out as far as I could on either side of him and Joseph flattened himself against me on my back and placed his prick at my asshole and pushed.

"Yes!" I gasped as my sphincter gave way and the head of Joseph's prick entered and started in deeper. Success at last!

Not! Just as Joseph's cockhead started into my ass, I spit him out.

I didn't mean to. The trouble was, I was too far along in the fucking to stop. Sid was under me, his cock all the way inside; when Joseph laid down on my back he trapped me, and I couldn't keep sliding my cunt up and down along the length of Sid's prick. My body couldn't stop fucking, though, so my instincts took over, and I continued fucking Sid by gripping and releasing his cock with my pussy, contracting my pelvic muscles and clenching my ass – clench, release, clench, release.

Every time I'd clench my ass, I'd expel Joseph's prick. It was prick in, clench, plip!, prick out, release, prick in, clench, plip!, prick out . . .

After several plips, Joseph said, "Fuck!" and climbed off.

Though I was trembling by now, close to coming, Sid and I were confused for the moment, and Sid scampered out from beneath me.

"No! No!" Joseph snapped at us. "Go! Go! Fuck her!"

I was on my knees. "Come on, come on!" I cried out, and Sid got on his knees behind me and put his cock under my ass; I reached for it between my legs and grabbed it and stuffed it into my cunt and said, "Yeah, fuck her!"

I put my head down on my forearms and shut my eyes tight and rammed my ass back to take Sid's driving prick. Joseph was standing by the side of the bed, watching us fuck. It must have been a magnificent sight, my ass high off the bed, Sid's big prick appearing, shiny wet from my soaked pussy, then disappearing back into my cunt. I knew we were providing audio to match, Sid's grunts and my cries in rhythm with the gooey-gushy sounds of prick-through-cunt and slapping flesh. We were giving Joseph a great show, but Joseph, I admit, was not in the forefront of my thoughts. This was a fabulous fuck, a heroic fuck, and my whole body was atremble; every stroke of Sid's prick sent signals to every nerve-end in my body, and the signals were getting hotter and I was going to come and when I came I was going to explode.

And when I was close my eyes fluttered open, and what they saw was Joseph standing there by the bed, by my head, watching, his erection fading. Though I was on the brink of the orgasm of my life and knew it, I couldn't help myself: I reached out for Joseph's cock, drew him down to the bed, and took his cock in my mouth.

Sid banged against my buttocks, froze, and shot.

I trembled around Sid's implanted prick and slid Joseph's prick through my hands into and out of my mouth.

Sid backed back, slammed into me again, shot again. I gurgled and sucked, blowing Joseph while the rest of me started to shudder with orgasm.

As Sid pumped the last of his cream into my pussy, Joseph came. I swallowed some, some shot about, some slid down Joseph's prick and into my hands.

I came with Sid's soon-to-soften cock still inside my pussy and Joseph's cock beginning to shrink in my mouth. I held them there – Sid's with my fingers, Joseph's with my lips – until I was finished coming. After a series of quivery shudders, I collapsed flat on the bed, and got rid of them both.

We took a swim. It wasn't that late. We didn't talk about what we'd done, but I didn't feel we were awkward or tense. We were relaxed and gentle, kissy and touchy, enjoying the sexy afterglow.

Was I disappointed? Well, a little. The evening's promises had not been kept. The imminent orgasm of my life had been close – but downgraded when we'd had to make readjustments. And of course my dream of being fucked pussy and ass remained a fantasy unfulfilled.

I'd had good sex with two men, yes, but it had wound up with me on my hands and knees, one cock fucking me while I sucked another. Just like college . . .

I woke up during the night. I had my nightie on; Joseph and Sid were wearing their boxer shorts; both had their arms draped across me, kind of trapping me. I couldn't see the clock without pushing their arms away. I didn't care what time it was. What I cared about, what I lay there thinking about, was the opportunity we missed last night. It wasn't as though we squandered it – we tried, didn't we? – but still I wondered if I wanted to let it go. Somehow I knew that we wouldn't have the opportunity again. Joseph and I would get married and have kids and I didn't know how much things would change. Fulfilling my fantasy probably wasn't even that important; it was just something I'd wanted to try, to do, to know I had done. Silly but . . .

All of a sudden I felt really determined. Lorna, this is your chance, don't blow it; important or not, do it.

I removed the guys' arms, climbed over Joseph, and got out of bed. I separated the Venetian blinds to look out. It was getting light; the sun would be up in a few minutes.

My gaze fell on my dressing table. It was an ordinary dressing table, lower than a desk or table, with a low stool in front and a mirror behind. I cleared everything off the top, then got a pillow off the bed, put it on the dressing table, folded it over the front edge. I looked in the drawers and found a small brown bottle of massage oil, put it on the table, then opened the slats of the Venetian blinds a little. Finally I found some music – a Chopin étude played on a synthesizer, schmaltzy but sexy – and put it on.

I leaned against the pillow on the dressing table and waited for the guys to wake up.

It didn't take long. The rising sun sent stripes of light into the room and across the guys, the music swelled, and Joseph's eyes opened and he saw me. He nudged Sid awake.

I smiled at them with both hands on my pussy, playing at my slit. When Sid and Joseph propped themselves up to watch, I lifted off my nightie and tossed it away. I poured oil into my hands and massaged my shoulders and tits, made them and my belly shiny, my eyes never leaving the guys. I soaked my pubic hair, found my slit, reached behind me with the other hand, found my asshole, and pushed.

Joseph and Sid couldn't take their eyes off me as my oily fingers disappeared into my pussy and asshole – masturbating, yes, but also preparing myself for them. They stroked themselves as they watched, pulled off their shorts, and showed me their cocks, which trembled with growth and hardness.

Presently I took my hands from inside myself and beckoned with a finger.

Joseph and Sid crossed to me. I stepped away from the table and put my arms around Joseph and kissed him, rubbing my oily front against him, massaging oil into his back and buttocks. I turned to Sid, kissed him too, then put my hands on his shoulders and backed him against the pillow on the dressing table. The table was low; Sid had to extend his legs wide as he rested his backside against the pillow. That's how I wanted him: halfway between standing and sitting, his erect cock lower than my hips.

I kneeled in front of Sid and held his prick in my two hands and stroked it. "We are going to love this, right?" I said, and took him in my mouth. The first thought I had was, *this is a big prick*. The size was more noticeable in my mouth than it had been in my cunt last night. I enjoyed it, though, and used my tongue to get even better acquainted with it, and when I stopped sucking it I got more oil and soaked Sid's prick with it, massaging it in. Then I rose to my feet, kissed Sid again, turned my back to him, placed his cock at my asshole, and pushed down.

"This is so good," I said, "so good, so good," and lowered my oiled ass onto Sid's oiled cock very, very slowly. I felt its hardness as I sank. Pressure, increasing pressure, more than pleasure, that was the feeling I was most aware of as more and more of Sid's prick filled my ass. When I had about half its length inside I gasped as the pressure took my breath away, but I said, "No, it's OK, it's OK," and put my hands back and gripped the front edge of the table on either side of Sid's hips and closed my eyes and continued pushing. The pressure was incredible. There were moments of discomfort and pain, but I held my breath and never stopped until every inch of Sid's prick was up my ass. When it was I exhaled and said "God." Neither Sid nor I moved.

I opened my eyes and smiled at Joseph. "Sid's cock is in my ass," I said, "all of it." And I reached for Joseph. He stepped between my legs. I took his cock in my fist and stroked it, spread oil on it, then placed the head at my nook.

"Fuck me, darling," I whispered, and Joseph pushed into my pussy. The deeper it went, the tighter it felt. It wasn't easy – but I wouldn't let Joseph stop. "Keep pushing," I chanted. "It's great, it's gonna be great, so great, I'm so full, so full up, it's so filling, keep pushing, keep filling . . ." And it was true; I felt so full and tight, and I wanted it, and I wouldn't let Joseph stop until the tip of his cock met the tip of Sid's cock on either side of the membrane inside me.

"So fuckin' full!" I sobbed, almost shouting the word *full*, and then I trembled. "Come on, fuck me!" I commanded, and I moved and Sid moved and Joseph moved, and their cocks started sliding in and out a little – not much; with two cocks in you, you can't pump the way you pump when you're fucking – but we got a rhythm, the guys sliding back together and pushing forwards together, prodding.

And then it did start – the greatness – and I began to feel everything, everything, not just the pressure but the weight and power of the pricks and the eagerness of my orifices – I could feel the ridges of their cockheads as they trailblazed through my gooey pussywalls and clingy asshole and the shapes and tumescence of their cocks as they filled me, packed me and plugged me, and I could hear myself chattering, softly and languidly at first, "Oh God, oh God, oh God, is this nice, this is so nice, oh I love it, oh God, it's so good, oh God, this feels so good, so nice." And as they thrust and backed off and thrust, my responses came faster and harder, I talked louder and faster, "Oh I just love this, I love it love it love it love it, do it do it, do it!" And we did. Forget greatness; greatness was transcended. Prick in my cunt, prick up my ass, my dream-come-true, fucked all over and fucked through-and-through, not just my pussy, not just my ass but everything; my intestines were being fucked, my belly, my brain. Pins and needles of pure pleasure oozed from my pores and made my skin tingle. I squeezed, I twisted, I fucked with my tits smashing into Joseph's chest; I fucked with my tongue shoving into Joseph's mouth; I fucked with my ass jamming my buttocks against Sid and twisting; I fucked body and mind and soul . . .

And then I lost it – or found it.

With a sound between a sob and a cry I lifted a leg and flung it around Joseph; then, without thinking, I lifted the other leg. I would have fallen except that Sid grabbed my ass and held me up and pushed me into Joseph; I clamped myself to Joseph, the back of my heels against his calves, my arms around his neck; I pushed back hard as I could against Sid and I squeezed, clenched and wrung my innards around the two pricks wholly buried inside me – and came – came with strange, almost animal growling sounds through clenched teeth. Pelvis, ass, cunt all contracted and shot stars through my body. I was out of control, I couldn't hold on, I flung my arms and legs outwards and bounced and trembled as if automatic rifle-fire were riddling me with pleasure bullets. My limbs flew and my torso banged and my skin buzzed, and I babbled a rat-a-tat-tat sound, part laughter, part choke, and part chant, "Fuck-fuck-fuck-fuck oh God fuck!" And then I screamed a real scream that shocked me when I heard it, but then I screamed again, froze, shuddered, trembled, dropped my legs back to the floor. I spasmed so hard I began to cramp, and I made noises I know I'd never made before, gurgling and groaning. I heard the *fuck-fuck-fucks* turn to *wait-wait-waits* because the cramping was catching up with the ecstasy, and then to *stop-stop-stops,* even though I was the one doing the moving, not the guys, and I had to make myself stop.

It took a while. Though I stopped wrenching myself around the guys' two pricks, my body continued spasming for a while, jerking and bucking, but finally the spasms became after-spasms, fewer and farther between, and I sank back and let it fade.

It was the orgasm of my life, the orgasm of the century, the orgasm of the millennium, maybe the orgasm of all time. The guys had been great – reading me right, really fucking me when I wanted to be fucked, letting me use them when I wanted nothing more than hard pricks. And when I came down from my orgasm, their pricks were still hard inside me, Sid's a guest up my ass, Joseph's at home in my pussy.

"God," I breathed. My breathing slowed, and I put my arms around Joseph again and held him and squiggled back against Sid. I don't know how long we stayed like that – it seemed a long time, though it couldn't have been, for the guys were still hard and implanted, and hard pricks in tight places can't stay still for too long. I felt them twitching inside me, and, God save me, I felt my inner walls fluttering around the pricks again and liking it.

It wasn't over yet.

I straightened up, slid one hand around under my soaking oily ass and found Sid's balls and pushed my other hand down between Joseph's greasy belly and mine and found his balls, and I took both sets of balls in my fingers and gripped them. "Now fuck me!" I barked, and squeezed. Sid and Joseph pulled back together and rammed in together.

"Faster!" I said. "Harder!"

They fucked me faster and harder, and this time, even given that there were two pricks, it was more like conventional fucking with a real fucking rhythm – in, back, pump, pump, fuckers and fuckee, fuck, fuck, fuck! It didn't take long; when I felt Sid climbing I commanded him not to hold back and he didn't; I squeezed his balls harder and he jolted and jerked and shot my ass full of his cream, and while Sid was still shooting Joseph thrust so hard the dressing table slammed against the wall and the mirror shook and I squeezed his balls and he let loose, filling my cunt with his cream, and I don't know who the hell was done coming or still coming when I came, a different kind of orgasm this time, more like a guy's orgasm – jerk-jerk-jerk and then a bigger, harder jerk, a huge Mighty-Mouse Here-I-Come-to-Save-the-Day finale with a big cry of triumph. And then, absolutely drained, I collapsed like a ragdoll between my men.

Sid and Joseph held me between them until they slipped out. Slid out, really. Don't even ask me about the liquids . . .

We slept till three o'clock in the afternoon.

So that's it. My fantasy fulfilled. It more than lived up to expectations. It was easily the greatest, most intense physical sexual experience I've ever had.

Occasionally Joseph and I relive the event. We recall the details; I tell him how I felt, he tells me how he felt, and every time we talk about it we get more deeply into the nuances of those feelings. We talk to turn ourselves on, and it always works.

Now and then Joseph fucks me in the ass, but not that often: it's always a novelty. Sometimes we do it when I have my period. Or when we're in Europe. There's no special reason for that: we're just in the mood for it in Europe.

Sid's with us in spirit then, but in body it's just the two of us.

Sitting Uncomfortably

Sarah Veitch

Model Tenants Incorporated had few rules, but the rules which it did have were strictly adhered to. Linda was told this when she applied for evening work there.

"Are you always punctual?" the interviewer asked.

Linda hesitated, then reminded herself that people invariably lied at interviews. "Oh, yes, Miss Breeson. I detest lateness in others," she replied, forcing her lightly-glossed lips into an amenable grin.

There was a silence. The interviewer seemed to be not so much looking *at* her as looking *through* her. Linda glanced at the desk and squirmed in her seat. "In fact, if anything I'm usually too early," she babbled on. "Sometimes I'm so punctual for my night class that I end up helping the tutor to arrange the chairs."

"At least you talk a lot," the older woman said drily. "That helps show potential burglars that the property is occupied. You can talk to yourself as much as you like while you work."

She went on to explain exactly what the *Model Tenants* agency did. "Basically you house-sit when a property's owners are away for a week or two. You only work for a few hours at a time so it's not too restricting, but you don't leave till another employee comes along to relieve you of your shift."

"And I just *sit* there?" Linda queried, unable to believe that she was to be paid so handsomely for so little output.

"Well, you switch lights on and off at irregular intervals. You put on the TV and radio in various parts of the house."

"Sounds like a home from home," the blonde girl joked. Again she saw that the vaguely masculine-looking interviewer wasn't smiling. Miss Breeson's demeanour spoke business, from the unadorned cut of her navy skirt suit to her feather-cut dark hair.

One week later Linda began her new evening job. It sounded foolproof. By day she worked her usual hours as a market researcher. By 6 p.m. she was ensconced in the otherwise unoccupied hotel or sprawling house. There she played music and switched on and off the conversational tapes and watched television. At midnight she went to bed. By 8 a.m. the next day one of the other guards arrived to start the day shift, and Linda left the house in his or her capable hands.

But excitement soon turns to apathy. Newness dulls into routine. After a few nights Linda was bored with looking at the oil paintings and Chinese statues she was supposed to be guarding. She wanted dancing, drinking, life. She could sneak out of the back door and hurry along to the Mon Ami Club for an hour, she told herself, brightening. Her best friend worked in the cocktail lounge there. If she kept the lights on in the house and left her car outside then potential burglars would never know she'd sneaked away.

She went. The music was soft but the drink was harder. The hour stretched into two hours, as it usually does when you're having fun. Half-laughing to herself as she remembered her friend's gossip, Linda eventually returned to the Tudor-style house. Quietly she let herself in the triple-locked front door and strolled nonchalantly into the living room – then she screamed.

Miss Breeson sat there on the long leather couch. She was staring off into the middle distance. "You've let the firm down badly, my dear. You'll have to be punished," she said.

"Miss Breeson! I didn't mean to . . . I . . . em . . . had a headache so went for a walk," Linda muttered faintly.

"If a guard needs to leave the house there's a procedure to follow, as you well know," her boss replied.

The drill involved phoning Head Office to ask for a replacement guard to be sent. Linda cleared her throat. "I . . . uh . . . didn't think about the rules for a few moments."

"And *Model Tenants* doesn't employ unthinking people. I'll have your P45 ready by next weekend."

Linda stood, dismayed, in the centre of the room. She stared at her boss's somewhat Teutonic features. She'd heard rumours that the woman was attracted to slim fair-haired girls like herself. Now she wondered if a little flirtation would make all the difference. She had to keep this job.

Slowly she sidled over to the elongated couch, shrugged her jacket and shoes off, then sat next to the older woman, thigh side to thigh side. Her sand-washed silk dress looked very girlish beside MissBreeson's black denim suit

"I'd love to make amends," Linda whispered ambiguously.

"In that case," the older woman retorted, "get that disobedient young arse over my knee."

There was a pause, an even more awkward pause than Linda remembered from her interview. The woman had unnerved her then – but she was positively shaming her now!

"You mean you're going to . . . ?" she started, but couldn't bring herself to add the words "spank me".

"I'm going to turn your arse the colour of a Macintosh Red apple," Miss Breeson replied.

Linda stared at the carpeted ground. She tried to think of some clever wordplay about fruit but her imagination failed her. Instead, she began playing desperately for time. "How about if you give me extra unpaid shifts?" she asked.

"You're incapable of meeting your current work tasks, so I hardly want to entrust you with extra hours," her employer answered.

"Dock my wages, then, Miss?"

"Either you accept that this is your *last* wage or you bare your bum."

Another laboured silence ensued. Linda looked at her boss's firm hands. She looked at the hem of her own silk dress and imagined it being lifted. She tried to remember which panties she had on.

"Just a . . . a few smacks and I keep my job?" she queried breathlessly, trying not to picture such a scenario.

"Just two well-thrashed cheeks and you get to continue working for me," Miss Breeson confirmed.

Linda knew that she really needed this evening job. It had lifted her out of debt and was indeed now providing luxuries. And how many people got paid to live in wonderful Tudor-style houses filled with intricate antiques?

"All right," she said in a dazed small voice. Then she quivered as the stronger woman rolled both her sleeves up and pulled Linda over her dauntingly muscular knee.

For a few moments she lay there breathing heavily as her employer told her how bad she'd been and stroked her dress-sheathed buttocks.

"I'd like you to answer 'Yes, ma'am,' when appropriate," Miss Breeson added sternly.

"Yes, ma'am," Linda muttered, gritting her teeth with humiliation. Her face burned at the thought of the spanking which was to ensue.

Miss Breeson was obviously thinking of the spanking too. Leastways she said, "Let's lift this skirt up." Linda closed her eyes more tightly as she felt the lower half of her dress being lifted away from her bottom and thighs. It was a warm August night so she wasn't wearing any stockings. Now all that there was between this woman's hard palm and her own soft bum was her lace-edged flimsy pants. "After the skirt goes up, the pants come down," the older woman continued matter-of-factly. The 25-year-old skulked ashamedly on her tummy as she felt her briefs being dragged down her thighs.

"Mmm, quite a spankable looking spread," Miss Breeson continued, hoisting Linda's backside more firmly onto her lap. "It's small, but those little round cheeks are nicely fleshy in the centre." She fondled both spheres as she spoke, and Linda groaned. "Ask me to spank this bum hard if you value your employment," the forty-something woman continued. Linda forced out the words then moaned some more. An hour ago she'd been laughing and dancing at a club – now she was across this woman's lap with a totally bare bottom. Her only consolation was that no one else could see.

But she herself could certainly feel. She gasped as a heavy palm lashed down on one fair cheek. She was just recovering her breath when the woman smacked her other pale round buttock. Linda automatically reached her hands back to protect herself as the woman started up a veritable tattoo.

"Ah, ow, that hurts!" she muttered, trying to pull her employer's hands away. Those same hands caught her wrists and brought them together behind her back.

"I'd hoped that you'd be obedient," Miss Breeson said softly, "but as you're not I'll have to tie your naughty hands out of the way."

"But that hurts my shoulders!" Linda protested as the woman started to wind something round both wrists, thus imprisoning her hands above her buttocks.

"I'll tie your hands in front, then," the older woman said conversationally. "The only thing I want to hurt is your bum."

She half-lifted Linda and set her on the floor, then took hold of her arms and tied them loosely before her. "That's better," she said with obvious satisfaction. "Now we won't have any little fingers trying to shield those naughty globes."

"Please don't make the other spanks so hard," Linda pleaded piteously as her boss hauled her over her firm knee again. Her rotundities trembled.

"When you've failed in your work duties and potentially brought my firm into disrepute? I have to make the remaining spanks very harsh indeed."

Miss Breeson raised her palm. Linda buried her face in the leather couch. She wished that her bum wasn't such a vulnerable target. She howled as her employer began to whack alternate buttocks again. "Oh, please," she spluttered, writhing helplessly on her silken belly. She kicked the little she could with her equally bare slim legs. Why didn't Miss Breeson fondle her breasts or peek at her blonde-haired pudenda? Why was she so obsessed with beating her disarmed writhing bum? Linda moved her hips from side to side. She pressed her belly into the ungiving lap beneath her. She tried to pull in her buttock muscles to make each cheek a smaller target, but to no avail.

Then suddenly Miss Breeson stopped. "I think this arse and I should have a little chat," she said coolly.

Linda nodded, then uttered a belated. "Whatever you want."

"Is the arse sorry that it left its post without permission?" the older woman murmured.

"Oh yes, ma'am," Linda said. She searched for the words which would grant her release from her supine state. "This bad bum is truly humbled and will never again leave a house it's supposed to guard."

"I'm glad to hear it," Miss Breeson said matter-of-factly. "Now we just have to punish it for its earlier lies."

Linda felt her heart sink. Her reddened hemispheres jerked of their own volition. They were already invested with a rosy glow.

"What lies did I tell, ma'am?" she whispered raggedly.

"That arse lied about having a headache," her employer retorted, "when in truth it went to a nearby club."

"You watched me?" Linda asked weakly, knowing that her bottom was in for a further warming.

"Of course I did. We at *Model Tenants* have to keep a firm eye on our trainees," the dominant woman replied. She reached for a plump cushion and pushed it under the younger girl's lower tum. "Let's get that backside raised to its very utmost."

"Please have mercy," Linda whispered, puckering up her anguished flesh.

But her boss seemed to have a pre-determined number of spanks in mind. Leastways she whacked at Linda's lower curves and at her middle cheeks, ignoring her gasped-out promises that she would do better. She spanked the dark divide of the girl's posterior. She smacked the delicate fold at her nether thighs.

"I'll do anything, ma'am," the failed house-sitter whimpered, tensing and untensing her smarting bare bottom.

"Do you mean that, girl?" the older woman replied.

She stayed her hand. Linda's brain raced with scenes. If she pleasured her boss she might get extra weekend shifts and become her favourite. And it was probably as easy to rub another woman to orgasm as it was a man.

"Yes, ma'am. I long to please you," she said gutturally. Then she whimpered with relief as she was hoisted from her boss's imprisoning lap.

Linda stayed crouched on the floor waiting for her employer to untie her hands. Instead, Miss Breeson just pulled off her own jeans and briefs then opened her strong legs widely.

"Lick thoroughly, dear," she said.

Linda stared at the pinkish-brown folds of skin. The woman's labia was darker than her own, the lips longer. Her clitoris was peeking from its hood. "I've never . . ." she admitted faintly, rocking back on her heels.

"I hope that you're not reneging on your word? You said that you wanted to please me," the forty-something woman murmured. She reached forwards and squeezed the younger girl's tenderized spheres. Linda gasped at the pain and jiggled about on the carpet, then she put her open wet mouth to her employer's oiled flesh . . .

For the next few weeks the *Model Tenants* agency had a model house-sitter who turned up for work early and who never went out. She earned herself extra shifts until she was house-sitting every spare moment. It was lucrative. It was uncomplex. Until she met Nick.

Nick looked and smelt like one of those tanned muscular men in an aftershave ad. He sat next to Linda at the bar and desire traced its paths through her wanton flesh. After a double gin she made it clear that she was a single girl in search of communal pleasure. They danced and flirted all night.

"Let me take you to dinner on Saturday," he suggested at the end of the evening as he called her a cab.

"I'd love to, but I'm house-sitting," Linda murmured.

"Next week then, please?" he pressed. She loved the fact that he cared enough to pursue her – but she was house-sitting the next week and the next. "In that case," Nick continued, "why don't I come to you? I'll order from that *Home Comforts* place in the high street. They supply the champagne, the crockery and the meals."

"Sounds idyllic," Linda said. In truth house-sitters weren't supposed to have guests on the premises. But no one would ever know.

He came. He stayed. She was deliciously conquered. She could still feel the memory of his manhood inside her when she opened the door to Miss Breeson the next day.

"You broke the rules by entertaining here," the older woman said.

Linda swallowed hard, but knew better than to deny it. "I've known him for years," she lied. "He brought us both a meal."

"He also took a Victorian jewellery box belonging to the lady of the house," Miss Breeson informed her.

"He wouldn't do that. He was so nice," Linda said, her voice rising to something resembling a wail. She realized belatedly that con-men *had* to be nice in order to fool people. Maybe he'd even known that she was a house-sitter and had followed her to the club?

She was still musing over the situation when Miss Breeson marched into the lounge and turned on the security tape. The film showed Nick sneaking into the house's dressing room at 3 a.m. and taking the jewellery box.

"I assume that he was gone when you got up?" Miss Breeson asked.

"Well, yes," Linda muttered, still unable to believe that she'd been duped so easily. "But he left a note saying that he would phone me tonight."

"The police picked him up as he left here. The only phone call he'll be making is to his solicitor," the older woman said abruptly. She sighed. "It's lucky that the guard in Head Office was reviewing all the in-progress tapes and saw Nick actually stealing the valuables. Otherwise he'd have gotten well away."

Linda knew when she was beaten – or when she was about to be. "Are you going to spank me again, ma'am?" she asked in what she hoped was a seductive little voice.

Her boss shook her head. "The spanking obviously wasn't severe enough so I'm going to have to cane you. Be at the training hall for 8 p.m."

At 6 p.m. Linda had a bath. By 7 p.m. she'd eaten a light meal and put on her tightest blue jeans and a classic white polo shirt. She wanted to look neat yet casual. She wanted the thick denim to protect her bottom if her boss chose to cane her over her jeans. The younger girl feared the prospect of the rod lashing down on her helpless buttocks, but she was endlessly grateful that Miss Breeson hadn't handed her over to the police. After all, she'd let a virtual stranger into a house filled with near-priceless belongings. They might consider her an accessory to the crime.

Crime led to punishment. So be it. Determined to accept her caning with good grace, Linda drove nervously to the spacious training hall where *Model Tenants Incorporated* trained its employees. She was very aware of her small hips pushing into the car's driving seat. Would she soon need a cushion under these same haunches? An ex-boyfriend had been caned at public school, and he'd said that it cut like hell . . .

Cut it out, she told herself, parking outside the *Model Tenants Incorporated* facility. She walked slowly along the corridors till she reached the training hall. After taking a deep breath, she walked through the door – and abruptly stopped. Miss Breeson stood just inside the hall, but there were twenty men and women sitting in the seats around the arena. Peering closer, Linda recognized three. "Meet your contemporaries," her boss said. "They are all here because they've broken the rules, like you."

Linda licked her lips. "You mean we're going to watch each other being . . . You'll chastize me in front of them?"

"I've found it helps to drive the message home," her employer said. She swished something lightly against her military-style khaki trousers and for the first time Linda saw that she was holding a rattan cane.

Lost for words, the 25-year-old looked around the well-lit room. There was a piece of wooden apparatus in the centre.

"Meet your punishment rack," said the older woman, following her gaze.

"You mean we . . . get strapped in there?"

"Well, *you* do."

"And get caned in front of everyone?"

"Only everyone who is here," her boss confirmed. She paused. "Remember, your audience is comprised of fellow wrongdoers, so they're unlikely to tease you. My other eighty employees have an exemplary record and will never hear of this day."

Linda looked at the rod again. It was wickedly long and thin with a thicker curved handle.

"Couldn't you cane me in private, then I could please you with my tongue again?" she asked in a soft low voice.

"Private humiliation obviously wasn't enough. I need to set an example," the forty-something woman answered. "Go to the punishment rack now and take down your jeans."

"And if I don't?" Linda muttered, her cheeks flaming.

"If you don't I'll inform the police that you aren't fit to be a house-sitter, and you can leave my employ right away."

She loved the job. She liked the evening hours. She adored the money. Resignedly Linda walked towards the wooden contraption, Miss Breeson in her wake. Every one of the watchers leaned forwards. Linda realized that when she got onto the rack they would all be facing her helplessly raised small rear. She couldn't let them see it being exposed or let them stare at its naked trembling. She couldn't bear them watching it take on the sizzling red lines of the cane.

"Just one thing – I get to keep my jeans and pants on," she said fiercely.

Miss Breeson put her head to one side. "Well, for now you can keep your pants on." She looked at the punishment rack then back at the girl. "That is, as long as you don't try to touch your punished arse."

"And if I do?" Linda muttered, fearing that she already knew the answer.

"If you do I'll have to cane you harder on the bare."

Linda nodded. She'd show the woman that she was made of sterner stuff. She'd take her thrashing without a whimper. Marshalling her courage, she stepped forwards and clambered awkwardly onto the unpolished long oak rack. "There are straps for the miscreant's ankles and wrists, but we'll only use the ankle ones, seeing as you've promised to control yourself," her boss said evenly. Moments later Linda felt soft thongs pinioning her lower legs. She put her face down in the velvet-lined hollow that was obviously custom built for just this purpose. Miss Breeson adjusted the machine and a bolster pushed up Linda's tummy to its fullest extent. She closed her eyes with shame and a low spread of desire as she felt the woman tugging her jeans to below her knees.

Miss Breeson walked around the rack and stroked Linda's

blonde hair for a moment. Next she turned towards the back of the room, obviously addressing the rest of her staff.

"Linda failed to protect one of the properties she was house-sitting. Then she let a stranger into another house," she said. "She's opted for corporal punishment rather than for dismissal. Be aware that you may meet the same fate."

"What do you mean that they *may?*" Linda muttered, twisting her head round to stare at her boss in panic. "I thought that I was just the first wrongdoer? I thought we were all to be caned?"

"No, they are all on their first warnings. They're only here to witness your own bum turning scarlet," Miss Breeson said.

God, the shame! Linda closed her eyes and mouth, and tried to close her mind to her increasing indignity. Then she sensed that Miss Breeson had pulled her arm back, and automatically tensed her bum in readiness for the first smarting stripe. She lay there in an agony of anticipation. Behind her one man whistled and a second man laughed.

"How many do you think you deserve?" her employer queried.

"Six?" Linda asked nervously.

"Let's make it twelve, seeing as you're getting to keep your knickers on," the older woman parried. "That is, unless you touch your arse."

She wouldn't touch her rump no matter how much this hurt. She just wouldn't. Linda summoned up all her willpower and clutched the front of the rack. Then she yelled, her voice trembling, as the first stroke made contact somewhere near centre of her pantied orbs. Linda cried out and her bottom jerked almost of its own volition. Then Miss Breeson announced that it was time for stroke two.

This stroke went lower than the first, though it felt as if it were parallel to it. Again, there was little protection in her cotton briefs. Forgetting that she'd promised to stay in control, Linda writhed upon the bolster. This time her fingers began to leave the front of the rack. Remembering just in time that she mustn't protect herself, she put her hands back in situ and waited breathlessly for the third corrective lash.

"Now where shall we put this one?" her merciless boss

asked. Linda had some suggestions, but they were too rude to mention. Instead she lay there trying to psych herself up for the next taste of the cane. It soon fell further up her spheres, and seemed to go slightly diagonal. "Stop wriggling, girl, I like a nice still canvas," Miss Breeson said.

"But it hurts," Linda moaned, twisting back her head to look at her employer.

"Of course it hurts. It's meant to ensure that you become a better employee," the woman said.

"Couldn't I just go on a course?" Linda murmured. Then she howled as her boss swished the rod twice in quick succession across her curved expanse. Beyond thought, she reached back her hands, spreading her fingers out and rubbing desperately at her punished buttocks. "Oooooh!" she moaned.

A few seconds later she realized what she'd done and quickly moved her palms back to the front again. Miss Breeson marched around and lightly bound her wrists in place. "What a pity that you disobeyed me," she said softly. "Now I'm going to have to pull down those pretty pants."

Bent over the ungiving punishment rack, Linda bit her lip. Her twin globes tried to cringe away from the humiliation to follow. Her colleagues were about to see her naked cheeks.

Miss Breeson seemed to be savouring the moment to the full. She walked slowly towards Linda's knicker-clad orbs, which were raised like a sacrifice upon the bolster. She traced the sore cane-marks through the taut white cotton, then she repeated the taunting touch again and again. "What a wonderful heat, " she murmured with obvious relish. "I hope they look as adorably red as they feel."

She seemed to take her time pulling the blonde girl's panties down. Linda groaned with shame and wriggled her sore hindquarters. "Easy," Miss Breeson murmured. "You aren't going any place till you've had seven more of the cane."

"I don't know if I can bear it," the 25-year-old murmured plaintively, trying to suck her nether cheeks in closer to the bolster.

"I've already bared it for you, sweetheart," her employer said.

Linda quaked as she felt the older woman pulling her briefs

to below her knees. She quivered as her glowing pained stripes were fondled. "They're a lovely scarlet shade, my dear. It's just a pity that some of the bands have merged into others. I wish that I could create separate parallel lines." She palpated the sore globes some more. "Oh, well, I suppose that all I need is practice. Maybe next time you're bad?"

Linda promised herself inwardly that she'd never be disobedient again. This caning would be her first one and her last. It was hellish being displayed like this, her red haunches exposed for all to see. She wanted so much to put her jeans back on or at least hold her helpless chastened cheeks.

But these same soft cheeks still had to endure seven more strokes of the rod. Miss Breeson ordered her to count them. "Thank you for stroke six," she gasped belatedly as the first of the thrashings on the bare whacked down. Her poor bottom puckered up then relaxed then puckered again as it tried to anticipate when the next stroke was due.

The strong-armed Miss Breeson took her time. She seemed to know exactly how to keep a nervous backside waiting. Linda sensed that she'd raised her muscular arm. In turn, the younger girl tensed her bottom. Eventually her buttock muscles tired and she had to let them relax again. The second that her bum returned to smooth-bottomed splendour she felt the cane bite harshly into both lower cheeks. She made a sort of yodelling sound, shoving her belly into the bolster as far as she was able.

"I don't hear you counting the stroke and thanking me for it," her employer said.

"Thank you for the seventh stroke, ma'am," Linda muttered into the velvet hollow. She shivered with shame and a low deep pleasure as the older woman fondled her upturned bum.

"Ask prettily for the eighth," the woman prompted.

Linda hesitated and sucked in her breath.

"Can I be the one to lay it on?" a hoarse man shouted.

Reminded of her audience, the blonde girl skulked upon the punishment rack with additional shame. Just five more strokes, she reminded herself. Five more and it would be over – hell, schoolboys took more than this. She'd get to keep this job with its attractive wage.

"Ma'am, I'd appreciate receiving stroke eight," she whispered, anxious that the man who'd spoken wouldn't lay the rod on. The thought of a male colleague whipping her bum was even more hateful than the thrashing which was already taking place. "Ma'am, please apply stroke eight to my rear end," she repeated as the worrying silence stretched and stretched.

"Oh, you can plead for it more nicely than that," her employer said. Linda hesitated, not wishing to degrade herself further. "Perhaps Thomas will change your mind?" Miss Breeson asked.

"No – don't let him. I'll ask really sweetly," Linda forced out. She squirmed as she thought up the words. "I . . . I've been a reckless little girl, ma'am. I've got a naughty bottom. It deserves to . . ." She choked back a sob. "Deserves to feel the cane on the bare."

"It does, doesn't it?" the forty-something woman said. "It really needs it."

Linda howled as she tasted the thin hard rod again. The blonde girl asked equally obsequiously for the ninth stroke, but her imagination and courage faltered when it came to asking for the tenth. "I'll have to give *two* swishes of the cane in the same place if you fail to please me," her employer murmured, stroking her flesh.

Linda moaned at her words and actions. "Please, no! I want . . . My backside's really red."

"Tch, tch," the woman said. "You're not sounding servile enough. You're really not trying." She laid on two gentler strokes above Linda's thighs.

They still stung and Linda moved her bum powerlessly about for what felt like hours. Finally she settled down.

"One to go," the woman said. "Now, I can cane you further up where the flesh is relatively unscathed, or I can make you taste the rod in that hugely sensitive place you've just experienced."

"Oh, please, ma'am, do it further up, " Linda said.

"I don't hear you asking nicely," her employer prompted. She traced the cane along the twice-caned area until Linda begged.

"I . . . I've got the sorest arse in Christendom," she said thickly. "It's so hot and red that I can hardly bear it." She sniffed loudly, then made herself continue, "But I know it needs to take one more swishy stroke so that I never lie to my employer again."

"And should that stroke be hard?" Miss Breeson teased.

"Very hard,'" Linda forced out piteously.

"You're pleading nicely now," the older woman said thoughtfully, "but I'd like to hear you beg."

There was a pause. "I beg to taste the cane," Linda said.

"Then lift your bum further up for me," her employer countered. Snivelling with shame, Linda pushed her lower body up the little she could.

"I beg you to cane me hard, ma'am," she repeated tearfully.

Her boss drew back her arm and obliged. This time the rod fell further up the blonde girl's tethered bottom. Linda let her body sag against the bolster with long-awaited relief.

An hour later Miss Breeson sent Linda home, having promised that she could keep working for *Model Tenants*. When Miss Breeson herself got home she saw that her younger brother was there

"Have fun?" he asked.

"Lots of fun," Miss Breeson answered. Her labia was still tingling from her employee's obsequious tongue.

"Linda's got a great arse, doesn't she?" the younger man continued. "I kept looking at it the whole time I was making love to her," he added with a knowing grin.

Miss Breeson smiled brightly at her ever-helpful brother.

"She does indeed, Nick," she said. She paused. "I'm through with Linda for now, but maybe next week you can start checking up on young Mandy. She's supposed to be guarding the Riverside Hotel but I'm sure she'd break her curfew if you asked her for a date."

Greek Fever

Anne Tourney

There weren't many men in my Bible Belt town who practised Greek love. One of the few was my father, Simon. The other was Gabriel, who was posing as our live-in handyman. My father believed that Gabriel, with his charmed hands and cock, could fix anything from a sinking roof to a rusted libido. I didn't believe anything about Gabriel except for one promise he made to me. And that was only because I had wrestled my lust into something resembling faith.

Simon and I had Greek fever that summer. We staggered around with Greece on the brain, the light of Athens burning our bodies from inside. But while Simon retreated into his fever like a trance, I was planning to act on my affliction.

My father didn't know that I was going to Greece with his lover.

Gabriel told me what to pack: only enough clothes for sunbathing, drinking, and fucking. We could have done all those things in Oklahoma, but in Greece, Gabriel said, you could turn a life of lazy horniness into a personal philosophy. In the town of Pawsupsnatch (pop. 3,007) that kind of slutty behaviour was just another reason for people to gossip about you.

The gossip would have turned into mass hysteria if the citizens of Pawsupsnatch had known what went on in our house. On my days off, Gabriel fucked me. Nights, he made love with my father. In the darkness, soft groans would drift from

Simon's locked bedroom. During the day Gabriel and I would tear the house apart as we banged our way from room to room, knocking over furniture and denting the walls. Terrified of the Baptists who ran our local drugstore, I made secret trips to Tulsa to buy condoms by the trunkload. Considering Simon's social status as a widowed high school teacher, I assumed he was doing some smuggling himself. After twelve years of exile, the spectre of sex had swooped back into our home, and that spectre was pissed-off and ravenous.

"It's your turn, Aggie," Gabriel would murmur, starting things off with moth-wing kisses on the nape of my neck. His lips would buzz my ears while his arms roped my waist from behind. I'd burrow back into the muscular cradle of his torso until I felt his cock rise against my ass cheeks. I started wearing short, flimsy skirts so he could get to my pussy with his fingers, cock, or tongue whenever the urge seized us. Betraying my father felt like stepping barefoot on a rusty tin can – agonizing and thrilling and toxic – but I couldn't help myself. When I came with Gabriel, mighty spasms cored my body, leaving me raving and senseless. I didn't have orgasms; I had seizures.

"I could fall in love with you in Greece," Gabriel once told me. Now that summer's long gone, I know he must have told my father the same thing.

At first I couldn't stand to hear Gabriel and Simon making love. My father's celibacy was a given part of the deal we made when I put my life in deep-freeze so I could look after him and his feeble heart. I knew he fell in love now and then and that, since my mother died, he'd given up the struggle to love women. I must have known that his abstract love for men could translate into sex. I just never thought it would happen in my mother's bed.

My mother and father had always been discreet in their passion. As a child I never wondered how they made love, but whether they "did it" at all. At the age of 28, I wasn't prepared for this variation on the primal scene: my father having sex – intense, audible sex – with another man. My mind reeled. I wrote down a list of words to describe what two naked men might get up to, then I repeated those words until they lost their mystery. *Fellatio, sodomy, cornholing, cocksucking.* The throaty male voices taunted me, their moans melting and swirling like butter and bittersweet chocolate. Rituals went on behind that door that I couldn't visualize. Did they kiss with open lips and tongues? Did they rub their erections together, like two scouts trying to start a fire with a pair of sticks? Did they suck each other's cocks with juicy abandon as they lay coiled in bed, each lover's heart thumping against the other's belly? Did they mount each other, penetrate and thrust?

From the shouts and pleas that rang through the house at night, I imagined they did all that and then some.

After Gabriel had been with us for a week, my fascination took on a harder edge. In my sexual starvation, I hallucinated that Gabriel was moving on top of me, and that the moans echoing through the walls came from my own lips, not my father's. My body ignored all taboos and began responding to the urgent sounds. My fingers stabbed my cunt in time to the squeaking bedsprings. I imagined Gabriel's mouth on my pussy, my mouth on his prick, our hands roving over each other's sweat-slick skin. In the daylight, I was mortified by the idea of being aroused by my father's lovemaking. But as I witnessed Simon's growing joy, I realized that the man sharing a bed with Gabriel was no longer just my father. With Gabriel, Simon was transformed into the man he was meant to be.

That's when I let myself start wanting Gabriel. I not only wanted him, I deserved him.

He came to us in June. Tornado weather – the sky was swollen with its own miserable promise. The air in the house felt as dead as dough that won't rise. Simon and I were reading on the front porch.

As soon as Gabriel stopped his battered Dodge and stepped out, my father and I were lost. We gaped as he strolled around the car, his hips rolling in frayed blue jeans. The tips of his savannah-blond hair were painted with sweat. His white cotton T-shirt sucked lovingly at his damp chest. A halo of black gnats circled his face and throat. Suddenly I wanted more than anything to be one of those miniscule insects, sipping at that man's juice, stinging, biting, living a flash of a life in the warmth of his body.

"Morning," he said. "Need any odd jobs done around here?" His voice was like his looks: bronzed, sun-creased, lubed with honey. In the bilious daylight his eyes were snake green.

Odd jobs? In a household consisting of a lonely, horny librarian; her lonelier, hornier father; and about three thousand books (half of them written in dead languages) I'd say there were a few odd jobs to be done. Yes, sir.

My father rose and walked down the front steps. Gabriel extended his hand (God, to think where that hand would end up that summer) and my father clutched it, for what seemed like forever.

"I think we could find you some work," Simon said.

Gabriel stayed for lunch. I prepared the food while my father and Gabriel got to know each other. As I carried the plates to the table, my father announced, "Gabriel just got back from Athens. Agatha, he lived there for a *year*. He speaks a bit of the *language*."

Around here, that just about made him Plato reincarnate.

Simon's face was a searchlight, casting its beam back and forth between me and Gabriel, but resting mostly on Gabriel. Barring death or disaster, there was no way this stranger was going to leave our house.

And he didn't. The first night, Gabriel made a nest for himself on our sofa. Early the next morning, while he was taking a shower, I went through his belongings. I found a few dirty socks and T-shirts and a wallet with nothing but seven dollars inside: no credit cards, no driver's licence. I held a shirt up to my nose and inhaled his smell, as dizzying as a stag's musk.

The water stopped running. I flung Gabriel's things back into a heap. I thought he would appear any second, padding barefoot into the living room. His brown body would be sparkling with moisture, his hair slicked back, water clinging to his nipples and welling out of his navel and trickling down through the dark gold tendrils that fanned his pubis.

From upstairs I heard voices: masculine, companionable, an intimate rumbling.

Love banter.

I buried my hand in the heap of quilts and felt no trace of warmth. Gabriel hadn't slept on this sofa; he'd slept in my father's bed. While I was trying to find out whether Gabriel was a travelling axe murderer, he and Simon had been showering together.

Over the nights that followed, as I lay in my bed listening to the ongoing seduction of my father, I developed a theory about Gabriel. I decided that Gabriel wasn't a man or a god, but a spirit who goes back and forth between the worlds, like the *daimon* of Greek myth. This spirit came over from Athens in some tourist's shopping bag, landed in the Bible Belt, and answered the cry for love that came from Simon and me. I never thought to analyze Gabriel's sexual preferences: whether he was gay, straight, or some hybrid of the two. From the first time I saw him, I knew that Gabriel could take on any shape you wanted.

Since my mother's death Simon had fallen in love a few times, but until Gabriel his loves were always wildly suppressed and embarrassing, like the crumb that gets stuck in your throat in a fancy restaurant. Simon had a disturbing tendency to fall for his students. He taught History and Driver's Ed at the high school, but long ago he had earned a Ph.D. in Classics, and he missed Ancient Greek with a pain that showed in his eyes. Every so often a male student would sidle up to him and confess that he wanted to read Sappho or Plato or Aristophanes in the original. Boom – Simon would be gone. He couldn't help it; Greek was the language he loved with.

This whole affair would have been easier if Gabriel had been one of my father's pupils, and my father had suffered with love for years, waiting for an illicit yearning to ripen into a legitimate romance when Gabriel came of age.

Nothing in our lives was ever that easy.

The first words Gabriel said to me outside of Simon's earshot were, "I love girls your age." The way he let the word "love" shimmy down his tongue, it sounded more like he wanted to say "crave".

It was late at night. Somehow, under the dense shelf of heat that had been building up all day, Simon had managed to fall asleep. Gabriel and I sat outside at the picnic table.

"How old do you think I am?"

"Stand up."

I stood.

Though I couldn't see Gabriel's eyes, I could feel him looking me up and down. My nipples stuck straight out and begged his eyes to linger.

"Eighteen?"

"I'm older than I look," I warned.

I wasn't about to admit that I was 28. My personal fashion profile hadn't changed much since I was 16, the year my mother died.

"Take off that top, and I could make a better guess."

I could sense Gabriel grinning in the darkness. He wasn't wearing a shirt himself. All day he'd worn nothing but a pair of cut-offs, so short that I could practically hear his balls chafing against the ragged hems. Spit crackled in my parched mouth.

"I'll take off my top if you answer a question," I said.

"What kind of question?"

"Does it matter?"

"Sure. If it's about the past, I won't answer it. And if it's about the future, I can't."

"Do you love Simon?"

Gabriel didn't answer. I longed to sit down again, to get back to the promising buzz that had risen between us. But I had to keep standing there, like a prosecutor waiting for testimony.

Then Gabriel asked me a question.

"Have you ever been to Greece?"

"No. I've never been anywhere."

"How come?"

I sat down again. "My father has heart trouble, so I've stayed close to home. After high school I got a job at the public library, and I've been there ever since."

When it came to life, I was a virgin in all but the old cock-in-the-hole sense. Hand me any book, and I could catalogue it even in a coma. I could find answers to questions about everything from ant hills to transvestism, but I sometimes woke up in the middle of the night, my heart galloping, and realized that I might die before I ever experienced cunnilingus.

"You should go to Greece, Aggie. You'd see things differently there. Simon knows what I mean."

"My father's never been to Greece, either."

"Even so, he understands me. He knows what I am."

"Do you think you might fall in love with him?"

Gabriel laughed. "I told you I couldn't answer questions about the future."

"If you don't love him, why are you here?"

"I like the way he stares at me when I'm naked. I like the way he touches me. And because I'm dead broke and he's letting me stay here for free."

I should have hated Gabriel for admitting that, but I didn't. I could see him in Greece, sunbathing naked in the rubble of a ruined temple, recharging his body in the light of an amoral sun. I could see myself there, too, emptied of everything but a desire for life. Free of taking care of Simon. Free of being Agatha.

"I want to go to Greece," I said.

"Me too. But I can't get there without any money."

"I have money."

"Sure, Aggie."

"I do! Not a fortune, but enough."

"Then we'll go," Gabriel said.

I believed him.

"You promise?"

"I promise," Gabriel said. "We'll go."

"When?"

"Whenever you're ready."

I didn't decide that night. I did my research, throttled my conscience, and decided we'd leave in September. By the time my father started the new school year, Gabriel and I would be in Athens. From there we'd travel to the islands whose names I murmured in my bed at night like incantations.

It started on a Monday morning. Simon was teaching summer school. Gabriel was mowing the lawn. I stood at the kitchen sink, sipping a glass of iced coffee and inhaling the fragrance of cut grass. I should have known something was up when the lawnmower's drone stopped.

"Aggie?"

I hadn't heard Gabriel enter the kitchen. Coffee spilled down my chin. The glass fell from my hand and shattered on the floor.

"Shit!" I grabbed a dishcloth.

Gabriel was on his knees, picking up the shards of glass. I knelt beside him. A ruby bead welled out of the pad of his thumb. I grabbed his hand and stuck his thumb in my mouth.

His thumb tasted of gasoline, grass, and the dangerous tang of blood. I closed my eyes and sucked at the digit as if it were a straw to his soul. I sucked greedily, drinking his experiences, his memories, the mysteries of his past. I didn't consider what I was doing until I opened my eyes and found him staring at me. His eyes were a clear, steady gold that morning. I could almost believe he was sincere when he said, "I could fall in love with you in Greece."

"I don't know if I could fall in love with you," I said, "but I sure as hell need to fuck you."

We stampeded upstairs like wild horses, tripping over each other to get to my bedroom, where we undressed in a mute frenzy. Naked, we slowed down for some sensual investigation. His skin was moist from working outdoors; my fingertips clung softly wherever they made contact. He cupped my breasts and suckled my nipples until I thought I'd cry from the keen joy. His hard-on nudged my thigh, but he wasn't in any rush to enter me. Instead he moved down, spangling my belly with kisses. A prayer took shape in my mind.

Oh, Lord, let him eat my pussy.

Oh, Lord, let this be better than that time in the truck with Hank Maples.

Then Gabriel was turning my cunt inside out like the cuff of a velvet sleeve, and his tongue was wandering through grooves I didn't know I had, places that hadn't been touched by anything more exotic than a washcloth. Gabriel's mouth had more tricks than a whole herd of circus ponies, and that morning he showed me all of them. The flutter. The clit-flicker. The figure eight, the labial lunge, the lick-out-the-slipper, the toad-in-the-hole. He licked me into a state I've only heard drug addicts talk about: a mindless, floating ecstasy.

The floating got turbulent when he started to suck on my clit. He slid one finger inside me, then two, then three, then an impossible four. Deeper his hand plunged. My body felt paralyzed from the waist down, except for the red zone between my thighs. I was wetter than I'd ever known a woman could be, until I hit my peak and unleashed a flood. My body arched so high that I could swear I saw Greece. While Gabriel rode me to his own climax, I watched a delirious light dance against a blinding blue sky.

After he fell asleep I explored him, inch by inch. Gabriel's skin was a map. His tan formed continents of bronze and seas of dusky rose. It was not the kind of tan you get working in an oil field or fishing for crappie. His body bore the imprint of ancient light.

But Gabriel wasn't interested in ancient light. He was more concerned with drinking beer and scamming free plane tickets and screwing outdoors. Yet in that sense, Simon would have said, he was as ancient as they come: the living, breathing soul of unreasoning desire.

As a teenager I'd read my father's copy of Plato's *Symposium*. Simon worshipped those dialogues; he'd have given his life to go back to ancient Athens and sit in on that dinner party with Socrates and his friends, drinking and laughing and talking about love. I didn't know what I was looking for in that book. Possibly a balm for the uneasiness I felt about my parents' marriage, or a map to the places Simon travelled in his mind when his body seemed so restless.

When I read what Diotima tells Socrates about love and procreation, my heart turned into a sack of wet cement. Love is creative, she says; it strives for immortality in different forms. A person can create with his body – have children with women, in other words – or reach for a more exalted love and produce children of the soul. It's the second kind of love that takes you from the physical to the spiritual plane, and finally earns you a ticket to see absolute beauty. I figured that second kind of love was what Simon secretly craved, what kept him awake at night, incapable of resting in my mother's bed.

I once asked my mother how she and Simon fell in love. She told me, for the hundredth time, the story of how they met. He was a graduate student in Classics, she was an English major who wrote poetry, both believed secretly in fate. Once they realized that they not only shared a passion for Plato, but had been raised in the same stultifying town, they started to see the handprints of destiny everywhere they looked. That same destiny brought me into being before they were married, and between my mother's longing for respectability and my insistent need to be fed, they went back to Pawsupsnatch to take reliable jobs at the high school and public library.

But that wasn't the information I wanted. I wanted a bulletin from the world of adult love, some succinct secret to the mystery of passion.

My mother took a long time to think about this. "In the beginning," she finally said, "we thought we were two halves of the same whole. Later we realized that we simply loved the same books. And we loved you, of course."

"You mean that was *enough*?" I squealed.

My mother looked at me, bemused. "Books and a child turned out to be plenty for me," she said.

When I was 16, my mother died of ovarian cancer. In some dirty nook of his conscience, I think Simon saw her death as the ultimate sign that he'd failed at love. Twelve years later Gabriel came along. My father didn't seem to care who he was, or what he wanted; he just clung to Gabriel's body as if it were the last lifeboat on a desolate sea.

Maybe Simon thought that at some point down the road, he would see absolute beauty through a drifter with hazel eyes and a brass ass.

The last week of August, I made dinner for Simon and Gabriel every night. Guilt stripped my appetite, but it made me want to cook like crazy. The china rattled in my hands as I set out the plates.

"Are you all right, Agatha?" Simon asked.

I saw something besides concern in my father's face, a plea, or a challenge: *Don't take him away from me,* or *Go ahead and try.*

"The catfish is terrific, Aggie."

Gabriel stuffed a forkful of fish into his mouth. He winked at me. I scowled and fussed with the napkin in my lap. An angry red lovebite marked the inside of my thigh. I had been coming when Gabriel gave me that bite. He had five fingers curved up inside my cunt like a funnel when he bit me in the softest part of my leg, and I went over the edge.

"Nothing like catfish fresh from the lake," my father said.

We had bought the fillets at Shop 'n' Save. Every time I lifted my fork I could smell Gabriel's musk on my hand.

That afternoon Gabriel stole a rowboat from the dock of someone's summer cabin, and we rowed out to the middle of the water. We had told Simon we were going fishing, but the only pole that came out on that expedition was about eight inches long.

We sprawled in the boat, our legs intertwined, and rubbed suntan lotion into each other's skin. If anyone had been watching, they might have wondered why we applied lotion mainly to the parts of our bodies that were covered by clothes. The ruddy head of his erection was nosing its way up through the waistband of his shorts, and the seat of my skirt was slippery with my arousal. My cunt must have known, even if my brain didn't, that life was going to take a peculiar turn in the next week. How else can I explain why I ordered Gabriel to eat me right there in the boat, instead of dragging him over to the sheltering trees along the lake's shore?

He grinned. "You don't care if we attract an audience?"

I growled, spread my thighs, and pushed him down.

Leaning back, I closed my eyes against the sun. Under the tent of my skirt, Gabriel's head bobbed as he tongued me. The boat rocked crazily, shivering with the pounding of my pulse.

"You've never been this turned on," Gabriel said, his voice muffled. "You're soaking wet."

"Shut up. That tongue wasn't made for talking."

But he was right; I'd never felt such a primitive, unselfconscious lust. The rude midday sun blessed us, the sexy waa-waa of the insect chorus mocked my sense of propriety, and I felt like the gods of desire were urging us on. I hooked a leg under Gabriel's thigh and applied a steady friction to his crotch. His cock, still trapped in denim, was a hot, dry bulge against my shin. Suddenly he groaned and pulled back. His spine arched. His body trembled. He bit down hard on my thigh as he thrust against my leg, spilling come onto the floor of the boat. I stared up into the sun as I climaxed, watching the light pulsate with my cunt's throb, knowing I could be bat-blind when it was over but not caring if I lost my sight.

Needless to say, the boat capsized. We had to slosh around the Shop 'n' Save like drowned rats to find our dinner.

If I'd known that would be the last time Gabriel made me come, I would have made him eat me till his jaw locked. I would have made him lick my pussy till his tongue bled.

Two days before we were supposed to go to Greece, I decided to leave work early and go home. I don't know why. I'd never had a premonition before, and I'd rather not have one again.

I found Gabriel crouched on the floor beside my bed. The mattress had been pushed back. His fingers shuttled rapidly; for a second I thought he was saying the rosary. But it wasn't beads he was handling; it was my money. I kept a cash hoard under my mattress, in case the bank ever got hit by a tornado.

Gabriel looked up.

"What are you doing?"

"Getting ready for our trip."

"Bullshit."

Gabriel clambered to his feet. His backpack dangled from one shoulder.

"Leaving already?"

"Yep."

"Without me?"

He sighed.

"Have you really been to Greece?"

"Sure," he said.

But I knew that even if he were telling the truth, Gabriel hadn't been to the Greece he'd promised me. He'd been to a scorched, sweaty place, crowded with disappointed tourists who couldn't find the Greece they'd imagined, either.

"Get out of here," I said. "Take the money and get out."

It took every ounce of willpower I had to say that. A rabid animal was clawing at my gut, frantic with need. Then there was Simon. I didn't even want to think about my father's fragile heart.

Gabriel let his backpack slide off his shoulder. I knew what was coming. He walked up to me, standing so close that his chest grazed my nipples. Wary as an animal tamer, he circled me with his arms, then let his hands settle on my waist. Through the fabric of my skirt his thumbs hooked my panties and slid them down. They slithered to the floor like something small and valueless drifting into murky water.

"One more time, Aggie," he said. "Let me fuck you one more time."

I unbuttoned his fly and pulled out his cock. He was already fully erect, as if my pain had turned him on. I didn't want that sorcerer's wand anywhere close to my core. I knelt and took him in my mouth. No seduction, no ceremony, just a hard, angry suck, the kind of release he might get from a stranger in a public restroom. I gripped the root of his shaft with one hand and tugged with my lips, letting my teeth scrape his skin. He yelped; I dragged harder. His body tensed.

I usually didn't swallow, but today I wasn't about to stop. I gripped his ass and drew him deeper than I'd ever taken him, so deep that I almost choked. For a moment he was absolutely still, then he bucked and yelled. I let him shoot his bitter sap down my throat, knowing it wasn't safe, but needing to memorize the flavour of his particular evil.

"I'll never forget the way you taste," I said when I had caught my breath, "you taste like a lie. Now get out."

Leaving, Gabriel didn't make a sound. I felt him depart, though. The *daimon*. The spirit who comes and goes between worlds.

After Gabriel left, I took a walk. I ended up walking all the way out to the lake where Gabriel and I had made love. I conjured my father's face in the water and rehearsed what I would say.

Gabriel's gone.

No, Daddy –

He's not coming back.

My father would know we were heading for an emotional shitstorm if I called him "Daddy." He'd been "Simon" to me since my mother's funeral.

When I got home, the house was dark. Simon must have found out already. He was probably halfway to Texas by now, driving madly through the darkness, searching the highway for Gabriel's Dodge.

All night I waited. As soon as a respectable wedge of sunrise appeared, I called the high school principal at home.

"Simon's gone," I announced, too tired to be frantic any more. "I'm going to need help finding him."

"Finding him? What for?"

"You mean you know where he is?"

"Why, Simon got on a plane to Athens yesterday! Took a leave of absence so he could travel in Greece. Big dream of his. I wasn't thrilled at the short notice, but with his heart, you know . . . Agatha?" The principal's voice rose to a dumbfounded squeal. "Where the heck have you been?"

Agatha?

Was that me?

Where *had* I been? So fuck-drunk that the town gossip hadn't reached me. Once I landed at the bottom of my shock, I looked around and saw sense in the depths. My father and I had a hard time with love, but we were even worse at dealing with pain. Of course Simon hadn't told me he was leaving. I'd never planned to tell him about my escape, either. We'd both gotten passports, purchased tickets. The only difference was that Simon got away first.

I could fall in love with you in Greece.

Father or daughter – the object of lust hardly mattered to Gabriel, who could pound everything sacred to a pulp with his magic cock.

This is the way I justified my father's flight, after I'd talked things over with the Simon who occupies my head. If Simon hadn't gone to Greece with Gabriel, he would have gone alone. But his destination would have been a Greece of his own making, and you wouldn't see him in this world again.

He'd be having dinner in some Athens of his mind, a world of immortal light. Every once in a while, a nurse would come by with a pleated paper cup and order him to swallow some pills.

Blood is thicker than water, yes. But you don't crave a glass of blood when you're dying of thirst.

Hell, I hope Simon earned his ticket to absolute beauty, grabbed Gabriel's cock, and took that gorgeous bastard with him. I have no idea where Gabriel is, but in my optimistic moments I imagine he's still with Simon, drinking retsina at some taverna by the sea and listening to my father weave his own theory of love.

Dirty Pool

Thomas S. Roche

"Are you listening?" Frenchy Carver smacked me on the side of the head, trying with only moderate success to get my attention away from the blonde, who had just smiled at me and made me the happiest man alive. Simple minds, simple pleasures.

I grabbed his wrist "Watch it, Frenchy. Don't get between me and the next ex-Mrs Brewster."

Josie's Gin Joint was packed six deep with wanna-bes, gamblers, and mobbed-up pool fans getting pickled in anticipation of tomorrow's big win at the tournament.

"Don't let your dick be your guide tonight, buddy. You got an amateur hour to win tomorrow morning." He pulled his wrist free and lit my Cuban with his Zippo.

"Just enjoying a little eye candy," I said, without taking my eyes off the blonde.

"Well, pay attention, Brewski, because me and Johnny Bourbon and Joey Donato got twenty yards apiece riding on you." He turned to Johnny Bourbon, who happened to walk by at that moment. "Hey, John, what's the name of the guy Brewski's up against tomorrow?"

"Blackie Snyder," said Johnny Bourbon as he walked by. He leaned down to pat me on the back. "The name of the black queen Brewster here's gonna wipe the table with is Blackie Snyder."

"He's a spade?"

"Course he's a spade. With a name like Blackie?"

"And how do you know he's a faggot?"

"He's from Frisco, ain't he?" said Johnny. "Jesus, Mike, don't you read the fuckin' papers?"

I shrugged.

"Look, don't fuckin' make a joke out of it," said Frenchy. "Why do you think I got you over at the Sands? Teddy SouthSide's got a lot of prestige riding on this spade, and so does Big Johnny Frisco. Those West Coast motherfuckers might try something."

"That must be why you got me loaded down like a one-man band, smartass." Frenchy had given me two guns – a compact Glock nine, which I'd duct-taped under my dashboard, and a little Colt .380 in my cue case.

"You'll fuckin' thank me if anyone tries anything. But I don't trust your shooting, Brewski – I saw you at the range."

"I shoot pool, not guns."

"That's why I got Sam and Dave following you."

"That's fuckin' crazy. It ain't necessary."

"Sixty Gs, motherfucker. That's how much we got on you."

"Tell those two Peeping Toms not to get too close."

"I'll tell 'em," said Frenchy. "You're gonna lay the blonde, ain't you, you fuckin' pussyhound?"

"If it's the last goddamn thing I do."

I was watching the blonde again. She had uncrossed and re-crossed her legs, giving me a quick view of the full length of those gorgeous gams.

"You won't try to lose Sam and Dave?"

"I won't try to lose them." I was already looking at the blonde, who had leaned forward against the bar just enough to stretch what little there was of her dress tight across her back.

"You promise," growled Frenchy. "You'll let 'em tail you so nothing goes down. Be serious here, Brewski."

"Yeah, yeah, yeah, I promise." I polished off my Scotch. Frenchy knew I played better when I'd had about two hours' sleep the night before and recently acquired carnal knowledge of some sweet young thing.

I saw the blonde lean close to Josie, the bartender, and then slide down off the bar stool. She started coming my way.

"I see you're about to receive a visitor," said Frenchy, and he and Johnny vanished into the crowd.

The blonde was even more of a looker up close and personal.

"Hello," she said – sexy, but with just a hint of timidity. "You're that pool player guy, aren't you?"

I chuckled. "I've been called lots of things, most of which I can't repeat in the presence of a lady. But 'that pool player guy', I'm happy to say, isn't one of them. Mike Brewster at your service."

"So it is you! I'm a huge fan," she gushed. "You're all over the news. Everyone knows about you – you're a heck of a pool player."

"Something else I've never been called," I said. "Have a seat," I offered her.

"Oh, I couldn't – I mean, could I? I saw you talking to your friends . . . I hope I didn't chase them away."

"Of course not," I said. "Have a seat. And you are . . ?" I asked, raising my eyebrows.

"Oh, God," she said. "I'm so rude! Sorry. My name's Ginny Mott. I'm from Florida, but I'm up here on vacation. I didn't think I'd ever get to meet you in person! But now that I have, I'm hoping I can talk to you a little." She sounded really nervous.

I nodded, smiled.

She blurted: "I'm a pool player, you see. I'm in town to see the tournament tomorrow – I just love watching really good pool players!" The girl was positively perky with enthusiasm. "I was wondering if you'd give me any pointers. I've been practising since I was a little girl, and . . . well, I hate to say it, but I'm awfully good."

"Your modesty is becoming," I ribbed her, and she blushed. "What do you want to know?"

"Well . . . I just . . . I was wondering how I know if I'm good enough to go pro." Now she was leaning close to me, and I could smell her perfume – something expensive.

"You must be mistaken. I've never gone pro," I said.

Ginny blushed again – this time, just a little. "Oh, I know that, well, I mean, everyone knows why that is."

"And why is that?"

"Oh, you make more money this way . . . you know, under the table money. Everyone knows you're mobbed up — "

She froze, blushed deeper, looked at the floor.

"I'm saying too much," she said. "I don't mean to be rude, Mr Brewster — "

"Call me Mike," I said, leaning back and puffing my cigar. "No offence taken. Where do you practise?" I asked her.

"My daddy runs a diner. It has a table – in the back room."

I chuckled. "It's no use telling you, of course, that pool is not an appropriate game for a lady to be playing."

Ginny got a wicked look on her face, and smiled.

"Tell you what," I said. "How would you feel about a little mini-tournament, between, say, you and me?"

"Oh, my God, are you serious!" She was laughing. "I could never – I mean, I would lose, for sure, right?"

I shrugged.

"Oh, Mr Brewster, I would love that! Me, playing against Mike Brewster! Would you really want to do it?"

"Oh, yes," I said, eyeing her upper thighs. "Only one thing. I have a minimum wager on every game."

"Minimum wager?" Ginny looked suspicious.

"It's modest. Five bills." When she looked blankly at me, I said, "Five hundred dollars."

"But . . . I barely scraped up enough money to fly up here!"

I chuckled. "Well, since you're a beginner, I would be willing to make alternative arrangements."

"Really? You'd do that?"

"No need for you to risk your money on a game of pool. I think we could find something a little less . . . painful for you to part with. In the event that you lose I think you've got something that's worth five hundred dollars."

I took out the five Franklins I'd won from Dakota Joe earlier that night and held them up as Ginny watched, transfixed.

"I'll gladly place my money against your . . . assets."

Ginny just looked at me, horrified, her eyes wide, her mouth open in an expression of shock and disgust. "You can't mean . . ." she began, then lost her voice. After a minute, she managed to croak out: "You mean if I lose to you, I have to . . ."

"If that pretty face of yours isn't worth five hundred dollars, darling, I don't know who is."

I saw the shiver go through her body, as she looked at the ground, pretending to be nervous and embarrassed. But she was enjoying herself, no matter how good a show of false virtue she was putting on.

I figured this was anything but a wager. Rather, it was a way to cut through the bullshit – a way for Ginny to get into bed with me without having to play the does-she-or-doesn't-she game I saw in our immediate future.

Ginny looked back down at the ground for a long time as if collecting her thoughts.

"You mean if I lose, then I have to go to bed with you," she said nervously, without looking up.

"That's right," I said.

"H . . . h . . . how many times?"

"Just once," I said.

"Would I have to . . . do anything . . . unusual?"

I laughed. "That one's up to you."

She looked down again, and it was ten seconds, twenty, perhaps thirty, before she looked up. With this dark, wicked grin on her face.

"All right," she said. "Let's play."

I gave my money to Bad Check Sammy to hold, so of course I had to tell him what the wager was. And that sonofabitch has the loudest mouth there is. Soon everybody in the bar was crammed into the pool room, standing on tables, pushed against the walls four and five deep.

As Ginny bent over to take her breaking shot, that dress rolled up a little and a series of cheers and howls went up from the crowd. Ginny reddened, glanced back. Then she smiled, obviously loving the attention.

She held her position there for a painful length of time, and with every second the tension increased, till it felt like the crowd was going to explode.

The break rang out like a gunshot. Balls rolled everywhere.

Two balls rolled in – both solids. I almost swallowed my tongue.

I was sweating by the time Ginny took her third shot. She'd downed a third solid – the four – with her second, and she now had a passable shot at the seven, but it wasn't ideal. She put one leg up on the side of the table – a move that wasn't, strictly speaking, necessary, but which pleased the crowd and distracted her opponent more than anything she could have done with that cue. She was wearing red panties, and there wasn't much to them.

She missed her third shot.

My first shot was the ten, an easy shot into the corner pocket. Then the twelve, into the side, and the eleven and thirteen into the same corner. I had practically cleared the stripes when I let my mind wander to the shape of Ginny's ass in that dress.

The shot I missed was an impossible bank, but it still killed me to miss it. I might have sunk it another time.

"God," squealed Ginny, seeming genuinely impressed. "You're so good! I've never seen you play in person! You're so much better than I expected!"

"I ain't the only one," I said with ice in my voice, eyeing her suspiciously.

She giggled. "You really think I'm that good?"

I backed down. "I'm just bullshitting the competition," I said. "'Scuse my French."

In reality, she was better than I thought she'd be – in fact, she was damn good. It made me more than a little nervous. I had lost about one game a year for the last ten years, and I didn't want this year's game to be lost to a college coed in fuck-me pumps.

Ginny had nothing but a crappy shot from one corner of the table to the opposite, having to bank at the far end to miss the eight. She took a painfully long time setting up that shot. She seemed to be doing all the calculations in her head, furrowing her brow and gnawing on her lower lip.

Then she bent over again, slowly, spreading her legs and hunkering down low. The dress rode up high above the lace tops of her seamed black silk stockings, exposing the lovely framework of her creamy thighs, and my head swam as I looked at those gorgeous buns in the tight dress in her next-to-nothing red lace underwear.

She made the shot. And the next one. And the next one – each shot giving Ginny a new opportunity to flaunt those assets of hers. To me, and to the crowd.

She finally missed a shot. I let out a long sigh. I was on the brink of a fucking disaster here. Ginny had exactly two solids left on the table and I had three stripes. She could wipe the floor with me if I didn't sink the next shot.

I sighed and lined up an easy fifteen-in-the-corner-pocket. Ginny slyly positioned herself exactly across the table from me, and half-sat on a stool so she could put one leg up, showing me what I'd be getting if I beat her, no doubt in the hopes that the distraction would make me fuck up. This girl was more of an evil bitch than she appeared. There might be some hope for her yet.

I missed.

I was fucked. Ginny had two more balls to sink and then the eight ball was all hers.

Maybe she *was* better than me. Then again, maybe I *wanted* Ginny to win.

OK, listen to me for a minute here. I had pulled the "wager-against-your-assets" scam with a dozen girls who happened to be dumb or horny enough to fall for it, and it had never failed. And I *never* felt guilty about it.

Women don't enter into that kind of wager unless they're prepared to put out already and want to do it in the first place. So it just cuts through the bullshit, the "did you have any pets growing up?" crap that nobody, woman or man, wants to waste time with when there's a good fuck waiting to be had.

But it doesn't matter how good a pool player a girl is, I'd never met a girl who could make any serious headway in a game of pool against Mikey Brewster. Not until now.

This shot Ginny had at the six was a real bitch – almost impossible. Nobody could have made that shot, except possibly me, and possibly Clint Boston, and probably Killarney

Sean, the craziest, drunkest Irishman I had ever met and one
mother of a pool player. Sean was doing time upstate for boot-
legging cigarettes. That Irishman could drink a bottle of
whiskey and still sink shots that would have made Minnesota
Fats drop to his knees and weep. He's the only sonofabitch who
ever took me three for three. And I didn't even think Sean could
have sunk that shot.

But Ginny did.

"I made it! I made it!" she shrieked, her ample breasts
bouncing as she jumped up and down in celebration She
bounced over to me and hugged me, her nipples hard against
my skin through my silk shirt. "Guess you'll have to find
another way to keep yourself occupied tonight," she whispered, and danced out of my grasp.

The mood around the table was mixed. A lot of guys had
money on me for tomorrow, and they were beginning to lose
their confidence, maybe think about changing their bets. But
they'd seen me wipe that pool table with so many asses, even
theirs, that it brought them savage pleasure to watch Ginny
beating me. They lavished affection on her and a few guys
even shoved twenties into her cleavage, earning them playful
slaps. That bitch loved the limelight. She giggled and bounced
away to take a drink from the blended margarita her friend
Lucy was holding for her.

Josie makes the world's worst margaritas, so that was some
small comfort to me.

Ginny lined up the last solid on the table. If she made this one,
it was all about the goddamn eight ball.

Look, I already told you, she wouldn't have signed up if she
wasn't prepared to do it anyway. It's not like it was gonna be
torture for her if she lost, goddamn it. Plenty of girls . . . oh,
fuck it. I was gonna lose this match to a fuckin' girl, and be
forever humiliated among wiseguys and hangers-on. In ten
fucking years, it was going to be, "Hey, Mikey, you interested
in playing some pool? 'Cause I saw some girls from the
Catholic school walking by . . ."

Ginny looked more gorgeous setting up that shot than she'd looked yet – maybe because I knew I wasn't gonna have her. I thought about taking my dick out and wagging it at her the way she'd wagged those thighs and ass at me – but that seemed like it would be undignified, at best.

Instead, I prayed.

God, I thought, *just let her fuck up once, God. Just let me take one shot, and I'll do the rest. Just one shot, Lord, I'll never swindle a twenty-year-old girl out of her virtue again, I promise. I fucking promise, I will be good and go to church and I won't screw on Sundays from now on. I swear it.*

Bending over, one leg up on the table, tight body poised in that tight dress, Ginny looked up at me, smiled, and winked.

I flipped her off, and she laughed, like I was the biggest fuckin' asshole in the world and she was only moderately embarrassed to have to humiliate me like this in front of my friends.

I fuckin' mean it, God. I fuckin' mean it.

She missed.

I leaned down low and lined up a bank shot.

Ginny was on her third or fourth margarita; I was still drinking Scotch, nice and slow, sipping it. Easy. Easy does it. Ginny sat in Lucy's lap, the two of them almost crushing Ugly Dave, who had a pained expression on his face but was looking like he was in heaven nonetheless. Ginny's legs were parted, practically flashing me as I tried to focus on the shot.

You're never going to get to see that for real, I thought. *You're never going to fuck this dame if you don't start playing some pool.*

Then everything fell into place. I sank the nine and the fourteen, just like that – easy as pie. Then I banked the fifteen in the side, a very difficult shot, without disturbing the eight ball that was just begging to be nudged. Ginny stared like she'd just witnessed a miracle. Then her face fell, and she frowned. She wasn't giggling any more. And she was gulping, not sipping, her margarita.

Now it was just me and the eight ball, and Ginny's fine, sweet ass wrapped around my cock. Bent over the table, I looked up

at Ginny, who was staring at me, looking incredibly worried –
like a sick feeling of horror had come over her. Like she was
about to puke, knowing I was going to dust her and take her
home and fuck her like she'd never been fucked before.

"Aw, come on." I smirked, and winked at her. "I'm not that
bad, am I?"

The eight ball went in nice and easy, and I had the gall to
laugh. I guess I'm a sore winner.

We took my Impala. I unlocked the passenger's door for her
and Ginny slid into the passenger's seat, her dress hugging her
the way I was gonna be before much longer. I climbed into the
driver's seat.

Ginny looked up and smiled at me, wistfully.

"I really thought I had you," she said. "I thought I was going
to win."

"You and me both," I said, just a little more coldly than I
intended. I started the car but didn't put it in gear. Instead, I
stuck my hand under the dash, nice and easy. Brought it back
out again.

Ginny gasped when she saw the gun.

"Who put you up to it?" I asked, my voice cold as ice. Ginny
looked at me from under those long eyelashes, looking afraid.
She pursed her lips, looked at the gun, then at me.

"I don't know his name," she told me. "He promised me a
thousand dollars if I would beat you at pool. He said there was
a match tomorrow and if you lost to a girl tonight, you'd lose
tomorrow. Something about confidence."

I laughed. "Who's 'he'?"

"I already told you," said Ginny, too quickly, "he didn't tell
me his name!"

"Describe him," I said.

She shrugged. "Real short, kind of fat. Dark hair. Ruddy
skin."

"You know his name," I told her

She nodded.

"All right. He said his name was Theo."

"Teddy SouthSide," I breathed. "He goes by Theo when he
thinks he's being sly."

She shrugged. "Could be. I don't know."

"That sonofabitch," I mused. "Where'd he find you?"

"I'm the college champion at Gainesville. One of his scouts saw me."

"So you tried to play out of your league," I told her, a little cruelly. "And you blew it. You bet your body against his grand and my half a grand. You end up with nothing. And I get you."

She shrugged. "But I'm not a cheater," she said. "I don't play dirty pool. You beat me fair and square."

Then she was against me, her mouth on mine, her tongue working its way into my mouth, her firm breasts against my body. My arms went around her, the Glock in one hand and one of Ginny's firm breasts in the other. The Glock rested easily on the back of her neck, its weight a comfort as she held me. Her hands were all over me, and I could feel myself reacting to her, feel my cock getting hard. I could smell her sweet, musky perfume and I thought to myself for the first time in about five minutes how much I was going to enjoy this . . .

I pulled away from her, put the car in gear, and floored it.

I finally lost Sam and Dave near the interchange. It just wouldn't be the same with a couple of wiseguys looking up my butt through the window as I screwed Ginny.

I took her to the Rest-Tite off of 95, got a room right on the parking lot. Took her in there and closed the door. Left the light off but the curtains open a crack, so the moonlight streamed in and lit up that body of hers as she stood there looking at me, as if waiting for me to make the first move.

But then she turned, backed up to me, showed me her shoulders as an invitation.

I unzipped her red dress, and she shrugged it off – as it had been begging to come off all evening. It shimmered down her pale body and piled around her ankles. Her red panties were slight, just a string up the back – hiding nothing of that gorgeous, wide ass and smooth-slung hips framed by black garters. Her waist was tiny; I could practically let my fingers meet if I put one hand on each side of it. I did, and pulled her close against me, kissing the back of her neck, tasting the salt of her sweat, and listening to her moan as I kissed up to her ear.

My fingers slipped up her back and deftly unfastened the clasp of her bra; I brought my hands up to feel her large, heavy breasts, pinching the nipples as Ginny turned her body so she could kiss me. She kissed hard, too, with lots of teeth, the way I like it, her tongue battling mine for dominance, her pearly whites nipping at my flesh as if trying to draw blood. I looked into her brown eyes and watched them sparkle – lust, or mischief? Then I felt her hand on my cock, stroking through my pants, and I didn't care. She unfastened my belt. I kindly slipped the Glock out of my waistband and put it in the pocket of my sharkskin jacket.

She turned, and I held her, and she pulled me roughly back onto the bed.

Ginny was worth every goddamn bead of sweat, every instant of terror, when I'd thought I was going to lose the game. Her body was soft, lush, full of smooth and beautiful flesh, and she gripped me like a Chinese finger puzzle. She rode me, I rode her, and she showed me what that smart mouth of hers could do. By the time we lay in bed together, I was exhausted, my eyes thick with the need for sleep. But I slept with one eye open.

Because even as I listened to her even breathing beside me, felt her naked body pressed against mine, something smelled wrong – and it wasn't the tequila on her breath.

I listened to the sounds Ginny made in the bathroom. Then I heard some other sounds – cloth, zipper. I sat up, looked for her dress on the floor, didn't see it.

She'd made it out of the bathroom and gotten the door open before I grabbed my jacket from the back of the chair and whipped out my Glock. Then I dove for her, willy flapping in the wind as I grabbed Blackie Snyder's hair and yanked her back onto the bed, pistol at her head.

I screamed at the top of my lungs, "Drop 'em or I'll kill her! I fucking swear I'll do it!"

Ginny froze, I froze, the shadows in the doorway froze. I could see them clearly – two of them. Trench coats, low hats,

Remingtons.

I looked down into her big brown eyes for a long instant.

Then, "Go ahead and do it, you son of a bitch," she said, and ripped at my eye.

I didn't mean to shoot. It just happened – as she scratched me, I pulled the trigger. Plaster exploded everywhere around me and everything went bright red as Ginny kneed me in the balls. The Glock came out of my grip, and as I grabbed it, some guy hit me hard in the face with the butt of a Remington.

I laughed my ass off, lying there on the floor with blood running out of my mouth into a sanguine puddle underneath me. I felt a boot on the back of my neck. Somebody hit the lights.

"Blackie Snyder," I laughed. "Blackie fuckin' Snyder!"

"I don't usually bleach my hair," said Ginny, lighting a cigarette. She sat down in the chair just in front of me, no underwear under her dress, legs slightly parted so I could see the pussy I'd just fucked – or had it fucked me? – still glistening with the remnants of our lust. "Truth be told, though, I got the nickname from losing pool games by sinking the eight ball so many times."

"You've come a long way, baby," I grunted as I felt the cold weight of a shotgun barrel on the back of my skull.

"Yeah, well, I was eight," she said. "I've had ten years to practise. All you had to do was lose to me tonight, and you would have walked out of here with your bones intact. I would have beat you tomorrow; and Big Johnny Frisco and Teddy SouthSide would have been happy. But no, you had to show you're the best fucking amateur pool player in the country. Well, not any more, mother-fucker."

"Talk about dirty pool," I said. "This shit's filthy."

"It's a filthy world," she said.

"Especially with you in it."

"You know what really fuckin' burns me, Brewster?"

"Knowing I would have skunked your ass tomorrow?"

Blackie Snyder laughed, shook her head. "You're a good fuckin' pool player. I'm sorry to have to do this." Then she nodded to the two guys holding me down, and I felt someone grabbing my wrist, and I tried to fight against his grasp and felt a boot in my kidneys, so hard I saw stars.

And that's when the one guy took my thumb and twisted.

I told myself I wouldn't scream; then I heard a snap, and screamed anyway.

I looked up, through the bleak pain, and saw Blackie Snyder putting on her shoes. She bent low and grabbed my hair, pulled my face up so I could look at her pretty face, at the way her upper lip curled in contempt.

"Nah," said Blackie, standing up. "Not even close. What steams me," she said, her lips a quarter inch from mine, "is that you're pretty goddamn cute, Brewster. I would have fucked your brains out even if you hadn't won the game."

"Thanks," I said. "I fuckin' appreciate that."

Then even through the agony and the sound of my own scream as the guy grabbed my other thumb and twisted that one, I heard Blackie Snyder's laughter.

The guys let me go. I looked up through bright stars of pain and saw one of them dump the bullets in my Glock into his pocket, then throw the gun down on the floor next to me. I lay there, hurting. They left the motel room door open.

Blackie paused in the doorway, looked down at me.

"It takes the soul of a killer to play dirty pool, Brewster. You should consider another line of work."

Then she was gone, and I heard a car start outside, heard her high heels click-click-clicking across the asphalt. I crawled, groaning in pain, across the floor to the chair where I'd laid my cue case; I saw and felt and smelled the detritus of her sweat and perfume on her panties and bra, garter belt and stockings, littering the floor between me and the case. I screamed in pain as I flipped the latches, and I had to hold the Colt .380 with both hands as I limped out, naked and blood-caked, into the night. I heard the car door slam, heard the tyres squeal, saw the headlights come on. I stepped in front of them and raised the .380, laughing my ass off.

"How's this for dirty pool, motherfuckers?" I laughed, and pulled the trigger.

Night on Twelfth Street

Marilyn Jaye Lewis

In the half-light before dawn, the double bed jostles me from sleep, shaking with a distinct rhythm, like riding the double L train from First Avenue into Canarsie. It's Manny jerking off again. Lately he seems to need this furtive sexual stimulation before dashing off to work at the last minute – strictly solitary sex is what he's after. Sex that doesn't involve me, that lands his jism in a T-shirt, the T-shirt winding up in the tangle of sheets for me to discover later when I'm alone. And I'm the one who he says is possessed by demons. Nympho demons, the kind of demons his aunt, the Mother Superior, warned him about when he was a teenaged Catholic boy in Buffalo. He's only twenty now, six years younger than me.

Manny came into my life almost as an afterthought, like an unwanted conception late in life, and I can't figure out how to get him to leave. Whenever I suggest it might be time for him to move out of my little hellhole on East Twelfth Street and find a home of his own, he punches me repeatedly and starts smashing dishes that are irreplaceable heirlooms from my favourite dead grandmother.

The one nice thing about this Catholic boy, though, is that he's so hung up on his Catholic upbringing that he's psychologically incapable of coming in a girl's mouth. I can suck him until the proverbial cows come home and never have to swallow so much as a drop of his spunk. The sin of wasting his seed in this specific way weighs heavy on his conscience. But all the other sins have found a home in him.

His soul is blacker than tar, mostly because his mind is so fucked up. Let's face it, he's too inquisitive to be Catholic, but he was raised by a father who beat him regularly, who alternated between using a leather belt on his ass and bare fists on his face, and a mother who was a sister to the top nun. It's left a seemingly permanent schism in his psyche. Four months ago, he was a straight-A student at the university, studying to be an architect. Now he works as a ticket-seller in a gay porno movie house over by the West Side Highway. It's run by the mob and it's the only gay porno house left with a backroom for sex in these days of AIDS.

There are a lot of things about Manny that don't make sense if you weren't raised Catholic, which I wasn't. Still, I've heard him babble on enough these last couple of months to put the pieces together. He started out a trusting little boy with a good heart, but dogma has doomed him to a destiny of sociopathic perversion. I try to tell him to get over it already, that this isn't Buffalo anymore, it's New York City. Here he can be whoever he wants to be. Sometimes he listens to me intently and makes love to me in the dark as if he's starving for a sanctity he believes he can find in a woman's body. Other times the black cloud rolls over his face and the fist flies out, connecting with my cheekbone.

It was never my intention to save Manny from himself, just to lead him to the vast waters of the variety of human experience and let him drink. But the variety proved to be too much for his conscience. Sometimes, without my knowing it, the things I'd want to do to him in bed would push him over the edge, and instead of succumbing to orgasm I'd end up dodging his fists. Lately I don't have the strength to wave so much as a white flag. I'm reduced to trying to read his mind and staying the hell out of his way.

I like it when Manny's at work. I like the fact that the movie house is open around the clock and that his shift in the little ticket-taker's booth is twelve hours long. It doesn't matter a bit to me that he's back to doing blow, either. Even though it makes me spit each time I discover he's stolen my hard-earned money from my wallet, I'd rather he spent all night in the horseshoe bar on East Seventh Street without me. Then he's more likely to skulk around the Lower East Side looking for more blow at four o'clock in the morning, increasing the risk of landing himself in the Tombs again. He hates the violence of the Tombs. He's come out of there sobbing. But having him locked in that mad monkey house is preferable to having his unpredictable rage lying next to me in bed.

I wish I could get him to give me back my key. I wish I could afford a locksmith to change the lock on my door. I'm going to find a way to get him out of here. I'm going to do it soon. Ruby's band is back from their tour of northern Africa and Marseilles. She's trying to quit junk again, which means she wants to have sex with me. It's her pattern, and I've come to count on it. I love her so much it's scary.

I can't explain why I love Ruby. We have next to nothing in common. We don't seek the same highs. We don't like the same music. When we're lying in bed together we run out of things to say. I don't hang out in dyke bars like she does. I don't wear black leather. Even our tricks are from different worlds. I don't venture into the park after midnight to support a heroin habit. A cheap handjob in the shadows is not for me.

My tricks are uptown men who shoot their spunk in broad daylight. Restaurateurs, or entrepreneurs, wealthy men whose emptiness is too complex for what can be gotten in ten minutes at 20 bucks a pop behind some bushes. Ruby wouldn't fare well in those uptown luxury apartments. She's not OK with being handcuffed. She doesn't own a pair of high heels. Holding onto a man's dick in the dark is the limit of what she can stomach. Pussy is where her heart lies.

The first time I made out with Ruby, in a toilet stall in CBGB's, I didn't know she was on junk. I only knew she was a good kisser, which was why I'd followed her into the stall. We didn't do anything wild in there; we didn't unzip our jeans or pull up our T-shirts – we just kissed. But kissing Ruby was enough to make me fall in love. Her face close to mine like that, her brown eyes closing when our lips touched, her dark hair brushing lightly against my face, then the soft groans in her throat as our bodies rubbed against each other in that suggestive rhythm. Only now do I understand why she seemed to be in slow motion. It wasn't some trance of Eros; it was the gold rushing through her veins.

I didn't want to compete with the junk. I wanted the whole girl. When I told Ruby that, we didn't kiss again for a year. I blew my money that year on the gypsies on Avenue C. Mostly on the youngest girl, the 14-year-old with the stray eye. I paid her to hold my hand in her lap, palm up, and tell me a pack of lies. I was too in love to leave anything to chance. I wanted my destiny spelled out for me. I wanted Ruby to come to her senses. She did, after three men in the park raped her one night. She called me collect from the pay phone in the emergency room at Beth Israel. She was ready to try it another way.

She moved back in with her mother in Queens. Six weeks later, she showed up on East Twelfth Street, doubtful-seeming, though her veins were clean.

If Ruby could find a way to keep off smack for good, there wouldn't be cracks in my world, where vermin like Manny could wriggle in when I'm blind on bourbon, crying for myself. It's not that I kick Ruby out when she's shooting up, it's that she stops coming around. So I plug up the holes with whomever I can find. But now I have this dilemma: I want Ruby back in my bed. Nothing compares to her.

The first night Ruby and I made love, it was the height of summer. Salsa music blaring from some Puerto Rican's boom box clashed with the tin calliope sounds of an ice cream truck parked under my open window. But in my double bed at the back of the flat, the intrusions of the neighbourhood faded. It was finally just Ruby and me – both of us sober.

When I saw her naked for the first time, I felt elation, the way an exulting mother must feel as her eyes first take in the body of her newborn, that unshakeable faith in the existence of God. That's what it felt like to see Ruby without her clothes on. How else can one's mind account for something so perfect, so entrancing, so long-desired? Her firm, upturned breasts with their tiny eager nipples. Her narrow waist, slim hips. The dot of her navel and the swirl of black hair that hinted at the mystery hiding under it all – at first, it made touching her a little daunting. But she lay down next to me and fervently wanted to kiss. The force of passion coming from her slender body made the rest of it easy. I didn't worry about how to please her; I knew intuitively what her body wanted. I could smell it coming off her.

Her nipple stiffening in my mouth needed more pressure. I twisted it lightly with my fingers instead. Tugging it, rolling it, pulling it insistently, while my mouth returned to her kisses. She moaned and her long legs parted. That's how simple it was.

I knew she would be wet between her legs. My fingers slid into her snug pussy, and her whole body responded. An invisible wave of arousal rolled over her that I could feel in the pressure of her kiss. The muscular walls of her slick hole clamped around my two probing fingers, hugging them tightly, making it too plain that the thick, intrusive pricks of the pigs who'd raped her could only have succeeded in finding a way into her through sheer masculine determination. I knew how she had suffered.

Struggling, succumbing, three times successively. It was hard to believe her body had withstood the repeated violation. I shoved the pictures from my head. I centred my thoughts instead on the rhythm of her mound, how it urged my fingers to push in deeper. They did. Feeling my way, my fingers found the spot inside her that opened her completely, causing her thighs to spread wider, then she held herself spread, bearing down on my fingers as her slippery hole swelled around them.

I kissed my way down her ribs, down the flat expanse of her belly. Following the wispy trail of hairs that led to the world between her legs. I wanted my mouth all over her down there. It was what I had dreamed of, ached for. At last, she was offering it to me, wide open and engorged.

Sometimes I think about how easy it was to make her come. Two fingers up her hole and my tongue on her clit, then the river of shooting sparks gushed through her. And because I loved her it made me happy to make her come, even though afterward we lay together entwined with nothing left to talk about. Ruby and I were always silent when we finished making love. With those wealthy tricks uptown, it's more compli-cated. They need to discuss each detail. They practically draw you a map: the tit clamps here, the enema bag there, the length of rope tied like this, the gag last. The timing must be meticulous, the monologue rehearsed.

And with an uptight, paranoid guy like Manny it's even worse. There is no plan, no map, no discernible guideposts. Each gesture, each word is a toss of the dice: will it lead to a kiss, or a bruised lip? I try not to lose sleep over it. If worse comes to worst, when Ruby arrives we'll shove the heavy bureau in front of the locked door. We'll go to my bed in the back of the flat, strip out of our clothes, and make love. Then I'll call the cops on Manny at last, when he's shouting obscenities out in the hall and slamming uselessly against the barricade.

The Hill

J. D. Sampson

The locals call it "The Hill", a dry dusty piece of God's country that was never meant to sustain human life. The map calls it Los Alamos and the government calls it Project Y, one of three parts of the Manhattan project. I just call it hell. The secret military compound was a virtual prison camp. Barbed wire topped the fences, guard dogs patrolled the perimeter and you couldn't take a crap without some pistol jockey checking the colour of your badge.

We all had to wear them, small round badges with a number instead of a name. Numbers were anonymous but it was the colours that kept us in our place. I was given a white badge the day I arrived. White was top of the line, an all access pass, the chosen colour of the eggheads. But women don't talk to whites, not the women I was interested in anyway. Soon as I figured out that fact I traded my white button in for a yellow; tech access but not top of the line.

Oksana didn't notice me when I was a white. Her husband was a white. A physicist from Poland, Bronislawa had a good fifteen years on his charming wife and he wore her like a brand new watch. She was a pretty girl, not beautiful and Los Alamos was ageing her. Rumour had it that her father was Russian royalty and was ousted by the current regime. Oksana was used to the good life. This wasn't it.

It was easy to catch her. I told her she looked like Jean Harlow and that I would know because I lived next door to

Harlow back in Hollywood. Like most of the foreign women, she was entranced by the glamour of movie stars and that made her keen to talk to me. It was just talk at the beginning. That's the only way to start. You have to take it slow or you scare them away. It's like breaking a horse, only a lot more fun. After a few short conversations I graduated to a hand on her arm, always an innocent gesture. Let me help you step over that puddle. Oh, wait, I think it's over this way. From there it was a hand on her back, then a whisper in her ear and finally she was mine for the taking.

We agreed to meet in town at the La Fonda hotel. It was a regular watering hole for residents of the hill so no one would pay attention to her or me, not that anyone ever paid attention to me, I was invisible.

Oksana was shaking like a wet poodle when she slipped into the room. "We shouldn't — " I didn't let her finish. I grabbed her then and kissed her, hard. She stiffened in my arms and I worried that she might nix the whole thing. "So beautiful," I said, with the cream in my voice. "So elegant." I ran my hand through her pin-curled hair, then drew my fingers along the side of her face. "Now that I really see you, I know I was wrong. It's not Harlow, it's Lombard."

"Carole Lombard?" Oksana sighed. "No, you lie." She ducked her chin and blushed a pleasant shade of red.

"If Clark Gable were here he'd slug me for making time with his girl." I slipped my finger under her chin and lifted, raising her eyes to mine. There were tears there and for a second I felt like a first-class heel. She was just a child.

"I've never been with a man." Then she corrected herself. "Another man. Not Danez. I've never been unfaithful."

She was thinking again. That wasn't good. I crushed her mouth like a ripe tomato as I cupped my hand around her breast. She gasped at that and I knew I had her back. That was the trick. Pleasure. No time to think. I slipped my arm beneath her thin legs and scooped her off the floor. "You deserve the best," I said, planting the seed. "You deserve to have all you desire." I laid her on the bed then knelt beside her. She was panting with a mixture of excitement and fear. "Take your blouse off."

"I can't. My hands." She held them up and I could see that they were shaking.

"Allow me." I stretched out beside her then began to free her one button at a time. She tried to contain herself but four buttons down her hips began to grind against the bed. Two more buttons and I could see bare skin peeking out around a sturdy and serviceable undergarment. "You deserve better," I said as I undid the fasteners. "You deserve silk and satin, nothing else against your tender skin." Two white mounds of flesh presented themselves for the taking. I took. My mouth latched on to the nearest breast while my thumb and forefinger twisted the nipple of the other. The combination of pleasure and pain soon had her mooing like a happy cow. I blew a warm breath on the hardened nub forcing it to stand at attention. Then I worked the other, fingers first, blow – pop. So sweet.

Her skirt was the next thing to go, then her panties. I left her stockings in place. There's nothing like the sight of a woman naked except for stockings and a garter belt. My dick agreed with my mind but I wasn't ready to let him out to play just yet. I took off my shirt and tossed it to the floor to mingle with her clothes. Then, crawling on my knees, I settled myself between Oksana's legs. I kneaded her thighs with my strong fingers, relishing the way she twitched and moaned beneath my touch.

"You deserve to be pampered," I said, reinforcing the thought. "Like a princess." I slipped my hands under her knees and lifted, forcing her legs open and back. She lifted her head, her eyes wide with wonder. I still had my pants on and that confused her.

"First you, then me," I said. She had no idea what she was in for until she felt the warmth of my breath on her pussy.

"No!" Her small body jerked, her hands reaching out as if to stop me. "Please. I can't."

"Can't? There is nothing for you to do but enjoy." I covered her soft folds with my mouth. She moaned louder and longer. There were words in there but they were too garbled to understand. I sent my tongue searching for the jewel in the crown and I knew I had found it when she screamed. I sucked and teased, biting tender flesh, then soothing it with my tongue, over and over rocking her body with wave after wave of ecstasy. My dick was not amused. It banged against my zipper demanding to be let out. Frustrated by my own lack of control, I sat back on my heels and worked loose my belt.

"No one," Oksana said between breaths. "Has ever done that to me."

"Poor thing, what you've been missing." I unzipped my pants then shoved the material down around my thighs. My cock unfurled like a flag on the Fourth of July. "Look at what you've done to me."

Instead of looking, she closed her eyes tight. I grabbed her hand and placed it on my hardened dick. She resisted at first but slowly she encircled the flesh with her long thin fingers. "That's a girl. Squeeze."

"I'll hurt you."

"And I'll love it." She made a noise deep in her throat and the lava began its rise.

"Squeeze. Work it with your hand." To help her along I slid two fingers into her pussy. She was the earth on the day Noah sailed the ark – flooded. Oksana pulled at my dick, an amateurish attempt but I had to give her points for trying. The last one wouldn't even try. She had lain there like a dead fish, waiting for me to fuck her. But not this one. Oksana was adventurous, perfect for what I had in mind. Damn it. "Stop. Let go." I pulled my fingers out of her wet cunt and replaced them with my dick. I slipped it into her like I slipped my gun into the holster. She was tighter than I expected or maybe I was just bigger. She gasped when I entered her and I saw her bite her lip from the pain. At least she wasn't a virgin. That was the good thing about the married ones, they arrived already broken in.

I lifted her legs higher and felt myself slide deeper into her channel. Then I settled myself into position to begin the retreat. Out. In. Out. In. I picked up speed, a jack-hammer with miles of road to dig up. She was crying, moaning, screaming. It was all mixed together and I knew she was going to hate me in the morning. Her husband never made her feel like this. Her husband never fucked her until she was too weak to move. Her husband never treated her to a finger in the ass just as she was about to come, but I did. I knew how to make a woman beg for more and that was what it was all about. Getting my rocks off was just a bonus. Perk of the job. The job. Damn it.

There was a low, wet sucking sound as I pulled my wasted dick out of her aching pussy. Her hands grabbed for me as if wanting to shove me back in but I was done. I climbed over her legs and dropped down beside her on the bed. Now was the perfect time. She wasn't thinking clearly. She was high on sex.

"If only," I said.

"If only what?" She took the bait.

"If only I could stay."

Despite her exhaustion she popped up to one elbow. "Stay? In town?"

"On the hill. I have to leave next week. I failed."

"I don't understand." She draped her arms over my chest and clung to me.

"I shouldn't tell you this but I'm not who I appear to be." Just like the sex, take it slow, lead up then wham. "This bomb they're building, it's wrong. People are going to die, innocent people."

"Our enemies. The Germans deserve what they get."

"All the Germans? What about the children and the mothers and the Jews? The bomb can't tell the difference. They'll all die when it's dropped."

She shivered and latched on a little tighter. "I don't wish to talk about it. There is nothing to be done."

"But there is." I set a reassuring kiss on her forehead. It was damp and tasted of salty sweat. "If the Krauts had a bomb we wouldn't risk dropping ours. It would be a stand-off."

Oksana shook her head. "No. It would be worse. Hitler with a bomb."

"Ten thousand dollars would make life very sweet."

"Ten thousand dollars? That's quite a lot of money. For what?"

I stroked her face with my free hand. "Documents. Plans. I can't get to the kinds of drawings and reports that they need."

"My husband," she said softly.

"His reports would do the trick. They don't need much. Drawings maybe, of the bomb."

"Ten thousand dollars?"

"If I had a pipeline, if I had access to documents then I could stay." I tipped my head downwards and licked her softened nipple. "We could make love every day."

"No. Yes." She closed her eyes as her nipple shaped itself into a tight square. "I have to think. I can't think"

I rolled over on her so my mouth was near her ear. "Did you like it when I sucked you down there?" The quick rise and fall of her chest was the only answer. "You came so hard I thought you might break"

"Yes," she said. "I never."

"But now you have. And you can have it again and again. Would you like that?"

"Yes." Another breathy reply.

"Then help me, baby. Bring me what I need and I'll take you back to paradise."

We met again a little more than a week later. I don't know how she managed to get a pass so soon after her last "shopping trip", but she did and she left me a message saying I should meet her. I, of course, had no trouble getting off the hill. Getting off was easy. Staying off was the tough part.

Oksana arrived at the hotel red-faced and breathless with anticipation. I could see that she had been thinking about our last encounter. She was shaking when she entered the room and it wasn't from nerves. She wanted it bad and that's why her face fell so quickly when she saw Calvin and Hume.

"He's the man with the money," I explained but she still remained disappointed. Their presence meant it would be that much longer before she'd have me between her legs.

"I understand you have something for me," said Calvin.

Without speaking, Oksana reached into her purse and pulled out a thick fold of paper. She handed it to him and we all waited in silence as he perused the pile.

"These documents are quite revealing," Calvin said as he flipped through the pages. "Won't they be missed?"

"No, Danez, my . . ." she had trouble saying the word, "husband is always scribbling on bits of paper, it is the way he thinks things through. I throw most of them away and he never asks for them again. I took what I could find. Some are written in Polish. I don't read Polish very well, not the science words, so I do not know if they are helpful or not."

"From what I can see, they'll be very helpful." Calvin gave me a look but I turned away. I hated this part. He dropped the papers into his open briefcase then took out a black leather badge case. "Oksana Bronislawa, you're under arrest for treason."

"Treason? But I don't understand!" She tried to look at me too but I kept my eyes on the floor.

"Selling secrets to an enemy, Mrs Bronislawa. You'll have to come with us. Hughes, take her downstairs. I'll be there in a minute." Calvin's man took her by the arm and then led her to the door. She called out my name but nothing more. No begging or pleading from this one. No anger, no tears, those would come later.

"So how many does that make?" Calvin asked when she was gone.

"Three out of six. The next one will be the tie-breaker."

Calvin shook his head. "What's your secret?"

"That's easy. Always let her come first, literally."

"Shit, if that's what it takes, I'll stick to arresting them."

Mrs Abigail Covington was the wife of a British explosives expert. She was an older woman with a classic style and expensive tastes. I told her she reminded me of Garbo and I oughta know, see I used to live right next door to Garbo in Hollywood . . .

Soho Square

Justine Dubois

For three difficult months he had worked patiently through the night. He was a big man, not only tall, but massively built. In his overalls, he still retained some of the ceremony and bearing of Detective Chief Inspector. He was also handsome in a darkly impassive, ample-featured way. His eyes were particularly striking, neither brown, nor precisely blue, but dark grey beneath heavily plumed brows; something severely beautiful about the wide set of his mouth. He had a manner of looking at each person with honesty, interested and direct, yet also fractionally formal, which lent his personality a nuance of mystery. He was, above all, intelligent. Not the intelligence of the bookish, but of those who live life fiercely, in the raw, as though instinct and action were all, but who then later have the wit to deduce intellectually from their experiences. He was with the Met, working undercover. He investigated murder. In particular, he was investigating a current spate of irregular, but identically patterned murders of prostitutes in Soho. His undercover job was as night-watchman in an apartment block in Soho Square.

Soho Square is like a tree that has rotted at its base, yet still retains the lofty magnificence of its rich, fruit bearing upper-most boughs. Below, in the gardens, with their central pergola, people and rubbish accumulate alike, indiscriminately at every corner. The street doors appear anonymous, almost unused. No one ever notices people either coming in or going out. The narrow, brashly lit foyers are undecorated and unpatrolled, giving no intimation of the lives lived above.

Bill's assigned apartment block was to the east of the square. Every night, at eight o'clock, he parked his elegant car several streets away, so as not to be spotted driving such luxury, and walked to work, where, from the first floor in a back room cupboard, transformed into a surveillance post, he monitored the 24 screens relating to the CCTV cameras, which tracked, in slow, wand-like dances, the lifts, the corridors and the individual entrances to all apartments.

In the past three months five prostitutes had been murdered, all murders bearing the same handwriting, a signature not yet revealed to the press. Ten of the apartments in this block were inhabited by prostitutes, with one exception, all of them shared between three pimps; three more apartments were rented to merchant bankers, clever, laddish men, who all worked for the same company; two more to film producers; one apartment was owned, not rented, by a famous middle-aged business woman, and another owned by a famous restaurateur. The eighteenth remained empty. It had been the home of "Gloria", original name Gladys, a young prostitute murdered three months earlier. Now, the other girls were superstitiously reluctant to move in to it.

Apart from a brawl between two men overlapping late one night at an apartment door, all had been quiet in recent weeks. Bill had had to argue forcibly with his bosses for the right to continue his surveillance of the building. "Give it up, Bill," they had said. "It is sending you to sleep." They had laughed the manly laugh of men who know all there is to know about human nature, yet remain unafraid of the truth, both brutalized and empowered by their knowledge, at once bitter and forgiving. The forgiveness they felt was both for themselves and for each other, for humanity in general. But its connotation for them was not that of turning a blind eye or of finding the edges blurred between right and wrong. For them, right and wrong were identical with the law, a code which they operated sincerely enough. However, beyond the law was life itself, and it is that which they had learned to forgive, knowing both themselves and others to be potentially corrupted by it.

Absent-mindedly, but with little true curiosity, his police colleagues wondered why Bill had fought so hard to retain this dreary job. Professional zeal, a hunch maybe? His private life, certainly, had been sacrificed to its nightly rituals. His girl-friend had moved out of the home, which she claimed they had never truly shared. The job was essentially disruptive and boring and, in fact, his pals had been right to tease him. He had long lost interest in the various inhabitants of the apart-ment block, with their specious vanities and their pomaded nightly charades, felt only tedium listening to the nightly tap on their idolatrous conversations. He was bored by them all, except for one. And it had become exclusively for her that he stayed awake and vigilant night after night.

Unlike the other prostitutes, she seemed not to be run by telephone contact from a central office. It was unclear whether or not she had a pimp. Bill had certainly never seen him. Her calls, when they came, came from the street, from the ticketed, felt flurried phone boxes at street level. Bill had seen her card. It was unusual, in that it listed no promises, detailed no "services", merely quoting her pseudonym, "Dana", and the casual invitation. "Call me, sometime." And, goodness knows, people did call. Numerous evenings Bill had listened to her breathless voice prevaricate over some assignation or other before agreeing to meet. Sometimes she slammed down the phone on her callers. Sometimes she left the phone off the hook and was not seen all night.

At other times, she simply took to the streets, teetering on her highest of high heels, through the windswept litter of the Square, usually on her way to the Mezzo bar. She was a tall girl, with a faultless figure, something Grecian and sculptural about the perfection of her proportions, something geometric in the clever balance of her small waist to the rounded charms of her hips and breasts. Only her face failed to match the perfection of her body. Not that she wasn't beautiful, just that her face had escaped the ideal of her body. In its place was a visible war of emotions, of rueful, almost forgotten, pride; of sorrow; of beauty gradually yielding to the stain of disaffec-tion; of delicacy broken by feisty hopelessness, all these strands knitted together into a tight weave and made central

by an unmistakeable intelligence. Her clients liked her
because, as well as responding to them, she habitually assessed
them, almost, for a cursory few minutes, befriended them.
Briefly in her arms, they experienced the illusion of compli-
ance and passion, as oppposed to coercion and dutiful transaction. She was good at her job. Nor did she dress like an
obvious "floozy'. As she paraded the street in her enviable
figure and high heels, or leant gracefully at the Mezzo bar,
men stopped to talk to her, naturally attracted to her, not
imagining her to be a prostitute. And, so clever was she at
befriending them in a short space of time that, as the truth
dawned on them of her true status, it became just another of
the things they liked about her. They would pay up willingly
and retrace her steps back with her, like joyful sheep, to the
confines of Soho Square.

All these "friendships" were quite easy and simple to her.
But, at the point of actually working, she was governed by only
two thoughts, neither of them friendly. Firstly, that these men
must never see the interior of her apartment, which was, after
all, private, and, in her mind, not designed for use by clients.
And secondly a concern for her own safety. She knew perfectly
well about the localized deaths of prostitutes. Most of the fools
who followed her to Soho Square were just that, sweet, indis-
criminate fools. But she knew that it would be insolence to
assume that she could encompass the nuances of all human
nature in the space of half an hour. The murderer she knew to
be clever; she had read the newspaper reports. He would, she
thought, be like herself, deceptive, and not altogether what
one was expecting. Consequently, she had evolved a self-
protective habit that depended on Bill, even though she had
never met him face to face. Although, unknown to him, she
had seen him.

Every night, in the small hours of morning, when the rest of
the building was quiet, the other prostitutes all entertaining in
their apartments, she brought her fellow revellers back to the
block, inhabiting the lift, so that Bill's camera wand would
remain full upon her. There, she habitually acted out the
various fantasies of being overcome by her many partners'
sensuality. She mimed hesitation and shyness, boldness and

ferocity, and finally the reality of initiating sex there and then, adroitly jamming the lift for ten, twenty minutes at a time, and always performing for the camera.

Bill liked her best in the white silk dress, that fell on her supple body like water, the one that cleverly dissolved open with the rip of a series of rouleaux ties. He marvelled at the way she remained elegant, no matter what actions she performed. The men, she allowed do anything that they pleased; to clamber her high-heeled height; to bend her over, stretching the white lace straps of her suspender belt; to slam her anonymously, sometimes angrily, against the cushioned wall of the lift; to lift her on to their waists or kneel her before them, anything, just so long as they remained within view of the cameras. When the pavanes of brief courtship were over, she would knowledgeably unjam the lift and deliver her clients back to street level, bid them a decorous "good night", then speed in the lift to her own fifth floor, returning alone to her apartment, her every action tracked by Bill. She would then re-emerge half an hour later, bathed and dressed in a new outfit, pale pink or baby blue, occasionally black, always newly made up and recoifed.

Bill admired her finesse, her beauty, cherished her confidence in him and his camera. He could not bear the idea of abandoning this job. Each night he sat in front of the screens and found himself aroused by her broken beauty and her trust, by her seeming remoteness from the ordeals she put herself through. He perceived that, in spite of her sorrow, she was also happy. He remembered something that his father had once said. "There are no women quite so happy as prostitutes," although he wondered if that were really true. He had considered accosting her, trying to get to know her, although that might prove difficult, as well as dangerous to his career. Increasingly he wondered what secrets her apartment held, why it was that she never took anyone back there. Nevertheless, the formal correctness of his police discipline prevented him. He had a loathing for unprofessionalism.

One Wednesday night, as he watched her, stroking his own member yearningly, as she took yet another man's penis into her generous mouth to whip at and soothe, her wide eyes intercepting with his on the screen, something seemed different. As yet, Bill could only see the man's back. The top of his head was a thick crop of blond curls, like an altar boy's, beneath which his shoulders appeared unexpectedly broad. He wore the unlikely combination of a lumberjack's check shirt above neatly pressed trousers and shiny American loafer shoes. Bill's camera searched the well of the lift, to reveal his jacket discarded on the floor, its Versace label exposed to the camera. Bill had not yet seen his face, but his voice, which came to him in distorted waves, struck him as reminiscent in some way. It was not a good voice; too nasal, curiously disturbing, even when speaking platitudes. In spite of his preoccupation with passion, the man was strangely talkative, mostly in catchphrases. "More haste, less speed", Bill heard him say. As Bill's camera tracked him, he seemed to be demanding more of Dana than was usual. Most men had one idea. This man seemed to have several. Bill watched as he spreadeagled her against the wall. She was wearing the white dress that he so loved. But, despite the easy unlace of its ties, the man chose to ignore them, lifting instead the hem of her dress to expose her buttocks, pulling the string of her thong aside as he did so, and entering her brusquely, his well-cut trousers already released at his waist, but now slipped to his ankles. "A stitch in time saves nine," Bill heard him murmur. To hold her firmly in place, he pinned the flat of her left shoulder to the wall with his outstretched hand, whilst, with his other hand, he encircled the root of his own flesh and watched, as if transfixed, as its stricture disappeared to and fro between the soft roundness of her flesh. Bill noticed how unnaturally large and loose-skinned the man's hands appeared and then, with a shock, realized that he was wearing fine, skin-coloured leather gloves. The man then turned Dana towards him and, placing his arms round her waist, again lifted her on to him. He made no attempt to kiss her, but Bill watched enviously as the blond crop of unruly curls mingled with the straight dark lengths of her own hair. The man appeared to be in no hurry. He was not only excited, there was something more deliberate in his actions as well. He seemed almost to rejoice in his own self-control, prolonging the moments.

Bill's hand moved along his own thigh. He toyed with the buttons of his overalls, releasing their constraint at his waist. He stretched his legs forward languorously. As the man took her nipple into his mouth, Bill continued to watch, teasing himself desirously. As he knelt her before him, the man's face was now in silhouette to the camera and Bill could see, for the first time, how his halo of curls was at variance with the harshness in his features. Not that the man was not good-looking, in a certain aggressive way that many find attractive, a way which denotes arrogance and brutality. Bill perceived that, in taking his pleasure, the man felt a need to watch, both himself and Dana equally; as though spectator and participator were for him two distinct, but identical pleasures of the same sport.

He also realized that Dana was disconcerted by the length of time the man demanded of her. In order to better observe his penis in her mouth, he held her hair in fistfuls above her head, so as not to miss a moment of his own event. Bill witnessed the look of desperation in her eyes. And then, as the man's excitement grew, he forestalled her, time and again, postponing his pleasure, before finally lifting her to her feet and leaning her against his massive frame. Although tall, she was suddenly rendered tiny by his gigantic height. He still made no attempt to kiss her, but he began to caress her, running his swollen fingers between her thighs, making it clear that he wished to pleasure her, before claiming his own fulfilment. Under the scrutiny of the lens, Dana began to look troubled and exhausted. He heard the man's voice say, "A bird in the hand is worth two in the bush," as though he had transformed the prosaic into some modern riddle of profundity.

Bill was, himself, also excited by now, an excitement which combined the heady mixtures of concern and dismay. His penis now rested open in his lap, like a flower, its flesh a blush of anger and animation. He considered pursuing his own pleasure before the man fulfilled his. Usually he allowed his excitement to coincide with that of Dana's partners, as though it was him and not them who made love to her; when, suddenly, the phone rang at his elbow, startling and disturbing him, his commander's voice at the other end of the line. "Just until the weekend, Bill, and then I am putting you on another case." The phone was replaced without room for debate. Bill's thoughts shuttered distractedly through his mind, his penis fading in his lap. He held his head in his hands, contemplating how to deal with this blow. When he turned back to the milky screen, the girl and the man had vanished. The screen was flickering.

At first, Bill could not understand how they might have eluded him. He scanned the other cameras, focusing on the apartment doors and corridors, but still failed to find her. He became frantic. He ran from the concealment of his office as the lift was descending, fourth floor, third. It stopped at the second. Above him, he could hears the electronic sigh of the lift doors opening, followed by the sound of feet running on the stairs. A faint, familiar scent assailed him – chloroform. In a swift spiral of understanding, Bill deserted his post. As the man leapt the final few stairs to the foyer, Bill grabbed his calf, tripping him up. The two men struggled. The man was taller, but Bill the stronger. He rugger-tackled him, fighting with his full weight upon him to shackle his hands. The man fought hard. He was uglier than Bill had orignally noted, his veneer of suavity and good breeding undermined by the menace in his voice. Eventually, Bill won, his wrists cuff-linked behind his back, his feet tied with a length of rope Bill carried in his overalls pocket. Bill left him trussed up in the hall, whilst he raced to the first floor to check the lift. She was lying in a pool of blood, the smell strong. The man had cut her wrists. It was the same pattern as before. Distraught, Bill tore off his shirt, fretting at the material to improvise some rough bandages with which to tightly bind her wrists. He then made a call, requesting backup and an ambulance. The voice crackling at the other end of the line reminded him that the West End was almost static with traffic. There would be a delay. He spoke again to his boss, explaining that the murderer was downstairs, trussed up and finally detained. As he spoke, he suddenly remembered where he had heard the man's voice before. It had been one of the unidentified voices on the answer machine of a prostitute murdered two months earlier.

The girl was weak, but still half conscious. She looked up as he cradled her head in his arms. "You are Bill", she said sweetly.

"How do you know?" he asked, mystified.

Her reply was elliptical. "I have been waiting for you."

"The ambulance will not be long," he reassured her.

"Take me back to my flat first," she begged.

He looked at her astonished. "You shouldn't be moved . . . the evidence." He stumbled. "More than my job is worth."

"Please", she pleaded.

He hesitated then pressed the button to the fifth floor. He carried her to her door. Her key, he knew, was on a long platinum chain around her neck. He had focused on it often.

He opened the door on to an apartment filled with white, beautiful light, empty except for an ornate brass bed, a wide white sofa, an easel and numerous canvases. On the bed, as if waiting for them, was a white poodle puppy.

"I wanted you to see my paintings before I die."

The dog sprang to greet them, skidding giddily on the exposed floorboards.

"I shan't let you die. You are very weak, but I have caught you in time." Bill bent to gently kiss her, his big frame congested with conflicted feeling. They could hear the siren of the ambulance arriving.

"Will I ever see you again?" she asked. "Can you come with me in the ambulance?"

He looked up, scanning the clever intricacies of her magnficent canvases, something familiar. "I have fallen in love with you," he replied.

"And I with you," she answered.

"But you have never seen me before."

"Switch on the television," she ordered weakly. "Quickly, before the paramedics arrive." She stretched impotently towards the hand change. He reached and operated it for her.

On to the screen came a four-piece view of his downstairs monitor room. "I have seen you every night," she replied. Suddenly, he understood the familiarity of her paintings, abstract, grand, and yet they were all of him, based night after night in his monitor room, stroking himself gently whilst falling in love with a broken-winged angel, who always seemed to trust him.

Edge

Conrad Williams

Quietly obscene, the taking of E here, where old women walk three-legged dogs along Loch Broom and you can order your fish dinner from the restaurant before it's even been caught. As if the mountains could fragment, the Loch boil with the indignation of spurning their natural high for a chunk of synthetic.

Pippa's eyes bloat black.

Blemishes are sucked into the TV colour of her skin. We talk too quickly, trying to keep a grasp of the mundane but even discussions of moored boats and gliding lights in the distance spawn gentle leaps into the fantastic. It begins. As does the rain, flecking her Gore-Tex and disappointing us with its intrusion. No soft-nosed needles bursting sub-apocalyptically on our flesh here: just rain.

Earlier, over open prawn sandwiches and beer at the Ferry Boat Inn on Shore Street (served by a tough, likeable ball of flab, hair like a razed band between tracts of Scots fir. The prawns had a glaze not unlike that of his right eye – which was glass), we wrote postcards home. Pippa's fingers dabbed at the McCoy's. My backside was blockish and numb from driving – we hadn't stopped since leaving Dunvegan that morning. Loch Broom flat and dull as a blade. A boat, permanently tethered, cringed in the expanse upon which it was resting, its rust-orange hull gathering fire as the sun spent itself on a rind of mountain.

Hello Mum and Dad. Driving like idiots. Warrington to Oban in a day! And then on to Skye where we walked a beach of black sand.

"Here?" she said. "Shall we do it here? I reckon we should because if we leave it till tomorrow we'll be fucked for the drive back."

"But Durness," I urged. "The North Sea. Fuck off waves. Imagine that."

Pippa flipped the last corner of her ham sandwich on to the plate. Dug for a cig. Which pissed me off. Kissing her after she's been kissing the filter of a Marlboro Light is like frenching an ashtray. Sometimes I wonder if she eats just so she can have a cigarette afterwards.

"Yes, chicken. Very romantic. But be practical. We have to be back in London in two days' time. A long way. And I don't want to be driving whilst wazzed."

Eaten a full fry-up every day. I'm beginning to resemble a fried egg. I'll try porridge tomorrow as long as they don't put any salt in it!

"All right," I conceded. I felt on edge. "Not too bad here, I suppose."

"It's beautiful."

"I love you," I said, for want of a better.

She smoked like a novice, watching the coal as it frenzied, the gust of blue as she exhaled. I suddenly meant what I said. In that green, waterproof huddle she looked so damned vulnerable and soft, as if the ruthless career Dalek she became back in the Smoke had been smothered. Her breasts were under there somewhere, sweating up: dough introduced to an oven.

"I've got a hard on."

Durness tomorrow, then back home via Inverness. Pippa is desperate for a fresh fish dinner and I'm going to make sure she gets it. See you soon.

"Do you reckon I could get both your bollocks into my mouth at the same time?" Another drag on the weed. Quite sexy, come to think of it. Bacall-ish. "I've never met anyone whose cock was so greedy before. You'd get a hard on at the drop of a hat. You'd get a hard on if I said 'Bangladesh'."

"Ooh, you sleazy minx. Take me now."

"Finish your beer. We've got bags of time." She gives me one of those smirks that brought me to my knees right at the start. Somewhere between a smile and a purse and a lippy shrug. Almost the kind of indulgent moue you'd give a child. I'm not entirely sure I know what I'm on about, but I can't describe it. She has these moments when she is utterly, incontrovertibly, fucking gorgeous. Nobody can hold a flame to her. When she's tired or angry or bored, she looks as compelling as an oatmeal cardigan. Spinning between these two poles, like a magnet torn, I'm kept on my toes.

Back at her Micra, we unload the bags. My briefcase looks conspicuous, absurd, but it's got a combination lock on it. While Pippa goes through the pleasantries with the woman in the B&B, I dump our stuff and pootle down to the Post Office with the cards. Pippa's handwriting is an object lesson in efficiency. Some of her letters are improbably joined due to a short cut she's found over years of writing essays and exams. Her energy expenditure is minimal. Thankfully, none of these cost-cutting practices have found their way into our bed. If she ever downsized her double-handed Turbowank into some streamlined, eco-friendly two-fingered jig I'd be more than a little miffed.

M+D. Ullapool beautiful. North tomorrow. Speak to you Monday pm. P.

But for the cheap WH Smith turquoise ink, her only indulgence, it's brutal and lizard cold. That's it with Pippa. She's got something of the robot, the replicant about her. On the way back, I toyed with the idea of asking if she's ever seen Demon Seed but I didn't think she'd appreciate the joke.

In our room. She's propped up against the pillows. One breast is free of her halter-top. Her legs are in a loose pincer shape, feet almost touching each other. One hand is sprawled over her mons, middle and index fingers spreading herself so I can see flashes of her liquefying cunt, like moments in a zoetrope, as her other hand blurs over her clitoris. Slowly she arches, her left foot twitching, mouth folding from stiff oval to flat, thin line and back. Eyes disappear to black slots. On the cusp, her features slacken to something like surprise, to the kind of surprise characters in films adopt when they've been shot or stabbed without warning.

"Some welcome back," I say, homing in.

And now.

I can feel the lobes of my brain fizzing. Every breath becomes cleaner, colder, more congealed, as if soon I might be able to chew on the air. We've had a Dove each. I want to go and run up Ben Eilideach, all 1,800 feet of the fucker. It's like a huge, beautiful dick. A dick tenting a bed sheet. And the sky is the mother of all cunts. A wraparound cunt mocking the cock with teasing, unattainable distance. I tell Pippa this and she falls about.

"How do you feel?" I say, through clenched teeth.

"Absolutely wazzed."

We leg up and down the loch front like we're trying to plough a furrow. But no matter how ripped off my face I might feel, I'm buggered if I'm walking to the end of the terrace. Something is rustling there and it isn't an empty bag of Golden Wonder.

"Look, chicken!"

I heard it before I saw it. The schuss of waves and a backbeat throb of engine. Then rounding the crown of land came the ferry; its lights pearlescent, like underlit smoke in the windows. If there wasn't a figure at the prow of the boat, twisting himself in and out of extravagant knots, slithering like oil along the railings, expanding like a blot of ink on bandage, there ought to have been: it was a gorgeous sight. Just the night though, no doubt, wanking with my mind. The night and the pill.

The rain on Pippa's face was a thin matting, like hoar frost. She was so still, my heart spasmed as if she'd died on me, while I was chuntering on about bush shapes lunging for me like servants carrying trays of food that they were zealously getting me to sample. Then she moved, holding my hand and pulling me towards the B&B. Inside, we held each other so tightly, it seemed I'd just open up and fold around her. The heat coming from her settled, a layer against my skin. She made glottal noises and shuddered occasionally. Her jaw spasmed against my cheek. She was off somewhere I couldn't yet know, despite the almost unbearable rise of the drug: a balloon inflating in my head and threatening to take off with or without me. I licked her gullet. I pulled her head down and kissed her. The kiss developed rhythms independent of us. Mouths melded, it felt I could slowly melt into her, without pain, until my mouth quested from the back of her head. I tasted, very acutely, her black stream of words which squirted on to my tongue.

We shall go to the very edge together.

"What do you mean?" I said, breaking away, a thin rope bridge of saliva looping between us.

"I didn't say anything."

We'd reached our ceiling. A few minutes later, I was reluctantly controlling things, even though great pollen-like clouds of wow were still softly exploding. We walked back to the pub and sipped beer by the fire. I couldn't look into the flame: it was too much like staring at ripped flesh.

I drove the next day, knowing that Pippa was always drubbed out after a trip. We made excellent time, bisecting the mountains while the tape looped The Breeders' *Hag* over and over till we got tired of it and played Radiohead instead. Pippa read out loud to me: Steve Erickson or Joel Lane or Patrick McGrath. She told me what she'd do to me once we arrived in Durness. We watched the fighters make languid arcs over Kinloss and Lossiemouth.

Travelling north seemed to be cleansing us of all the city dirt and impatience. Pippa looked more relaxed than I'd seen her for weeks, the lines and shadows round her mouth gone, a rose bloom to cheeks which had been waxen and livid for too long. We hadn't discussed work (or in my case, the lack of it) since the first ten miles of our holiday. Her irritability where I was concerned had been sucked back into its shell.

It seemed almost feasible that we'd spend the rest of our lives together.

On the final stretch of road, a stream at the bottom of a glacial valley beneath us caught a lozenge of sunlight which chased the car: a blip on an ECG. A T-junction loomed;

beyond was a bluff of land and little else, save for the ocean which unfurled towards a whitish, ill-defined horizon.

"Welcome to Durness," said Pippa. "End of the line."

We parked by the information centre, which was closed for the winter. Luckily, the souvenir shop opposite was open and, while I picked out a pair of gloves, Pippa asked about likely accommodation. Outside, she took on a grotesque approximation of the shopkeeper's accent and repeated to me what she'd heard, dressing it up and sounding more like a hysterical Frazer from *Dad's Army* the more she progressed. "Och, ye might try the Smoo Cave Hotelllll the noo. Mind how ye gooo."

"Ayyyyyyye." I got in on the act. "You'll nae be stayin' looong in our neck of the woods, I'll be bound. D'ye hear what they say aboot the people who dare to stay in the old Smoo Cave Hotel?"

"Ye might gae in," mugged Pippa, turning on me with a leer. "But ye shooor as heeell won't come oooot!"

I creased up, trying to steer the car up a sheer portion of road which ran along the perimeter of the beach. It took but a single slow pass along the front of the Smoo Cave Hotel for us to sober up, ruffled by how accurate our badinage had proved. The hotel was little more than a single-storey B&B, scabrous and shallow as a Hollywood façade. There was even a door that wasn't shut properly, slamming to and fro in the wind.

"You go," I dared.

"My arse," Pippa said. "Let's see if there's anywhere else."

Small place, Durness, but we found a farmhouse advertising bed and board as soon as we U-turned out of the grounds of Castle Grim. A pleasant, open-faced girl of my age answered our knock and I thought, yes, this'll do. Olivia led us to a room upstairs – a bit pokey – but I was so jiggered that a kennel would have sufficed. Pippa handed me a temazepam and I necked it with a glass of peaty water, watching her do likewise. We kissed and snuffled around each other for a while, until things became more serious, perhaps encouraged by the warm spread as the jellies kicked in. We undressed each other, revelling in the comfort of blankets which would have been starchy but for the downers.

She took me into her mouth, sucking just the head of my cock, her tongue lolling against it, eyes sexdrunk slits. Her hand worked me furiously. Occasionally, I'd slip from her lips with a Schpluh! before she plugged me back in. Reaching round, I felt for her sodden cleft and strummed gently at her from top to tail till she was trying to back up and swallow my fingers. I was losing myself, all of my feeling and heat racing to the purplish bulb which was being roiled around the delicious vacuum of Pippa's mouth. She sensed the twitch and, in extremis, moved her head away, replacing it with her left breast, which was slick with my spit, pulling on my cock till I gouted a great jet of come over her chest. I pushed her back and chased the pearly glut around against her nipple with my tongue before turning her over and moving into her.

I fucked her with her head into the pillow. She yowled but I was past the point of caring whether it was pleasure or pain. She was too, her hips bucking, hands clawing the mattress till it tore. The edges of the bedsheet curled back like a smile and showed me a black hole beneath that appeared so deep as to have no end. I felt myself being gulped into it, as slickly and effortlessly as into Pippa. A vertiginous rush eclipsed the core of my pleasure and I thought I was going to lose my balance. It suddenly seemed important that I be able to see what was watching us through the window: it felt as though I was out there, looking in. When I came again, thrashing to free myself rather than out of any recourse to pleasure, my head was totally banded by darkness and I felt, with the conviction that only dreams can muster, that I was dead, or close to death, and I would never see Pippa again. On the edge of my dissolution, however, the night dissipated and Pippa was stroking my backside, asking me what I thought of Flann O'Brien's *The Poor Mouth*. The window was misted: sex ghosts. Something hulked beyond. I walked the three paces and placed my hand against the glass. A deeper mist sprang from the edges of my skin. When I removed it, I saw, through the black star that remained, an ancient man, hair rioting in the wind. His eyes were wetted black grapes thumbed deep into the dry dough of his head. Through the slit of his mouth, his tongue jutted a moment. He said something. I read the movement of his lips: *Walk with me.*

"Wassup, chicken?" Pippa's voice syrupy with sleep and trancs.

"Nothing." I went back to her. I wasn't afraid. Sex worked its palliative magic, working at the knots in my muscles, and freeing my brain of worry. But I couldn't sleep. Pushing through the comfort and the warmth was the cold prickle of something not right. I could sense something brewing inside Pippa. I wanted to unhinge the top of her head and peer beneath the lid.

Persistent, murmuring voices in the room abutting this one I used as the reason for my insomnia. At one point they became heated, although I couldn't make out what was being said, so muffled was their anger. I slipped from bed, but Pippa was too dead to the world to notice. Opening the door a crack, I spied a sliver of light bleeding through the bottom of the door next to ours. Pacing shadows disturbed it: a man and a woman. Something terrible in their voices, not so much anger as misdirected passion which twisted them into gross human spoofs. Yet there was something in their spiteful gainsaying which made something in me feel liberated. I don't know what it was. I could hear only fragments of argument: plosive words such as *betrayed* and *bitch* and *kill* from him and blistered reason from her: *on the cards,* I heard. And, in a moment of clarity: *don't be such a fucking stupid childish bastard.*

I left them to it, hoping it would blow itself out before any of their dark promises were kept.

Sometime after midnight. Me, eyes wide as peeled eggs. Pippa says, in a voice thick with desire: "Oh, Jeff. Suck it. Come on."

"What are you having for breakfast, chicken?" she said. "How about my tits on toast, hmm?"

I slid away from her yawning legs and ducked my head under the tap, blasted my tired, tired face with cold reality. She didn't notice my standoffishness and that suited me fine, because I wasn't ready to talk about it. I didn't know how to talk about it. Or whether I should talk about it at all – it was just, apparently, a dream. But that specific name. Jeff. Fucking Jeff. Jeff-rey. I hated the cunt. And I didn't even know anyone called Jeff-bastard-rey.

Olivia was preparing toast when we came downstairs. "No breakfast for us," I muttered.

"Great," she returned. "I suppose I'll just eat all this by myself."

"Give it to the folks in the room next door. They wasted enough energy bawling at each other last night. They'll need a good breakfast."

Her frown disarmed me and I hoped I hadn't heard her properly as I hurriedly shepherded Pippa outside:

There are no other guests.

Despite being wrapped in thermals we kept banging our heads against a wall of frigid air built by the seafront. Huge boulders in the sand provided enough shelter for my ears and from prying eyes while Pippa lit a huge spliff. Her hair was savagely drawn back from her scalp, tamed by a simple green hairband made of elasticated fabric.

She took a few tokes and passed the J to me. I shook my head. Soft grey shapes emerged on the horizon, like thawing fossils from ice. Oil tankers probably. Pippa took a last drag and stuffed the roach into a crack in the boulder.

"Lets go and check out the cave," I said. A figure had breasted the prow of land to our left, next to the shell of a burned-out Allegro. He was looking towards us, hands deep in the pockets of a mackintosh, hair like a wreath of white smoke. Even from here I could see him hook his index finger. Beckon me. On his wrists, a curve of green. The detail made me wonder for a minute if there were still traces of MDMA sprinting around my brain but then I heard Pippa's measured tread on the stone steps down to the beach and I dismissed the thought.

There are 88 steps down to the shingle beach which provides access to the cave. I counted them to give me a distraction: black words were ganging up in my head. I didn't want to unleash them before she had a chance to defend herself against my initial question, which I asked as we reached a rusted winch, bolted into the ground like a sculpture. A few sheep watched us from the hillside upon which rocks had been placed to make messages. "LIAM LOVS LUCY," I read. "KOL+FIONA DID IT HERE."

"Jeff?" she said. "I don't know . . ."

She's a fucking abysmal liar. I just looked at her. Her face changed, losing its expression of doughy victimisation and finding instead a resilience. OK, it seemed to say, let's thrash this out then. I'm probably more fucking ready than you are.

"Jeff's someone I met at a conference in Brighton. We meet sometimes. We go to bed. That's it."

"That's it? As if there's nothing wrong in what you're doing?"

"Whats wrong? I fancy him. He fancies me. We fuck each other. Big deal."

"So why pretend you don't know him?" My hands were fisting like I was testing someone's blood pressure.

"Because I knew you wouldn't be able to handle it."

"You're fucking right I can't fucking handle it. You've been coming home to me, filled to the fucking brim with some other fucker's seed?"

"Oh, come on," she said, using the Grade A patronizing tone a teacher will reserve for a dimwit child. "Jeff and I obviously use a condom."

"Jeff and I," I mimicked, not giving a shit if I was being cruel or puerile. "And I was speaking figuratively, anyway."

The cave seemed to deepen as we breached the lip; a muscled gullet distending as it drew us in. Our voices bloated and took on an echo to make it seem no pause for digestion had followed any sentence. Behind it all, a frenzy of water helped keep my adrenaline pumping.

"So where does that leave us?"

She shrugged, made a bow of her lips and looked at me with a kind of pleading scrutiny as if trying to both examine my feelings and get me to draw my own conclusions. When I simply stood there, like all the pathetic pieces of shit in the world stuck together, she shrugged again and took a Marlboro Light from her pocket.

"Is this it?" I finally snapped. "Are you finishing it?"

"I think so. Yes. I am."

"How can you do this? How can you betray me like this and then act as if it was such a fucking drag, a real bore for you?" Funny how, despite the beefy acoustics, my voice sounded wheedling.

Another shrug, another suck on her stupid little tube of grass. "Dunno."

"So are you going to go with this Jeff?"

Shrug. Suck. "Might."

"Aw, you bitch," I spat. "You miserable, heartless bitch. I should fucking kill you for what you've done to me." I went into the cave, relishing the cold that swarmed at my shoulders. A small bridge led to the waterfall which was causing such a racket. I walked it, squeezing past a tethered dinghy. Wondering what the hell use that was in a little pond like this; I didn't hear her step up beside me.

"It was on the cards, honey," she said. Soothing sentiment but it might have been Davros delivering it. I watched the water till its constant motion seemed so unchanged that it froze: wax ropes. I backed away, not least because I saw, filling the hole in the ceiling of the cave, his head as he leaned over to watch us.

Green lamps bolted into the heights painted the limestone an eerie hue. A boom, like thunder, filled the cave and I ran, not caring if Pippa was anywhere near me. I kicked at the stone messages as I climbed the incline. Sheep, tolerant of humans to the point of boredom, moved desultorily out of the way.

Another boom echoed moments later by a larger, nearer explosion.

The sea's limit hove into view above the severed foreground of land. I rushed to meet it, enjoying bitterly Pippa's beseeching yells. I stopped at the crumbling edge of the cliff and turned round. The Smoo Cave Hotel's doors clapped as if part of a participating audience. The old man had moved away from the hole and was drifting down the steps to the winch; his face turned up to mine. Any shiver he might have generated in me was lost to the general discomfort of cold.

"What are you doing?" she asked, in a wavering voice filled with either panic or ire. I couldn't guess which and I couldn't give a monkey's uncle.

"I'm going to toss myself off, if you know what I mean."

"Oh, don't talk cock," she said. "Don't be such a fucking stupid childish bastard."

Another boom. Those grey shapes had found their form: battleships on training, firing shells into Cape Wrath. Dangerous Area. Keep Out. War Games.

She reached out to me and clasped my hand. "OK then," I whispered. Turned. Grabbed her throat and her hair. Swung her over. Let her drop. She didn't make a sound. Her hair-band came off in my hand: I let it slip over my fingers. Something to remember her by.

"Suck on that, Jeff," I said, and sent an unexpected, fiery jet of vomit after her.

Trudging back, through the tears of my nausea, I saw him moving up the incline towards me. He paled as we neared each other, misting before my eyes so that, as we softly collided, the weight of his arrival became nothing but a sigh, settling against me.

We went for a walk.

Essence of Rose

Poppy Z. Brite

The city of Nashville straddles its polluted stretch of the Cumberland River like a lover, nestles into its fertile patch of Tennessee land like a cluster of rhinestones sewn onto a rich cloth of earth brown and malachite green. The streets of the downtown area are brick, dating from the early days of the city. Above these cobbled paths, towers of glass and chrome soar up and up, some for 30 storeys or more, elegant hotels and shopping centres and temples of commerce, catching the southern sunlight by day, reflecting the million coloured fairy lights of the city by night. Many of the tallest buildings have glass elevators that can be seen from the street after dark, ascending the sheer faces of the buildings like shimmering insects climbing towards the moon.

Or spiders, thought Anthony, going up to spin a web between the few stars that were faintly visible through the haze of city light. Yes, he could paint that: white and silver spiders, spinning gossamer threads between points of light in velvety purple-blackness.

But he thought Rose might paint it better. The image was more suited to her style.

He stood naked at a window on the 31st floor of a grand hotel, pressing his body to the cool glass so that a foggy outline began to form around him – his body heat made visible – and gazing out over the city. Only the faintest shadow of his reflection was visible in the glass: sharp-featured, big eyes staring, skin very pale and hair paler still. He was backlit by the Christmas lights strung around the room, the candles burning, the tiny orange eye of an incense stick smouldering here and there. A room lit by juju.

From what Anthony had seen, the hotel staff consisted of impeccably dressed black men with gleaming bald heads and big-haired white ladies who wore their make-up like an extra face, so thickly applied that it seemed to hover a fraction of an inch above their actual features. They would certainly suspect juju or worse if they saw the room now. But they never entered, nor did the housekeepers, not during this week. Anthony met them at the door to receive towels and soap for the long, steaming baths he and Rose took. The bed could not be changed because it was in constant use, so that by the end of the week it would be a swirled, jumbled confection of sheets and pillows and small creamy stains, rich and ripe with the many scents of love. And, this year, with the faintly sour tang of spilled champagne.

All the rest of the year Anthony was a sherry drinker. He had never been able to make himself like the taste of beer, and liquor mutated his personality, made him a mad thing, unable to paint. Rose always drank champagne. This year she'd begged him to drink it with her, and he had given in. It produced a strange drunkenness he'd never known before, balloon-headed, almost numb. It made him want to obey her, to please her more thoroughly than ever, no matter what it was she wanted. Yesterday she had wanted to urinate on him in the empty bathtub, and though every fibre of his fastidious being shrieked its revulsion, the very dirtiness of the act made it more thrilling.

You're mine, she had whispered as the recycled champagne flowed out of her, over Anthony's chest and stomach in a pale yellow stream. *You're mine, no one else's, not hers, only mine now.*

Her words, as much as her act, had given him a jolt. Rose never referred, even so obliquely, to the uncomfortable fact of Anthony's marriage.

He placed his hands flat against the glass – two perfect, long-fingered handprints limned in a nearly phosphorescent

mist – then pushed himself away from the window and
reached for the ice bucket. A half-full bottle of champagne was
chilling there. *Magie Noir,* the strange brand Rose always
brought with her. She said it came from a winery near New
Orleans, where she spent the rest of her year.

"Cajun champagne?" he'd asked, a little nervously, the first
time she had poured it for him.

"You'd really have to call it *sparkling wine,* I guess," she'd
said. "But that sounds as if it ought to be pink and served in
Dixie cups. *Magie Noir* is a *potion.* "

Now Anthony poured some of the potion into a tall fluted
glass and sipped slowly. Bubbles exploded against the roof of
his mouth. There was an underlying spiciness, a slight burn
like the essence of Tabasco without the garlic and vinegar, like
oil of cinnamon, a subtle heat stitching across the tongue.
Still, he could not detect all the flavours Rose said were in the
bouquet; she knew the names and tastes of herbs he'd never
heard of.

Anthony drained his glass and turned to look at the woman
who shared this room and this week and this city with him.
The woman who slept the sleep of the sated, sprawled across
the white expanse of the enormous bed. Every year the beds
seemed to grow huger, softer, more enticing. Every year their
bodies seemed to fit together more precisely, their hearts
seemed to bleed into each other more willingly.

Rose LeBlanc.

He knew so little about her, knew not even whether that was
her real name; the symmetry of its syllables seemed too
perfect. But he could imagine no name that would suit her
better. And that was what it said on her Louisiana driver's
licence, next to a tiny snapshot, all disarrayed hair and fierce,
camera-hating eyes: Rose LeBlanc of New Orleans.

They had met in Nashville, two up-and-coming young
artists invited to exhibit paintings in a museum show.
Anthony's wife wasn't with him; his career did not interest
her. He'd been at some cocktail party sucking down the free
sherry, and suddenly there was Rose wrapped in black lace
and silk, hair in a wild purple cloud around her head, a glass of
Magie Noir already in her graceful, gloved hand. When he saw

her work, Anthony knew he had to sleep with this woman.

Rose's paintings seemed ready to crawl off the canvas and twine tendrils round your wrists, almost too beautiful and too morbid to bear. Psychedelic washes of colour twisted into intricate, mandala-like patterns, seeming to swarm on the wall. Black-green swamp scenes so lush and organic that you swore the leaning tree trunks could be made of bone, the draping foliage and shadow a thin network of viscera, of stretched flesh and trailing, looping vein. Her paintings glistened and seethed. It was as if she mixed quicksilver into her tempera, LSD into her watercolours.

They made Anthony think of creation and destruction, sex and voodoo, of broken skulls resting on candlelit altars, eye sockets blazing dead black light. Of the thousand ghost stories that must pervade any block of her native French Quarter, of the thousand deaths and pains inflicted there daily. And of the sodden, decadent pleasures.

Looking at Rose's work – even the Polaroids of new canvases she occasionally sent him between visits – was like being in a hotel room with her, her tongue working him over or her legs wrapped tight around his hips, burying him deep inside her. Sometimes Anthony felt stupidly, nigglingly jealous of the other people who must see her work, wondering if it made love to them in just the same way.

But they did not hold her tight as she laughed and cried with pleasure. They did not bite her throat and lick her nipples, they did not spread her thighs and drink the sweet nectar of her cunt under a rainbow of Christmas lights, 31 floors above the city. They did not drink *Magie Noir* with her.

At least, Anthony hoped they didn't.

He approached the bed. The folds and ripples of the white sheet caught all the colours in the room; they spread like a watercolour wash over the hills and hollows of Rose's body. A corner of the sheet was draped across her face, trembling with each breath. He took hold of the sheet and gently pulled it away.

Flawless skin paler than his, pale even against the white sheet. Mouth raw from the days they had already spent together – from kissing and the sandpaper rasp of Anthony's scruff, since he did not often leave the bed long enough to shave – too dark in the pale face, like an overripe plum. Lashes smudgy against cheeks, twin streaks of charcoal. Hair of a curious purple-black, the colour of a bruise, teased and tangled around her head; there were a couple of patches at the back where it had begun to knot up into dreadlocks. The soft bush of hair between her thighs was the same strange colour; when wet with his saliva or sperm, it glistened nearly violet.

Rose was thin and lithe, the upper part of her body almost boyish in the hollowness of its shoulders and collarbones, its small, vivid nipples, the subtle framework of ribs visible beneath skin white as parchment. But her hips were wide and strong, and her ass was as round and heavy as fruit, delectable. With the tips of his fingers Anthony brushed her cheek, then ran his hand down the side of her neck and cupped the small swell of her breast in his palm. The nipple puckered at his touch, and Rose opened her eyes: all great black pupil and glittering purple iris, hectic even at the moment of awakening. Huge, wild eyes; feral eyes.

"How long did I sleep?" she demanded.

"A couple of hours."

Next he expected her to ask, *How many more days do we have?*

It was the only thing that disturbed the flow of their time together each year: halfway through the week, Rose would start counting off the days until they had to part, then the hours, and finally the last, excruciating minutes before Anthony boarded a plane for the other side of the continent, back to the wealthy wife he could not bring himself to leave, and she hopped a southbound Greyhound. The diminishing time seemed to twist inside her, to cause her actual physical anguish. At the end she could not even bear to lose time to sleep. If Anthony slept, she would sit awake watching him, studying the tightly drawn, compact lines of his face and body as if memorizing them for another year.

But she didn't ask the question, not this time; just pulled him down to her.

In lust her voice became thick, clotted, like slow southern sap, like sweet oil. Her sobs and her cries of pleasure were curiously muted, as if her strongest emotions burned pure and hot enough to drain the air of oxygen. "Come into me," Anthony heard her say faintly. "Come to me now. *Come into me now . . .*"

He descended into the moist, fragrant world of the bed and the body of his lover. Nothing mattered but Rose's tongue in his mouth, his hand between Rose's legs, sliding up and down the wet length of her cleft, then sinking two fingers deep inside her. It felt like wet silk in there, like the slow rippling muscles of a snake. She groaned way down in her throat and moved hard against his hand, forcing it deeper. For a moment his fingers found her rhythm, heightened it.

When he pulled away, Rose caught at his hand. Anthony brought her fingers to his mouth, kissed their small, sharp tips. Then he pulled her legs wide. *A passage more ancient than the river, with a stronger pull than the ocean's tide . . .* He lowered his face to her, ran his tongue around the swelling bud of her clit, then let it slide into the rubypearl depths of her vagina. Her smell was like flowers crushed in seawater, her taste like fruit ripened and slightly fermented. Anthony thought he would die before he could drink enough of it.

Soon, though, he burned to be inside her. He tumbled Rose onto her back and found the heart of her womb with one liquid thrust. Her scream was like a crystal knife falling, splintering. Time went away; he might have spent minutes or hours inside her; his orgasm seemed to stretch the fabric of reality to the breaking point, then beyond.

Afterward they lay tangled together, too spent to speak. Anthony's penis felt as if it were melting inside her. In fact, his whole body felt ready to melt. He slept.

When he woke again, he could not move.

The slight, pleasant numbness he'd felt earlier had grown to vast proportions. It weighed down his body, his thoughts. His brain buzzed dully. He could not twitch a finger or an eyelid, could scarcely remember his own name. He hadn't drunk enough to feel this bad, had *never* drunk enough to feel like this.

Rose was sitting up in bed beside him, her huge eyes shining. She smiled when she saw he was awake.

"Sit up, darling," she said.

Anthony knew he would not be able to obey. But even as he thought this, he felt himself bending at the waist. He looked on as if from a distance as his body levered itself into a sitting position.

"I'm afraid you won't be going home to your wife this year. I get so lonely, Anthony. I haven't painted anything for months and months. I spent all that time perfecting my recipe . . . my *potion*."

She held up a bottle of the champagne.

"*Magie Noir,* darling," she whispered. "Black magic. *Bufo marinus* . . . itching pea . . . children's bones . . . and datura, the *concombre zombi.*"

Zombie, he heard dumbly. The word ought to mean something to him, but he couldn't think what.

"I don't have much money, but that's all right. You can go out and work while I paint. You can do anything I tell you to do . . . *and not a damned thing more.*

"Now come here and fuck me again."

He would not move. He would simply refuse to move, would exert every ounce of his will to resist her. He strained against his own treacherous musculature. He was losing the battle.

"*Fuck* me," Rose said again. Her voice was more urgent this time, and edged with the slightest hint of danger.

Helplessly, Anthony took her in his arms and entered her. He couldn't feel a thing, and soon the buzzing filled his skull so that he couldn't think either.

"*Perfect,*" Rose sighed beneath him.

Rarebit and Other Foods

Bill Noble

Rarebit

Argue about whether it's "rarebit" or "rabbit", though you've had the same argument before. Do it for the joy of watching him glower like a little boy and then burst into laughter.

Melt a tablespoon of butter *as you lick his ear.* Two tablespoons. *Lick both ears.*

Whisk in a bit of flour and dry mustard – *goose him in time to the whisking* – and pour in a cup and a half of ale.

Simmer and whisk for ten minutes *while kissing him. If you lose track of time the ale will boil away and scorch the butter.*

Grate and add a half-pound of sharp cheddar, a bit of horseradish and a clove of garlic. *Lick the inside of his lips with horseradish while you pinch the tip of his cock through his pants.*

Slice and toast homemade ryebread *and insist that fresh-baked bread smells exactly like good sex. Unzip his pants. Take him out. Don't stroke him, though, until he agrees with you.*

Place each slice of toast on a cobalt blue plate. *He does this part while you kneel and suckle him. It's deliciously awkward, his reaching the toaster, then trying to get the rye on the two plates, desperate for you not to stop.*

Garnish with green apple and walnuts.

Scramble to hide in the pantry.

Spy through the doorcrack as he undresses his wife and serves what you've cooked. Analyze your feelings as they argue "rabbit" or "rarebit". Ignore the maddening seep between your legs, the outrage.

Spaghetti

Her husband left for Detroit with no clean shirts; the shampoo bottle fell on her toe; little Willie broke out in chickenpox; and the Toyota ran out of gas on the ramp to the Bishop O'Connor Expressway. Triple A had changed their telephone number, and the first call took the last of her spare change.

She was left with an almost desperate horniness, and she knew as well as you do that penises respond in a sense exactly backward to that of spaghetti, but still, at lunch, it seemed unfair that half an hour on her knees in the darkened stock-room couldn't coax Averill, earnest and balding, much beyond *al dente*.

Tapioca

"Tapioca beats anything."

"It's lumpy and fattening."

"This tapioca's non-fat, and so creamy you won't worry about the lumps. Kiss me?"

"OK." *She kisses.* "What's first?"

Get a big double-boiler, an egg-beater, and a wooden spoon.

"Gap-toothed women are definitely the best kissers."

"You're pretty good yourself. Now what?"

Two-thirds cup of sugar, a third of Minute tapioca. "I like the way you use your tongue." *Then a quart-and-a-half of milk.* "Do they make bras like this to frustrate men?"

"I'm pretty sure they do. But don't forget the tapioca."

"I want to watch you do the next part. It's pretty sensual." *Break four eggs, but just use the whites. Whip the ingredients to a light froth.*

"Hey, silly, take my shoes off first – jeans won't go over them. You're distracted."

"I'm paying attention to everything important. Can you reach the stove?" *Boil the water in the pot before you put the double boiler on.* "Gap-toothed women taste best, too."

"Now *I'm* getting distracted. Get a chair?"

"You sit and stir while I . . . ?"

"Uh-huh."

It takes 20 minutes to bring the tapioca to the edge of boiling.

"It's thick and hot."

"The tapioca?"

"Mmm. You're very silly. How long till it's cool?"

"The tapioca?"

"Hey, is your wife going to walk in on us again?"

"You want the secret?"

"What?"

"She's in Seattle for the weekend." *Twenty minutes after it comes off the stove, add a teaspoon of vanilla and a splash of almond extract.*

Can't You Write a Story Without a Penis in It?

"So, Giselle, whadda lesbians do for Beltane?" Amy was finishing the crossword puzzle.

"I dunno, same as everybody, I guess. Hey, be OK if I ask Melissa to sleep with me? Cuz it's Beltane, I mean? – Fuckaduck, I burnt the toast!"

"That lipstick gal with the unicorn tattoo?"

"Yeah. Pass the bread?"

"Wanna sleep with her here?" Amy passed the OJ.

"Hey, bean-brain, the *bread.*"

Amy tossed her the loaf. "Sorry."

"So, OK?" Giselle was burrowing for the sandwich wrap.

"Can I sleep with her, too? What's four letters for 'fiduciary'?"

"Jeesus, Amy. Ask her yourself. You're such a penis."

Kissingwine

"You can only make this in July? Jeez, this feels good!"

"That's when you harvest the flowers. Just lie there. Close your eyes and let me kiss."

"It feels . . . dangerous, doing it in your wife's bed. Flowers?"

A gallon of elderflowers and dandelion petals. Just flowers, no green parts. "It's my bed, too. You put them in one of those gallon jugs in the pantry – with the little airlocks."

"Elderflowers. Mmm, a little more tongue. Is she in Seattle again?"

Add half a five-pound bag of sugar and the juice of one lemon and one orange. "Does dangerous make it sexier?"

"Yeah."

Boil three and a half quarts of water, and cool it until you can just hold your hands on the pot, then add it. In an hour, add Sauterne, yeast and nutrients. "After five days you strain the petals out."

"I can't last five days with what you're doing to my breasts!"

"Silly."

"So, Seattle?"

"No. After that, it's a matter of time." *Ferment until it almost stops, then rack it, top off, and go another six weeks. Do that twice.*

"Twice? Promise? Then where is she?"

Sweeten to taste, and go another two weeks. "This is the critical part. Spread your legs wide and relax, completely."

"– *What the fuck is that?*"

"It's Karen, honey, licking your clit. I'm not in Seattle."

"*Karen? KAREN?*"

"Mmm-hmm."

Bottle and cellar for at least six months. Complex and subtle, this is the perfect wine to drink with a lover. Or two.

Tea Time

She set out jam and biscuits, then turned for the teapot in its flowered cosy. *Too handsome for a minister. Such yellow hair,* she thought. *Strong-lookin'. Be out in the world, he should. Them big hands!*

He watched her move through the afternoon kitchen. *As if she weighs nothing at all.* His eyes caressed the pale turn of her ankle. He felt the flare of his nostrils, the bump of his heart. As she came towards the table, his eyes rose to her bosom. *Smallish nipples,* something whispered inside him. *How would I ever know such a thing?* he objected. *Like fruit,* it said, *like berries.* He flushed as she sat across from him.

"Welcome to Pemberton," he said with his best pastoral smile, "and to the parish."

"Wouldn't you have tea?" *Kissin' lips on that man.*

His hand brushed her small hand as they each reached for the pot. *Warm,* she thought. A ripple tightened along her spine. Unbidden, she pictured his hands cupping her breasts, broad thumbs brushing her nipples.

He held his cup as she poured. "This seems a small house for two people," he said, hoping for more information. So easy to long for her to be unmarried, to picture leaning forwards and kissing her neck, there, at the pulse.

She thought of her dour brother, away long hours at the harbour. "It's comfortable for us," she said. *Ah, t'slip that collar off him,* she thought, *t'unbutton the shirt and put me hands against his skin.* She nearly upended the cup with the teaspout. "Gracious!" she said. "Did I spill it on you?" *Such thoughts about a man of the cloth!*

"Not at all," he said. The hot tea sent a jolt up his arm; he surged with arousal. He saw her concern, grey eyes translucent in the late light. *I want to kiss her.*

"I did scald you!" She dabbed his hand with the tea towel. Perhaps she held his hand a moment too long, perhaps not. *What is it t'kiss a man with your mouths wide open?* She contemplated that, looking at his rough, ruddy cheek, the incised lines beside his mouth. *And if me tongue touched his?* A gasp escaped her.

He couldn't move from her touch. The urge to slide his hand into the fine hair at her nape, to pull her face towards him, was overwhelming. He was beginning to engorge. *God in heaven.* He scrambled up, and then, afraid his arousal would be apparent, sat heavily back down. He imagined her naked, pressed the length of him. He had imagined for years the exalted movement of his body over a woman's body. His hips pressed against the table-edge.

I saw a man once. Molly Hantle and I watched from behind bushes. Is this one like that, huge and red? Could I wrap me hand round him? Would he growl in his throat? She snatched her hand back and shrank into her seat.

He gulped the tea and pushed the cup towards her. "I . . . I must go," he said, "I've just noticed the time." *If I stripped her clothes, would she beg me to take her? How does a woman smell, there? Would I feel her heart?* "We hope you'll visit the church sometime, come to Sunday service." He rose and stepped towards the door.

S'pose I gripped him right through his trousers? S'pose I asked him to make me a woman? Her belly contracted. "Surely," she said, alarmed at his departure. "Would ye take a biscuit with you?" *S'pose I bit his lip with my hand on 'im?*

"No, no, thank you." He groped for words, found none. Well, then . . ." he said. *Would she cry my name? Would we sweat and call out?*

"Have a care," she blurted, "the roads go icy this late of the afternoon." *Would his seed leap the way that man's had?*

He went down the steps to his car, clumsy with his tented pants, at the wet staining the heavy black cloth. He imagined her fine, even teeth seizing his lip. He felt her hand close around his flesh, and shook in the winter chill.

She leaned against the closed door, eyes shut, hands wandering over her apron. An unfamiliar moisture inched down her thigh. She turned back with a sigh towards two chairs askew in the late sun, towards the small disorder of the table set for tea.

One Thing About Chocolate

Sex with Susan always made Roger crave chocolate.

The last customer in Bubba's, he was propped dreamily by the midnight window. The freckled waitress brought his UltraFudge.

She dipped a finger in his hot fudge and smeared it over his lips. "Can I sit down?"

He grinned at her generous breasts.

She grabbed his spoon and dug into the sundae. "I spent an afternoon boinking Gary. Boinking makes me crave chocolate."

"Me, too. And then the chocolate makes me . . ."

"Me, too," she laughed, and opened her mouth for the fudgy kiss that was sailing straight at her.

Embracing

Lucy Taylor

In the heat of midday, I set up my easel at the edge of the Decatur Street garden, dab paint on my palette, and wait for the man with skin the colour of Cuervo Gold to come strolling. I saw him yesterday and the day before. Last night I glimpsed him inside his house, making love to another man behind the lacy shades. There were others, too, men and women both, their limbs intertwined like the vines of wisteria and ivy that crawl over the exterior of the fine old Greek Revival house with its two pairs of columns, Doric below and Ionic above, and the black wrought iron balcony that overhangs a great exuberant festival of rose bushes.

I tell myself I'm coming here to paint the garden, the jungle-like greenery interspersed with bright blossoms, and the raised flower borders where the many blooms, most unfamiliar to me, are identified only by tall bronze plaques that bear no English words, only strange hieroglyph-like symbols. But I am lying to myself, and I know it.

The wet heat of the New Orleans August nuzzles next to my skin. I open some buttons on my lavender blouse, where a strand of pearl-like sweat shimmers in the furrow of my cleavage.

When I look up again, the man is standing on the opposite side of the garden, bending to inhale the fragrance of some roses. Tall and sinewy with a glistening hairless dome, like the knob on some giant-sized cherry wood bedpost. He wears white cotton pants and a saffron-coloured shirt. A gold hoop embedded in one earlobe glints in the sun. He's humming some soft, lilting tune with echoes of samba and reggae. But for all his grace and dignity of bearing, it's also clear there's something wrong with him, which makes me watch him all the more intently, for, being one myself, flawed people fascinate me. The studied, halting way he lifts his ivory cane, the slight hitch to his gait, as though once on this very path he might have twisted his foot and so treads decorously even now. He leans so far into the flowers, sniffs so deeply, that you would think they must be giving up their secrets.

Setting my brush aside, I imagine him sniffing as deeply into me and ask myself, what would Kevin do if he were in my place? What clever phrase or artfully languorous pose would he employ to convey his lewd intentions? If seduction is an art, then Kevin might have rivalled Renoir. We were married, but we never fucked. Not till the end at any rate. We weren't to each other's taste – but then that was the whole point of the marriage. It gave me the freedom to study art and Kevin the liberty to revel in the joys of flesh other than his wife's.

By now, the man in the garden is very close. I open up my blouse completely and let my breasts loll forth. They make a tiny smooching sound as they sigh against the slope and swell of my belly, but the man never turns away from the flowers. A fluttery sensation and a surge of sharp inner heat sizzles through me – like I've just eaten a huge meal of boudin and jambalaya – as I, who haven't removed my clothes for anyone of either sex in close to a decade, sit bare-breasted in the sunlight.

But I like the feeling of doing something illicit, forbidden, so much in fact that I go a step further, hike up my flowing skirt and part my legs. A puff of breeze slithers up beneath the fabric and flutters against the lips of my pussy. Wetting a finger on my tongue, I touch myself, smiling as I do so at the image I must make – a partially clad Venus of Willendorf posing obscenely, pussy spread wide open like a mouth grinning at her own audacity.

Now the man turns, lips parted quizzically, and comes towards me with one large, veined hand extended. "You?" he says. "You were here yesterday. I like the way you smell. Like orchids."

But the garden is a sea of competing fragrances; of ripples and currents and eddies of scent. How could he possibly detect, amid this profusion of olfactory stimulus, the dab of perfume that I applied this morning or the musky undertones of my sweating skin?

And then, as I deliberately shift my position, my nipple brushes the palm of his hand. His fingers curve beneath my breast and for a moment I've an image of a man at an open-air market, judging the heft and weight and ripeness of a honeydew.

His voice is low and gravelly, his accent flavoured with the tang of the Caribbean as he says, "This is a private garden. You shouldn't be here."

"I only came to paint. I thought visitors were welcome in the French Quarter gardens."

His hand, still fondling my breast, now moves up to my neck, my mouth, then skims across my eyelids and explores the corners of my eyes. More harshly now: "You don't belong here. This is a private garden. This is a garden for the blind."

I could make it simple and say that after Kevin died, I moved to New Orleans because I wanted to get laid, but I could have done that in New York. Just because I wasn't getting any and wasn't going after it didn't mean sex wasn't on my mind much of the time. In the Village, I knew the bars where the leather dykes loitered like panthers, in heat and hungry, and the bars where the Marlboro Men wannabes parked their Harleys in hopes of parking their dicks later that night in some sweet warm piece of cooze and even the trendy uptown cafes where some future Donald Trump might be showing off his stock portfolio while the scars from his liposuctioned love handles healed.

But I wanted to be in New Orleans for the heat, torrid and swimmingly thick. New Orleans, where the crawfish etouffee is succulent and burningly hot and the Pimm's Cups potent with gin, where everyone's skin seems hungry all the time, and the cloyingly sweet odour of gardenias and wisteria and

jasmine are enhanced by the underlying fragrance of lust. I
wanted to simmer and stew in my sexual juices, to explore the
places where Kevin went with impunity, but where I never
dared go.

Ours was a marriage of affection and convenience, Kevin's
and mine. I believe we loved each other. Tried to, anyway. We
went to movies together and ice hockey games and had brunch
at Sardi's. All the things other young couples do, everything
but make love. We had grown up together in a tiny
midwestern town and got married right out of high school.
Kevin was small, bookish, and effeminate – the butt of the jock
kings' cruelties. To change his image, he bulked up with
weights and acquired an impressive array of tattoos. To
change his image even further – and to my everlasting shock –
he asked me to marry him.

I was an even more obvious outcast – when other kids were
experimenting with sex in the back seats of cars and downstairs in their parents rec rooms, I was armouring myself with
fat, developing relationships with Godiva Chocolate and
exploring the exotic sensuality of halva and baklava.

I feared sex as much as Kevin feared being openly gay. Our
marriage and subsequent move to New York was an alliance
against those fears, a safe harbour, an island of mutual respite.

Over the years, though, Kevin changed, while I did not. In
the beginning he was cautious and chose his partners with
care. A handful of lovers came and went, a couple of them
serious enough that I offered to move out, get separate living
quarters. He said no way. But gradually his lifestyle grew more
reckless, his short forays into promiscuity became extended
and obsessive. I knew he sometimes connected with strangers
in the back of sex shops or in public parks, that sometimes he
took money. What I didn't know until later was that he also
attended parties where the practice known as barebacking –
unprotected sex with multiple partners – took place.

He came home one morning with a new tattoo. Some sort of
Celtic scrollwork on his upper arm framing a symbol that was
almost ominous in its simplicity. Inside the empty patch of skin:
a single horizontal line. The design looked unfinished, incom-
plete. "You're going back, aren't you?" I said. "It isn't done."

"Not yet." Then he explained what the tattoo meant. When I stopped crying, I told him he was crazy, that if he wanted to kill himself, why not just use a gun like any normal suicidal maniac? He got angry, said he was tired of being afraid all the time, tired of watching his friends die, tired of condoms and tired of tests – *will I or won't I, is he or isn't he?* Embrace what you fear and fear is vanquished, he told me. Say fuck off to fear and you're free.

Bullshit, I said, all that happens is you die.

So be it, he said.

He died last year, and I was left with fear I had no desire to embrace. His death, though, left me no choice. That's when I decided to move to New Orleans.

Wonder of wonders, the man who didn't want me in his private garden seems to have changed his mind. Perhaps somewhere between my nipples and my inner thighs this change of heart occurred.

Already I've learned his name is Martin, he's from St Croix and that his cock is long and rapier-like, hot and hard as an andiron fresh from the fire.

I haven't had a man inside me in so long, not since that one night long ago with Kevin. I hadn't realized how much I missed the feel of it, the squeak and friction of hot, hard sex, the intensely pleasurable pain when I'm first stretched open, penetrated.

I close my eyes for privacy, then open them again, remembering Martin's eyes are closed forever, although I can see thin, milky crescents below the lids. He's drenched in sweat, I can taste the salt on his skin. The muscles of his shoulders bunch and knot as he penetrates me with the same exquisite slowness with which he meandered in the garden earlier, more mindful in his blindness of this new terrain that he traverses.

The sun slides behind a cloud, then pops back out, throwing a checkerboard of light and shadow across our bodies, his naked, mine still clothed – sort of – blouse open, skirt rucked up in a silken sash around my waist. I do very little, but let him proceed. I watch his mouth as it closes around my nipple, his

hands as they knead and squeeze my breasts, big hands but
not nearly big enough, even when he splays his fingers wide,
trying to contain the flesh.

His penis is a different colour than the rest of him, deep
purple at the crown and lighter, rosy-brown at the root. Up on
his arms now, thrusting, I watch him slide inside me, pull back
out, and resubmerge.

I bend forwards so I can scoot my tongue along his flat, hard
belly, see him flinch a little as though the sensation has
surprised him.

I remember that he cannot see me.

I feel beautiful.

I am not beautiful.

I'm a big woman, *very* big, tall and well over two hundred
pounds. Amply proportioned and generously endowed.
Lusted after by that small, but dedicated subculture of men
addicted to what the magazines that cater to them euphemisti-
cally describe as chubby chicks. I was once offered a thousand
dollars to pose for photos for a magazine like that, where the
women are all three hundred plus and recline split-beavered
on satin love seats like an obscene parody of an Ingres odal-
isque.

I turned it down. Not because I oppose such things in
principle – men who love fat women need stroke books, too –
but because – and this is the absurd part – someone I knew
might see me on display like that and *realize I was fat.* Amazing
how the mind deceives and tricks us, how we fall prey to our
own insanity. As if no one had noticed before, as if the tent-
like, brilliantly-patterned dashikis and swirling caftans and
bedouin-like robes I wore were merely some kind of eccentric
fashion statement and in no way indicative of the girth of the
body concealed beneath.

Over the years, I convinced myself I didn't really need or
want sex. After all, I had my art, a form of sensuality and self-
expression I loftily placed above mere crass carnality. Besides,
whether consummated or not, the fact remained I was a
married woman.

But when Kevin died, the years of celibacy caught up to me

in a tidal wave of longing and wanting and fierce, unrequited lust.

A few years into our unconsummated marriage, Kevin and I had vacationed in New Orleans. What a lush and sensuous city, at once vampish and aristocratic, coquettish and campy. I remembered eating Beignets covered with heaping drifts of sugar at the Café du Monde, licking the sticky sweetness off my fingers, the smell of hot chicory coffee, the cool darkness of the interior of St Louis Cathedral on Jackson Square. I remembered the lithe, half-naked women offering brief, teasing glimpses of themselves from the doorways of the strip clubs on Bourbon Street and the winsome, smooth-chested young men who caught Kevin's eye and mine. Most of all I remembered the odour of flowers, a hundred subtropical blooms overflowing the flower boxes along the Moonwalk and the Farmer's Market and Pirate's Alley, growing wild among the tombstones in St Louis No.1.

It was the flowers, I tell myself later, that drew me to the garden in back of the Greek Revival style house on Decatur Street, where I set up my easel that first day. The smell of olive and jasmine and the swelling masses of shiny green foliage scraping the side of the pale, mint green house.

It was also the dark man I saw silhouetted behind the frills and lace, the two women I glimpsed embracing behind one of the magnolias. And others who passed along the cobblestoned path, embracing, nibbling, fondling and caressing as they made their way to the portico of the house and disappeared inside. All sightless and all of them in lust.

It was the odour of their lust that drew me.

The night after Martin fucks me, my pussy burns and throbs so intensely I can imagine he is still inside me, that he lies behind me, cupping my breasts while his cock moves slowly, like the sweat that, despite the best efforts of the ceiling fan to cool me, still trickles between my breasts, along my thighs.

When I finally sleep, I dream I am inside the mint green house, which breathes like a human body. Smooth cool-looking columns stand at intervals in every room. I can see the columns breathing too, convexing and concaving, before reforming into long white supple arms and legs and heaving ribcages. Not columns at all, but bodies intertwined. Blind bodies whose limbs coil upwards together like plumes of smoke, bodies whose ability to know and touch the world comes from between their legs.

When I wake up, the soreness between my legs only serves to goad me into moving more quickly as I shower, dress, and make my way back to the garden.

But I've misjudged the time. I thought it was mid-morning, but by the time I reach Decatur Street, it's already early afternoon. The sky dulling down, crowded with long, streamlined clouds the shape and colour of low-swimming sharks. Grey blurry cirrus clouds, like small waves, lap at the horizon.

The two women that I've seen before are here today. Unlike Martin, neither carries a cane or walking stick, but each drags her fingertips along the edge of the wall on either side of the path. At the places where the Braille markers identify the flowers, they pause and touch and bend over to inhale the aroma of the blooms.

The taller woman's hair is caught back in a flowing honey-coloured ponytail. Orangey freckles dot her small, deeply tanned face. Her friend is shorter and plump, with large breasts that stretch the top of a yellow sundress. She looks up into the sun without seeing it, caresses her lover's face, and murmurs something. Her hands glide down along the blonde woman's hips to caress her between her thighs. Then she retreats back towards the house.

Alone, the blonde woman approaches me. When she's within a few feet she stops and cocks her head like a small, inquisitive bird. "Natalie?"

"I'm over here."

She smiles. "Yes, Martin said you would be. My name's Lily. Are you painting?"

"Yes."

Her full lips curve into a smile. "I thought as much. Come here and let me look at you."

I walk beside her and she touches my face, fingers penetrating slightly between my lips. Her fingers smell faintly of saffron and oranges. Her hair brushing my arm feels silky and cool, like a Siamese cat's.

In the centre of the clearing there's a stone sundial with an inscription that reads: *The kiss of the sun for pardon, the song of the birds for mirth, one is nearer God's heart in a garden, than anywhere else on earth.* It isn't in Braille, but the letters are engraved deeply enough into the stone that I'm sure the non-sighted can read it easily.

A little farther back, there's a kind of grotto where the palm trees and banana trees crowd so thickly they block out the sun. It's here that she starts to caress me. Our clothes slither and whisper and slide to the grass. Our breasts and lips mash together. She is sleek and well-muscled, like a horse bred to run. Her blind eyes are beautiful, slitted and cloudy like water frozen into a pattern inside an icicle.

"You feel wonderful," she tells me, as she explores with her hands and her tongue, "plush and bountiful. You feel like a feast."

Which is what she makes of me, lapping and tonguing and nibbling her way from nipple to cleavage to belly to thighs, strumming and sucking my clit, tonguing her way up inside me. We lie on the grass, getting drunk on the lush, syrupy odours of gardenias and iris and cunt. Much later, although it seems like only minutes, I watch the sun shimmer and set behind the fiery gold coils of her hair.

"Do you live here with Martin?" I ask her.

She nods yes.

"I'd like to sleep here with you tonight – inside the house."

She shakes her head, sadness or regret or something else tinged with the tang of despair, freighting down the corners of her mouth. "You must go," she tells me. "This place seduces all who stay here. You won't be able to leave."

"I don't want to leave."

She sighs and shakes her head. "Go home, Natalie. Before it gets too dark for you to see."

The night I learned the truth about Kevin I had stayed up painting. A dark canvas, full of blacks and muddy greens the colour of faded hedges and moss-encrusted tombstones. Kevin came home and showered, preparing to go out again.

When I came into the bedroom, he was changing. Quickly he reached to put his shirt on, but I saw it then, what had been added to the tattoo. Where before, inside the Celtic framework, he'd had the single horizontal bar, now a vertical one, exactly the same width and length, crossed the first.

Making it a plus sign.

The sign for positive.

I'd been holding my breath and I let it out. "Kevin, no."

"I found out last week and had the tattoo finished."

"But why?"

"So the others will know now that I'm one of them. That I have nothing left to fear any more."

I remember walking up to him and staring at the tattoo, wanting to touch it, but afraid. As though what it symbolized would somehow rub off. But then I did touch him, I touched the plus sign and from there my hand closed around his biceps and slid up onto his shoulder, and I found myself caressing that splendid body, the body of my handsome husband whom I had never fucked. For the first time in so long, I wanted sex. From a man, a woman, from someone, anyone, but most of all, from Kevin, who had touched the face of death.

'No, Natalie," he said, pushing me away.

"I want to."

I dropped to my knees and took his cock in my mouth – it was cool and dry, white and hard as marble. I wanted it inside me. I wanted his sickness, too, and his greed. Sexual greed, a bottomless neediness, demanding more and more and always more.

Something I came to New Orleans to try to fill.

"You please me, Natalie," Lily says. "That's why I don't want you to come back here. I'd rather imagine you painting in some other garden, far away."

"It's too late for that," I tell her. "My husband fucked himself to death. I want to understand what could possibly have driven him to make that choice."

"You'll get your chance." The voice is Martin's. He's crept so stealthily through the vegetation that, until this moment, I didn't see him at all. The clouds are crowding in so thickly, the sky so very close to dark.

Martin takes my arm as though to guide me. "Can you find your way home tonight?"

A strange question. The blind leading the sighted. I nod, tell him of course, and start walking the short distance between the Decatur Street garden and the apartment I'm renting on Dumaine Street.

To my surprise, however, I realize at once that his concern was not without foundation. The street lights have gone out – a power failure, I assume, probably brought about by too many air conditioners working at once during the day's heat – and a dull haze seems to hang over the city. The damp, sweltering air is murky, sluggish, tinted with tones of sepia and purple. When something smooth and tickly soft brushes my forehead, I recoil, gasping and swatting at it with my hands, then realize it's only the long tresses of the Spanish moss that overhangs the sidewalk. I pick up the pace – aware that beneath the fragrant hothouse surface lurk a plethora of dangers, that strolling alone on a darkening street courts mugging and worse – but night is coming on so rapidly that I trip on a tree root poking up out of the sidewalk and would go sprawling, easel and all, were it not for the wrought iron railing my fingers manage to curl around to catch myself in time.

I scarcely sleep at all that night, so excited am I by the prospect of being allowed inside what I now consider a secret sanctuary, the mint green home with its tangle of wisteria vines and ivy and eager, hungry human limbs. Before the sun is up, I'm on my way back to the garden, moving slowly in the pre-dawn darkness, stumbling now and then over the tree roots I don't see.

In a few minutes, when the sun is up, I'll start to paint. Meanwhile, I sit in the warm, plant-shrouded dark, forming images in my mind, waiting for the sun.

What I'll paint, I've decided, isn't from the garden, but something from my memory and my heart. Kevin's face. His perfect body. Kevin when he was strong and straight and healthy, before the minus sign tattooed on his arm was changed into a plus.

I feel desire heat my skin and realize, then, that the heat isn't coming from within me, but is beating down on me from outside. The sun is starting to come up. I feel its gentle singing on my face and its kiss, tinged with fire, on the backs of my arms. The sun is up, but the world is still dark. I can't see my hand or my brush or the canvas a few feet in front of me.

I hear the sound of Martin's cane clicking on the paving stones, then punching into the loamy earth.

His mouth finds mine. His tongue is avid, greedy, like my own. I'm too hungry for his touch to feel afraid just yet. That will come later, I suspect. Lovers and lovers later.

"Come inside the house with me," he murmurs as his fingers brush my open and unseeing eyes.

The Afternoon of a Venetian Chambermaid

Andrew L. Wilson

On weekday mornings she drove over from Mestre into Venice in the thin, pale hours before dawn, parked in a garage in the Piazzale Roma, then walked a few streets and took the vaporetto n.1 to the San Marco landing. She used the service entrance to the Hotel Giorgione and changed into her uniform in a cramped room among other maids, most of them quite younger than she, who stood around in states of partial undress chattering as they puffed on cigarettes. At the Hotel Giorgione she made as much money as her husband made at his factory work, and much less than her grown up son was making dealing in shady exports. She was not yet worn out by the work.

She changed into her white shoes and straightened the hem of the starched pink uniform, then smoothed her black hair back and clipped it behind her neck. Like this, her face had a more severe expression than usual. She had a few white hairs which flashed in the dark, smoothly rounded shape of her swept-back hair, but these didn't show when she put on the bonnet. Then all you saw were her searching, sad intelligent eyes and her smile. When she bent her head, you saw that her neck was as smooth as a girl's.

The Hotel Giorgione rang in the mornings and afternoons with the voices of the tourists who came to stay there having been drawn by descriptions of it they'd read in novels, perhaps, or seen on television. At first, she was cowed by the sheer massiveness and beauty of the place – a 16th-century palazzo with wide, gleaming carpeted halls and vaulted ceilings on which the frescoes of another age had recently been restored to startling life. But she had quickly learned to keep her eyes on the job.

She loaded her cart with fresh towels and linens and with cleaning supplies. She took the freight elevator up to her floor and pushed the cart slowly down the hall to the end, looking for doors which showed the sign asking for the maid to please make up the room. Sometimes the tourists went out early, but sometimes too they stayed, at least the passionate couples on a romantic vacation did, in their rooms making love loudly all morning.

In the rooms that had to be made, she worked with a swift, ruthless efficiency she never showed in her own household. She had learned how to clean a w.c. in ten minutes flat. Most days, as she worked steadily, she was able to detach herself by remembering things that had nothing to do with the cleaning of hotel rooms.

That morning, as she stood in the hall with an armful of dirty sheets, about to stuff them into a laundry bag suspended by a hook to the rear of her cart, a large man stepped out of a room just in front of her. He looked at her and gave her a wide, pleasant smile. She smiled in return.

He said something in English. An American.

She shook her head. He beamed at her and said, *Va bene, grazie.*

What was this man thanking her for?

She smiled again but, as she did, she raised one hand to her face and touched the side of a cheek with her fingertips.

He looked at her, it seemed, with a sudden sharpness. Then he blinked and smiled again and, turning on his heel, strode off in shoes that squeaked down the corridor to the elevators.

She stood there, holding with one arm the mass of soiled linens, her other arm raised – and she found herself blushing.

At first she thought, It's easy to know why that happened, this man reminds you of your husband. But it wasn't that.

Then she thought that the feeling that had pierced through her probably had nothing to do with this man for himself but with what she had been thinking, or fantasizing, just as he stepped out into the hallway. She turned her mind back to try to recreate those thoughts, whatever they had been, but she could not. She shrugged theatrically to herself and dropped the sheets in the bag.

From the wide mouth of the laundry bag rose the smell of bodies and of spilled semen.

At noon she took her break. She walked to a small, narrow park nearby the hotel and sat on a bench under the yellowing plane trees. She hugged herself with one arm as she smoked a cigarette and watched the people strolling through the park. At one end was a large statue in sunlight of Garibaldi on a horse, his sword upraised.

There was plenty of cleaning work that day, many of the rooms having cleared out after the long holiday weekend. As she worked, she smelled the scent of her own body rising through the maid's uniform. She remembered smelling herself like that as a girl – a thought that made her smile

She saw an image of herself swimming with her husband. He was thin then and had the body of a god. After their swim, they'd always go up into the dunes and make love. She remembered once, in a spasm of passion as her husband lunged in and out of her, licking her own shoulder, as if licking her own flesh were somehow no different than licking his.

Recalling that day made her wet between the legs. She shut and locked the door to the room, went into the toilet and, sitting on the curved edge of the bidet with her legs spread and her stockings rolled hastily down and her panties around her knees, masturbated swiftly. She bit the back of her hand as she rose up, up, up into her orgasm.

She was trembling as she hurriedly pulled up the panties and refastened the flesh-coloured stockings. She smelled her fingers – the smell of sex on them was pungent, like the smell of the lagoon around Venice. She patted her dress down front and back.

* * *

Who should be walking in the hall but the large man with the clear, pleasant smile? He was dressed in a suit and was holding a large bottle of mineral water. She swept a hand over her forehead to get off it a clinging strand of hair and smiled demurely at him.

Scusi signorina, he said.

She smiled at that. *Signorina!*

Signora, she said.

Ah, he said, *Mi scusi, mi scusi. Signora, io voglio* – He suddenly stopped and let his fluttering hand fall.

You can speak English, she told him. *I speak some. From my school.*

Ah, he said. He shook his head, smiling. Then he looked at her with the sharpness of this morning and said:

Please. I want to know your name.

She stared at him with her mouth open in an O.

My name? she said.

Yes. How do you say that in Italian? I knew but I've forgotten. I'm sorry.

Come si chiama?

That means?

It means: What are you called?

Ah.

He looked at her. He had blue eyes.

I am called Gabriella.

He held out a wide hand, which she shook. It was fleshy yet not unpleasant.

Mi chiamo, he said, stumbling a little and pursing his wet lips –

Buono, buono, she said with forced warmth, encouraging him.

Harold.

She beamed. He let go of her hand.

Piacere, she said. *It means, With pleasure to meet you.*

Ah, he said. *Piacere, then.*

Are you in Venice on some business? she asked. She was impressed to hear her own speech, realizing that her English was in fact very good, and the fact of her English being good gave her a kind of superiority over him, even though he was in a beautiful suit and she was wearing her slightly wrinkled maid's uniform.

Yes, yes, he said, pursing his lips as if he were trying to speak his English the way that she spoke it.

Realizing all at once that the hand he had just shaken in his hard, firm grip was the same hand with which she had just finished masturbating herself on the bidet in the locked room, she laughed.

Well, she said to his enquiring look, *I hope you have a good stay here.*

I will. And thank you. Ciao.

Ciao.

He raised his hand and, waving slightly, passed by her as she stood there in the hall. Watching his back go, Gabriella felt a sadness that thrilled her body like pure elation.

The Dinner Party

Emma Kaufmann

When Stewart arrived at the dinner party with a life-sized mannequin tucked under his arm, Stella asked him if he would care to deposit it in the cloakroom where the rest of the guests had left their coats.

Igoring her, Stewart marched down the hall to the dining room. Stella scurried after him. The conversation stopped as he set the mannequin – dressed in a red satin evening gown, which was split to the thigh – next to the fireplace. All eyes were drawn to one of her legs, which jutted out from the slit. The guests held their breath as Stewart arranged her so that she balanced against the mantelpiece, then gave a collective gasp as the mannequin toppled to the floor. From her prone position, legs sticking up stiffly into the air, it was clear that she wasn't wearing panties.

How to handle this? wondered Stella, as Stewart lifted the mannequin back to a standing position. She watched in amazement as her husband, Graham, walked over to Stewart and handed him two martinis.

The mannequin, thought Stella – from her gazelle-like limbs to her parted mouth, that gave the impression that she was permanently poised on the verge of saying something witty – was the epitome of everything that Stella had strived for and failed to achieve during tortuous sessions at the gym. As Stella walked towards her husband, a wave of anxiety rising in her chest, she had the distinct impression that the mannequin's eyes were following her.

She tugged at his shirtsleeve. "What on earth are we going to do?"

"Do?" said Graham, a tall man in the latter stages of baldness. "About what?" He speared an olive and plopped it into a glass.

"About Stewart. Don't you think he's behaving a little oddly?" She looked over to the mannequin's martini glass, which Stewart had lodged between her fingers, where it remained untouched.

Graham chuckled. "Yes, quite amusing, isn't it?"

"Well, I don't know," said Stella, feeling a little faint. The mannequin was still looking at her, this time she was certain of it. Her head had twisted to the left, and her gaze was trained directly on Stella.

Stella walked backwards towards the kitchen, tugging her fitted black dress towards her knees, wishing she had worn something looser. She usually considered her legs to be her best –well really, only – feature and had worn the dress to show them off, but since the mannequin had appeared on the scene she was convinced that the tight dress only emphasized the world of difference between her hippo-sized backside and the mannequin's slender haunches.

She shut the door behind her, took a gulp of air and began to stir the cassoulet, which was bubbling on the stove. What on earth, she thought, licking the spoon absentmindedly and setting it aside, had compelled her to put on a pair of black hold-up stockings this morning, as well as a rather provocative thong?

As she began to mix up a chocolate soufflé the question continued to niggle. It was hard for her to admit her motives to herself but, if she was honest, the donning of the outfit had been a practical response to Graham's recent lack of sexual interest, and she was nothing if not practical, she thought as she whipped up the soufflé a little too vigorously. She could only hope that after the guests had left the sight of her saucy undergarments might bring forth some sort of response from him.

She poured the soufflé mix into individual serving dishes

and slid them into the oven, flushing as she thought of the mannequin's eyes and the way they had followed her. She hadn't felt this way since she was 14 and had had a crush on Miss Charlton, the gym mistress. Her insides felt all gooey as she put the soup tureen onto the hostess trolley and wheeled it into the dining room.

To her dismay, she saw that the only seat left at the dinner table was next to the mannequin, whose chin was now propped in her hand, her head turned expectantly towards the empty chair.

She could hear Stewart say to Graham, who sat beside him, "I've not known Carla long. It's very much early days . . ." Graham was indulging Stewart, Stella noticed, nodding attentively as he talked.

Stella poured the soup into the bowls and put them in front of her guests. Because her friends had impeccable manners, no one had dared to ask Stewart directly why he was so insistent that this dummy – Carla, as he called her – was his girlfriend. But, mannequin or not, both the other men besides Stewart and her husband were transfixed by the perfect cream orbs that spilled out of Carla's low-cut gown.

Not wishing to make a scene, she set a bowl in front of Carla. She would humour Stewart as if he were a child with an imaginary friend.

As she leaned over Carla to put a bowl beside Stewart she felt a hand brush the back of her leg, so that she almost dropped the soup into his lap. She looked at Stewart. Had he just touched her? No, it was impossible. He was still rambling on to Graham, "The thing about Carla is, she actually listens to me. Whereas with Dorothy – " his ex-wife – "I could hardly get a word in edgeways . . ."

Stewart turned back to Carla and tied a napkin around her neck. As Stella sat down beside her she could scarcely believe her eyes as Stewart lifted her spoon, filled with cream of mushroom soup, to Carla's lips and tilted it. Some of the soup ran into the hollow between her lips, the rest spilled over her chin.

"OK, darling," he said, as if responding to an imaginary voice. "If you think you can handle it on your own." He let the spoon sink back into the soup and turned back to his conversation with Graham.

As she looked at Carla, at the viscous globules of soup that stuck to her lips, at her bright, vacuous eyes, she was vividly reminded of an image from one of those magazines that Graham kept hidden under his golf clubs in the wardrobe, of a girl who had just had a man ejaculate on her face. She would never let Graham do something like that to her, of course, although she had read somewhere that it was quite good for the complexion . . . She froze. Amidst the chatter that swirled around her she felt that touch again, and this time she was quite certain whose it was. Carla's hand was cupping her knee, then slipping under the hem of her dress.

She turned to look at Carla, whose blank expression provided no answers. She clamped her thighs together over Carla's hand, which was surprisingly warm, quite lifelike in fact, not stiff and cold as she would have expected. She felt quite flushed as she gazed at Carla's nipples, clearly visible through the flimsy fabric.

"Go on," said a voice. "You know you want to." Stella's heart began to pound. Had Carla actually spoken to her? She reached down and pulled Carla's hand out of her skirt, trying to decide what to do. She was not one for making a scene in public. No, the best thing to do would be to take Carla into the kitchen and get to the bottom of this, woman to woman.

She leaned across Carla to Stewart. "I'm just taking her to the kitchen to clean her up. She seems to have got a little soup on her dress."

Feeling rather self-conscious, she helped Carla up. She was startled to find that Carla's limbs felt not only like human flesh but smoother, baby soft, and hot, as if there were molten liquid fizzing and bubbling beneath the skin. Despite the fact that her head was spinning and she felt unsteady on her feet, she put her arm around Carla's waist and carried her across the room.

As soon as she pushed open the door to the kitchen, Stella was hit by a heady gust of chocolate. The chocolate soufflés! She had completely forgotten about them. Leaning Carla awkwardly against the washing machine she pulled the tray out of the oven, turned off the stove, then, flustered, spun around.

"Now, what's all this about?" she asked. "What did you mean by touching me?"

In response, Carla took a step towards her and pressed her mouth onto Stella's, prised her lips open and poked her tongue in. Stella was surprised to find that it was enjoyable – extremely enjoyable in fact – to have Carla's tongue in her mouth, darting about like a snake. She felt her body respond urgently, as it once had with Graham, many moons ago. A tingle ran over her skin as she felt herself becoming wet, very wet, down there.

"Do you want to experience something different," whispered Carla, "or do you want to end up like them in there – " she nodded in the direction of the dining room " – dead from the waist down?"

It was no longer strange to Stella that Carla had been transformed into a pliable, fleshy entity, that right now Carla was pulling off her dress to expose the hairless expanse of her pussy. Stella, without knowing why, disrobed, ripped off the thong and, clad only in the stockings and heels, pulled Carla towards her, a reckless passion coursing through her as they sank to the floor.

"You like me, hmm?" said Carla, kneeling up and scooping up a handful of the soufflé, then placing her fingers in Stella's mouth so that the warm chocolate melted on her tongue and dripped down the back of her throat.

Carla took another dollop of soufflé and began to smear it across her chest, laughing recklessly while Stella crawled over to her and began to lick off the soft goo that flowed between Carla's breasts. Then, breathlessly, she pushed Carla down onto the floor and started to probe Carla's pussy. Even after many evenings surreptitiously scouring Graham's naughty magazines she had never seen a pussy as pale and glistening as Carla's. As she licked at it she was surprised to find the taste had a remarkable similarity to cake batter, a mixture of vanilla and musk, with a light dusting of cinnamon. Her mouth tingling with anticipation, she started to devour her with her tongue.

"Ooh," moaned Carla. "That feels sooo good." She lay flat on the floor, her chocolate-smeared fingers squeezing her breasts together, as Stella probed her clit, drinking in the nectar that ran from it, until she felt an enormous surge of heat in Carla's pussy, followed by a tremendous shudder that shook Carla's body.

Carla moved on top of her and Stella felt a silky soft length of leg, dripping with soufflé, slip in between hers.

"This is so much more fun," said Carla, her hand moving over Stella's pussy and slipping two fingers inside, "than that boring old dinner party."

Stella was so excited that she found herself shouting, "Fuck me!" as she closed her eyes, felt Carla's fingers twist inside her, then pull out to be replaced by a cold, hard object.

"Sorry it's so cold," said Carla. "All I could find in the fridge was this zucchini." But Stella's pussy didn't seem to mind one bit about the coldness, as Carla plunged the zucchini in and out until finally Stella flailed against the slippery floor, her climax crashing over her.

Stella opened her eyes and looked up at Carla, her eyes no longer blank but sparkling with lust. Her long white body was now completely smeared in chocolate.

"What about my guests?" asked Stella, suddenly regaining her composure.

"Oh God, yes," said Carla. "Quick, let's get cleaned up. Stewart mustn't know what happened. He's never seen me like this." She ran a tea towel under the hot faucet and began to wipe herself clean.

"You mean, he thinks you're just a mannequin?"

"Of course. He fell in love with me when he spotted me in a shop window."

"You're having me on!"

"No, seriously. He just marched right in and bought me from the shop manager." Carla wiped her neck clean of chocolate. "I was grateful. All that standing around behind hot glass can get very tiring for a girl." As she started to run the hot towel over Stella's shoulders, Stella felt her pussy begin to throb.

"So Stewart doesn't know that you can come alive?"

"No, and I don't want you telling him either. It's an easy life, just acting like I'm made of plastic. He likes to look at me, show me off to his friends, and doesn't expect much in return." She shrugged. "It suits me just fine."

When they had both cleaned up and dressed, Stella leaned over to give her one last kiss, but even as she did so she felt the life leaving Carla's body, saw the eyes glaze over, felt Carla's limbs stiffen in her arms.

She pushed open the door. "Sorry I took so long." All heads swivelled towards her as she carried Carla back to her seat. "The main course is just about ready to serve," she said, flustered by the fact that everyone was still watching her, their mouths hanging open like dead fish. Then, finally, the silence was broken and conversation resumed.

"What is it?" Stella hissed in Graham's ear as she picked up his empty bowl. "Why did everyone look at me like that?"

"It's your dress," he whispered back. "It's on inside out."

Dive Inn

O'Neil De Noux

Go ahead, ruin my fuckin' weekend!

Goddamn FBI Seminar starts this afternoon, 14 hours after I caught my latest murder case, a girl of 17 found strangled on the second floor stairwell of a Philip Street tenement, just off Tchoupitoulas Street.

Her name was Priscilla Lewis. Sprawled on her back on the stairs, her light brown hair tangled around her face, there was a thin rope twisted around her neck. The rope had cut into her throat which bulged obscenely around the particularly crude murder weapon of rough hemp.

As she lay pretzeled on the stairs, I studied her, noticing how her flowered dress had been repositioned neatly around her legs. Her torn panties lay 20 feet below on the first floor landing, next to three bent-up soft drink cans and an empty pizza box, residence of two cockroaches and a host of those small in-door roaches. What struck me was the print on her panties. They were Little Mermaid panties. That's right, from the movie.

Tiny for 17, Priscilla measured an even five feet on the autopsy table.

When I spoke to her mother at three a.m., she said Prissy was "slow in the head". Not retarded, but slow. Prissy loved going to movies and riding the streetcar to the Audubon Zoo. She liked to walk too. That evening she went out to catch the Jackson Avenue ferry to Gretna to take a bus to Oakwood Shopping Centre. *Pocahontas* was playing.

It was the third murder on that steamy Thursday New Orleans evening, this one discovered by a gas company crew checking the area for a possible gas leak. One of the men vomited. The other's eyes were red and vacant. Death'll do that to you sometimes.

I spent three hours processing the scene with the crime lab, while my overworked partners canvassed the area. I spent an additional hour searching the stairwell and surrounding area for Priscilla's missing left shoe before heading for her autopsy.

After her post-mortem, in which we discovered she was killed between seven and nine p.m. and wasn't raped, I managed to get about four hours sleep. Reading the notes from my partners' canvass over coffee, I found several interesting leads. We lifted a number of decent fingerprints from the scene. We also secured prints from Priscilla's body using that new DuraPrint system.

Only I can't follow up the leads. Hell, any good homicide detective knows the first 24 hours after a murder are the *most* important. No. I have to go to an FBI Seminar.

Ruin my fuckin' weekend! *I have a murder to solve.*

"You have to go," my lieutenant ordered me. "It's been scheduled for six months. Don't worry about your case. Your murder will still be there Monday."

So Friday afternoon, I park my unmarked Chevy Caprice in the 4400 block of Dryades Street, 50 feet from one of the great New Orleans restaurants, Pascal's Manale. I look across the street at a pink stucco building with rows of tinted windows and recheck the address in my notepad. Apparently this is a bed-and-breakfast known as Dive Inn.

Tucking my notepad into the coat pocket of my navy blue suit, I toss my coat over my shoulder and readjust my black canvas holster, riding high on my belt at the small of my back. In the holster is my new stainless steel 9 mm Beretta.

Crossing the street, I can't help thinking how only the FBI would be dumb enough to schedule a major crime seminar in

New Orleans during Jazz Fest. We've had to stash the 200 cops in town for this seminar in every small hotel, bed-and-breakfast and rooming house we could find.

The relentless New Orleans summer sun draws perspiration on my freshly-shaved face. I find the door to the place around the side. It's ornate, wooden and locked. So I ring the bell. I'm buzzed into a small foyer with four steps. Turning right, through an archway, I hesitate as I take in the view.

To my left is a large swimming pool of turquoise and brown tile. Overhead, a tinted glass skylight bathes the wide room with bright sunlight. A small sitting area to my right is crowded with high-back rocking chairs and a long wooden pew that must have come from a church.

Across the pool, behind a large, U-shaped bar, stands a bald bartender with a reddish-brown goatee. Just this side of the bar, closer to the pool, is the only other occupant, an elderly Japanese man in all white. He stands next to a waist-high exercise bench.

As I round the pool for the bar, a door opens to my right and a naked lady strolls out of a bathroom made from what looks like a gazebo. I freeze as she walks past, giving me a little mischievous grin. About five-five, her shoulder-length brown hair hangs in long curls. For a petite woman, she has nice full breasts and an even nicer, round, voluptuous ass.

She waves at the bartender and walks straight to the exercise table. The Japanese bows to her and she climbs on the table and lies there on her belly. The man pulls a bottle from under the table and pours a thick slurp of oily liquid on the woman's back.

"What can I do for you?" the bartender calls out to me.

Still watching the naked lady, I move to the bar and ask, "Did I just step into another dimension?"

The bartender laughs and nods to the exercise table. 'Naw. That's just Mr Yokura and one of his clients."

The bartender is about my size, about six-two, but has a good 100 pounds on me, and ten or fifteen years. At 27 I still weigh what I weighed-in as an LSU quarterback – 175. My dark brown hair, in dire need of a haircut, reaches past the collar of my dress shirt.

I look back at the woman as Mr Yokura rubs the liquid on the woman's shoulders.

"Want something to drink?"

"A Coke would be nice." I pull a buck out of my pocket.

"No charge, officer," the bartender says as he fixes me a fountain Coke. Even in civvies, I act too much like the police, I guess.

"I'm ex-police myself." He puts the glass in front of me and reaches his hand out. As we shake, he tells me his name is Bruce Wayne – no relation to Batman – and how he once worked the Second and Sixth Districts. A car wreck ended his career. "I'm on partial disability."

I leave the dollar on the counter and take a sip of the icy Coke.

"You here to pick up Detectives Norling and Palmer?"

I nod as I watch the naked lady. Yokura's hands massage the small of her back, just above her ass.

"They're kinda peculiar," Bruce Wayne says.

"Huh?"

"Norling and Palmer. Where are they from?"

"Union Parish."

"Well, they'll be out in a minute." Bruce Wayne leans forward and lowers his voice. "That's Mrs Sucio. Husband's a neurosurgeon."

Yokura pours liquid on the beautiful ass. I have to readjust myself as I sit. The blue-veiner between my legs is a full hard-on now. The spindly hands began rubbing the ass, working the liquid into her creamy skin.

I hear footsteps behind me, turn in time to see a tall man in a tan suit and a white cowboy hat come through the door that must lead to the rooms. He rounds the bar and I watch carefully as he spots what's on the exercise table. He stops and grabs the bar for support. Leaning forwards with mouth open, he leers at the naked lady getting her ass rubbed.

I have to ask, "Feel like you just walked into The Twilight Zone?"

He nods slowly.

"It's real," I tell him as I turn back to Yokura who moves the lady's feet apart to massage her thighs.

"Jesus H. Christ!" The man in the cowboy hat has a north Louisiana drawl, which sounds like a rural Texan. He stumbles to the stool next to me. He's breathing so heavily, I have to turn to make sure he hasn't whipped it out.

"Norm Norling," he says, extending an empty hand which I shake. "You Detective Ravenboo?"

"John Raven Beau." I pull my hand away.

"Raven? You some kinda Injun or somethin'? Choctaw or somethin'?"

I wait for him to look at me so he can see the anger in my eyes, only there's no way he's looking away from Mrs Sucio.

"I'm half Sioux," I tell him flatly. "Call me 'Injun' again you can walk to the fuckin' seminar." No need to tell the idiot I'm half Cajun.

Norm slaps my shoulder and chuckles. "Don't mind me, padna. I'm an asshole. That's why I went into law enforcement in the first place."

How'd Bruce Wayne describe him? Peculiar? I finish my Coke and Bruce refills it immediately, asking Norm if he wants something to drink.

"Got any Calhoun beer?"

"No."

"Budweiser, then." Norm taps my shoulder and points a thumb at Mrs Sucio. "Does shit like this go on a lot 'round here?"

"All the time," I lie. "It's New Orleans."

Mrs Sucio rolls over on her back. Norm lets out a high-pitched whistle. A smile crawls on the lady's face as she lies with her eyes closed.

Yokura pours oil on her belly and proceeds to rub it in neat circles. He pours more between her breasts, which rise with her breathing. Slowly, he works the oil across her breasts, kneading them softly, rubbing her pink areolae, twinking her pointy nipples.

"Motha-fuck!" Norm says. "What kinda show *is* this?"

"Nude body massage," Bruce Wayne answers.

I egg him on. "Y'all don't have this up in Union Parish?"

Norm points his Bud at the woman. "Who *is* she?"

Bruce explains as we watch Yokura's hands work their way

down to the top of her pubic hair. He pours oil on her bush. Mrs Sucio opens her feet as Yokura rubs the oil in, his fingers slipping around the sides of her pussy. I finally catch my breath and take another hit of Coke.

Norm climbs off his stool to get a better look at her pink slit.

Mrs Sucio raises her knees, then lets them fall open as Yokura's fingers slip inside her pussy. When she starts rocking her hips, it's time for me to readjust my diamond-cutter dick.

Jesus!

Mrs Sucio moans and gasps a breathless, "Yes. Yes. Yes!"

I turn to Bruce Wayne whose elbows are propped on the bar as he watches the show. I have to laugh at the way we're leering, like schoolboys, until I hear another pair of footsteps approaching. Looking at the doorway to the rooms, I spot a young woman enter.

In a grey business suit, her shoulder-holster rig obvious beneath her jacket, she must be Detective Palmer. I'm surprised she isn't wearing a Dale Evans outfit. I tap Norm on the elbow.

"This oughta be fun," he says as he looks over his shoulder. "Here comes Ms Prude."

Seeing us, she comes around the bar and stops immediately. Her face blushes and she looks at Norm, then at me with an accusing look.

"Whatsa' matter?" Norm says. "This is *New Orleans*!" He laughs and goes back to leering at Mrs Sucio.

Standing between her legs, Yokura's face is only inches from her pussy as he stays his course, fingering Mrs Sucio through spasmodic gyrations.

"She's gettin' close," Norm announces.

I turn back to Detective Palmer who stands there as if quick-frozen. Stepping off my stool, I move next to her.

"I'm here to pick y'all up for the seminar."

"What?" Palmer's blue eyes flash at me.

I take a step back, hold my hands up and introduce myself.

She pulls her large purse up to her chest and wraps her hands around it.

"Jane Palmer," she says.

Kinda pretty up close, she has a plain, natural beauty. She's lanky, thin with a nice figure and thick, blonde hair streaked with brown and red highlights. She appears to be in her mid-20s, maybe younger.

Behind me, Mrs Sucio hits a high note. Detective Palmer looks around me, so I look too as the woman on the exercise table goes through a loud climax, her ass bouncing on the cushion.

"Damn!" Norm says.

"She sure likes an audience," Bruce Wayne adds as he asks Detective Palmer if she'd like something to drink.

"Think I'll go over and introduce myself," Norm says, climbing gingerly from his stool, heading for Mrs Sucio.

Glancing at my watch, I tell him we don't have time. "We have to go."

He waves me away. "One minute, Detective." Removing his stetson, he approaches Mrs Sucio.

Jane Palmer is already backing away, looking at the pool now. I start to follow, turn and tell Norm we're leaving. He can catch a cab.

He waves me forwards with his stetson. "This here is Detective John Raven Beau of your own New Orleans Police Department."

Norm steps aside to give me a clear view of Mrs Sucio, who's leaning up on her elbows, her legs wide open. I try not to stare at her wet pussy.

She smiles at me and lies back as Yokura pours oil on her feet and begins working her toes.

I walk away with Norm following slowly.

He calls out to Bruce Wayne, "You better let me know when the next woman comes for a finger wave."

Jane Palmer, sunglasses on now, waits for us outside. I point to the Caprice and lead them across the street. Norm insists on the back seat where he can recline because he can't bend properly, not with the "stinger" in his pants.

Donning my own dark sunglasses, I drive off. No one talks. When we reach downtown, I ask Jane where is Union Parish, exactly?

She crosses her legs, tugging at her skirt which is only a few inches above her knees.

"It's up against the Arkansas border," she says without looking at me. She still looks zoned out. "South of El Dorado. Huttig more precisely."

Jesus! Huttig? That explains it nicely. I have no fuckin' clue.

"Any cities in Union Parish?"

"Farmerville. It's the parish seat."

Farmerville? Where the fuck is Barney Fife when you need him?

I look in the back seat to see if Rod Serling has hitched a ride.

Norm grins at me. "Hope this stinger wears off 'afore I gotta climb out."

As I turn on to Poydras, heading towards the river and the Convention Centre, where our seminar is to be held, Jane surprises me.

"Thanks for picking us up," she says.

"No problem. We take care of the police here."

No longer blushing, her complexion is peach coloured. She doesn't seem to wear much make-up and doesn't need to. She bats those big blue eyes at me.

"Y'all caught a plane down here, I hope."

She shakes her head and tells me they drove.

Poor thing. All that way with the wonderful Norm Norling.

"Y'all ain't gonna believe what we saw," a detective with a Claiborne Parish Sheriff's Office badge clipped to his suit coat shouts as we crowd into the large auditorium. "Women up on balconies showing their titties for carnival beads."

Norm Norling, finding a soul-brother, stops to tell everyone about Mrs Sucio and the finger wave at Dive Inn.

I move past them to sit in the last seat, in the last row. Jane Palmer follows and sits two seats from me. Wish I'd have brought a pillow. I put my dark sunglasses back on.

A dozen neatly dressed FBI special agents pass out folders for everyone. When they reach our row, they pass two to Jane and suggest we move up closer.

"I can't," I tell them. "Nose-bleed."

"My nose bleeds too," Jane says.

I gleek her, peeking at her over the top of my sunglasses. She doesn't look back.

Across the outside of my folder, emblazoned in blue is: Department of Justice, Federal Bureau of Investigation. Below, in red, is: Seminar on Sex Crimes. It's the same class I took in Homicide School last year at the Southern Police Institute. I told my lieutenant. But what the fuck do I know? I'm just a worker.

I recognize the lead lecturer. Interesting guy, for a fed. He starts out with the standard "murder among friends and associates" spiel, how 80 per cent of murders are committed by people who know the victim.

Jane writes furiously. I peek over and see she's taking shorthand. Nice. Wish I could take notes that fast at a crime scene, or during an interview. She sure is conscientious.

Leaning my head against the wall, I close my eyes and drift back to Philip Street. I envision Priscilla walking, walking everywhere. I can see her approach the ferry on her way to see *Pocahontas*. Wonder how she was led up those stairs? She wasn't dragged. There were no drag marks on the dirty stairs.

My steady breathing lulls me and I see Mrs Sucio lying there with her legs open and those soft, silky pubic hairs around her pussy lips.

Ah!

I hear Jane Palmer's voice. "Wake up."

My eyes snap open.

She's leaning over me. "We're adjourned."

Everyone's moving toward the exit.

"Are you the only one from NOPD here?" Jane asks as I stand and stretch.

I point to a motley group of ill-dressed detectives across the aisle and tell her they're from the Sex Crimes Unit. "We also have a couple Juvenile Detectives here, but I'm the only one from Homicide. I have all the luck."

On our way out, she tells me how I missed three good lectures. I tell her I took the same classes last year. She's confused. So am I.

It's still daylight outside. I look around for Norm and Jane tells me not to.

"You can just bring me back to Dive Inn." I can see her mind's made up. I was thinking of maybe a nice supper, but who am I to argue?

As I pull up alongside Dive Inn, she turns to me and says, "Just what the hell was that by the pool, with that woman?"

I try to explain as nicely as I can about Mr Yokura and his client, Mrs Sucio and what Bruce Wayne calls nude body massage. "I've never seen anything like it, either."

"You didn't set it up as entertainment for the out of towners?" She glares at me.

"Nope." I climb out and go around to open her door.

She's out before I get there, slamming the door as she walks away. Watching her, I have to admit she has a nice figure. I start to follow, in case Mr Yokura has another client, but I have a better idea. I head straight for Philip Street. I've got work to do.

Bruce Wayne is behind the bar Saturday morning when I walk in. The place smells of cooking – bacon and eggs. Yokura is nowhere to be seen. I almost miss Norm Norling as he lies draped across the church pew. Wearing the same tan suit, his stetson covers his face.

Bruce smiles at me and calls out, "Breakfast?"

I don't realize I'm hungry until I get close enough to see the bacon sizzling on the gas stove along the backside of the bar.

"This *is* a bed-and-breakfast," Bruce says. He nods toward Norm. "He isn't eating."

I sit on a stool and watch Bruce flip the eggs in the second skillet.

"Last night that fool brought a shitload of country-ass cops back with him. They got drunk and tried to get me to call Mr Yokura, as if he can get a client over here for a nude massage any time."

I laugh.

"Yeah. Well, good ole Norm isn't going anywhere today."

Jane Palmer, smart looking in a navy blue suit, comes out. Looking cautiously at the exercise table, she seems relieved when she sees it's empty.

"No suit?" she asks me as she sits in the next stool.

Today I wear a black T-shirt and faded jeans, my gold star-

and-crescent badge clipped to the front of my belt, my Beretta in its usual position at the small of my back. I have a dark grey dress shirt in the car that I'll wear unbuttoned like a coat, to cover my weapon in public.

Bruce puts our plates in front of us, along with icy glasses of orange juice. He serves himself up as I start in on the first breakfast I've had in months. Usually coffee's it for me in the morning.

Saturday at the conference is a re-run of yesterday. I grab the seat next to the wall, Jane sits one seat over and takes notes in shorthand.

Her skirt is higher on her thigh and she doesn't pull it down. The audience is at least a quarter smaller than yesterday. Friday night'll do that in New Orleans. Even fewer will be here tomorrow.

I start to doze off before the first lecture is over.

I'd spent a good deal of the night talking with the people along Philip Street between Tchoupitoulas, Annunciation and Jackson Avenue. Of course, I came up with nothing. Two of the men I was looking for couldn't be found.

As I slip into slumber, a Homicide cliché comes to mind, "Good detective work is in the details, not in broad strokes."

The dream comes to me in snap-shots at first, as if I'm taking pictures of Mrs Sucio walking out of the gazebo-bathroom. Her full breasts move slowly up and down. I focus on her pink areolae and nipples that grow hard as she moves to the table. My fingers rub the oil into her skin, fondling her ass, rubbing it, sliding into the crack.

She rolls over and I knead her breasts. I'm not massaging, I'm feeling her up, fondling her boobs as she breathes heavier. My hands glide down the sides of her body to her hips. She opens her legs and my fingers move through her soft, silky pubic hair.

She gasps as I lightly brush my fingertips across her clit.

The sound of shuffling feet wakes me.

Jesus! I'm at the seminar!

I stretch and look at my watch. It's almost one. Jane comes in the back door and sits next to me.

"I was going to wake you for lunch, but you were sleeping so soundly." She has something wrapped in a paper towel. "I brought a chicken salad croissant for you."

"Thanks." I take the croissant on my way past her.

"Lecture's about to start," she tells me.

"I'll be back."

My hard-on slowly fades as I cross the street toward Poydras Street. On my way to Mother's Restaurant, I give the croissant to a homeless man carrying a black garbage bag. He doesn't bother to thank me, but eats it on the move.

After a nice, sloppy roast beef po-boy, I finish off my second icy Barq's root beer then slowly make my way back to the seminar. Jane's taking furious notes as I plop next to her.

Thankfully, the afternoon goes by quickly. I force myself not to think of naked women on exercise benches. I actually listen to a forensic lecture on toothmarks. It's interesting, only I've read a shitload of books on the Ted Bundy case, not to mention watching investigative specials on cable TV that replay every few months. Famous cases, like Bundy and Richard Speck and The Boston Strangler seem to be favourites of investigative reporters.

Jane is ready to leave as soon as the seminar adjourns. Walking next to me, she thanks me again for driving her around. She's quiet in the car, her legs and arms crossed.

I take her straight up St Charles Avenue, pointing out the fine mansions of the Garden District to her. She looks but isn't paying attention, not even as a streetcar rattles by along the neutral ground.

"Damn," she says, uncrossing her legs. She pulls her skirt up. There's a run in her hose, from her knee up her thigh. To my surprise, she pulls her skirt up as far as the run goes, almost to her crotch. I get a good view of her pink panties beneath her pantyhose.

My hard-on's back that fast.

She pushes her skirt down, but not too far. Looking up with those large blue eyes she says, "I'm not a prude, no matter what that asshole says."

I guess the fuck not.

She uncrosses her arms and looks out at a passing mansion,

a Victorian painted sky blue.

"I've been thinking about that naked woman," she says.

I glance in the rear view mirror. Nope, Rod Serling's not in the back seat.

"Can't get over a married woman getting finger-fucked like that."

I try not to run into the car in front of me. Guess I stare too long at Jane, because she squints her eyes at me.

"What?" she snaps.

"You didn't see Bruce Wayne carrying any big seed pods around Dive Inn last night?"

"Seed pods?" She crinkles her nose.

Looking back at the traffic, I tell her, "I don't know who the fuck you are, but you're not Detective Jane Palmer. You've been body-snatched."

Her face reddens and she looks away. "Why, because I said the 'f' word?"

"Yeah. And you showed me your panties."

She folds her arms again. "You didn't see my panties."

"They're pink."

She clams up, but doesn't pull her skirt down.

Climbing out quickly when we pull up at Dive Inn, she thanks me once again as she hurries inside. I'm about to call out, ask her if she'd like some real New Orleans food for supper, but she's through the door.

Time for me to head back to Philip Street.

Sunday, the last day of the conference, and I'm wide awake and bored to hell. Two seats away, Jane Palmer sits with her legs crossed. Her black wrap skirt, opened nicely in front, shows almost as much of her sleek legs as I saw yesterday. She wears a white blouse today and barrettes in her hair, pulled up on the sides, giving her a more sophisticated appearance.

I'm all out of leads on Priscilla's murder. Often, promising clues lead to other clues, not solutions, but these led to nothing. I still hope it's a neighbourhood thing, someone seeing her, pulling her into that tenement. If it was some douche-bag, cruising around in his car, then it could be anybody. Fuck!

I don't realize I'm listening to the lecture when my mind reminds me of the homicide cliché again, "Good detective work is in the details, not in broad strokes."

The lecture's about "organized" and "disorganized" serial killers. The lecturer, a balding man with black glasses, is discussing the link between victim and murderer.

"Their interaction can be a lone encounter. Or they could know each other, well or slightly. You see, the victim is a complementary partner to the killer . . . the good side of a coin while the killer is the bad side."

What? I look at Jane and she's jotting away.

Complementary partner?

As if I'd asked a question the lecturer goes on to explain how the killer selects and interprets communication clues from the victim that the victim may be unaware he or she is giving.

"If a victim is passive, this may provoke the attack. If the victim resists, that may provoke the attack. Certainly, for the brief period it takes for the murder to occur, there is communication between victim and killer. They are partners in death."

The lecture goes on to explain the two basic behavioural patterns of murders. The first is premeditated, intentional, planned and rational killings. The second is killings in heat of passion or slaying as a result of intent to do harm, without specific intent to kill.

Communication. The word rattles around in my head and I remember something from one of the interviews the night Priscilla died. Someone living nearby. Something about the way Priscilla walked.

Looking at my watch, I see it's only ten minutes to our lunch break, but I can't wait. I get up and step past Jane who looks up in confusion. Digging my briefcase from the trunk of the Caprice, I locate the statements taken the night of the murder.

It's in a statement by a neighbour, one Henry Hyde, white male, 28. Hyde lives around the corner from Philip St on Jackson Avenue. He claimed he didn't know the victim, however, he'd seen her strolling around. Strolling. It's not much, but he didn't say *walking*. He said *strolling,* which means a leisurely walk, as if he'd watched her. It's a subtle thing, but sometimes that's all we have to go on. Did she communicate that to him, that it was a leisurely walk?

Jesus, am I reaching or what?

I crank up the Caprice and spot Jane rushing across the street. The wind catches her skirt and it opens, showing her sleek legs and shapely thighs. I roll my window down.

"Where are you going?"

"Work on my case."

She pulls her hair away from her face. "You'll miss getting your diploma."

"They can mail it to me."

She looks over her shoulder at the mass of cops streaming out for lunch. Turning back, she says, "Mind if I come along?"

I unlock the front passenger door. She climbs in, fastening her seatbelt, but leaves her skirt open.

"You'll miss your diploma," I tell her.

"Stuff it. Let's go."

No one answers the yellowed door of Henry Hyde's apartment. Nestled on the side of a three-storey home long ago converted into apartments, Hyde lives a block up from Tchoupitoulas.

A warm breeze filters up from the river as Jane and I walk slowly from Hyde's house down to Tchoupitoulas. Checking garbage cans and alleys, we look for Priscilla's missing black shoe.

Passing a particularly smelly lot between two dilapidated buildings, I tell Jane, "Welcome to the inner city."

"Smells like a cow pasture," she says, "after a long rain."

As we turn right on Tchoupitoulas, we almost walk past a blue dumpster in an alley. Half hidden behind an abandoned green Ford with no wheels, the dumpster has no lid.

I climb up on the Ford's trunk and spot the shoe immediately. My heart races as I lean closer. It's a left shoe all right. I pull my radio out of the back pocket of my jeans and call headquarters for the crime lab.

"You serious?" Jane says as I climb down.

I rub her arm. "You're good luck."

She smiles and bounces on her toes.

It takes the crime lab an hour to arrive and another 40 minutes to photograph, secure the shoe, dust it for prints and lift one print. Turning to leave, I spot a man standing on the sidewalk across Tchoupitoulas. There's nothing but the grey seawall behind him as he stands leering at us, hands in his pants pockets.

As I approach the man, he presses his back against his seawall and stands stiffly. I pull out my credentials and show them to him.

"What's your name, mister?"

"Henry Hyde."

I feel the hair standing on my arms. "We have to talk," I tell him.

He's about six feet tall with prematurely greying hair that hasn't been brushed in God knows how long. His smooth, pinkish face is almost adolescent looking. His grey T-shirt is two sizes too small and his pants cuffs end a good inch above his black, high-top tennis shoes.

Jane is definitely good luck.

While Henry Hyde festers in a tiny, windowless interview room, I locate an old buddy from the academy, now one of our ace fingerprint technicians and call in a favour – on a Sunday. Thankfully, Hyde has a criminal record, arrests for shoplifting and cruelty to animals.

Sitting at my desk in the wide Detective Bureau squad room, Jane and I sip the fresh coffee I made.

"How long do you think it'll take?"

"With this new computer equipment, not long I hope."

Just as we start on our second cup, my phone rings.

One of the prints lifted from Priscilla's body and the print lifted from the missing left shoe are positively Henry Hyde's right index fingerprint. Two of the others look promising too.

I lead Jane into the interview room, turn on the video camera in the corner and sit next to Hyde at the small table. He bats his eyes at me like a myopic goldfish.

I tell the videotape the date and time, then, "I'm Detective John Raven Beau, New Orleans Police Homicide Division. Also present is Detective Jane Palmer of the Union Parish

Sheriff's Office and Mr Henry Hyde." I read his date of birth and address aloud, then read him his Miranda Rights. After each right, I ask if he understands. He answers yes in a high, shaky voice.

Henry stares into my eyes, but won't look at Jane.

"Well?"

He shrugs.

"You might feel better if you tell us how it happened."

His chin sinks and he closes his eyes.

Over the next two hours, I become Henry Hyde's friend. He doesn't admit it, not at first, but describes how Priscilla strolled around a lot. He'd seen her several times.

He gets choked up and I press in closer, talking in a low, controlled voice. Priscilla did communicate with Henry Hyde. She ignored him. I press on, eventually explaining to Henry about his fingerprints.

Tears form in his eyes and, like a good plains warrior, I pounce.

"You were ashamed, weren't you?"

He starts crying.

"That's why you straightened her dress, isn't it?"

It takes a while to get him to stop crying and even longer to tell the story in narrative form. He'd followed Priscilla several times but never too closely, until this time, until she turned suddenly and almost ran into him.

"I didn't mean to hurt her!"

"I know," I say unemotionally.

Eventually he explains that she didn't resist. That made him madder.

I control my natural inclination to strangle this bastard. I keep remembering Priscilla's twisted body and her Little Mermaid underwear, torn and lying on that filthy landing.

At 7 p.m., Jane and I walk out of Central Lock-up after Henry Hyde. She grabs my arm and says, "That was exhilarating!"

I feel it too, the natural high from solving the case, from putting it all together.

"You are definitely a good luck charm," I tell her. "How about a nice New Orleans supper?"

"Absolutely!"

I drive straight to Pascal's Manale where we feast on alligator soup, barbecue shrimp, spicy crawfish etouffée and a bottle of Burgundy. She tells me what it was like growing up on a farm with a hard-working father and a stern, Bible-preaching mother. She's very curious when I tell her how I grew up on the swamp next to Vermilion Bay with a Cajun father and a Sioux mother.

Walking across the street to Dive Inn, Jane tucks her arms around mine. Probably the wine. She drank most of it. She thanks me again for dinner and especially for letting her work on the case.

We spot Mr Yokura immediately as he works his magic fingers along the backside of a long, lean blonde woman on the exercise table. Bruce Wayne, elbows up on the bar, watches Yokura work. Norm Norling, *still* in the same tan suit, sits on the stool next to Bruce, his stetson up on the bar.

"Join us," Bruce calls out.

I hesitate, but Jane, staring intently at Yokura and the blonde woman, pulls me to the bar.

Norm turns to us and almost falls off the stool. Giving me a bleary-eyed stare, he says, "Shit. Why ain't you the Jap?" He picks up his latest Budweiser and finishes it off.

"You mean him?" I point to Yokura.

Norm looks over his shoulder and blinks as if he's noticed the show for the first time. He lets out a loud moan, stumbles away from the bar, does a little spin and crashes flat on his back, spread eagle.

Bruce puts an icy Coke in front of me.

"You live here, or something?" I ask Bruce.

"I own the place."

Still watching the Yokura show, Jane asks for a glass of Burgundy.

Bruce obliges as I turn and watch. The woman rolls on her back, Yokura pouring oil between her round breasts. She arches her back when he starts rubbing the oil in.

We watch in silence as the hands work the woman to a heavy-breathing high. Yokura's right hand moves from breast to breast as his left hand slips between her legs, rubbing through her slightly-darker-than-blonde pubic hair.

"That's Mrs Panemy," Bruce tells us. "A widow."

Jane takes a drink of her wine.

Yokura moves between Mrs Panemy's open legs and uses both hands, one fingering her clit, two fingers from the other hand slipping inside. He takes his time, but she's bouncing already and crying out.

"He's good," I hear myself stating the obvious.

Jane lets out a long breath. "Very good, I'd say."

Just as Mrs Panemy's groaning and gyrating seems to reach its peak, Yokura backs away and bows to her open pussy. It takes her a few seconds to catch her breath. She leans up on her elbows and looks our way.

"Excuse me," Bruce says as he passes us. He extends a hand for Mrs Panemy and pulls her up off the table. She wraps an arm around his waist and they walk back past us on their way to the rooms.

"Well," Jane says as she finishes her wine. "Can't say I blame him." She reaches over the bar for the bottle of Burgundy.

I notice Yokura moving our way. Jane doesn't see him until he's next to her. When she's finished pouring herself another drink, she turns to face him.

"Would you like to be next?" he asks her with only a hint of accent in his voice.

The blue eyes widen. She softly bites her lower lip and turns to me. And I can see it in her eyes. She's thinking about it.

In life there are pivotal moments where we can go one way or the other.

Yokura steps aside and opens his hand towards the exercise table.

Jane's chest rises as she stares at the white, cushioned table. She takes another drink of wine, hands me the glass and climbs off the stool. She takes a hesitant step forwards, her back to me now. I feel a surge of excitement as she unbuttons her blouse and hands it to me. I lay it on the bar away from the wine glass.

She wears a lacy white bra. Unfastening the lone button at the front of her skirt, she pulls it away and hands it to me. She steps out of her heels and works her pantyhose down. Her panties are also lacy white.

Turning to me, Jane smiles and reaches back to unhook her bra. She hands it to me, her eyes staring into mine, daring me to look at her breasts. I smile back and look down at a pair of beautifully formed breasts, not too big, not too small. Her pink areolae look so soft and kissable, her small nipples hard and ready.

Jane climbs out of her panties, steps around me and drops them on the bar. Scooping up the stetson, she walks over to Norm-the-unconscious. Standing naked over him, she sneers, "Prude, huh?" Bending over, she covers his face with the stetson.

Yokura already has his bottle of oil in hand as he stands next to the table. Jane gives me a sexy look as she moves over and climbs on, face down. I step off my stool and straighten my swollen dick.

Her skin looks extra pale under the fluorescent lights, Yokura's hands darker and gnarled like magnolia branches. He works the oil across her back and up to her shoulders. Moving down to her hips, I watch as he rubs her ass and then works the oil into her thighs.

I finish my Coke, walk over and ask Yokura how much. In New Orleans, we pay as we go. He tells me 20 and I drop a 20 dollar bill into his open case.

Jane turns over. I'm breathing heavy now.

"Come here," she tells me as Yokura pours a thick slurp of oil between her breasts. She cranes her neck up, her lips pursed for me. I bend over and kiss her lips lightly as Yokura starts rubbing the oil on her breasts.

She lets out a deep breath and presses her lips against mine, her tongue in my mouth. We French kiss while Yokura rubs her breasts. When he moves down her body, pouring oil on her belly, Jane takes my hands and moves them to her chest.

I come up for breath, Jane gasping as I start feeling-up her breasts, rubbing them softly. My fingers rolls over her nipples, tweak them and rub them.

Yokura moves between her open legs. Kneading her

breasts, I continue feeling her up as I watch Yokura's fingers work the oil through her thick mat of pubic hair.

Breathing heavily Jane lets out a series of tiny squeals. Yokura's fingers slide into her.

She cries out and tells me not to stop. I've slowed down my squeezing. I knead her breasts a little harder.

"Kiss me!"

I kiss her – a maddening, tongue-probing, hot kiss. Her body rises, then falls. Her hips gyrate in long, smooth strokes to Yokura's fingering. She has to pull her mouth away to breathe.

Yokura leans forwards and blows on her pussy as his fingers continue working in her. She cries out. I reach down and run my finger through her pubic hair. I reach her clit and rub it softly. She presses it against my hand, bouncing now.

Yokura motions to me with his free hand, then suddenly steps away.

I move around quickly and stick my tongue into the folds of her wet pussy.

She shudders and grinds against my tongue. I lick her clit and work my tongue in and out and up and down. I taste her juice and feel the heat from her pussy as I continue Frenching it.

When I stick a finger deep inside, my tongue not missing a stroke, Jane screeches and pulls at my ears. I don't stop, moving my finger in a tight circle inside her, moving my tongue in quick licks across her pussy lips.

Jane's back arches, her hips rising high. Gasping, she holds it there for a second, then goes through a withering climax, an ass-bouncer, a legs-squeezing-my-ears, loud orgasm.

I think she calls me God, or maybe just calls his name.

She tries to pull away, but I won't stop, which sends her hips bouncing high. I don't stop until she finally collapses in a heap on the table.

It takes me a minute to catch my breath.

Jane sits up and pulls me forwards, wrapping her arms around my chest, her legs around my waist.

"That was *soooo* delicious," she gasps. "Take me to my room, Mister, and I'll get rid of those blue balls for you."

Scooping her in my arms, I wink as I pass Yokura on our way to the hall. She points to the third room on the left. The door's unlocked. I place her on the bed. Jane grabs my belt as I pull off my over shirt, pull out my Beretta and place it on the end table.

She yanks at my T-shirt and has me naked in two minutes, holding on to my diamond-cutter dick as she pulls me atop her. She guides it to her pussy and I work it in slowly, feeling the hot, wet walls of her tight pussy. Sinking it all the way in, I stop for a second as Jane gasps and pulls my mouth down to hers.

I fuck this girl, riding her, grinding my dick in her, pumping hard and then not so hard and then hard again. She pumps her hips in rhythm to my humping. When I get close, I stop. She won't and keeps pumping against me. As soon as I've got it under control, I start again and she increases the pace until I can hold back no longer. I come in her in long, deep spurts, my legs shuddering. I jam her and continue until I collapse atop her.

The air-conditioned air feels good on our sweaty bodies. We lay in the scent of our sex, arms and legs around each other.

"I don't believe this," Jane finally says. Her voice doesn't indicate regret, but incredulity.

I tell her she's hot, an incredibly hot woman.

"I don't mean that. I don't believe how I've felt ever since I got here." She snuggles her face against my chest. "This place got to me."

"Dive Inn?"

"The *city*. I've been turned on since I got here."

"I've been that way since I was fifteen."

She pinches my side.

"OK. I know what you mean. There's something about New Orleans. Maybe it's the air or the humidity or . . . I don't know."

Jane runs her fingers across my chest.

"When you're ready for seconds, let me know," she says softly.

And it occurs to me, this didn't turn out to be a bad weekend after all.

Tell Me a Story

Susannah Indigo

"Take a deep breath, Rikki."

She smiles, inhales, and tries to relax.

"Now, slow down and tell me again," Alex says with a laugh.

"Oh, Alex, I won. I really won! I got the letter today, and I'm going to Italy. Thank you for all of your help."

He leans back in his chair behind the big mahogany desk and watches as she is barely able to sit still in her seat.

"Rikki, you look like 16 when you're this excited."

She blushes. "I'm glad that I'm not. I never could have written that story without my years of experience. I can't believe it."

"Come here, Rikki. I haven't seen you in almost a month."

She looks up in slight surprise. Dr Alex Russ has always been friendly to her, but he's never looked at her in quite this way before. She steps over towards his desk, still bouncing with excitement, unable to quite discern the look on his face, that handsome bearded face that has cajoled and laughed with her through so many of her writing struggles.

"Sit up here on my desk. Let's talk about what you wrote."

Rikki blushes again. A tale of sexual obsession was her choice of subject matter for the winning entry. The theme of the contest had been "The End of the World", and what would truly matter when that time came near. She had ditched her original ideas about survival and gone for what she knew.

"I'm pretty sure I was the only one to turn in an erotic story of domination and possession for my entry," she says. "But what else is there, when you strip away all of our pretenses?"

"Rikki, I have to tell you – talking about sexual obsession for those two months with a 32-year-old woman who just dropped in to audit my class has been the highlight of my year.

Perched on his desk, she pulls the folds of her full forest green silk dress over her stockinged legs and crosses her ankles primly in front of him. "Well, you helped me a lot. Like we talked about, the only themes that really matter are sex, religion, death, and art."

"I've thought about you and your story day and night, and I have a secret to share with you."

Forgetting the writing contest for now, she begins to notice Alex's deep voice reaching her in strange ways.

"A secret? I love secrets," she says, trying to laugh it off

"Look at me. I'm quite serious. I want to act out your story. With you."

"Oh, my."

"Yes, exactly. It's all I thought of every time you left my office."

"I don't know, Alex, what are you saying?"

His eyes lock on hers, and she begins to feel the need for his hands on her, somewhere, anywhere.

"I want to feel it. I want to know if one person can truly possess another. Your writing is so clear, so erotic. We're going to take that journey together. Nothing else matters. We can think of it as the end of the world."

"Maybe it won't work in real life?" she asks, feeling the wetness growing between her legs.

"Rikki, I can see it on your face. You want it as much as I do. Ask me to act out your story with you."

"We both have real lives elsewhere. And, we both know how it ends."

"It doesn't have to end that way. We can stop whenever we want to. We can create our own little secret world. Go close the drapes."

Alex lights a single candle, places it on the coffee table, opens a bottle of wine and pours two glasses.

"Do you like Coltrane, Rikki? You must."

"God, yes, I listen to him all the time when I write."

He starts one of her favourite CDs, "The Last Giant."

"Come sit on the floor with me, Rikki, and let's talk. You look nervous – tell me what you're thinking."

"Oh, you know. You know. I don't know if I can do it."
"Unbutton the top button of your dress."

She pauses.

"Do it."

She slowly reaches down and undoes the first button.

"That's not near enough. Undo another one."

She unbuttons the next pearl button on her dress, exposing the top of her cleavage.

"That's beautiful. Tell me you can do this."

She just smiles.

"You'll learn, every time you come into this office."

"Yes."

"Much better Now, tell me what you're wearing beneath that lovely dress."

Rikki looks down shyly and says, "I'm wearing a white lace bra."

"Does it fasten in the front?"

"Yes, it does."

"Good. Never come to me again wearing any other kind of bra. Reach inside your dress and unfasten it."

She reaches down and unclasps the bra, freeing her breasts, feeling the hardness of her nipples against the silk of the dress.

"Beautiful. Now, what else are you wearing underneath?"

He still hasn't touched her. She tries to move over towards him, reaching for a more comfortable level of normal affection.

"No, Rikki, stay right where you are. I want your eyes on mine while we do this. I want you to be uncomfortable, to find an intimacy that's so easily bypassed by everyday sex."

She sits back down crosslegged, looking directly across the coffee table into his eyes. "Yes, Alex."

"Answer my question."

"I'm wearing thigh-high stockings, and panties that match the bra."

"Stand up."

Another pause.

"Do it."

Rikki rises and stands in front of him. She begins to sway to the music, to follow the rhythm as he talks.

"Lift your skirt up to your waist and hold it there."

He sits before her and watches as she gathers the full skirt up around her waist, exposing her ass.

"Take your panties off for me."

She reaches down and slips off her panties, dropping the dress from her waist.

"No. Lift it back up. And spread your legs."

Hesitating only for a moment, she follows his instruction.

Alex lays her panties aside. "Here are the rules, sweet Rikki." He finally touches her thigh, stroking gently up and down, never touching her pussy. "You will come to me twice a week, just as you did when we were working on your writing. But you will come in the evening, and you will plan on spending the night. You will bring nothing with you." Trembling, she stands before him, as he kneels, stroking and examining her.

"You will never wear panties. You will never wear jeans. You may wear any kind of skirt that you choose. When you enter my office, you will walk over and close the drapes, then come to me wherever I sit. You will lift your skirt, for inspection, without a word. Do you understand?"

"Yes, I do." The wetness begins to flow and she closes her eyes for the moment.

"If I call you and ask you to dress some other way, you will. You will tell me erotic stories when I ask. You will make them up on the spot if I so choose."

"Yes."

"We're going there, Rikki, we're going where the couple in your end of the world story went. We're going to where nothing else in the world matters but our desire for each other. No matter what it takes. And we will give each other everything."

His fingers are dipping into her slowly, withdrawing, coming to his lips as he tastes her wetness. He stands up next to her, holding her with one arm, and places one of his wet fingers deep into her mouth, running it around her tongue. "Taste, baby. Taste my finger." He opens her mouth wider with the force of his finger, running it across her teeth and down into her throat, fucking her mouth with his finger as though it were his cock. Her head drops back, lost in the intimacy of a single finger invading her mouth.

"Drop your skirt down, Rikki."

She opens her eyes in surprise as he withdraws his finger.

"That's all for today." He blows out the candle, walks away, and opens the drapes.

"I'm so proud of your winning that contest. I'll see you here on Tuesday at six sharp." He picks up her white lace panties from where they lay and tosses them in the wastebasket.

Rikki sits in her car and shakes, feeling her bare bottom touching the leather seat. *This is crazy – this is the craziest thing I have ever considered. We both have lives. It was just a story. Just fiction. I'll write him a note, that's what I'll do. I do have it in me to do this, but God, if I do, if let go into this kind of sensuality, I'll never get back. I'm going to go home, get out my stationery with the roses on it, write him a note thanking him for everything, and then I'll never see him again. It was just a story.*

By Tuesday evening at 6:30, Alex is sure she's not coming. He's debating the virtues of calling her when he finally hears the knock on his door.

"Come in."

Rikki ambles in, obviously a bit tipsy. She dances over to him and poses on his desk, kicks off her shoes and places her feet in his lap.

"Hi, Alex."

"Rikki, aren't you forgetting some things?"

She wriggles her toes in his lap.

"Do as you were told."

With a flounce of her skirt, she hops down and heads for the drapes.

"And you're late. Where were you?"

She pulls the drapes closed and turns to look at Alex. "Oh, you know, I just stopped down at the pub for a minute and had a glass of wine." She watches him from across the room, feeling rather like a pawn in a chess game, unsure of her next move.

"Come here."

She pauses, then joins him.

"What are you to do when you enter?"

"Close the drapes and then come to you.

"And then?"

Blushing, she reaches down to the hem of her black cotton skirt and lifts it up to her thighs.

"Not quite. Keep going, baby."

She sighs and lifts the soft skirt up around her waist.

The tops of her black stockings perfectly match the jet black colour of her pussy hair. He reaches out to caress her soft hair and she moans.

"Yes, that's better. Now turn around."

She feels shy and slutty all at the same time. The two glasses of wine helped just enough to get her up to his door, but she suspects she needs the whole bottle to carry on much further.

He bends her over the desk. "Make yourself comfortable there, baby." She looks back over her shoulder as he starts to caress her legs and her bare ass, talking to her the whole time. Her hands find the far edge of the desk and hold on.

"Was it hard to come here to me tonight?"

"Yes. I was scared. I almost wrote you to say I couldn't do this."

"But you didn't."

"No. No, I kept putting it off, and then I had a drink downstairs, and here I am."

Alex kneels down and starts to kiss her black-stockinged legs from the ankles up, slowly. "I'm glad you were scared. It means you take this as seriously as I do."

He spreads her legs a little wider with each kiss rising up her thighs. "You're all I've thought about every minute of the day, baby. I've thought about what we're doing. About where we're going. About what I need to do to you."

Moaning and giving into his touch, she whispers, "It's all I've thought about too."

His hands slide up over her ass, slowly exploring every

opening. "I have two surprises for you tonight," he says, with his fingers buried deep inside of her. "First, something for your body. Relax, this won't hurt at all."

She feels something hard and cold pressing against her pussy lips.

"It's just something to keep you warm inside for me while we take care of the second surprise. They're small silver balls, and they will gently roll around inside your pussy while we're out." He pushes the second ball in. "How does that feel, baby?"

"Oh, God. It feels very full and wonderful. Out where?"

Alex leans hard down on her back as she lies over the desk, pressing his stiff cock up against her ass. "You love it, don't you."

"Yes."

"Good. Then we're going out to dinner with a friend of mine. Let's get ready."

He helps her straighten up her skirt, keeping his hands on her ass while she catches her breath.

"I don't know if I can walk anywhere with these inside of me."

"Yes, you can. Let's go."

Walking down the street on his arm, Rikki realizes that although he hasn't even fucked her yet, she still feels completely possessed by him.

Waiting at the table in Sostanza's, Rikki says, "You know, Alex, there are things in my end of the world story that I don't want to do."

"Yes? Like what?"

"Some of the more dangerous things . . ."

She's cut off by the arrival of Alex's friend, Jonathan. After greetings and polite chatter, Alex brags about Rikki's prize-winning story

"You wrote about sex at the end of the world?" Jonathan asks.

"Yes," she answers, "Sex and intimacy and stories and passion." *Give me another drink*, she thinks, *and I'll even tell you the ending.*

"Rikki's a great storyteller," Alex says. "Some night we'll all have to get together and let her enchant us with her tales."

He leans over, whispers to her, "How do the balls feel deep inside of you?" and watches her blush.

They continue to talk of her story as though it were a scholarly work, dissecting what could truly happen and what couldn't. She listens in fascination while Alex keeps his hand high on her bare thigh.

"I was just telling Alex before you came," Rikki interjects, "that some of the things in that story are just fantasy, and people don't really do them."

"Like what?"

"Oh, just some of the more dangerous things, involving control and possession and physical harm."

"Rikki and I have been thinking about trying out some of them ourselves."

She looks quickly to see if perhaps she misheard. She didn't, he's smiling. She excuses herself and flees to the restroom.

Alex meets her there in the hallway five minutes later. "Jonathan's gone." He pins her up against the wall, kissing her deeply. "He's an open-minded guy, don't worry about him."

"How could you?"

"I could." He whispers fiercely into her ear, "I need to fuck you, baby, here."

"No, not here."

"Yes, here." He pulls her out into the dark alley behind the restaurant. "Lift your skirt and bend over."

"No."

"No? Let me help you." He does it for her. Pressing her fast up against the railing, he shoves her skirt aside and unzips his pants. "Tell me, Rikki. Tell me you want me to fuck you hard." He can feel her breathing fast, and reaches for the hardness of her nipples. "Tell me. Tell me how much you want it."

His cock is hard against her bare ass. "Oh God, yes. Yes. Yes. I want you." He spreads her legs and enters her pussy hard and fast, feeling the metal of the silver balls inside her against his cock. The heat builds until he's fucking her fast and furious and she no longer cares who can see or hear them. His arms are wrapped around her tight and they both come violently into the night.

As they begin to recover, they straighten each other's clothes and laugh. "You make me feel like a teenager, Alex."

"You are, baby, in your heart. Let's go home. I need you to tell me a story."

Lying on the carpet in front of the single candle, Alex slowly removes all of Rikki's clothes, and then all of his own. He ties her wrists together with one of his red neckties, leaving her feeling vulnerable but not seriously bound.

She recognizes this as one of the scenes she has written, and is amazed at his attention to detail, right down to the colour red and the single candle. She's also amazed that it feels exactly the way she thought it would, purely and wonderfully sensual.

"Tell me a story, baby."

She laughs. "Do you know where I got that whole thing from?" She's beginning to melt under the slow and gentle massage of his hands on her back.

"No, where?"

"It's a silly rhyme from my childhood –

> *Tell me a story and sing me your song*
> *tend my heart gently to keep us both strong*
> *make it a tale full of love and romance*
> *or spin me the truth*
> *and we'll each take a chance*"

"That's not silly, it's great." He pours lotion into his hands and starts in on her thighs.

"Now, baby. Tell me a story. Make it a true one."

She sighs with pleasure. "This is wonderful. OK, a story of my past."

His fingers press and probe gently as she begins to talk.

"This is the story of where all my tying-up fantasies begin, I suppose. Once upon a time I had a boyfriend, when I was quite young and neither one of us knew much of anything about sensuality, who liked to play around with tying me up. He liked it, I liked it, it was pretty harmless. Mostly he'd just tie my wrists to the bedposts and fuck me. And he wanted me to do the same to him sometimes."

"How old were you?"

"Oh, probably 20 or so . . . oh, my, that feels great. You are the sexiest man on earth."

He turns her over and places her tied hands behind her neck.

"So what happened?"

"It was fun, but not great, probably because we weren't that great together to start with. But then he got a little weird on me. He liked to tie me up and just leave me that way, all evening. He liked to sit me on a hardback chair with my wrists and ankles tied tight and just watch me. It was sexy in a way, but also scary and strange."

Alex straddles her waist and begins a serious massage of her nipples. She can feel his cock growing hard at her words.

"He would come by the chair and tease me every now and then, you know, touching me, caressing me, pinching my nipples. But he wouldn't say much, and we were so young we could hardly talk about what we were doing. It was like we knew what we liked, but we had no idea where to go from there."

"Not like now, where you can write stories that take you straight to the end of the world."

"Yes."

He slides up to her mouth and begins to stroke her face with his cock. "Tell me more. And keep your hands right where I put them behind your neck."

She squirms under the caress of his cock. "So, I often found myself sitting on this very uncomfortable chair, tied up for hours, just to please him. After the first hour or so like that, the stiffness of my body overcame any erotic feelings I might have had."

Alex slides the tip of his cock into her mouth, watching her close her eyes and run her tongue deliciously around it. "More story," he says, and withdraws.

"God, yes. Then, one night, he got kind of cruel about it. He not only tied me to the chair, he blindfolded me. Then I heard him leave the apartment. I was terrified. What if something happened? I think about it now, and I think it could have been sexy if we could have talked about it, if I had any idea what was going on."

His cock is hard in her mouth now, halting her words. She sucks him until he is ready to withdraw again and hear the rest.

"So, he left. And I admit, I was turned on in spite of it all. But I was angry too. It's dangerous to play too fast and loose in the realm of the senses like that. He came back hours later and I was exhausted from crying. But . . ."

Alex's cock is fucking her mouth hard now, stopping the story, his fist wrapped in her hair. "Finish," he says finally, withdrawing.

She takes a deep breath. "But . . . I admit we had the hottest sex we'd ever had that night. It was like he owned me. He left me blindfolded and held me on the ground and fucked me every way possible. I learned some amazing things about my body that night."

The story stops as he buries his cock deep in her throat, coming with force. "Yes, baby, yes."

She takes her time and licks her lips and swallows all of his come, and he leaves his cock near her lips so that she can lick him clean also. Untying her wrists, he holds her tight and begins to rock her towards sleep in his arms.

"That was a great story, Rikki."

"But you never heard the end. I left him the next week. It was all too much."

"You will never leave me, baby. You are the bridge to my darkest desires."

"But what happened to stopping whenever we wanted to."

He holds her close. "We can. But you will never leave me. Never."

Tuesday and Thursday nights come and go in the fog of sensuality. Rikki starts showing up on time without the previously required glass of wine. Some evenings she even shows up early. They experiment with schoolgirl clothes, with candle wax, and with spanking. Meetings stay as planned, but the phone calls begin – two, sometimes three times a day.

"Rikki, I want you to wear your prettiest dance clothes tomorrow night," Alex tells her one day on the phone.

She shows up in a deep purple chiffon skirt and black

leotard, long black hair down and flowing, with no idea where they're going. She enters, closes the drapes, and comes to him for inspection. Lifting the swirling skirt and hopping up on his desk, she spreads her legs wide and tucks her toes around his waist.

"Hi."

He thinks perhaps he could die right here, watching this lovely woman be so free and open and sexual with him, so far into their intimacy that she no longer has any hesitations.

"I love you, Rikki."

"Oh, Alex." She's speechless beyond that. This is not exactly in the story they are supposed to be acting out. "Where are we going dancing?"

He runs his hands up over her legs, stroking her pussy through the leotard. "I don't even mind that you're not quite accessible in this, you look so beautiful."

She slides down onto his lap, holding him close, feeling the hardness of his cock beneath her.

"We're not going anywhere, Rikki. We're staying right here." He lifts her back up onto the desk and opens the bottle of champagne he has brought for them. "No glasses, we'll just share." He takes a long swig and then kisses her, delivering champagne directly to her mouth.

She laughs at the idea of being all dressed to go out and having only their own private dance. He lights the single red candle, they pick out music together and begin to dance slowly, wrapped around each other. He steps back from her.

"Dance for me, Rikki."

"A little more champagne, please."

More long kisses deliver the champagne.

Rikki begins to dance, swaying, swirling her skirt, trying to remember every move she's ever seen in strip shows. More kisses bring better moves, until she is standing right in front of him as he sits in the armchair. She removes her leotard completely, leaving only the long chiffon skirt and her black high heels. Her breasts move freely as she dances, over him, on him, for him, for her own sensuality, full of passion and power.

Alex strokes her breasts when she leans over him, then just

lets her go. She dances over to the stereo and puts on Mickey Hart's "Planet Drums," and begins to dance and caress her body in the middle of the room as he watches.

"God, Alex, this music always makes me just want to lie down and be fucked hard."

"No. But you may touch yourself all you want while I watch."

He feeds her the rest of the champagne. She begins to perform a dance that involves fondling herself everywhere. She has no idea where this comes from, but she continues until she collapses in front of him and reaches an over-whelming orgasm while he watches.

"God, Alex."

"Yes."

They spend the rest of the night teaching each other every dance they know, from the tango to the Sugar Shack dance to an elegant waltz.

In the morning, Alex says, "Don't leave."

"I must."

"Never leave me."

"I won't."

Rikki calls him late that night at home at midnight.

"I need you."

"Meet me by the fountain in the Quad. Ten minutes."

She's there when he arrives, and he wraps her tight in his arms and holds her.

"Alex, this scares me. I need you so much."

"And I need you. We need to move forwards. We need to complete our story."

The following Thursday Rikki calls him. "It's your turn tonight, Alex."

She enters promptly at six, wrapped in a long trench coat.

"You look rather like a secret agent, baby," he says, smiling.

"I have a surprise for you, Alex."

"I'm ready."

She closes the drapes and comes to him in ritual fashion. "You sure you're ready for this?" she asks.

"Yes, Rikki, I'm ready for everything."

She strips off her coat, and Alex sits back in surprise and admiration. She wears thigh high black suede boots, a red and black corset with matching garters and black stockings. The corset pushes her breasts high. She also wears a red and black lace collar.

"Rikki, you look like every man's midnight wet dream," he says, regaining his composure. "You actually drove here like that?"

"Yes." She's amazed how far she's going, how little she cares about anything in life but pleasing him.

He lifts her up and carries her across the room, laying her down in front of their candle.

"No, Alex, it's your turn."

He's fascinated by the tone in her voice.

Rikki undresses him slowly and guides him to lay down in front of her. She ties his hands above his head with one of her red silk scarves.

"How does that feel?"

"Rikki, I don't know about this."

"Just give in to it, you'll love it like I do."

She stands over him in her high-heeled boots with her legs spread.

"Watch me."

He watches as she strokes herself, trying to reach up and touch.

"You need something more, I think. You're much less well-behaved than I am."

She ties the ends of the scarf to the leg of the coffee table. "Don't pull too hard or you'll tip the candle over and we'll be on fire."

He holds still.

"One more thing." She wraps another silk scarf around his eyes. "Do you like that?"

"I don't know, Rikki, it's strange."

"Yes, it is. When you're deprived of two of your senses like that, though, the seeing and the touching, everything else gets more intense. You've taught me that."

Rikki lowers herself until her bare pussy rests on his chest.

"Now, Alex, tell me a story."

"Oh, man."

"Make it a true one."

"All right." Alex breathes deeply and tries to relax.

"Let me help you relax." Rikki starts to stroke and kiss him starting from his toes.

"Yes, yes, I'll tell you about Paris."

"Paris?"

"Yes, Paris. I was there when I was in graduate school, just for a summer. There was a woman. She was pure sex. Pure abandonment. In fact, sometimes you remind me of her."

Rikki laughs. "I have nothing that exotic in me, I'm afraid. In fact, I'm only French in my kisses." She kisses him long and deep.

"God, Rikki, how can you ever tell stories and do this at the same time?"

"You've made me an expert."

"Anyway, I met her in a cafe one afternoon. She had dark short hair, she was very tiny, and not terribly pretty. But there was something about her that fascinated me."

"What was it?" Rikki moves down to his cock and begins to lick slowly.

"I didn't know when I met her, but I can tell you now. She lived in her senses. She was totally impractical. There was nothing she'd rather do in life than fuck."

"Yes," Rikki whispers, her face buried deep between his legs.

"And she wanted me. But she wasn't aggressive at all. She just let me know. It started out fairly normal, as young love affairs go. Lots of time in bed, lots of late nights. Then one night she told me what she really desired."

Rikki spreads his legs wider and starts exploring down the inside of his thighs.

"I need to see you while we do this, Rikki."

"No, you don't. Go on with the story. What did she want?"

"She wanted me to command her. To possess her, to own her. To tell her what to do. To use her, to abuse her. To completely dominate her."

"That sounds right up your alley," Rikki says with a kiss.

"It may be now, but I wasn't sure then. I loved it, but it felt bad. You know what I mean? The things she asked me to do shocked me. She was older, maybe 30, and she'd had experience with this."

Rikki straddles him above his hard cock. "What did she want you to do?"

"She wanted to call me 'Sir' all the time. She wanted to serve me. She wanted to be on her knees for me. She wanted me to spank her. She wanted me to hurt her."

"And did you?"

"Yes."

"Tell me about it while I fuck you." She lowers herself down slightly, so that just the tip of his cock enters her pussy.

"I don't know if I can talk about it."

She slides down all the way, and holds him inside of her.

"Oh, man, Rikki. That's wonderful."

"Tell me what you did. I want to know all the good and the dark things about you."

Alex tries to move his hips up to meet her, but she holds him still.

"OK. She would kiss my feet. At first because she wanted to do this. Then because I wanted her to. And finally because I made her do it. You know *The Story of O*? It became very much like that."

'And you loved it."

"Loved, and hated."

Rikki slides slowly up on her knees until just the tip of his cock remains inside of her. "Tell me more," she says as she slides back down and leans over to kiss him deeply.

"I don't know, she just found something in me that I didn't know existed. The need to dominate. The need to be cruel. I often didn't want to even see her again, but I would. It only lasted a few months or so."

"What happened?"

Alex takes a deep breath as Rikki begins to ride him slowly to the rhythm of his words.

"It scared me to death."

"What happened? You can tell me."

"It just went too far."

Rikki leans over and unties his blindfold and his wrists. "God, I need your hands on me . . ."

He reaches for her breasts, then slides his hands down to her hips and raises her up. "Come with me, Rikki. Ride me hard. Come with me."

"God yes." Rikki reaches her climax at the same time that he explodes deep inside of her, and they collapse together on the floor.

Entwined together by the light of the melting candle, Rikki asks one more time. "Will you please tell me what happened?"

"No. I'd rather show you."

"What?"

"Next weekend we're going away. We're going to break all the rules."

"Where?"

"You don't need to know. I will take care of everything. And I will take care of you."

The following Thursday Alex calls Rikki in the early afternoon.

"Meet me tonight, on time, at El Chapultepec. Wear that red short dress with the black leather belt."

"Yes, I will."

She arrives to find Alex and his friend Jonathan in a back booth in the jazz bar, deep in conversation. Rikki begins to slide into the booth, but Alex stops her.

"Aren't you forgetting something?"

Rikki laughs. "What? – there are no drapes here."

Alex looks at her with that look that Rikki thinks he must practise in front of the mirror. It makes her melt every time – it's a look of absolute passion, yet absolute control.

"Lift your skirt."

"Alex!"

"Do it."

"Alex! Not here, not with him . . ." She looks at Jonathan and blushes. He seems to just be sitting back relaxed, expecting this. "What can you be thinking of, Alex!"

"Look around you, Rikki. Not a soul is watching you. Except for us. Do it."

Options float through her mind like the jazz riff she hears in the background – *fright, fight, freedom, flight?* All seem like a dream, for she knows that this act is in her story and that she is caught hopelessly in the descending rhythm of her own writing.

"Yes, Alex."

Rikki looks one more time over her shoulder, avoids Jonathan's eyes, looks directly at Alex, and slowly slides the front of her red linen skirt up her thighs.

"Isn't she beautiful, Jonathan?"

"Yes."

Alex reaches out and touches her soft lips gently, making her flinch. "You may lower your skirt, Rikki, and join us." Alex rises to let her slide in between them.

Rikki knows there isn't enough wine in this place to help her get through what she suspects is coming. She hopes perhaps he will alter her story and head in a different direction, as he has occasionally done in the past.

They chat about the blues singer in the spotlight, and Rikki tries to look at Jonathan and talk as though she hasn't just bared her pussy directly in front of him.

"I have a gift for you, Rikki," Alex says. He pulls a jewellery box out of his jacket pocket and presents her with it.

Rikki opens it slowly, and there it is. It is so close to what she described in her story that it brings tears to her eyes. "Oh, thank you, Alex." She lifts the choker up to examine its beauty, and finds her name inscribed elegantly in script across the golden underside of the heavy clasp.

Alex takes it from her and lifts it up toward her throat. The delicate filigree chains shimmer in the shadows and the candlelight.

"It's beautiful."

"It was designed just for you, Rikki. There's another piece that matches it, which you will receive this weekend."

Rikki kisses him with passion. "Thank you."

"Jonathan has read your story, Rikki."

"He has?"

"Yes, and he knows exactly what this means. When I place this on your lovely neck, there's no going back."

Alex pulls the intertwined chains snugly around her neck, and fastens the heavy gold clasp beneath her hair.

"You are mine, Rikki. You are never to take this off without my permission."

"God, yes, Alex, I do belong to you."

Rikki dances with Alex, and then she dances with Jonathan, losing herself in the music of the evening.

Sandwiched between the two men back at the table, she feels warm and safe and loose and free, almost ready for anything. "It's time, Rikki. Jonathan's going to be so kind and lend us his cabin in the mountains for the weekend. I think we need to repay him for his generosity. Tell her about the cabin, Jonathan."

"It's pretty small, but comfortable," Jonathan responds, "and very, very isolated."

"It will be perfect for us," Alex says with a smile. "Now, Jonathan, what would you like her to do?"

"Only one thing. Tell me a story, Rikki. Tell me a story full of sex and romance. Oh, and just like in your writing, raise your skirt and let me watch you touch yourself while you tell it."

Rikki blushes until she's sure she'll die. "I cant."

"Let me help, Rikki," Alex says.

He turns her back towards his chest, so that she's looking directly at Jonathan. "Sit here, move in between my legs, that's it."

Alex slides her skirt up above the black stockings, just above the soft black curls of her pussy. "How is that, Jonathan, do you have a perfect view?"

Rikki closes her eyes, pretends this isn't happening. Yet she feels herself on fire.

"Perfect. Tell me a story, Rikki."

By the end of the evening, Rikki's told several stories, always stroking herself to orgasm at the end of each one. She's told the story of the teenage finger-fucking episode in explicit detail, and the complete story of the three candles. Nestled safely in Alex's arms with her legs spread wide, yet discreetly, behind the table, she's made up a wild tale of a woman named

Annie and her dancing and her Daddy. Jonathan's entranced, and Rikki imagines he wants her to go on through the night this way.

"Alex," she whispers, "I'm exhausted, and I need you. Can we go home?"

"Yes," he responds, stroking her hair softly.

They all leave together, and Jonathan hugs Rikki goodbye. "Thank you, Rikki, that was incredible. Take care of her, Alex."

"I will."

Rikki and Alex barely make it inside the door before they are tearing each other's clothes off, desperate to make love. They collapse on the floor in passion and wrap themselves tightly around each other and never let go.

They fall asleep immediately afterwards. Alex awakens her in the early morning with his tongue deep inside of her, letting her come to life slowly as he devours her.

"Oh God, it's late, Alex, I have to go," she whispers after recovering.

"Twelve hours, Rikki. In twelve hours we'll be leaving for the mountains. In twelve hours you will be completely mine in the wilderness for three days. Do you remember your instructions?"

"Yes, Alex. I will bring nothing with me. Nothing."

"Close your eyes tight," Alex tells Rikki as he guides her to the car.

"Why?"

"Close them."

She closes her eyes and lets him seat her in the passenger seat and fasten the seat belt for her. The aroma of flowers is overwhelming.

"Alex! What is that?"

"You may look."

Her eyes flutter open and the sight outdoes even the smell. "Look at all the roses! I've never seen so many roses together! How gorgeous, Alex, what a beautiful thing to do."

The back seat is full of roses. Huge bunches of yellow and orange roses, piled high and wrapped several dozen at a time, all tied with pale orange and yellow ribbons.

"Those are my favourite colour roses. But why so many?"
She picks up one small bunch and inhales. "They're
gorgeous."

"Because you deserve them. We'll figure out something to
do with them all," he says with a smile.

"You are just too good to be true, Alex. I'm going to miss
you."

"What do you mean?"

She puts the roses down. "Oh, you know my trip to Venice
is next month." She realizes that this is the first time they've
ever talked about the future.

"Are your plans all made?"

"Yes. I have a place rented for the month, and they have the
conference all scheduled."

He's silent, and she peers at him through the dim light,
trying to determine his feelings as they travel up the winding
pass into the mountains. "We did say we could stop any time."

Alex pulls the car to a stop at a visitor observation point.

"Let's go for a walk, Rikki."

They climb up to the top of the deserted viewing platform.
The lights of the city can be seen twinkling in the distance.
The valley spans below them beyond the 500-foot drop-off.
He guides her close to the edge, with his arms wrapped tightly
around her waist.

"Take another step, baby."

"No, it's too scary."

"Do you trust me?"

"Yes." She steps forwards.

"Another one. I've got you."

She trembles in his arms, but steps forwards, wondering
how far she'll go.

"I need you, baby. You have to trust me that I know what's
right for us. I've reached the edge where I wanted to be. I can
never let you go."

They stand together and watch the lights. Rikki has no
words.

Driving miles down a private dirt road brings them to
Jonathan's cabin.

"Wow," is all Rikki can say when she sees it. A small log cabin with a wraparound porch sits a hundred yards from a small lake that is only discernible by the shimmer of the mist reflected in their headlights. Small groves of aspen trees surround the cabin.

"Have you been here before, Alex?"

"Yes."

"This place looks like paradise."

"Wait until you see it in the daylight."

He guides her inside, where she gasps again. The ceiling soars to a peak of heavy logs, making the single room look huge. A narrow spiral staircase rises in the middle of the room to the loft bedroom above. One entire wall of the cabin ensconces a multi-coloured stone fireplace. The far right side of the room holds an old-fashioned ten-foot-long pine dining table.

"Sit here at the table, Rikki, and put your feet up. I'll bring everything in."

"I can help. I'm a feminist, you know," she jokes, feeling rather helpless.

"So am I. Stay where you are."

Alex brings in the groceries and the one large suitcase. It takes him five trips to bring all the roses in and lay them before her across the table. He gets the fire going, lights the candles on the mantle, and puts some music on the CD player.

"The roses are not nearly as beautiful as you are, Rikki. Stand up."

She catches her reflection in the enormous picture window that has no drapes.

Alex turns her so she can watch herself in the glass. "Take your skirt off."

She unbuttons the long straight denim skirt from the bottom, and lets it fall at her feet. She stands bare except for her shirt and sandals and the glimmer at her neck.

"Yes. Now the shirt and the shoes."

Rikki strips off the shirt and kicks away the shoes. Only the filigree chains remain at her neck.

"Yes, baby, yes. That's how I want you. That's how I want us here." He removes his clothes while she watches in the glass, and runs his hands down over her hips. "Civilization stripped away, all our pretences gone. I want you to stay like this all weekend."

She's lost in his touch, in the glancing reflection in the window of him standing behind her stroking her, in the aroma of roses that are strewn across the table. She can hear Joni Mitchell singing about "dancing up a river in the dark" in the background.

"Come lie across the table for me. This table was made just for us." Alex clears a spot for her amidst the roses. "On your belly." Her breasts press down into the hard pine.

He climbs up next to her on the table and begins to unwrap the roses. "Close your eyes and just feel, baby." Roses run up and down her body, petals and thorns and then petals again. He caresses her everywhere, and she can only feel hands and softness and hardness and sharpness, until she cries out for him in need. He moves on top of her, hard cock pressing against her ass, entering her and fucking her hard, until nothing remains for either one of them but the fragrance of roses and love.

Hours later they are laughing and dancing around the kitchen area, trying to find enough glasses to put all the roses in. They line up the glasses down the middle of the table, finish putting the groceries away, and cuddle up together in front of the fireplace under a heavy blanket.

They tell each other stories, the silly and the serious, the important and the whimsical, until they fall asleep to the rhythm of their words.

In the morning Rikki wakes up shivering, and Alex gets up and finds her one of his big white cotton button-down shirts to wear while he cooks her breakfast. They relax in their closeness while gobbling down the scrambled eggs and toast. She tucks her bare feet up into his lap.

"This is the most breathtaking place I have ever seen, Alex. I want to set the next story I write here. Maybe I'll write about a couple with minimal clothing and an absolute obsession for each other. And lots of roses."

After breakfast, Alex finally takes her upstairs to show her around. There's just one room, with a big four poster pine bed with lovely old quilts on it. It's irresistible – they crawl under the soft quilts together and quietly make love one more time until they are momentarily satiated.

"Come with me, baby, let's find out what it's like to be bathed in rose petals."

Warm water and bath oil, Alex's hands and a thousand rose petals seem perfect to Rikki. Afterward they sit on the bed for a long time, curled together, while he brushes and dries her long hair.

She starts to put his white shirt back on but he tells her not to. "I want you like we talked about last night, Rikki, with no clothing here. We'll keep the fire going all the time in case it gets cold. But we're not about to have any visitors here who can see us. You look just perfect the way you are, except for one thing."

Alex brings out a jewel box, and Rikki opens it to find another set of chains that match the ones around her neck. He kneels down in front of her to show her where it goes. He wraps the first section around her waist, and then runs the fragile chain down across her clit, teasing her and taking his time. The chain runs back up over her ass and fastens on the back of her waist.

"God, that's just gorgeous. Thank you so much."

She walks down the spiral staircase feeling completely open and vulnerable, shimmering in gold like an Egyptian princess.

In the afternoon it's perfectly sunny and they lounge on the porch in the soft chairs with no clothing and their feet kicked up, drinking lemonade. They talk and observe the crystal lake in front of their cabin, and finally read each other erotic stories from some books they find tucked away on a shelf.

"Jonathan must be kind of a kinky guy up here," Rikki says, looking at the stack of erotic books piled up next to her.

"He doesn't get to come up here much any more. Rikki, I wish we could stay here forever." He makes her read some of his favourite dirty passages over and over. "You look tired, let's go back in."

He takes her back upstairs to the big bed. "Lie down and hold still for me."

She flops down on the bed, hearing the chains around her body clink together. Alex brings out the rope he brought in with the groceries and ties her wrists to each corner of the bed.

"You look so perfect there." He covers her with the turquoise quilt. "I'm going to go out for a walk, and I want you to just rest here for me like this."

"You're going to leave me like this?"

"Yes. Do you trust me?"

"Oh, God . . . yes."

She hears the door close, and begins to drift off. She finds herself wondering dreamily about what they're doing.

Is this just meant to be? Is there any way to simply escape and live like this forever? Would it work if we did it all the time? What really happened to him in Paris that he's going to try and show me? Is he safe? Am I in love with him? Do I really trust him? She finds that just thinking about him like this starts to make her nipples get hard and the wetness flow between her thighs. Being aroused and alone and bound is frightening, and she pulls at the ropes in frustration. *What if he never comes back?*

A few minutes later she hears the door downstairs. "Oh God, I got scared after a while, Alex. Please untie me."

"Yes, baby, but we both know what happens in your story after this, don't we? Do you think we can change the ending? Does being scared turn you on?"

She shivers. "Yes, oh, yes, it does."

"We have two more days here, Rikki, I want you to stay as you are, naked and bound in some way for me the rest of the time we're here."

"For two days?"

"Yes. Just let me take care of you."

He unties her briefly to let her get up, and then reties her hands behind her back. He helps her down the stairs and seats her comfortably on the bench at the table.

He feeds her dinner. "I feel like a child."

"Yes, but I may not always be so gentle here."

After dinner and wine, he takes her out for a walk on the patio with her arms still bound, slipping a jacket over her shoulders.

"It's so quiet here, Alex, it's like the end of the world."

They experiment that night with every possible way to use

the roses and their petals while making love. Rikki imagines she will smell these roses for the rest of her life. She's beginning to lose track of where she is and why she's here. He finally unties her for the night, and she feels lost.

Alex finds a way to help keep her comfortable and close and safe. He wraps her arms around his upper leg and reties her wrists, nestling her in between his legs to sleep. They both fall asleep with her head resting on his belly and her mouth gently on his cock. She awakens the next morning to find it's already noon. Alex's been up and gone out already. Rikki tries to stretch, only to find that he has quietly retied her hands above her head while she was sleeping.

He returns and brings her breakfast in bed.

"Alex, you're spoiling me rotten."

"I know." He feeds her.

As the day goes on, she notices his mood changes slightly.

"Baby, I want you to feel what it's like to be deprived of your senses, slowly but surely, until you are left with nothing but love and trust for me. I love you, Rikki. This is not just a story. We're going all the way. I know it scares you some. It scares me too. But I have to do it."

They go outside before the sun sets, and he reaches over and plays with her chains.

"I think we'll skip dinner tonight, and just dine on champagne. Take a good look at the beauty of the lake, baby."

She does, and then looks to him in trust. He brings out a black scarf and blindfolds her with it. Walking back in to the big leather couch, she gets a bit dizzy at the loss of both her hand movement and her sight. He lets her sit there comfortably on the couch, stretched out, feet up. "Tell me a story, Rikki. A truth. Tell me where you think we're going. How you feel about me."

She can't reach for him, or even see him. "I love you, Alex. I do." She pauses. "But I'm afraid we're going to consume each other and lose track of the line between what's real and what's not if we keep going."

He reassures her, and they talk for a long time. She notices that the apprehension over what they're doing often alternates between the two of them.

"One more sensation, Rikki. Are you ready?" Another scarf. He wraps this one around her mouth, stopping her cry of surprise.

"That's beautiful, baby. You should see yourself, so helpless, so vulnerable, so trusting."

He doesn't touch her, just lets her spiral into the loss of movement and sight and speech. He sits down next to her and tells her his story.

"This is the kind of thing I did in Paris so long ago, but we did it all the time, and there was too much cruelty in it and not enough love. It was more like a contest to see who could go farther. To see who could be more evil. There wasn't enough trust, not like with you. You're soft and loving and imaginative and full of desire."

She struggles to say something.

"Just listen to me." Alex begins to play with the chain around her waist again. "The night you asked me about. She brought a knife out, and wanted me to use it on her body. It was the night it ended. I ended it. It went too far. I started to do what she wanted. I did. But I was afraid I would hurt her too much, and I was afraid I might like it. She knew what she liked. I wonder if she's still alive."

Rikki's getting slightly nervous at this story. She leans slightly away from him the best she can.

He holds her chain tight. "Don't ever pull away from me, baby. We're on the edge here, but we can stay there. I want to control you, I want to own you, but I will never cause you serious harm. Will you trust me?"

She nods slowly, struggling with the gag and the blindfold, scared, wet, excited, anxious.

"You just need to stay with me tonight, just let yourself go. Let yourself go for me, baby, there is no other world, there is only us and our passion. There is nothing more intimate in the world than giving yourself over completely to another human being. I want you to feel me tonight, I want you to know I am on you for ever."

His words are becoming hypnotic to her.

"You've been bound since last night, but you've been able to move most of the time. Let me show you what control really is."

Alex lifts her off the couch and lays her down on the floor on her back. Spreading her legs wide, he ties each ankle to a leg of the couch. Her wrists are pulled over her head and tied across the carpeting to the armchair. She can only feel the warmth of the fireplace, and the smell of the roses that permeates the cabin. She's almost glad she can't speak, because there are no words for this feeling.

"Are you all right, baby? Just nod if you are." She nods. "Now, there is one last sense I can take from you."

Her body jerks involuntarily, with no idea what it could be.

"Before I do this, just know that you are nothing but the sensations of your body, and that you can trust me completely. I will always treat you like a precious object. And it will make us both strong."

Alex places tiny earplugs underneath the wrapping of the blindfold, and continues to talk to her, knowing she can no longer hear him. "I love you, Rikki. Good God, look at you. And now I am without a voice also. We are reduced to exactly where we should be. This may just kill both of us eventually."

As he begins to command her body, she gives herself over to him completely, feeling the pleasure, the ache, the withdrawal, the new sensations. Every opening and inch of her body is being explored and entered. There are strokes and there are slaps and she can barely tell them apart. Kisses begin to feel like bites and bites feel like sex. She hears stories in her head and they are like dreams, stories being told by someone else, someone who has total control over her and knows her from the inside out.

When Alex turns her over and reties her on her belly to begin working his way up and down her back, she's lost in the dance on the line between pain and pleasure. With no sight, no sound, no control, no power, she finally gives in to the absolute sensations of love and abandonment and her own wild hunger for passion and silently begs him for more, and then more, and then even more.

The return from the weekend had been very quiet between them. Alex calls her on Tuesday to say he needs to cancel that night, and wants to meet her for lunch the next day.

He holds her tight when she arrives at the restaurant. "Rikki, this is killing me. I wake up craving you. I think all day long of ways to hurt you and love you and own you. I forget to do important things, like pay bills. I can't get my work done. I can't find my way back across this bridge we've created."

She just listens. "We can stop whenever we want to."

"Rikki. Rikki. The weekend was incredible. I'm sorry. You were right, we're going to consume each other if we keep going. And I can't handle it."

"You loved it. And so did I."

He's near tears. "But I've lost the line. The line between fantasy and my own darkness. I'm falling apart, Rikki. If I stay with you it may kill me. It may kill you. We can't live in this secret dark world forever."

She watches him calmly, trying to figure out what to say. She's never felt stronger in her life.

"I have to stop, Rikki. God, I have to stop."

She rises to leave and drops her second airline ticket to Italy on the table in front of him. "I understand, Alex. It will be all right. But I have a surprise for you, just in case you change your mind. July first. Take care."

After three weeks away from him, Rikki's amazed at how strong and happy she still feels. She tries not to think too hard about why this is. She misses him. But their power shifted somewhere, and it satisfies her deeply. There are things that she wants and needs and now she knows how to get them

Leaving for Venice, she writes him a short note on her rose stationery. She asks him only to take care of himself, to be well.

Sitting on the airplane gazing out the window, she fingers the filigree chains that she still wears tight around her neck. Shortly before take-off, Alex arrives, out of breath. He looks thinner, worried, a little older. She just smiles, reaches over, closes the windowshade, crosses her legs, lifts her white sundress up to her waist, and presents her bare pussy for his approval.

Alex watches her, surprised, enchanted. "You knew I'd be here?"

"Yes."

His hand is strong on her thigh as they take off. "Tell me a story, baby."

The Minyan

Lawrence Schimel

Simon felt self-conscious as he walked down East 10th Street. He wondered if everyone could tell that he was going to a sex party, which was a ridiculous thought since it was a private party being held at someone's apartment. It wasn't as if he was going to one of those clubs where anyone watching him enter or leave would know what he was up to.

Still, he felt like it was obvious. Which may have simply been because he was nervous. He didn't usually go to sex parties, but one of the guys from congregation, Uri, had invited him. Simon had spent the rest of the service wondering which of the other guys Uri had invited as well. He'd found himself mentally undressing the men around him, wondering what they would look like naked, how big their dicks were, if Isaac was hairy all over, thick mats of fur covering his body. He'd imagined them in all sorts of sexual poses and situations.

As if he didn't feel that these thoughts – so improper in *shul* – were sacrilege enough, Simon had been embarrassed by his body's behaviour, the fact that he'd had a hard on pressing its way outwards in his pants every time he stood. He'd felt like he was back in high school, getting a woody on the way to class and holding his schoolbooks in front of his crotch, as if everyone – especially all the other guys – didn't know what that meant. The instinct to shut the *siddur* and hold it protectively in front of his crotch, to shield his erection from view, was still strong, but Simon resisted. He recited the responses from memory, his vision blurring as he nervously glanced to his left and his right, trying to see from the corners of his eyes if anyone had noticed his arousal. He was grateful for the fringe of his *tallis,* which hid his boner behind its white veil, although he was afraid that his hard-on was making the fringe stand out as well.

Although he was not certain who among the congregation was also invited – the way one did not know who exactly the *lomed vuvnick* were – Simon had skipped services two nights ago because he felt too ashamed about seeing those men there and knowing what they planned to do this evening. Or what he imagined they planned to do; Simon wasn't quite sure what it would be like, since he didn't often go to this sort of party. In fact, he'd never been to one like this, although he had once been to a "sauna" when he was down in Puerto Rico on vacation. He'd been fascinated to be in the presence of sex, to watch men around him sucking and fucking in public, but he'd been too nervous to let anyone touch him, let alone do anything more. Men did touch him sometimes – the rules seemed to be touch first, ask later – but Simon always shied away from the groping hands, the men who tried to sink to their knees before him. He'd fingered his own dick behind the protective curtain of his towel, too afraid to show it off in public despite the naked bodies all around him, and he came almost immediately, shooting into the terry-cloth fabric. He went back to his little cubicle room and turned the towel inside out, so that the come-stained side was not against his skin, all sticky.

But he did not leave.

He had felt a compulsion to stay as long as his time would permit and to watch as much sex as he could. It had taken days of rationalizations and justifications to talk himself into coming there, and he'd done it only because he was so far from home – almost in another country, for all that it was technically a territory of the United States. He'd always been curious about the sex clubs back home in New York, but he was always afraid that if he went to one he'd run into someone he knew. It didn't matter that they would both be there for the same reason; Simon would just die of embarrassment if that were to happen.

So now that he'd convinced himself to finally visit one, he stayed in the bathhouse in Old San Juan for hours, pacing the halls, exploring every room and alcove, always watching, silent, not talking to anyone – whether they spoke English or not. He just wanted to be there.

Hours later, in a back room that was pitch black, Simon did let them touch him. He didn't know how many men there were – he couldn't see them, couldn't see anything. Somehow, as long as he couldn't see them, it was OK. It was like his friend Eric who talked faster and faster whenever he lied, as if he hoped that somehow God wouldn't hear his falsehood if Eric talked so quickly.

It didn't make any sense, Simon knew, but he stopped thinking about it. When a hand had touched him in the darkness, he did not jump back. He let it explore, slowly working its way down his chest to the barrier of his towel, tightly wrapped around his waist. The fingers pulled on the flap tucked away, and Simon grabbed the towel before it fell to the floor, clenching it in hands – to give him something safe to hold onto as the fingers continued to explore, and touched his cock.

Because he couldn't see anything, Simon was able to imagine whatever and whoever he wanted. He was too afraid to do anything to anyone else, although he did from time to time reach out with one hand to feel the bodies of the men around him, the invisible men whose hands and mouths were touching his body, and there were always too many hands or mouths on him, always more than one man. His fingers would venture forth (the other hand still tightly clutching the towel like his own version of Linus' blue security blanket) and touch flesh, drop down to feel the man's cock, then retreat back to the safety of the towel, wiping off the droplets of precome that had clung to his palm.

Simon had wanted to pull back, when he came in someone's mouth – he didn't know whose – thinking, "This is unsafe, you shouldn't do this, you don't know who I am." But it was too late. Before he knew it he had crested over into orgasm, his hips bucking his cock deeper into the stranger's mouth, and the man grabbed his ass, pulling Simon towards him, not letting go until his body had quieted again and his cock had begun to grow soft in the guy's mouth.

Stumbling over the bodies around him in his hurry to get out of there, Simon had practically run to the showers and scrubbed his body pink, then went back to his hotel. That was all nearly two years ago now, and he had never been involved in any sort of group sex before or since. Until tonight.

Because he was nervous, and had been building up this moment in his mind for so many days now, Simon was sure that everyone could tell that he was on his way to have sex.

He was also horny. He hadn't jerked off for the past two days, even though he normally jerked off at least once a day. But he had developed this sort of superstition about not jerking off on the night before he was going to have sex, or when there was the possibility of his having sex, such as if he were on a date. Or going to a sex party.

Part of it was simply performance anxiety. By "saving up" he felt more secure that he would get hard quickly, no matter how nervous he was, and also that he would have an impressively thick come.

He arrived at the building and stood before the door. This was his last chance to turn back.

But Simon wanted to be here tonight. For all his wanting a boyfriend, looking for a mate who'd be his life partner, for all his reticence at the sauna in Puerto Rico, Simon knew that he could so easily become addicted to such promiscuous sex. There was a part of him that craved that wild abandon, to have sex with many men in a single night, to not know or care who they were or ever see them again.

He hoped that tonight, among these men who he knew and who, moreover, were his people in so many ways – fellow Jews, all with the same sexual desires he felt – that he'd be less nervous, more willing to let himself try things he'd only fantasized about. To be part of the groupings of bodies he had only witnessed last time.

Simon cleared his throat, hoping his voice wouldn't crack when he had to say his name, then pressed the buzzer. After a moment of waiting, he heard the click of the door being electronically unlocked, without anyone asking him who he was.

This made Simon a little more nervous. Just how many men were invited to this party, that they let anyone up? Or was he simply the last invitee left to arrive?

He rode the elevator wondering if men were already having sex or if they'd waited for him before starting. As he stared at the floor numbers going up and up, he shifted his hard-on in his jeans, willing it to go down. He thought it would seem improper to have one before he arrived and disrobed, as if he were so hard up and desperate that he couldn't control himself.

Arrows indicated which wing each set of apartments was in. He pulled the invitation from his pocket and checked the number, then put it away again. He stood before the door and rang the buzzer. Simon could hear men's voices inside chatting. He wondered if soon the neighbours, anyone passing by the doorway, would be able to hear their sounds of sex.

Simon heard the flap on the eyepiece being lifted. He smiled, although he always felt he looked ridiculous through those warped fisheye lenses. He took his hands out of his pockets. Uri opened the door.

It's strange to be greeted at the door by someone you know only casually who's wearing nothing but his BVDs. Especially when you're not used to seeing them in this state, such as if you went to the same gym and saw each other in the locker room all the time.

Simon couldn't help looking him over, up and down, staring at Uri's body. He was short but solid, with thickly muscled arms and legs. His skin shone like burnished bronze, and he had wiry black hairs in a line down his chest and covering his legs, like sparse grass poking up through desert sand. He'd grown up on a kibbutz in Israel before moving to the US five years ago.

"*Shalom!*" Uri cried, leaning forwards to kiss Simon on the lips in the typical gay greeting. "The party's just getting started," he continued. "Come on in."

Simon reached out and kissed the *mezuzah* on his way into the apartment. Uri lived in a nice one-bedroom condo. He had a large abstract painting over the living room couch, under which sat three men, also naked except for their underwear. They all looked sort of nervous, and sat separate from each other even though they were all on the same sofa; nowhere did skin touch skin. Simon nodded to Benji, who he knew, and then looked away, blushing because of how Benji was (un)dressed and what they were planning. He had to suppress a barely controllable urge to giggle.

There were other men, also in only their underwear, standing with their backs to Simon, looking at the books on Uri's shelves. Two of them had *kipahs* on, pinned to their dark hair.

Uri led him into the kitchen. "Take your stuff off," he said, pointing to the stacks of neatly-folded clothes on the countertop. "What do you want to drink?"

At other apartment parties, everyone took their coats off and left them in the bedroom, then congregated in the living room. But tonight, the bed was going to be put to better use. And so, for that matter, was the living room.

There were six other guys there so far, besides Simon and Uri. Simon knew three of them from *shul* – Howard, Stanley, and Benji – although he'd never seen any of them naked – or nearly naked – before. They hadn't been among the guys he'd been mentally undressing that night Uri gave him the invite, but they didn't look bad without their clothes on, just sort of average: dark-haired, dark-eyed Slavic Jews who didn't get much sun.

Of the rest of them, there was one guy, Darren, who Simon had met before at a gay Yeshiva dance. He was tanned like Uri, but his body seemed hairless. It was only later, when Simon was closer, that he realized Darren had shaved it, even his crotch.

The other two guys, Ezra and Joshua, Uri knew from when he lived uptown and went to the gay congregation up there. Joshua was a redhead whose arms looked too thin. Not at all Simon's type, but then he'd never understood the fascination many men seemed to have for redheads. Ezra, on the other hand, was the kind of boy who might catch his eye on the street, with his dark eyes and goatee and v-shaped torso. It was a surprise to Simon to learn that Ezra was so shy and unsure of himself, sort of nerdy, hiding behind his glasses the way Simon felt that he, too, did quite often.

Everyone was in their late 20s or early 30s. And they all seemed nervous, or unsure of what they were or should be doing. Everyone except Uri, the mastermind of this little get together, who walked about with complete comfort, unconcerned about his near-nudity and the sex that was on everyone's mind. He played the host, but also seemed completely at ease, chatting with his friends as if this were any ordinary get together.

Since few people knew each other, no one knew really what to talk about.

"It's funny," Howie said. "My mother is always after me, since all my boyfriends are blond and blue-eyed. If you have to have sex with other men, she asks, couldn't you at least find a nice Jewish boy? And here I am, in a roomful of guys she'd approve of, only not about to do anything she'd approve of!"

It was the wrong thing to say, really, Simon thought. No one wanted to be reminded of what their parents would think of what they were about to do, for all that everyone there was eager for it all to begin. But what would happen when they ran into these men again in their regular lives? How could Simon ever go back to *shul* if he saw Stanley, tonight, with a stranger's fingers up his butt? He would never be able to see these men again without remembering what they looked like naked.

The silence stretched on uncomfortably.

Darren told a joke: "So this kid comes home from school and says, 'Ma, Ma, I got a part in the school play!' And the mother says, 'That's nice dear, what part did you get?' So the kid tells her, 'I got the part of the Jewish husband.' The mother stops what she's doing and looks at her son. 'What's the matter,' she says, 'you couldn't get a speaking role?' "

Everyone laughed.

The buzzer rang. All noise stopped suddenly and everyone turned to stare at the door, even though whoever it was had to come all the way upstairs before they got to the door. They were all wondering the same things, Simon knew: would it be someone they knew or a stranger? What if this new guy was ugly? What if he was unbearably cute?

Even though only Uri knew everyone there, it was like they were all tired old regulars at some bar, just waiting for fresh meat to show up. Was that how things would happen: one time someone would come in and catch someone's eye and make their move, breaking the ice for everyone else to start having sex? Who would be the first to do something?

Uri looked through the peephole of the door, then opened it. Simon could see from where he was that there were two people on the other side of the doorframe.

"Aaron," Uri said, "what a pleasant surprise. You should have told me you were bringing someone."

" It was sort of a last-minute thing," Aaron said. "Jorge, meet my friend Uri. Uri, this is Jorge." He smiled at Jorge, then looked back at Uri and winked. "We met at Escuelita last night."

This was one of those moments of sex party etiquette. Or perhaps simply party etiquette. What to do if someone brought someone who hadn't been invited? At a normal party, this sort of behaviour was usually more forgivable.

Uri looked over Aaron's friend and evidently decided he made the cut. He invited them both in and led them to the kitchen to unclothe.

The whole nature of the party seemed to change with Jorge there. It was the presence of foreskin in a roomful of circumcised gay men. It was the presence of a non-Jew.

Simon remembered how his uncle Morty used to always joke, "*Shiksas* are for practice," whenever he asked if Simon had a girlfriend yet.

Simon didn't doubt that this *sheggitz* would get as much practice as he wanted tonight, since every guy there seemed to be utterly entranced by Jorge's smooth dark skin as he stood in the doorway of the kitchen – to show off, still visible to the rest of us? – and peeled out of his clothes.

Once stripped down to their Calvins and briefs and holding their cocktails, they came back into the other room. There were ten men now crowded into the small area, sitting or standing around awkwardly.

"Hey, we've got a *Minyan* now," Howie said. You could tell he was happy to be the first one to notice.

"Actually, we don't," Ezra said. And technically he was right; Jorge didn't count.

But that was for prayer. For a sex party, ten bodies – regardless of their religion – was enough critical mass to get things going. Uri circulated, introducing people and drawing them into conversation. Not everyone could fit comfortably in the living room – at least, there weren't enough places to sit. So some of the guys had drifted into the bedroom where they'd stayed to get it on while no one – at least, not everyone – was looking.

Of course, the moment one of the living room group noticed, everyone rushed to the doorway of the bedroom to watch.

Somehow this didn't seem to be the right sex party etiquette but it didn't stop anyone.

Simon watched the back of Joshua's head bobbing up and down before Stanley's crotch, as if Josh were *davening,* and perhaps this was like prayer for Joshua, lost in a trance of cocksucking.

With all of them crowded there at the door, growing hard from their voyeurism if they hadn't been already, it didn't take long for the rest of the guys to start touching one another as well. A hand on thigh or belly, fingers cold with nervousness. A hand cupping an ass-cheek through the fabric of his underwear. Simon didn't really know who was who but it didn't matter. His heart beat faster, he felt a tight constriction in his chest from nervousness, then he took a deep breath and relaxed into the sensation of his ass in some man's palm.

He thought for a moment back to that bathhouse in Puerto Rico, where even though he'd wanted to he wouldn't do anything except in the concealing darkness of the backroom, as if sex were something too shameful to be seen. Among these ten men, these other gay Jews gathered together for the worship of the body, he no longer felt guilty about his desperate yearnings for sex with other men, as he had on the walk over here and on so many occasions previously. He looked around him, at the men who were so like him, now lost in their pleasure, the giving and the receiving of it, and he smiled. He was not alone, and he was glad to be part of something bigger than himself, this Minyan, which for him is what it was even if one of the men was not Jewish. A Minyan of desire, men who no longer needed to congregate in clandestine secret to worship, but who could love and pray without shame.

"Amen," he whispered, and pressed himself back against the man who cupped his ass, no longer holding himself apart.

Glossary of Yiddish words:
daven Ritual bending of the knees during prayer that causes the body to sway backwards and forwards.
kibbutz A type of agricultural commune in Israel.
kipah Another name for yarmulka, the ceremonial head-covering worn by Jewish men to show respect for God when inside a temple, or in general for Orthodox Jews.
lomed vuvnick The 36 ordinary people who are so pure of heart that God does not again destroy the world with flood or fire or so

forth. Because no one knows who these 36 are, one is taught to be kind and offer hospitality to all people, in case they are one of the lomed vuvnick.

mezuzah A small tube containing a scroll with Hebrew prayers, placed on the doorframe of all Jewish households, to commemorate the escape of the Jews from Egypt and the Angel of Death's passing over the homes of the Israelites during the 10th plague.

Minyan The minimum number of adult males (10) necessary to maintain a temple and pray.

shalom Salutation meaning hello, goodbye, and peace.

sheggitz Male form of shiksa, less commonly used.

shiksa Derogatory term for a non-Jewish girl.

shul Temple.

siddur Prayerbook.

tallis Ceremonial scarf.

Pornographic Story

Rebecca Ray

I'm not lying now. I'm going to tell you this story and you have to listen, you have to listen close. Because I've waited a long time for a story like this one to tell. All right? This story is pornographic, you have to listen closely and you have to believe. Just to enjoy it, you have to suck the whole thing out of reality, you see? You turn the lights out to watch one on television, so the shadows only flicker over silhouettes in your room. It's like that. It's the story of how I fucked a cab driver at two o'clock in the afternoon, parked up in the archway between Air Street and Regent Street, Piccadilly Circus end.

I love London, loved it from the first day. London's full of people like pornography's full of sex. I thought that, the first day. I used to sit in this cafe on Charing Cross Road, watch the people walk past. And they never meet your eyes and you never meet theirs, but they're walking to be watched. They know you're sitting there, they feel you like the softest touch on the side of their face. They wet their lips and smell the exhaust fumes, and they know you're sitting there. They feel the contours of their own features, their own body under their clothes, all the more clearly for your eyes. They feel themselves. London's full of people, full of fingering glances and sounds. A man told me once, touching my stomach in bedroom light, that my body was a landscape: a jungle and mountains, desert. All bodies are like landscapes maybe, with a city for the mind.

London's full of fantasy, people come here and they leave their names behind. My boyfriend, he grew up here, he doesn't feel it maybe. But I've never felt it as strongly as I did that afternoon. Air Street is this little passage, right? It runs you from Regent Street into Soho, from one side of London to the other in the moment it takes you to pass under the arch. That's how close the two sides are: silk gloved fingers and dirty fingers, interlinked and gripping tight. Does that sound stupid? Does it sound right? When it rains, the water pushes trickling fingers between Air Street's broken paving stones, under the arch and out. Into Regent Street's bright sky. Into its open road. London is everything, it's the pornographer, it's the audience, and it just breathes with being them. Full of fantasy, and never more so maybe, than when you open a black cab's door. You could be anyone then. You could be a princess then, you could be spending stolen five-pound notes. Or you could be ten minutes away from fucking a man whose name isn't given to you. London allows fantasy, needs it like a camera trained on people without clothes.

We love each other, London and I. I could put my hands down on the street and grey my skin with it. I could stand in its centre, my eyes closed, and feel every sound and every movement like things I've always needed to feel. I came here, I left my name behind. I never went home again. And, parked up under that archway in Air Street, we fucked that day, London and I.

A November day, it was, the sort that blows people and litter before it like it doesn't care which it moves. The sort that bruises every face. And this is how it happened: on Embankment, me standing there with my arm stuck out and no idea, no idea. I saw the cab slow, standing there. Cold air and breath and traffic fumes, caught in the river wind. I was going home.

This guy, he was early 30s maybe, dark hair and brown eyes. He poked his tongue into his cheek, looking up at me, like he didn't give a fuck if I was beautiful or ugly, didn't give a fuck where I was coming from. Like I shouldn't expect him to. They like to talk, cabbies, but they only talk through the glass and they don't look back at your face. And I talk, and it's

London I'm looking at. There's something very free, I think, something absolute, in speaking to a stranger without ever meeting their eyes. He had brows that almost met in the middle, this guy. He had a wife, two sons and a daughter, he told me. He had a life, somewhere else. He asked me if I was going home.

"Home, yes," I said. On the other side of the glass, I saw him nod. "My boyfriend'll have the kettle on by now."

"That's the best thing, isn't it? That's what you need, cup of tea when you get in. Just sit down with someone for a bit." He told me that he didn't like to talk when he got in. He just liked to sit with her, relax without having to talk. He told me, sometimes the talking gets on top of you, doing that job. Always having to talk. And one of the best things about being married was that you could sit in silence, without coldness, without awkwardness.

"I could never get married." I looked out through the window: Embankment and the shadow of the footbridge, moving over us. People moving, everything moving, like the wind could rattle and shake every person in London, and no one would ever come loose. "I'm not the right sort of person."

He told me that you didn't have to be any kind of person to get married. Marriage, he said, was a good thing for anyone. I looked at him, his neck, his shirt collar, and my reflection was painted across the glass, in shadow.

"I don't know. You get married, you'd have to be the same person every day. I mean, you wake up, he's the same . . . he makes you the same." I looked away from his back, and I said, "He'll have the kettle on when I get in now, but we're not like that, see? You get married, you're always the same."

"No, it's not anything like that. Everyone changes. You spend a few years with someone, both of you are going to change, aren't you? Try having kids. No, I mean, my wife, she's a completely different person from the one I married. Totally different, like. But she's still the same underneath. Anyway," he said, "you've got a boyfriend, just the same with a boyfriend."

"I came home, a couple of months ago, I'd just got paid. You know what I said to him? I said, 'Let's go to the airport.'

And you know what he said? He said yes. We went to Rome that weekend. You get married, you don't do things like that anymore." I looked at his eyes in the rearview mirror. "How's she different, then?" I said. "How's she changed?"

"Lots of ways. I don't know, lots of ways. Got a different job, hasn't she? Different friends."

"What does she do?" I said, "Your wife." And London was going past us in low gear. I listened to him answer and then I said, "My boyfriend, he's got a different job every six months, and we're always skint. And you know what? I don't care. I don't give a fuck. Because he's never the same, week to week. But that's not it anyway, it's not that they're always the same. It's that they make you the same." I looked at him. "You know?"

"I know what you mean. Course I know what you mean, but – "

"See, you do have to be the right sort of person for marriage. I couldn't handle that. I couldn't be the same person every day, you know? That's what I love about London," I said. "You can put on your make-up and clothes and be someone different, any time you want to, any moment, you know? You can walk out the door and meet somebody and be a different person." I met his eyes then, and we were smiling at each other, but I couldn't see his mouth. "I like that," I said. "I like to have that, you know?"

She imagined the sort of wife he would have. She imagined his wife reaching up, the tiniest touch with the tip of one finger, where his brows met in the middle. His eyes would be closed, she thought.

Through the glass, I could see his arms moving. And we were turning now, and all the grey streets turning too. He stopped to let a woman go past. In London's winter, people move as if they can't stop for the wind. And I saw her look in through the windscreen, maybe she saw me. I met her eyes.

We were eight minutes from Air Street then. He had dark hair, just like his eyebrows, thin on the back of his neck.

I said, "How old are your kids?"

I've never found people attractive by their faces or bodies. The look of someone is a blank thing, dust on a TV screen. It's the way that someone wets the corner of their mouth, it's what's in their eyes when they take you in, and you can imagine the sound they might make as they come. It's the way that they would hear your sounds, and feel the need to move, hearing them. The smallest things, do you know what I mean? I want you to know.

I watched him answer. And outside: Londoners walking. Londoners, brushing against each other, and feeling the touches without a flicker of expression. The engine ground as hard as the wind out there, through Charing Cross and onto Haymarket, filthy grey.

No one here seems to look at each other. No one needs to look, everyone knows that it might break the spell. Everyone in London walks as though they're walking alone, but they can only keep that expression because of the people by their sides. This place, it scrapes people against each other, until they could crackle and scream.

You have to believe in London to love it, like you have to believe in pornography so you can let it make you come.

I said, "I couldn't do it, marriage, children. I have to be able to get up in the morning and know, I can do anything I want to do." I saw his shoulders move, shrugging. On the glass between us, my reflection was still. "It's playing," I said. "That's what it is. It's the best kind of playing in the world, to pretend, to do something really new, you know? To do something mad. I'm the sort of person, I couldn't live without that."

She imagined how he'd sit with his kids, how he'd go home to them. She imagined them on the sofa, crowding round him, all grabbing for a little piece. He would look out over them, trying to find the television screen with his eyes.

I said, "How do you live, without that?"

Coming up to Piccadilly Circus then, where every street spits people onto the road and lets them press together there.

I said, "When was the last time you did something mad?"

She imagined the flickers of anger on his face, trying to find that television screen, the way his hands would push them away. And on the screen, she could imagine it, people fucking. She could see how it would be.

Here on Piccadilly Circus, with every person pushing dryly

against each other, I can see it all: Soho's ragged edge. The clean, tall shops. The traffic. The sky. Here, this is where I'd stand and close my eyes. This is where I'd put my hands down onto the pavement and let them come up grey. There is a noise here, there is a feeling. Do you know the feeling where everything strains? Back arched, muscles tensed, and eyes closed like that, everything in your landscape body tries, everything in your city mind. London is the fantasy; it shows you what you want in every window, in the reflections sliding over every car; it gives you everything that you want to believe in. It gives you yourself.

I said, "When was the last time? Something you've never done before? Something that was nothing like you at all?" He had big hands, I could see them on the wheel in that grey afternoon light, changing as he drove through shadows. He laughed, told me that he didn't remember. And I asked him then, if he wasn't afraid, just having to say that out loud.

I said, "My boyfriend does what he wants, I don't ask him. It's better that way."

He looked in the mirror and he asked me, "Oh, yeah?"

And I told him, "Yes."

She knew how he must be looking at her now. She could hear it in his voice and see it in the glance of his eyes. But when he spoke, she couldn't tell what words he said, through the taxi intercom. And when she spoke herself, her hands were sweating. She could have wiped them on the vinyl seats and seen her palm prints there. They might have faded slowly after she got out. There might have been a trace left by the time that someone else opened the door.

I looked at him then. I said, "If someone asked you to do a mad thing now, could you do it? Would you do it?"

His eyes were half caught with all the traffic, the lights, and with trying to look at me. There wasn't any trace of going home in them now. No trace of silence with his wife. And on every side of us, the people walked without looking. No one looks in London, but everyone sees. London is the pornographer. It gives you the fantasy, holds steady all the things that you need to believe in, long enough for you to take what you want.

"Would you do it?" I said.

"I don't know. Depends what, doesn't it? Depends — "

"If it was something that you'd remember for the rest of your life? Something that you might never have the chance to do ever again? Would you do it?" I said. "Now?"

He looked away from my reflection, out at London and every person moving there. He looked back at me. And then he said, "What?"

I've used pornography, used it with people, used it on my own. I like it put that way, in the same way that London will never be home, but you can use it to shape your life. I like the films though, not the magazines. A page doesn't cast light and shadow in your room, there's nothing to believe in on a page. Pornography shows you people, just the way that London shows you them. I like to think, when I watch it, that the people on the screen are watching me back. They could be the audience, as much as I am. And London, fantasy, pornographer, must be the audience as well. You could vomit on the street in London, and people would run their eyes over you, just like fingers. London is the audience, because it breathes and wets its mouth with fantasy, and every fantasy needs an audience to live.

I asked him, "How long is it since you had sex with someone apart from your wife?"

And while he laughed and sputtered, we were stopped at the traffic lights, caught between other black cabs, caught between other people's glances. Maybe they saw us.

His hands shifted on the wheel.

"I mean it," I said.

"What do you mean? You mean what?"

In front of us, the traffic lights changed. Traffic needs to move, we jolted forwards.

I could see his shoulders and his tense neck, the way his hair shifted against his collar every time he shook his head. And I didn't care what his body would look like, and I couldn't really remember his face. I told you, we fucked that day, the city and I.

"How long?" I said, "You could do something now, and you'd never forget it."

What is it about the things that aren't handed to you, that you want them so much more? And he was still laughing, still shaking his head, but there was something new in his movements now. I watched him. The things that aren't handed to you keep you running. Maybe people, like engines, just need to be moving, and in London, no one stops. It's built to show you the things you want, the things that keep you moving. Try watching a porn movie, there's always someone who's just about to come.

Let me tell you how we parked up on Air Street, how he looked both ways, every way, before he got into the back of his cab. He wiped his hands on his trousers once he'd closed the door. He looked at me like he was scared, but I could have told him, you could have told him, there was nothing to be scared about. It's only fantasy, only porn.

Let me tell you, I want you to hear.

She saw spots of rain on the windows then. It would be raining on the little path that led to her front door. She thought, watching him shift as he tried to find answers to give her, of that little path, that door. When she looked out from there, the only view showed houses. There seemed to be a million of them, a million little paths. And she thought sometimes that, if London was the flickering screen, then all these houses she saw, they must be the silhouettes, the shadow shapes of a room, waiting to be seen in daylight again.

I said, "Pull over. Get in here."

"I'm not going to pull over, fuck's sake. You want to go home or not?"

"I told you what I want. Pull over, and get in here. And when you go home tonight, you won't be looking back at another day at work – " I wanted to tell him, it was only a fantasy, and how often do you get that chance? The chance to live one, to actually be one. I wanted to try and explain, this place was full of fantasy, and it was only right to live it, when you had that chance. It was right to try and be a part of it.

She kept thinking: London fucks you. London fucks everyone, every chance it gets. She kept thinking: Either you take it, or you take part.

The floor of a black cab is hard rubber, relief patterns, and I looked at it then. I drew my legs up. That floor would put marks on my knees, patterns in just the same shapes. And if there hadn't been glass between us, I would have reached out then, ran my own finger over his hairs. Tiny, soft little things on the back of his neck. I would have dug my fingernails into his skin. There was glass, though. And when I put my hand up and touched it, it was cold as a television screen.

She had touched the television screen once, she had put the flat of her hand against it and felt no flesh, no breath. The screen had been dry. Static electricity had flicked at her like a parody of movement.

He looked at my hand, pressed there. He could see it in the rearview mirror. And he was driving still, flicking glances from the road, to me. From London, to me. My hand must have been only three inches from those soft little hairs. Maybe the glass didn't even matter. He was tense now. Under his clothes, his shoulders were hardening up. On either side of us, London moved in grey rainwater, with grey, hunched bodies. The pavements, the roads, they felt like they could have squirmed with it. Air Street was there, up ahead.

"Pull in," I said. I didn't move my hand from the glass.

"Look, you don't understand. Fuck's sake, I can't — "

"You see it? There. Pull in there." I put my other hand up, framing his head with my fingers, on the other side of this glass. I swallowed. "I want to go home, see my boyfriend, and know that nothing about today was ordinary. I want to think about this, remember it. I want to do it, and go home and write every detail down. I want to write down, that you got in the back here, that you looked at me, reached out, touched me. I'll write, that you put your tongue in my mouth. That you put your fingers in my mouth. Pull over. There."

When he looked around us then, all he saw was London. There was nothing to stop him in what he saw. There was nothing out there that could break apart the things that I'd just said. What was out there, it made true the things that I'd said. It made them real.

And when he turned the wheel, his movements jerked, quick enough that he couldn't change his mind. I saw the side of his face for a moment as he pulled the cab in, but I didn't look at it long.

From Regent Street's bright, reflected sky, we came to a stop. The arch of Air Street, damp, dark stone and broken pavements. And when he turned the engine off, I could hear the sound of people walking there. I could hear their voices in the traffic's noise, and they were shopping, walking, moving. London shows you the next thing, and the next, they couldn't stop. Think of a porn movie, five people fucking on screen. None of them can stop. You build a fantasy so fast, so constantly, that no one can step out. Are you ready to hear it? I'll show it to you, I'll tell you how it was.

I watched him turn the engine off, and he didn't sit for even a second. In front of the windscreen, Air Street closed us in. Dripping stone and scaffolding, buildings pressed almost close enough to touch. If their walls were faces, bodies, they would have been close enough to catch each other's breath.

I watched him get out and come around to my door. I ran a hand across my mouth and it was wet and my tongue wanted to move. My whole body wanted to move. They were built to move.

I opened the door for him, his face down, not looking at me. And that was when he ran his hands on his trouser legs. He stooped inside. He closed the door behind him. He sat on the seat next to me, and

She saw his dark eyes were lined with long lashes. The sort a wife might know well, might touch so gently as he slept, watch them flutter and be still, as he rested again.

I slid up to him. I put my hand around the back of his neck, the place that I'd seen, that I hadn't been able to touch for the glass. His skin was warm there, those soft little hairs tickled. And I did dig my fingernails in.

Outside, around us, there was rain. There was noise. Everything in this place strains like a muscle strains, reaching for something that can't be touched. I dug my nails in, I

moved across to him and I could hear his breathing. Quick,
like he might jolt forward. Like engines, restrained.

I put my face up next to his face, and then I could feel his
breathing. Another tiny inch, and his skin would be up
against mine, his mouth would be up against mine. But I
didn't move. I looked into his eyes, so close that there were
no contours to his face. I held him there. I held myself there.
His mouth was as wet as mine. I saw it on his open lips.

I said, "Put your tongue out, the tip of your tongue, let me
see."

His lip was shaking, oh so slight. And when he did it, I felt
my own tongue move, like something in a mirror. Like we
could echo each other, and still nothing but breath could
pass between us. I would be the audience for him, I would
watch every small movement his mouth made, and he would
do the same for me, and still nothing would pass between
us.

She had come, as some woman on the screen came, some
woman with blonde hair. And her own fingers had moved too fast
and too hard. They must have both felt the same thing then. The
same straining, wanting thing.

So slowly, so perfectly slowly, I moved my mouth closer to
his. Even his breathing was wet then. I put my hand on his
leg.

"OK," I said. "OK, OK. Touch my mouth with your
tongue. Gently, touch my lips, OK?"

He tilted his head to do it. And when he put his face
against mine, I could feel the stubble there. And when he
put his tongue against mine, I could taste him, like static.

He moved his body closer, strained it closer. Twisted
towards each other in the cab's back seat, his chest pressed
on mine and I could feel the rub of skin underneath his
clothes.

I pulled my hand from the back of his neck, scraped his
skin as my fingers fell away, and then his hands were in my
hair. Grabbing at it, like he could hold me still if he could
only get enough of it in his hands. And my hands – my
hands were under his shirt then. My fingers were on the
hairs there, on the sides of his rib cage, breathing, breathing.

The kind of rising, falling breath that makes you want to claw, grab, dig in hard enough that
there's no distance any more
you're eating each other, mouths and skin and hands, eating away at each other, like you can't ever bite enough out. His tongue was in my mouth then, right the way in, all of it and I could feel his teeth and the softness of his lips, and all of it wet. Sharp or soft, all of it wet. All of it wanting.

I moved my fingers up his leg, other hand scraping fingernails on him. And he was trying to get closer. Pulling my hair. Kissing everything, mouth and cheek, uncaring, unaware. I moved my fingers up his leg, and through the cloth of his trousers, I felt it.

He arched.

Through the wetness on both of our faces, I pulled back. Just enough to speak, just enough for him to hear me through our breathing. You want to fuck me? You want to fuck now? Do you
do you want me?
You want to fuck me now? Baby? I can feel you, you want to now. I can feel it. Baby.

And outside this metal and glass, every place around us, London strained. It reached. It wanted. It scraped with the noise of the cars and the buses, it was wet with the rain, with our kissing mouths. Outside Air Street's archway, there were people pressed so close. Close to each other, feeling it, not allowed to show the feeling. And close to us, to the shadows and reflections across the back window, so close to the place where we moved.

Fuck me now, yes, you want to. I know you want to, it's all right, you can do it. I want you to. It's all right, baby. It's all right to want it, I know you do. I can feel you wanting.

London fucks, all day and all night. It bucks with the movement of a million people. It fucks them, every single one of them, every moment that their eyes are open, it puts its fingers into them, its many tongues, and fucks them while they can't move or show that they feel it. While they can't even let their breathing change. And every grey, impassive face can feel it. It's in the flickers of doubt. It's in the way that they want to meet your eyes and have to turn away. London fucks every person here, while it holds their faces to the street.

I pressed my fingers there, into his crotch and moving oh so slightly, under his balls, cloth itching him. Around his dick.

That's it, baby. That's it. It's all right.

He strained. In his chest and his legs, in his mouth. And then I moved my fingers to his trouser fly. And he stopped straining. He stopped breathing. For a moment, I could feel him wanting nothing but

me

my hands.

I undid the button. Slow. So slow. I stopped. I reached up under the line of my skirt, as he sat, immobile, watching only. In front of his eyes and his open lips, I pulled my underwear away. I dropped it on the cab floor, in shadow there. And then I moved to sit on top of him. Both fingers in his fly, unzipping, both hands inside, and my mouth all over his mouth again. His fingers in my hair, needing me.

That's it. That's right.

Do you want to hear it now? I'll tell you how it felt.

She couldn't get his dick inside her, sitting up on him like that. She had to pull him down onto the floor, where dirty shoes had left smears of cold water, her own shoes, and other people's.

I went down on all fours, with his hands still in my hair that way, and I felt him pull his trousers down, felt the prickle of the hair on his thighs. He put his fingers on my hip, trying to find skin, trying to find something he could grip and hold onto. And when he'd found his grip, he could push himself in. And he did. Kneeling, I felt him. In a little. In a little more, and then he was fucking me. A little more. Again.

She had to let him do it from behind, too dry to be fucked in any way but the easiest. With her head down, she saw the ridged patterns on the floor of the cab. She let him fuck her, too dry to feel anything but pain. Somewhere underneath those patterns, the paving stones let filthy water trickle, out under this arch, and into Regent Street, under other people's feet. Like tearing, that was how it felt as she let him do it. She thought about the woman on screen, the woman with the blonde hair. They have drugs, for making porn movies, pills that send the blood down into the crotch and give a penis an erection, fills the walls of a vagina with enough blood to make it swell. She didn't look like that on screen, like she might have taken drugs. On screen, everything was very brightly lit. Watching it, she hadn't been able to see the line where the set ended. There was a line, though. The carpet in shot was taped down to a hard floor, scuffed around the edges by the shuffling feet of soundmen and cameramen and the boy that brought the coffee in. London shines with dirt and chrome, like every part of it is lit with stage lights. But there is a line where London stops, and only houses carry on. A million rows of houses, like an audience, gathered to watch, hands up against a glass screen. She lived in that kind of row. The kind where grass and weeds struggle around the path and there are four locks on every door. Her front door was painted blue, it was heavy, made of metal. There were skips parked outside, rainwater running now down their sides. Grey sky showed in the windows where she lived. It reflected there, with no lights on in the rooms inside. Behind her front door, the carpet was dim, mail strewn in piles. Behind her front door, there was silence. It settled like cold, in rooms where no one else had ever talked or fucked or slept.

In the kitchen, there was a photograph, stuck to the fridge. It showed the place where she'd grown up.

I felt him, moving faster. On my hips, his fingers gripped and loosened, every time he moved. And the sound of his breathing was little groans now. Little moans, and I was telling him, yes, you move, you moan, it feels good, doesn't it feel good? Little needful groans that got faster. And he fucked harder, and he was saying things, saying words then, saying yes. I want it. Let me come. I want to come. He was swearing over and over then. Fuck. Yes. Yes. He was coming, and he told me. I'm coming. Now. Please.

Fuck.

Outside, they must have seen us. They must have heard us and felt us. And knowing, they must have walked past, trying not to let it show on their faces that they could feel themselves, all the more clearly for his dick in me.

He shivered when he came. He purred. He let it go.

That was how it felt. Can you feel it? I want you to feel it, I want you to know. How many chances are there to be part of a fantasy? I was part of a fantasy that day. Every fantasy must have an audience, it must have one, just to live. To be real. This one was mine. Tell me, please. How do you feel?

When He Was Good

Marc Levy

He stood in the parking lot. The black asphalt shimmered like tarmac used on chopper pads. Annette was late. When the Land Rover pulled in he called to her.

"Looks like a tank."

He kissed her extended cheek.

"Lovely day," she said. "Isn't it gorgeous?" Her British accent always new.

He winked at her and stepped in. She slipped her right hand from the clutch to his thigh, then back, pulled into traffic.

"Right, then. Happy to see me?"

He leaned over and kissed her behind the left ear.

"You're such a naughty boy, aren't you?"

Annette fiddled with the radio, searched for music, news, anything.

"That's fine," he said. "Right there."

Martin flexed his body in time to the pumping beat, eyed her blouse, the inviting curve of her breasts. Annette was not pretty, he thought; her features were hard, as if she were a salmon that survived the run up river.

"Sometimes I think you work too hard."

"Really? But you do put up with all my sass."

"I figured you'd call sooner or later. I missed you," he said, fingering the clefts between her knuckles as if they were his own.

"I read all your letters. I was absolutely delighted . . . delighted by what you wrote." She turned to him. "Sexual love is . . . is so much easier to sustain, don't you think?"

She snared his hand in hers, then turned the radio mute. He smiled at the distorted reflection of himself dancing in the opaque lens of her sunglasses.

"Frankel says there are three kinds of love: impersonal, personal, and irreplaceable," he said.

The light changed. Annette accelerated, overtaking a lumbering van.

"Did I tell you my neighbour's tree smashed into the side of my house last night? He had the nerve to say it was my fault. Mine!"

She swerved into the fast lane.

"Did anyone get hurt?"

He spooled the volume dial clockwise.

Annette turned right on Warton Street; a parade of ornate homes and well kept lawns soldiered into view.

"Oh, have a look. Have a look," she chortled, pulling up the driveway. "The workmen must have come." She pointed to the dismembered tree, its trunk and branches neatly stacked to one side. " 'You're so lucky no one was injured,' " she mimicked, tugging back the emergency brake. "Well, have a look at my lovely garden!"

Stepping out of the car, she pinched the remote alarm on her key chain. The horn beeped once. He thought it sounded like a great metal goose shot in the wing.

"It's the deer," she said, pointing to the wilted stalks and bald patches of earth. "They come down from the reservation. I've already called the Mayor." She looked at him mournfully. "Julian, those animals are positively ruining my land. You absolutely must set out poison or have the hunters in.' He said he would look into it. Now this."

He estimated the garden measured ten metres by twelve; the backyard, one acre. Trees and shrubs edged the sides of her property. There was no fence to ward off intruders. A Victorian house peeked through a line of sycamores thirty metres ahead. He noticed the deer tracks, exaggerated a frown, then stepped behind her, embraced her body, nuzzled her neck.

"It looks different," he said, pointing past the ominous tree line.

"Oh, that. They painted it last week." She dug her backside into his groin. "I rather liked it when it was blue. Now it's just . . . Oh, I don't know . . . who would ever paint their house solid red? Can you imag . . ."

Martin closed his eyes, saw the pith helmeted blur figures running past. His neck snapped left to right.

". . . or suppose they installed one of those dreadful mosquito-killing machines?" She paused. "Are you all right, darling?"

"Yes, everything is under control."

He began undoing the hard plastic buttons of her blouse. He dipped his fingers inside, toyed with the lacy bra, dotted the nape of her neck with kisses until she quivered.

Annette turned round and faced him.

"You naughty, naughty man. In front of my nosy neighbours, will you? Inside, or I shall have to call the police."

"Fancy something to eat?"

"Maybe later. I need to work up an appetite." "You rascal. Come with me."

She led him by the hand as they walked from the well-appointed kitchen, its walls lined with gourmet utensils hung from dainty hooks, to the immense living room. A hand-frosted bay window overlooked the lawn and the cobble stoned gas lanterned street

"Isn't it just lovely?" she said, gesturing to an exquisite glass table and leather bound chairs, the black plush sofa, an array of exotic wall hangings and marble statues. "Mum left it to me. None of it's really mine. Well, I suppose it is."

She planted her fortyish chin on an upturned palm.

"How old was she?"

"Nearly ninety. I never told you? 'I simply must have my own bed and bath, Annette. Really. How perfectly dreadful, those horrid American elder farms.' Elder farms! Dear Lord."

"Do you miss her?"

He drew her hand away from her face and thumbed the curve of her mouth.

"Good gracious, no. Nothing ever suited Mum, darling. Nothing. But . . . all that's past now." She led him forwards. "What do you think? Charming, isn't it?"

On one side of the room two bookcases stood packed with grade school reference volumes, toys and games, each item tucked precisely in place. He imagined not one item missing.

"Very nice," he said, fingering the well worn spines.

"Those are my favourites," she said, pointing to an orderly shelf crammed with jig-saw puzzles. "I absolutely adore them. Sometimes the girls and I spend hours on the silly things . . . Don't look so sad," she teased, looking past him.

Stepping forwards, Annette pushed Play. The blinking answering machine whirred to life. A young man's voice, coy and energetic, spoke.

"Hi. It's me. Wondering when we can spend time together. I've been working out . . . hard. I think you'll like what I've got to show you. Tomorrow I have tickets for . . ."

"Oh, you and your bloody tickets," Annette shouted, shutting off the machine.

He knew of her lovers. Once, she had written him: As to my young stallions, well, in fact, how shall I say this, there is one chap I am rather fond of. We tryst weekends, when the kiddies are with their Dad. And, well, dammit, yes, there is a youngster I occasionally visit, a client, but it's simply puppy love, darling. At least Frederick is gone. The bastard. Martin, I will not be intimate with these two any longer if we have a go at it"

He thumbed a shelf full of encyclopedias; below it, a tin-cased biology set complete with specimens and microscope. Two adult frogs, vacuum packed in formaldehyde, stared at him, their large black eyes unblinking.

"I thought you weren't seeing him any more."

"It's nothing . . . nothing, I assure you, sweetheart. Can you believe he sent me flowers, with a card, hand written by the florist, for God's sake. 'To my busty Brit. Love, Kisses, Yours ever so deeply, Robert.' Bastard!"

" 'I'm whole again,' " he said, reading from a sheet of torn paper found wedged in Volume Seven, Renaissance Literature and Art. " 'Harpooned by a private doctor the other day. He slipped an illuminated plastic eel down my KY jellied cock and determined I will need only minor surgery. This is good news, Annette. The procedure will not incapacitate my ability to make a certain woman ooze with delight. Yours sincerely, Martin.'"

"Whatever will I do with you?" she said, rebuttoning her blouse.

He took her hand away and held it. She continued to speak, her voice trailing after him as they walked up the spiral staircase to her bedroom.

It was their tenth meeting in four months. This time he hoped things would be different. Her response to his personal ad had been straightforward and provocative. What I wouldn't give for a good and virile lover. Whatever is one to do? Have any ideas? Yours, A. But their encounters were flaccid, uninspired and boring. She had no sense of play: sex was a business deal to be discreetly obtained and offshore harboured, her executive orgasms a curated series of stifled yelps and well-mannered postures. He wished she would just once relax and let him make love to her.

Hand lightly tapping the staircase banister, he imagined her slowly undressing in front of him, heard the soft rustle of silk against her lambent skin, her blouse and skirt falling to the hardwood floor. "Leave your shoes on," he would say, and watch as she unclasped the lacy bra, slowly unshouldered it and leaned forwards her nipples erect, the full breasts plump and radiant.

"Look what she's done now," said Annette, sweeping her hand across the room. "I've told Marcia at least a dozen times, solid colour sheets on Monday. Solid. Honestly . . ."

He shrugged.

"Right, then."

She kicked off her shoes, undressed quickly, folded her clothes over the back of an antique chair, then slipped into bed, not once looking at him.

"It's a gun," said Martin, leaning over her, hoping she would tease his pleasure.

She looked up and frowned. "You know I don't go in for that sort of thing. Besides, the children will be back from school at three-thirty. It isn't as if we had all day, darling." She lowered the covers, her body a target. "You do understand, don't you? Say yes."

Unzipping himself, he took her right hand and guided it between his legs.

"You devil," she said, fondling him.

Martin undid his belt, uncoupled his pants, let them drop to the floor. Annette pulled his briefs down.

"Good Lord," she said, reluctantly drawing him to her mouth. "Slowly," he said, watching her lips encircle him. He traced delicate patterns around her ears while rocking her head back and forth.

"My turn," she said. "You're on top. Come along, darling. Well, come on."

Annette threw herself back, parted her legs and waited. Martin sheathed himself.

Embracing her, he gently pulled himself inside, pinned Annette down, pushed softly, then hard, then plunged himself full forwards into her body.

"You . . . you demon," she stammered. "Wherever did you learn that?"

"Shh . . ." he said, prompting her legs around him. She tried moving her hips in time with his. Shifting sideways, he guided her, suckled her breasts, kissed her, gripped her buttocks, felt the tingling sensation begin.

"Slowly . . ." he whispered, and cleared his mind.

Annette was driving; traffic lights blinked red-green-red. She eased the huge vehicle into the drive way, carried on about her garden, the foliage; he glimpsed the village beyond the wood line, heard bodies run past, smelt the foul enemy scent, shook as machine guns fired, flinched as the wounded screamed. Am I all right? Doc? Am I all right? How bad is it? How bad? Beneath him, her body arched and trembled; her lips formed an involuntary exit for the moaning sound. He watched her jaw clamp shut, stunting the pleasure. He groaned. They slept.

Annette kissed him awake, short, lacklustre pecks on one side of his face. It had happened again. The frustrated lovemaking; the war inescapable.

"Well, aren't you the quiet American?" she snickered.

He remained motionless.

"Are you all right, sweetheart?"

She fluffed her pillow as though spanking a child.

"I was thinking of something. Would you like to hear it?"

"Oh, bloody hell, why not?"

Curling up next to him, she twirled the hairs on the back of his neck. He nearly turned to kiss her.

"It's always good to travel in pairs," he said. "Backpacking. Ever done that?" He nibbled her hand.

"All that muck and filth? Good heavens, no."

He continued speaking.

"We found a cheap place with an air conditioner, flush toilets, mosquito nets . . ."

"Mosquitoes? Where on earth were you?"

"I'm getting undressed, Alex is stepping out of the shower, towel wrapped around him, in walks this girl. 'Boom boom? You want boom boom?'"

Annette lifted her head from the pillow, slapping the bed as she spoke.

"What the bloody hell is 'boom boom'?"

"Sex."

"Really? What kind of people would call the most intimate expression between two people boom boom? Dear God, that's absolutely horrid."

Lying back, she caressed him.

"The Americans," he said.

"And how would you know?"

She stretched with anxious pleasure.

"We spoke that way during the war," he murmured, wondering why he had told her.

She paused, eyebrows knotted in puzzled concentration.

"Not in that awful mess . . ."

He trailed his finger tips up and down her arm.

"She was pretty. Better-looking than the woman in Phnom Penh."

"Goodness, you do get around, darling. Isn't that the capital of . . ."

"Cambodia," he said, recollecting the event.

They had choppered into an enemy base camp. No one expected to live.

"In June we were overrun," he heard himself whisper.

She drew his hand to her breast, at the same time turning opposite, her backside pressing against his manhood, making him big.

"Well, don't stop now, darling. This is absolutely delightful!"

The blood rushed into his face.

"She wanted ten dollars," he said. "A lot of money for what I wanted."

"What on earth?" she shrilled with excitement.

"They have a problem with AIDS," he said, and felt her stomach tighten. "Alex got dressed and went out for a walk. We bargained in sign language."

"He flashed the fingers of his right hand directly over her head.

"You beast, you absolute Minotaur!" Annette shrieked. "Go on. Oh, do go on," she squealed.

The girl had kicked off her clogs and perched on the spring coil bed, squatting Viet Cong style. He pantomimed; she removed her blouse.

"She didn't understand," he said, tracing a phantom arc of confused and awkward movements in the space between them. "Pulled and pushed my cock every which way."

Perplexed, the girl had closed her eyes, making her more beautiful.

"It was awful."

Annette shook with laughter.

"This is too much, darling. You are absolutely precious! A hand job, was it?"

She wailed with delight.

"I had to show her," he said.

His voice was not pleasant.

Annette curled the O shape of her thumb and forefinger around his swollen cock.

"Like that?"

'Yes. Like that"

He kissed her harshly on the mouth.

"This is brilliant . . . brilliant! Oh, go on! Go on!"

He pushed her tight clenched fist away.

"I stopped her," he said. "Just held her in my arms. Even travellers get lonely. Know what I mean?"

"Are you trying to tell me something, darling? Don't you think I'm sexy? Well? Don't you?"

She was impossible.

"Maybe. Maybe not"

Annette wagged a school marm's finger in Martin's face. He swatted it back.

"What then, darling?" she tittered.

"What then?" he mimicked. "I kissed her breasts, her mouth, pinched and rolled her nipples between my fingers until they were hard. You should have seen the way her eyes lit up." He had held her close, smoothed and kissed her hair. She had spoken to him while dreaming.

"Well, don't stop!" Annette commanded. "What happened next? Oh, do tell! Do tell!" Hours later, in the musty bathroom they had showered and towelled each other dry. Dressed, they went out for food.

"You-good-me," she had said.

That night he bought clothes for her children.

"So the little bitch couldn't wank you," Annette crowed.

He shrugged indifferently.

"Oh, darling, this is priceless. Better than Waugh . . . than Lawrence. Have you read them? Surely you've read Frank Harris?"

She paused.

"Darling, did you ever see her again?"

"No," he said, turning away.

"Well, after all . . . she was just a tart," Annette stammered, "A slut, really. It was business, for God's sake."

For several minutes they lay without moving. Martin watched the second hand of the bedside clock swerve past the illuminated roman numerals. The memory always stopped at the clouds of cordite smoke spewed forth by their weapons. There were ten of them. They lay where they fell, bodies perforated, the death agony having lasted all night. Sometimes the scream sounds made him weep. A machine gun burst decapitated one survivor. The Lieutenant shot the second at close range. He saw it now. The platoon scavenging the dead for souvenirs. Now the woman moved, her uniform brain spattered. She groaned, then raised a feeble arm, clawing at his canteen. The others bickered how best to kill her. He knelt down and tipped the plastic jug to her dreadful lips, watched as she suckled herself back to life. He shielded his eyes so the others would not see.

Still blinking, Martin removed the wet hands from his face. Annette stared at him; wordless sounds spilled from her mouth. Except for his lowing sobs, which rattled and shook both their bodies, for a very long time they did not move.

69 Love Songs

Maxim Jakubowski

1 It begins like a movie. With a white screen and a wash of music, massed strings or more likely synthesizer chords, rising to a majestic crescendo. Images coalesce and a melancholy melody emerges from the unshaped wall of sound . . . *Porcelain* by Moby maybe, or the soundtrack for an imaginary western whose ending will turn out to be particularly bittersweet. A tune that aims straight for the heart but hints at sadness to come. Sadness, yes; because tragedy is too strong a word. The credits roll and then shapes emerge out of blurry chaos throughout the rectangular geometry of the once silver screen. Panavision format. A woman's voice is heard, plaintive, across the fading sounds of the music. Is she singing? Has she a quaint, somewhat exotic foreign accent?

2 Like all men with talent, he had many flaws. But his worst trait was how he romanticized over women time and again, never learning from experience. How the emotions they created inside his head and body skewered his perception of them and coloured all his relationships. He was aware of the fact, but knowing the existence of this Achilles' heel didn't help him avoid the same old mistakes over and over again. Was it the way he was brought up; the fact his father never had the guts to tell him all about the birds and the bees? How he mentally stored and interpreted the distorted facts about the way men and women coexist and war from tell-tale stories

circulating amongst school kids? How he was savagely wounded by the unknowing betrayal of the first girl he felt longings for?

3 Her presence in a world of men had nagged her from early teenage years. They fascinated and attracted her, but at the same time there was something fearful about these other creatures. They were different. She had always been accepted as a fun person by the groups she wove in and out of, at school, at play, mingling with her elder brother's friends. Always rough and ready for a game, a tumble, she was treated as an equal. Her breasts came late and were never quite as opulent as many of her girlfriends. She would eventually grow into a B cup, barely. But from the moment those bumps made their bow inside her blue school shirt, the young men, the older men she would see in the street or in shops seemed to look at her in a new way. Thus did she discover lust.

4 Catherine Guinard was not the prettiest young girl in the class during his first year in a mixed school. Nowhere near; Rhoona DeMole, Beatrice, Elizabeth and Jacqueline ruled that roost. But something about her touched him inside, where it mattered. Maybe that was his main flaw: he thought with his emotions, not with his cock. She was small, had thin, mousey light brown hair and slightly crooked teeth. But you know how it is, it's not just the way they look that does it; it's the way they laugh or their eyes sparkle at a given moment. He worshipped her from afar. Helped her with her class work. Then, one night, at a friend's party, Pierre what's-his-name in a game of Truth or Dare revealed he had already fucked her and, compounding the injustice, said she wasn't even that good in bed. His heart had dropped a thousand vertical paces to the ground at the unexpected news.

5 Her parents were anything but intellectuals; her father installed shower units and her mother worked in a local government office, but they both loved opera. So she was called Mimi, in homage to La Bohème. It puzzled her for a long time. Nobody in Estonia seemed to be called Mimi apart

from her. That's because you're special, her mum and dad would say to her. Which became, as she reasoned it out, a reason for great satisfaction: her brother was just plain Pavel. When unhappy days ended and she lay in bed listening to the silence invade the room and darkness take over, she would invariably remind herself that she was special. I am special. Then fall asleep with a smile on her face. That expression later became almost permanent, and her lips always appeared to be smiling, whether she was happy or not. That was one the thing that attracted men to her like fireflies.

6 Catherine Guinard was the first to carve a deep notch across his damaged heart strings. Others would follow. Over 39 years, it became a gentle litany of hurt. Many of them were blonde. So he did learn to approach blonde women with the utmost caution. Maybe he wasn't good enough for blondes, he reasoned. Or they were too good for him. And sometimes, juggling memories, tried to balance his past sexual statistics by hair colour. The results never made sense.

7 Men liked Mimi. But they wanted more than she was willing to give them, she soon realised. As much as she enjoyed their company, dancing across the smokey floors of youth clubs and downing endless glasses of vodka, she knew that the roving hands caressing her body, clumsily fingering her, were just an overture to fucking her. And she also knew she wasn't ready to be fucked. As much as sex attracted her, and mad thoughts of its horrors and delights flew across her dreams and nights, something inside also told her none of the callow boys she went out with was right for her yet. Sex must mean something.

8 He also had dreams. Dark-eyed, always elegantly dressed, Pierre was fucking Catherine. She lay passively on her back, legs held wide apart by the young man's weight while he thrust in and out of her. The scene was always silent. It brought tears to his eyes, but it also made his cock hard as he strained to move closer and observe the movement of the

penis breaching her entrance. But he could never see enough. He would have to wait until his first trip to Scandinavia where hardcore films were legal to witness the copulation of others at first hand and on a large screen.

9 He was not a violent person, but he reasoned Pierre should die. But at 17, you have neither the imagination nor the means. His betrayer being run over by a bus seemed to be the best option. But it didn't happen. Next time, he decided, maybe he should take matters into his own hands, and began noting methods of murder and execution in his notebook, gleaning necessary information from the crime paperbacks he was reading: James Hadley Chase, Brett Halliday, Peter Cheyney, Claude Rank, Jean Bruce. Although the latter seemed to be more interested in the minutiae of sexual torture. Which also provided him with regular erections.

10 Catherine Guinard was quickly forgotten after the school year ended and she returned to France. He followed her to Paris a year later, but by then the world was full of blondes.

11 At first, Mimi estimated the men would be satisfied if she consented to let herself be kissed. Real kisses, of course, with tongues. It pleased them briefly, but failed to satisfy her. They tasted of stale alcohol and tobacco and she found the experience of kissing her dance partners and boyfriends definitely unpleasant. And still their hands, encouraged by their locked lips, would venture further and they would suggest full sex; almost demand it. She confided in friends and the consensus was, if she wished to retain her popularity within her circle of friends, that she should give in or at least accept to provide the men and boys with blow jobs.

12 Elizabeth was the first blonde to break his heart. Well, you have to begin somewhere. She was much more sexually experienced than him, and years later, he would marvel how in hell he had managed to hold on to her for all of six months. Her pubic hair was short and curling, thus initi-

ating another of his obsessions, and a shade or two darker than her mid-shoulder-length straight blonde hair, which puzzled him mightily, ignorant as he was then of hydrogen peroxide. They fucked like rabbits. She found him fun but he made the capital mistake of falling in love with her. One day while she was sleeping, he read pages from her diary and discovered to his disappointment that he didn't even rate very high in her sexual pantheon.

13 Mimi had never before given too much consideration to men's cocks. She knew they had them; had seen enough of her brother's dangling genitalia, even her father's. At first, the idea of taking one inside her mouth felt a bit ridiculous, but she was also curious to know what it would feel like to experience one swelling up and growing under her lips, tongue or ministrations. Would a penis have a specific taste? A particular texture? The thought intrigued her.

14 When Elizabeth finally tired of him, she broke the news gently. After all, she had a good heart. Not ready for commitment and all that. Naturally, he took it badly and, melodramatically, a couple of weeks later slashed his wrists, cunningly arranging for her to discover him just in time. Which didn't bring her back to him. She even left the country to avoid seeing him again. Another lesson learned.

15 So, while some of her girlfriends were losing their virginity time and time again in the back of cars or in the badly lit backyards of local jazz clubs or in the fields that bordered the fun fair near the chemical plant, Mimi became the blow job queen of their home town. After all, she reflected, it's only a piece of flesh, harmless in this form, and even though some men seemed overly keen on pushing their cocks too far and made her gag, she knew she was always in control. And however many cocks she sucked, she was still a virgin, waiting for the right man to come along. The one who would at last matter. Wasn't too keen on swallowing their come, though . . .

16 Even though his attempt had been far from earnest, he also developed an unhealthy fixation on suicide and death. And years before Woody Allen came on the scene, already equated love and death in strange juxtaposition. Even began making listings of how famous people, actors, writers had committed suicide or been killed. Columns for poison, knives, guns (broken down into manufacturer and calibre of course), car and other accidents, etc. But then he was a far from cheerful young man. The gloom surrounding him would not dissipate much until he turned 30 and had made love to further blondes in various countries.

17 Cocks had no taste per se; come did. They came uncircumcised or cut, although the latter were few and far between since the local Jewish population had been decimated in WWII. Each one was different in length, thickness, appearance and smell. Mimi was unconcerned. It kept them out of her pants and, her nipples proving particularly insensitive, she didn't overly mind their rough, often drunken hands grazing, twisting her nipples or kneading her small breasts. It made her popular, paid for drinks or cinema or club tickets. A cock was a cock. In a way, she felt, it wasn't even connected to the man. Just a transaction. You want to be sucked; so OK, I'll suck you but don't expect any more. She had no regular boyfriend, just men whose cocks she didn't mind taking in her mouth for the comfort of their company.

18 Beretta.
Sig Sauer.
Colt.
Luger.
Smith & Wesson.
Sawn-off shotgun.
Digitalis.
Cyanide.
Strangulation.
Smothering under a pillow.
Swiss army knife.
Asphyxiation.

Carbon monoxide emissions.
Death by drowning.
Methods of revenge.
In search of the perfect murder.

19 She'd suck their cocks with her eyes closed. Almost pretending she was blind, her tongue moving over the head, licking the ridge, imagining the shades of pink, brown and purple of the aroused mushroom inside her cheeks. She would tease the opening, the slit, with the pointed tip of her foraging tongue, feel the tremor of lust surging through the man's body as she did so and retreat in time before he came so that the flow of hot ejaculate would either fall over her tongue or, preferably, outside her retreating mouth. Some guys came too fast, some couldn't and she would learn to finish them off by hand. But she learned to enjoy sucking cock. Even took some pride in her growing skills and the occasional compliment proffered.

20 Then came Nicky. She was the sister of one of his best friends and they somehow drifted together. Light brown hair and cheekbones to kill for. Short and square-assed and prone to awful mood swings. At first, she was head over heels in love with him; he advised caution and patience. By the time he realized he loved her too, her own ardour had quietened and they faded apart following summer holidays spent separated. Bad timing, he reckoned and began writing crime stories in which the perfect crime always came undone because of a lack of attention to small details and deep-seated psychological flaws.

21 Of course, she pined for actual sex, but Mimi was determined to wait for the right man, the right occasion. She wanted it to be so absolutely right. Even a blow job queen can be romantic. And six years is a lot of blow jobs and cocks in your mouth.

22 After Nicky, there were others. After all, he wasn't unattractive and was particularly fluent and articulate, even displayed a witty sense of humour when the darkness didn't dominate his soul. There was Marie-Jo, followed by Anne and then Danielle, who was absolutely wild and insatiable and even, ône night, moved from their shared bed to join an ex-boyfriend who was staying over in the next room where their noisy sex kept him awake for the rest of the night. His first two men a night woman. For weeks, he would mentally kick himself for not having joined them which he realized she wouldn't have minded. Another obsession took root of a threesome with two men both servicing the same woman.

23 So Mimi drifted through the final years of her teens, desultorily moving from school to menial part-time jobs with a live now, pay later attitude to life and that infuriating smile ever draped across her face. Often doubting her purpose, neither happy nor unhappy, aimless in a quiet way. Somehow inside she knew there was something better waiting for her around the corner. So, she made her way down the road. Life wasn't bad after all: there was music, there was vodka, there was the flattering attentions of younger and older men, there was the beach at Nidas with its fine yellow sand, and the never unpleasant feel, texture and sensation of warm cocks as she swallowed them and offered a willing harbour to men's lust. Mimi was patient, seldom worried about tomorrow.

24 He tried whores but they never engaged his heart and their embraces were too mechanical and unfeeling. He travelled. Prospered. Even one day married and settled down. The epiphany and beauty of babies briefly assuaged his unhappiness, but children grow and always disappoint to some extent, he discovered. And that hole in his heart, first opened by Catherine Guinard's treachery, kept aching and reminding him of all the roads never taken. Often, he would serenade himself to sleep with a monotonous litany that endlessly conjugated all the "what ifs" of his life so far.

25 Mimi had been mixing with a group of friends attending the science faculty of the local university and, one balmy summer, met up with a bunch of young Belgian students who'd come to the city for exchange summer classes. Serge was the first man to make her heart leap. They paired off most evenings and she even introduced him to her family and he became a regular guest at their dinner table. She liked his cock, long and thin, somehow devoid of the rough vulgarity of most of the local boys' penises, she felt. One night, she invited him back to her room but somehow couldn't find the courage to go all the way with the Belgian boy and, after fellating him, found herself content with sleeping naked against him in the small bed, feeling his warmth permeate her to the core. Drifting off into the lands of sleep, she swore to herself that this was the first man she would let herself be fucked by.

26 Serge returned to his studies in Belgium when summer ended and they began corresponding in broken English.

27 She took a job in the administrative offices of the chocolate factory and took night classes in English in order to communicate better with her foreign boyfriend. She would still suck other men's cocks on Saturday night after the dance, if they really insisted, but Mimi felt detached from the act now, already planning a nebulous sort of future. Serge wanted them to spend the following summer together after his graduation. He wrote that he was saving his money up for this already. She had agreed.

28 He drifted into his first affair almost by accident. Then further opportunities for unfaithfulness arose. An American tourist one night in Athens with whom he had anal sex (Danielle, albeit willing, had been too tight). Someone at the office. Another woman at a trade fair. The satisfaction of illicit sex was transitory, and never lasted very long, but what surprised him most was that he felt no guilt.

29 The Belgian boy sent her a plane ticket to London and met her at Gatwick. When she noticed him waiting for her outside the luggage hall, she somehow remembered him as sweeter and more attractive. Mimi sighed. But she was now committed to this holiday. He had liquidated all his savings and had arranged a package to a Thai beach. The plane to the Far East left in 36 hours; in the meantime, he had booked a hotel room in London. So, Mimi lost her virginity in Bloomsbury. She was too tight and screamed in agony as she lowered herself onto his jutting cock and tore herself apart. She bled profusely and felt no pleasure this time. The water in the bathroom when she washed afterwards was tepid. Sleeping against the snoring man, she felt no affinity with him any longer. He had already become a stranger.

30 He dreams of death. In dark alleys, in western shoot-outs, in soiled beds. He remembers his mother's cancer and darkness like a cloud settles over him. Publicly, he is affable and successful, always has the right turn of phrase to make a woman smile and get into bed with him. But he's on automatic pilot, wanting ever more out of life.

31 The beach was a sheer vision of paradise following the long, dusty journey by bus from Bangkok. Lying in the sun wearing the brand new green bikini he had bought her in London, Mimi lives again. The sex with him, every morning and afternoon and night, is relentless. She no longer feels pain, has been stretched enough to accept his cock inside her, but he is always the one to initiate it. At the end of the first week, her cunt is sore, inside and outside from all the pounding she has to submit to. She realizes she is now paying the price of the holiday. He seems happy, unworried that all his money has gone and has been spent on her and this tropical idyll. She knows she is using him, but the thought comes easy. He doesn't even want blow jobs, goes straight for the missionary position and fucking her.

32 He meets Edwina at a professional function and, despite his better judgement, the uncontrollable lust he feels for her turns to head over heels passion following their first fuck. She is tall, blonde of course, also married, but the sex between them is both wild and tender and out of control. For the first time, he feels fulfilled and loses contact with the emptiness that was laying waste to his guts. She takes him into her mouth on the first occasion they go to bed; they make love on floors, tables and in hotel bath tubs. He ties her hands and she flushes with delight. He breaches her sphincter ring with two fingers and she squirms and moans like no woman ever has before for him. He makes plans. Wants to take her to Cap d'Agde, New York, Barcelona, Bangkok. Promises her the world and more. He loves to watch the scarlet pool of her orgasmic flush spread from cheeks to chest while she lies there still dripping his juices in the penumbra of the room, the smell of their exertions and the echo of their whispered obscenities still hanging like a stain in the atmosphere. He is reborn.

33 Following Thailand, Serge accompanies her back to Estonia before returning to Belgium where he is due to begin his apprenticeship in a lawyer's office. Mimi's family are delighted by the fact she has a good-looking, responsible foreign boyfriend. Arrangements are made for her to visit him and his parents for the Christmas holiday. Mimi acquiesces, allows others to make all the decisions. When he is gone, she doesn't miss him and goes back to her routine of bestowing blow jobs on Saturday nights to her escort for the day. One Saturday, she drinks too much at a party and a Pole fucks her roughly in the tunnel near the railway station. But she goes to Bruges for the holiday. On Christmas Eve, her Belgian boyfriend introduces her to a Dutch acquaintance of his. The next day, Mimi moves out of his place and follows the Dutchman back to Holland. He has a beard, works for a business magazine and is ten years older than she is. Six months later, she is pregnant by him. Even precisely remembers the occasion it happened: the day they were both drunk and he had mounted her at the bottom of the stairs and smacked her bottom until it hurt. After she announced her pregnancy to him, he would use this as an excuse to fuck her repeatedly in the arse. But she wanted the baby, she really did, so she kept silent and allowed Marcel, the Dutch man, to dominate and use her.

34 Edwina returns to her husband and breaks off the affair. He is gutted. Never even saw it coming, or rather intentionally misread all the signs. He drowns his sorrow by listening to melancholy music with the volume turned up to maximum, conjuring a soundtrack for his imaginary tragedy and he dreams of death. Her death in a thousand and one circumstances, as he'd rather she was dead than no longer his. Her husband's death in cunningly plotted scenarios. His own wife's, even. But the thoughts of revenge come to nothing. He is aware he is too much of a coward to do anything about it.

35 Following the birth of her baby boy, Mimi declares to Marcel she is no longer in love or even in the least attracted to him any longer. She refuses all further sexual contact. The authorities give her Dutch nationality and a passport and benefits. Everything about Marcel now disgusts her and she sleeps with the child in the spare bedroom of his canal side house, half an hour's drive from Amsterdam. He has lost his job in a reshuffle and now pens freelance pieces from home while he attempts to start up a small business. He doesn't understand her change of attitude and resents it. Secretly she plots to leave the house they uncomfortably now share and applies to the council for her own place. He strongly opposes this.

36 Still emotionally damaged by the affair with Edwina, he stumbles almost by mistake onto an Internet chat room and soon begins new affairs with women he meets there. He is a man to whom words come easily and his voice over the phone was knowingly seductive. There was an overweight opera singer in New York. Then came an American banker in Paris who delighted in cybersex of the highest and kinkiest calibre but lied about her identity and never turned up for their assignment before disappearing altogether from view. Later came a woman in the south of France, who had five children, no husband, but looked too much like his own sister for him to even contemplate seeing her again following their sweaty weekend together.

37 Mimi loved her baby dearly but still she knew something was missing from her life. While Marcel was out, she would play around on his computer and, after typing in the words "sex" and "love" into a search engine, landed in an adult chat forum and began flirting with other men there. In her naivety, she never lied to them, always revealing who she was, her approximate whereabouts, even on occasion her mobile telephone number and the nature of her circumstances. They came running. Even faster once she scanned a colour photo of herself taken the previous summer on the deck of Marcel's canal boat.

38 All the men Mimi met on the Internet wanted to meet her. Although her written English was halting and riddled with mistakes, she enjoyed cybersex and graded her suitors by the imagination they displayed in their virtual embraces and sundry penetrations and variations on positions. She had never realized before how much the power of words could affect her imagination, and was surprised how wet she would often become, sitting there at the keyboard, her mind racing from situation to situation, imagining what the sex would be like in real life. She met a banker from Zurich. He was particularly imaginative. He amused her. He came to Amsterdam. She arranged to meet him, leaving the baby with Marcel. After dinner, she followed him back to his hotel room at the Krasnapolsky and they fucked.

39 Muted rumblings from the brass section emerge towards the back of the normally plaintive melody, interrupting his smooth, sad flow. The pace of the song, the music quickens.

40 They meet online. He is "melancholy", she is "estonian girl". He declines her offer to have cybersex. She is surprised. He explains how words alone don't make it for them. They talk. His curiosity is piqued. She tells him her story. He tells her his. They speak daily, although there are times when she ignores him when he pages her. No doubt too busy indulging in virtual sex with others to pull herself away.

But the dialogue continues over several weeks. He is being cautious, doesn't want to run before he can walk. She is intrigued by his reticence. The day after her Hotel Krasnapolsky tryst, she reveals excitedly that the man in Zurich wishes her to come live with him in Switzerland, and she can even take the baby with her. Will she? he asks. Yes, she answers, no one has made a better offer and it's a chance to start all over again maybe. He nods, facing the lines on his computer screen scrolling up and up until they are out of reach. He wishes her good luck and absent-mindedly hopes they will somehow stay in touch. He files her photograph away in an old folder, believing this is the last he will hear of Mimi.

41 Marcel is furious when she informs him she is leaving to live with another man in Zurich; he makes dire threats, forbids her to take their child. He hits her on the face in the heat of the argument. She waits until he goes shopping to leave and takes a cab to Amsterdam Central railway station. The apartment in Zurich is beautiful and for a few days Mimi feels she has taken the right decision to travel here. But soon, the sexual demands of the Swiss banker become more extreme the moment the child has fallen asleep. He wants her to become his submissive. This goes against her nature. He orders her to keep her sexual parts shaven at all time although it sometimes brings her out in a rash, and buys leather harnesses and enjoys taking photographs of Mimi in revealing positions. He wants her to wear a dog collar and announces he will take her to parties as his slave, and might actually allow her to be used by other men in his presence if he feels so inclined to share her. Reveals that her cock sucking talents are indeed superior and should be demonstrated to the world at large. He gets uncommonly angry when she moves furniture or things around in the apartment. She finds him increasingly petty, and dangerous. She leaves Zurich in haste and lands back on Marcel's doorstep in Holland only two and a half weeks following her initial flight

42 Severely addicted, he continues to haunt the Internet chat rooms. Fascinated by the number of people who profess to be bisexual online, his mind wanders over risky waters and, one day, out of sheer curiosity indulges in his first man to man oral experience. It is not totally unpleasant.

43 Mimi apologizes profusely to Marcel for her escapade to Zurich but stands firm when it comes to resuming sexual relations. Her ex-boyfriend and father of her child just no longer attracts her in the slightest. She will accept his hospitality until the day she is given her own accommodation by the authorities, and remain in his house for the sake of their little boy. His anger gets out of control. She has to flee his blows several times and one day, furious at having to listen to her flirt over the phone with an internet acquaintance, he attacks her and rapes her. Mimi stays passive and when he finally withdraws from her, Marcel is in tears and begs her to have another child with him. She refuses.

44 Mimi sends an e-mail to the man in London. Somehow she still thinks of him warmly. Explains that Zurich didn't work out after all. He answers and they resume their conversations, online and over the phone. He makes arrangements to stop over in Amsterdam for a night and a day on his way to an academic conference in Warsaw. He books a small hotel by a canal near the station through his travel agent. They agree to meet for dinner nearby. He, naturally, hopes for more but doesn't count on it. Mimi tells Marcel she will be away overnight staying with a girlfriend.

45 She is taller than he expected. Conversely, she finds him shorter than she somehow thought from their conversations and mutual self descriptions. She is also prettier. There is a delicacy about her, a gentle sadness also, which allied to her peculiar accent and ever-present smile, make him feel all shy. The meal comes and goes, spoiled only by the boisterous company of a large table of office workers nearby. They walk back to his hotel. He doesn't ask her up, but she follows him silently into the lift. The door closes and he slowly moves his lips towards hers and they kiss. She remains standing as he undresses her, slipping off her panties and burying his nose and mouth in the short, matted hair of her cunt. He likes her taste. She thrills to the firm but gentle caress of his tongue opening her up. She comes. He is still fully dressed. They move to the bed.

46 Her body is pale and her breasts slight. Her hips are high and firm like a Russian peasant's. He surveys the pale expanse of her flesh as he spreads her out beneath him, noting every mole and blemish scattered across the whiteness of her warm skin. A brown stain on the left side of her left breast, a hardened mole in the small of her back, a spot of darker pigmentation blending into the darker pink of her right nipple. He licks every exposed inch of her. She devours his cock with ardour but also delicacy, her clever tongue darting across his shaft, her hot mouth cupping and then swallowing his heavy, dark balls. He notes that her nipples are not overly sensitive. "How do you prefer it?" he asks. "Doggie style," she answers quietly. He turns her over, holds his cock aloft and directs it to her entrance. The view is breathtaking. The puckered hole of her anus darker, inviting, vulnerable. He positions himself at her lower entrance, parts her now wet lips as she raises her rump further upwards, face buried in the blanket, her breasts hanging firm from her supple body. He thrusts himself inside her. She holds her breath and exhales with a deep sigh of pleasure.

47 He would later reflect how much she enjoyed taking her pleasure. He woke her in the morning by sliding below the bed covers and waking her with his tongue and teeth inside her still damp cunt, in which he could still taste himself. Other women always washed themselves out after sex; Mimi was the first since Edwina not to do so and retain his juices inside her. Her whole body spasmed and she came. He then rose up, pushed her legs apart and inserted himself between her swollen cunt lips. While he moved in and out of her, her eyes locked on his, imploring, screaming silently, watching him as he fucked her, both wordless. Something about her touched him deeply. Before they rose for breakfast, he managed another erection and she sucked him off to completion, his thin, tired come jetting into her mouth. She said nothing and afterwards rose quietly to move to the bathroom where he heard her spitting it out and gargling.

48 What affected him most about Mimi was the way she kept her eyes open throughout their lovemaking. A silent stare that spoke a thousand words. And how she joked that her eyes were now all shiny and glazed and Marcel would know, without the shadow of a doubt, that she had been fucked. That it was written all over her eyes and would stay that way for days. And reassured him by stating that it didn't matter in the slightest. She remained with him for the whole day, his guide to Amsterdam on a cold and windy December day. He remembered her in the throes of sex; she, cheerful that this man could make her laugh so much, with his dry, almost absurd jokes and wit. They parted at the train station, both refraining from any kind of promises.

49 She had told the Englishman of her dreams and plans. She couldn't stay with Marcel forever. Maybe she should advertise herself as a potential mistress for a rich man to subsidize and keep in comfort. After all, it would only be sex. A commercial transaction, but not as compromising as being a whore. The way his eyes clouded over when she said this, she realized he disapproved so she dismissed the idea as a joke. But she did place an advertisement in a newspaper a few weeks later.

50 She received a handful of answers to her advertisement. She met some of the men. A drink, maybe a meal, at worst a blow job, she reckoned, even if they were unsuitable. Kept her out of the house for a few hours, looking after the ever growing baby, away from Marcel's clutches. There was another Englishman. Commercial traveller across northern Europe. He'd fuck her in his rental car, not even bothering to take her to a hotel room, but she kept on seeing him several times. The asshole, she kept on calling him, and afterward she would cry because she knew he was just using her, and treated her like dirt. Why was she punishing herself in this way? She confessed to the man in London. She knew it gave him pain, but he absolved her. So she saw the jerk again. He didn't even bother to undress her, ordered her skirt up above her waist, roughly pulled her thong off and indicated the back seat of the car to her. They were parked by the side of a small regional road. Anybody could have seen her moving bottomless to the back of the car. He positioned her on all fours and savagely entered her with no preliminaries. He grunted as he came, then, pretexting an important business appointment, excused himself from dropping her back to the bus station where he had picked her up and left her standing there in the countryside, his come still dripping down her thighs and legs. Never again, she swore, but deep inside was uncertain how long her resolve would last. Maybe she needed this humiliation?

51 He called her every week and told her how much he missed her and how he liked her and just felt so natural and comfortable with her. Mimi agreed: it wasn't just the sex, they did feel good together, walking by the Rijksmuseum, the canals, Kalverstraat and across town, smiling in front of the window of the Condom Shop or nervously giggling at the windows of the Red Light District. Yes, we must meet again, they both agreed.

52 She had told him how the man in Zurich had insisted she shave her sex, and this thought obsessed him and kept him awake, and hard, at night. She has a lovely cunt, hair straight and brown and thick lips pouting through the growth. When she positioned herself with her rear thrust towards him and on her knees, the spectacle of her cunt was better than any porn movie. Straight gash punctuated lower down by little hills of darker, protruding flesh which he liked to chew on, pull gently, play with, opening her cunt like a flower, unveiling the nacreous pink of her damp insides.

53 Through the ad, she also met a younger Dutch boy. He was too good-looking by her standards but liked the baby and didn't mind her bringing him along when he took her for drives. They would help the child fall asleep and then would go to bed in his bachelor apartment. He worked in computers. The first time he undressed in front of her, she was shocked by the size of his penis. Seemed so enormous. She was really scared how much it would stretch her, but surprisingly he fitted inside her like a glove. However, he often had difficulty coming and would thrust away inside her for ages until she had lost all feeling and she would then have to tire herself out until her jaw ached helping him climax with her mouth.

54 Her eyes, below me, inches from my own, as I move inside her. Watching me. Judging me. Asking questions I have no answer to. Listening to the shortness of my breath as my climax approaches. Glazing with joy, shiny, luminous. Moving the thousand shades between grey and blue. Mimi's eyes. She's getting to me.

55 They decide to meet again and he FedEx's her the money for the train journey to Paris. They arrive at the same station a half hour apart. He has booked a small, picturesque hotel on the South Bank with a view of Paris roofs and migrating pigeons. They walk, see movies, shop on the Champs Elysées, eat too much and make love with great abandon when their stomachs are not too full. Enjoying ice cream at the Haägen-Dazs terrace on the Boulevard Saint-Germain he cracks a joke, and Mimi laughs so much she pees in her knickers. Back at the hotel, he licks her clean. She is still laughing. The sound of her happiness alleviates his darkness. But the weekend quickly ends and there are trains home for the two of them, separate trains, separate lives.

56 He knows she is partial to words and whispers indecent suggestions and dirty deeds into her ear as they fuck and feels her whole body strain and react as her cheeks colour even further at the thought of what he is outlining. He intimates at another man joining them in their activities, watching this stranger mount her as she fellates him and then both males simultaneously investing her holes. He improvizes a story in which they are both captured by pirates or gangsters and made sexual slaves and in which he has to suck to hardness the cocks of their male captors and then guide them manually into her and is made to watch as they despoil her repeatedly; to cap it all, he is then himself sodomized in her presence and gladly sacrifices his anal preserve out of love and affection for her. She listens in rapt silence, but the heat generating from her body, her cunt, her skin betray the story of her lust and her eyes acknowledge her increased excitement.

57 He wants her again. By now, she has left Marcel's house and lives alone in a small cottage with the baby. A friend comes from Estonia to stay and arrangements are made to leave the little boy in her care. They meet up in the bright arrivals hall of a small airport by the Mediterranean. She has cut her hair shorter and coloured it auburn. She wears faded jeans and a burgundy chenille sweater. He hires a car and drives to a nearby port where someone has recommended a pleasant hotel. The room has a balcony overlooking the sea and he fondles her arse while they take in the view. He undresses her with all the slow, lingering ritual of a religious ceremony. He trims her pubes. Jokingly suggests she should not wear any underwear for the duration of their stay here. She smiles and agrees to his whim. They eat, they fuck, they talk, and neither of them wishes the week to ever end. One afternoon, he takes a short nap and she decides to go for a walk in the town. In her absence, he delves into her handbag and finds a photograph of her and another man, a good-looking younger man by whose side she is smiling blissfully into the lens of the camera. He knows it is not Marcel. Or the English asshole or the Dutch computer man. He guesses she is still seeing other men in the intervals between him. He says nothing to her.

58 He knows it doesn't make sense and the relationship has no future. She is 20 years younger than him and there is no way he has the mental fortitude to even try and believe he could try and bring up another child, even more so that of another man. He knows she likes sex too much and will eventually tire of him. He knows she uses him, and the sex she grants him is her unethical, if Eastern European way, of paying him back for the gifts, the money, the travel. He often awakens at three in the morning in his marital bed at home dreaming of her, fantasizing of the warmth of her body, of witnessing her being fucked by total strangers while he holds her head in his lap and wipes her feverish brow He imagines taking her to a nude beach and exhibiting her to the unflinching gaze of others, her nipples and sex gash highlighted by scarlet lipstick, showing her off, maybe piercing her parts, and organizing her ravishing in some sort of pagan ceremony. He plays with himself when he thinks of the way her eyes always betray her sexual pleasure. He pictures her with her erstwhile Dutch friend, he of the uncommonly large penis, and in abominable close-up watches the monstrous cock impale her to the hilt, stretching her apart like a piece of raw meat. In dreams, he has no shame.

59 She sends him a birthday card in which she assures him he is special. You are my treasure, she says. Two weeks later, she calls him, desperate for some money. He obliges, relieved she didn't phone advising him she was pregnant. Apart from the first evening in Amsterdam, they have never taken any precautions.

60 Christmas comes and Mimi has made arrangements to return for the festivities to her family in Estonia. She cannot afford to fly so is hitching a lift to the German coast at Kiel to catch a ferry with one of her girlfriends who is married to a Dutchman. Even though she hasn't asked, he sends her money and a gift for her little boy, whom he has never seen outside of photographs. The two-year-old is blond.

61 He misses her intensely. Wants her like hell. Since she moved out of Marcel's house, she no longer has access to a computer so their rare conversations take place over the phone. In Estonia, her mobile is out of reach. Out of sheer stupidity, he logs on to their familiar Internet chat room under her old handle "estonian girl". Within minutes, he is deluged by calls. The majority of them are clearly just attracted by the reasonably exotic name, particularly the Yanks, and have no previous knowledge of her. It's been months after all since she had last been online. But some clearly know her well. He improvizes his way through a half hour conversation with an architect in Brooklyn who has seemingly extended her an open invitation to come to America. Visibly they have often spoken on the phone. As he probes further to unveil any possible intimacy, he is rumbled and the other man disconnects.

62 He compounds his mistake the following day and assumes her Internet identity again. He gets a call from "infinity and beyond". Another man who knows Mimi, and through a process of deduction he uncovers the fact they are still in contact and have exchanged pre-Christmas text messages on their respective mobile phones. The man has just returned from a trek to Tibet and wishes to meet her again. He blunders his way through the conversation by pretexting her mobile's battery is low and elicits more information. It is quickly apparent Mimi is fucking this guy on a regular basis; in a hotel in a place called Aalmark. He logs off angrily.

63 He knew he wasn't her only man. How could he expect to be? But the smug assurance by "infinity and beyond" that she was a great fuck and why didn't they have another session after Christmas, in the obvious expectation of an enthusiastic response, damn hurt. A lot. And made him so angry at Mimi.

64 Between the rage, the haunting images of her with others. Men as well as women (although he'd never been the sort of man who gave undue thought to women together). He remembered how during the course of evening meals in restaurants on the Mediterranean port, she had often remarked on the sexual attractiveness of, one day, a waiter who limped and the next evening a waitress who enjoyed using her poor English while serving them but was otherwise dreadfully plain-looking. She said she took pity on them, but he knew her interest was also to some extent sexual and her mind was still excited by their bedside patter about a third person between the sheets.

65 Still under the empire of anger, he felt the need to confront her. Tracked down her parents' address through directory enquiries and booked himself on the first flight to Estonia. He just had to confront her. On one hand, something unhealthy buried deep within his head or loins, hankered to share her touching beauty with others, but not this way. Not without him. The jealousy burnt a hole inside him.

66 He'd kept watch on the apartment block for half a day when she emerged. She held the little boy's hand and made her way, holding a heavy suitcase in the other, towards the nearest bus stop. He hailed a cab and followed her.

67 Mimi and her son arrived at the docks and, standing 50 yards back, he observed her negotiating passport control and walking the gangway with another woman dressed in thick winter attire on to a large passenger boat. He checked the destination: Kiel. She was on her way back to Holland. He had over an hour to get his own case from his hotel room, check out and purchase a ticket for the boat. He saw her, the boy and her girlfriend eating at the ship's snack bar that first evening but decided against making contact. The next day, the ship held a large dance after dinner and, sitting in a remote corner of the cavernous room, he observed Mimi from afar as she kissed the child goodbye and her friend returned to their cabin. She sat at the bar, alone, slowly sipping a drink. The music began, loud and formless, a frantic aggregate of beats and naked rhythm. A man invited her on to the dance floor. She was smiling. Damn, why did she always smile? Another drink, then another dance partner. Midnight came and she was visibly drunk. But happy. He watched as her last dance partner whispered something in her ear and took her hand and moved towards one of the doors to the lower deck. He followed. He was already seasick and what he saw didn't help. There was Mimi, in a dark corner of the deck, on her knees, sucking the man's cock with an appetite that looked mighty indecent. The man gripped her hair between his hands, forcing her to take him ever deeper. From his hiding place in

the shadows, he couldn't see whether she kept her eyes open or not. He turned and vomited over the wooden deck.

68 The man she had been voraciously sucking off had finally returned inside and Mimi stood on the deck, leaning over the guard rail, watching the sea at night, lost in her thoughts. What, he wondered, was on her mind? Did she feel there was poetry in the landscape of the night? Sadness in the oppressive silence, broken only by the clapping sound of nearby waves? He moved quietly towards her, her silhouette highlighted against the brightness of the pockmarked moon. He gently put a hand on her left shoulder. She turned round to face him. Thinking maybe the other guy had returned for more. She was crying. "You?" she gasped. "Yes," he answered, a knot gripping his stomach. "What are you doing here?" The faint trace of a smile spreading across her cold lips. "I loved you," he said, "didn't you know that, didn't you realize it by now?" She lowered her eyes, accepting her fate.

69 He raised his other arm and pushed. Mimi offered no resistance. Her body toppled over the rail and disappeared into the darkness and the sea. He looked at the illuminated face of his Tag Heuer: it was one in the morning. The distant horizon was 200 miles off both the coasts of Denmark and Germany. A time and a place for love and death.

[I acknowledge stealing the title of this story from Stephin Merritt's and the Magnetic Fields' wonderful triple-CD set]

Surrender Dorothy

Lisa Montanarelli

Dorothy was my best friend in college. When we first met, she was, by her own definition, "straight". But her definition of straight changed like the wind. Dorothy was the first woman I had sex with, and vice versa. She framed this event as an act of charity – to help me determine whether I enjoyed having sex with women – as if she somehow represented all women on the planet. After having sex with me, she decided that she also had to sleep with her best friend from high school, who would be crushed if she ever found out that Dorothy had slept with any woman other than her. Thus one charitable act led to another, and soon Dorothy was shepherding me into sexual configurations of various numbers and genders. Since I was the shy one, I was happy to rely on her to organize our sexual forays. Until she finally came out as bisexual, she had a way of organizing group sex, then fleeing the scene, racked with guilt. As I later discovered, Dorothy fantasized about having sex with virtually everyone she knew, and my burgeoning bisexuality provided an opportunity for her to test-drive some encounters that would otherwise have been difficult to rationalize, given that she still called herself "straight".

My first threesome was orchestrated by Dorothy and a guy she was fucking named Matt, who happened to be my ex-boyfriend's roommate. What I remember most about the experience was Matt's effort to make sure everyone felt included by mentioning both our names as he came: "Oh,

Dorothy . . . oh, Lisa." As I fell asleep that night, I couldn't help feeling as if I'd just had my first bisexual experience, even though I'd already identified as bisexual for a year and had sex with both men and women individually. Nonetheless, if I had sex with a man at 7 p.m., and a woman at 8, who's to say I didn't go through a heterosexual phase at 7 and find my true lesbian identity an hour later? After my first ménage à trois, I felt as if I'd jumped through the final hoop of true bisexual identity.

We finally cornered Dorothy into coming out as bisexual. It was a bit like gang warfare, and it happened during a surprise party that I organized for her 19th birthday.

Several months earlier Dorothy had confided her core childhood masturbation fantasy in the wee hours of the morning, when our inhibitions were down. Since the age of seven, she had fantasized about crawling through a paddy wagon of authority figures, consisting of her grammar school teachers, camp counsellors and babysitters. Eventually, she came to the last link in the chain – the school principal, who would spank her hardest of all. That was the part of the fantasy that made her come.

I admired Dorothy's sexual precocity. But I also realized that she was telling her childhood fantasy from the perspective of her present 18-year-old self. She was thus embellishing this particular fantasy with a knowledge of sexuality that she couldn't possibly have had as a seven-year-old. I concluded that the paddy wagon was a present fantasy, which Dorothy was unconsciously projecting onto her childhood – probably because she felt less guilty telling it in the past tense.

In any case, spanking was Dorothy's biggest turn-on. She wanted to be punished. Unfortunately, she had a hard time asking her sex partners to whack her on the butt. After all, we were only 18, and most of us hadn't evolved much in the way of sexual communication skills. Organizing group sex, then fleeing the scene, was a circuitous and ultimately unsatisfying route to getting what she wanted. I decided to make it easier for her by giving her a surprise paddy wagon for her birthday.

I got stuck on the question of which authority figures to invite. We were in college at the time, but professors were out of the question. Graduate students, on the other hand, were predatory beasts, lying in wait to seduce young undergrads, hoping to gain some semblance of respect, which the university denied them.

So I invited Megan, my neurotic girlfriend, who just last week had been studying for her PhD exams while Dorothy, Matt, and I fucked in my bedroom several blocks away. Megan would have been happier if I had forewarned her of the threesome, or even asked her permission. But at the time I was unpractised in the ways of polyamory, which is a nice way of saying I was cheating. I also invited Megan's best friend, Michael, who was Dorothy's former teaching assistant. Megan and Michael had slept together, I knew, but Michael was primarily attracted to men. His boyfriend, Daniel, was an undergraduate and a mutual friend of Dorothy's and mine. (Dorothy had engineered a threesome with Daniel and Michael the summer before.) So I invited Daniel too. I also invited Chelsea, my quiet bisexual roommate, and her loud boyfriend Jeff, a graduate student in the French Department, who wanted to be bisexual for political reasons. Martin was Jeff's best friend and a local drunk. He was capable of brilliant conversation and occasionally fucked my girlfriend, but was otherwise generally useless. Jeff and Martin were 30 and 32 years old, which seemed ancient to me at 18, so I thought they'd make good authority figures for the paddy wagon. Finally I invited my ex-boyfriend Tom, who could be a stick in the mud. Dorothy didn't really like him, but since I was inviting Matt, and Tom was Matt's roommate, I had to invite Tom too.

I told all the guests about the paddy wagon, although I didn't tell them it was Dorothy's masturbation fantasy. I just told them she'd like it a lot. I was secretly hoping the event would turn into an orgy – although I didn't tell everyone that, either. To decrease the likelihood that people would stomp off in disgust, I tried to invite bisexuals, or at least people who were willing to have sex with both men and women.

The night of the surprise party, I invited Dorothy and Matt to come over at around 8, just to hang out and celebrate her birthday, perhaps with another threesome. The guests arrived an hour early. They were supposed to stay in the living room, so Dorothy wouldn't see them when she first walked in. When the doorbell rang, they quickly got into paddy wagon formation – standing in line with their legs spread so that Dorothy could crawl through. I opened the door for Dorothy and Matt. We chatted in the kitchen for a few minutes. Then I quickly led them into the living room, so that the guests wouldn't get leg cramps from holding their paddy wagon positions too long.

"Surprise!" they yelled, as I opened the door.

Dorothy's jaw dropped. "O, my God, what are you all doing?"

"You have to crawl through our legs!" shouted Jeff, who was at the front of the line.

It took a few seconds for Dorothy to get it. Then she blushed deep red and ran out of the room.

"Hey, wait!" Matt and I grabbed her arms and dragged her back in, virtually kicking and screaming.

"Come on! Crawl through!" the guests demanded. "We can't stand here all day, you know." They were starting to fidget.

"No," Dorothy insisted. "Not unless everyone else does."

"You first. It's your birthday."

Dorothy blushed deeper, but finally got on her hands and knees in front of the line. She hesitated. Matt and I stood right behind her in case she tried to bolt.

She looked back at us. "I can't believe you're making me do this," she said.

Dorothy started to crawl. As soon as she was halfway through Jeff's legs, he administered a loud whack on the butt, then drummed on her ass with both hands.

"Ouch!" she wailed. "Ow, ow, ow." I'd positioned Jeff at the front of the line, because I knew he would spank hard and bold – demonstrating to everyone else how it was supposed to be done. Chelsea came after Jeff. Her spanking was tentative, but Megan's was hard and stingy – she was a mean hardass, when it came right down to it.

Michael was next in line. To everyone's surprise and delight, he grabbed the elastic waistband of Dorothy's sweatpants and pulled them down, exposing her bare butt.

"Oooooh," we cooed.

"Hold on. That's not fair," Dorothy protested. But Michael and Matt were already caressing her naked ass.

"You don't want us to stop now, do you?" Michael asked, as he spanked her ass with one hand, stroking it with the other.

Dorothy didn't say anything. But she was sighing and wiggling her butt, clearly enjoying it. I could see Matt's cock swelling under the zipper of his jeans. He knelt down beside her, and they kissed. Dorothy was still on all fours between Michael's legs. Michael was still spanking her, and there were three people left in the paddy wagon line: Michael's boyfriend, Daniel; my ex-boyfriend Tom; and Martin, the drunk.

Then mayhem broke loose. Daniel spanked Michael, Megan spanked me, as about five hands stroked and spanked Dorothy's butt. Michael slipped his fingers between Dorothy's wet pussy lips. Dorothy was squirming. Matt unzipped his pants.

"Hold on," Dorothy interrupted, standing up. "I'm not fucking all of you!" Michael, Matt and I exchanged glances.

"Oh, yes, you are!" we said in unison.

Matt and I grabbed her and held her still on all fours.

Dorothy screamed, but there was no one to save her. My next-door neighbour was deaf, and the people upstairs were insane. They were building a bomb shelter on the second floor. Screams were nothing out of the ordinary.

Michael took off his pants. Daniel stood behind him, grinding his crotch against Michael's butt. "Why don't you fuck her while I fuck you?"

"Hold on there. Ladies first." Megan sat down beside Michael, wearing a strap-on, which she must have grabbed from my bedroom when she saw where all this was going. Meanwhile, Dorothy had stopped screaming. Matt put several fingers inside her, as I caressed her butt.

"You OK?" I asked.

"I guess so. For the moment." Still on her hands and knees, she wiggled her ass in the air.

"She's really wet," said Matt. I stroked her clit. She was

dripping. I moved my fingers back and forth, then in circles. She moaned and squirmed.

Megan was wearing a huge red dildo. She covered it in lube and pressed the tip against Dorothy's cunt. When it was all the way in, Megan waited as Dorothy adjusted to the huge dildo.

Meanwhile Michael and Daniel had positioned themselves in front of Dorothy. Daniel stroked his cock right in front of Dorothy's face. When he was really hard, he put a condom and lube on his cock. Michael got down on all fours, and Dan entered him from behind. Dorothy, Megan, and I all got excited, because we love watching gay porn; it was an even bigger turn-on live.

Megan pumped the big red dildo in and out of Dorothy's cunt.

"Harder!" Dorothy demanded. The live gay porn had apparently transformed her from a quasi-resistant gangbang victim into an insatiable slut. As Megan thrust harder, Daniel did too, and for the next fifteen minutes, the loudest sounds in the room were those of pelvises slapping against butts. Matt and I stood by, administering random whacks to Dorothy's ass. Chelsea, Jeff, Martin, and Tom had retreated to the side-lines and were providing a running pseudo-intellectual commentary, which I could barely hear over everyone's groans.

Just as I noticed Matt had a condom on his cock, he threw me down on my back. I'd gotten so absorbed in spanking Dorothy that I hadn't even realized how wet I was. Dorothy looked up as Matt entered me, and I recognized that furtive gleam in her eyes. I dragged myself closer to her, as Matt lay on top of me thrusting. Dorothy leaned over and licked my nipples. At that point, my ex-boyfriend Tom stomped off, slamming the door loudly. I didn't know how he and Matt were going to live together after this, but at that moment, I didn't care, and I don't think anyone else did either. Meanwhile, Chelsea, Jeff, and Martin the drunk retreated to my bedroom to have comparatively boring sex with each other.

After an hour of hardcore fucking and multiple orgasms, we

collapsed, exhausted. As we were lying around in a sweaty, pulsating heap, Michael asked, "So Dorothy, does this mean you're finally a card-carrying bisexual?"

"I guess I'm not in Kansas any more," she sighed. A big satiated grin spread across her face.

Among the Beks

A. J. Horlick

Many people find it quite shocking that my husband bought me. Oh, it is not as if Jzhat'lan women are not admired by the Beks. Our delicacy excites them, certainly. Like fine glass statuary, we are easily broken. The Jzhat'lan brothels on Post 3 are always full of Beki traders and mercenaries, and it is an uncommon Beki man who would not welcome a woman like me to his bed.

But as a wife? That is a different thing. I can never bear my husband's child. I will never give him heirs.

My husband, my master, is soft-spoken, slow to anger. On those occasions when the gossips cease talking behind his back and confront him to his face, he merely smiles mildly. "My sister's children can have my trading company when I am gone. I will, at least, have died a happy man." *Can you say that?* hangs unspoken in the air.

I have other disadvantages as a wife, of course. Here on Mrw-Bek, I must sleep most of the day. Even slathered in lotions and shaded by heavy clothing, my fragile, pale skin would blister quickly under the twin suns. I am almost blind in the bright glare of midday. While my husband goes about his business, I doze amongst the piles of pillows in our bedroom, the draperies pulled tight, dreaming of the greyish-blue mists of Jzhat'lan. During the first long dusk, I bathe and scent myself for him. At first sunset I am out in the market, doing what few errands I don't entrust to the staff. By second sunset

I am home, kneeling on the cool tile, the windows open, the evening breezes blowing my curled and braided hair back from my face, my pupils wide and black. I have never not been waiting to serve him when he returned home.

He says he has nothing to complain of.

In the deep of night when he is sleeping, I slip from our cushions to read, to write, to valet his clothes, to walk the vast high-walled gardens, or view the disks of new trade goods he is considering. But on occasion the restlessness comes on me. With his permission I swathe myself in layers of tissue-thin silver cloth and slip through the silent night-time streets to a tavern in the merchant's district. Behind my veils, I can do what Jzhat'lan women are born to do. I sing the *drzaliin*.

I am always back naked on the cushions ready to lick him awake at the glimmering of first sunrise. And those of his friends who have heard the *drzaliin* no longer question his wisdom.

I have spoken of the Jzhat'lan brothels on Post 3, but do not be misled. My husband did not find me in some brothel. No, my father was his senior trading partner on Jzhat'lan, brokering carpets and pharmaceutical botanicals, optical lasers, and the finest beadwork. My husband caught glimpses of me in my father's house – pouring tea for my sisters, studying under the bower of vines in the side yard, passing shyly in the hall. Then one day he heard me laugh. He says it was that which bewitched him. He wanted to be the one to make me laugh. And whimper. And scream.

It's not our way to sell women, but my father took the funds readily enough. He said he wouldn't disrespect the customs of an honoured business associate. I think he almost believed that. To this day, when I pray at my little altar on the Days of Purification, I thank my ancestors that my father was not burdened with too many scruples.

The marriage ceremonies were done on Jzhat'lan while the contracts and documents had already been filed on Mrw-Bek. I was already my husband's property when he took me through the portal to his home world. He had kindly timed it so we would arrive just before full darkness and as we stepped out of the arrival building into the street, I had to gasp at the strangeness. The buildings all low and wide and made of lustrous white stone, the air thick and just beginning to lose the day's heat. And the people, oh, all the people, Beks, all of them at least a head taller than I, smooth sleek hair where I was hairless, chattering in Beki dialects that sounded to me like low growls.

I could feel the covert glances on me as well, some admiring, some merely curious, sizing up the rich brocades of my Jzhat'lan marriage robes, the elaborate twists and corkscrews and braids in my waist-length hair, the painted good-luck markings on my face. I clutched my new husband's hand almost involuntarily, and he squeezed back in reassurance and wrapped one of my braids firmly around his other fist. He whispered to me in the trade language, his voice as seductive to me as mine had been to him. "I should have thought to bring a leash for you. But this will do for now."

I shuddered slightly. And felt, for the first time, a very different, new emotion.

He had procured Jzhat'lan fruits and cheeses for me and sparkling pale green wines. And on my bridal night he fed them to me from his own hand, held the goblet to my lips himself as we reclined upon the pillows. All the while he spoke to me in that same honeyed voice, vowels thick as syrup, telling me what he would expect of me. "You will call me 'my master'," he said, using the Beki word. It meant nothing to me. I nodded and licked a droplet of wine from my lower lip.

"My master," I tried to repeat and the word caught in my throat.

He smiled. Or bared his teeth.

I have asked him on occasion, in the years between then and now, whether he knew. Whether, even before he had asked my father for me, he had seen something in my face, heard something in my voice, that made him sure I was unlike most Jzhat'lan women. "I wish I could say yes," he had answered, rubbing his soft-furred face across the taut flesh of my belly, pricking that flesh with his incisors, raising little red welts. "It would seem more noble were I to say I recognized that I could give you what you needed, what a Jzhat'lan male would likely not." Tiny bites on the inside of my thigh. Then soft laughter. "And it would be a lie. You were beautiful. You had a Jzhat'lan woman's voice. I knew you would moan exquisitely both when I beat you and when I pleasured you. That was enough." A sharper bite, enough to draw blood, and the sound he wanted to hear escaping from my lips. "I wanted to own you."

He owned me from the time the papers were signed, but on my bridal night he took possession just little by little. After I had nibbled the fruits from his hand, after the wine cups were empty, he gave me my wedding gifts. My tutors had tried, half-heartedly, to teach me some Beki customs once my father – and I – had consented to the marriage. As my new master placed the pile of boxes wrapped in delicate metallic tissue in front of me, I remembered Lady Vutlael stammering, playing with her hair, looking out past the courtyard gates as she murmured something about "traditional marriage present . . . jewellery, and, um, other things." As I began tearing open the tissue at my husband's behest, my face grew gradually more flushed and other parts of me warmed, and I realized with amusement why the Lady had been so uncomfortable and so vague.

The first box contained a beautiful rope of many fine platinum chains twisted into one heavy cable. Just long enough to lock around my throat. My husband purred as he clicked the clasp closed and fingered the ring attached to the lock. "Where the leash attaches."

Jewellery, indeed.

The second and third packages contained whips. Each was made of a long strap of fine leather split into two pointy tongues and attached to an intricately carved wooden handle. One, however, was heavy and slightly stiff and studded with just the tiniest knobs of metal; the other made of the softest hide imaginable. "Another custom," he said. "One to punish you, one to give you pleasure." My tutors had neglected to mention any Beki sexual practices. I cannot even begin to imagine what expression was on my face, but my husband continued in the same calm, seductive voice.

"I could never use a regular Beki instrument on you, of course. Even a Beki pleasure-whip would injure you, and just a few strokes with a punishment one would flay the flesh from your bones. I had these made to order." Another ambiguous smile. "The craftsman enjoyed the challenge, I think. Finding the right material for a disciplinary tool that might leave you screaming and sobbing and very well marked, but without damaging your delicate body. As for the other tool – " He made a slightly dismissive motion, but even then I could see the wickedness gleaming in his eyes. "Who even knows if you will respond as a Beki woman does?"

I ran my finger over the carving on one of the handles, just for an excuse to avert my eyes. It was in Beki script. I couldn't read a word of it. Later, I found it was customary to inscribe both the couple's names and a proverb on each whip. The punishment whip would generally contain some adage about a woman's need for a firm hand, the pleasure instrument one about the wisdom of keeping a woman well-satisfied. Much later, when I had become fluent in my husband's tongue, I read our names on those whip handles. And the phrase he had chosen for both.

I will not deny.

I learned the touch of that pleasure whip on my wedding night. I learned . . . so many things. My body was like a neighbouring country, one I had heard so much about, yet never visited.

He reclined me back against the cushions first, his hands firm and gentle as he guided my shoulders down. The discarded wrappings from my gifts crackled as we moved against them and the spicy bite of the scented candles above us tickled my nose. My new collar was heavy against the hollow of my throat.

He murmured, a low purr in my ear, using a Beki word which means, alternately, "toy" or "wife" or "property". The tone was clear, if not the meaning. My loins felt heavier than the fine chunk of metal about my neck. As he began to unbraid and untwist my hair, my lips parted. I wanted to call him by the title he'd taught me. I couldn't speak.

Later I would see the irony in my voice failing me.

Unsheathing a claw, he drew a finger down the front of my marriage robes, neatly slitting them open. He parted the clothes from my body, held me down against the cushions, and began to touch me. He was an experienced man, my new husband. He knew a woman's body, even a Jzhat'lan woman's body, all the pleasure spots, all my secret places. With ruthless efficiency, he rubbed and kissed and licked them.

I began to moan and squirm. Then struggle outright. The urge to sing the *drzaliin* was strong, yet instinct bade me hold my tongue. His restraining hand was not cruel. It was firm. Gentle. Unyielding. His tongue and fingers kept up their onslaught. I closed my eyes then and let my body melt into the cushions as I gave myself over to the pleasure.

The stroking turned to pinches, scratches, the kisses to the most mild of bites. I was almost keening then, the slight pain intensifying my arousal. I clutched at his body, twining my fingers in the softness of his pelt, wanting something I had no knowledge of. He lifted his head from the inside of my arm. His hands stopped their motion. "Turn over," he said then, in the trade language, his voice even thicker. *Turn over,* a throaty command, and I obeyed, pure instinct once more.

Imagine, I might have told my sisters. *Imagine, me, responding to the voice of a man.*

I was shaking as he lifted the pleasure whip, tucked it against his body. My keening trailed off into a low steady moan. He slipped an arm under my hips, raising me, and shoved a bolster beneath me to bend my body slightly. Goose bumps formed on my skin, yet I was hot all over.

His hand was in my hair. "Slave . . . wife," he murmured, again in the trade language. ". . . mine." The words seemed to come sluggishly, from far away. I know now, of course, that he longed to speak Beki. There are words in his native tongue without precise equivalent in any other language.

He grabbed my head up. "Please," I whimpered. "Please."

I didn't know what I was begging for.

He shoved my head back down into the cushions. The whip smacked across my thigh. I screamed.

I smile now to think of it – screaming at a lash from that soft, velvety leather, screaming at a lash that was more a kiss than a blow. But my nerve-endings were awash in sensation, confused, and I screamed more from shock than pain.

My husband crouched beside me, laid the pleasure whip gently down on the plane of my back, and shushed me. "Don't be afraid," he said softly, one hand firmly in my hair again, the other once more tweaking a pleasure spot with casual adeptness. "Punishment should frighten you." The tweaking fingers grew busier and he leaned to brush his mouth against my hair. "But this isn't punishment . . . it's pleasure."

I was moaning, almost keening, again when he took the pleasuring hand away. Something dropped in my belly and I felt a great emptiness, a yearning. Somewhere in some corner of my mind even then was the knowledge that I could sing the *drzaliin,* but the wish to do so, to this man, to my master, was obliterated. "Please," I repeated instead, and this time I had a small inkling of what I was asking for.

He lifted the whip from its resting place on my back then and started peppering my thighs and buttocks with soft, quick, stinging lashes, heating every inch of skin.

Later he told me how wondrous it was, beating a Jzhat'lan woman for the first time, watching the colour come up on my pale, smooth flesh. And the noise I was making, a continuous musical wailing, passion tinged with suffering, was the most beautiful sound he'd ever heard. He was, he said, almost overcome with the exquisiteness of his pleasure. It was all he could do not to try to enter me right then.

He didn't, of course. He was far too large to use my body sexually without weeks and weeks of patient dilation and further weeks of harrowing training for me. Instead he kept whipping until my flanks were a perfectly uniform shade of dusky red and the sounds that were coming from my throat were ones I had never made before. Then he tossed aside the pleasure whip and manipulated my most pleasurable spot of all, until my body convulsed and I let out another scream.

As I trembled in his arms afterwards he whispered a mix of Beki endearments and compliments in the trade language. I was so beautiful, so pliant, so sexual. He was so pleased with me. I would be such a good slave, a wife to be proud of. As my breathing slowed to normal, he brushed his mouth along my hair again, buried his face in it, chuckling quietly. "Now I know," he murmured, "that you do respond to the whip as a Beki woman does."

"Yes, my master," I murmured back. The words rolled smoothly from my mouth.

I was not my father's eldest daughter, but I was his most responsible, and I came to my new husband's house with an expectation. If there were obligations to my husband, my master, I would of course fulfil them. If there were commitments, I would honour them. I would be as I had always been. Dutiful. Conscientious.

As the first weeks and months of my marriage unfolded, my husband undertook to shatter that expectation. I would not obey out of mere duty. I would not follow the mere letter of the law. He wanted something different. Something more.

He spent the long evenings and well into the nights of those early months lavishing his attention on me. Slowly and patiently, he taught me his language and his customs. Taught me to serve him, to care for his needs and provide for his pleasures. Talked to me about his days, the business, the news of the city. Asked me endless questions about Jzhat'lan, about my family, myself. Worked on my dilation, and then the arduous process of training me to take something as large as his member into me, giving reassurance but never mercy as I wept and pleaded in my agony. Walked with me in the gardens and, on occasion when I was restless, snapped on my leash and took me out into the streets, the public parks, once even to see the pale orangish ocean. Laughed with me. Brought me to ecstasy in ways I didn't know existed. Held me in his arms when the homesickness poisoned me. Learned to know me. Began to love me.

He stayed up far too late in those days, got far too little rest – though I couldn't, at the time, recognize the signs of exhaustion in his slightly dulled hair or heavy lids. It was well worth it, he tells me now. By the time of my first storm season on Mrw-Bek, he had begun to see what he wished to see. I was beginning to be bound to him by something stronger than law, obligation, or chains. That he would have my obedience was a given. Slowly he was capturing my devotion.

Devotion is, of course, something that might well be tested.

You might think my "opening" proved to be a test for me, but in truth, somewhere in the final phases of my dilation or the beginnings of my training, the whole process became easier for me. I still cried tears of pain as I was stretched and plugged. There was no denying it hurt. But at some point, my fear of the pain had been superseded by my wish to please him.

I no longer begged mercy when he told me to fetch the instruments. I brought them quickly and without complaint, positioned myself however he ordered, spread my legs wider or bent myself more as was his whim. Sometimes, when I saw he meant to advance to the next longest or thickest instrument, tears would start running down my cheeks before he actually forced it into me, before he began to move it in hard, rhythmic thrusts, but I no longer wanted him to spare me. Every painful session was a step closer to my being able to please him completely.

I sometimes contemplated the final instrument in the set with horror and longing. It was as large as his member and as cruelly barbed. When I was opened enough to take that into my body, when I could bear to have him work me with it for more than a few moments at a time, then I would be ready for him to use as any Beki man might use his wife. That night was fast approaching. My belly tightened as my pleasure spots tingled, thinking about it.

"It will hurt you, my property," he whispered when he saw the direction of my gaze. "And I'll enjoy that."

"I know, my master," I whispered back, desirous.

No, it was not my opening that tested my devotion. It was something else altogether

My mother died when I was just a small child, and my two elder sisters were only several years my senior, too young to serve as surrogates. It fell mostly to my female tutors to teach me of the *drzaliin,* of my powers and responsibilities as a Jzhat'lan woman. The Lady Vutlael, she who was later so squeamish about Beki customs and sexuality, was dry and factual about our own. "The *drzaliin* is the power of your voice to entrance and enrapture a male. The man who hears you sing it will, for a time, wish for nothing more than to do your bidding. The pleasure he feels from it will be so overwhelming, it will be stronger than even his wish to copulate."

I had a thousand questions the first time she addressed the matter, but she gave me no time to ask them. Instead she went on lecturing about my moral obligations not to misuse the *drzaliin* – to use it only for the mutual pleasure of my mate and myself – and then started in on evolutionary theory. How our pregnancies are so long and copulation was so dangerous to our unborn in the days before technology, scientists thought the *drzaliin* had developed as a way to keep our mates bonded to us. I'm sure it was very fascinating, but I was a young girl, interested in more practical, immediate matters.

"Lady," I said finally, tugging on her sleeve to forestall more lecturing, "how will I know how to do it? How will I know *when* to do it?"

She allowed herself a small dry smile. "You won't need to be taught, girl. As you come to womanhood, hundreds of thousands of years of instinct will guide your sweet voice. As to when . . ." She paused. "When you are with your mate and, ah, amorous, you will sometimes feel the urge. Perhaps at other times as well. It is up to both of you how often you yield to it. If you are unmated . . ." Another long pause and a slight frown creasing her face. "A mature woman who goes too long without singing the *drzaliin* will begin to feel irritable and conflicted. For unmated women, there are other outlets."

Apparently she felt that she had said too much, been somehow inappropriate, for she sat up straighter then and shook her head, almost. "Enough of this for now, girl. Get your astronomy and botany texts. Your father will be much displeased if you fall behind."

That particular aspect of the subject had never been touched on again. Not even whilst she and Lady Truio were preparing me for my marriage. Why would it have been? I was going to be mated.

Of course, they failed to take into consideration that my marriage would be rather different from their own. I would be mated. I would be owned. I would be tested. There were things I might have benefited from knowing. Experience is, after all, the hardest teacher.

When the irritability came upon me, the nagging feeling of wrongness and unease, I failed to understand what it was. My husband noticed it, of course, but he too failed to glean the significance. Homesickness, feelings of confinement, even the oppressive humidity of the storm season . . . it could have been any of a thousand things which had put me out of sorts.

Even when I began to baulk at his orders, he wasn't much concerned. Slaves usually rebelled, fought their own submission, at some point in their training. He would simply repeat the order in a cool, low voice and give me a look suggesting it might be unwise to make him speak a third time. His face would remain impassive as I forced myself to obey.

And eventually the feelings would pass, the crawling sense of confusion and peevishness would leave my belly as quickly as they came on and, lying on the cushions with him, I would want to say *I'm sorry, my master, so sorry . . . I don't know what is happening to me.* But his hand would be in my hair, stroking, the slow thud of his heart beneath my face quieting me, and I never spoke.

We went on that way for several weeks, through the worst of the storm season. The winds would suddenly whip through, a few minutes of darkness and blinding rain, then back to the heavy, sullen, sticky air, unmoving and barely breathable. My moods were much the same, quickly upon me and quickly gone, but leaving unpleasantness in their wake.

One night my husband came home to find me, as he always did, kneeling on the tiles, prepared to greet him and to serve. I hadn't bothered to braid any ornaments into my hair, nor had I perfumed myself. I bowed my forehead to the floor and recited the greeting he'd taught me with what might well have been a touch of sarcasm. As I raised my head, I saw he had noticed all these things, and I saw he was weighing whether they were worth a reprimand. I felt insanely pleased.

"You'll want tea?" I asked in tones of supreme boredom as I stood to take his cloak. My voice grated in my own ears. He handed me the garment and I placed it – tossed it, almost – on its hook by the outer door, not troubling to shake it out or smooth its creases.

As I turned around, he was there, immediately in front of me. I gasped in surprise, and gasped again as he grabbed a fistful of my hair. "What I want is you back on your knees."

So. I had done it. I had made him lose his patience finally. I felt even more insanely pleased. I bowed my head as I slipped back down to the floor, letting my hair cover my face and my smirk.

"Crawl to my chamber, slave." I noted the word he used, not the affectionate one, not the one that connoted "my property" or "toy" but the one that meant, quite simply, "slave". I deflated a bit. He was angry then, really, seriously angry, not just annoyed. I began to consider that perhaps, just perhaps, my little show of rebellion was childish and ill-advised.

"Crawl." He nudged my flank with the side of his foot, and I did. Halfway to our bedchamber, my irritation came flooding back. Let him be angry with me. I didn't care. I was angry, too. The fact that I couldn't think of a single rational reason why I should be angry only served to make me seethe.

He stopped me just inside the bedchamber. "Stay there," he said in a low, clipped growl. I understood enough Beki now that he rarely had to resort to the trade language. "I'll be back."

I heard him exit the room, leaving the door ajar, brisk footsteps echoing in the hall. It sounded as if he were heading to the kitchens. Good, I thought, another nasty smirk on my face. Let him fix his own tea. Let him serve himself. Let him think me miserable, kneeling despondently here, grieving over his reprimand. I pulled myself up from my hands and knees, and plopped onto my bottom, shaking my hands out and stretching, telling myself I didn't care about his orders.

The wind was picking up outside, seeping through the shutters I'd latched earlier and making them rattle. I lifted my face to it, welcoming the marginally cooler, fresher air, even as it tangled my hair. Perhaps, I thought sourly, perhaps my husband was so irritated he would go out for the evening. Perhaps he would leave me here, alone, thinking to punish me with his absence, and I would go out into the gardens and stand in the rain just to feel it soak my hair and cool my skin. Perhaps . . .

"I thought 'stay there' was a phrase you understood."

I turned quickly to the sound of his voice. He had removed his own boots; his footfalls were silent as he padded towards me. In one fist were a handful of scraggly twigs and his eyes were colourless. "Hands and knees. Now."

I slid back into position, angry and ashamed and angry with being ashamed. My lips parted. I wanted to make some scathing remark. I wanted to hurt him. He took absolutely no notice, just crossed to the platform where our cushions were and sat, that odd bundle of sticks in his lap.

"You've gone too far, you know," he said. His voice was as colourless as his eyes, as cool and detached as I was angry. Apparently during his little walk to – where? – the little patch of garden beyond the kitchens? – he had composed himself. "Your behaviour has been insolent, provocative. Like an ill-mannered child." He fingered that bunch of twigs in his lap. "You don't deserve the dignity and the respect of being disciplined with your own punishment whip, like a woman. I'm going to spank you with this bundle of *clatha* switches instead.

My head snapped up and my mouth dropped open, unreasoning outrage colouring my cheeks. "Oh, no, you're not," I spat. Then I called him the vilest insult I could think of. In the Jzhat'lan tongue. He took my meaning anyway.

He didn't react. We stayed that way, staring at each other, for long moments, the rattling of the shutters as the wind rose even higher the only sound in the room. Finally he motioned to me. "Come here, my property," he said very quietly. "You needn't crawl."

Something broke inside of me. My anger drained away in that moment, replaced by the shame I'd been fighting. Tears started as I rose shakily and walked to him, head bowed. "I'm sorry, my master . . ."

He shook his head. "No. Not now. You'll apologize after your thrashing." His voice was not unkind. It had, in fact, lost some measure of its coldness.

He positioned me, not as he did for a pleasure whipping, comfortably bent over the bolsters, but draped over the side of the platform instead, my head and torso hanging down. He gripped one of my lower legs firmly to hold me in place, and tapped my upper thighs with the bundle of branches, apparently judging the angle of his stroke. Then the spanking started.

The switches were considered an appropriate, mild chastisement for an impudent Beki youth, but on my delicate flesh they had a more extreme impact. Each stroke burned and scratched my thighs, the skin soon fiery hot and covered with tiny, hardly bleeding cuts. On and on my husband spanked me, bringing the bundle of twigs down over and over, and only on my thighs, as I moaned and sobbed. No keening sexual cry. Just tears of humiliation and frank pain.

At some point I realized the rain had begun, and at some point, that it had ceased. Still the punishment continued. Every time my master stopped, every time he paused momentarily to rest his arm, I thought he was going to end the beating. And every time, the switches would snap down again and I would sob harder. A few times, a switch would break and he would halt the thrashing just long enough to remove it from the bundle. After a while, my tears were not just from pain and shame, but from hopelessness.

An hour must have passed before he finally ended the spanking. My face was as swelled from my tears as the backs of my legs were from the *clatha* branches. He helped me up off the platform and back onto my knees. My head swam momentarily from the change in position. "Make your obeisance," he said.

I lowered my head to his feet, splayed my upper body against the tile. I raised my buttocks high. He hadn't switched them at all and they felt strange next to my throbbing, swollen thighs. "I'm so sorry for my disrespect, my master. For my disobedience."

"I know you are," he said softly. "And you are forgiven." He raised me up and held me to him. Then gently and thoroughly, he licked my face, cleansing it of my tears. When he was finished, he kissed the top of my head. "Now say what else is in your heart, my property."

I looked at him, confused, but in a moment I knew he was

right. Things were not quite settled between us. I had apologized. He had forgiven me. I had taken my punishment. A child's punishment.

The colour leached from my face as I realized what I was going to have to ask for. But he was correct. It was in my heart. I had to finish this. I took a deep, shaky breath and lowered my eyes. "Please . . ." I said. "My master, please . . . please finish my correction. Give me a woman's punishment. Treat me as your slave, not as a child."

He nodded, and trailed a hand down my cheek. "I will." His voice was tender. "My property."

He allowed me over the bolsters this time. I watched him, my head turned and my eyes half open, as he fetched the whip from the closet. The cruel metal studs shone in the dimmed lantern light and I shuddered. What had I asked for? How much more pain could I take?

He whispered a number to me. My face grew even paler, but I nodded, a small movement of my head, as if giving consent. The first stroke knocked the breath from me. The second made me scream. The third made me scream even louder.

My husband stopped after the sixth stroke, though we were nowhere near the number he had mentioned, and waited for my howls to stop. "Just because your thighs have already been welted," he murmured, "doesn't mean that I intend to spare them now." Four strokes then, incredibly hard, the stiff, studded leather tongues of the whip cutting into my swollen skin. I clutched at the cushions and shrieked, my keening not as musical as when my husband used me, but even more heartfelt. I wanted this over. We weren't close to being done. But I wanted it over. The hopelessness I'd felt before hadn't returned. I felt, instead, panic.

He reverted to whipping my bottom and my lips parted. What came out was not a scream nor a sob, but the notes of the *drzaliin*. My face was turned to him. I saw his eyes glaze. I saw an expression of confusion and pleasure come over his face. He raised the whip halfheartedly. The *drzaliin* continued to pour from me. All I had to do was tell him to put the whip down . . . all I had to do was to say "Stop."

I looked at him. Suddenly I understood it. Everything. I

stopped singing and began to cry again, great racking sobs. He shook himself as if coming out of a dream and dropped the whip.

He lifted me from the bolsters and held me. "Tell me," he whispered. "When you are ready, tell me." I indulged myself with a only few more minutes of tears before regaining control.

"It's the *drzaliin,* my master. I need to do it. My body needs it. That's why I have been so . . . so *wrong.*" I lifted my eyes to him, pleading. "But not with you. You are my owner, my One. I don't want to gain control of you. Not even to avoid a punishment." I sucked in a big gasp of air. I was on the verge of tears again. "Especially not to avoid a punishment."

He hugged me to him, murmuring reassurance and cursing himself. "I should have known," he said. "It's my responsibility. I should have known." Then he laid me down on the cushions, gently, but not caring that I flinched as my lacerated flanks met fabric, and covered me in possessive kisses. "I've been a fool, my property, but I promise, I'll rectify my errors." He kissed me some more.

My devotion had been tested. And proved.

We didn't finish my punishment whipping until the following night.

It took some time, much talk and research, letters back to Jzhat'lan and to one of the brothel owners on Post 3, but we learned to deal with my need. My husband found a tavern owner, a man discreet and trustworthy, who would let me perform for his customers when the need struck. He would even pay me in coin, as if I had need of such. I stayed heavily veiled, anonymous, safe, tucked into a corner of the stage. I would captivate a roomful of men, leave them stunned and panting. When they were in my power, I would gently suggest they drink some more wine and then go home and pleasure their own women.

One of those suggestions was to repay the tavern owner's discretion. The other is just a little whim of my own.

It has worked well for all these years, this small arrangement, as have all the other facets of my life here on Mrw-Bek. I remain my master's joyful property. Our love has grown through the years till we can no longer, either of us, imagine a life not bonded to each other.

I tease my husband quietly sometimes about the gift of prophecy he never knew he had. The phrase so beautifully engraved on my marriage presents, now engraved in our hearts. "I will not deny," I whisper to him softly.

He cups my chin in his hand, purring. "I do not deny," he whispers back.

Bob & Carol & Ted (But Not Alice)

M. Christian

"What are you afraid of?" Not spoken with scorn, with challenge though. This was Carol, after all. His Carol. The question was sweet, sincere – one lover to another: really, honestly, what are you frightened of?

Robert fiddled with his glass of iced tea, gathering his thoughts. He trusted Carol – hell, he'd been happily married to her for five years so he'd better – but even so, it was a door he hadn't thought of opening in a long time.

They were sitting in their living room. A gentle rain tapped at the big glass doors to the patio, dancing on the pale blue surface of the pool beyond. In the big stone fireplace, a gentle fire licked at the glowing embers of a log.

Carol smiled – and, as always, when she did Bob felt himself sort of melt, deep inside. Carol . . . it shocked him sometimes how much he loved her, trusted her, loved to simply be with her. He counted himself so fortunate to have found the other half of himself in the tall, slim, brown-haired woman. They laughed at the same jokes, they appreciated the same kind of jazz, they both could eat endless platters of sashimi, and – in the bedroom, the garage, the kitchen, in the pool, car, and everywhere else the mood struck them – their lovemaking was always delightful, often spectacular.

"I don't know," Bob finally said, taking a long sip of his drink (needs more sugar, he thought absently). "I mean, I think about it sometimes – it's not as if I don't like what we do, but sometimes it crops up. A lot of the time it's hot, but other times it's kinda . . . fuck, disconcerting, you know. Like I should be thinking of what we're doing, what I want to do with you" – a sly smile there, hand on her thigh, kneading gently – "instead of thinking about, well, another guy."

Carol leaned forwards, grazing her silken lips across his. As always, just that simple act – one glancing kiss – made his body, especially his cock, respond with desire. "Sweetie," she said, whispering hoarsely into his ear, "I don't mind. I think it's hot. I really do."

Bob smiled, flexing his jean-clad thighs to relish in his spontaneous stiffness. "I know – it just feels weird sometimes. I can't explain it."

"What do you think about? Talk to me about it – maybe that'll help a little bit." Her hand landed in his lap, curled around his shaft.

"Pretend I'm not here," she added, with a low laugh.

He responded with a matching chuckle. "Oh, yeah, right," he said, leaning forwards to meet her lips. They stayed together, lips on lips, tongues dancing in hot mouths. Bob didn't know how to respond, so he just followed his instincts – his hand drifted up to cup Carol's firm, large breasts. Five years and she still had the power to reach down into his sexual self – to get to him at a cock-and-balls level. But there was something else.

"I think it's hot," Carol said again, breaking the kiss with a soft smack of moisture. "I think about it a lot, really. The thought of you with . . . what was his name again?"

Bob doubted Carol had really forgotten, but he smiled and played along. "Charley. College friend." Charley: brown curls, blue eyes, broad shoulders, football, basketball, geology, math, made a wicked margarita. Charley: late one night in their dorm room, both drunk on those wicked margaritas, Charley's hand on Bob's knee, then on his hard cock. "We fooled around for most of the semester, then his father died – left him the business. We stayed in touch for a year or so, then, well, drifted away. You know."

"I think it's wonderful," Carol said, smiling, laughing, but also tender, caring, knowing there was a Charley-shaped hole somewhere deep inside Bob. Carefully, slowly, she inched down the zipper on his shorts until the tent of his underwear was clearly visible, a small dot of pre-come marking the so-hard tip of his cock. "I think about it when we play – when we fuck."

Bob suspected, but hearing Carol say it added extra iron to his already throbbing hard-on. Carol normally wasn't one to talk during sex. This new, rough voice was even more of a turn-on.

Bob felt a glow start, deep down. Even to Carol, Charley was something private – but, hearing Carol's voice, he felt as if he could, really, finally share it. "He was something else, Charley was. Big guy, never would have thought it to look at him – that sounds stupid, doesn't it?"

Carol had gotten his shorts down, quickly followed by his underwear. Bob's cock had never seemed so big, so hard in his life. It was as if two parts of his life had met, with the force of both working to make him hard . . . so damned hard. Carol kissed the tip, carefully savouring the bead of come just starting to form again at the tip. "No, it doesn't. You're speaking from the heart, sexy – since when is anyone's heart logical or fair?"

He smiled down at her, taking a moment to playfully ruffle her hair before allowing himself to melt down into the sofa. "I wouldn't call him 'sweet' or 'nice' – but he could be, some-times. He just liked . . . fuck," the words slipped from his mind as Carol opened her mouth and – at first – slowly, carefully started to suck on his cock. "Fuck . . . yeah, he liked life, I guess. I don't even think he thought of himself as gay or anything. He just liked to fuck, to suck, to get laid, you know. But it was special. I can't really explain it."

"You loved him, didn't you, at least a little bit?" Carol said, taking her lips off his cock for a moment to speak. As she did, she stroked him, each word a downwards or upwards stroke.

Bob didn't say anything, he just leaned back and closed his eyes. He knew she was right but that was one thing he wasn't quite willing to say – not yet. He'd come a long way, but that was still in the distance.

Carol smiled, sweetly, hotly, and dropped her mouth onto

his cock again. This time her sucking, licking, stroking of his cock was faster, more earnest, and Bob could tell that she was aching to fuck, to climb on top of him and ride herself to a shattering, glorious orgasm. But she didn't. Instead, she kept sucking, kept stroking his cock, occasionally breaking into a whisper, then said, in a raw, hungry voice: "I think it's hot . . . not him just sucking your cock . . . but that you have had that. I bet sometimes . . . we look at the same guy . . . and want to know what he'd be like . . . to suck . . . to fuck."

Even though Bob was somewhere else, damned near where Carol wanted to be, he knew she was right. It was hot, it was special, and he recognized that. He wanted to haul her off her knees, get dressed, and bolt out the door to do just that. The kid who bagged their groceries sometimes at the Piggly Wiggly, that one linebacker, Russell Crowe: he wanted to take them home, rip off their shirts, lick their nipples, suck their cocks, suck their cocks, suck their cocks –

Then something went wrong. Just on the edge of orgasm, Carol stopped. Bob felt slapped, as if ice water had just been dumped into his lap. He opened his eyes and looked, goggle-eyed, as Carol got up off the floor, straightening her T-shirt over very hard nipples. "Didn't you hear that? Of all times for someone to ring the fucking doorbell."

Tugging up his pants, Bob rehearsed what he'd say: Mormon missionaries? Slam the door in their faces. Door-to-door salesman? The same. Someone needing directions? "Sorry, but you're way off," then do the same . . .

Just as Bob got to the door to the living room, he heard Carol – who'd been a lot more dressed to start with – saying, "Ted! How's it hanging?"

Bob rounded the comer, a smile already spreading across his face. Of all the people to have knocked on their front door, Ted was probably the only one who would have understood.

Ted and his charming wife, Alice, lived just across town. Normally, Bob and Carol would never in a million years have crossed paths with them – but it so happened that Ted worked in the coffee place right across the street from where Bob worked. After six months of going back and forth, Bob finally struck up a conversation with Ted and found out, much to his delight, that the tall, sandy-haired young man and he had a lot in common: the Denver Broncos, weekend sailing, and Russell Crowe movies. Bob and Carol felt very relaxed and even sometimes sexually playful around Ted and Alice, even going so far as to have a kind of sex party one night, when they all got way too wasted on tequila and some primo green bud that Ted had scored the night before. All they'd done was watch each other fuck, but it had been more than enough to blast Bob and Carol into happy, voyeuristic bliss – and to fuel their erotic fantasies for weeks afterwards.

"Low and to the right," Ted answered, smiling wide and broad and planting a quick kiss on Carol's cheek. Bob gave Ted his own quick greeting – a full-body hug that only when he finished did Bob realize had probably given Ted more than he expected in regard to Bob's still rock-hard dick.

Bob and Carol smiled at each other, feeling relaxed and still playful in the presence of their friend. "Where's Alice at, Teddy? Somewhere in the depths of Colombia?" Bob said. Alice was the other half of Bean Seeing You, their little coffee-house, and was often away trying to wrangle up all kinds of stimulating delicacies – not all of them coffee-related.

"Worse than that," Ted said, playfully ruffling his friend's brown locks. "Nope: deepest, darkest Bakersfield. I'm kinda worried about her – the last expedition down there vanished without a trace."

Everyone laughing, more out of released tension than Ted's weird brand of humour, they retreated back to the living room and the couch. As Bob and Ted sprawled out on the couch while Carol got some drinks, Bob couldn't help but wonder if their friend had figured out that they'd been almost screwing their brains out a few minutes before. The thought of it made Bob grin wildly.

"Come on, bro," Ted said, picking up on the smile. "Out with it."

Suddenly tongue-tied, Bob was glad when Carol walked in with three tall, cool drinks. "One for the man of the house" – Bob – "one for the handsome stranger" – Ted – "and one for the horny housewife" – Carol. "Cheers!" she concluded, taking a hefty swallow of her own drink.

Bob and Ted toasted her, Bob almost coughing as he drank, the drinks being stiff, and then some. He smiled to himself again as he sank back into the sofa. Talking about Charley made him feel as if a secret had been released from some dark, compressed part of his mind. He felt light, airy, almost as though he was hovering over his body, looking down at Ted – tall, curly-haired, quick and bright Ted – and Carol: Carol, who even just thinking of made his body and mind think of their wonderful lovemaking.

Sneaking a furtive glance at Ted, Bob looked his friend over more carefully. In his new, unburdened vision, Ted looked . . . well, he wasn't like Charley, but there was still something about Ted that made Bob think of his college friend – no, his college lover. Something about their height, their insatiable appetite for life, their humour.

"Is it hot in here or is it just me?" Carol piped up, laughing at her own cliché. Bob and Ted laughed too – but then the sound dropped away to a compressed silence as Carol lifted off her T-shirt and theatrically mopped her brow.

Bob's mind bounced from Carol's beautiful breasts, and her obviously very erect nipples, to Ted's rapt attention on them. He was proud of Carol, proud that she was so lovely, so sexy. He wanted to reach out and grab her, pull her to him. He wanted to kiss her nipples as Ted watched. He wanted to sit her down on the couch, spread her strong thighs, and lick her cunt until she screamed, moaned, and held onto Bob's hair as orgasm after orgasm rocketed through her while Ted watched. He wanted to bend her over, slide his painfully hard cock into her, and then fuck her till she moaned and bucked against him as Ted watched. He wanted Ted . . .

Carol's shorts came off next. Naked, she stood in front of them. Like a goddess, she rocked back and forth, showing off her voluptuous form. But even though he loved her, and thought she was probably the most beautiful woman he'd ever seen, Bob turned to look at Ted.

Ted, with the beautiful Carol standing right there in the room with him, was, instead, looking at Bob.

Bob felt his face grow flushed with . . . no, not with what he expected. It wasn't embarrassment. Dimly, he was aware of Carol walking towards him, getting down on her hands and knees again, and, in a direct repeat of only minutes before, playfully tugging his cock out of his shorts and starting to suck on it.

Still watching Ted watching him, and Carol sucking his own cock, Bob smiled at him. In Carol's mouth, his cock jumped with a sudden influx of pure lust.

Carol, breaking her hungry relishing of his dick, said, "Bob, I really think Ted would like you to suck his cock."

Now Bob was embarrassed, but not enough to keep him from silently nodding agreement.

"I'd love that," Ted said, his voice low and rumbling. "I really would."

"Take your pants off, Ted," Carol said, stroking Bob's cock. "I want to watch."

Ted did, quickly shucking his shirt as well as his thread-bare jeans. He stood for a moment, letting Carol and Bob look at him. Bob had seen his friend's cock before, but for the first time he really looked at it. Ted was tall and thin, his chest bare and smooth. His cock was big – though maybe not as big as Bob's (a secret little smirk at that) – but handsome. It wasn't soft, but it also wasn't completely hard – but with Carol and Bob watching, Ted's cock grew firmer, harder, larger, until it stuck out from his lean frame at an urgent, 45-degree angle.

"Bob . . ." Carol said, her voice purring with lust, ". . . suck Ted's cock. Please, suck it."

Ted crawled up on the sofa, lying down so that his head was on one armrest, his cock sticking straight up. His eyes were half-closed, and a sweet, sexy smile played on his lips.

Bob reached down, turning just enough to reach his friend and not dislodge Carol from her earnest sucking of his dick, and gently took hold of Ted's cock. It was warm, almost hot, and slightly slick with a fine sheen of sweat. He could have looked at it for hours, days, but with Carol working hard on his own dick, he felt his pulse racing, his own hunger beating hard in his heart.

At first he just kissed it, tasting salty pre-come. With a flash of worry that he wouldn't be good, first he licked the tip, exploring the shape of the head with his lips and then his tongue. As his heart hammered heavier and his own cock pulsed with sensation, he finally took the head into his mouth and gently sucked and licked. Ted, bless him, gave wonderful feedback – gently moaning and bucking his slim hips just enough to let Bob know that he was doing a good job.

As Carol worked him, he worked Ted. They were a long train of pleasure, a circuit of moans and sighs. Time seemed to stretch, distance to compress, until the whole world was just Ted's dick in Bob's mouth, Bob's dick in Carol's mouth – all on that wonderful afternoon.

Then, before he was even aware it was happening, Bob felt his orgasm pushing, heavy and wonderfully leaden: down through his body, down through his balls, down through his cock, and – in a spasming orgasm that made him break his earnest sucking of Ted's cock – to moan, sigh, almost scream with pleasure. Smiling at his friend, Ted followed quickly behind, with only a few quick jerks of his cock as Bob rested his head on Ted's knee.

Bob felt . . . *good*, like something important, magical, and special had happened. The world had grown, by just a little bit, but in a very special way. Resting against his friend's knee, Carol kissing his belly, he smiled. Everything was all right with the world.

Later, the sun set, and as everyone was very much exhausted by many more hours of play, Ted stumbled to the front door, Carol helping him navigate through the dim house. "Thanks for coming," she said with a sweet coo, almost a whisper, so as not to wake the heavily slumbering Bob in the next room. She kissed him, soft and sweet, smiling to herself at the variety of tastes on his lips.

"I was happy to – very. Thanks for asking me to . . . come," Ted said, smiling, as he opened the front door.

Carol smiled. "Thank you for giving him such a wonderful gift. Next weekend, then?"

"Definitely. Next time I'll bring Alice."

Another gentle kiss, a mutual "Good-night," and the door closed.

The Back of the Store

Nola Summers

I took the afternoon off and drove all the way to the next county as a precaution against anyone seeing me. The farther from home, the better. I even waited until the store was about to close, so there would be fewer people to see me, or – my biggest fear – to know me.

We were bored, Jack and I: same positions, same time, same place. He didn't seem disinterested yet, but I knew it was getting to that point. I didn't really want someone new as much as something new.

The store was on a side street, off the main run through town. I parked down a few doors so I could watch people coming and going from the store. Some people came out with nothing at all, and some with discreet black bags. Nobody had secretly taped signs on their backs saying "I've Been to a Sex Store". They all looked as if they were just out shopping.

I was on the verge of chickening out and driving home when I thought of Jack – of me on top of him, and Jack watching the TV while I bounced around on him. That had actually happened last Saturday night. Dammit! I wanted Jack to watch me, not the TV.

Already red-faced and horribly self-conscious, I got out of the car, took a deep breath, and walked towards the store. The little bell that went off when I opened the door sounded deafening, but the one shopper inside didn't appear to have heard it at all. The store clerk looked like the girl next door. She smiled at me. I grinned like a fool and then marched to the back of the store as if I knew exactly what I was looking for.

I found myself facing a wall of vibrators and dildos. I had no idea I'd have such a wide choice. So many colours, shapes and sizes! I heard the little bell ring again, and hoped it was the man at the checkout leaving. I couldn't bring myself to look at anything or even to turn around until he did. When Janice – that turned out to be her name, Janice – asked if I needed any help, I dropped the rubber cock I was holding. She bent and picked it up for me.

"That's a pretty big one," she said, placing it back on the shelf. "You seem a little nervous. Is this your first time here?"

"It shows, doesn't it?" I said.

She just smiled and walked away.

Janice brought me a glass of wine and told me to relax and look around. The store was closing in 20 minutes, she said. She'd lock up and we'd have the place to ourselves. She'd help me find what I wanted. A few more people came and went. I managed to avoid them all. I heard the bell ring as the last customer left, and then the turn of the lock.

Janice brought out a glass for herself and refilled mine. "Ready for the big tour?" she asked. "Let's start here."

She explained how the store was laid out. Novelty items up front, cards and things like that. As you walked to the back, the merchandise became progressively more hardcore. The furry handcuffs were in the middle; the real ones were at the back.

I told Janice why I had come to the store and admitted I didn't really know what to get. I was open to any suggestions.

She said we should go back to the lingerie rack and see if we could find something that might tear Jack away from the TV. She picked out two items: a red, lacy bustier-style teddy and a white babydoll nightgown. She handed me the white one and told me to try it on. Two glasses of wine and no one to see me. Why the hell not?

The changing room was small but mirrored, and I thought I looked pretty good. Very risqué. The bra had holes for my nipples and the panties were crotchless.

Janice asked me through the changing room door how I

looked. "I don't need the other one," I said. "The white one is fine."

She said, "Let me see – just to make sure it fits right."

I opened the door.

I was stunned. Janice had put on the red teddy. The blonde hair that had been tied back now flowed over her bare shoulders. The bustier left her breasts completely exposed. They were full and heavy with deep pink tips. The legs on the bustier were cut high, leaving the lacy front pointed south like a red arrow, drawing attention to her obviously shaven pussy. She wore red gloves and matching high heels. She stood with her legs apart and her hands on her hips.

"Would you like to see the back?"

I nodded dumbly.

Janice turned around and bent over. A thin red line snaked up between the white cheeks of her round ass. "Do you think Jack would like this?" she asked.

"Uh-huh," I said. I sure liked it. I wasn't thinking of how it would look on me. I liked the way it looked on her.

Janice walked towards me. "Let's see if this fits right." She walked around me, adjusting the sheer material. "It needs to hang right," she said.

I couldn't speak.

She smoothed the material over my breasts.

I couldn't breathe.

She gently pulled my nipples through the holes in the bra top and I felt them harden under her fingers.

Janice turned me around to face the mirror. I closed my eyes. She stood behind me and separated the two halves of the panties between my legs, barely touching me. "That's better," she said.

I felt her move to adjust the front. I couldn't look. She pulled the lace to the side, exposing my dark curls. I still don't know if she opened my legs herself or if I helped. So much easier to say that she did it: made me want her, made me start getting wet.

She knelt and held my hips in her soft hands, and slipped her tongue between my downy lips. My head fell back. I gasped, shocked at the heat of her mouth and the depth of my own desire.

"Look in the mirror," she said.

If it was a turn-on to feel a woman between my thighs, it was overwhelming to see it. She knew the effect it was having on me. I saw her beautiful ass framed in red lace. I saw her head bobbing as she sucked on me and I did what anyone else would have done. I took two big handfuls of her long blonde hair and held on.

Janice looked up and asked if I wanted her to stop. I shook my head no. She parted my outer lips, exposing my hardening bud. Her tongue flicked back and forth with a directness and purpose I had never experienced before. It was as if she knew my body, as if her mouth knew its way.

This was for me. Nothing was expected of me but to accept pleasure. I felt the waves start deep inside me, washing down my shaking legs. My eyes did close, but not before I saw myself in the mirror. I watched myself coming with a woman.

I watched myself liking it.

I never touched her that time, besides the handfuls of hair, and I didn't kiss her. I changed and bought the red teddy right off her body. "It will help you remember," she said. "Come back any time. If you need any more help."

I realize now how smooth she was. Is, I suppose. I have been back to Janice's store lots of times.

We play the same game each time. I go late, and pretend it's my first time. I don't need to act nervous, because I still am. Each time, it's the first time for something. We're working our way back to where the real handcuffs are, but we always end up in front of the mirror. "You need to have a clear image of us in your head," Janice says. "It will help you remember. Jack can have the benefit of that." She likes to teach me things that Jack has asked for.

Janice brought out some pillows one time and piled them in front of the mirror. We had a little picnic there on the floor. We lay naked in each other's arms, giggling like children as we fed each other. I painted trails of melted chocolate around her nipples, over her flat stomach, and down between her pouting lower lips. I had paid attention to what she did when she licked me and wanted to return the favour, so for the first time I centred myself between her thighs and eased her legs up and out, exposing her sticky chocolate mess. I knew what I liked when she was washing me with her tongue and I wanted to make her feel as good as I felt on the receiving end.

"Taste me," she said.

I was as nervous as a first kiss. The one you want but are afraid to take. I bent down and gently licked her inner thighs. I worked my way closer to her.

Janice stopped me and pointed to her face. "Just pretend you're kissing me up here," she said.

I bent down again and she opened like a mouth accepting a lover's tongue. My taste buds enjoyed her salty chocolate flavour. Question answered: she tasted good.

I wanted more. Janice pushed a pillow under herself and pulled her legs apart. I took my time exploring, pulling the folds back and exposing her hard little clit. I watched the juice ooze out of her, catching it with my tongue just before it ran down between the divide of her soft, white backside. I felt in control and enjoyed playing with her, bringing her to the edge and back several times before letting her come.

I lay there with Janice, thinking that we were equals at last. I had done something for her.

She waited until she had caught her breath before rearranging the pillows. I thought it was my turn next, and it was. "You did really good," she said. "I moved these pillows so you'd be more comfortable. Lie down."

I lay back as if I was going to get my blue ribbon for coming in first, all proud of myself.

"You need to turn over."

I was a little confused but Janice helped me turn and pushed the pillows underneath me, forcing my ass up in the air.

"It's a good day for first times," she said, as she moved around in front of me. She knelt and tied my wrists with a silk scarf, then tied the end to a ring set in the floor by the wall. She tied both ankles the same way, leaving me exposed and vulnerable.

"I'm not going to gag you because I'm not going to hurt you. You won't have any reason to cry out," she said. "But I want to hear you when you come."

Janice knelt behind me. I thought that she was going to take me from behind somehow. She let me think that as she fingered me and I found myself pushing back to meet her thrusts.

"Nice, isn't it?"

"Yes," I managed to gasp. "You've never tied me up before."

"Oh, this isn't the new part. That's coming now."

I felt my cheeks pulled apart and Janice's tongue probing my rear.

I was tied down, so I wasn't going anywhere. She told me I was very pretty back there. "Has Jack ever had you here?" she asked.

"No."

"Good," she said, "because I want to be the first. You can be my virgin."

Janice took her time that day. She started with her tongue. Licking and sucking me until my ass was covered with her spit. She took some lubricants from the shelf and brought them to me.

"Pick one."

I told her which one I wanted and she moved behind me and greased me. It was cold but I could feel it warm with my body heat. She knelt in front of me and began to grease the fingers of her hand. She held her hand in front of my face.

"Pick one. You're going to feel them all, eventually, but which one do you want me to start you with?

I said I didn't want to pick. She said I had to. They all looked big to me. I felt myself tightening. Her red lacquered nails glistened obscenely with their layer of grease.

"The thumb," I said. It seemed like a good choice: it was shorter. I didn't realize, that first time, how much thicker it was.

Janice moved behind me again. I felt her thumb resting at my opening. She began to exert a steady pressure to ease herself in, circling inside me. I could feel her widening the arcs, stretching me slowly open. I watched in the mirror as she began to move her hand back and forth, violating me further. Janice withdrew for a moment, but only to insert a different finger. First one, then two, and sometimes three. She never left me empty longer than it took to decide which combination she would use, or to apply more grease. She used her other hand to cup my pussy and play with my swollen bud. She had been truthful about not wanting to hurt me. Tying me down was just to make me feel helpless.

True to form, she made me look when she felt me start to come. I still had chocolate on my face from being between her legs. My ass was up in the air, so I could see her fingers disappearing between my cheeks. I looked like a bad girl that had been caught in the cookie jar. Offered up for punishment. There was nothing I could do but give in to Janice as she filled me front and back with her thumb and fingers and stroked me till I came.

Janice wants that part of me. She says it's hers now. My ass. No room for Jack there.

That was last time and now I've come back again. I hear the bell tinkle as the last customer leaves, and hear the lock turn.

We stroll around the aisles and stop at the wall display that still amazes me with all its shapes and sizes.

Janice kisses me and fondles me through my top. I put down my wine glass, unbutton her shirt, and slide it over her shoulders. I unhook her bra, leaving her naked from the waist up. I like to have her this way sometimes so I can concentrate on whatever is exposed. I cup her ample breasts in my hands. I push them together and lick the crease where they meet. I turn her around so I can hold them from behind, kneading and gently pulling her rosy nipples. I have her hair in my face and I inhale the female scent of her that I cannot smell on myself. I face her again and bend to suck one hardened bud into my mouth and roll the other between my fingertips. The skin around them is flushed pink and warm. Janice knows how much I enjoy her body; she lets me take my time. She'll tell me when it's time to move on.

She helps me undress. She is very loving tonight. When she's like this, so tender, it always means that at some point she will take complete control, and I will allow her to do whatever she wants. She knows. She takes her time plying my body with her fingers and tongue, and I lay there waiting.

She stands up and walks to the wall. She picks up a

harness with attachments, one for me, one for her. She tells me to help her put it on; I do, tightening the straps so they fit over her hips. It's small but thick. I separate her blonde lips and find that she's already dripping, so it slides in easily. I bring her up to her knees and adjust the straps that hold it tight inside her.

My turn. I get down on my hands and knees in front of the mirror. She takes her time fingering me, spreading my juice on the rubber cock that bobs between her legs, joined to the one I've put in her. She asks me if I'm ready. Asks me if she's bigger than Jack. I answer yes to both as she pushes inside me. She knows exactly what to do. She waits after she fills me, just a slight rocking of her hips, barely noticeable. When I can't wait any longer, I ask her to fuck me. She asks me if I'm sure, and my answer is to push back on her.

She starts slowly at first. It feels good. Each stroke forces Janice's plug deeper inside herself. Our tits bounce in unison as we moan the same song. I want to turn around. I want to look in her eyes; I want her to see me when she makes me come this way.

Janice withdraws and I turn around to face her, easing her onto her back. I want to taste myself on our cock, and bend to take its pussy-slicked length in my mouth. I feel Janice's hands on my head, establishing a slow steady rhythm. I leave our phallus and lick around the base of the plug buried in Janice. My tongue probes around the hard leather straps that contrast with the soft downy folds they force open. I suck up her generous juices, then rise to lick a tongueful into her waiting mouth.

"I need to fuck you," she whispers as she trades places and slides up between my legs. She grinds against me, forcing our plugs deeper. I gasp with the unexpected rush. I am fuller than I have ever been. Her sex-swollen breasts brush my face and I catch a nipple, sucking her in as she swings above me. I grasp the other nipple in my hand, kneading and squeezing as she moves in and out of me. "Look in the mirror with me," I say. It is a wonderful sight: my long legs as far apart as they can go; the muscles of her ass straining as she pumps into me; our breasts sweating, pressed together.

She tells me I've come a long way. I tell her I'm going to come.

"Good," she says. "Let me help you."

Just a little bit harder, just a little bit faster.

Just a little bit closer to the back of the store.

First Love

Hubert Selby, Jr.

You comfortable?

   I guess so.

   Would you like to start?

   I suppose.

   I realize this must be difficult for you, so any time you would like to stop just say so.

   Yeah . . . But I don't think you know how I feel.

   I assume I do not know exactly how you feel, but I would think that you feel self-conscious talking about the events –

   No, no. That's not it. It's her, not me. I'm concerned about what you'll think about her.

   I see.

   No, you don't . . . not really. You see, I love her. With all of me I love her. She opened up a world I never knew existed.

   Yes . . . love can do that.

   Yes, and beyond.

   Would you like to start?

   Yes.

   How did it all begin?

   It began with her mouth. She had a way of moving her mouth that stimulated every muscle and bone in my body . . . and my mind. At first I was just amazed at the feelings —

   Do you remember what you were thinking?

   I don't think I was thinking. I was totally overwhelmed by

the feelings. But I do remember having trouble breathing for a few minutes. It was that overwhelming.

What did you do then?

I don't really remember doing it, but suddenly . . . my ah . . . my thing was in her mouth and I almost passed out.

The sensation was stimulating . . . erotically?

Erotically? I don't know. I had never been with a woman before. It was my first time. I only know part of what happened —

Only part?

– the feelings seem to surround me . . . sort of wrap themselves around me and I don't remember where I was or where I went but the feelings more and more kind of swallowed me and I remember I could hardly breathe and I couldn't really see —

You lost your vision?

No, no, it's not like that, it's just that I couldn't focus on anything, it's like the air was spinning and I wanted to yell and scream and cry and I was spinning around and the feelings sort of ate me up and I sort of disappeared into the feelings and that's all there was . . . was this . . . this feeling . . . I was just one big feeling . . . yeah, it ate me up.

I see. How long did this . . . experience last?

Don't know.

Well, what time did it start?

I don't know.

Let me try it this way . . . what was the last time of the day you remember?

It was daylight.

Daylight. What time in the daylight . . . morning, afternoon, what?

I don't know . . . daylight —

Come now, there must be something you can remember that will give us a point of reference with respect to the time of day. Really!

Well . . . I did eat lunch . . . yeah, I'm pretty sure I ate lunch . . . I think. Hmmm . . . yeah, peanut butter and jelly sandwich. Yeah. On Graham crackers. Not really a sandwich I guess, but —

Yes. Well, that does give us a point of reference. So it was afternoon. I assume you do eat lunch in the afternoon.

Oh, yeah. One o'clock. Lunchtime, you know.

Yes . . . lunchtime. What time did you regain your memory?

It was dark. I mean sort of.

Of course. "Sort of." That narrows it.

You know, it was dark and it looked like the sun had just gone down.

Well, apparently you were in ecstasy for at least four hours.

Ecstasy?

Never mind. What happened when you awoke?

Well, I just sort of lay there . . . I mean it took a while to realize where I was —

In what way?

Well, it's sort of confusing. I didn't recognize things at first. It took a little while for me to realize it was home. But when I tried to move I was weak, very weak. My body felt wobbly.

You felt drained?

I guess. I tried to move and I realized my arms were still around her and my thing was still in her mouth and she was looking at me with her big pretty eyes and –

Your "thing" was still in her mouth?

Yeah. And she looked at me . . . you know, sort of sideways. And when I tried to move she started sucking on it again.

I see. And you had another . . . memory lapse?

Well, sort of.

Sort of. You either did or didn't.

Yeah . . . but see, I remember it was dark and I went to my house . . . leastways that's where I woke up.

I don't suppose you know what time that was?

Sunrise. I remember lying in bed and watching the sun and she seemed to sort of wiggle out of the sun . . . sort of.

Wiggle out of the sun?

I mean it really wasn't her, but you know how you can see the sun when it first comes up and she seemed to wiggle out of it and her breasts were like two suns and beams of light came right out of the nipples into the room and started going up and down on my body and my thing got all big and hard like concrete and it hurt . . . an itchy sort of hurt and she came right through the window and at first I had to close my eyes the light was so bright, but it got dimmer and I could feel her sucking and licking my thing and her tongue was warm and wet and her lips were so soft and she just kept doing it and my thing was so big but she put it all in her mouth and I kept trying to move but I was so weak and her tongue was licking me all over –

All over?

Yeah.

What do you mean by, all over?

You know . . . everywhere. Ah . . . *those* places.

Be specific. You ashamed to tell me exactly what she did?

Yeah, sort of. I'm afraid you'll think bad things about her.

I wouldn't think bad things about her. Tell me everything . . . in detail.

Well . . . She would bend over me and rub her lips all around the top of my thing and look at me with those . . . her eyes were so soft and sweet –

Yes, yes, but what did she do?

Well . . . she would put her lips around the top of my thing and rub it and twirl her tongue around it all at the same time, then put it deeper and deeper into her mouth looking at me so sweet and twirling her tongue and I could feel my thing hitting the back of her throat, all the way in, and she sang a song or hummed and something kept rubbing the tip of my thing and her tongue kept licking and then she would slowly oh so slowly raise her head –

Still using her tongue?

Yes. Her tongue. And she slowly raised her head until it was just the tip in her mouth, then she would slowly put it all in her mouth again, over and over and I felt like my heart would stop and she took it out of her mouth for a moment and smiled then started running her tongue up and down and around it and then she . . . she kept going.

Kept going? What do you mean?

Well, she kept moving her tongue all the way down my thing and then started licking my things and –

Things? What in the hell do you mean?

My things . . . my . . . sacks.

Oh. Go on. Continue.

Well . . . You won't think bad things about her?

No, no. What did she do next?

She kept licking and kissing the inside of my thighs then down to my . . . you know, my . . .

She stuck her tongue in your asshole? She rimmed you?

Rimmed?

Never mind, never mind. Keep going.

Well, I can't hardly be sure.

You what?

I kept forgetting sort of . . . like I was out of my body but lost in it or something. I never felt anything like this. She kept doing these things to my thing and then my tummy, then back to my thing and sacks and bottom and everywhere and I was going in circles and all the time those big eyes were smiling at me and then it would seem like everything, every part of my body, all the feeling would go into my thing and it felt like it was swelling up and huge and was going to burst and she would always put it back in her mouth and rub it up and down with her beautiful lips and I would explode and she would keep going and –

She swallowed it.

It?

Forget about it, go on, go on.

Well I just seemed to float away and I think I screamed or something and I just seemed to collapse but then I would hear her sort of humming and feel her mouth around my thing and then her finger was rubbing my bottom-hole –

Ahhh . . .

– then she put her finger in and out as she kept rubbing up and down on my thing with her mouth as she sucked and licked all the stuff from my thing and then I would explode again –

How many times?

Huh?

How many times did you come?

Huh?

Explode, for God's sake?

I don't know. It just kept happening, over and over, all day.

All day?

Yeah. Then she just held me for a while and kissed me and let the gooey stuff from my thing drip into my mouth then put her breast in my mouth and told me to bite her nipples and she squirmed and moaned and I kept biting and squeezing and something came over me and I started kissing her everywhere and biting her and she put my hand in her thing.

Your whole hand?

Yeah, she just –

You fisted her.

Fist –

Go on.

And she moved around and up and down on my hand and it slowly went up her thing and all my fingers went in, and then my knuckles disappeared and she kept moaning and squirming and pushing down on my hand and I was in past my wrist and she kept squirming and pushing and moaning and saying yes, yes, harder, fuck me, fuck me and I was feeling squirmier and squirmier and rolled around and my thing was all big and hard and felt itchy sort of and she pulled my hand out of her and I didn't want her to and shoved it in further and further and chewed on her breasts and she rolled around and around and finally slid off my hand and sat on my thing and I lay there watching it going in and out of her thing and it was all wet and dripping and I wished I could lick both our things while she was doing it but she shoved me down and bent over me and stuck her breasts in my face and told me to chew on her tits and I did and I kept biting harder and harder and I could taste blood in my mouth and she sat up and moved around on my thing and pulled the lips of hers apart and pointed to some little thing in there and told me to rub it and I did and it sort of flapped back and forth and she started moaning again and saying yes, yes, o fuck, fuck, yes, yes and I pinched it and rubbed it harder and harder and it seemed to get bigger and soon I was getting all jelly again and she kept bouncing up and down harder and harder and I felt so weak but I felt like I wanted to tear her thing out and pinched harder and harder until I exploded again and I couldn't rub it any more but she kept moving, but slowed down and soon she just sat there and every few seconds she would sit up and I could see all the gooey stuff on my thing and dripping from hers and then she finally got off and rubbed her thing up and down on my tummy and then licked my thing and sucked it until all the goo was gone and then she kissed me and I could taste it and I sucked it out of her mouth and my thing started getting itchy and then she rubbed her thing on my chest then knelt over me and put her thing on my mouth and told me to open my mouth and I put her thing in my mouth and she peed in my mouth, real slow and it was warm and made my thing itch and get hard and swollen and then she moved her thing slowly down my body and peed all over me and put my thing in hers and kept peeing and told me to pee and I did and I stopped when she said to and she got off and closed her thing then knelt over my face and let the pee drip all over me then told me to pee in her mouth and I peed too fast and she grabbed my thing and squeezed it so hard I couldn't pee and she . . .

Why do you stop?

I don't want you to not like her.

Believe me, I like her. What else did you do?

I don't know . . . lots of things.

How long were you doing this?

Don't know. Seems like the sun came up and went down many times.

How many times did you . . . explode?

Didn't count. Lots I guess. Over and over and over.

What else did you do?

All kinds a things. Can't remember everything. Ropes and things . . .

Did she look like the women in those magazines you have?

Sort of I guess. Not really sure what she looks like. Think she's prettier.

How long have you been collecting those magazines?

Couple of years. Since mother died.

And you have been living alone since then . . . since she died?

Yeah.

You can't remember everything you did?

No . . . But I think there was a lot of biting. Seems like I remember her saying over and over to bite her nipples . . .

Biting her nipples . . . Did you also kiss them and lick them?
Oh yeah, lots of licking . . . yeah.
And you fondled them and stroked her pu – vagina?
Vaa . . .
Her thing.
Uh huh. Lots.
And it got wet and . . .
Oh, yeah. It got wet and slippery like and it dripped all over –
And you licked it and kissed it?
Uh huh. She pushed me down on my back and kneeled over me and told me to stick my tongue out and she'd spread her thing open and slide it up and down on my tongue then just sit on my face and tell me to bite her thing and sometimes she'd pee and rub her thing all over my face and tell me to keep licking and biting . . . yeah, over and over.
And you nibbled her clit during a golden shower . . .
Huh? I just bit where she said.
And she turned over and you licked her ass.
Oh yeah. She kneeled over me and spread it open and told me to put my tongue in there too and everything made my thing get big and she'd put my thing in her mouth while she moved around on my tongue and wiggled and I started biting her even when she didn't say to and it made me dizzy and my body would jerk around and everything was yelling, even my toes, then I'd explode and I'd feel like my body was going to snap like a twig, then I would feel like jelly, all wishy-washy like jelly.
And she kept your thing in her mouth.
Yeah . . . oh yeah, and kept doing things and I got all hard and swollen and –
And you kept biting her tits and nipples and ass.
Uh huh. She kept saying like you, bite my ass, bite my nipples. Yeah.
And you kept biting and it felt good to sink your teeth into her ass and nibble on her pussy.
I kept biting even when she was bleeding. I think I bit one of her nipples off . . . or almost. Maybe.
Oh Jesus, you bit it off, just bit the fucking thing off her tit?
Don't know. Maybe . . . Why you taking your thing out?

Show me how she kept your thing so hard.

Oh, you got that gooey stuff dripping out . . . Hm, my thing was bigger and harder.

Put it in your mouth and do what she did . . . oh . . . oh . . .

How did you feel after you killed her?

I'm not sure. I woke up holding her and I thought maybe it had been a nightmare, but there was blood and she was dead.

Why did you kill her?

I don't know. Couldn't think of anything else to do, I guess.

What did you do then?

I ate her.

You ate her.

Well, I didn't just eat her like she was. I wouldn't do that. It wouldn't be right. I baked her first.

Baked her.

Yeah. Sorta slowly. Then I ate her. It took a long time, days I guess . . . many days it seems like.

What did you do next?

I don't exactly know. Seems like I slept a lot.

Then what?

I think I called the police.

Why did you do that?

Seemed like the right thing to do.

Do you know where you are?

Police station – some sort of jail, I guess.

You're in a hospital.

Hospital?

Yes. And I am a doctor. Specifically, a psychiatrist.

Why would I be in a hospital? I didn't get hurt.

The police checked your story and there's no evidence of a crime.

What do you mean?

There was no woman's body or . . . remains.

But I ate her.

Yes, that is what you said. But all they found were the bones and hide of a lamb.

What are you talking about . . . this is crazy . . what do you think I did with her?

There was no woman. It was all a hallucination.
Hallucination?
You made it all up in your head.
She was real. I just think about her and my thing gets all hard.
I know you believe it.
It was real . . .

Now, tell me again how you put your thing in her mouth and tickled her tonsils, then bit her nipple off . . .

Triptych

Helena Settimana

My friend Lynette and I are lying on our beds in a hotel on
Lancaster Gate. We can see Hyde Park across the street with
its massive, winter-naked oaks standing like wild-armed
sentries. The room has red velvet drapes and gold and red
flocked wallpaper. I suspect it is supposed to look sumptuous,
but the effect is more like a second-rate whorehouse. It is
raining outside, and I have been watching the beetle-black
cabs and a mounted policeman passing along the slick street. I
am telling her seriously that I will kill myself if I ever lose "it"
before I am married. Lynette looks at me like I have three
heads. She has dark-rimmed, cat-green eyes that open wider
in disbelief, but she is too wise or too dumbstruck to say
anything. I just might be the last virgin in my senior year, but
it is all too much to absorb, so I vow self-death as an antidote
to the roil inside me, brought on by the fact that a boy I have
met on this March Break excursion has stuck his muscular
tongue in my mouth and provoked a hormonal crisis. I rushed
to brush my teeth, but felt helpless to brush away the throb
that lingered between my legs. The feeling is potent and
threatens to overwhelm. Death is a limited solution.

He is anxious to please, this boy, and anxious to advance
his cause. He has unruly jet-black hair and pale, freckled,
Scottish skin. He has been a figure-skater, is muscular and
lean, and comes from another school, stuck on the same
itinerary. Craig follows me, alternating puppyish flirtation

with macho posturing. On the night after we meet we all go out to a play and in the dark he gently draws his thumb across my palm and ventures a hand on my thigh. My breath is suspended. I feel incapable of rising to my feet at the end of the first act, slick and damp. He remains seated for a while after I excuse myself to find the bathroom. My friends are watching me closely. To this day I don't remember the name of the play.

I try to remember my vow.

He sees me to my hotel room door, where Lynette has disappeared discreetly inside. He kisses with his tongue again and ventures pressing himself, hard, into my belly. Panicked, I wiggle a goodnight, but the next day, and the next, my resolve begins to unravel in this miasma of newfound passion. Still, I allow him no room to go beyond.

On the tenth day we sit together riding the plane home. As the lights are dimmed he calls the flight attendant for a blanket, and wraps me discreetly beside him. The imaginary barrier is drawn between us and the rest of the world, and in this seclusion his hands wander to my breasts and carefully fondle me between my legs. Craig has taken my hand and guided it to him. I feel him hard the first time I have ever touched a boy, a man, there. If anyone is aware of what we are doing, it goes unchallenged and our fondling continues, unchecked. When one finger slips beneath the scalloped edges of my panties, my breath catches again. I know he can't "go all the way", and so I let him slide one sturdy finger inside me, opening my legs and pushing my hips onto his hand before sudden panic strikes again. The exploration ends. When we emerge from our hiding place, I feel the eyes of other passengers on us. They know! Somehow I feel triumphant.

I hold him at arm's length. My parents love him, adore him, trust him. They retire and leave us alone one night. He succeeds in putting his cock in my mouth. Weeks later he tells my friends, in front of me, that we are getting married but we will live together first. He hasn't mentioned this to me. It is the beginning of the end. I can't imagine settling for one man right now when this wicked new world is waiting to be discovered. I find I have a cruel heart. Just to make sure, I fuck the next guy I meet.

I'm still alive.

Leigh is standing beside the window in a cheap hotel room in Victoria. He has carried my luggage in from the curb and up two flights of stairs. I was not anticipating the Ritz, but perhaps something more on the measure of the hotel by the park. This is closer to a flophouse and is fortunately only a stopgap until I can find an acceptable room of my own. The hotel seems to crawl with the dregs of London: whores and pimps and pushers. I wonder how I am mixed in with them, and remind myself that it is only a temporary thing and that lodging here, unlike home, is exorbitant. I am a poor student and I did not book this part ahead. The heater hangs askew on the wall, broken wires dripping out, the victim of a previous tenant. The door is missing from the wardrobe, and extra linens are tossed carelessly inside. I don't want to look closely at them.

I have put aside my life to be here – to see if this is the man I want for keeps. I am now being dragged slowly into this sagging, creaking bed, stripped of my clothing, jewellery, underthings. For a while I feel as if I have come home and I collapse under his weight, grateful for the warmth and familiarity of his body. He smells good, his mouth burns on me, his teeth rake the fine surface of my skin. I finger the crucifix around his neck and bend, push up into him.

The whores are fighting in the street. It's distracting me from coming. Eventually, Leigh sidles to the window to watch the show. He's blue-grey-black-and-white-TV-coloured in the streetlight, bronze lined with silver. He seems distant. When he sees the management toss an unpaying visitor out into the road, he hastily dresses and leaves with a promise to return in the morning.

Early in the morning, he comes to my room and takes his sweet everlovin' time pulling the rings from my fingers, then the blouse, the slacks, the snappy bits of bra and panty off me, and lays me down tender as you like, and rubs all of the red marks out of my skin. He makes me cry out and whisper, "I love you," and when he has finished he gets this sad look on his face and says, "I'm sorry," and "It's over," and walks out, just like that – out into the dirty street. He told me that he has reconciled with his wife. Suddenly I see I am at home in this place after all.

From a phone box in the road I call Mireille in Islington and ride the train underground, walk the warren of alleys and roads that lead to her basement flat, and cry at her door as if bereft of life.

His wife. I can't believe it.

Mireille is good at serving tea and sympathy to me but is merciless with Leigh and pronounces a hex upon his cock for good measure. This makes me laugh a bit.

She says, "He will never be the same after this, but what does not kill you will make you stronger, and you will be very powerful indeed." I am giggling and hiccoughing sobs at the same time.

I've been dreaming every time I sleep. Mireille tries to rub the red marks out of my eyes, after I tell her about the rotten heel. Mireille kisses my swollen eyelids, my mouth, down the side of my neck, draws me backwards into her body with arms that are deceptively strong. I am paralyzed with shock, then eased by resignation, then loosened by desire. The glossy dark hair that curled out from under her cotton shorts shocked me into arousal – so did the hair that peeked from under her arms. Weak, weak, I feel weak. She says, "How could he make you feel bad, how could he? He deserves to be shot."

I find myself propped like a broken doll on her hand, desperately twisting my leather-brown, nubby nipples while she moans over the three fingers I had managed to slip inside that sopping mouth.

The sound of my breath caught in the air sounds rasping, ragged. It hangs in the dark like frozen vapour emitted on a winter's night: small crystals of ice colliding. The noise is shattering in the tiny room. I am afraid that if I look on the floor I will see bits of my orgasm lying in jagged pieces: an *A* here, an *O* there. Curls of *G*s and fragments of *F*s. I fear we'll waken the neighbours. The sound has brought me to consciousness:

my insides clasping frantically, the sharp images in my mind are shredded by wakefulness. I resolve not to panic.

Mireille rolls over, nuzzling her face into the pillow. What can I say? I feel different, new – not exactly fixed. It is too soon for that.

I think I shall never return.

The woman sprawled on the settee is staring at Jack. She looks like a young Melina Mercouri – brassy dyed-blonde hair with black roots and a single eyebrow. I look away. If the one we find looks like a Greek, it had better be like Irene Papas – my idea of a goddess. Jack is looking the other way at this leggy sylph of a thing with golden-brown hair and a dimple that makes her look a bit like Kirk Douglas, if Douglas were a woman and a delicate, skinny one at that. The dimple drops her eyes – not her, either.

It's a dare. He's got me teetering into this place on dangerous heels. I'm still madly in love. It's our tenth anniversary, and all he wants is to live his fantasy at last. We have been together so long that in the moment it seems not only safe, but exciting. I am to find an agreeable partner, ignoring the boys on the way. Jack is an adventurer, though he likes me all to himself.

In the end I spy a golden gazelle of a girl sitting in a dark corner, watching. She has a purple slash of a mouth. Jack presses himself into my ass before sending me off to broach the topic. I buy her a drink, light her cigarette, drop a strap off my shoulder, swing my pointed shoe with studied non-chalance, brush her arm as if by accident. Then she says, "Are you coming on to me?" and I have to tell her yes, and wait for her eyes to shutter, but they burn instead with a kind of smoky light and it is OK. We sit in the shadows, her skirt hiked a bit, my hand exploring the juncture of her legs. She pushes herself on my hand, her purple mouth open. She says her name is Amira. She is Kenyan and speaks with a trilling, exotic timbre to her clipped colonial English.

Jack appears like an apparition, his cock veiled in the linen of his trousers. I whisper the invitation to her and wait again for her to say no, but her mouth opens in a tiny *O* and she nods. Jack calls for our coats and leads us to the curb, hails a cab. I watch the furtive glances of the driver in the rear-view mirror as we sit flanking our new friend, probing hands on her thighs, teeth on her neck, tongues in her ears. She massages Jack's cock, and a stain begins to bleed through the fabric of his pants. I am so hot that I am out of body.

He pays the driver, who looks a little bit disappointed at our departure. Our hotel is a good one this time, decorated in dark wood and forest green, brass, Chinese vases. Amira is like a miracle shining naked on the bed. I've gently parted her lips, pulled the mouth of her sex open. She is tidy, neat, her hair trimmed, her lips understated – the colour of aubergine. I wonder if she has been clipped a bit, but it's hard to tell. Seawater oozes from her pink interior.

I think of Mireille's strong arms as I pull her back into my body, laying her on top of me, stroking her blackberry nipples, brushing her belly while Jack searches for her teeny clit with his tongue. She rolls off me and offers her ass to him, pulling intently on my breast, nuzzling down into the thatch between my legs.

He fucks her. This is not exactly in the plan, at least not the one he shared with me. I'm aroused, overcome, transported by this fantasy into one of my own. I am nowhere, I am every-where, I am he, and I am she. I inhabit their bodies and think and feel for them, make them do my bidding. She's so tiny – narrow and almost adolescent-looking – vulnerable. I offer help: help to hold her down, to spread her legs, to penetrate her. I never feel what she feels, only what he feels as she twists and moans and flails narrow avian arms and legs while he buries himself into her with force. His cock, shiny with latex and juice, is thicker than her wrist and he holds her over his lap, facing me, making sure I see as she jerks like a meat mari-onette on him. When they come I come too, my hand cram-ming my quivering hole. Jack is staring me in the eye. He whispers, "I'm the luckiest man in the world."

He may be right.

Pinkland

Graham Joyce

The two had been ethereal lovers for almost six months before Nat admitted to Sammy she was a woman. Sammy had to go out of the room just to, well, fan the face, draw breath, squat down and mull over the irony of it. When Sammy got it together to squeeze an inflating skull back into the room Nat was still waiting for some kind of a response. Winking, as it were.

>Still want to meet?< Nat was asking.

Hair on fire, fingers atremble, Sammy typed >Yes, of course I'll meet you. Why wouldn't I?<

A woman! A *woman*! Sammy knew some of the dangers involved in conducting a relationship on the Net. Truthfulness was the first casualty in any sustained campaign. You meet someone in a chat room, establish a few details and move breezily on to other things. Nat (Natalie? Nathaniel?) had simply typed in abbreviated style: *male, 31, single* in answer to early questions. One always predicts, suspects and occasionally encourages dissembling along the way – hell, thought Sammy, that's what modern communication is all about, isn't it? – but after six months of spinning out a serious electronic mating game Sammy felt comfortable in the knowledge of who and what was vibrating the other end of the line.

Wrongo! Double-double wrongo!

What the hell had Nat been playing at? All that wasted time webflirting and chatting about music, yeah, check it out; and films, catch this, catch that; and what's your favourite drink, say daiquiri to conjure enigma. But Nat had made Sammy laugh out loud when he – drat, she – had said *pre-coital cocoa*. This was all long before their first nervous, faltering Internet kiss.

According to Nat, Sammy was a natural. A linguist.

>A cunning linguist you be.< Nat typed.

>Slippery slidey tongue.< Sammy tapped back. >Moist, hot, furry, slidey, slightly saline, semen-bearing . . .<

>Stop stop stop!< Nat replied that first time. >You're making me hot, and I haven't been hot in . . . < The cursor faltered, winking, > . . . in ages.<

And then the new ages, endless hours logged on constructing their own website home together, dubbed Pinkland; carefully choosing the decor, *nouveau* naturally, Nat; filling it with favourite books, nothing post-modern, also Nat; installing works of art, anything abstract, Sammy. Building a life together, all while Sammy squirmed, typed, and double-entendred towards getting Nat naked, before finally abandoning broad hints altogether:

>Nude. Naked. Stripped. Buff. In the skin. Peeled. To the pink.<

Which, after all was what an Internet relationship was all about. Flesh. It became conditional upon creating Pinkland that clothes should be discarded at the virtual door, consigned to a decorously described heap. Sammy, at least, was always faithfully nude at the keyboard.

Then without preamble one day Nat produced the silver handcuffs. >See how they wink in the indigo light? Slip your hands behind your back, darling. That's good. Don't you love that icy breath of cold, cold steel, the intimate clink and click of chain and catch? Now, don't squeal. I'm going to fuck you savagely from behind.<

And Nat had done exactly that. In retrospect, and now that Nat had confessed to being a woman, Sammy failed to see what pleasure that afforded, and felt abused by the fact that Nat couldn't do it in *restricted* time. (Sammy and Nat never referred to *real* time. Was not time on the Net real? Was not their relationship between real people? Not as if, they both agreed, the Net was a dream or anything.)

But now Sammy had agreed to meet Nat to confront her at the Orbit Café in South Kensington. Sammy wanted to gloat, to study minutely Nat's response. Natalie, you see, having made her own confession, still thought Sammy was a man.

Sammy certainly didn't go along to denounce her or anything. They had lied to each other, that was all it amounted to. Each deception – of pretending to be a man – was neutralized in turn by the other's deception of pretending to be a man. No one had any right to be furious. Or aggrieved. Or to feel cheated. Or anything.

Favouring a feminine, clinging satin skirt and wearing a nimbus of flowery perfume, Sammy deliberately arrived half an hour early, taking up position. It was a dead-hour zone. The place glowed with amber light and the smoky loneliness of mid-afternoon. A few couples leaned together and two single men sat alone, one at the bar and one at a shadowy table. Sammy was already having second thoughts.

Supposedly a drinker of Brandy Alexanders, Sammy hadn't got a clue what they tasted like, didn't drink alcohol as a rule, and so ordered a cola. Three-quarters of an hour later Nat still hadn't showed up. Sammy began to nurse suspicions about the two single men. Maybe Nat had lied, was a man after all, had got there in advance, to get the drop.

Sammy took a deep breath and approached the man at the bar. >Are you drinking daiquiri?<

>What does it look like?<

Sammy wouldn't know a daiquiri if it squirted from a nipple, but it was exactly the evasive answer Nat might give. >Looks like you got here before me.< Sammy gave the lips a polish with an extraordinarily versatile tongue, knowing that drove Nat wild.

>Wanna fuck?<

Only Nat would be so upfront: Sammy knew it was him. >Can I finish my drink first?< It was important in this game to appear *cool*. Something Nat and Sammy had fallen into from the beginning, out-cooling each other, but like the sugar-frost cool of the rim of a cocktail glass. Sammy said nothing concerning his lie about being a woman, and Nat said nothing about the sudden discovery that Sammy was a woman too. Weird but exciting. Neither alluded to the fact that they'd known each other for six months on the Net. They were playing the *strangers* game: you crack, you lose.

Drinks finished, Nat took Sammy back to a shabby one-room bedsit. Nothing like the penthouse suite overlooking the Thames he'd often described when they set up Pinkland. Sammy was about to protest before being bundled, quite roughly, against the wall.

Sammy took a deep breath of him, a gulp, almost a lick. He smelled good, earthy, natural. No resistance was offered as Nat pushed up Sammy's vest, slaking himself on the small, boyish breasts. Sammy's nipples hardened instantly at the lashing of his tongue. Soft noises of encouragement seemed to make him rabid with excitement. He pulled up Sammy's skirt, exposing a smooth midriff and the fur purse. Whenever they'd had Internet sex Sammy had never worn underwear but Nat seemed slightly surprised this time. Sammy felt his fingers probing, slithering inside, deep, up to the third knuckle. Then Nat crumpled to his knees, pushing his tongue where his fingers had been, swaying slightly as if made dizzy by the brimstone-and-honey odour of sex.

Because the air was seeded, streaming, drenched with genital perfume. They had irresponsible and delirious unprotected sex, though Sammy complained when, losing control and with fingers tangled in sweat-matted hair, Nat inadvertently pushed Sammy's head against the wall as he ejaculated. >Easy, Nat,<Sammy said. >Easy.<

He flickered as he recovered his breath. As soon as he was able to speak, he said, >Who the fuck is Nat?<

Sammy hurried back to the Orbit Café. It was beginning to fill up, but by now there wasn't a single person, male or female, sitting alone. There was nothing to do but hang around for a while, feeling naive, humiliated and furious with Nat.

Next time they were online together, Sammy gave him (or her, since now it wasn't possible to trust a single word Nat said) hell. >You could at least have left a message, to say you weren't coming.<

>I'm sorry. Something came up. I couldn't make it.<
>You put me at risk!<
>Why? What happened?<
>Nothing happened. Forget it.<
>Are you sure nothing happened?<
>I said forget it.<
>I promise I'll be there next time.<
>Next time? There isn't going to be a next time. Listen Nat, after what happened to me I'm never going to trust you again. Final.<

But that was all talk. Sammy didn't want it to end. What Nat got from the relationship was a mystery; but Sammy got insight, Sammy got experience, and most of all Sammy got *language,* the exotic kind that squished on the tongue like choux pastry or stung like liquorice.

Nat was endlessly critical of the shortcomings of the English language. >I don't know how we're expected to be erotic with these shoddy goods. I mean how erotic can a language be when there's no word for the most tender and erogenous part of the leg? Or for the natural genital perfume of a clean woman? I don't know why I bother.<

But bother Nat did, and Sammy learned that the Germans had a word, *kniekehle,* for that fold at the back of the knee, the erotic cleft to which Nat referred; and the French too were unafraid, in naming the *cassolettes* she so delighted in. And it was when Nat started talking dirty, foreign dirty, angelic dirty, that Sammy knew they were about to have Internet sex.

What Sammy truly appreciated was Nat's sensitivity, a knowledge of when tenderness was required and when rough handling might be in order. Sammy was mightily impressed by this verbal dexterity, and Nat's hoochy-coo was like a sexy English lesson, demonstrating a virtuoso's ability to switch smoothly, despite his complaints about the language's shortcomings, between the polysyllabic caresses of the Romance-root and the good old-fashioned hard-thrust Anglo-Saxon.

Nat was the perfect Internet lover. One hand on the keyboard, the other dipped at the thigh, it never took long for Sammy to come. Oddly, it was always the keyboard fingers

Sammy sniffed for residual fuck after the event.

For Sammy, the imagined scent of Nat lingered there for hours. There was none of this so-called post-coital *tristesse* after Internet sex. Just the longing. And a back-brain howling, like the wind moaning through circuits girdling the planet.

So of course Sammy agreed to meet Nat again, though flatly refusing to return to the Orbit Café, certain that the rough lover was there even at that moment, laughing, regaling the waiters and customers, making a bonfire of the needs of the naive and the desperate.

Nat, of course, had indeed been joking around, and was a man after all. They met in a hotel lobby this time. Sammy, to get revenge, declared manhood. Nat was easy to identify because he kept approaching other men.

It was a laugh to see him hitting on passing strangers. >Are you Sammy?<

>No. Nope. Noedy. No sir. And no sireeee.<

Sammy's smirk was a mile wide. Nat just wasn't looking for a woman.

Finally Sammy tipped the wink. Trying to stay cool, Nat merely levitated an eyebrow. After six months on the Net, the joke was on him. Sammy enfolded long, slender arms about him, inhaling the scent of him.

>You smell good.< Sammy said. >Just like I knew you would.<

>How do I smell?<

>Sugar almonds; lychees; the wet earth. In fact you smell just like the taste of your come. <(It was what the rough lover from the Orbit Café had said: his words exactly.)<

>Very poetic. Want to go to a room somewhere?<

>No. I want to do it right here.< It was true. That's what Sammy wanted, still slightly sore from that recent experience, but aching for excess and still fixed on exacting some revenge. Making his zip rasp and hooking his trousers down around his ankles, in one deft move Sammy had a hand inside Nat's boxer shorts. Not until Sammy's mouth was clamped around Nat's fattening cock did either of them notice the conversation in the lobby around them had gone completely dead.

>Can't we go to a room?< Nat wailed.

>Why bother?<

>I can't do this.< Nat said.

>Just relax.<

>It's too weird. I'm going.< And logged off. Leaving Sammy's knees indenting the virtual carpet, as it were, sucking on air and mouthing noises to a lobby full of blasé onlookers, quite accustomed to acts of public sex. Realising Nat had withdrawn, Sammy hurriedly logged off too, and shut down the computer.

It was days before Sammy spoke to Nat again, having twice now been left in embarrassing and faintly ridiculous situations. Trust was at an ebb. Sammy sat contemplating Pinkland, reviewing all of the books and the music and the artwork built up there, thinking about destroying it all with a keystroke, when Nat appeared in an Instant-Message Box.

>I've had it with you.< typed Sammy.

>Why? You in Pinkland?<

>Yes. You don't take this relationship seriously.<

>I'll call it up. How can you say that? We've been together for over six months now. We've got a good thing going haven't we?< Then he typed >g<, which in Net communication means grin, and that absolutely *sickened* Sammy.

>You don't turn up when we arrange to meet. You log off when we're in the middle of something. Why don't we just forget it?<

>Sometimes, Sammy, I think you take things too seriously. It's only a game.<

>IT'S NOT A FUCKING GAME!< typing this in capitals, even though it was considered bad form to shout on the Internet. Sammy *wanted* to shout. To scream. Instead, Sammy started deleting music they'd carefully downloaded to their room in Pinkland. The Pet Shop Boys. Deleted. Tom Jones. Deleted. The Monkees. Deleted.

>What are you doing?<

>What does it look like? I'm ending it. If it's all just a fucking game I can't win then I'm hooking over the chess-board.<

It was their first real Internet fight. Then, after a while, Nat started cooing, and finally he said *kniekehle,* and incredibly he got Sammy to agree to do it all over again; though Sammy did exact a promise that The Monkees would stay deleted. After all it was Sammy's favourite Internet sex game, keeping Nat guessing over the current gender. Many times they'd agreed to meet up outside the safety and exclusivity of the Instant Message or the private Chat Room, on some preselected Internet site where other net users of any stripe were at large, and to behave as though they were meeting for the very first time.

The point of this game was to preserve the excitement of novelty. Although they'd known each other on the web for six months, they could still surprise each other this way. They could, and often did, pretend to be someone of the opposite sex. Both of them.

Deep down, Sammy suspected Nat of being a woman.

Sammy had tried, over the last couple of weeks, to look for deep clues. Little mistakes, insensitivities, gaps in knowledge, things a woman should know, things a man shouldn't. But the Net allowed for such a range of improvization that one's persona could easily become subsumed by the alter-ego. There was always, and in everyone, a shadow just aching to come out and play, to don the leather trousers or the frilly frock, to taste the whip, to pop the amyl, bind the cord, lick the cream, crush the fruit, sting the skin and to stretch the neck right up to the hissing wind of mortality's scythe.

Sammy's preference was for coming on as a man, set upon by a small crowd of rampant women, stripped and molested and then re-clothed in somewhat tarty women's gear before they began a systematic programme of mild abuse, leaving Sammy aching, and sore, and spent.

Even on the Net this fantasy was difficult to deliver.

But then Nat shocked Sammy. >I'm not talking about meeting on the Net any more.<

>Any time, any place.< Sammy said, pretending not to have grasped the significance of what Nat now proposed. A meeting in *real* real life. Beyond cyberspace was another country.

>Stop it!< Nat said sharply. >Stop making out you don't

know what I'm talking about. Things have come to a head, as you knew they would. That's what all this pouting and complaining is all about. If you want this to be a real relationship – and I mean a corporeal, physical, off-line thing, a caring relationship where yes means yes and no means no, where people have flu and sour breath in the mornings and where we have to endure each other's black moods and we do all that 'cos we genuinely love each other – then we have to meet. Engage. We have to press flesh, Sammy. Press flesh.<

Love? thought Sammy. Who said anything about love? This was getting weird. There was a hierarchy of steps to be taken before making the thing corporeal. A file transfer here and there; a telephone call; an exchange of the kind of mail which requires a postman to come whistling up the path; a trading of photographs; gifts even. Love wasn't something you just downloaded.

But Nat hadn't finished. >Just be clear, I'm not talking about faking it all over again and again and again. I've been thinking about this for a while. I don't know what happens to you when we go off-line, but me, I'm left alone, trying to guess whether it really is just a game. Totally alone. Longing for you. And if you've felt me retreating lately, that's why. So there it is.<

Long pause while Sammy's cursor blinked, waiting for a response. >Can't we keep things as they are? We've got a good thing going, haven't we?< Sammy typed those words fully aware of how weakly they echoed Nat's earlier remarks. Even in typescript it was possible to make words curve, wail. >Can't we just stay in Pinkland? Aren't you happy here?<

>Do whatever you want with Pinkland. But on your own. If we don't meet, we don't no more greet. That's it. That's what it means to me.<

Nat would brook no argument, and since they both lived in London there were no practical constraints. He proposed that they flesh-rendezvous the following Saturday in a bar just off Soho which he said was quiet, where he sometimes went alone. He said he'd be there whether Sammy showed or not. >Now I'm logging off. The choice is yours. Forever Sammy.<

>But how will I find this place?<

>Got a tongue in your head, haven't you? Lingual, aren't you?< A sneer in the words made Sammy afraid.

>Wait, wait, how will I know you?<

>You'll know me.<

>I don't even know if you're a man or a woman!<

Pause. >You'll know me.<

Sammy agonized about going. They'd played this game too many times on the Net, with dire consequences, for it to be merely intriguing.

The journey in on the Tube was awful. Sammy's pulse rate rose and fell with the approach and departure of the underground trains. On the Internet it was always possible to touch a button and scuttle away. Real life has no keypad. Throat dry, hands trembling, Sammy kept asking what was to be gained from doing this. But the answer was the same every time. Sammy didn't want to lose Nat. The thought of life without him was worse than the thought of meeting him.

Not only was Nat Sammy's demon lover, Nat was number one best friend. Nat was the only person who could make Sammy fall from a stool laughing, whenever at the keyboard. Sammy had never met anyone half so witty or funny. Presented with a problem, Nat always had something for Sammy. When Sammy's Dad died just five weeks into the relationship, and Mother was useless and remote, Nat was the one who brought Sammy through it, weeping at the keyboard sometimes; and Sammy suspected he was weeping at his end of things, too. Nat was the only person in this world who treated Sammy as an adult, with respect, with recognition, with responsibility.

On reaching the nominated bar Sammy dithered outside for a while, trying but failing to peer through the semi-frosted glass; finally stiffening the sinews and finding the courage to enter. It was dark inside, with a double row of tables lit by soft amber light. A candle burned at each table.

An irritating couple, hopelessly in love, sat holding hands in the corner. Apart from a barman crunching an ice-machine behind the bar, there was only one other person, deep in the gloomy recesses of the bar. Sammy knew instantly it was Nat.

Nat looked up at Sammy, and exhaled a rich blue plume of cigarette smoke. Betraying no sign of recognition, Sammy marched up to the bar and ordered a daiquiri. The barman turned slowly and winched a single eyebrow very high. Sammy tried to outstare him. The barman notched his eyebrow a fraction higher still. Sammy coloured and muttered something about accepting a Coke.

Taking the Coke and sitting at an empty table, Sammy tried to take a drink, the glass colliding with teeth. Nat gathered up cigarettes, lighter, drink and handbag, clearly preparing to come over. For Sammy, everything went slow-mo.

Nat was very tall. Sammy simultaneously marvelled at and was horrified by the extraordinary length of Nat's legs. The calf-muscles were too large. They were exaggerated by stiletto heels and an excessively short skirt. Even under the dim light Sammy could see that Nat wore too much make-up.

When Nat slid into an adjacent seat, Sammy felt suffocated by the scent of cheap perfume. Sammy looked round wildly for that keypad, that escape button. But on this occasion there was no way out. Nat lit another cigarette, offering one for Sammy to decline before extending a hand that wanted shaking. Sammy accepted the hand. It was very large with prominent blue veins, highly manicured and with brightly polished fingernails.

"Sammy?" Sammy nodded an answer. Nat's voice was rather husky. "Does your Mother know you're out?"

"She thinks I'm at a friend's."

"Thought you hadn't got any friends."

"I invented one."

"You sure did." Nat let out a sigh and a lungful of smoke altogether, on which cloud Sammy heard Nat float the word *Christ.* Then, "I'm surprised they even let you in here. If I'd known I'd have arranged to meet you at a milk bar or something. Did you qualify for half-fare on the train?"

"Sorry."

"I suppose that's it, then. Over before it's begun." Nat whisked a compact mirror from his handbag, smoothed an eyebrow and plucked at something in the corner of his eye.

"Is that a wig? You're a – "

"Don't!" Nat said sharply. Then more gently, "It's only words. And I can be anything I want."

Sammy saw the light from the candle starbursting in Nat's eye. "Are you upset?"

"Upset? Listen, kiddiwinks, I've been upset by the best of them. It takes more than a fucking teenybopper to get me upset."

"Shall I go?"

"Yes. Run along. Run along, for Christ's sake."

Sammy got up from his seat. He tried to offer a handshake but Nat wasn't having any of it. He wouldn't even make eye contact. In the end Sammy got out very quickly. In fact he didn't even finish his extremely expensive Coke.

The ride back was a nightmare. Sammy spent the entire journey from Leicester Square to Hounslow with his ears between his knees and the palms of his hands pressed against his flaming cheeks. The other passengers just thought he was a sick boy.

Sammy knew what he had lost. He also felt he had let himself down in a way quite mysterious. Because at the same time he knew it was hopeless. He had, during this brief encounter, stolen a glance at Nat's *kniekehle*. The blue vein in the fold at the back of the knee had pulsated in a manner quite threatening. It was not at all erotic. Indeed it made him feel slightly queasy. The thought, too, of Nat's *cassolette* made him want to faint away.

Some days later he resolved to try to find a new partner, and not on the Net either. But real life wasn't the same. It wasn't possible to converse in the same way. He discovered, with a girl his own age, that ordinary relationships often consisted of spending large blocks of time together saying nothing; whereas on the Net the convention was always to be saying *something*. Even if it amounted to nothing.

Some nights he cruised the chat rooms back on the Net, hoping to stumble across Nat. He suspected Nat had given up, or was going under a different screen name. Once or twice he thought Nat was there, hiding behind a new persona, toying with him. But if it was the case, Nat never let on. After a while Sammy simply let go and stopped looking. But he always knew that he'd been tested, right at the confluence of technology and the flesh, and he'd failed.

Some nights Sammy dreamed of ghosts on the Net, but on waking the dreams made no sense. There are no ghosts of ghosts, he thought. He often considered going to Pinkland and deleting all the music and the pictures and the books. But he never did, even though it hurt him to think of Pinkland unvisited, untenanted, and echoing strangely on the Net forever.

Closer to God

Heather Corinna

They say she came because she heard the singing, say she heard't o'er the cliff on the edge of the Beeks' field, right down under the waves. They say none of us saw her for what she were.

What they say, isn't right, but they'll never know't – I saw what she were, and Alan saw what she were, and I saw the both of them and did naught to stop't, didn't say a word, couldn't even whisper, wouldn't dare. I've sat here outside the church now, each day of 20, watching John carve her face into the pew as they asked him to, and never said a word, not even to tell how her cheeks were a bit more round, nose a bit more sharp, lip more full. Never will to none but myself, not even save God, not even to ask for forgiveness.

Asking the empty air instead that she chose not Alan, but myself, and knowing for all of't, I'd not be forgiven if any knew. I cannot ask God for forgiveness, cannot bear to step foot in that church, knowing myself a traitor, and knowing what I know of perhaps angels, perhaps demons. I cannot be sure, still.

But I can be sure I saw what she were the minute she showed up here, on that Sunday morning, the choir with their faces scrubbed clean and voices sweet. 'Twasn't a soul in town that'd come to church, past ten, but sure as the sunrise, that door opened at half-past and in she came. As a girl, I'd buried myself in books and Bibles, studied the paintings of demons and angels, and never had a doubt in my mind which be which until she came to church at half-past ten that day. She'd slid in right behind me, in the very last pew. Usually, I'd be further up in the rows, but that morning we'd had the tail of a storm that knocked down one solid wall of the barn, and we'd had sheep spread out o'er our hills like a pox.

But you couldn't have missed her coming in, not if you were as close to her as I were. Not if you knew. John and me'd spent half a morning out in the rain, but the smell of salt and sea was nowhere near to as strong on me as 'twere on her. When you're a child, first learning to swim, and you've no sense of when to breathe and when not to, the water gets up in your nose and your throat, the taste of salt near to fills your veins it's so strong, and that's how the scent of her were.

I tried not to stare, less from courtesy than from the matter of being in church and't being Sunday, but it were of no use. Her hair was knotted and damp, but the colour of acorns in fall, her blue eyes bright against the pale white of her skin. She was wrapped in only a blanket, and naught else, and that was hard to ignore, to be certain.

But clearer than day – or than a girl near bare in church who wore the sea instead of her best frock – was that her eyes were on young Alan the moment she came in and sat herself down. Now, Alan was hard to ignore, I confess't. I myself have been drawn to him now and again, but he is, or he'd been, the brother of my eldest friend, and having known him since we were small, even a glance too long felt a bit strange, like staring at a brother. But he does – did – have the sweetest voice of any in the choir, the voice boys have before they get gruff, sweeter than any girl can sing. You could close your eyes when the choir sang and listen to none but Alan – his voice sailed out o'er all of the others, higher and clearer. Closer to God, I truly feel 'twas. Closer to God, even in light of all that happened, and forgive me for thinking so much as to know what God is, to speak such blasphemy, but 'tis the only way I can describe't.

And that day, whether 'twere just his glad spirit – or whether 'twas because she came – 'twas Alan were the angel, and he sounded more lovely than any angel could have, even in dreams.

I heard her behind me weeping, quiet, like a child would weep that didn't want none to know her sorrow. She wept as the choir finished and, when the sermon were done, Alan walked right to her and took her hand, and they stood like that for a good time.

"No!" I'd heard myself shout, not sure why, and slapped my hand to my face just as quick, humiliated I'd shouted in church.

But not a soul'd heard me. Catherine – my closest friend and Alan's sister, as I said – and their folk all went to her, fawning ov'r her, worried for her sad state, and wrapped her up like a parcel with them before I could even catch my breath.

Did they not see? I'm not one for superstition, never have been, and anyone'll tell you I'm a sensible girl, always have been, but she – she wasn't one of us. She wasn't anything I'd seen before and was everything I feared I never would see, and I wanted no one else to have her. I wanted her for my own, and I wanted for her never to have appeared all at once.

Were a handful of Sundays came and went just like that: she'd slip in late, and Alan would sing to the heavens, better and better each time, and she would weep and fill my breath with salt and sea and sorrow, and something else I cannot name for want of't.

But one Sunday, she didn't come. Alan didn't come neither, and then – then – they knew. But I'd known the night before, and I wept with the rest of them, not saying a word, because though they wept out of sadness for losing Alan, I wept out of jealousy.

I wept for not having an angel's voice and the young boy's rosy cheeks that brought him, not myself, to her favour.

Most of all, I'd wept out of shame, feeling my own cheeks burn and turn ashen at thoughts of what I'd seen – or what I'd done, I'll never be certain – the night before. And the shame in knowing there weren't nothing I wouldn't do to do't again.

I'd gone to see Catherine, the sleep still in the corners of my eyes. Though't were early, I'd been trying to finish some mending and had broken my last good needle, and Catherine and I had many times rapped on one another's doors for this thing or that, neither of us being heavy sleepers.

But then I'd heard him, passing the cliff, sweet as a lark, singing high and soft. I wasn't at all sure't wasn't myself daydreaming, and so I'd climbed down a bit, looking, and there he were. There he were standing on the low rocks, tide high, singing to the waves.

Singing to her.

She came out of the waves like an angel, and curled herself upon the cliff at Alan's feet, eyes full of tears or full of salt, I well couldn't say.

I sat still as a stone as I watched Alan halt his tune and kneel down to her, as she took his face in her hands and covered't with her lips, and wrapped her shiny arms round him, pulling the wet clothes from his body, and oh, his eyes glittered like glass, they did.

I tried to turn my face for shame, knowing he were but a boy, but the sight of the ebbing moon o'er his skin, sleek as a selkie, and the roundness of his backside in the dim dawn light pulled my eyes to the scene and wouldn't be letting them go. But he was little to behold in comparison to the sight of her.

'Twere as if she wasn't of the waves, but were the waves herself. I'd swear to't there were more than one of her, but I couldn't say for certain; could only say her lips and arms and tail – that glittering tail of a million bright jewels! – were on him like a thousand currents, all't once. She washed o'er his face, then the smooth swell of his boy's chest, brushing her breasts o'er him, their buds redder than any rose I'd ever seen and there were music to't, too. The crash of water on stone, and then his sighs, high and clear, and her pretty laughter – so loud I were sure all the town'd come running at any moment.

But they could not have heard, for none came. None came as she wrapped her mouth o'er his tall rod and suckled't, milking the thing until cream and water ran down her chin, and I watched dazed – silently cursing myself, for no good Christian woman'd sit and watch such things – but I couldn't move from my place, I was drawn to the scores of arms and limbs from beneath the water covering the boy.

The longer I watched, the more I felt a heat inside me that made me itch and hunger, and the more I watched, the more't seemed that I wasn't watching the creature – or creatures, as't seemed there were many – moving o'er Alan, but moving o'er myself.

My nose were full of salt, but I could feel those cold arms, and sodden hair moving o'er me, a thousand mouths on my lips, my breasts, o'er my stomach and in the cavern between my legs. I could feel the coarse sting of icy spray on my face, and the crags piercing my back, but I could not move, stricken as sure as if I'd been hit by a thunderbolt.

I watched each thin finger weave in and out of every warm crevice, each snakelike tongue dart and lap hungrily and my ears were filled with the sweetest music; sighs upon sighs, as the angels do sing in Heaven so was the sound on that cliff.

I looked for Alan from behind my closed eyes, but I could not open them again, dizzy as I were, and then I felt't upon me – a wild pulsing deep in my belly, and my own heartbeat rang loud in my ears as a drum. Lips pulled at my breasts as the mouths between my legs locked on some hidden place there, nearly drawing my breath from my lungs as't coaxed the heat full from me. I felt I would scream from the intensity of't, but the only cry I heard was Alan's as I floated apart from myself, limbs light as feathers, and I shuddering like a child with the fever.

And then't stopped, as quickly as a dream when you wake up sudden, and 'twas none but me on that cliff, silent and cold, with none but the sound of the waves.

And Alan's voice soft beneath them, carried by laughter. And me, alone, red with shame and green with jealousy, for I was left behind.

They say she came because she heard the singing, say she heard't o'er the cliff on the edge of the Beeks' field, right down under the waves. They say none of us saw her for what she were, as she sat in that last pew but every Sunday, blanket o'er her legs, they say that even Alan didn't see until 'twas too late. They say – now, they say — that surely 'twas a curse upon us, but if 'twere, then I am a heathen, for how I long for those demons again. Some few say 'twere a blessing, but if that be so, I ha'been passed o'er for heaven by the angels themselves. In any event, I cannot step into church again, knowing I be either scorned by angels, or am in thrall with devils. They say I am simply too heavy with grief about Alan. What they say 'tisn't right, but they'll never know't.

They say to John to carve her face into the last pew, so as to warn others that might come that we know of them, and will not be fooled again. I say naught a thing – but watch as he carves her beautiful face, hoping they come again, and mistake't instead for a welcome, and I spend my Sundays instead on the cliffs, learning to sing, closer to God.

The Notebooks of Gatling Wessex

Larry Tritten

Volume I

Where pornography ends and literary merit begins is a question that has long vexed scholars of literary erotica. It can be answered graphically with several pages from *The Notebooks of Gatling Wessex,* the work of a self-avowed pornographer who has written about sex with an intensity and poetry that would rank him as a great writer in any other field. Wessex's career has been distinguished by an extraordinary level of craftsmanship. From the ambitious searching of early novels such as *A Legend in His Own Pants* and *Knee-Deep in Nectar* through the mature perversity of middle-period novels such as *Blondes in Brass Brassieres, Pig-Iron Panties and Galvanized Garter Belts* and *Slaves of the House of Pancakes* to the experimental boldness of *Post-Holocaust Proctologist* and *Corgi and Bess,* his work has always illuminated sexuality with literary deftness. Here, for the scholar of eroticism – or the merely horny readers – is a selection from his recently published notebooks.

Stray Thoughts
- Extrasensory perversion – "Don't come in my mind!"
- What does it say on the bottom of a Coke bottle on Lesbos? USE OTHER END.
- Woman raped by ghost, impregnated with ectogism.
- Ambition – To be the 50-Foot Woman's gynaecologist.
- Poetic fetish – Eating food left on plates in cafeterias by

beautiful women.
- Some women are born to greatness, others have it thrust into them.
- Dream – In Museum of Modern Art, he enters candlelit room labelled MÉNAGE À TROIS in which two people are making love on a couch.

Scenes
"Ouch!" he gasped.

"Relax," she whispered. Her tongue made its debut below his waist. It seemed as if a mouthful of hummingbirds had been released upon his shaft. He watched wide-eyed, then narrow-eyed, and then with his eyes squeezed shut but his mind's eye resuming the view as her tongue whirled, swirled, skipped, skittered and flickered across the pulsing catwalk of his cock. As the sensation sweetened, the nerves in his cock began a tactile tinkling, like wind chimes in a sirocco. His buttocks oscillated. Her nostrils flared. She suckled him with vivid passion and, as he watched, her mouth became a churning vortex into which he feared he might be drawn and vanish, cock first. In the meantime, time froze solid, then a few aeons thawed slowly, one at a time; and the next thing he knew, he was climaxing with a series of sensations like high hurdles leaped against a driving wind, and she was making a sound like a somnolent turkey backed into a table fan.

"I say that man is *innately* sensual," Colander said, unzipping his pants and waggling his fingers with comical vulgarity at his hostess across the crowded room as he spoke, "that as long as he has an appendage, he'll look for vacancies to fill; and as long as he has access to an orifice, he'll look to its tenancy. After all, nature *abhors a vacuum . . .*" He left the sentence resonating in our minds and, as if to demonstrate his point, drew a throbbing erection into view and soared off in its wake toward the nearest blonde.

During the 60th second of their lovemaking and with the 120th stroke of his phallus (each one embellished by a stylish sideways twist on the backstroke), Karen had an orgasm so powerful that she felt totally subsidiary to it, which meant, she supposed, that the orgasm had really had *her* – she was its, its clearly subservient and spectacularly sentient servant; and then, all at once, the neural whirlpool into which her senses spun her became more chaotic as another and continuing orgasm jerked and jolted her this way and that, reminding her of the clunky banging of an unruly washing machine's rotator near the end of a spin-dry cycle. Yet she herself was no more dry than monsoon earth – she was in a briny sweat, and all of her vulvar musculature was vividly wet with interior leakage, like the inside of a pink submarine whose seams are beginning to burst inwards from skilful depth-charging.

"Say it," she said.

"I want you," he gurgled.

"On your knees, litter brain," she cannonaded. He was there at once, and she extended one leg, the sole of her leather boot directly at his lips. She had been to the theatre, and the bottom of the boot was brindled with dried cola syrup, a single jujube bonded to its surface, the ruby candy crushed and blackened from her walk through the slums.

As his affenpinscher might, he tugged at the candy with his teeth and would have had it, too, if a sudden Charley horse hadn't seized her, spasming her leg and throwing her to the floor, where she went through a series of thrashing convulsions, massaging and hammering at her leg frantically until the pain slowly dissipated.

"Time out," she whimpered, and he knew the mood had been lost.

"Who's your favorite analyst?" she asked.

"Rank," he said, smiling. "Otto Rank. Who's yours?"

"Horney," she said, returning his smile. "Karen Horney."

"Rank," he mused.

"And Horney," she grinned.

They gave each other a nosebleed in their rush to fuck.

In the Cimmerian darkness, he would have to find her by the scent alone, that was the game; and in a 40-room chateau, it would not necessarily be easy – yet the moment it began, his olfactory nerves were tingling with the distant bouquet of her sex, that ineffable fragrance of burnt sugar, shellfish buffets and storm-flagellated dahlias when the winds bore away and a pale gilding of sunlight brightened them. The molecules of smell seeming to sparkle in his nose like the effervescent bubbles of a carbonated drink, he was virtually drawn along by his nose, and he found her finally on the second floor in a bedroom, supine and ready, the hot magnet of her redolence pulling his face into the palpy shoals of her cloven vulva with a soft adhesive bunting of lips and chin; and it was in that glorious moment that he sprained his tongue yearning for her cervix, for his tongue was, alas, somewhat shorter than any other part of himself with which he had also failed to touch the gossamer bottom, the ultimate oyster with its apocalyptic pearl just beyond reach in the sodden abyss of the cozy chasm.

"Oh, wow," she gasped in the aftermath, her face ashen, cunt rumpled, her eyes bluer by a shade. "Where'd you learn to give head like that?"

He grinned. "Took lessons," he said. "From a lesbian yogi. She could tumble a hassock with her tongue. Why? Ya like it?" But he was already talking to a corpse.

Novella had a penchant for duplex sex (as she called it): taking one penis into her mouth while another impaled her vaginally or anally. She'd come a long way, she thought, since those virginal days when her sex had been like a studio apartment visited only by a familiar thumb or forefinger, which loved the ambience and stayed for hours on end.

During timeless nights, she taught him all she had learned from the Incarnadine Countess and her Carnelian Acolytes. Where once he had startled her by buffing his penis on a razor strop while readying for a set-to, now the tricks she could show him made that seem like a trivial novelty: her cloister had become a veritable machinery of agile musculature whose soft wheels, resilient rollers and subterranean gizmos commenced a turbulent pulsating and clutching that astonished him with its precision – it was like a gilding of the very lily of sentience, and in its throes it seemed as if his penis were a celestial cud being worked and reworked by the mouth of some divine bovine; he felt as if the neurons all along its sultry length were being irradiated and marinated in a sort of effervescent salt brine. She belaboured him with her cunt: her mobile vulva chewed him over methodically, like a loving dog with soft electric teeth, and when she had achieved her own orgasm, which he recognized by a gaudy cry like that of a peacock flushed from cover by a Fauvist gamesman, she brought him off as well with a sudden series of muscular tugs and primpings analogous to those of a mother urging her son onto a public school stage for a holiday performance.

She came for the first time not with a bang but with a whimper. But by the end of their honeymoon, she would bring psychic luggage for each orgasmic journey, monogrammed and covered with travel stickers from Xanadu, Shangri La, Valhalla and, of course, Baton Rouge.

Concussion! Convulsion! Haroldine undulated with orgasm, coming in great whopping spasms, coming, coming, coming, coming, coming, coming, coming and coming again (after all, the sign on the door had suggested it!), and as the roaring waves of release carried her onto the hot beach of fulfilment, she felt more erotically pleased than she had ever felt before, as if she had just stepped from a solitary confinement cell, been ushered into a lilac Rolls-Royce and driven along a jungle highway where all the trees dripped sperm in the aftermath of an extraordinary storm that would have every bird and animal staring skywards for days to come.

It was in her night-time dreams that her daydreams came true. There, freed from the cold bondage of her priggish upbringing, her hothouse fantasies blossomed in candy colours: she crawled through an orgy in a pitch-dark room, tasting everything she touched until the flavours made her brain ring like a holiday bell; she performed a fantastic cartwheel through a constellation of stars and blue moons onto a cosmic buffet table where she lay amid the viandes and desserts, dappled with sauce, prinked with flecks of celestial mayonnaise and meringue and sweet adhesive gravies, herself the *pièce de résistance* for the gods and goddesses who began to jostle one another in competition to taste her hot and savoury corpus; she drank ginger beer from the black-leather boot of a countess while the lovely lady's toe tickled sparks of orgasm from the tender tinder of her clit; and she swung on a braided golden rope across a huge ballroom where a host of naked lords and ladies played a roistering parlour game on all fours, dropping herself carefully and with unerring accuracy onto an uptilted erection that her plush sex encapsulated as smoothly as a velvet glove did a well-manicured hand.

Without women, Grayson learned, men do strange things. In the twilit yard, he came upon a heayy-set man from Prague who had tricked up his penis in a little dirndl and sketched a likeness of a female face on his glans. He was engaged in the act of trying to bob his mouth down low enough to kiss the minuscule face and that with a bad back, as Ivan would later point out in the infirmary.

Volume II

Where pornography and literature intersect is where we find Gatling Wessex, the author of such novels as *A Legend in His Own Pants*; *Blondes in Brass Brassieres, Pig-Iron Panties and Galvanized Garter Belts*; *In Vulva Veritas*; *Buggering Heights*; *The Hershey Highwayman on the Cadbury Canal* (and 116 others!). A self-confessed pornographer who has said that he "considers arousing the reader sexually no less important than the self-consciously arty inkslinger's goal of cozying the critics", Wessex has been described by John Updike as "a writer who brings up refreshing quaffs of briny liquor from the well of the libido" and by Norman Mailer as a writer "whose work is a form of psychosexual football full of primal scrums and prurient scrimmages."

Here, for the scholar of erotica, or the one-handed reader, is a selection from the recently published *Notebooks of Gatling Wessex*, Volume II (Onan & Sons, $14.95).

Ideas, Thoughts

- Horror story – Man who returns to the womb, is subsequently evicted and forced to move into anus.
- Science fiction – Woman has appointment with extraterrestrial gynaecologist.
- Closing line – Up yours truly.
- Breaches of sexual etiquette – Masturbating under mistletoe; Kneeling to kiss the bride.
- Male child of couple who named daughter Chastity – Celibacy.
- Laws – Law of Contraception – Invention prevents the necessity of motherhood.
    Theory of Bisexual Relativity – $E=AC/DC^2$.
- Characters names for western – Spread Eagle; Split Beaver; Little Big Tits; Head Over Hooves.
- Censorship, sunk off Virgin Islands, with no survivors.
- Monogamy as symptom of disease misogyny.
- Two subliminal messages – The penis is mightier than the sword.
    The rapist.
- Modern love story formula:
  Boy meets girl or boy or boy/girl (transexual or bisexual)
  Boy loses girl or boy or boy/girl
  Boy gets girl or boy or boy/girl.
- Sex organs of Irish women – Labia majora, labia minora, labia begorrah.
- Militant feminist sexual position – Woman on top, man overboard.
- TV Shows – *I Dream of Genet, The Santa Barbarians, The Bel Airheads, The Sherman Oakies Parallel History Playhouse* (Première – Japanese bomb Pearl Bailey) *A Streetcar Named Desire Under the Elms The Invisible Nudist History of Elements* (Première – Curie's radium & Dworkin's feminesium).

Scenes

Not for nothing was he a mathematician. He divided her legs and added his body to hers, then began to do immeasurably pleasurable things with their figures, multiplying sensations, faster than any computer, losing himself in the soft geometry of her vital statistics, their libidos mutually entwining like an exercise in hot topology. His cock was harder than advanced calculus.

"*Soixante-neuf, soixante-neuf!*" she begged, reaching for the ceiling as he plowed her like the proverbial north forty. But, alas, he did not speak French and thought she was sneezing.

Later, in the aftermath, she would reach for his abacus and only half playfully attempt to lodge it in an uncomfortable place, while whispering to him a bit of advice on the value of learning a little about Language Arts.

Dr Spender followed the guttering candle flame through the musty corridor, glancing carefully about at the walls and ceiling for spiders or whatever other cryptic horrors might lurk within the vault. Alicia was close behind him and he reached back his hand to touch hers lightly as if to impart assurance.

The corridor yielded into a larger area and they found themselves standing in the funeral chamber itself, a room dominated by a great stone catafalque upon which rested a casket of gold which even in this tenebrous atmosphere shone like the light of the sun. Dr Spender held the candle aloft and saw that the walls had been decorated with *bas relief* cunts in an amazing profusion of styles – cunts like orchids and roses and hyacinths and African violets, all in a riot of gaudy efflorescence, each labial fold and interior petal beautifully articulated; cunts like the entrances to sinister caves and alluring seaside grottos; great menacing cunts like the thirsting maws of mythical beasts wherein might lurk viperish tongues or carnivorous dentation; cunts like the portals and doorways to palatial rooms and rich storehouses; wondrous cunts like magical mathematical vortices into which one might plunge like Alice down the rabbit hole into a subterranean wonderland. They were surrounded by bouquets and tableaux and displays of fabulous cunts.

"Well, we certainly know what he liked," Dr Spender understated, spellbound by the sight.

"Marvellous," Alicia breathed, and her voice, void of any professorial detachment, was like that of a child on Christmas morning.

"Indeed," Dr Spender said. And "I . . . I . . . I seem to be having some trouble with this zipper, Alicia. Could you give me a hand?"

In his twenty years of knocking around the civilized galaxies, Filbert had done it *all*, he thought with quiet satisfaction as he reviewed his sex life. He had been to interspecies orgies, triple moon singles bars, extraterrestrial brothels, android swing parties, and incarnadine carnivals in all of the sexiest constellations. He'd suckled lactating ladies all throughout the Milky Way, done it Dog Star doggiestyle, and made both moons of Uranus revolve during the Anal Spelunkers Ball on Buttworld. He'd tried all of the water sports on Oceanus with bisexual (literally!) mermaids. He'd had a Jovian fellatrice with an extensible tongue give him a blow job from around the corner and gone to a bicolour orgy with a colourful lady with kaleidoscope eyes, piebald hair, and plaid erogenous zones. He'd had a mutant girl introduce him to green showers, clump humps, and drool jobs. He'd experienced Venusian pinatas, methane sponges, pink smorgasbords, and blob jobs. He'd gone down the sluice tube and had the jelly wallow with Megadork on Cygnus IV and submitted to black and blue bondage on the fabled Planet of the Blondes. He'd been mindfucked by telepaths, tried the Big Hot Softy with Zug Zug, and ridden the sodden subway with pinkheads and mutables on Little Old New Sweden.

At least Filbert *thought* he'd done it all. But that was before Scrump and Bunny *****berg spazzled into the room, making him realize that everything that had gone before was in all likelihood mere prologue.

Normally a somewhat restrained, if not downright phlegmatic lover, Mullings found that the aphrodisiac gave him incentive to fuck with a flamboyant panache, delving into Pammy with strokes so impassioned that each one banged her head against the bed's headboard, making her intermittently cry "Oww!" through bitten lips and whoop like a distressed crane beached in the wash of an oil-spill tide. At some point Mullings seemed like a mere addendum to his dick, which definitely had its own notions about how to fuck, ranging from banging away nonstop like a Bofors Gun to veering and twisting at odd angles like a carnal divining rod seeking the secret flume of Pammy's G-spot. Coming, normally a quick businesslike spritzing and subsequent falling away, was this time more analagous to the Big Bang theory of the creation of the universe, and Mullings lost consciousness as he pitched from the bed in the manner of one of the Flying Wallendas executing a triple somersault. Moments later, waking, he would discover Pammy tugging at his arm and asking in a dazed voice if he had any spare change, the ceiling sprinkler system showering them with water, and the sound of his car's alarm ululating urgently from the nearby garage.

"Fuck you!" Rorketon said, putting both hands on the bar and staring at the stranger.

"And fuck *you*, too, buddy!" the stranger replied in a voice with no humour in it whatever.

"Fuck ewe!" the shepherd called cheerfully from his table across the room.

"*Fuck you!*" both Rorketon and the stranger shouted simultaneously at the shepherd.

"Fuck Hugh," said a fellow at the end of the bar wistfully, for that was his lover's name.

"Ah, good old Fuck U," another fellow at the bar said nostalgically. "Class of '69. Good times. Co-educational in all the best ways. No wonder I ejaculated when I matriculated." And he blew the foam off his beer to emphasize the statement.

Plimsoll did not consider it successful cunnilingus unless when he finished he had a milk moustache, a sprained tongue, a duplex smile, and a tendency to swing his head involuntarily to and fro like a bass following a zig-zag lure. Retention of sentience was mandatory, and perhaps the best proof of a superior session was a mind whose thoughts were as successively blurred as the figure in Duchamps' *Nude Descending a*

Staircase, although a hard on you could bend horseshoes on was pretty good, too.

An inveterate leg man all his life, Drupes switched preferences in a fraction of a second after his first sight of Fancy. She swayed across his line of vision with that seemingly slightly buoyant stride of hers induced by a pair of breasts so aerodynamically implausible that the combination of convexity and resilience could only be accounted for by some mystical collaboration of physics and biology, and as she lilted past, evoking subsidiary visions of London beneath flotillas of barrage balloons and the Macy Thanksgiving Day parade, he thought: I wonder if she's leaving her body to science fiction. Hitherto a certifiable leg man who could either take tits or leave them, Drupes' mind was suddenly ravished by the zestful palindromic *bounce* of the word *tit*, and as Fancy hove to like some earthbound UFO he felt himself being drawn along in her wake as if by some preternatural force. And as he followed her, seeming to walk on air himself in response to her virtually levitational gait, he knew one thing for absolutely certain: Tit City was where he planned on dwelling from here on in.

Some of Harry's ideas, like the novelty fake semen blot, Spanish fly paper, and the scratch & sniff centrefold were, Melton felt, ambitious but crazier than roller skates on a race horse. On the other hand, *a pussy-flavoured soft drink . . . !* The more he thought about it, the thirstier he got, and before he knew it he was writing a cheque and drawing up a partner's contract. After all, the success of pet rocks was enough to give any investor the boldest of hopes.

In recurring dreams Custody was repeatedly seduced by Rambeau, a renegade militant lesbian lover who worked her over so skilfully with a Browning Automatic Dildo and Gatling vibrator that she died from the pleasure, tongue extruded and a little puff of steam rising from her riddled cunt. In the next scene she was either awarded the Purple Heart by Eros at a ceremony in Washington AC/DC and/or given a heroine's burial at Arlington, with Cupids firing a 21-arrow salute as she was lowered into the ground in a pink casket and wearing a smile no mortician could ever erase.

"Have you ever *seen* an orgasm?" she asked him with a bemused smile, speaking to him as if he were a child.

"That doesn't mean they don't exist," he said. "Have you ever seen atoms? Molecules? The Easter Bunny? Spokane? No, but we know that they exist."

She looked away sceptically, but she was already remembering the wonderful chocolate and candy eggs that had always been waiting for her on Easter morning and the time when a cousin of hers who claimed to have been to Spokane talked about missing a connecting flight there and having to wait for so many hours that there could hardly have been any doubt at all that such a place really did exist.

Geranium had written a series of erotic stories for the German men's magazine, *Schwank*, using the nom de plume Tse Tse Ella Mare, stories with titles like *Sans Panties Andante*; *Scumbunny*; *Rumpler*; *Pumpernickel and Wurst*; *Groceries in the Dark*; and *Lesbian Thespian Aphrodisiactors*. At first she had confronted writing the stories as a task, but in no time at all she had been seduced by the vicarious pleasure of rendering her sexual fantasies in prose that waxed from purple through platinum to burgundy and bice, and as she really went with the flow she had found herself typing with one hand only, each printed syllable seeming to simmer in the wake of the stroking keys, every comma seeming to waggle like the tongue of a salivating satyr as she piled her prose into orgiastic clumps, licking her lips and flexing her toes as she raced every fictional orgasm to a collaborative climax with the action in her lap.

Each day at lunchtime the dyke in the serving line whose breasts filled her grey prison blouse to voluminous capacity like two basketballs (and who had the name Tinker Bull tattooed on one bicep) would give Snook the eye and exhibit a series of little mouthing gestures and enticing moues like someone practising a Marilyn Monroe impression. On this particular day the dyke was serving hamburger patties with tongs and as she plopped a patty into Snook's compartmentalized tray, she reached out with the tongs and deftly snared one of Snook's nipples through the thin fabric of her blouse, holding it in delicate abeyance and staring straight into Snook's eyes. "Say *uncle*," she said. It was precisely the wrong thing to say, for one of Snook's pet peeves was the fact that there is no term in English the equivalent of the word avuncular that means "like an aunt". She caromed her tray off the dyke's head and lunged over the serving line, seizing her by the throat. The two writhed wildly on the floor, biting, kicking, and scratching, and probably would have killed each other if by some curious twist of fate Snook hadn't fallen deeply in love halfway through the fray.

Chi Chi gurgled like an emptying sink as her orgasms abated, and she clawed at the sand as if to anchor herself to the earth. Her expended body smelled like a newly opened package of fragrances: her sweat had the scent of an aphrodisiacal champagne fermented in the nuclei of her pores by some mystical erotic alchemy; an odour of ripe sylvan herbage rose from her excavated asshole; and her cunt gave off the wondrous redolent fetor of seaweed strewn surf and tangerine reefs and lilac sea beasts languishing in tidal pools.

She could only have wished for one thing more, and that wish was granted, at least metaphorically, as the bank of lavender-blue clouds overhead yielded up a shower of warm rain, golden in the sunlight, a gift from the water spirit Undine to whom the whole world was a bathroom where no towels were needed.

"Smell my fingers," Gala said, thrusting them at Bruin. "Where do you think they've been?"

Bruin looked at the peachblossom-pink fingernails, then took a sniff, tentatively. "Making tuna salad?" he guessed.

"Nope."

"Uh, picking anchovies off a pizza."

"Nope."

He tried one more time. "Baiting hooks?"

"Nope," Gala said, grinning. "Giving starfish artificial respiration." She laughed, and gave Bruin a punch on the arm that propelled him off of his stool.

Sam

Cheyenne Blue

I inherited Sam when I moved into my crumbling apartment. Most people find cockroaches under the sink or a stray cat in the back yard. I found a ghost who liked to fuck.

I was living alone for the first time in my life. There wasn't much money after the divorce and my credit rating was so bad that it was hard to find somewhere to live. The decaying concrete-block apartments were on the wrong side of Broadway, so the managers were less fussy in their choice of tenants. They let me live there; and apparently, at one time, they had let Sam live there. Most people eventually left. Sam stayed on.

At first I thought he was a dream, a sensual sojourn, a fantasy. Light, barely-there fingers caressed my skin one night, just the hint of their touch, just enough to raise the fine hairs into awareness. The rustle of the sheets as they were lowered to bare my breasts, the kiss of the moon and the streetlights shining through the narrow window: it all felt like part of my somnolent state.

Open questing lips drifted down from my neck to nestle in the valley between my breasts. A whispered sigh. I shifted slightly to encourage my dream lover to explore my nipples, already hardening in anticipation. I kept my eyes closed. I did not want to wake from this sensual lethargy in a hurry. I pressed my legs tightly together to build the ache of climax. I knew that if I moved to rub myself I'd wake up – and I didn't want this beautiful torment to end.

The mouth moved to my nipples and circled around them, hot and wet. When the mouth started meandering down my belly I couldn't hold back any longer. Even if it meant waking up, I had to masturbate. I dropped my hand to the clutch of hair between my legs. It encountered a brief resistance, as if the air were denser somehow. When I moved my fingers into my slick-oil folds, the mouth moved back to my breast.

Even through my spiralling arousal, my fogged brain realized something wan't right. I was awake, no doubt about it. Yet lips still closed over my nipple. I raised my head and looked down over my body. Nothing. The air seemed to distort slightly, to ripple and coalesce into a denser pattern, like mist floating in from the sea. It drifted upwards and my skin shivered with the absence of touch.

"Who's there?" I cursed my voice for wavering.

There was no answer, of course.

My arousal withered and dried. I was spooked enough to get dressed, turn on the light, and sit by the open window nursing a cup of cold coffee until morning.

Next day I asked Marisa, my neighbour, if she had heard of anything strange ever happening in my apartment.

She grinned her wide, white smile. "Met Sam, have you? Annie, who lived there before you, swore she'd never move out! Said that ghost was better lovin' than any man she ever had." Marisa rolled her eyes. "And hon, let me tell you, she had a few men!"

"Ghost?" My voice was surprisingly steady.

Marisa shrugged. "Nobody knows for sure," she said. "What else do you call a phantom who makes the sweetest love this side of heaven?"

"He made love to her?" My curiosity was roused.

"Oh, hon, he did! Some mornings Annie walked bow-legged. She said," Marisa's voice dropped to a confiding whisper, "that no one gave her orgasms like Sam did. Three, four times a night. He doesn't come every night, but when he does, he doesn't leave until morning."

"Why's he called Sam? Was he someone who lived here once? How did he die?"

Marisa shrugged. "Don't know," she said. "Annie called him Sam. Said she needed a name to call when she came; Sam seemed as good as any."

"Why did Annie leave?"

"Didn't do it willingly. She didn't want to leave Sam. But her mom got sick and she had to move back to Cleveland. She kinda hoped Sam might follow her there, but I guess he didn't." She kicked the doormat with her toe. "Guess he likes Denver."

"Did Annie have a boyfriend?"

"She did when she moved here. He didn't last long. She said Sam was better than any flesh-and-blood man, but when she brought someone home he didn't seem to mind. Said she sensed him watching." She giggled. "Not the jealous kind. The perfect man – or ghost."

I was beginning to like the sound of this.

Marisa winked. "Hon, if you move out, tell me. I might just switch apartments."

That night I stripped and climbed into bed, the sheet bunched down around my waist, my breasts invitingly uplifted. He didn't come. Not that night, nor the ones after that. I was beginning to think that it was all my imagination.

That was when he came.

It was midnight, and I was in that hazy stage between sleep and consciousness, that elusive floating stage when the soul leaves the body and pirouettes around the room. When the mind can finally make random leaps to solve impossible problems. The weary end of the day when every muscle liquefies, so that you sink into the mattress, bonelessly, until the edges of your body blur.

I felt a soft touch on my mouth. A welcome-home kiss. I waited, my heart pounding in anticipation, to see if it was repeated. Again, the merest brush whispered over my lips. I opened my mouth slightly, trying to breathe silently, and I felt a tongue insinuating itself into my mouth. It twisted around my tongue and withdrew.

"Hello, Sam." I whispered the words into the charged air.

There was no answer, but I could feel the corners of his

mouth turn up as he smiled against my skin. He lapped his way down my neck, pausing to lave a collarbone before trailing his way down to my breasts. I turned slightly, encouraging him to take my nipple. He didn't disappoint; I felt the warm wetness as he closed over my breast.

With a shock, I felt a disembodied hand cup my other breast. It hadn't occurred to me to wonder if Sam had hands as well as a mouth. My acceptance must have encouraged him to become bolder. His hands slid over my skin with the drifting touch I preferred; not rough human hands with their too-heavy press, but a reverent glissade of sensation.

The mouth moved down my belly, lapping, sucking me with open-mouthed kisses that had me writhing as I realized his ultimate destination. I reached to tangle his hair, to steady his head and direct that mouth where I wanted it most, but my hands passed through a slight heaviness in the air, nothing more. Sam didn't need direction, though; crawling fingers nudged my thighs apart, and those same illusionary fingers crept up my inner thigh to touch the damp curls of my sex. Just when I thought he would push his finger into me, it retreated, to walk its way up the other thigh. It skated briefly over my clit and fell back.

It was a carefully planned assault. Advance, retreat, push forward, fall back: taking me on a roller-coaster ride to release. I don't know when I started begging, when I wanted the promised orgasm more than pride, when the soaked and twisted sheets under my fingers bunched and wound around my hands – but when the promise alone had become too much, I felt Sam's mouth on my sex, felt the damp rasp of a tongue as his mouth closed over me. I felt the cat-like flicker of his tongue lapping my clit until I howled, sobbing with release.

I took a shuddering breath, and another, and I felt his whole mouth descend once more, slurping and suckling, fierce and demanding, until my whole body shuddered through a second climax, shocking and sudden. I'd never come twice. Not until Sam.

I lay and let the aftershocks wash over my body. How do you thank a lover who wasn't really there? I could hardly offer him coffee and lead him to the door. But Sam wasn't finished. I sprawled in wet abandon on the mattress. My body was already missing the touch of his mouth when I felt the briefest whisper of a kiss on my lips. I dipped my tongue into his mouth, missing the taste of myself when a lover kisses after going down on you. But then . . .

There was not the weight of a body lying over me, nor the rasp of wiry hairs on the insides of my thighs. There was simply the unmistakable feeling of fullness, of a fat, turgid penis pushing inside me. I gasped and angled my pelvis to better accept his thrusts. He continued to push, slowly, until he was sheathed all the way. He was large. He was thick and firm. I clenched to see if I could feel contours, to see if his fatness was illusory. He swelled inside me and I felt the glorious friction of real sex as he began to move slowly in and out.

I reached between my legs, curious to see what he felt like. I missed encountering hairy sacks, but I ran a finger around my stretched opening. This was no illusion: someone, something, was inside me, fucking me to a steady rhythm. I moved my hand, unsure of where to place it. There were no buttocks to grasp, no back to run my hand along, no balls to tease. I settled for grasping the mattress on either side of me, and let him fuck me.

He held a relentless, slow-building tempo. The sensation of one-dimensional sex was initially unnerving. The only sensation was that of limited touch; there was no body resting on mine, no musky male sweat; the only scent was my own sharp arousal. There weren't the grunts and groans and creaks of lovemaking. There wasn't the visual stimulus of a body lost in pleasure. No, it was more like masturbating with a vibrator – except that I didn't have to do the work.

My analytic fancy shattered as he brought me sweetly towards climax. I was amazed: I'd never come from penetration alone. Sam moved faster now in my wetness. His thrusts disintegrated into the jagged spurts of a man on the brink. As I spasmed around him, I felt his unmistakable wet, spreading warmth inside.

I relaxed. He relaxed. I could feel him softening; his spend, viscous and hot, trickled onto the bed. I put a finger down to catch it but, like the phallus, it was an illusion.

"Sam." I spoke his name out loud. "You can come back any time."

His head was between my legs again. I was wrapped in the cocoon of his satisfaction.

I stayed in that apartment for seven years. Sam stayed with me all that time. Even when I had a near-serious, near-permanent relationship with Richard, I always made sure I was alone at least one night every week for Sam. Eventually Richard left, but Sam stayed.

The eviction notice came as a shock. I knew my rundown neighbourhood was becoming trendy as real estate prices in Denver soared, but I hadn't expected it to change that quickly. They were pulling down the old apartments and building modern condominiums. Luxury buildings, ridiculous prices.

That night, after Sam's loving had made me weak from more than sex, I told him. "Come with me," I said. "I don't know where I'm going yet, but please, come, too."

There was no answer. There never was on those few occasions that I had addressed him directly, but I thought I detected a palpable sadness. I knew then: Sam would never leave this space.

I live on the other side of Broadway now, in a sleek modern condominium that echoes with loneliness, especially on the hot dry Denver nights that remind me most of Sam. His apartment is long gone, but I've studied the block that has risen in its place. Apartment 3C. That is his space. I never knew the exact boundaries of his realm, but apartment 3C contains the space that used to be the bedroom. In the five years since its construction, that apartment has come on the market six times.

I've saved and have the deposit now; the next time apartment 3C is for sale, I'll be ready.

I hope Sam remembers me.

Madam Petra

Mark Ramsden

Veins full of warm champagne. A warm, honey glow spreading through the midriff. A reason to smile on a grey, winter morning. I never leave Petra's place without fond memories, and a presence that stays with me through the day. This spirit double seems to be compounded by her big pussycat smile, her scent, and her big, beautiful body. Her hour glass figure was once thought to be the ideal female shape – and still is in hotter parts of the world. (And why isn't there a better ready-made expression for "woman-shaped"? You still have to use "hour glass". Although we don't tend to measure time with sand any more). She has blonde hair hanging in thick thatches down to a joyously deep and full bosom. She's big. Weighty. Broadly luscious and amply bountiful. Big-brained, big-hearted, big-chested and big-mouthed – although she may prefer to be described as assertive. She is a substantial presence, most especially when sat on your face. And hard to miss anywhere else.

She is earthy, rich and mulchy. Fertile soil, which responds well to diligent prodding. Something to dig your fingers into. Real food for real men. Not so much comfort food (the Magnificent Petra is never merely comfortable) – more like the hottest chili on earth; a meal that challenges you to finish it. Some prefer sushi (or pretend to like it, or need to be seen eating it). But there are times when warriors need to feast. And there is nobody better to gorge upon than the pouting

Petra. She is a ten-course banquet, washed down by tankards of foaming ale. She is richly rewarding. And fortifying – if you have the strength to take her on in the first place.

Petra and I used to be a guilty secret, then something my wife could join in with. And now we're inseparable. All of us. Cosy as this is, it's not generally a good idea to try to praise two goddesses simultaneously. If you value your life. So we will leave my wife and Petra snuggled up together for another time. In the fervent hope they will still let me in. It can't be too long before they start to wonder: what do we need the bald guy for? Despite her strength and magnificence even Petra has occasional problems with self-esteem. Anyone big has to have a problem while too many men seek skeletal women as trophies. Hoping to enhance their status. Among other drips. But real men feast on flesh. Well, that all sounds bracingly manly; in the old sense of hale and hearty. We just need the drunken cry of "I am a Genius!" and we might have the start of a Henry Miller pastiche. But it's hard to resist trying to be epic when one is haunted by Madam Petra.

Maybe that's the secret; she is not merely human. How else could a working lawyer learn sword-fighting, hand-to-hand combat, spell-casting, accurate divination and the extremely esoteric practice of High Art textile-weaving? As you enter her boudoir you will be awed by the large loom, a rickety wooden structure that looks more dangerous than the rack of teasers and tweakers hung next to her St Andrew's Cross. Petra produces her art on this contraption (although most of the public, including me, is more interested in what happens on the St Andrew's Cross). Her textiles perform no useful purpose other than looking interesting – if you know what to look for, and have done a bit of weaving yourself. Even then you still might find the viewing an uncomfortably intense and harrowing experience.

But I'd keep it to yourself if I were you. She has a bit of a temper. Which is not enhanced by the current indifference of the world in general towards avant-garde textile art. Your average skill-free conceptualist would say, her work is "merely decorative". She is "only" a craftsperson. For whatever reason she never wanted to be a foul-mouthed drunk shooting cack-handed videos of nothing much – a reliable indicator of genius in the art business, as we speak.

Her day job is the law, practised for the good of the people, most especially women who have suffered rape and domestic violence at the hands of men. She's been doing it for about 20 years. And a couple of decades watching what happens in the courts and working with the abusers and the abused . . . she is not short of righteous indignation. Some of this gets taken out on submissive men and sometimes it is her weaving loom which gets a sound thrashing. The loom is right next to the bed: both wooden structures that creak a lot. If her partners ever pall she swings her legs out from under the duvet and seats herself in front of some hapless fabric and proceeds to rattle out a challenging new creation.

She mutters curses as she weaves – the loom clattering and seething. Germanic magic does involve whispering spells while knotting rope – sometimes around people's necks – but it's best not to know too much about this. There's few enough seekers on the path as it is, without accidental fatalities further thinning out the flock. You may think I'm a bit cowardly for refusing to sample oxygen-deprived sex. I just keep remembering all those guys who get the mathematics wrong – and there are only two seconds in which you can decide whether you are experiencing the best rush ever or is that the grim reaper knocking on the door? Maybe it is. I'll just . . . Oh Dear . . .

You may disagree. If so, why not contact the British Auto-Erotic Asphyxiation Society? They're usually looking for new members. All you need is the annual subscription and a suit that looks good at funerals.

As Petra weaves, her blonde hair dangles over the whining wood, perilously close to becoming part of the woven fabric. Somehow, she is never dragged into her threshing machine. Perhaps it is because she is a witch – an initiate into most current covens. She has danced with the Druids and swung with the sorcerers. And once you've done all that you are less likely to want to pretend that flower remedies work. Or that your Native American spirit guide is always watching you. Or that "issues concerning power caused your boiler to collapse" (advice, from a reputable medium, during the cold snap of 2001). Let's face it, if New Age remedies fixed anything, sweet Diana Spencer would have been well. Instead of quite ill.

Some flowers get trodden underfoot but no one is going to step on Petra. She is a warrior – hot words and cold steel. After a few years with Petra it was becoming clear that all this crusading lawyer stuff is a just a cover story. She is actually one of the three Germanic goddesses.

Petra is the one who weaves the future.

If ever your life seems to be sabotaged by an unseen assailant you can always blame her – Petra, the weaver. Your Viking warriors would sometimes cite Odin as a trickster God – it came in handy when far too many of the opposition turned up and overwhelmed the lads with the horned helmets. But it's not him – grumpy old blokes with beards are less in demand these days. You can put sudden reversals of fate down to the Weaving Woman. The loon with the loom. Her. The Goddess. Petra.

As a long-time playmate I was recently invited to watch her favourite tranny slave serve tea. I was wearing an Ozwald Boateng red pinstripe jacket, a shimmery lilac houndstooth shirt by Thomas Pink and some charcoal trousers that seemed to cost far too much at the time. I mention this lest anyone suspect I had attempted to cross-dress. Not that I haven't tried. Who wouldn't want to be dressed up in Madam's extensive theatrical wardrobe? But we eventually gave up on the attempt to feminize me. I tend to look like a biker's bitch or a rock chick who can't quite kick Jack Daniel's. It feels great. But it looks terrible. So I leave all that to Tracy these days, Madam Petra's most faithful slave.

Mistress/slave relationships often crash and burn. Slaves are usually far from slavish in their demeanour, often demanding far more than they deserve – or offer in return.

"Do I really have to care about someone's emotional health just to get my dishes done?" asked Ruby, another Dom who is always looking for slaves to manage her domestic chaos.

Indeed so. You might as well be married, my dear. So this must also be in praise of Tracy, a good-looking bloke who makes a better-looking woman. And actually behaves like a slave, instead of an Argentinian dictator whose shoes don't quite fit. As many of his rivals do. Tracy's thing is forced feminization. Punished in panties. But it is doubtful whether we should use words like "punishment" for this process. It often appears to involve a greedy little slut getting what he really wants. Or it may be having a licence to be a slut for a few hours. Even better, someone else is forcing you to do it. So you get to do what you want, except that it is someone else's fault. No more decisions, or responsibility. A holiday from who you have to be to cope with the outside world.

I first knew Tracy in the context of a five-way exchange of sexuality in a night club. She was on all on fours offering herself to those approved by Madam Petra. It was hard to ignore Tracy's immaculate rump, two peach halves immaculately clad in flawlessly white panties. Tracy arrives at clubs looking like a sixties' pop goddess; thigh boots, mini-skirts, hair reminiscent of Sandie Shaw. As a French Maid, dressed for service, she is even more attractive. It sometimes seems a shame that someone of refined birth and exquisite manners should be lumbered with "Tracy" (it's a tribute to a former mistress).

But perhaps this humiliation is exquisitely painful for such a delicate flower, a further way of revelling in being downtrodden. Tracy managed to serve Petra and I tea, behaving impeccably despite Madam Petra's lewd banter and wandering fingers. But it wasn't long before her impossibly high standards required that punishment be administered. Perhaps she thought Tracy was flirting with her guest. The little minx did seem to be over-hospitable with Madam's gentleman caller. And Madam does not like being ignored, even for an instant. There is only one God. And her name is Petra.

"It is obviously far too long since I have punished you," said Petra. "You filthy little slut."

"Yes, madam. Thank you, madam." Tracy leaned forwards, offering herself, big eyes imploring.

Petra smiled, all too familiar with her slave's little fads and fancies.

"I know you want to be over my knee," she said. "But this is a punishment. Your head would be far too close to my shiny black stockings. It would be far too easy to drink in Madam's scent."

We were already gratefully aware that Madam was wearing Angel by Thierry Mugler. And that it was floating around the room on a cloud of sex hormones pulsing from her gorgeously fleshy body. Tracy turned away from the face she so adores and bent to touch her toes. Madam flipped Tracy's skirt up and patted the seat of her knickers.

"I'm relieved to see you have grasped the concept of whiteness at last. My arm ached for two days last time. Not as much as your bottom hurt, though, did it?"

Someone else was with us now. A firm but fair matron who will stand no nonsense. Petra can credibly impersonate Marilyn Monroe, a stuck-up duchess, a Victorian street-walker, wenches in general and teenage minxes in particular (with choice of regional accents and accurate period detail. Favoured epochs: Victorian, Restoration, Dark Ages). And her bossy lady with slutty little slave is absolutely flawless. But then so it should be, after all these years.

She checked Tracy's posture, straightening one of her legs before patting the seat of her knickers approvingly. She reached for a wooden spoon, an implement chosen to emphasise domestic servitude as well as an effective tool for inflicting bruising, scorching pain. She stood and measured the spoon against her target, using it on each cheek in turn, taking time out to examine her slave's flushed face, to pinch her nipples. The punishment became more intense. Soon there was a fierce red glow visible through the thin white panties. Although Tracy was silent her breath came thick and fast. There was an occasional sigh as the spoon thrashed the same spot repeatedly.

"You may stand," murmured Petra eventually. She was flushed, a faint moist glow on her formidable cleavage.

"Thank you, mistress," said Tracy, sincerely. She curtsied as Petra has taught her, although there was the occasional unavoidable squirm as Madam's lecture continued. Finally she held the spoon for her to kiss. Eyes downcast, Tracy planted a long kiss on the implement before Petra took her chin by its point and tilted it upwards. She stared down at her slave for a while, imprinting her dominance deep inside her. Then Petra clutched the bulging erection in Tracy's knickers, kneading and massaging the throbbing mound while the sighing slave jiggled from foot to foot. We watched her hop for a while. It was entirely cute.

"You may rub yourself," granted Petra.

Tracy mewled in relief as she strived to lessen the harrowing sting in her well-beaten bottom. It was some time before she recovered her composure. She then needed considerable strength and endurance to comply with the rest of Madam's most unreasonable demands. Never able to forget that failure meant another punishing session with the wooden spoon.

When Petra was satisfied she had pushed her slave just that little bit further than last time, she gave Tracy some more domestic tasks. And we were free to talk once more. Assam tea arrived. A strong, full-bodied brew. Just right for a strapping lass like Petra. It even sounds like s/m. As we sipped at its dark strength I asked Petra if I could write a story about her.

"I thought you were burnt out," she said, with a smile appropriate for this piece of self-pitying amateur dramatics. "Why write 'another erotic story'?" I let her mock me for a moment. Which is fair enough, considering how much material there is to work with.

"It might be nice to bring a beautiful woman alive," I said, hoping that it would please her. She smiled. And glowed. And we felt the space enclose us. Sometime, somewhere, we are always together. Exchanging fragments of dreams and whispered prayers. In the long, slow, sweet dance of love. Warmed by a pussycat smile.

Stage

Mari Ness

"I want to get fucked on a stage," she said, extending a long, graceful leg towards him, curling her toes. He took the foot, bringing it up to his mouth, and examining the toes carefully before putting it back down.

"Hmm," he answered.

"Thoroughly fucked."

"Where?"

"Stage centre. Three feet from the edge, so they can see every tiny, juicy detail."

"They?"

"The audience. Five hundred of them, maybe. A select group."

"Do they know you?"

She considered that for a moment, drawing her feet up under her, fiddling a bit with her sweater. "No. I'm a complete surprise to them – they haven't even been told what's going on."

"What stage?"

She bit her lower lip, played a bit more with her sweater. "Hmm. Well – I guess the Winter Garden Theatre. Where they're showing that musical – 'Cats'. You know, maybe I can even get all those various hunky cats watching. Maybe licking themselves or something."

"Real realistic."

"What's not realistic about it?"

"That you could ever get a booking at the Winter Garden while that show is going on."

She sighed, moved her hand towards her left breast, pinching it a little under the sweater. "Oh. OK. Well, some other New York theatre, then. Medium size. Lots of showy lights that can go off and on, depending upon how excited the light guy gets."

"Is he going to get excited?"

"When you start ramming me, yes. And even before that. This isn't going to be a fast thing, you know."

"Oh, am I included in this?"

"If you want to be," she said. "But you'll have to be incredibly ready. Incredibly horny, incredibly hard. I'm going to be using you, hard."

"How?"

"Well, the show's got to last – what, two hours? You won't be fucking me all that time, of course — "

"Do we get an intermission?"

"No one will want one."

"I don't know," he said, putting a doubtful tone in his voice. "I'm not entirely sure you'll be able to keep up."

"You're the one that has to audition for this."

"Haven't I already?"

"That wasn't on a stage, though."

"Why don't you just give me my stage directions?"

Her lips pursed again. "OK. This is Broadway, right? So, you come on. You're dancing. Just like it's a regular Broadway show. You're doing – I don't know – 'Forty-Second Street' or something like that."

"You have to be kidding."

"It's not for very long. The audience is like – what is this? Because of course you don't dance well – "

"Understatement – "

"But then you suddenly stop, and as the music is playing, you slowly take off your shirt. To the beat of 'Forty-Second Street'."

"And the audience falls over laughing."

"No, they don't."

"Yes, they do. Start over."

"Anyway, as you're dancing, I come out on the stage. From the left. I see you, and I giggle, and I announce that you're going to have to pay for that."

"God."

"OK, I don't really. I see you, and I start to breathe hard. I let the audience see my chest moving, and I move a hand up to my throat and start to unbutton my blouse."

"You're wearing a blouse?"

"Yeah. Black. Silk. And a long skirt – black. It flares out. And fishnet stockings, of course."

"No originality, huh?"

"What'dya mean?"

"Never mind." He shifted his chair so that it was touching hers, so that he could reach out and touch her body simply by extending his wrist. "I'll tell you later."

"Anyway, I tell you that since you can't dance on the stage, you're going to have to dance all over me with your tongue. Artistically, of course."

"Of course."

"The audience judges. It they think your tongue's performing well, they'll clap, and then you can go on to the next section. But only if you do it artistically."

"How can you tell?"

She shook her head. "I won't be able to. That's exactly why it'll be up to the audience. I explain this, letting the spotlight shine on me as I tell them that they'll have to watch your tongue dancing all over me and tell me how good you are. A few of them giggle nervously – they're not really up to this kind of thing – but a few of the others get real hard or real attentive. They take a long look at me, and they start to clap when I take off my blouse."

"How?" he asked, flicking a hand close to her chest, almost, but not quite, touching her. He brought his hand back and placed it on his thigh.

She breathed hard, swallowed, then touched her tongue to the top of her lip. "What do you mean?"

"Are you just ripping off the blouse, or taking it off slowly?" His fingers began stroking his own thigh, lightly, gently. She saw him; he watched her eyes widen slightly, stare at his legs.

She breathed deeply. "Slowly, I think. After all, this is Broadway, and they've been promised quite a show. So I undo the buttons one by one, staying with the music." Her hands danced down to her own thighs, touching them briefly before returning to her chest, to touch her sweater where buttons might have been.

"What am I doing?" he asked, continuing to run his fingers up and down his legs.

"Watching. You've stopped dancing, of course – although you're still tapping your feet. But, like everyone else, you can't take your eyes off me. You start to pull off your shirt, and come up behind me. When your shirt's off you put your arms around me. I lean into you, and you begin stroking me with your hands, getting me ready. My nipples jump to attention."

"Like this?" he asked, moving his hands to his own chest, making swift circles around the nipples, and suddenly pinching a nipple, hard.

"Yes – but slower. Much slower. I want this to last, after all – I want the audience to get ready with me. I want them to be getting excited and – "

"And this gets you ready too damn fast." He suddenly moved one hand away from his chest and snapped his fingers together, grinning. She shook her head; she almost laughed, but she recovered herself, keeping her hands on her breasts.

"Exactly. So I step forwards, pushing away from you a bit, and suddenly turn to the side, so the audience can see you clearly. The spotlight suddenly shines on your pants. You're bulging. You look at me, and I nod. I can't have you too uncomfortable, after all, and I let you take off your pants and your boxer shorts. The spotlight illuminates every single detail. You're huge – huger than you've ever been before, you're so turned on."

"Am I?"

She nodded. "Three of the women in the front row pass out."

He laughed. "Stop it."

"No, really. They're, like, nuns or something. Anyway, I let the audience take a long, slow look before I pull you to me. You've got work to do, after all. I point to my breast." A slender finger on her left hand pointed at a breast as a thumb moved towards the nipple, stroking it. "You're so turned on that you forget about the whole thing – that your tongue's supposed to be dancing over me. Instead, you grab the breast with your whole mouth, taking in the entire nipple, and begin sucking on it. I let you do this for a bit – it feels pretty good, after all – before I remember the audience. I push you off."

"Ooh," he said, with a pathetic pout.

She put her hands on her legs, rubbing gently. "I remind you that your tongue's supposed to be doing the dancing, not your teeth. The audience laughs . . ."

"Are we miked?"

"Yes. So they can hear everything we say or breathe. Anyway, they laugh, and then I let you start working on my breast again. Only this time, you just use your tongue, nothing else. I let us swirl around a bit so that the audience can see every angle."

"Right. You'd be moaning helplessly and you know it."

"I would not."

"Right." He flicked a careless finger towards her right nipple. She gasped, almost on cue. "I know you, remember? Since when have you ever been able to focus on anything once I've even noticed your breasts?"

"If that were true, I'd get nothing done. You're fixated on them."

He gave her a long look, touching his tongue to the top of his lips as she took a deep breath and allowed her hands to wander back to her sweater. He hid a grin. Not that everyone would notice, but she had moved one or two fingers under the sweater – and they were wandering towards the edge of her panties. "True. Not that anyone can blame me . . . So, you're on the stage, moaning, I've got my tongue dancing over you — "

"In rhythm – "

"Rhythm?" he said, unable to move his eyes from her dancing fingers. He lifted an eyebrow. She smiled back.

" 'Forty-Second Street' is still playing. The sound guy's so turned on that he's forgotten to change the music." The fingers moved a bit lower.

"I glare at him." He had, he realized, his own problems now. But he couldn't stop watching those fingers. And – she couldn't be. But she was – three fingers slipped in, even as she kept on talking.

"No, you don't. You're dancing your tongue over me, over my breasts, my nipples, my stomach – over every single inch. You're trying to make me beg for you. But I'm managing to hold it in — mostly. I let out a few moans, and the audience starts to clap. You suddenly grin, and remind me: if the audience claps, you get to go on to the next stage."

He watched her fingers moving up and down just inside her jeans, even as her other hand continued to play with her breasts. He covered up his groan with rapid speech. "Which means that I turn to the audience and shout, 'Right?' and they all scream back at me. Right?"

"Pretty much. You yell out to the audience, and they start clapping and cheering. You grin back at me, and ask me if that was artistic enough. I can't really come up with any witty repartee – I just moan, and the audience cheers. I spread my legs out wide – sorta like an Olympic gymnast – and let everybody have a good long look." In the chair, her legs opened, gaping; her fingers snuck out from under her jeans and moved back to the tops of them, still rubbing lightly. "I hold that for maybe 15, 20 seconds, even while you're panting behind me begging me to let you fuck me. The audience is loving this – a few of them are even cheering you on, or cheering me on, telling me they want a longer look, even while most of them are remembering that they are on Broadway, after all. So they just clap politely."

"They're clapping politely?" He allowed his fingers to trail over his own erection, never taking his eyes off her.

"You can't stand it. You're hearing the audience and seeing my legs spread and hearing your own voice begging me to let you fuck me and all of a sudden you go nuts. You grab me and move me forwards and suddenly ram into me from behind. You pull my butt up, getting me into doggie position. I can't resist; you're filling me up so hard and so well that all I can do is hang on to the floor. I groan, and the audience is cheering."

"Oh, yeah." He kept his movements as slow, as discreet as

possible, but she saw him, and gave him the tiniest of grins.

"It totally, totally gets you off. You keep pounding into me, going deeper, deeper, shouting out to the audience how hot I am, how tight I am, how no other woman could ever do this to you. I don't let you stop. I make you keep going and going — every position, every angle, left, right, front. You on top, me on top. Doggie style, sideways – you name it. For hours."

"Hours?" He tried to slow his own fingers, found this impossible.

"We're so turned on by this time that we can't stop – it becomes endless. It tortures the audience. The men have their fingers up and down their dicks and the women are playing with their clits, aching for me to come. Waiting for me to release it. And when I finally do, they gasp out, and come too. Almost at the same time. Five hundred simultaneous orgasms. It's wonderful. It's art. They're gasping and cheering and calling out to God."

"Do I get to come, too?"

"Oh, yes, just after I do. While the audience are still recovering from me. You come, and when you do, they all come, every one of them, all over again. Five hundred people coming at once. All because of me." She circled her hands around her breasts, looking up at him through her eyelashes. "Their moans go right through my body, making it vibrate and shake."

"Because of you."

"Well, and you too. A bit." She gave her nipples a sudden pinch; he watched blood rush into her cheeks. She placed her hands carefully on the sides of the chair, drawing her legs together. "What do you think?"

"That's your idea of art? Basic fucking?" he asked.

She leaned back in her chair, the picture of calm domestic comfort. "What else? How would you do it?"

He mimicked her movements, sinking back into his black chair, placing his hands on the arms and gripping them firmly. "Well, for one, you never described the set."

"I was just thinking a bare stage." Her grip, too, he noted, was fairly tight. He kept his grin to himself.

"Oh, come on. For one thing, it's too hard on the knees.

We've gotta have something there – some type of elegant Oriental rug at least. It's the only old thing on the stage, though. Everything else is absolutely modern – black leather couches, those real ugly black lamps, you know. Everything in black. Except us."

"We're not wearing anything, right?" A few of her fingers lifted off the chair's arm.

His own hands stayed tight. "We're in costumes. But the costumes don't fit."

"They don't?" Her fingers moved back down.

"No. When the audience first sees us, they think there's something wrong with our costumes – that we've stepped onto the wrong stage. We look like figures from the Commedia D'ell Ante – you in a soft pink gown and a butterfly mask, me in a Harlequin costume. Almost. The mask is right – slightly primitive, a leather one rather than that plastic crap you see on stages – but the patches on the costume aren't diamonds, they're dicks. Red against the black."

"Erect?" Her hand trembled.

"Of course. Not that I'm giving anyone time to study the costumes. The stage goes dark almost immediately. Five seconds of total darkness, and then the spotlight comes back on. Two tiny narrow spots that just illuminate our masks, nothing more. The audience watches, puzzled and just a bit bored. They can't see that, behind your mask you're beginning to moan, and they can't see that in the darkness, I've flipped up your skirt – it's cut short in the back – and I'm running my hand up and down your clit."

He took his hand off the chair, moving it towards her, keeping just inches away from her hand. "The audience is starting to get a bit suspicious though. Even though you've been told to keep absolutely still, you can't help breathing more deeply, can't help moving your face a little with my fingers, a movement that makes your mask dance in the cool spotlight. And they're starting to hear something as well. You're trying to stay absolutely quiet, but my fingers just happen to strike that one place on you, and you start to moan. Loudly. You tilt your head back, and suddenly another spotlight comes on, aimed directly at your hand and my fingers.

The audience blinks, not quite sure what they're seeing at first, and then suddenly gasps. When I hear them, I stop."

"Hey." Her fingers backed up along the chair, away from his.

He extended his arm. "It's only for a moment. I show them my hand, still dripping with your juices, and let it shine in the spotlight for a moment, before I lead you to the table, making you sit on its edge. I want to make sure that they have a good view."

"No cushions?" The arm crept back out.

"You don't care about cushions; all you care about is getting my fingers back inside you. You sit up and spread your legs out on the table and grab my hand. The audience is mesmerized. They watch my fingers dance on and in you in total silence. The only thing they can hear is your moans, which are filling the theatre by now, especially since I won't quite let you come. Not yet. The audience starts to mutter. They know I'm torturing you, know that I'm keeping you right at the edge, and they can't decide if they like it or hate it. As they start to mutter, you start to beg for it. Softly at first – with the music, only I can hear you – but then louder and louder."

"Like you'd be able to resist for that long."

"Surprisingly, I can. Maybe it's the audience, maybe it's something else. But whatever it is, I keep you going for a long time before I suddenly twist the table so that the audience will get a good side view and, before anyone quite realizes what's happening, I've slid into you, and you're coming, moaning through your mask."

"What's the audience doing?"

"Masturbating. They can't help it. Even the ones who've seen live sex shows before have never seen anything this primal, this forceful, on the stage. They're used to bored people licking each other and going at it like porn stars. This is different. This is real. Maybe more real because they have no idea who we are, because we are two faceless people behind cold masks. They breathe with me as I tear into you, as I thrust myself completely into you, trying to become one with you even through the masks. They breathe with you as you reach up to grab my back, to dig into me, to push me into you. They can't believe the energy that we're creating, the energy that's going throughout the stage and throughout the theatre. And they can't believe how long it takes us to come."

"Do they come with us?"

He considered that for a moment. "No. They've waited, and they continue to wait, not one of them coming until they can clearly see that it's over, until they can see you draped across me, spent. We don't move for a moment, wondering what they thought about it. They can't tell us; they're all too busy fucking themselves and moaning."

He paused, and looked at her. She placed tapered fingers against her lips. "That's your form of art? Something totally fake?"

He shrugs. "Seems to be pure Broadway to me."

"Not that you've ever been to a Broadway show, of course. And Cats doesn't count."

"Why don't we let an audience decide?" he offered. "Pure applause. Whoever is louder wins. And no cat-calling, either. Pure clapping. For you – " he paused, waited, smiled broadly " – and for me." He paused again, and grinned at her. He took her hand, and they stood, side by side.

His pants were still bulging; her face was flushed and open. He raised one hand, pointing at her, and waited for a few minutes. She grinned again, and he pointed at himself.

"I think I win on loudness," she offered, after a moment.

He shrugged. "Maybe." He allowed a doubtful note to enter his voice. "It's very close. But I definitely win on length."

"Length wasn't the criterion."

"Point taken." He bowed mockingly to her. "Shall we call it a tie?"

She bowed back, and gave him the hand that had been so recently playing under her jeans. He realized again that he should have worn looser pants. It was too late now. With a final smile at each other, they turned and bowed.

In front of them, the audience of investors applauded again. He noted with a grin that several of the men should have worn looser pants as well, and that at least one woman was doing an odd sort of one-handed clapping. His grin got even broader when he saw that at least three of them were reaching for cheque books.

They might be able to turn this from art into reality after all.

Persona Non Grata

Dominic Santi

I was persona non grata at the Torelli household. Not that I particularly blamed them. Cancelling a wedding three weeks before The Event of the local social season was bad form even in my book. Tony, Marcella's older brother and my former best friend, had offered to rearrange my facial structure far beyond the rather sizeable swelling he'd initially planted on my chin. I didn't want to think about what her younger brother, Greg, was going to do when he showed up for his week of requested-six-months-in-advance leave from the Marines.

"How the fuck could you not know you can't live without dick until this close to the wedding?" Tony snarled when he was rubbing his sore knuckles. He'd knocked me flat on my ass.

"I thought I didn't need it," I growled back, rubbing my hand over my very tender jaw. "I really thought Marcella was going to be enough for me." My head was swimming, and I had the good sense to stay down. He's bigger and meaner than I am. But I refused to look away from him. "I love her, Tony. No matter what it looks like, I love her. This whole fucking mess is tearing me to pieces."

Tony just gave me one of those looks. After all, it was a rhetorical question for him anyway. It was one of his tricks who had gotten me going. I let him vent while I tried to clear my head. Tony and I had fucked around as far back as I could remember. Other than a few mutual JO sessions, we'd never gotten it on together. But he knew how much I liked sex with men. I liked sucking cock and getting my cock sucked, and when I got a wild hair up my ass, the hunger stayed with me until I got fucked until my eyes crossed. I couldn't count the times I'd watched his thick Italian meat ploughing some bottom-boy's hole while I massaged my tonsils on a well-hung stud's swollen shaft.

For me, sex with guys was just good old fun, horny *sex.* When I fell in love, it was always with women. I loved their softness and their high voices and how half the time, I couldn't understand what the fuck they were talking about but I didn't care, so long as they kissed me. I loved sucking warm, heavy breasts with big nipples and burying my face in hot, fragrant pussy. I could eat cunt until my tongue was numb and my hair hurt from being pulled and my ears rang with screams. But most of all, I loved sinking balls, deep in Marcella's quivering cunt and fucking until I came so hard it felt like my heart had exploded. I could spend hours on the couch with her, kissing and sucking and fucking while we pretended to watch TV. Shit, I even liked the way she gave head. She took me deep and wet and she used her hand when her throat bottomed out, and she sucked hard when she pulled off. Even when we weren't in bed, we had so much fun just doing shit together. Man, I just plain loved *her.* I wanted to marry her and have kids with her and make a life with her. I hadn't known it was possible to care for someone that much.

Which was why I'd called off the wedding. Until last weekend, I'd thought I'd loved her so much that my passion for her eclipsed even my need for dick. I thought that right up to the moment Tony's latest blond, blue-eyed, twinkie boy with the well-toned swimmer's build and the bulging dick strolled into Tony's apartment. Golden boy winked at me and wrapped his arms around Tony. They started swallowing each other's tongues and grinding their crotches together. When they tipped towards the couch, I had to leave. All I could see was golden boy's cock snaking down my throat. I went home and beat off, trying to concentrate on my upcoming date with Marcella. But when I tugged my balls and squeezed my dick and my come spurted through my fingers, it was his climax I was seeing, not mine. I wanted golden boy so badly I could hardly breathe. Even after I came, my dick wouldn't settle down.

Marcella had made it plain that while she didn't care that I thought I *was* bisexual, an open relationship with her was not an option. She said she was not going to share her husband with what she called The Competition. I remembered that all evening long, when we were laughing at the movie and later on when I was fucking her deep and hard and it felt so good, so fucking good, and I was getting off on her so fucking much. Even then, in the back of my mind, I kept seeing golden boy's heavy dick swinging in front of my face. And when I finally came, when Marcella's wet, clutching pussy spasmed around me so hard it felt like her cunt was sucking the come right up out of my balls, in my mind, I still imagined golden boy's velvety soft cock flesh sliding over my lips and down my throat. I spurted into the rubber buried deep in her shuddering pussy and I let the tears flow down my cheeks as I came and came and came until it felt like my soul was shattering into her.

The next morning, over a breakfast of peanut butter toast and coffee, I told her I was too queer to get married and I broke off the engagement.

I hadn't mentioned it to Tony, but Marcella packed a back-hand that had my cheekbone throbbing damn near as much as my chin. And her voice was a helluva lot more shrill. When she finally calmed down enough to ask just why the *fuck* I'd waited until now to tell her, I reminded her that I'd told her I thought I was bisexual and that I'd sometimes "experimented" with guys. I told her that I could only hope she believed me when I said what I felt for her was so overwhelming that I'd truly thought it was enough to overcome my need to be with men. OK, so fuck it, I was crying when I finally told her that nothing about my feelings for her had changed and that breaking up with her was ripping my heart out. But I said I understood, really understood, how important monogamy was to her. I loved her, and myself, too much to end up cruising the parks after work ten years from now while she was at home alone with the kids, suspicious and hating me.

This time, though, when Marcella had calmed down enough to talk rather than scream, she put her hands on her hips and told me to explain to her just what the hell I'd meant when I'd told her I'd "experimented" with guys.

"Specific details, Brendan. I mean, paint me a fucking picture." So this time, I told her, in explicit, graphic detail.

"My fucking brother!" she yelled.

"We didn't fuck!" I snapped. "We just, well, we fucked around, OK? I've never sucked his dick or had his cock up my ass, or anything like that. We just beat off together. And we had sex with other people in the same room." I dragged my hand through my hair.

Marcella got quiet then. She leaned back against the refrigerator and sighed. "But you had sex with other men, right, Brendan? You didn't just 'experiment'. You did it a lot. You sucked their cocks and you let them suck yours, and you fucked them . . ." Her voice trailed off as she rubbed her hands over her eyes.

"I didn't fuck them," I said quietly. Not that semantics really mattered, but if we were clearing the air, I didn't want any more innuendo. When she looked at me, I shrugged. "They fucked me, in the ass. And I liked it so much I came." I felt like I was watching a 25-year-old woman age in front of my eyes. She took a deep breath and let it out very slowly.

"Did you at least use a rubber, or do I have to worry about that, too?"

My eyes flashed hot. "I said I was queer, not stupid."

Before I could say more, she nodded and held up her hands. "I'm sorry, Brendan. That was mean, and I shouldn't have said it. I'm feeling really hurt right now and I just realized that you'd always used a rubber with me, and I wondered if that was why."

"Actually, it's not." I lifted my shoulders and let them fall. "I'm just a responsible kind of guy, you know? And we didn't want kids yet." I closed my eyes, trying hard not to think about the kids I now wasn't going to be having with Marcella. I didn't want to start crying again. So, I looked at her and answered the question she hadn't asked, but that I figured she had a right to hear the answer to. "I've always used latex, every time, with everyone, even for sucking. My tests have always been clear."

I tried to smile, but I couldn't quite make it. "For what it's worth, I haven't been with anyone else, male or female, for almost two years – since we started going out." I took a deep breath and decided to come clean on everything. "Though, for the record, Tony and I did beat off together in your grandfather's garage a year ago New Year's Eve, when we got drunk with the rest of your family and we were the last ones up after everybody else had gone to bed." As fire flashed in her eyes, I shrugged. "That's pretty much it."

"I'm going to kill that son of a bitch," she snapped. Things went downhill from there. The whole scene was pretty emotional for both of us. She hugged me when she left. But I wasn't all that surprised when Tony stomped in the door two hours later and planted his fist in my face before he even said hello.

I'd agreed to let Marcella handle telling everyone about the cancellation in her own way. So I lied to the people at work and told them I'd been in an accident, which wasn't that far from the truth. Three days later, I still hadn't heard anything. I missed Marcella so much it hurt to breathe, and I was horny for her and pissed at myself that even with all the shit going on, I was still thinking about golden boy's dick. I even missed Tony, despite how much my chin still hurt. It was Friday night, and I didn't want to run into any mutual friends at our usual haunts. So, I settled down for a rousing evening of feeling sorry for myself with a selection of action adventure flicks and some microwaved popcorn and a six-pack of beer. I'd just popped the first top and poured some real butter on the popcorn when Tony walked in the door.

"You got a gun this time?" I sighed, only half joking. He shrugged and shook his head. Everything else I was going to say died in my throat when he stepped all the way into the room. Golden boy was right behind him, wearing a tight white T-shirt and pair of clean but well-worn jeans that outlined his dick so clearly that I could tell for sure he wasn't wearing underwear and that he definitely was circumcized. When he saw where I was looking, he ran his fingertips over the outline of his shaft, thrusting his hips none too subtly as the bulge started to grow.

"I hear you want this, bud."

I put the popcorn bowl down so I wouldn't drop it. I didn't know what the hell Tony was up to, but I was getting pissed, and my dick was already straining against my jeans. To buy time, I carefully licked the butter off my fingers.

"I suppose it's too much to hope that there's a logical reason for this visit, oh former brother-in-law-to-be."

Tony's smile was dazzling, as always, but for the first time I noticed he had a bruise on his cheek that looked remarkably like the one I was sporting. I smiled. Marcella didn't take a whole lot lying down. Tony noticed where I was looking. He rubbed his cheekbone and shook his head.

"I do not try to figure out women, bro. It gives me a headache." He fingered the slightly discoloured area. "When Marcella finished screaming and crying, she got real pissed off. Bottom line is that she's not giving you up without a fight." I stared at him, and Tony smiled nastily.

"Marcella says she wants to know what she's up against, what a man can give you that she can't, and if she can live with it. Since we are 'such fucking good friends', I have been instructed to set things up with you so she can see what, as she put it, you feel you have to do with 'the competition'. Adam here is agreeable, so long as he doesn't have to touch women. Your cock-sucking reputation precedes you." As I stood there with my jaw hanging open, Tony waved at the smiling-faced golden boy, who was still fingering his now thoroughly engorged cock.

"I'm to tell you to strip naked and wrap your throat around this guy's dick. Anything after that is up to my baby sister." He picked up my beer and drank the rest of it in one pull. "Whatever she has planned, I don't want to know about it." He set the bottle back on the table with a loud thump. "I'm outta here. You guys figure things out, and I'd suggest coming to an agreement before Greg rolls into town. He's likely to do us all in if he's used up some of his precious leave time for nothing." He leaned over and gave Adam a long wet, crotch-grinding kiss. "Damn, but you can kiss, boy."

Tony stepped back and gave me one last, nasty smile. "Good luck, pal. You're going to need it." Then he was gone. I was suddenly alone with the Adonis I'd been lusting over so badly my balls ached. I wiped my sweaty palms on my thighs and sighed heavily, preparing to give myself the coup de grace I'd no doubt regret for a very long time.

"I am not going to have sex with you under these circumstances, Adam, though I do appreciate the offer." I didn't know who I was more pissed at – Tony or Marcella, or myself. I wanted Adam so badly I could almost taste him.

I'm not sure what reaction I'd expected, but his grin caught me off guard. He was even more gorgeous when he smiled. "I'll stop if you say to, dude." As I stared at him in disbelief, he moved to my side and unbuttoned my shirt. "This sounds like it's going to be one really kinky scene." He pulled my shirt off and tossed it on the floor. I couldn't help shivering as he ran his hands up my arms. "A couple of the guys at Troubadour's said you give fantastic head." His fingers were fast. Pretty soon my pants and socks were on the floor and I was naked. "I want to fuck your face."

Then his hands were in my hair and his tongue was in my mouth, and I was having trouble breathing any more. I was so pissed. I was certain we'd all lost our minds. But more than anything in the world, at that particular moment, I wanted to suck the cock of the man holding my face in his hands. Precome leaked from my dickhead and my face flamed.

"This is nuts." I was trembling, and I didn't want to be.

"But you want it, don't you?" He whispered the words right into my mouth.

I felt tears sting my eyes, but I didn't break away. I nodded. As his hands held my face and his mouth ravaged my lips, I undid his belt and shoved his pants down to his knees. Before I could manoeuvre us towards the nightstand, he reached into his shirt pocket. He pressed a condom into my hand and shoved down on my shoulders.

"Suck it," he growled.

For just a second, I closed my eyes, wondering what the fuck I'd gotten myself into. But by that point, my cock was thinking for me. I did the one thing I could. I dropped to my knees on the rug, and, in one motion, I had the soft pool of latex unrolled and my lips were kissing their way down Adam's dick. I kissed and licked, slobbering him full of spit as I inhaled the smell of horny man crotch and rubber. My tongue feasted on the taste of his swollen dickhead and his long, smooth shaft. With a moan, I gave it up and took him in my mouth. I let my throat slide down over his shaft until I gagged against him. I stayed there, my throat muscles choking and squeezing against him until even I had to come up for air.

"Fuck, man!" Adam gasped as I sucked in air beside him. "Do that again!" He pulled me on to him again. As my cock filled to the wonderful feel of his flesh moving into me, the door opened.

For a moment I panicked. Adam held me on his dick until I was desperate enough for air that I could only kneel there panting when he let me off. When I could finally breathe again, he pulled me back on until just the head of his dick was between my lips. Marcella laughed softly in back of me.

"Brendan, you would not believe how incredibly fucking hot you look kneeling there with a dick in your mouth." As I twisted to try to see her face, Adam let me up just enough that I could see she was smiling. She was wearing a short black miniskirt with a deep V neck and four-inch heels that showed off her long legs and her cleavage. It was usually my favourite outfit. Tonight, the toe of her shoe rubbed over the head of my quickly shrivelling dick.

Marcella knelt beside me, her hand trailing over my cheek, just below where Adam held my face firmly against him. Her finger trembled, and I saw the tears sparkling in her eyes. She looked as pale and scared as I felt. I cocked my head at her, as much as Adam's grip allowed. Her finger moved along my sore jawline, curving around to where my lips were wrapped around his dick.

"I want security in my marriage, Brendan. I am still so fucking pissed at you. But I've been thinking a lot this week, about you and me – and Tony and this jerk." She frowned up at Adam. He grinned. Marcella took a deep breath.

"I've been thinking about a lot of things, starting with that maybe your having sex with men isn't competition." She smiled, but her voice was shaky. She carefully chose her words. "We can call it quits if that's what you want – I'll even make Greg back off. But I'd like to try to work things out, if you want to. I really do love you."

I closed my eyes for a moment, trying to keep the room from spinning. My brain was overloading and I still didn't have quite enough air. But as I waited in the quiet, I was suddenly so very aware of the warm, living, latex-enclosed shaft between my lips and the musky smell of Adam's crotch and the feel of his hands on my hair, and of Marcella's finger resting on my cheek and the cool leather of her toe moving over my slippery dickhead. In my mind's eye, I saw my precome sticky on her shoe, and wondered what she'd do if it stained. Probably yell, I thought. My lady didn't take shit from anybody. As my lips twitched, my tongue moved almost on its own over the bottom of Adam's shaft. He moaned appreciatively, and I felt my cock hardening under Marcella's shoe.

I kept my eyes on her and I started to suck. I sucked deep and hard, letting the shaft slide out until only the head was between my lips, then taking it back in deep, in and down my throat.

"God," Marcella whispered. "You look like your jaw is unhinged."

This time I did choke. As I gagged around him, Adam yanked me off his dick, and we both laughed until I had tears running down my face. Marcella knelt down next to me and stroked my chin.

"I want to watch."

I was beyond being surprised by anybody in the Torelli family. I looked up at Adam, who shrugged.

"As long as she doesn't touch me, man. I am really not into chicks." He pulled me back onto his dick. "You, though. You suck cock as well as everybody says you do."

I ignored Marcella's snort. I settled into giving Adam a blowjob that let my mouth live up to all the fantasies I'd had about having him between my lips. But when I took my dick in my hand, Marcella pushed it away. I turned to stare at her, Adam's dick poking out into my cheek.

"He said I can't touch his dick. I'm sure as hell going to touch yours, babe." I watched, stunned, as she opened that huge fucking purse she always carries and took out a hand towel. She laid it on the floor. Then she took out a pair of gloves, a huge tube of lube, and a very realistic looking and definitely more than realistically well-endowed dildo and laid them on the towel. Adam burst out laughing, his abs bouncing against my forehead as Marcella snapped on the glove.

"You're going to fuck him?" he laughed.

"You bet your ass I am," she said. "I'm not into open relationships. But if I'm going to 'share', then he better get used to me being in on the action."

I tried to move back to say something. I'm not even sure what, I was pretty much in shock. But Adam pulled me firmly towards him and said, "Suck!" Marcella's hand moved over my ass and into my crack. I couldn't think of anything else to do, so I sucked.

Oh, God, did I suck. While Adam's wonderful warm cock slid in and out of my spit-filled mouth and over my lips and tongue and into my throat, Marcella slathered my asshole with cool, thick, slippery lube. She worked me open, one slow, sensuous stretch at a time. I groaned against Adam's shaft, trembling as he moaned at the vibration on his dick.

"I stole some of Tony's porn videos." Her hands pulled in opposite directions, moving around and around my sphincter in bigger and deeper circles. "There was one on how to give anal massages." Her finger pressed deep, right up into my prostate. I arched up to meet her. "Am I doing it right, sweet cheeks?"

I nodded vigorously, shaking as precome leaked through my dick tube. I sucked frantically on Adam's dick.

"You're sure as fuck doing something right," Adam groaned, holding me even tighter to him. "He's fucking swallowing my cock."

Marcella laughed, deep and sexy. "Let's see if this helps." Her weight shifted as she picked up the dildo. The lube was cool as she squeezed another huge glob onto my asshole. Then she stopped.

"His ass isn't at the right angle. Lay down, Adam, so

Brendan can lean over to suck you. That way, he can stick his ass up into the air for me at the same time." She pressed her fingers in firmly. "You wouldn't want to argue with a man's fiancée, would you, Adam?"

Adam's belly rumbled against my forehead again. "Far be it from me to get in the way of a man's fiancée's dick." In one movement, he'd pulled me off him, flopped down onto the floor, and kicked his pants off the rest of the way. Then he yanked my head down onto his crotch. "Suck, asshole!"

My ass felt like it was waving up at the moon. But, instead of being nervous, my whole body seemed to be concentrating on the feel of the word "fiancée" moving over my ears. Tears filled my eyes and I moved over Adam to 69, so I could take him at a good, deep angle. Then I opened my throat, and I worshipped that man's cock. I licked and kissed and sucked while the tip of Marcella's dick loosened my sphincter. As the huge head popped through, I took Adam deep. I worked every inch of his glorious shaft while Marcella slowly and surely slid her thick, heavy cock deep into my ass. She fucked me until my eyes crossed, laughing when she found just the right angle to hit my joyspot and make my dick drool. My nuts were climbing my shaft when she grabbed my cock. Her hand closed around me and she twisted up in one long, slow, squeezing roll.

I came so hard I thought my spine was breaking. As the come erupted through my cock, my ass-muscles clamped down hard. Marcella pressed deep, grinding her dick into my prostate. I groaned around Adam's cock, swallowing him until he stiffened and the viscous heat of his jism filled the tip of the rubber.

I was shaking so badly and the dildo was so deeply embedded that Marcella just left it in my ass when she lay down and pushed Adam out of the way. His dick slipped free of my lips and, as he lay there panting, Marcella hiked up her skirt and I was face to face with her pantiless, glistening, musky cunt.

"Eat," she snapped. And, God almighty, I dove in and I ate her cunt until my tongue was numb. Adam had barely caught his breath when he said, "Sorry, dude. I can't watch this pussy business."

"Lock the door behind you," Marcella gasped. I flicked my exhausted tongue mercilessly over her clit. The door clicked closed, and she buried her hands in my hair, arching her pussy into my face. I shoved my fingers into her sopping, hot cunt and I licked her until she screamed. As her thighs squeezed my head, my ass-muscles finally loosened and the dildo slid out of my asshole, pulling me open even further as the heavy toy fell down and the head finally fell free.

My arms gave out and I lay there with my face smashed into Marcella's pussy. When she'd finally caught her breath, she pulled me up until we were wrapped in each other's arms. We talked until almost dawn. When Tony called in the morning to see if we were still alive, she told him the wedding was back on.

We eventually came to an understanding that works for both of us. I can beat off with Tony any time I want, so long as we don't touch. She said that would just be too weird. Beyond that, whenever I want to suck cock or have mine sucked by a male throat, I have to bring the guy home, and the three of us retire to the bedroom when the kids are asleep. And when I want a dick up my ass, it has to be Marcella's. She's too worried about a rubber breaking to go along with other men fucking me, but I found I can live with that. Even in a three-way, when I'm kneeling on the bed with a latex-covered cock buried balls-deep in my throat and rough, male hands jerking me off and a gravelly voice telling me what a beautiful slutty bottom-boy I am, the fingers tickling my sphincter open are my wife's. She fucks her huge, rubber shaft up my hole, and I come for her. Oh, God, I come.

Pleasure Domes

Kathryn Ptacek

In Xanadu did Kubla Khan
A stately pleasure-dome decree:
– From *Kubla Khan*, Samuel Taylor Coleridge

Alexander Ivanovich Tamaroffsky – Sasha to his friends and family – had been riding bloody well all night, and he was damned weary, hungry, and very lost. But he couldn't stop now; he had to travel when it was cool. He knew at least that much about the country. That much his guides had told him before they had abandoned him.

He had awakened one morning to find all his trunks, his photographic equipment and money, and his native guides and their pack animals gone. At least they'd had the decency to leave him his horse, what he wore upon his back, and the meagre contents of his saddlebags – the few volumes of Burton's *The Arabian Nights* that he'd brought along, a few personal items, and the letters of introduction Uncle Vanya had prepared. Not that those were going to do him any good, he grumbled to himself, not out here anyway.

This was to have been his Grand Tour in this year 1894, a coming-of-age present from his uncle, a time to travel throughout the world, notably in the East, and to sample the exotic – in sights, in food, in drink, and in women. It would be, Uncle Vanya assured him with a knowledgable wink, an education to make him a man. It was his uncle who had told him from an early age of the earthly delights to be found for a young man such as himself.

Only now Sasha found himself in some damned backward country where they didn't even have the decency to speak French – as all well-trained young ladies and gentlemen did in his native Russia.

He had been riding for two nights now, using Venus as a guide, always keeping the star to his right. It was the only way he knew how to navigate through this sea of sand. Surely he would come to some form of habitation soon. He recalled hearing one of the guides whispering about a town or something far ahead in the desert; the others had all shaken their heads when he'd mentioned it. Sasha would come to it eventually, he supposed, as long as he wasn't riding around in circles.

His horse was thirsty and exhausted, and even now the poor beast wobbled slightly; he was sore and hungry, and he wanted nothing more than to slip into a comfortable bed and sleep for hours without swaying in a saddle. He was tired of the desert, tired of his adventure, tired of being on his own this way, and he wanted to go home.

But home was hundreds of miles away and, even as he thought of Moscow and the cool spring nights his sister and mother would be enjoying now, he realized that his head had nodded forwards onto his chest. He jerked upright and peered into the black distance.

Wasn't that a light? He rubbed his gritty eyes. Was it close to dawn? Surely not. Surely he had a few hours of cool darkness left?

A mirage, perhaps. But he thought that one only saw those during the savage heat of the day. Perhaps he was asleep and dreaming.

He ground the heel of his hand into his eyes again, and then blinked. The light remained.

He kicked the horse, but the animal, already at its limits, could go no faster. They plodded forwards, and Sasha forced himself to quell his growing excitement.

Even as dawn broke, he continued riding in the direction of the light, which he could no longer see. He rode on through the heat of the day, with the sun blazing down on his bare head, because he knew he *had* to reach the light. Sweat poured from his body; the horse staggered even more; but Sasha couldn't stop.

He rode for days. Sasha was barely conscious now, yet somehow the horse continued heading toward the beacon.

Finally the sun, red and angry, set in the west, and as a cool breeze rose to caress his blistered skin, Sasha saw the light gleaming in the dusk.

For a moment the light disappeared behind the rise of a dune. He reached the top, and then looked at what lay below.

Light radiated from a huge pearly white structure that was Oriental in design. It seemed all willowy columns and graceful domes and minarets, and for a moment he was reminded of the onion domes of his homeland. The structure seemed fragile, as if made of spun sugar, and he wondered that it could withstand the fierce desert windstorms.

The light seemed to emanate from the entire building, rather than coming from one window or another. One part of his mind questioned how that could be, but his eagerness to reach it quelled any suspicions he had.

He urged the horse down the incline, and beast and man half slid, half fell down the dune. The horse collapsed, dead, and Sasha stumbled towards the building. Nothing would keep him away. Now that he was closer he could see that the long ghost-white draperies billowed out from between some of the pillars, and he thought how refreshing they looked. He wanted to wrap himself in them, mummy-like, and soak up their coolness, let them soothe his fevered body.

I must be delirious, Sasha thought, as he pitched forwards into a faint at the foot of the steps leading to the building.

He awoke once in darkness, his body cradled by silk sheets, while hands, as soothing as ice, moved across his face; he cried out in pain because his skin was so roughened by the cruel sun and wind. The hands withdrew; a moment later something cold trickled down his throat, and he gasped gratefully at it. He was so parched . . . so fevered . . .

He thought he detected the fragrance of some spice . . . anise, but he couldn't be sure, not now, not when all he wanted was the sweet water.

He slept again.

When he awoke it was still dark, yet he could see because of the moonlight streaming through the latticed windows. He tried to rise up on one elbow, but fell back; he wasn't strong enough yet. He didn't feel as feverish as he had before, but he didn't didn't feel well, either.

"You are awake," said a voice, and he blinked as a woman slipped into his range of vision. The scent of anise drifted towards him, and that of oranges and cloves. They were pleasant bouquets, and he inhaled deeply.

"Yes." He swallowed roughly, aware that his lips remained cracked. His voice was husky from his ordeal in the desert. "Where am I?"

"You are in Xanadu," the woman replied.

"Xanadu?" The name seemed faintly familiar. Xanadu. Now where had he heard of that? Ah, yes from the poem by the English poet Coleridge. *In Xanadu* . . .

He frowned slightly. "That was just a poem," he said. "Xanadu isn't a real place."

She smiled. "Everything has some kernel of truth. Have you not found that to be so?"

"I guess."

She knelt beside him and, with his eyes adjusted to the half-light, he saw how beautiful she was. Her hair shimmered down her back like the night sky. Her face was oval, with high slanting cheekbones, and she could almost be one of his countrymen, he thought. Her eyes were smoky, liquid, dark, and he thought they held more than their share of amusement with him. She wore a kaftan-like garment, and it was almost sheer, for he could see the tip of a dusky nipple as it pushed against the material. He ran his tongue across his lips. Strings of pearls wound around her neck.

In the distance he heard the muted splashing of water. A fountain nearby. He closed his eyes and imagined the water, imagined the soothing water on his fevered skin . . . imagined the woman bathing in the fountain, the moonlight glinting off her skin . . .

"Here, you must drink," she said, and she cradled his head

against her breast and helped him to drink. The liquid tasted faintly of grapes and anise.

"What is it?" he asked her, as he lay back down on the pillow. "It's delicious."

"Raki. Almost like Greek ouzo. You know this?"

"Not personally, no, but I've heard of it. My uncle's told me of it."

She smiled, and her lips were red, very red, even in the moonlight. "It will make you strong again." There was no mistaking what she meant by strong.

His body stirred, and once more he fell asleep.

Her name was Aina, she had explained, and she had lived here for many years. Before that she had lived in Greece, but that had been a lifetime ago.

"But how do you manage?" Sasha asked when he had recovered even more. Surely no woman could live by herself – much less in this barbaric country. How did she obtain provisions? How did she stay sane with the loneliness?

"I just do."

He was now able to rise from his bed and move about the room without assistance for hours, although she always stayed with him. The corridors and rooms of this place were labyrinthine, and Aina had cautioned him against wandering around by himself, in case he should get lost. He seemed to sleep during the daylight hours and wake only at night, but in this country that made sense, he told himself. It was too hot during the day to do anything else but sleep. He was content with his schedule.

Every day he rose at dusk and bathed in water scented with jasmine, and shortly afterwards Aina would join him, bringing him a tray. The food and drink were for him only; she always explained that she had eaten before he awoke. He had no reason to disbelieve her. Occasionally she joined him in a glass of wine or raki. The food tasted delicious – he ate tangy rice with almonds and currants, tiny pastries filled with cheese or meat – borek, she named them – or leblebi, roasted chick peas.

Sometimes he remembered his camera and photographic equipment and wished he still had it. He would have liked to have her sit for him. She would make a beautiful subject. He would dress her in the sheer kaftan, perhaps with one shoulder bare, the material trailing down her white arm. Perhaps he would arrange the material sliding down past one breast, one long strand of pearls laying against her dark areola.

He wondered what she did to keep herself from boredom. "But what do you do here?" Sasha asked her finally.

"I read and study. I paint. I wait."

"Wait?" He frowned, puzzled. Wait for what? Perhaps she was a member of a harem. His uncle had told him about such things. Of sultans and their numerous women, all given to pleasuring one man. It was, he thought, too much to hope.

She smiled, and he forgot about his camera, forgot about his uncle.

The following night Aina took him on a tour of the palace, for that was precisely what the building was. It contained hundreds of rooms, far more than he could keep straight, and he understood then how much bigger it was than when he'd first glimpsed it. Each room was decorated in the most lush of furnishings – thick handwoven carpets of scarlet and gold and cobalt upon the tiled floors, tapestries with geometric designs hanging upon the walls, latticed windows draped with delicate curtains that billowed inwards at the slightest breeze. The furniture was low to the floor, sometimes nothing more than thick cushions, although here and there he glimpsed a divan or two, and low tables whose wood gleamed darkly. Every room was lit by candles that gave off the most golden of light he'd ever seen. The scent of spices hid the smell of wax.

In all of this he heard few sounds beyond the musical splashing of the water and the occasional twittering of a bird outside.

There were just the two of them, he believed, although once or twice he thought he had heard other women's voices, but he couldn't be sure. He was too shy to ask the woman. He was afraid that he had simply dreamed it.

He wanted to see more of the palace, wanted to see what it looked like outside, to see the courtyards and gardens. In due time, Aina said.

Once more a warmth spread throughout his groin, and he wondered what she meant.

She came to him that night, gliding across the tiles to stand by his bed, and he blinked in the semi-darkness, almost convinced he dreamt. He wondered if she had been giving him opium; he drifted in and out of sleep so easily . . . it was hard to tell what was real, what was dream.

She pushed the diaphanous robe off her shoulders and it whispered to the floor, and shyly he studied her body. Her pale breasts jutted out, firm and full, and her waist was narrow, her hips curved, the triangle between them dark.

He had never seen a woman naked before – not beyond the etchings his uncle had shown him, and this was not at all the same. He wondered how soft her mound would be, and he put a hand out to touch her. She clasped his hand, rubbing his fingers against her triangle and the damp curls there. He moaned.

Aina bent over him, a cool breast brushing his face. Reflexively Sasha opened his mouth, then felt the firm nipple being pushed into his mouth. He sucked at it, and it tasted of dusk and moonlight, of ice and fire, and as he licked and sucked at it, he felt her hands pulling away the silken sheet on his bed.

His penis throbbed; he was already fully erect.

Her eyes slid to his manhood, then back to his face. "You are ready, I see."

He nodded, not trusting himself to speak.

He reached up to fondle her breasts. Twins in beauty. So perfect, so wonderful. Pleasure domes, he thought, and smiled languidly.

He fondled her cool nipples as she caressed and stroked his thighs, his stomach, his manhood, and once he thought he was about to explode, but she drew back quickly, and his body trembled but did not betray him. Then once more she was there, moving so that she was atop him, her lips kissing his chest.

He fumbled, trying to ease into her, and she breathed into his ear, "Do not be so hasty, Sasha." He groaned, as she slid from him. She kissed his cheeks and lips, and sucked at him hungrily, as if she could draw his very breath from his lungs. For a moment he panicked and fought against her, but she held him down and soon his struggles ceased.

Then her mouth slipped down his chest, to his stomach, past, and he felt her mouth on his hardened shaft. Voluptuous pleasure rippled through him as her mouth slid up and down on him, and blindly he reached out, but hands – not hers, but another's – pushed his away and held them against the silken sheets. He tried to turn his head, but someone held it in place. Yet another pair of hands gripped his ankles, and for a moment he bucked at being captured so, but Aina murmured to him, and he relaxed.

It was dark, too dark to see anything; he could only feel.

A breast touched his cheek, and instinctively he turned his face to it. The nipple grazed his teeth, and he licked it with his tongue, felt it harden beneath him. Aina continued to suck on him, and now he felt another mouth on his chest. Someone – something – nibbled delicately at his nipple, and the pain, mixed with fiery pleasure, shot through him. He arched his back, and cried out wordlessly, and Aina opened her mouth wide and took him inside even more.

He panted, hard, and clenched his captured hands. This was like nothing he had read about, nothing he had heard about from his uncle and the other men.

He bucked and pumped, and his penis slid moistly into another mouth, and that one licked and sucked at him, and the thin tongue curled around him, like a cobra squeezing its victim.

They murmured wordlessly as they ran their expert hands across his thighs and arms, stomach and face, and he felt satiny breasts brush against him, tasted the moistness of their cunts, and even as he opened his eyes all he could see was Aina's face. But was that real, or only in his mind? He didn't know. He didn't care.

Teeth tore at his chest and groin, and he bucked and ground his hips and thrust wildly, trying to fill *something*, trying to come to full release, and pumped and pumped until he thought he had nothing left to give. Exhausted, drenched with sweat, his hair plastered across his forehead, he fell back onto the bed. He was now limp, and so winded that he nearly choked from lack of air.

"You are so handsome," Aina murmured, and kissed him on the lips, and she tasted of anise and something faintly salty that was not sweat.

He woke later than usual the following night, and he was groggy, almost as if he had been drinking. But he knew he'd had nothing more than raki, and that had never bothered him. He put one hand to his forehead, and his skin was warm, almost feverish. He moistened his lips.

"Good evening," Aina said, as she brought his tray into the room.

He managed to sit up, but all he could do was nod at her. His head ached, and he was tired, so very tired. Almost as exhausted as when he'd first arrived there. He wondered what had happened? Had he suffered a relapse of some sort?

"Are you giving me opium?" he asked Aina as she handed him a cup of raki.

"No," she said simply.

But he wasn't sure he could believe her. He pushed listlessly at his food with his fork.

"What's the matter?" she asked.

"I'm not feeling well."

"Perhaps you should sleep."

"I sleep too damned much," he said sharply. "That's why I think you're giving me opium." He knew he sounded petulant, but he couldn't help it.

"There are things other than opium, dear one," she said, as she trailed her fingertips across his forehead, "other drugs." She kissed his lips, and he realized then how swollen and sore they felt, almost as if they had been bitten. He put his hand up to his mouth and when he stared down at his fingers, blood glistened there.

After Aina left him, Sasha drifted back to sleep. He woke to see the moonlight coming through the windows. The moon's rays painted pale designs upon the marble, and he wondered what time it was. He realized he never knew the time, only that it was either night or day. He decided then that he ought to get up and explore while the woman wasn't there to stop him. Where did she go at these times? Maybe he would find out.

He rose and pulled on his clothes. He looked around for a candle to light, but found none. He would have to hope there was enough light to see during his exploration.

He walked quietly down the corridor. Rooms lay to the left and right of him, but all were deserted. Once he heard the flowing water, then that went away, and he was left in the dark silence. This corridor led to another one, then still another passageway, and behind him and in front were dozens of rooms. All empty.

Finally, he thought he heard a voice – no, two – and crept forwards carefully and peered around the doorway.

Half a dozen women lounged in a chamber that seemed to be nothing more than one enormous bed that extended from wall to wall. A carpet – no, a mattress, it was so thick and luxurious, with silken sheets – covered the floor. Gossamer draperies, like webs, hung in the corners, while richly hued tapestries decorated the walls.

He saw Aina, reclining against a mound of brocade pillows. She was naked, except for the strands of pearls at her neck, and her knees were slightly raised. He realized then with a shock that a woman, her braided hair the colour of burnished copper, crouched with her head between Aina's legs and she was kissing Aina in her most private parts. Aina moaned with pleasure, and pushed the woman's head hard against her.

He swallowed hard and his hand crept to his crotch. Two very young women, who could have been twins so alike were they in appearance, embraced and kissed, sticking their tongues in each other's mouths. They kissed each other's breasts, then giggled, and turned to another woman, a blonde who lay on her stomach, as if waiting. One of the twins pushed a pillow under the third woman's hips, elevating them, then the other twin strapped a leather belt around her waist, and Sasha blinked when he saw that the woman had grown a phallus.

The dildo was long – impossibly long – and of gold-veined marble. She oiled it with a pungent gel, her fingers rubbing in long caressing strokes, then thrust the phallus deep between the raised rounded buttocks of the blonde woman. They laughed, and the second twin reached out and deftly slipped her fingers between her sister's legs, and the girl gasped and ground her mound down on her sister's hand, while the woman across the pillow pounded her fists against the cushion and whimpered. The woman with the phallus thrust in and out, in and out, each time going faster and faster until finally the three cried out together, then collapsed in a heap. The twins languidly kissed each other, while the blonde buried her face in the lap of one of the sisters.

Nearby another woman, much smaller than Aina and with hair much darker, sat propped against a cushioned wall and kneaded her erect nipples. Harder and faster her fingers went as she first flicked the nubbins, then squeezed, then rubbed them hard again and again as she mashed them with her palms, and she bucked against the wall. She raked her nails down her heavy breasts, leaving angry red welts, and she laughed, then thrust the marble phallus into her cunt, and fucked herself until blood glistened on the marble. She gave a great shuddering sigh of release, then crawled over to the others, and they began to bite and pinch her. All the while she laughed.

Sweat trickled down Sasha's temple. His breath was short, and he could feel the hardness in his pants. His penis pulsated, pushed against the material, and he slipped his hand inside, touching his moist skin. He rubbed himself, stroked, and his breathing quickened. The room was redolent of musk, and he licked his lips. He was hot, so very hot. He wouldn't need much more for release. At that moment Aina opened her eyes and looked at him and smiled. The copper-haired woman between her thighs never looked up.

"Come join us," she said, extending her hand.

He did.

He was awash in a sea of curling legs and grasping arms and voluptuous bodies. Half a dozen mouths caressed him with their lips, their tongues, and he reached out, stroking randomly at breasts. There was muffled laughter, and one of the women – he didn't know who – began licking him. He felt himself enlarge, felt the blood pumping through his body, and realized he had never felt more alive than now. Desire and something more – life, a vitality that he had never had before in Russia – coursed through him. Something soft – a feather, perhaps? – touched his arm, and a physical thrill raced down his side. The feather danced its way down to his groin, and he laughed when it brushed across his penis. A woman's lips, hard and demanding, fastened on his mouth. He realized it was the small woman and she sucked his breath until he thought he would pass out. He reached out for someone, and one of the twins captured his hand and began licking each finger, slipping it into her mouth and sucking on it.

He exploded violently, and again he heard the muffled laughter. The blonde ran her tongue down his chest, all the while the other woman continued to run her tongue up and down his manhood. He felt himself beginning to harden again. He tried to caress Aina, touched the firm buttocks of another woman, ran his hand down her smooth thigh. He slipped his fingers inside her, and she was cold, as cold as ice, and he pumped his hands, and she ground her hips down onto his hand.

He took a deep breath.

Aina lay curled, close to his head, and she stroked his face with one languid hand. She whispered to him, and he smiled, not understanding the words but knowing their meaning.

He came time after time after time, and hours later when he lay on the sheets, exhausted, Aina uncurled, and drew herself across him, her mouth fastening on him, and he had no choice but to satisfy her.

He awoke the following night, not convinced that he'd really seen the women. Surely it had been a dream. Or had it? He was exhausted, as if he hadn't slept in days, and he remembered vaguely a woman with copper hair kissing him, while twins took turns mounting him. There was something about Aina and the blonde . . . but what? . . . He wondered why he couldn't remember. If it had actually happened, that is.

Wishful thinking, he told himself while he smiled. He rose after a moment and went to the washstand across the room to splash water on his face. Perhaps that would make him feel better. He squinted into the mirror, then stumbled back in shock. The face there wasn't his. It couldn't be. It was the face of a man many years older.

How long had he been here? he asked himself. Days, perhaps a week or two at most.

No more . . . no more than that, surely.

But there lingered the doubt that it might have been more. No, it couldn't. He could remember each night, could account for his time . . .

But can you? asked the silent voice within, and he knew he couldn't. The days . . . the weeks . . . the months? . . . had become a blur to him.

So much time . . . lost forever now.

He was well now; he must leave and go home. As much as he would have liked to stay with Aina and her sisters – for surely that was who those women were – he had to return home. His parents would be worried. His uncle would be worried. And he had much to tell his uncle.

"Stay with us," Aina said, and he realized he hadn't heard her approach. But then he rarely did. She walked . . . glided . . . so quietly, so carefully, as if she were a cat creeping up on her prey.

Her arms slipped around his waist, and as he stood there, he felt her tug at his trousers.

"No," he started to protest, but she drew his hand away, and he could say no more, as she pushed his pants down and led him back to the bed.

Aina straddled him, and, heavy-lidded, watched him. He pulled her down by the chains of pearls. The strands broke, and hundreds of pearls went flying, some pelting his chest. She smiled and pushed herself down onto him, and Sasha felt her coldness sucking at him, drawing his warmth, his life, his youth, and willingly he gave himself up to her.

He opened his eyes to see the face of the small woman, and she too was smiling at him. He cupped one heavy breast in his hand, and she bent down as if to kiss his shoulder, but instead bit him hard, drawing blood.

He cried out and squeezed her breast in response, and she bit him again. He squeezed harder, pinching her nipple, and her smile widened.

She reached down and raked her nails across his penis. He gasped from the pain . . . and the pleasure it brought, and she kissed him hard then, bruising his lips.

When he came, it was like a thousand barbs tearing into his body.

And he liked it.

When next he saw himself in the mirror, he was even older.

Or looked older, he thought. He couldn't have aged all that much, he rationalized. It was from doing too much at night, too little otherwise, he told himself. He must awaken during the day and walk around the grounds a little. He needed fresh air, he needed . . .

. . . needed . . . the women.

They came to him, melting out of the shadows, and he felt their hands fondling him, stroking, arousing him, awakening his desires, delving into every crevice of his body until he thought he would go mad with delight, and he sobbed, and leaned with his arms propped against the washstand as they took him there, and sweat and come and blood flowed freely.

He didn't know when the pleasure and the pain had become entwined, and it frightened him. He couldn't have one without the other now, and each time he fucked, it hurt beyond belief. And yet he wanted more. He had to have more.

And the women knew it.

"I must go home," he whispered to Aina, who lay next to him. She was caressing his chest, twining the greying hair there around her fingertips.

"You are home," she said.

"My parents . . ."

"Gone."

"Gone?" He couldn't figure out what she meant. "Gone?" he repeated dully.

"They are dead, Sasha."

"My uncle . . ." he began.

"Vanya is also dead."

"Dead?" He blinked. "But how? . . ."

"It has been a long time, Sasha. A long time. They are but ashes now." She rolled over onto him, and slid down, pushing his penis between her breasts. She rode her breasts up and down his penis, the friction making him erect. As the tip of his penis emerged from the cushion of her breast, she gave his glans a quick swipe of her tongue. The pain tore through him like red-hot pincers.

"Dead?" he wondered aloud, then thought no more of family or home, as he came violently, and she smiled down into his agonized face.

"You are a vampire," he said. He was familiar with such a creature, for there were tales of vampires in his country.

She shrugged. "A lamia."

He had heard of that, too. There might be a difference, but he couldn't see it. Not now.

She laughed, a lilting musical sound, and the fear and desire rose in him.

His lips raw, bleeding, he kissed her, and tried feebly to push her back onto the bed so that he could mount her. But she was far stronger, and she flipped him onto his back, and automatically he opened his legs, and she grabbed him and jerked hard, and he begged her not to stop.

She didn't.

He came hour after hour after hour, and finally slept like the dead.

As she crouched above him, running her mouth across his chest and down to his groin to suck at him once more, he realized there were vampires who took more than blood from their victims. Succubi or lamia. Those who sucked out the very soul or essence – or youth – of a man.

"And what does "Aina" mean?" he murmured.

"Always, until the end."

And she smiled as he screamed, but whether in pain or in pleasure, he could no longer tell.

Glyph

Simon Sheppard

Antigua, Guatemala is a town entrapped, haunted by its own past, in the shadow of volcanoes, left desolate by earthquake, catastrophe, surviving. I was staying at the best of the town's cheap hotels. The man in the next room was exceptionally beautiful. From the moment I first saw Ben, I longed to ask him two questions. First: how did it feel to be so handsome, to live behind a face that drew all eyes? And: what would it take for him to condescend to having sex with a man like me?

Even if these were questions that could have been spoken easily to a stranger, something about Ben's aquiline features, a certain impassiveness, discouraged asking the questions of, in particular, him.

For two days, I watched him greedily as he sat in the hotel garden, writing postcards and drinking bottled water. When he went back to his room, I would retreat to the bathroom of my own. Our baths shared a common vent which readily transmitted sound. I'd sit on the toilet in the dark as the music of his pissing filled my ears. I stroked myself into a frenzy, imagining the sight of hot liquid coursing from the inner recesses of his body, jetting from the tip of a perfect cock. Better still, I could hear him shower, hear the subtle changes as water flowed over his muscled torso, between impressive thighs, down the wiry, tanned legs his shorts had revealed. I imagined the water swirling around his feet, myself face down on the floor of his shower, lapping up the liquid that had cleansed his flawless body. I was lost in envy and desire.

The second night, Ben spoke to me, asked about a new restaurant in town, the only place in all Guatemala to get good Thai food. I cautiously suggested we go there for dinner. He accepted.

Conversation, over spicy yum-na and local beer, was polite, safe. I could feel myself straining to maintain the right balance of formality and friendliness. Watching that face, hearing him speak to me, was a privilege and a gift. The slightest sign of the urgency of my desire might scare him off. All the while, I wanted to yell: *You are one of the most beautiful men I've ever seen.* I wanted to beg him to use me as he saw fit.

On the way back to the hotel, through cobblestoned streets shadowed by the ruins of antique cathedrals, he stopped to buy some beer and invited me to his room for a drink. I followed him up the stairs, watching his muscles shifting beneath the thin shield of his clothes.

His open suitcase was on the room's only chair. We both sat on the unmade bed. I could look past him, into the bathroom where he'd been naked. I caught my breath.

For several long minutes we sat wordlessly, drinking the slightly sour beer. He complained about the lingering heat of the day. Rising from the bed, he kicked off his sandals and, standing just feet away, unbuckled his belt and let his khaki shorts fall to his feet. Opening another beer, he sat crosslegged on the bed. His white boxer shorts gaped open at the fly. I had no choice; I stared at the thatch of black pubic hair, at a patch of smooth white flesh. He shifted slightly. The base of his cock came into view.

Ben reached over, put his hand under my chin, firmly raising my head until my gaze met his. His beautiful face gave nothing away. I stared into his eyes. He took my hand in his, pulled it over to him, to his crotch, to the gap in his boxers. To where he was warm and hard.

As he unbuttoned my shirt, I felt vaguely ashamed of my body. I touched his cheek, ran my fingers over his perfect profile, his nose, his mouth. Leaning over, he opened my lips with his tongue. He pulled off my shorts, releasing my swollen dick. I was naked, a poor gift for his perfection.

He took off his boxers. His dick was much bigger than mine and oddly shaped, massively thick at the base, tapering to a smallish head where precome glistened in his piss-slit.

He reached over to his suitcase, pulling out a rubber and a small tube of lubricant. He unrolled the latex over his stiff cock and covered it in lube. He put both his hands on my shoulders and shoved me back on the bed. I wrapped my legs around him and he lowered himself into me. I gasped as he slid in, opening me with the thickening shaft of his cock.

As he fucked me, his face remained expressionless. And he was still wearing his T-shirt. Even as he thrust into me, he remained somehow armoured, half-hidden from view. But I was wide open. I needed to bridge that gap.

I reached to his waist, running my palms up under his T-shirt, over his flat, hairless belly, the flawless torso I'd imagined as I'd masturbated. His nipples were small and hard. And his chest . . . What was that? The flesh of his chest was textured, a network of ridges running across what should have been perfect skin. My fingertips found their way along a welter of intersecting scars.

In that moment, Ben's face had altered radically. Gone was the frozen mask. In its place was grief and something like anger. He pounded harder and harder until it hurt, until I had to grit my teeth. Just when I thought I could take no more, when I was about to beg him to stop, he came with a shudder and a shout.

He pulled out and went to the bathroom to peel off the rubber and wash up. Left alone on the bed, I pulled at my dripping cock until I shot hot flows of come over my sweaty chest.

Ben had returned, was standing over the bed, his face had softened. He took off his T-shirt. His beautiful chest was scarred, lighter lines against a deep tan. Someone had carved into his flesh, inscribed three Mayan glyphs, geometric symbols the ancient Indians had used as their writing. I must have gasped. Ben smiled, wrapping his arms around me.

"I have," Ben said, "a story to tell you . . .

"Javier and I had been together six years. I thought he looked like a Mayan prince. Smooth brown skin, that incredible profile. His family came from the highlands of Guatemala, almost pure-blooded Indian, but Javier had never been further south than Tijuana. We loved each other a lot.

"Javier was HIV-positive when we met. I remained uninfected. From the first, we'd made plans to visit Central America, see the village his parents came from, tour the ruins at Tikal. But we were both always busy with school, and then work, and when we did find time for vacations, we'd end up on Maui or Key West.

"Then one summer, symptoms started to appear. Nothing much at first – Javier got tired more easily, got rashes on his beautiful skin. But his bloodwork wasn't promising. We realized that if we were going to visit Guatemala together, time was growing short.

"We landed in Guatemala City, came here to Antigua, went on to Lake Atitlan. Visited Sololá, the Indian village his family was from. Got my wallet lifted on market day.

"By then, Javier wasn't feeling all that well, occasional fevers, was losing a little weight. Still, we were able to finish our trip. We'd saved the best for last. Took a plane from Guat City to Flores, made our way to Tikal.

"Have you been to Tikal yet? You'll love it. It's the most incredible Mayan ruin of them all, a huge lost city in the middle of deep, lush jungle. In the centre of it all is the Great Plaza, a huge open space surrounded by ruined temples. Two huge pyramids, Temple I and Temple II, stand at the plaza's east and west ends. With special permission, you can stay in the Plaza after dark, until eight o'clock. Well, Javier and I had something else in mind, so as the sun went down and the full moon rose over Temple I, we climbed the hill to the Central Acropolis and hid in the shadows. The stones of Tikal turned a misty white in the moonlight.

"Finally, at eight, the last loudmouth tourists headed back to their hotels and the guards' flashlight beams vanished in the distance.

"We made our way down across the Great Plaza, all alone beneath the hulking ghost-white pyramids, their staircases leading to the heavens. You know, I used to have an idealized picture of the Maya; they were this peace-loving civilization destroyed by bloodthirsty Spaniards. But it turns out that on festival days the Mayan high priests would stand atop the pyramids and sacrifice enemy warriors to the gods, cutting out their hearts with obsidian blades and letting their still-warm, bloody corpses tumble down the stairs.

"On the north side of the Plaza there's a long row of sacrificial altars. At one of them, a large carved column shows Yax Kin, one of the greatest rulers of Tikal, standing on the body of a bound prisoner. At its base, a round altar stone is carved with the image of another prisoner lying on his back, arms and legs tied with ropes, awaiting sacrifice.

"There, in front of Yax Kin's altar, we stripped off our clothes. Javier put on a loincloth he'd made. I lowered myself onto the altar stone. I can still remember the coolness of the carved stone pressing against my naked back. Javier took some ropes from his backpack and tied me down. Rope around my ankles, my wrists, rope tight against my thighs. Lying there, head thrown all the way back, I could see the upside-down shape of Temple II. Everything was inverted. The great sweep of the staircase, which had been aimed at the heavens, now seemed to lead downwards toward some darkness that had become light. The night was anything but silent; the scream of the jungle filled my ears. As Javier tightened the ropes, my dick grew hard. He put his wet, hot mouth on it, took me down his throat. I arched my back, pressed myself against the comforting restrictions of the ropes.

"He let my throbbing dick slide from his mouth. I could hear him rummaging through the backpack. I couldn't see him, but I knew what was coming.

"Javier put his face to mine, whispered that he loved me, and cut into my flesh. I lay there, feeling the sting of the sharp blade, as my lover traced out three glyphs: the Mayan symbols for Tikal, for the god Smoking Mirror, ruler of fate, and for the phrase *Na-wa-ah,* which means the gaining of merit through the sacrificial shedding of blood. As the moments passed, the pain became something other than itself, as though time had ceased to exist, as though there were no distance at all between the days of the Maya and that full-moon night amidst the ruins. I was in my body and yet not in my body; I don't know if that makes any sense to you. I'm not sure I understand it even now.

"When he finished carving the glyphs, Javier took my dick in his mouth again, quickly bringing me to the brink of orgasm. Then, just as the ancient Mayans had done in their bloodletting ceremonies, my lover took a sharp needle and pierced the underside of my swollen dick. The love I felt for him at that endless moment was greater than anything I've felt before or since.

"Finally, as we'd agreed beforehand, Javier removed his loincloth and straddled my body, stroking his uncut dick until he came all over my bleeding chest. He lay upon me, smearing together my still-warm blood and his stinging hot come, and sobbed as he held me in his arms. Dawn lit the sky above the temples of Tikal.

"In a way, it all seems like a dream I had a long, long time ago. Javier's gone now, but he left me with these warrior marks in commemoration of that night. Here, just over my heart, I carry the glyph for *Na,* which means 'to feel, to know, to remember.' And I do."

His story finished, Ben fell silent. He stared at the white-washed wall of the hotel room, toward some far-off invisible volcano. I stroked his beautiful face, running my hands down his throat to the marks on his chest. In each other's arms we drifted off to sleep, my hands still resting over his heart.

We became sometimes-lovers after that night in Antigua. Back in the States, we tried living with each other for a while. But Ben wasn't the easiest man to know. There was often something remote and frozen about him, a place where my caring couldn't reach.

And Ben was HIV-positive. I assumed it had happened that night at Tikal, that night with Javier. But he always refused to talk about it. Speculation was futile, he said. In just those words. "Speculation is futile."

As the months went on, Ben's beautiful body became gaunt. Lesions appeared on his once-perfect skin. Eventually, the doctors put a catheter in his chest, right through the symbol commemorating blood sacrifice. And somehow, as he seemed to become translucent, as I could see the skull beneath the skin, I desired him all the more.

Strange how a random encounter in a foreign town can change your whole life. How it changed mine. How different things might have been. But speculation is useless. We go on, I guess because we have no choice.

And that, since you asked, is the story of these scars of mine. Ben is gone now, as Javier before him, but he passed his markings on to me, left me with these warrior marks. These scars over my heart. The central glyph reads *Na-wa-ah*. To feel, to know, to remember.

Here, run your fingers over them, and then we'll go to bed.

Seducing Storms

E. M. Arthur

Low, grey clouds pound my ancient Ford wagon with tinhammer rain.

"Should we move?" Kate asks. She's one of Doc Brandon's grad students. It's her first time with me. She thinks she wants to be with the other storm chasers, the PhDs with expensive equipment.

"No," I say. I look her over. She's maybe 25, not much younger than me. Too young and pretty for serious academia, she's got something to prove. She's watching the storm through the windshield. Her eyes are dark grey, like the clouds.

"We need to head south," she says. "I want to be there if this one spawns a funnel cloud."

Money and study got her on Brandon's storm team. Knowing him got her put in a car with me. He must like her.

"We're fine," I say. She's afraid she's missing something exciting. She probably fell in love with movie and TV visions of storms.

She doesn't feel the storm like I do.

She leans forwards to catch my eye. I'm already watching her. She realizes it and blushes.

I wonder if she thinks she looks more serious with her red hair pulled back tight and braided into a tail that reaches to her shoulder blades?

"Mr Martin," she says, "I want this storm."

I smile. "Andy," I say.

Her hair only accents her grey eyes and high cheeks. She wears a too-big flannel shirt. Humidity makes it stick to her skin, outlining the perfect breasts she probably wants to hide. The extra rolls of fabric above her waist only make her jeans seem tighter, her ass higher.

I expect her to pout. She has the lips for it. Instead, her lips get thin and white like cirrus clouds running before a front.

"The heart is going to miss us," she says. "The radio says it's headed towards Mt Vernon." She holds up our walkie-talkie like it proves she's right.

I nod. I parked us on a dirt lane between two cornfields. It's nearly night dark even though the sun won't go down for a couple of hours. Beyond the corn, a lightning-scored black stripe crosses the belly of the clouds. That flashing band of black is where the power is, and it's moving south fast.

"Damn!" she says. She pounds her fist on my cracked vinyl dash.

"There'll be other storms," I say.

She looks at me. Anger flashes in her grey eyes and heats my blood. It might as well have been real lightning, striking next to the car.

Her look reminds me of Angela. For a moment, I wonder if Kate might be able to feel it, if she might share the storm passion.

The radio squawks. Doc Brandon's voice says, "Barometer's dropping fast. It's a big one. Everybody on it?"

She responds, "We're too far north, Dr Brandon. My driver won't move."

If she had the passion, she wouldn't need the radio.

The voice comes back, "Andy's your driver?"

"Andrew Martin," She glances at me. "He's a local." She says it with contempt. The lightning in her eyes is gone. I decide she doesn't understand storms.

"Kate, get your camera ready," Brandon says. "You do whatever he tells you."

"Dr Brandon?"

"You want to see one up close, right?"

"Yeah, but it's going south fast."

"You do exactly what he tells you." His tone leaves her no room for argument.

"Yes sir." She frowns. She's confused. She doesn't know me.

"Andy?" Brandon asks. She hands me the radio.

"Here," I say.

"It's an Angela storm, Andy."

"I feel it," I say. There isn't much else to say. "Out." I turn off the radio and put it on the Ford's bench seat.

Brandon knows me. Brandon, his sister Angela, and I chased storms when we were kids. He still loves Angela, too.

Kate and I watch the storm slip south. Hail clatters on the roof and bounces off the windshield. Outside, corn leaves dance under the assault.

Kate's disappointment fills the car. It's the cool emptiness of a meadow after a summer shower. Her eyes follow the distant squall line. The grey is darker, more distant.

"Have you ever been close to a tornado?" I ask.

"They sound like a freight train," she says. "They can put a two-by-four through the wall of a house."

There's no fear in her voice, no respect. She's just repeating something she heard or read.

"That would be never," I say.

She flushes red. She squirms on the bench seat and pulls at the legs of her jeans. Finally, she looks at me. "I was so excited," she says. "I thought tonight would be my first time."

"Brandon tell you that?"

"I begged him to let me ride chase," she says. "I told him I wanted to get closer. He said he understood. He said he knew someone like me once." Her voice shakes with regret and desire.

I see a little of Angela in her, Angela when we first met. I start to like her. "He does understand," I say.

"I'm with you, and he's in the chase van," she says.

"I grew up with trains and tornadoes," I say. "With trains, the ground vibrates just enough to soothe."

For the first time since Kate got into my old Ford wagon, she sees me. Her grey eyes show a little black, a little interest. She picks her sticky shirt loose from her breasts.

The windows are steaming up. I crack a window. Rain-cleansed, cool air brings the smell of wet corn into the car.

"When the storm comes," I say, "that flannel will feel like a wet dog wrapped around you."

"Your cotton's better?"

I look at my light denim shirt. It's sweat-soaked and plastered flat to every rib and ridge of my belly. "It's just lighter," I say.

The storm line is black and lumpy, like coal hanging from heaven. Forks of white fire flash in and around the lumps. It's still just a storm, though. It hasn't smoothed out into the deep-sea green wall of cloud that spawns twisters.

"Brandon put me with you because I'm new," Kate says. "He isn't going to let me get near a tornado, is he?"

"Maybe he likes you," I say. "Maybe he thinks you have a feel for the storms."

"He made me go with you, and he went in the chase van."

"And I'm just a local, right?"

"No offence," she says. "The chase van did go south, and the storm is heading south."

"True," I say. I look her in the eye. She's lost her anger. The grey of her eyes is deep and uncertain.

She looks down at her hands. She picks up the small video camera from the seat.

"Nobody can tell a woman or a storm what to do," I say.

Her laugh is a soft, spring shower falling on a freshly mown lawn.

The hail stops.

I like her laugh. I wonder if it stopped the hail.

We watch through the windshield for a few minutes. Finally, she says, "If it doesn't sound like a train, what's it like?"

"You really want to experience one close up?" I watch desire darken her eyes.

"Yes," she says. "More than anything."

All her professional reserve can't hide her breathlessness. She wants the storm. She does have Angela in her.

Brandon saw it. I trust him. I trust my instincts. She's more than some TV-fed kid that thinks she might like storms. "Lock your camera into the plate on the dash and start recording," I say.

"There's nothing – "

"Do everything he tells you," I mimic Brandon.

She laughs and sets up the camera.

The record light goes on.

"Relax," I say. She settles back into the seat and crosses her arms over her breasts.

I close my eyes. I let out my breath and inhale heavy summer air. "Listen to the rain," I say.

I wait until I hear her sigh. "Listen to my words," I say. "I'll call the storm to you."

"Bullshit!"

"Everything he says," I repeat.

"What the hell," she says, and I hear her settle back and relax.

I go to work. "Tornadoes sound like a pounding heart tearing itself in two, like a screaming bag of demons coming to end a way of life."

"You've been hit?" she asks.

I open my eyes. Her eyes are wide. Her arms unfold.

"Angela and I," I say. "Listen to the rain."

She closes her eyes and leans back.

I stare through the windshield into the storm, "God, Angela loved tornadoes."

"Your wife?" She doesn't open her eyes. Her lips are moist and red.

"Not married," I say. "She was a lover a long time ago."

Kate relaxes into the seat a little.

"They had a lot in common, Angela and tornadoes. Her eyes had the deep green of a wall cloud descending from the belly of an overripe storm. Her moods rose and fell like hail cycling up and down through the core of a storm.

"Once, we were parked on a road like this one. We were kissing in a storm like this one." I pause.

Kate's eyes open again. They reflect the darkening sky outside.

"Lightning hit the car," I say.

Kate turns toward me. Concern and fear twist together in her eyes. "You both lived?" she asks.

"Better than that," I say. "The power of it passed through us. It filled our love."

I smile. "Before that, we chased storms with Brandon. Beer and adventure. After that, Angela and I chased alone. On summer nights like this one, we drove endless miles together. I was the only one she knew with equal passion for both her and the storms. We made love over and over on the cold steel floor in the back of this station wagon."

"I'm not sure I want to know — "

"It's OK," I soothe. Kate's forehead is flushed. I touch her arm. Gooseflesh rises on her skin. "The storm will come. She'll come for the story. Let her fill you."

Kate looks at me sideways, but she nods.

"Angela wanted to feel the mood of the storm through the steel floor: the chill, the electricity, the damp and dryness coming and going with the ebb and flow in the air around us.

"Eventually, storms weren't enough. Lightning wasn't enough. She wanted tornadoes; she wanted to get close. I'd look into her eyes. I'd see the cold green there, and I'd look for the lightning, for the green darkness that made our sex something supernatural.

"Angela would urge me on, 'Closer, Andy. Take me there.'

"I always did. I searched the sky for us both. I learned to search for the power with my eyes, my ears, my nose, my skin. Eventually, I just closed my eyes and felt the storms."

Kate's hand worries the top button of her shirt. The interior of the car is muggy. I point at the squall line.

Kate's eyes follow my finger.

The black line is moving straight towards us.

Kate gasps. She turns to me. Her eyes flash excitement. "That's impossible," she says.

"Even at night," I continue, "a wall cloud is darker than the blackest sky. It captures light. It makes the air still like some great monster inhaling everything and waiting. On our last night, I felt for a storm. My ears stretched towards it. My skin went cold. Angela's voice became thin, like a voice through a wire. The hair on my arms stood. I pointed the car towards the biggest storm we'd ever found. The car seemed to expand around us as we got near the heart of power."

"You had sex in a tornado?" Kate asks. "What was it like?" She's a little breathless. Her eyes take on roiling depths that match the rising power beyond the cornfield.

I nod. I don't take my eyes off the storm. "Angela," I whisper. The billows in the belly of the squall line smooth to a single green-black wall. I point again.

Kate leans forward. "Oh, my God," she says. She reaches for the radio.

I take her hand. "No," I say. "I'm calling the storm for you."

For a long moment, she looks into my eyes. Her hand is damp in mine. Her desire battles her training. Finally, flecks of green appear in her grey eyes. "What happened?" she whispers.

I pull Kate's hand to my lips and kiss her fingertips. She slides closer on the seat.

"Angela wanted more than me. She wanted the undersea silence. She wanted lightning and horizontal rain. She wanted the electric fire she only got from fucking on metal in the heart of a great storm." I open my window more. I inhale cool pretwister air. "She wanted to ride a long, twisting shaft into the sky."

Kate squeezes my hand.

I look up. The wall is not far off. My ears are tight. Even though we're shoulder to shoulder, Kate's breath sounds far away.

"That last night, she told me I was afraid of the storms.

"I turned down Davis Road, not far from here, trying to get a bearing on a wall cloud to the northwest. I told her I was trying to get closer.

"She said, 'You're afraid to be under a funnel. You're afraid the storm will kill you.'

"I stopped the car. 'Fuckin' A right!' I said.

"'I want to give myself up to the sky,' she said.

"'I want to live through my senior year.'

"She asked me why.

"She looked at me with those green eyes. I saw the storm there. I felt the draw of her, of the sky, of the screaming demons, and I couldn't answer her. I turned off Davis onto a farm road. We headed between corn rows straight for the dark and the green wall."

Kate presses against me "Oh, shit," she says. Her voice comes to me through a wire.

The undersea silence is on us. The wall has come, the wind is gone. Even with the window open, the windshield bows outwards.

"A wall cloud is enough to scare most folks," I say. I put an arm around Kate and kiss the softness behind her ear.

Her hand comes to my neck, but her eyes are on the green darkness above us.

It hangs low like God's squeegee scraping the muck from the farmlands. It's the colour of drowning in deep sea. It smothers light. It smothers thought. It promises oblivion. And it moves with magic in ways you can feel but not see. From thought to thought, it's never the same.

"The first spiral descended from the cloud." I say it, and outside the car it happens.

Kate claws at my arm.

"Angela gasped with pleasure," I say.

I take the rubber band from Kate's braid. Her red hair unwinds in my fingers. It's damp and soft.

"Angela grabbed my arm," I say. "I nearly went in the ditch.

" 'It's going to be a big one,' Angela said. 'I feel it.'

"She glowed. Maybe it was luminescence from the dashboard. Maybe it was my own excitement, but I swear she glowed. Her skin was light green, her white-blonde hair took on a ghostly luminescence, and her eyes. Oh, God, that was the thing about her. I swear her eyes held the lightning and wind. She smiled. She touched me with her eyes.

"I was hard."

Kate caresses my bulging crotch.

"I pressed the accelerator to the floor, and we fishtailed along the dirt track towards the storm.

"Angela called out and pointed. Tendrils reached downwards, braiding themselves together, pressing towards the ground. For a long moment, they hung suspended above us, joining and founding the rhythm of the storm. The funnel spun like the tail of a cat about to pounce on a barn rat."

I pull Kate's lips to mine. They're salty with her sweat. Her tongue is quick and hungry, and the kiss is long and urgent. When we break, I see the green in her eyes growing, taking over the grey.

"Finally," I say, "the funnel stabbed down directly in front of us. It became a tornado.

"Angela pulled at her shirt. Buttons ricocheted off the windshield. She clawed at my shirt. 'Andy!' she screamed. 'God, Andy!'

"I slowed the car to keep control.

" 'No!' " She clawed at my belt. 'Don't stop!'

"I hit the accelerator. The car jumped forwards.

"Dirt and debris exploded from the track half a mile in front of us. A small tree spun past the windshield and disappeared into the cornfields.

"Somehow, still driving, I found myself naked from the waist up. My pants were open. Angela's lips were on me, hot, wet, urgent.

"Twisting like the storm, she managed to get her clothes completely off. Her perfect ass was high and glowing green. Her hair danced across my lap. She was the tornado trying to suck me up into her.

"I drove hard into the storm.

"The tornado grew wider, fat with power, fast and full of the debris of the farmlands. The thing grew too fat to undulate, too pregnant with dirt, barn shingles and trees to do anything but spin.

"It filled the windshield.

"My ears popped. 'Angela,' I said. 'I'm . . . Oh, God!'

"Her head came up. 'Closer,' she said. Her eyes were darker than I'd ever seen them.

"Angela lifted a leg over me and slipped it between the seat and the car door. She guided me into her, settled her weight onto me. 'Go,' she screamed over the wind. 'Go fast, Andy! Take me there!'

"God, she was alive inside."

Kate kisses me quick to get my attention. She points. The twister is down. It's moving along the road ahead. It rips at the cornrows. "It's coming," she says.

"Angela wrapped her arms around my neck and buried her

face in my shoulder. I could barely see the road, but I kept the pedal down.

"She rose and fell with the pulse of the storm.

"Darkness surrounded us. Lightning shattered it. The rear glass of the station wagon exploded."

Kate pulls at my belt. I work my fingers through her hair to the back of her neck. The twister outside grows. It undulates. It slips back and forth across field and road, feeding on corn and dirt. The scream of the demons makes it hard for Kate to hear me.

"Angela screamed in my ear," I yell. "I barely heard her over the deafening storm.

"I screamed, too. I couldn't hear my own voice.

"Hail shattered the driver's window. Glass and rain pelted my face.

"Angela rode me tight and hot and hard. Her hair danced with electricity, straight out, and up, bending against the roof of the car. She lifted her head from my shoulder. Her eyes were black-green. They were holes through her head, and I could see the heart of the tornado through her."

Kate frees me. Her damp, warm hand wraps around my shaft. She says something, but I can't hear her.

"The car twisted," I say. I'm no longer telling the story for Kate. It doesn't matter if she hears me. "It tilted, lifted, and fell.

"She screamed. Her orgasm grabbed me, pulled me deeper into her heat.

"A spasm squeezed my ass and thighs. I exploded into her. My foot drove the accelerator to the floor. Lightning struck. The windshield exploded.

"She spoke into my ear. Her whisper was one with the wind, and I heard her. I heard her love and satisfaction. She said, 'I'll always be here for you.'

"Then the invisible hand of her lover lifted her into the sky."

I take a deep breath of heavy air.

Kate's head comes up from my lap. Her full, moist lips part. She stares. She blinks green eyes. "No!" she says. "Don't stop now."

Kate's eyes are the storm. Sweat holds her loose hair to her forehead and neck. She slips off her flannel shirt. The white curve of her breasts heaves in time with the wind buffeting the car.

The tornado moves towards us.

"I don't chase storms," I say. I take her face in my hands.

We kiss.

She tears open my shirt.

I caress one smooth breast, slide a finger across her hard nipple.

She shudders, smiles, and cradles my balls in her hot palm.

I touch her lips with mine again.

The storm screams.

Kate moans.

I help her wriggle free from her jeans.

My lips to her ear, I say, "Only seduction can open the heart of a storm."

"Yes." She slides a leg across my lap.

She leans back against the steering wheel. Her eyes are drowned green. Her skin glows. She guides me into her. She's hot-oil wet. Her insides are alive like boiling clouds.

"I'm here, Andy," she says. "Take me there!"

"Angela," I whisper.

The Perfect O

Cara Bruce

I never knew I liked pain, or how much I liked it. I've had fantasies and my bookshelves are lined with romance novels involving Victorian classrooms and harsh punishments. But I didn't *know*. What I have always known is my love of jewellery. When I was little it started out as a fascination with my mothers'. I would sit for hours holding up long earrings to my tiny lobes, shaking my head so they would brush against my seven-year-old shoulders. Then it became the junk they sold in the dollar store at the mall, fluorescent parrots, rubber oranges – anything bright and fancy attached to a metal post. Every special event in my life has been marked by the gift of earrings: topaz for my 18th birthday, aquamarine from my first serious boyfriend, diamonds for my college graduation and a pair of black pearls from my grandmother when she passed away.

I still have each and every pair. Mark, the lover before this one, bought me a beautiful mahogany jewellery box, lined in deep brown velvet and speckled with tiny holes for the thin posts of my treasures. Small, pull-out boxes ran along the bottom – the perfect place for safe storage of rusting faux silver and chipping gold. After Mark left I thought of putting the box back in my closet with the pop-up white ballerina box my father bought me years ago for my 16th birthday. The typical gift bought by a father who has no concept what 16-year-old girls need or want, a father still desperately trying to clutch on to the passing away of youth, theirs and his, by a twirling, plastic figurine. But then I opened Mark's mahogany box, ran my finger over the shiny remnants of my life, and decided what many women before me have tearfully accepted: that just because the men are rotten doesn't mean their gifts are.

I didn't think that Kyle, the man I had been seeing for the past three months, had ever noticed that I even had my ears pierced. So the night I met him for a drink and he tenderly ran his fingertips over my tiny, silver hoops, I was pleasantly surprised. Kyle was what my mother would call "a real catch". He had no particularly bad habits, dressed well, was gainfully employed and naturally good-looking. It was enough to make me wary and I was beginning to grow fearful that he was so perfect he would soon grow dull.

Kyle ordered us another round of drinks. He seemed distracted, fidgeting, glancing at the clock, tapping his fingers, and adjusting his seat. His behaviour made me nervous, typical of a man who has something to tell you but doesn't quite know how to put it into words. Finally I had to say something; if I was going to be dealt a blow I wanted to meet it head on.

"Kyle, what's on your mind?" I said, forcing him to look into my eyes.

He took a moment before he sighed and said, "Your earrings."

"My earrings? You don't like them?" This was not what I expected.

"No, no, they're fine." He fumbled in his briefcase for a moment and brought out a plain brown paper bag, which he slid to me across the table. I opened it up and withdrew a glossy magazine. On the cover was a gorgeous woman wearing an expression of unbridled lust. I opened the slick pages and was met by various shots of women pierced – in every possible location. I flipped the pages silently – my heart beating faster and my crotch growing wet. I looked up at Kyle and comprehension flooded me. His gaze was steadfast and even though I had never known these hoops to hang anywhere but from my ears, I knew I was about to.

I placed the magazine back in its wrapper and instead of returning it to him I slipped it into my purse.

"Let's get out of here," I whispered.

We drove in silence to his house. The faint pitter of evening drizzle drummed against the top of his car before it exploded into rain as we pulled into the driveway. We made a dash for the front door, dripping as we entered the front hallway. Without a word Kyle led me upstairs to his bedroom. I was nervous. My palms were sweaty and my cunt was throbbing. I began to ask him a question but he motioned with a finger for me to be quiet. He stood me in the centre of his room and took a neatly wrapped gift box off the top of his dresser.

Inside lay a single needle.

As I slowly brought my palm up to examine it my heart stopped. He began to look a little uncertain.

"That's OK, isn't it? I went to the piercing shop and asked about the gauge. That's what they told me."

"No," I murmured, turning the delicate instrument in my hand, "it's fine."

He smiled, instantly relieved. He placed his hands on my shoulders and gently massaged them. Then, without another word, he began to unbutton my blouse. I felt light-headed and my legs were simulating freshly made Jell-O. He slipped the white cotton over my shoulders and stood staring at the front-clasp white bra, slightly padded and frayed at the edges. I was embarrassed. If only I had known, I would have bought some new lingerie.

He took a deep breath and unhooked it, slowly, reverently. I was afraid to breathe. But he slipped it off, and smiled.

"Perfect," he whispered, and took a step back to examine these two mounds that I have carried with me all my adult life yet have never heard the word "perfect" used to describe them. My breath came back and without a single touch my clit sprang to life.

He was like a schoolboy enraptured, gently rubbing his forefinger over the brown nipple, which had already hardened by its sudden exposure to fresh air.

I closed my hand tight around the needle and moaned. In that moment all hope for my nipples' virginity was gone. He bent down and kissed me, his strong mouth parting mine just enough to allow his tongue to slip tenderly across my teeth.

Our bodies remained slightly apart and it took all of my willpower from pulling him close to me and pressing his pelvis against my aching cunt.

"Sit down," he said, moving away and exiting through the bathroom door.

I had not known I was one for pain.

"Why don't you take off your clothes and get comfortable?" he called. My body moved without my brain, unzipping my skirt, rolling down my stockings, trembling, quivering scared . . . and wanting.

He came back in, naked except for a pair of white boxer shorts that showed the line of his erect cock pushing against the thin fabric.

"The alcohol," he said, and held up a bottle and cotton like a track star with a trophy.

He came over and knelt before me, placing his toys upon the bedside table. I sighed as he gently kissed the point where my calf began to curve. His mouth worked its way up along the soft inside of my leg, pausing on my thigh. He parted my legs slowly, forcing me to bite my lip to keep quiet from anticipation, and attached them to leather buckles that must have been previously secured on the bottom of the wooden posters.

I jolted at the feel of the cool buckle against my ankle. "It will be easier if you can't move," he explained calmly. He reached up and took my right arm, bringing it to the post as well. The buckle was secured against my right wrist, then my left. Not only were the restraints keeping me still, they were making me terribly aroused. I sat on the edge of his bed: wet, wanting, and spread out for his needle.

He uncurled my hand which was still clenched around the instrument. Then, with careful precision he wiped it clean with the alcohol. He blew on my nipples. They were so hard they looked as if they could have been popped off by a simple flick of his thumb. I gasped. He drew the soaked swab across and smiled as they amazingly grew another millimetre. He looked into my eyes. "Just relax," he whispered.

I felt the needle as soon as it touched the edge of my breast. He was teasing me, tracing the curve of my falling bosom with the cool metal. He traced my areola, then brought it to the edge of my hard bud. I moved against the restraints but they were too tight.

"Relax," he said. "I'm just going to push the needle in, leave it for a moment, pull it out and replace it with the hoops. Then, once they are in, I'm going to kiss you all over. I'm going to make circles on your clit with my tongue, I promise you are going to feel good."

As he spoke he began pushing the needle in. It was cold then burning hot. I heard him telling me how he was going to fuck me, I felt the metal piercing through my tender flesh, the endorphins from the pain flushing my face and making me woozy. It was almost orgasmic. And it was in.

"There, that wasn't that bad." He stood up and surveyed his handiwork, slipping out of his boxers and allowing his thick dick to spring fully to attention.

He opened the drawer of his bedside table and brought out another, matching needle. Then he knelt again.

"Are you OK?" he asked me. His eyes were sparkling.

Through my reverie I managed to nod. He smiled, white teeth shining. He came towards me, bringing his mouth down over the untouched breast. I felt his tongue caressing the brown skin made smooth by excitement. My other tit was straining itself against the metal lodged inside, increasing my pain and arousal to a point where I was again dangerously close to climax. He removed his warm mouth and cold air blew in, then, slowly, so slowly, he began pushing the other needle. The pain made me high and his voice hypnotized me. He was agonizingly slow and I imagined with what tenderness he would glide his huge cock into my wanting cunt.

The second needle was through.

He slid his hand over his long dick. "Beautiful," he whispered. I had stopped breathing long ago.

From the bedside table came two matching heavy silver rings. He held them up for me to see.

"Do you like them?" he asked. "I went to three different shops to find these. They're perfect for you."

I nodded, wondering how my old bras would rub against that heavy silver, afraid they would look so obvious against a white T-shirt, excited at the thought of him gently tugging them as he pulled me close.

He slid the needle out quickly. The sharp pain was replaced with a rush that forced me to cry out from the intensity. He pushed the pointed spike of the earring through and hooked the loop. I moaned. My nipple was dragged downwards by its heaviness. The pain faded into a dull ache. He did the other one with the same quick yet precise care. My entire body seemed to hang forwards with the weight of the metal. He lifted my chin. Now even his touch was electric. I was over sensitized, ready to come in an instant. His tongue was so warm in my mouth. His hands so firm as they undid the buckles.

My head was spinning as he lifted me and laid me back on the bed. Every nerve-ending of my body led directly to the metal hoops. I was a magnet waiting for a charge.

"You are so beautiful," he said, and reached down and pulled on one of the hoops. I cried out in that fine mixture of pain and pleasure. He smiled. He began to lick inside the silver circle, opening my hot pussy with his cock. He picked up a ring with his teeth and he entered me. I no longer knew where I was. My body was flooded with the most acute sensations I had ever experienced. I thrust my hips to meet him as he plunged in deeper, his tongue finding the sore bud beneath the silver. With his mouth on one breast he lifted his hand and began rubbing the other nipple with his fingers. All my blood followed his fingers.

I yelled, ripping at his strong back. He moved into me, fucking me hard and fast. My entire body was on edge and I had never hurt so bad, yet felt so good. As he plunged once more I began to come, but this was different. This didn't begin in my stomach and burn through me, this orgasm was centred around those two metal rings, just like a perfect silver O.

The Beach Boy

Rich Denis

My wife's breasts stand proud as she sits up, stretching her arms towards the burning midday sun. I feel the familiar warm surge of affection. At 35, she is only a slightly more generous version of the statuesque showgirl I found, sequinned and feathered, in a Vegas chorus line. She is blind now, but I love her no less.

She reaches for the suntan oil, pours a rich stream across her chest, then spreads the coconut-scented liquid over her body. Occasionally a slippery hand strays into her bikini bottom which, in showgirl style, is pulled up high on her hips. The shred of fabric becomes oily, defining, rather than obscuring, what it barely covers. She releases a satisfied sigh and reclines again, her skin shining. She has already turned chestnut brown.

The young beach boy, his eyes hidden behind cheap mirrored sunglasses, leans on his rake, mesmerized. His sole purpose in life seems to be cleaning the soft white sand, to make a small portion of this Mozambique paradise neat for tourists like us. For this simple task he earns two dollars a week. Today, I know he would have worked for free.

Though other guests are scattered along the beach, he has spent most of his time close to us, a moth attracted to the flame of my wife's almost naked body. Each time she's performed this ritual with the oil, she has noticed that the rake falls suddenly quiet. I've described him to her; his age, his height, the bulge in his tattered shorts.

The sun is vicious, too hot for me. I dart across the powdery sand and wade out into the ocean. The water is tepid, its colour absurdly blue. I break into a gentle breaststroke and taste salt water on my lips. A hundred feet offshore, I stop swimming and tread water, surrounded by silence. I can see my wife. She sits up, and the beach boy walks across to her. I know that she's called to him. She is propped up on one elbow; he squats beside her, close enough that she could lick the sweat from his ebony skin. Her hand moves reassuringly to rest on his thigh as she speaks to him. Their heads turn towards me, sunlight glinting off their dark glasses. I kick into a fast crawl and swim farther out, excited and horrified at the expectation that tugs in my gut. My reaction is still the same after two years, and over a dozen of these . . . little incidents. We have long lost the logic of whether she does this for me, or if I allow it for her. It doesn't matter.

When I wade back to the shore, she is gone. The boy is gone, too. I relax in my beach chair, and take a cold beer from the cooler. Third world holidays are wonderful, away from the predictable tourist path. What is luxury, if not this? Beer, burning white sand, an impossibly blue ocean, and people you'll never see again.

I finish my drink and wander back to our tiny hut. Thick bushes with yellow blooms cluster along the pathway with a sickly, heavy scent. Freshly whitewashed, the hut nestles amid the fat, ridged trunks of towering palm trees. And there are two windows, framed in blue. I move palm fronds aside, and step close to one.

She is bending over the back of a wooden chair, her legs spread. Her perfect rump, with its minute pale vee where the bikini nestled, is pressed to the boy's crotch. He stands naked behind her, and fucks her.

I light a cigarette.

Her breasts sway and the muscles in her long legs flex beneath the skin. Her fingers clutch the seat of the chair. The boy is teenage skinny. The shaft of his cock appears and disappears with his thrusts. I wonder if it feels different to her, his shaft. Do they all feel different, and like Braille she can recognize them? If all the cocks she has ever known were lined up, and she walked slowly past them grasping and stroking each one, would she put a name to each? I'd have no idea if each woman I'd ever had were slid onto my cock, each breast I'd felt were put in my hand.

Shiny lines of sweat trickle down the boy's spine. I suck on my cigarette and wait.

Soon her head begins to nod; her drawn-out "*Yes*" comes clearly through the window as she rises to the tips of her cerise painted toes. For a few seconds, she remains on point, then she sinks down and turns around. Her blank gaze passes over me. She is grinning.

The boy's cock sticks straight out. Its angry purple-black colour is at odds with the pink condom. His cock is long and thin – probably the thinnest one I've ever seen. She reaches out to find him. Her hand connects with his hip and moves down. She tugs off the condom and leans closer. Her pink tongue appears. She licks at the tip a few times, then her mouth slides over this licorice dick.

Am I fascinated or horrified? I'm not sure, but something in this scenario makes my own dick lumber to middle-aged attention. I drop my cigarette and leave the window.

The door is unlatched. I walk into the room with my best reassuring smile in place. The boy jumps back, his eyes widening to saucers. I gave him a thumbs-up, and tell him to relax. Uncertain, torn between pleasure and escape, he glances down at my wife, then back at me, then at the door. I hold up a ten-dollar bill and nod my head vigorously to re-inforce my generosity. He stares at the money and remains where he is. I step out of my swim shorts and drag the small table away from the wall.

Lying across the table on her back, legs spread on one side, head hanging on the other, she provides perfect access for the boy and me. His cock, now level with her face, slides neatly into her mouth. She cups a hand around his balls, controlling his thrusts. Each time he withdraws her teeth scrape along the length of him, the way I've watched her eat an artichoke. From the other side of the table, I lift her legs onto my shoulders. Her thighs are slick and wet from the boy's previous efforts. I push into her.

In our normal life, sex is efficient and satisfactory; far better since she became blind, but still merely pleasing. We have eliminated the unnecessary and the frivolous. Like eating, we do it often and sensibly. But occasionally we want something different, a treat, and all treats become boring if one indulges too frequently. So we save this, or variations on this, for vacations. And for lucky strangers.

Like demented lumberjacks, the boy and I saw at her from both sides. His eyes catch mine, and I wink. He frowns. I settle into a rhythm that matches his. Small cries of pleasure seep from her. We are a fucking team, the three of us.

She moves her free hand to a nipple, rolls it between her fingers, and immediately jerks and squirms harder. On my shoulders, her legs squeeze my head and begin to tremble. Trapped and impaled between us, she arches and twists as she comes.

Her body relaxes. I slide out of her. His cock slips from her mouth. But she is still for only a moment before she flips over, grabs for him. Says, "Help me here." Her expression is serious and wild.

I take her wrist, guiding her hand towards his dick. She strokes him a few times, and then says, "Now you."

I put my hand on him. Her fingers close over my knuckles, feeling what I'm doing. I check his reaction. His lips slide back to reveal white teeth. I kneel and begin to work at him. His eyes close as I tighten my grip, rubbing him harder. His cock twitches, and her hand squeezes mine. Her head is tilted away from us, hearing and feeling what we cannot, living in a sexual world I'll never know. I envy her.

Suddenly he squirts two pearly jets of come. I hold tight, point him at her and milk another spurt from him, then another.

Sticky white lines are streaked across her face. She laughs as she sticks out her tongue and licks a lingering drop from her lip. "A flood," she says.

I stand and pull her up, and tell her that kids always have a lot of spunk. And as I say it I feel him grab my own cock. I take her hand and let her feel this happen.

She pulls me closer. "Let him, please."

"But . . ."

"Please."

This is our game, to pretend I am reluctant. That I allow it only for her pleasure. Already hard at work, he has understood nothing of this. His roughened hands are surprisingly adept. She squats next to us, listening, a small smile on her face as her own hand moves between her legs.

Until two years ago, I'd never had a man touch me. At first I was shocked at how much I liked it. I had no idea men did it better, that their careless aggression was so exciting. I have no interest in what label this attaches to me: gay, bisexual, who cares? It gives us pleasure. Life is for living.

My pale shaft swells between his dark fingers. The swollen ruby head disappears and reappears as his fist slides over me. I feel young again. I wish she could see.

As if reading my thoughts she reaches out. Her fingers are wet. "My stud," she says. "Tell me it feels wonderful."

I tell her, between groans, and she laughs with delight.

Her pleasure makes me swell even more. The muscles in my thighs harden. Warmth spreads slowly along my spine. The boy feels my reaction and speeds his stroke. The heat moves faster and accelerates, until it burns through me with a rush, and my juice makes a small arc onto his arm. My legs relax, but his hand continues to move on me with no less insistence. I am at that contradictory place where I desperately want the exquisite agony in my cock to end, but never stop. To my surprise, I pump another white stream across his hand and then the pleasure is too much. I pull away from him and sink to the floor exhausted.

My wife leans forwards and kisses me. "Thank you, baby."

Too spent to reply, I gesture to the boy. It is time for him to go. He pulls on his tattered shorts, takes his money, and turns towards the door.

My wife and I sit together, entwined on the warm cement.

The Boss

Jazz Lloyd

He's tall, dark and distant.

Just like my daddy.

And just like daddy – he's just out of reach.

He's got daddy's eyes. Black and dirty like marbles in the dust.

He's got my daddy's big clean hands. Clean on account of having counted money all his life and pushed cold hard pieces of paper around his big leather desk.

He smells like daddy too. Though I couldn't tell you how daddy smells. I know it when I smell it. It's like the BBQ going on next door. It triggers your appetite but you're not invited to share the meat. Don't get me wrong. I never did my daddy. We were a respectable household. There was never any suggestion of doing daddy. That would be a disgrace. But I never met a man I loved as much as daddy. I never knew a man I wanted more to impress and I never thought I would. That was before I got the job at Swelter Inc.

That was before I met Tom.

Tom is my boss. He tells you to call him Tom but he still wants you to think of him as Mr. He dresses like a Mr, with his Armani suits and his shiny, shiny shoes. If you stood close enough to him and looked down you could see your reflection in those shoes. I have an ongoing fantasy where he lifts his foot onto a stool so I can clean his shoes before a very important meeting. I imagine that I lift my power suit, squat down on those shoes and rub the juices from my wet and sticky pussy all over them. Dirty the image, muddy the reflection. Leave my scent all over his feet so that with every step he is reminded of my sex. I want to start my own BBQ.

I don't know whether he reads my filthy thoughts. Sometimes I imagine he can.

And I am humiliated at my own depravity. If daddy only knew just what I'd like to do to him he might even invite me to sit on his lap, behind his big wooden desk. He might take me over his knee, lift my little skirt, pull down my little white panties and thrash my pretty white arse.

He might give me 20 strokes. He might leave his handprint pink and rare all over it. He might, you know, if he knew what I was thinking. But only to absolve me of my wicked thoughts. Only because he loved me.

I like to think of my job as a role. That makes it more fun. If I pretend I'm in a movie then even boring jobs like filing seem less monotonous. I can pretend that the camera's moving around me on a dolly and I'm checking out the key lights to make sure I'm well lit. I'm not worried about how I look because, when I'm the star of my movie, I'm always gorgeous. Mr Tom is my leading man. He doesn't know that's what he is. If you asked him about the movie, he'd probably say that he was the star and everyone else had vignettes and character parts. If you asked him to show you his script you may even find that you didn't have a role. That's what I'm afraid of. That I don't have a role in his movie.

I am so afraid of that knowledge that I have to make a conscious effort to disguise my obsession. But the smell of him is enough to throw me off balance. I attempt to keep some distance so I can think, even though I want to be near him all the time. I would sleep in the office if he'd let me. I'd sleep on his big black chair and cover myself with his long woollen coat. The one that lives on his hat stand. I'd bury my face in the leather and breathe him into my dreams.

In my dreams I do the forbidden. I touch him. There is no touching Mr Tom in real life. He is untouchable. On account of the woman that he married to forget. And his two baby girls who frolic in a burgundy frame on his desk. When I go into his office, early in the morning, before anyone has arrived I turn that frame to the wall just for a few minutes. I don't want to bring them into this. In my fantasy he has no children. There is only me. Through his window Sydney spreads out in front of me. She is wild and beautiful. If I look down I feel vertigo. I imagine that Mr Tom has come early. That he silently walks up behind me and slips his arms around my waist. I imagine those arms embracing me. Exploring my forbidden arse, forbidden breasts, forbidden flesh and how I would open up to him. I imagine him bending me over the windowsill so I had to look down so I had to feel the vertigo and slipping his hard cock deep inside me. Without foreplay, without hesitation, unmercilessly fucking me. So hard, so deep, that I find a moan in the bottom of my belly that I didn't know I'd housed. And when I throw back my head and throw that moan right through the ceiling it vibrates through every floor of the tower. And the entire glass palace shudders with the impact.

"Good morning, Julie."

Unmercilessly, hungrily, so hard, so deep.

"Good morning, Tom. I'm checking out the view from your window. It's beautiful this time of the morning. I'm making coffee; would you like one?" The morning sun is streaking through the windows and the day is already charged.

This is how I start every morning. Charged. I no longer eat breakfast. Some mornings I ache for him so bad that I have to lock myself in the cubicle and massage my swollen sex. Everything feels like a caress. My dress brushing against my thigh. Water running over my hands, the sound of my own breath. My nipples are always hard and they ache for release. I want him to lead me around the room by my nipples. I want to watch him suckle and play with my breasts. And when he grabs for my arse, a hand around each cheek. I want him to own it. I want to be his.

"Julie, can you ring my wife please and tell her you'll send a courier to pick up the Lyman papers? They're on the dressing table beside the bed."

I pick up the phone and ring his wife. I'm imagining her getting the girls ready for school.

I'm imagining the bed unmade and the sheets unstained and the papers that he studied all night strewn out over the pillows. She talks to me as if I'm her assistant too. She talks like the Master's wife. I talk to her as if I don't really exist. As if I'm an automaton or a wind up doll. As if I'm stupid and insignificant, just another cog in the wheel of business. She doesn't hear the dirty great whirlpool going on under my skin. She doesn't know what her husband does to my pulse when he walks in the room. She doesn't see him that way. Maybe that's because he's not her daddy. Maybe she married the wrong man.

I married the wrong man. I married a man with faded eyes and downy blond hair and skin as hard and cool as a pumpkin. A man I can beat in an arm wrestle and tear up slowly with my tongue. I don't want to tear him up. I don't even enjoy it. But he begs it from me and, ever the whore, I oblige. Still I lay untouched by even the most passionate of his attempts to conquer me. I flatten myself out and lay myself limp so as not to intimidate him. So as not to give him the sensation of being devoured. It is I who wants to be devoured. Not he. He wants to devour me. So when he is lying on top of me, the veins on his skinny arms bursting with the effort, I think of Tom. I imagine him opening his arms like a hawk and enfolding me within them. I imagine myself naked and small and lost in his flesh. I imagine his breath on my neck and his voice in my ear. He says, "You're mine. You've always been mine. Open up. I want to fuck you . . ."

I say, "Here's your coffee, Tom."

He is sitting on his big leather chair, behind his big leather desk. He is wearing black and his body is open, his arms stretched out behind his head as he talks on the phone. He smiles at me and motions for me to wait. I stand on the other side of the table watching him, animated, talking to a client. I know what will happen. He will not cut the conversation short for me. He has motioned to me and it is I who have to wait. Wait for him with my throbbing cunt and my nipples alert until I have been given my instructions. I will stand very still. I will not squirm. I will not wipe the trail of juice that's inching down my thigh. I will not unbutton my blouse and expose my breasts or squeeze and pull at my nipples. I will not find my well-marked spot on the left hand corner of his desk and massage my ache on its leather mound. I will stand there for five minutes? Ten minutes? Fifteen minutes . . . ? I will stand there until he has finished his conversation. I will stand there all day if he wishes it. And I will write the next chapter in my script.

The carpet is new. It smells like wool. I roam it, naked, on all fours. I'm the office panther. They let me stay because I'm beautiful. I roam the offices on every floor of the tower. I'm therapy for all the office workers. I give them permission to touch a living thing. All the love they cannot show each other they give to me. I raise morale so management allows a wild thing a home. And although I am adored by both men and women I have taken a fancy to Mr Tom.

I like his carpet, I like to bury my face in its pile, roll on my back with my legs in the air and purr with satisfaction.

I like to slink around his ankles and/ leap onto his desk without reprimand.

"Thanks for the coffee, Julie."

He takes the cup in both hands and leans back in his chair. He takes a long sip of the strong milky brew and observes me without wavering. I don't know if he wants me to stay or go. I smile and turn to leave the room. I am unable to talk because I know the break in my voice will betray me. I make a beeline for the door but his voice halts me mid journey. "Julie." He says my name. And when he says my name I imagine him wrapping his mouth around it. Swallowing me whole.

I turn to face him. He just looks at me, looks through me. Burns holes into me with those dusty black eyes and smiles. The silence is a test of will. I want to raise the white flag and admit defeat. I want to throw myself at him, rip off my clothes and parade myself for him naked, fan myself across his desk and mess up his paperwork . . .

"Julie, there's something I have to say to you. Can you shut the door please?"

He is sitting on his big leather chair and his cock is slowly mushrooming in his trousers. I can't keep my eyes off it. He's speaking but it's not his words that I'm listening to. His voice fades out as his cock grows and takes form in front of me. I imagine myself crawling under his desk and unbuttoning his stiff black trousers and taking that powerful muscle in my mouth. I imagine sliding my lips hungrily up and down his shaft, pausing to run my tongue behind his balls and take each one, like Chinese fruit, into my mouth. He no longer has any control. He is completely at my mercy. I tease and flick his straining member with my tongue. I take his huge cock in my mouth and feel it sliding down my throat. He's gripping the sides of his big leather chair. He bucks and thrusts, his arse sliding down towards my open mouth, his pleasure mounting as my warm wet mouth takes him further and further inside. His ecstasy builds until he loses all sense of his own boundaries. He throws back his head and releases his pleasure in a howl that shoots right through the ceiling, echoing through every floor of the tower and the entire glass palace shudders with the impact.

Suddenly his voice fades back in.

"So, Julie we've decided after this three-month trial period that we're going to let you go. You'll be given a fortnight's payout but we'd like you to finish on Friday."

"OK, then."

He nods his black eyes, cold, unmoved at having had to play the henchman. He's already onto his next task for the day. "If anyone rings I'm not here. I'm just going to check my email." He turns on his computer and begins going through his in-tray.

I leave the room. He does not call me back. He does not follow me to my office.

He does not throw himself at my feet and beg my forgiveness.

He gets back to pushing cold hard pieces of paper around his big leather desk.

He gets back to business.

Yep. Just like daddy.

The Devil and Mrs Faust

Ian Philips

Yer never gonna believe this story. I don't blame ya. I have a hard time believin' it an' it happened t'me. I mean, how often does the Devil talk with a Jew?

What? Oh, sure, Pat Buchanan an' half of Idaho want ya t'think it happens every day. Right after the Devil calls one of us, we triangulate with our other cells in Moscow an' Jerusalem. Actually, if ya play a video tape of the Academy Awards – any year – backwards, all his instructions are there for the year to come.

Trust me. Whatevuh y've learned about Jews an' the Devil in Sunday School or yer Rotary Club an' yer Junior League meetin's is all wrong. We're talkin' total crap here! This don't happen every day. T'be honest with ya, I think this was the first time. An' first time out, he *shtups* one of us.

Actually, I *shtupped* the hell outta him.

All right already. Stop with the eye-rollin'. Hear me out an' then close yer mind. Just listen, will ya?

In the beginnin', there was this fuckin' *schlimazel* an' his saint of a wife. That's me. My name's Ruth. Ruth Faust.

Again with the eye-rollin'. Wait an' hear my whole name an' then roll away. Ruth Faust, née – that means "born" if yer a girl – Ruth Marie Vitale. What gives? yer askin' yerselves. Whoeva heard of a Italian girl named Ruth?

My mutha, née – don't ya just love that word. It sounds like somethin' outta Shakespeare. What? Ya don't think I ever read the bastard. Hey, don't let the plain speakin' ways of my people fool ya. What people? New Yorkers, ya *schmo*. Greenlawn, Long Island, t'be exact.

Anyways, I've read the complete works of Mr William Shakespeare three times in the last year. That's right. I said "year". OK, OK. Hold the phone. I'll get to that if you stop rushin' me.

My mutha's name when she was born, in case yer still interested, was Estha Rosenbaum. Guess what? She's a Jew. An' 'cause of that, I'm a Jew in the eyes of good ol' *Eretz Yisrael*. I could make *aliah* – that's Hebrew for returnin' to the muthaship – in a second an' be putzin' aroun' Tel Aviv's equivalent of the Walt Whitman Mall t'day.

My *tata*, Sal – that's Sal, not Saul – his family came over on the boat about a hundred years ago from Palermo. That's in Sicily, by the way. That's right. I'm a *Sicilian* Jew. Don't fuck w'me. Unless ya want yer bed, yer house, an' yer world t'be seriously rocked. Even the Devil'll vouch for that.

I wasn't always so in ya face, though. Actually, I'd never talked back to anyone till two years ago. Honest to Gawd.

Hey! I said enough already with the eyes.

Na, since I was a kid, I've always been the good little girl. The problem was that, on the inside, I wasn't really good. It's just that I was afraid of gettin' caught doin' all the dirty stuff I was thinkin' about doin' – *all the time*. An', on the outside, I wasn't ever little. That's right. I was fat. I still *am* fat. The only difference is that now I'm fat with a fuckin' vengeance. But I'm gettin' ahead of myself here.

Back then, I was just fat. An' shy. An' a girl. It couldn'ta been worse. Except at home. I mean, me an' my parents didn't hold hands all day an' skip aroun' the house. But they loved me. I think they worried about me bein' so quiet 'cause they weren't. No way, no how. But that didn't matter. In their eyes, I was their beautiful daughter, Ruth Marie. An' as for the fat, they were unusual for the time. They never said a word. I mean, how could they. The food don't fall far from the table, if y'know what I'm sayin'.

So, home was allright. Hell was anywheres other kids where. Gawd, kids can be such fuckin' shits. Like at school, durin' recess, in the third grade, I'm finishin' up my lunch, bitin' into my Charleston Chew an' dreamin' of what it'd be like to touch Bobby Randall down there, an' Joey Fusaro comes over an' starts in on me. Don't ask me what he said. Either yer fat an' y'know or yer not an' y've said it. Or whaddabout every afternoon in tenth grade, after gym an' after fingerin' myself to the point of no return – twice – in the showers while thinkin' about Scott Jacobs bonin' me, an' I have to walk back to my locker past Mary Kilpatrick an' hear her wonderin' aloud to her *girls*, Brigit O'Shaughnessy an' Shannon McQuaid, about why it takes so long for me to shower. Y'know. All that *blubber* needs time to hose off or some freakin' shit like that.

You'd think things woulda gotten better in my junior year when I gave up on food an' just swallowed pills an' washed 'em down with Diet Cokes. I lost 70 pounds by senior year.

T'be honest, I lost many things by senior year. That's when I met my future husband Kurt. Kurt Faust. A little too Aryan Nation, I know. But I fell in love with him, not his name. Trust me, the last name coulda been worse. Thank Gawd, it wasn't Waldheim.

Actually, he's *Dr* Kurt Faust. He'd want ya to know that. What my *schmuck* of an ex-husband – I'm gettin' to that – wouldn't want ya to know is that, after ten years of tryin' an' failin', he had to make a deal with the Devil t'get his tenure at S.U.N.Y. The one in Stony Brook.

I'm not shittin' ya. I swear. The original Slick Willie. Lucifuh.

So where was I? Oh, yeah. Senior Year.

Kurt'd just transfered in. Instant misfit. We met for the first time when we sat next to each other in band practice. What instruments? Trumpet. Don't laugh. I had amazin'ly strong lips. Still do, just a lot lower.

An' did I mention he was cute? Little did I know he was a *putz* in *mensch*'s clothin'.

Lookin' back, it's so obvious I was naive. Not in the stupid way where ya get what ya deserve. But in the sad way where ya settle for somethin' that's so-so 'cause ya can't believe you'll ever get anythin' better. If y've been there, y'know what I'm talkin' about. If ya haven't, forget about it.

When I saw Kurt all I saw was the *mensch*. This really kind,
gentle man. He wasn't the first guy to kiss me. C'mon, my life
was never *that* pathetic. But Gawd, could he put his
embouchure to good use! An' no, he wasn't the first guy to
fuck me. But he was the first to really look at me while he was
poundin' away. Askin' me is this good for me? Do I like this?
How about that? An' he was definitely the first to go down on
me. I bet he's still got little dents in his head where I dug my
nails in.

Maybe that was all show. He gave me head so I'd give him
one of my "famous" blowjobs. Yeah, I had a reputation, at
least among the football team, for doin' things their girlfriends
wouldn't. That's right. No gag-reflex. No shit. I musta practised my way through a field of cucumbers the summuh before
my senior year. *An' I swallowed.*

Or maybe the reason he was so sweet was 'cause he still
believed he had everythin' ahead of him. Hell, he was 17. He
hadn't failed yet. He'd never even fucked up. Never lost
anythin' really special.

Not till April 3, 1977. That was the day the doctuh told my
mutha, who told my fathuh, what I'd already learned two
weeks before, pissin' on a pink plastic stick in the bathroom. I
was pregnant. Go ahead. Say it. Y've been dyin' to.

Oy!

Feel better?

Yeah, there was lots of tears. An' shoutin'. An' more tears
when I finally told Kurt. But he did the *mensch*ly thing an'
asked me to marry him. An' I was 17 too an' wait-listed at
Hofstra – can ya believe it? Hofstra!

An' I was scared. I was in love. I said yes.

In May, we graduated. In June, we got married. In July, we
got our own apartment. Both our parents helped with the rent.
In August, I miscarried an' I lost my baby.

OK, I don't mean t'be flip or nothin', but let's just say I
knew about Hell long before I met the Devil. An' that's all I
plan to say ahout the "Summer of 77".

Kurt got his first degree. I got a job as an office manager for
this lame-wad office supply company. I also got back the 70
pounds I'd lost an' then some. Next Kurt goes an' gets his

master's. An' then, in the four years it took him t'get his doctorate, my mutha – Gawd rest her soul – died of cancer an' my fathuh – Gawd rest his soul – lasted about a year longer before he died of grief. That left just me an' Kurt. In other words, I was alone.

I missed 'em somethin' fuckin' awful. Still do.

So, yeah, right. Where was I? Right. Kurt gets his doctorate. In what? History. With a special emphasis on that magical moment when the gawd-awful Middle Ages turned into the ain't-it-friggin'-swell-t'be-alive Renaissance. What was the word he used all the time? Oh, yeah. "Liminal". It was a *liminal* moment. I think it means "doorway" in Latin. You know, "threshold". Like what you carry a bride over. Or that invisible boundary you have to cross t'get from bad to worse.

Which Kurt an' I did some time in 1997. Our 20th anniversary – can you fuckin' believe it? Twenty fuckin' years.

Now'd be a good time for ya to roll yer eyes.

Thanks.

I don't know why we stayed t'gether that long. I mean, I guess in the beginnin', even after the baby died, it was 'cause I was in love with him. But from August 17, 1977, Kurt Faust hated me. I mean, in his *cockamamy* mind, I was the fuckin' cunt – his words, not mine – who trapped him in marriage an' then killed his child. But he needed a maid so he kept me on. I see it now. I didn't wanna see it so much then. I told ya I used t'be very different.

Take sex for example. Not like I wanted to have sex for a long time after the baby, but at some point the jones comes back. I mean, it's part of bein' human. I used to try all the time t'get him as hot-an'-bothered as I was. But he'd push me away. An' then, for some gawddamned freakin' mysterious reason known only to him, he wouldn't. An' when he was done, I wished he hadn't bothered, the *schlub*. You know. Like I'd be goin' down on him an' right when he's about to burst, he goes an' pulls it out an' shoots all over himself or the bed. The same with fuckin'. It's like he never wanted his precious gawddamned fuckin' seed anywheres near me again. An' goin' down on me? Gettin' *me* off? You can *so* forget about that.

Right, 1997. By then, we'd been livin' in Smithtown for almost ten years an' Kurt'd been teachin' in the Department of European Languages, Literature an' Culchah at Stony Brook where he spends alla his time runnin' the tenure track like a rat in a wheel at the pet store. We'd stopped havin' sex altogether an' didn't even talk. Wheneva he was home, he lived in the downstairs den: *his* office, *his* study, *his* space. Occasionally, he opens his door an' shouts out some command, which I ignore, or some complaint, which I also ignore. Why bother? I'm mean, it may take milk a few days to go sour. But, with Kurt, it took 20 long years. An', Gawd, by 1997, he was the foulest *farbissener* there ever was.

What? *Farbissener*? You know. A bitter ol' fuck.

Oh. What's with all the Yiddish? ya ask.

Now ya ask.

Yeah, yeah. I've heard it all before: if I'm a *Sicilian* Jew, how come I never go an' blurt out a really killuh insult about my ex in Italian. I mean, it's obvious I'm not too fond of him nowadays. For good reason too. An' the language has got some fuckin' perfect words for a man like Kurt Faust.

The answer's simple.

Pretty much everythin' was *verboten* – you know, *forbidden* – in Grandma Renata's house, 'specially swearin'. An' my dad's dad, Grandpa Giancarlo, died when he was just a kid, leavin' him alone with his five olduh sisters, each one a nun from birth, an' his holy terror of a Mutha Superior. An' the rest of dad's family lives in Jersey an' he only saw 'em wheneva there was a funeral or weddin'. Sure, he learned a few dirty words from his cousins. What teenage boy can't say "whore" in at least two languages? *Gabiche?*

Gawd, I can hear him doin' it now in my head. He's yellin' from the reclina in front of the TV to my mutha in the kitchen about his cousin Vito's third wife, Concetta. "You like *her*? I *hate* her. What? Huh?! 'Cause the *butanna*'s a freakin' hoo-uh, Esta, that's why!"

Yeah, my *tata* Sal could curse with the best of 'em. But he never learned how to swear the way yer supposed to in Italian. Rapidfire. Arms an' fingers shootin' off in the air. Which means I never learned how to swear like an Italian, like a

Sicilian. Which is too bad, cuz Italians can curse as good as they cook. *An'* fuck.

But, boy, whadda mouth Bubbe Rachel had on her. That's my mutha's mutha. An' if ya wanted to talk to her ya had to learn to give as good as y'got. By the time I was six, she had me swearin' up such a blue streak, I could make even *her* blush every now an' then. I wish she were still alive to see just how much *chutzpah* her little *bubeleh*'s got now. She'd totally *kvell.*

That's Yiddish for "cream in yer jeans". An' ya will too if ya let me finish my story. OK?! So, one night in 1997, Kurt comes all the way outta his office an' speaks to *me.* OK. Speaks *at* me. He tells me he knows that I think I'm some hot-shit witch. Which I never said or thought, yet. But it was no secret either what I was doin' in my freetime. An' there were all those trips an' cheques to the Magickal Childe in New York. Who knew the *schmendrick* still paid attention to the outside world? An' then he goes an' says the most fuckin' outrageous thing eva. He says he needs *my* help with a research project of *his.*

Yeah, I looked just like ya. My mouth all open wide. Oh, did I forget to tell ya I'm a witch?

Well, *bubeleh*, I am. I'm a fuckin' amazin' witch. An', maybe, if ya keep bein' a good listener, I'll give ya a ride on my broom when I'm done tellin' ya my story.

What? When did I turn into a witch? Listen, ya don't just turn into one. What are ya? From California or somethin'? This ain't *Bewitched* we're talkin' about. Ya can twitch ya nose all ya want, but you'll look like a friggin' rabbit with a coke habit an' that's about it. Na, it's just like everythin' else. Y'gotta start out knowin' nothin' an' then work yer ass off.

For me, that was when I joined this monthly women's encounta group. The year's 1981 an' I'm 22 an', as ya can imagine from what I've told ya so far, very lonely. Yeah, we did that rite of passage for the repressed housewife. Y'know the one: ya squat over a hand mirror an' read between ya lips. Gawd, I can see the rest of their faces now. Some of 'em look so shocked, like they'd just been asked to go down on the woman next to 'em (a request that, at the time, I'm sorry to say, would have had me runnin' for the car). Actually, Mrs

Scaduto does. Run for the car, that is. I'm already hikin' up my dress an' pullin' down my panties before I hear her car door slam. By the time she's floorin' the car into reverse an' then grindin' the gears over to first, I'm done wedgin' the slightly steamy mirror between my thighs.

You'd think I'd be all hesitant to do this shit in front of strangers. Wrong again. First, the mirror was nothin' new. The summuh I was 13 I wanked off in front of the mirror every day. An' takin' a peek at my twat. No problem. What? Yeah, I know it took me a long time t'get over how others saw my body. I was there, Einstein. But I never was ashamed of my twat. Don't ask me how or why the Angel of Penis Envy passed me over. All I know is that me an' my twat have been best friends since I was four.

What's with the face? Oh, don't even try. A lot of well-meanin' women over the years have "counselled" me – that's Joyce's word – Joyce Krieger, she's the one that started the group. Anyways, they've counselled me to call it by any other name. Sorry, "ladies". Sorry, Joyce. But I'm gonna call my "female mystique" a "twat" till the day I die.

Why? That's easy. I hate all the other words. "Vagina." It's too clinical. It makes me dry up every time I hear it. All I see are stirrups an' cold, shiny speculums. An' "vulva". It's a great name for a drag queen an' that's about it. An' "pussy". Puh-leez. If I was a size two, maybe. But t'me, it sounds so high-school, y'know. An' "cunt", y'gotta scrunch up yer mouth just to say it. It's too tight an' angry. An' that ain't my twat. No ways, no how. "Twat." Y'gotta really stretch yer mouth to say that. Wide. An' it is. An' deep too. Especially mine.

So, after a year, the group kinda turns into this witches' coven. Or, as Joyce, who's known to witches far an' wide t'day as High Priestess Morganna Moonblood, calls it, "a circle of goddesses". The first meetin', I feel kinda stupid. Joyce keeps wanderin' aroun' the room with that same damn mirror an' makes us tell our reflections, "Thou art Goddess." But it's still better than waitin' aroun' for Kurt to come home from classes an' pick an' complain his way through whatevuh I'd cooked. Which, at that point, he's done every night since our weddin', unless it's somethin' *über*-german like bratwurst. Then he *fresses* his way through it like a pig at a trough.

Finally, after months of *kibbitz*in', we go an' "celebrate" our first ritual. The minute we get sky-clad, y'know, naked, my twat's hooked. But it ain't till we're spinnin' aroun' the room chantin' to the witches' gawddess Hecate an' I can feel the encouragin' laughter of Bubbe Rachel that the rest of me lets loose. It was the closest I'd come – in 23 fuckin' years – ta the Big O without havin' to use my killuh hands.

An', even if I don't believe much in the high ritual mumbo-jumbo (*O sea-swept watchtower of the watery West* . . .), I really took to the idea of spells. It's just like cookin'. I started borrowin' all of Joyce's Llewellyn books. Ya probably have no idea what those are. They're like those ol' time school books for "Today's Wiccan". Y'know, see Jane cast a spell on Dick.

Wiccans? Jeez, I need a freakin' vocabulary list here. More Yiddish yer thinkin'. Wrong. Y'know, Wiccans. They're like the Unitarians of pagans. A pinch of this an' a dash of that with lots of so-so songs an' endless conversations filled with bad, really bad, puns, thrown in for good measure. I'm sure you'd know who I'm talkin' about if ya saw a big gatherin' of 'em. There's always some ol' hippies who like to do arts an' crafts when they're stoned an' lots of middle-aged formuh Dungeons & Dragons warriors who wander aroun' in home-made armour convinced they're extras on the set of *Excalibur* an' tons – literally – of some of the ballsiest fat women, like yours truly t'day, in search of finally gettin' the respect an' righteous bonin' we so deserve.

Sorry. I'm gettin' way off track here. Where was I? Oh, right. Spells.

I kept it kinda simple in the beginnin'. Y'know, a little prosperity spell – a few green candles slicked up with some fast money oil – ta have enough cash t'get the shoppin' cart through Waldbaum's without havin' to *schlep* the Tupperware bin with all the coupons in from the car. Or my favourite – one I made up myself – the be-there-now spell. I'd use a little incense, the cigarette lightuh an' ashtray, an' start chantin' as I'd head the car toward Burguh Haven. An', nine times outta ten, by the time I drove up to the winduh, that gawd Rick –

Jesus, I can see his face an' his plastic name badge even now an' I get wet – Rick would be waitin' to hand me my double cheeseburguh an' fries.

Hey, stop lookin' at me like that. I told ya I was "happy" in my marriage. *Real* happy. I was fuckin' giddy by the time my 20th anniversary hits me. Come to think of it, it was a week after that blessed day when Kurt goes an' asks *me* for *my* help.

"What's the project?" I asks.

"You wouldn't understand, Ruth. It's very complicated."

"Try me," Isays.

Boy, does he look pissed. He knows he's gonna have to tell me.

"I've translated this text in medieval German . . ."

"When'd *you* learn medieval German?"

"In graduate school. When do you care? Just shut up and listen, OK?"

"Y'know," I says glarin' at him, "you got a fuckin' attitude!"

"What now, Ruth?"

"Forget it!"

"Fine."

"Fine! Y'know what, yer right I don't care."

"Good. That'll make this all the easier."

"Sure will, 'cause I'm not helpin' *you* with nothin'!"

"For fuck's sake, Ruth, don't go and fly off the handle. Jesus, you're always so emotional. Just listen. This could help us both. And you know we need help."

"No shit, Sherlock. I mean, *Dr* Sherlock."

Now he's givin' me that frosty stare he's gotten so good at.

"All right," I says. "I'm listenin'."

"It's a ritual for summoning the Devil."

"The Devil," I laugh. Then I look at him. "Oh, for Gawd's sake, Kurt. The Devil? What are ya, some teenage delinquent?"

I was nervous. Not hysterical, but spooked. I mean, I didn't really believe in the Devil or Gawd or any gawds or gawd-desses then. What can I say? My family was only half-Jewish. An' that half was so Reform we was non-practisin'. The other half was classic recoverin' Catholic. In fact, if it hadn't been for the time Grandma Renata got all worked up to have me baptised an' confirmed, I never woulda known enough about the Devil t'be scared of him now. I had to spend a bunch of Sundays goin' to Mass with my aunts an' havin' to sit at their kitchen table for hours afterwards learnin' all about "my father's faith". Then Grandma Renata died an' they got all distracted. But those Sundays was enough to creep me out for years.

"Go ahead," he shouts. "Think I'm crazy. I don't give a shit. I'm not the one who plays witch with a bunch of frustrated housewives on the weekend while my husband's out in the real world busting his hump to make something of himself."

"Poor baby," I says but he don't hear me. He just starts pacin' back an' forth.

"No matter how hard I work, nothing comes of it. No matter how many articles on the quattrocento I publish, no matter how many stupid freshmen humanities courses I teach, I can't get those assholes to notice me. Ten years. Why can't they see that I'm this century's Walter Pater?"

"Who?" I says. I'm gettin' scared 'cause now Kurt's standin' talkin' to the wall.

"My career's in the toilet unless I get tenure. I can't transfer. I can't do a frigging thing. And those old farts just keep passing me over. They're hellbent on passing me over. Hellbent! So, fine. I've tried everything else. Now, I'll get Hell to help me for once.

"Here," an' alla the sudden he turns back t'me an' throws a piece of paypuh on the floor. "Get me all these things by this date at this time . . . or else." Then he storms off an' I hear his door slam shut.

I got him what he wanted. Yeah, I was afraid. I told ya before I was very different from how I am now. But mostly, I was curious. I knew there was no way he could pull this off. But maybe it would calm him down. An' I'd never been in his sacred space since the day we moved in.

The list was pretty simple. A lot of plants an' spices with names you'd imagine for summonin' the Devil: hellebore, devil's dung, poison parsley, dragon's blood, toad flax, ghost flower, hag's tapers, bad man's plaything, clove root, puke-weed, naughty man's cherries, witches broom. I ground up a bunch of 'em for a powda an' the rest I boiled down into this oil that fuckin' reeks. It took a week t'get that smell outta my kitchen.

By a few minutes before the witchin' hour, I'm ready. I'm sittin' at the kitchen table tappin' my nails so fast it sounds like machine guns are goin' off. Finally, the clock says it's midnight. Midnight, Saturday night. The Devil's open for business. Don't that explain a helluva lot, I thinks.

I grab the Tupperware with the incense an' the jar of oil an' walk through the livin' room an' down the hall to the den. I knock on the door. It's real warm. What the fuck is he doin' in there? I asks myself. Then I hear all this fumblin' an' the door opens just a crack an' I see the forehead of my no-goodnik husband, all pasty white with his thinnin' hair plastered to it. Then his little bird-like eyes. He's all squintin' an' shit like I've shined a flashlight in his face. But all the light's comin' from the den. He musta bought every fuckin' black candle in the tri-state area.

"What?" he barks.

I almost sound off. Then I check myself. I wanna see more. So, I says, real polite, "Here. It's all the shit ya wanted for callin' the Devil."

"Oh," he says an' opens the door wider. I push the Tupperware into his hands an' try to wedge my fat ass into the room. Kurt stumbles an' the door flies back. But I just stand in the doorway. Not 'cause he's put a curse on me or some-thin'. It's the smell. Gawd, it's like a moldy gym bag someone took a crap in. He musta painted the winduh shut when he painted all the glass black. I look aroun' an' there's books stacked in piles everywheres – on the desk, on the TV, on the couch, on the Lazy-Boy – an' paypuhs an' boxes of paypuhs stacked on top of 'em an' pohstuhs an' cut-out pitchuhs of all these paintin's of fat women. That fuckin' *schlub*. An' then there's all these candles. I never seen such a fire hazard. I can't believe the house ain't burnin' down right that gawddamned minute. I'm gettin' ready to blow an' let him know just what I think of this toilet when I look at the floor.

I almost bust a gut laughin'. But, by some miracle, I keep a straight face. He's used like a hundred cans of Morton Salt to make this complicated circle in the carpet. There's a pentagram – big surprise, huh? –an' some real crazy symbols I never seen before.

"Give me the oil," he screams now that he's back on his feet. He's shakin' an' flappin' his arms over his head. Gawd, he's even thinnuh than when I first met him.

"Sure. Here. Take it." I hand him the jar. Thank Gawd I put a lid on it or he woulda spilled it all over the carpet. He's twitchin' somethin' awful. Like he's got the DTs.

"Leave," he says in this creepy high voice. "Leave now. And don't open this door no matter what happens. Heed my warning, woman, or be damned."

"OK, ya fuckin' freak," an' I pull the door shut so hard the frame rattles. I decide to go upstairs an' pack before the place catches fire.

I guess somewheres in the middle of packin' I fell asleep. Outta nowheres, from far off, like in a dream, I hear this awful classical music blarin' away. An' it keeps comin' closuh an' closuh. Then it hits me. It's not in the dream. It's like that moment in yer sleep when ya figure out the noise is comin' from yer alarm clock an' ya wake up. The same here.

Shit, Kurt, I think. I roll over. It's friggin' five in the mornin'. The music's even louder now that I'm awake. "Gawddamn it, Kurt," I shout at the top of my lungs. But it sounds like I'm whisperin'. I sit there waitin' for the sirens. Someone musta called the cops by now. Nothin'. Just this music that sounds like some kinda demonic John Philip Sousa march.

"Fine, at least the house's not on fire, ya bastard," I scream. An' I stomp, skyclad, all the way downstairs to his door. I think I'm gonna have a seizure 'cause the hallway light's all wonky an' flickerin' on an' off real fast. I yell for him to turn the fuckin' music off. I yell for him to come out. To go to hell. I'm coverin' my ears an' I'm still goin' deaf here between all the brass an' timpani an' me screamin'. Then I decide to bang down the door. I try an' nearly burn my hand off.

"Kurt Faust, what the fuck are ya doin' in there?"

Alla the sudden, silence. But now it was too quiet. Somethin' really bad musta happened, I thinks. An' when the gawddamned strobe light ovahead lets me, I start seein' these little wisps of smoke comin' out from unda the door. An' I smell more of that awful reekin' gym bag. "Christ, Kurt, ya set the house on fire!"

I guess the "C-word" set somebody off 'cause the music comes back. Not so loud, but you can still hear it thuddin' away from anywheres in the house. An' it goes on for two weeks like that. That damned music an' little clouds of smelly smoke. A full freakin' fortnight as Shakespeare would say. Come midnight Saturday I start gettin' worried. I'm thinkin', maybe that smell's from a dead body? What if it's Kurt's dead body? How'm I gonna explain that to the cops?

Next day, Sunday mornin', the music stops again. For good. I know 'cause I can hear my nails – the ones I haven't bitten off – rappin' against the outsides of my coffee mug. An' alla the sudden, this little man appears. He looks sorta weird.

Oh, yer back to the eye-rollin', huh? All right already. I know, I know.

Weirda than all that's happened so far? Kinda.

First, he really *is* little. No talluh than Bubbe Rachel was. We're talkin' 4′11″ here. Secondly, he's dressed all in black: little shoes with silvuh buckles, some kinda panty hose or tights, these silk lookin' shorts that come to his knees an' are wrapped tight aroun' his legs with little bitty bows, an' this fancy jacket with all these buttons goin' up the front. But best of all, he's wearin' this huge white collar aroun' his neck. It looks like this cheese wheel made of lace or somethin'. An', on top of that, there's his head. It's kinda shaped like an olive. Y'know, pointy. But not the colour of an olive. Na, it was – what's the word? oh, yeah – "ruddy." A little bit of mud mixed with a little bit of red. He's mostly bald with some white hair an' a goatee. An' he's got these sparkly little green eyes. Like he was a real handful when he was young. Y'know, some sophisticated ladies' man. Or a really classy *faygeleh*. I can't tell for sure.

I guess I coulda been frightened or startled even. But I was just relieved. The fuckin' music had stopped. He wasn't Kurt. An' he didn't smell like a gym bag. Not at all. More like lemon verbena. Y'know, like he'd gone an' splashed Jean Naté all over himself. Like I said, he was classy. An' he was real polite.

The first thing he says t'me is "Do you mind if I smoke, madam?"

"Knock yaself out," I says.

Next thing I know, he's pulled out this long silvuh cigarette holduh, like a silent movie star. Outta thin air, he takes a cigarette. Puts it in the holduh an' touches it with the tip of his finger. It starts to glow. He comes up to the table, motions with his hand if it's OK to sit, I motion back "sure," an' he sits down an' smokes.

When he's done, I find out he's this nice little ol' Greek man named Mr Mephistopheles. An' then he goes on to tell me he's my husband's servant. That's when I freakin' *plotz*.

That's Yiddish for "shit a brick".

"Yer his what?" I says. An' I goes an' hits my fist on the table so hard the coffee sloshes outta my cup. "Tell me this, Mr Mephistopheles, what does my *schmo* of a husband need with a gawddamned fuckin' servant when he's got a gawddamned fuckin' slave?!"

"Mrs Faust, have I offended you?" he says as he takes out this big frilly white hanky an' wipes it once over the table an' it's like it's some magic paypuh towel 'cause the coffee's all gone.

"*Mrs* Faust? What am I? His mutha? Listen, Mr Mephistopheles, ya can either call me Ruth or Yer Majesty but never call me Mrs Faust, ya hear?"

"Yes, Your Majesty." An' the little flirt winks at me while he pockets the hanky.

After I get us a plate of Stella D'Oro Swiss Fudge Cookies an' some fresh coffee, he proceeds to tell me that Kurt really went an' pulled it off. He got the Devil to show up in *our* house. An' that, Mr Mephistopheles points out, is very rare. The Devil usually sends him to do all the bargainin' an' the paypuhwork. The Devil told him that Kurt was one of the most promising hellbounds he'd met this year outside of George W Bush.

"So where's Kurt now? In Hell?" I says all hopeful.

"Oh, no, Your Majesty. Not for quite some time. The master is in Florence for the next year with his girlfriend."

"What?" I screams an' I drops my cookie into my coffee. "Mastuh? Florence? Girlfriend?"

"Oh, I am sorry, Your Majesty, but your husband has a lover named Gretchen." Then he goes an' puts his hand in the arm of his jacket an' pulls out a friggin' polaroid. "This was taken here in the house. In the master's study," he says as he hands me the photo.

I know I'm gonna shit anotha friggin' brick when I sees the photo but I look at it anyways. There's Kurt, about to fuckin' burst with joy. An' there she is. Gretchen. This blonde *shiksa* dressed like she's workin' Oktobuhfest. Swear to Gawd. Big boobs in this tight blouse an' dirndl.

I wanna kick over the table or rip up the gawddamned photo or somethin'. But I don't. I just hand it back to Mr Mephistopheles.

"So all that music an' noise was the Mastuh an' his girl-friend?" I says.

"I am afraid so, Your Majesty. I do apologize for the loud-ness. That was my doing. Only inside the Master's study could one hear Master Wagner's operas in their titanic glory. I did a little bit of sophisticated necromancy to prevent any words from within being heard without. But, as always, the sin of Pride in my work blinded me. I had not taken into account that cries of pleasure are not always words. So, I had to increase the volume on your side to drown out the Master and the Mistress."

"The Mistress," I says, slumpin' over my coffee. "Thanks, Mr Mephistopheles, yer a real pal."

"I truly am sorry, Your Majesty. While I understand the Master's desire for power and glory and tenure, I cannot fathom how he could ignore a woman of your calibre."

"Me either, *bubeleh*. So the Devil gave him his tenure?" I asks.

"Why, yes. Not only does the Master have full tenure now, but he is also the leading light in Renaissance Studies as well as an authentic Renaissance man."

'Well, fuckin' A for the Mastuh," I says. "He's finally got his stinkin' tenure." Thank Gawd, I whispuh all silent to myself. I never have to hear that *alter kocker* bitch about that again. Maybe I never have to see him either. That perks me up.

"Hey, Mr Mephistopheles."

"Yes, Your Majesty."

"Ya wouldn't get in any trouble if ya showed me the contract, would ya?"

"Well, I'm not supposed to do so. First, may I ask a question of Your Majesty?"

"Sure," I says.

"Is Your Majesty considering offering her soul to the Devil as well?"

That stumped me. I hadn't thought about it. I'd just wanted to see how long before Kurt was roastin' away.

"Maybe? How much worse could Hell be than here, huh?"

"I'm afraid quite a bit much."

"Yeah, I figured. But ya still don't mind showin' me the deal?"

The sweet little ol' man smiles at me. Then he puts his finger to his lips an' digs aroun' in the arm of his coat again. He pulls out this little plastic box an' puts in on the table. The minute he does it swells up into one a those fancy schmancy laptop computuhs. He opens the lid an' turns the screen t'me so I can read while he goes an' lights up anotha cigarette for himself.

A course, it's all written in fuckin' lawyer. So, I have to scroll down an' down t'get to any good stuff. Well, good stuff for Kurt. As I'm readin' it, all I can think is, "I'm dyin' here." Basically, it says as long as Kurt's alive, he's got all Hell's demons at his friggin' beck an' call. He can have anythin', no matter how awful. Tenure. Blondes. World domination. Worst of all, he gets to live t'be a 175. The only good part for me comes after he croaks. That's when he gets the four-star treatment in Hell – foreva.

But 138 years – 37 from 175; y'do the math – is nothin' compared to all eternity. Boy, he really got screwed.

"What a stupid *schlemiel,*" I says out loud. "I can't believe he signed this. Wait. Yes, I can. Jesus, Kurt!"

Once I say the "J-word", Mr Mephistopheles starts gettin' all fidgety in his chair. "Sorry," I says. "Hell's friggin' bells, Kurt! That better?"

"Quite, Your Majesty. I personally do *not* have a problem with you-know-who's name, but *He* does," he says, pointin' at the floor. "It has been written into all of our contracts that we writhe and moan at the merest utterance of Our Lord's latest Arch-Rival. At the risk of appearing vainglorious before Your Majesty, I must admit that I used to be quite good at it. I would even toss in a round or two of hissing. But, after a thousand or so years, I have grown weary of trembling with fear. Now I merely wriggle."

"Ya did fine, *bubeleh*."

He smiles again an' takes a long drag on his cigarette.

"Mr Mephistopheles."

He nods his head all eager an' smoke shakes outta the cornuhs of his mouth.

"I gotta question for ya. Ya really gotta do whatevuh Kurt says till he bites the dust?"

"Yes. Quite so, Your Majesty."

"I'm not talkin' the typical deal-with-the-Devil stuff like invadin' Poland or gettin' an Oscar. I'm talkin' the really pissant stuff."

"Yes, yes, that too!"

"Ya mean if he asks ya to cook him his food, clean his clothes, even flush the toilet for him, y'gotta do it."

He takes anotha long draw from his cigarette an' stares up an' out through the winduh above the sink, as if he's really interested in the new shingles on the Nachmann's roof. Smoke's curlin' slowly outta his nose, like the little roots ya see when ya repot houseplants.

Then, he sighs an' goes an' says, "Yes."

"Oh, ya poor *farchadat dybbuk*," I says. "Do I know how bad a job that is!"

An' once I'd said that, I got t'thinkin'.

My life's a freakin' shambles. Kurt – the *putz* – has sold his soul to the Devil an' is gettin' it on in Italy, of all places, with some bimbo named Gretchen an' Gawd-knows-what-else.

But that's not the worst of it. Now I'm even more alone than before 'cause I don't go to the coven no more. Joyce an' I had a little partin' of the ways about a month before Kurt gave it up for the Devil. I – always the *meshuggeneh* – thought we could take turns bein' the high priestess. Y'know, rotate it. My "sistah goddesses" ended up takin' her side too. So I told 'em they could all rotate *this* an' left. Which means now the only person I can talk to other than myself is a demon named Mr Mephistopheles.

Not that he ain't nice an' all. But he works for Kurt. So I goes an' decides right there I need a demon of my own. Someone who'd do all the wifey crap I'd been doin' for years an' was sick to death of.

Hell, I think some more to myself, if Kurt can do it, why can't I? I mean, I'm the witch in this fuckin' madhouse. *An'* I'm a *Jew*. I know I can finesse a way better deal outta the Devil than that clunkuh Kurt settled for.

So, the next Saturday night at midnight I'm settin' up an altar in the kitchen. It's a little cramped over in the breakfast nook by the table 'cause my altar's three TV trays crammed with gawddessey *tchotchkes* an' red candles an' four or five of my spice racks with all my incenses an' oils.

I was just gonna pick a few an' mix 'em up in a bowl. The problem was I didn't have a free bowl anywheres on the altar. So, I goes an' turns t'get one off the kitchen table. That's when my big, fat *tuchis* hits the trays an' knocks everythin' to the floor with a big crash.

The sound scares the shit outta me an' I nearly ram the table through the swivel chairs an' the half-wall where the side counter is. An' I can feel all this heat behind me. The room's gettin' all smoky, quick. "Gawddamned freakin' dammit," I scream, smashin' the bowl on the table. I turn expectin' to see the wall on fire or somethin'. But instead, there's this really butch dyke commando starin' back at me.

She's about an inch or two talluh than me. Y'know, like 5′5″ or 5′6″. Her hair's black like mine but she's cut hers real short. In a crewcut or somethin'. Actually, since my hair's been down to my ass since I was 13, I put it up that night 'cause I didn't want it t'get in the way. If only I coulda done the same thing with my ass.

Anyways, she's got these fuckin' beautiful, light brown eyes with dark eyelashes. An' the most gloriously Semitic *schnoz* since Barbra's. An' this skin that's as tanned as mine is pale, somewheres between the colour of a garlic-stuffed green olive an' a perfect black Kalamata. Speakin' of stuffed, she's gotta this brick shithouse of a body that's nearly burstin' outta this dusty ol' beige muscle T-shirt an' these black-brown-an'-grey-spotted camouflage pants. I mean, we're talkin' fuckin' killuh biceps an' great breasts an' this beautiful little belly – she was probably aroun' a hundred pounds lightuh than me, about a 180 – an' wide hips an' monster thighs an' thick calves that were laced up in a fierce pair of boots.

Sounds like I had the hots for her. I checked with my twat. We did.

Whoa, yer thinkin', when did that happen? I thought ya said youse was gonna run for the door, like Mrs Scaduto, if yer women's group asked ya to chow down on anotha of yer sistah gawddesses.

I did. That's all true. If she'd'a grabbed me then an' there an' pushed my face into her crotch I probably woulda bolted. But I wasn't that surprised by my attraction. Hell, I was 37. In my friggin' sexual prime. Still am. An' let me tell ya, that many hormones makes ya honest. I mean, I could admit I was curious. Christ, I'd thought about foolin' aroun' with other girls as far back as high school. An' since I hit my 30s, I'd even gone to bed a few times an' wanked off thinkin' about doin' it with a room full of hot women. So, like I said, it didn't surprise me – t'think about it.

A course, I was still sorta in a bad mood from knockin' everythin' over an' a little shook up from havin' yet anotha person appear in my kitchen outta nowheres. So, I kinda lit into her.

"Who the hell are *you*?" I says.

"Your mother, Ruth," she says.

"Right, right. Sure y'are. My mutha always dresses like she's chasin' after Rommel."

"No, really. I *am* your mother."

"Great. I'm tryin' t'get a devil of my own an' instead I get some *meshuggeneh* dyke with maternal instincts."

"*Bubeleh,* the name's Lilith."

"Oh, fuckin' Christ Almighty. A course, I get Lilith the baby-killer!"

"Ruth Marie," an' she goes an' grabs my face in her hands an' says all serious, "I'm only going to say this once. OK?" I nod. "I'm no baby-killer and neither are you."

An' then I goes an' starts t'cry an' then she does an' we're huggin' an' bawlin'. Jeez, it was so freakin' *Lifetime*. But, honest to Gawd, somethin' did change right at that moment.

We talk for a few hours while I make us cups of coffee an' we work our way through a Entenmann's pecan ring. By the time we finish off the second box, I've told her as much as I've told youse so far.

"Oh, *bubeleh*," she says, pushin' away her plate, "he's worse than the first one."

"What? Y'think I'd do this a second time an' pick *him*?" I says. "Trust me. Kurt's my first *an'* my last husband."

"No, no," she says. "The first man. Worse than Adam."

"Listen to *you*. That a dyke like *you* should know from Adam."

"Trust me, I do. I told you I'm Lilith. I was his first wife."

"No shit. Ya really *are* her? Ya don't look anythin' like I imagined ya would."

"Most deities don't."

"Oh," I says. I mean, how the fuck do ya respond to that?

"I've changed my look some since the last time someone summoned me."

"Oh."

"Yes, it's been a while. Congratulations."

All I can do is shrug my shoulders an' smile. What a *schnook* I am!

"This is also the shape I take in dreams nowadays. Do you remember any of them?"

"Huh? Ya mean we've met before?"

"Yes. I come in the night to women who dream of regaining their lost strengths. I show them just how they can do this. I also keep them warm while they sleep. Very warm."

"Oh, really," I says an' my voices goes an' squeaks. "But I read that all ya did was run aroun' givin' head. Great head. Come in the night an' drink guys dry."

"Our pasts have a lot in common."

"No shit," I says, noddin' my head.

"Our futures have even more."

Omigawd, I'm thinkin', she's makin' a move on me. An' what do I do? I blush. That's it! My twat knows what's in store an' she's sittin' tight. Well, actually, she wasn't tight at all.

So Lilith pushes away from the table an' comes over t'me. She stretches out her arm. Y'know, invitin' me to take her hand. My twat says, "Take it, ya *schlemiel.* " I do it. She pulls me up into her arms an' gives me this fuckin' tender, wet kiss. By the second one, I got my tongue in her.

Next thing I know, she leadin' me upstairs to my bedroom, undoin' my hair, strippin' my dress an' my bra an' my soakin' panties off of me between kisses, an' then she pushin' me back onto the bed where she licks her way down to my breasts an' aroun' an' aroun' my nipples, takin' these little hurts-so-good bites into my high beams, an' then she's lickin' her way over my big sighin' gut an' into my twat.

Fuckin' A!

Even Kurt, when he loved me, was never this good. She sucks her way aroun' my lips. She pushes that tongue of hers into me to drink up every drop of my juice. That tongue! *Oy!* Does she know how to use it. Even how to put just the right amount of pressure for just the right amount of time on my clit. Listen up, people. Too much an' I'm gonna kickbox yer head away. Too little, an' I'm gonna fall asleep with my thighs wrapped tight aroun' ya. Gawd, I sound like freakin' Goldilocks here, but it's true. An' all the squirmin' in the world won't wake me up once I gets a good snore goin'.

A course, none of that's happenin' with Lilith. Not on yer life. Goldilocks is takin' her lickin' 'cause it's just right. An' then, it gets even better. I have The Big O to end all Big Os. I'm shakin' an' screamin' like a porn star. But I really mean it.

"Feel better?" she says as she slides outta my twat an' up my belly.

"Um-hum," I muttuh. We kiss.

"But . . . ?"

She's like a friggin' mind reada or somethin'.

"You haven't been fucked in five years."

"Six."

"I think I can definitely help you out there." She pulls this duffle bag outta the air an' takes it into the bathroom.

Boy, do I start gettin' excited all over again. I'm imaginin' she's gonna go an' get Rick for me. Or maybe take his shape. Then she comes out with this harness strapped aroun' her ass like she's ready to climb a mountain or somethin'. An' there's this big, fat dildo wavin' at me from where her twat used t'be.

I musta made a face. A pretty bad one too. Somethin' that said, "Yer kiddin', right?"

All I could think to say was, "Nothin' personal. But I like boy bits for fuckin'. Y'know, real ones."

"I know."

"Oh, OK." I was confused. "So, then, ya don't mind, y'know, gettin' me some or, um, maybe turnin' yerself into . . ."

"I don't do men any more."

"Oh, sure, right."

"I'd seen so much of that pillar of salt that the other goddesses used to call me 'Lot's Wife'."

"Oh, o-ho, yeah, pillar of salt, that's clevuh," I says, stallin', tryin' to think of what to do. Then, I figures what the hell an' goes for broke.

"But ya could turn yerself into one, right?"

"I've done it a few times. Parties mainly. But," an' she starts to walk towards the bed, her dick floppin' ahead of her, an' I'm slowly scootin' on my ass back towards the headboard, "that's not your fantasy."

"Oh, it's *not*," I says all surprised 'cause I *am*.

"No," she says. An' she crawls up on the end of the bed an' wades on her knees through the sheets an' blankets an' gets to my legs which I got drawn up against my chest an' she pulls 'em down an' then pushes 'em apart with her knees an' rubs her dick up an' down my twat's fatter-an'-juicier-than-eva lips. "Not tonight."

An' was she right. What can I say? If ya get the right demon with the right dildo, anythin's possible.

So, later, we're snugglin' in bed, talkin' about my idea to make a deal with the Devil but keep my soul by bettin' him I could give him the best blowjob he's ever had. Lilith's holdin' me from behind in her big arms, just listenin' t'me go on about what I'm gonna do when I win. Then, she kisses my neck an' I forget what I'm sayin'.

"Bubeleh," she says, "the devil's dick is cold. Icy cold."

Somewheres I remember someone else warnin' me about this. Right. It was Auntie Teresa. She was the smartest of my dad's sisters. I mean, she's read Dante's *Inferno,* for Chrissakes, an' that's how I learned the Devil lives on the ninth floor in Hell. An' it's freezin' cold. Like an eternity of Januarys in Minnesota or somethin'.

"And," she says loudly to catch my wanderin' attention, "whatever you do, don't let him stick it up your ass. That's his favourite. You'll never melt him that way."

"So, I'll just microwave him with my twat," I says.

"It's a hot one, I'll grant you that. Lots of juice. But, it won't be enough."

"Get outta here."

"Trust me. But I think I have just the plan to put the *kibosh* on him stealing your soul. We'll have to tag team him . . ."

"We?" I can barely say the word. I'm gettin' all *farklempt* here, an' fast. Thirty seconds till I'm bawlin' again. I mean, she's bein' so freakin' sweet t'me an' it's been so long since anyone's talked t'me like this. Not since my parents died. But I gotta know what her plan is. So I take a deep breath an' stifle the waterworks for t'night.

"Won't the Devil recognize ya?" I says.

"I doubt it. We travel in very different circles," she says.

"Oh."

"Hey. You want to hear my plan or what?"

"Sure. Let me have it."

"You're insatiable, Ruth Faust." She kisses me an' slips me her tongue an' then – guess what? – we fuck for the second of thirteen times that night.

Hey! What'd I tell ya about the eyes? It'd been six long, *dry* years.

The 13th time was the craziest of all. She asks me, all nice an' everythin', to eat her out an' I do. This from the woman who says she only likes boy bits. Well, like anotha crazy Jew once said, we're all a bit polymorphously perverse.

So, I push Lilith off of me. I chew aroun' on her neck some more an' do a bit a nippin' an' tuckin', if y'know what I mean, on her breasts. Hey, great tits are great tits! No shit. I've always gotten kinda warm when I spot an awesome rack. But my twat knows I should be pokin' my tongue somewheres else an' she drags me down to Lilith's dick. I deep throat it on the first go – I told ya I have no gag reflex! – an' give it my high school special. A heavy suction swirlie. I grip the dick really firm between my lips – no teeth – an' every time I get to the head I let my tongue go wild. A few bobs on a teenage boy an' he's creamin'. Shit, the last time I did "Fat Ruth's Special" on a guy, Kurt *was* a teenage boy.

I'm startin' t'get nostalgic here, so I stop before I bite her dildo in half.

I pull it outta my mouth an' help her get it off. Boy, fuckin' a girl ten or eleven times in one night can make ya ripe. She smelled like a big, hairy wild animal an' dirt ya just dug up in yer garden after a really light rain. It was makin' me wild. It was makin' me wanna dig.

I look up at her an' grin. *"L'chayim,"* I says an' she laughs. Then I press my mouth, my tongue, my nose – hell, my whole gawddamned face – into her shakin', steamin' twat an' go to town.

Despite all my enthusiam, I gotta admit I didn't do so hot. The first time. I didn't suck neither, mind ya. Na, wait. I did suck. A lot. But I fumbled here an' there. I kept gettin' all shy with her clit. I mean, I know what I like. I just never done it from that angle before. But I got better. Lilith's a fuckin' amazin' teachuh. *Oy,* my tongue got so strong an' so fuckin' suave, if it was possible an' it wouldn'ta hurt like hell, I coulda gone back in time to that night an' tied a knot in her clit just like a cherry stem. Yeah, I was that good. Actually, I'm even better now.

Remember that, OK? It's important. 'Cause eatin' twat is the key to Lilith's plan.

Next Wednesday, it's gettin' close to about four. The usual time that Mr Mephistopheles an' I get t'gether for coffee an' cake. Lilith thinks he might recognize her an' blow everythin'. So, she takes off to visit a few of her musician friends. I'm puttin' the pecan ring out on the table when I can smell him comin'. I take in a deep breath. The room's startin' to smell like pecan ring, cigarettes, an' Jean Naté. I'm feelin' better already.

After our second slice, anotha cup of coffee, an' a cigarette for us both, I'm finally feelin' relaxed enough to go for broke.

"So, Mr Mephistopheles," I says while I exhale, "ya remember when ya asked me if I wanted to sell my soul to the Devil?"

He's mid-drag so all he can do is arch his eye-brow an' grin.

"Well, I'm ready. T'day. Ya ready to write up my deal?" I stub out my cigarette. Next thing I know, his silvuh holduh's cigarette-down in the ashtray an' he's pullin' the laptop outta his sleeve.

"I'm ready, Your Majesty," he says.

So, I goes an' tells him what I want an' he types it all into his computuh.

Basically, I want all Kurt got. But I wanna live t'be 300 years ol' an' I wanna be in my sexual prime – y'know, 35, for the rest of my life. An' when I kick off, it's gonna be all peaceful like. In my sleep. With all my great-great-great grandchildren aroun' me.

An' when he's done typin' all that I says, "There's somethin' else but I gotta tell it directly to The Man."

"Oh, my, Your Majesty. I would advise you against that. I promise you I can arrange all the details of a soul transfer. Not to boast, but I am quite good at it. Legendary, if I might add."

"I believe ya, Mr Mephistopheles. It's nothin' against ya. It's just that I don't wanna give the Devil my soul."

"Oh, dear me. He's not going to like this. No, not one bit."

"I wanna make a wayjuh. If I lose, he gets my soul. If I win, he gives me all I asks for an' that's that."

"I see. And what kind of wager is Your Majesty making? A contest of wills, bodies, minds, appetites, depravities . . ?"

"Alla that. It's sex for Chri – " an' he starts to scrunch up his shoulders an' quiver so I stop myself. "For Satan's sake. I'm bettin' I can make the Devil come."

"Oh, Your Majesty, that will never do."

"Whadda ya mean?" I says all nervous now. He has to agree to my wayjuh or I'm royally screwed.

"It's just that, well, it doesn't take much effort for My Lord to – how does one put this to a lady of your calibre? – achieve his ends."

"Ya mean, come, right?"

"Exactly." An' he goes an' leans across the table to whispuh into my ear. "The Great-and-All-Powerful Satan has a bit of a problem with what mortals now call 'premature ejaculation'. It has actually proved quite convenient over the ages. Oh, my, especially when the Borgias were in the Vatican! Why, every gala orgy Pope Alexander VI threw, the more and more Borgias would show up to make a wager much like yours with Him.

"I personally would have been exhausted. But not My Lord. A few minutes with a hundred or so people meant he could be done in hours instead of days or months. And when he was through, he was more refreshed than when he had begun. Why, that rascal Cesare, even after he'd lost his soul, was still begging My Master to sodomize him as often as possible. And, kind soul that He is, the Bright Star would oblige and ream that rakish boy 15 or 20 times at every one of his father's bacchanalias. Yes, My Lord may be a tad hasty with his delivery but he has no problem whatsoever with recovery . . ."

At this point, I'm so fuckin' lost, I have no idea what he's talkin' about. I don't know nothin' about the Borgias yet. So I decide I have to clarify myself or give it up. Now.

"Hey, Mr Mephistopheles."

"Oh, oh. I'm sorry, Your Majesty, I was waxing on. Do forgive me."

"Forget about it." He bows from the waist an' I watch the lace cheese wheel tilt to the table an' back up. "I meant to say I can make The Devil come after his longest go-round ever . . ." Here I remember somethin' Lilith told me so I adds, "An' there'll be warm fluids."

"Well, well. That's a wager after all. I can't see him passing that up. It's never been done before. A very bold move, Your Majesty."

"Sure. Thanks," I says.

An' the ol' man starts to type away again, mutterin' aloud "warm fluids" an' gigglin' to himself.

That Saturday, aroun' midnight, Lilith an' I are waitin' up in my bedroom for the Devil to do a walk-on. I look over to the clock by the bed. It says 12:01. I turn back an' there's this little green ball in front of me.

It's like this tiny thundercloud. All bubblin' an' shit like someone's tryin' to boil it. I wanna start laughin' my ass off 'cause all I can think is this *schmekel* of a cloud *is* the Devil? It musta read my mind 'cause next thing I know, it's growin'. An' the bigger it gets, the worse it smells. "Christ," I yell an' the cloud freezes for just a moment. Now it stinks even worse. Like a fuckin' dump – I mean a honest-to-Gawd garbage dump – filled only with rotten eggs an' rancid garlic. I scream to Lilith to open the winduh. As soon as I do that, the *farshtinkener* cloud goes poof an' it's like it blew up. There're just pieces of it floatin' aroun'. Same goes with the stench. An', in the middle of *my* bedroom, there stands none other than the Devil himself.

T'be honest, I was expectin' a real lump. A bug-eyed golem with waxy skin an' big tufts of hair sproutin' from his shoulders. Instead, I get this curly headed, blond *boychik* with hypnotic blue eyes an' these red lips that beg t'be chewed, wearin' this *schmatte* of a red robe that barely covers any of his skin. Creamy skin ya wanna lick from head to head to toe an' back to head, if y'know what I mean. He looks like a cross between a Hitla Youth an' Christopha Atkins in *Blue Lagoon*.

Gawd, I wore that video ragged one summuh.

Anyways, this *pisher*, once he's shook loose his cloud of shit-stinkin' smoke, goes an' drops the robe an' I see he's got the biggest *schmuck* I ever seen. Swear to Gawd! Makes Kurt's look like a dinky *schmendrick*. All I could think was, Jesus Christ, if he sticks that thing in me I'll fuckin' *plotz*. My twat, on the other hand, she don't give a damn. She's already droolin' through my panties onto my inner thighs. An' in the end, I always agree with my twat that what she should want, she should have.

"So, you're the next contestant to best the Devil," he says, just oozin' smarm.

"Yeah, I guess I am," I says.

"Splendid."

"Y'know, my girlfriend fucks me up the ass all the time. She likes to pretend we're *faygelehs* runnin' aroun' the woods on Fire Island."

The Devil grinned.

"Don't get me wrong. I'm with the *faygelehs* here. I think butt-fuckin's hot."

"It *is*, Mrs Faust," he says, comin' as close as his all-of-a-sudden-stiff as-a-two-by-four-*schmuck* lets him. Believe me, it was close enough 'cause poster *goy* has got day-ol' vodka breath. We're talkin' cheap vodka. The Maneschevitz of vodka. "Just wait till I'm inside you. No one does it *quite* like I do."

"Oh, sure, sure," I says, backin' away from the fumes. "I've heard yer great. Hell, my girlfriend says she'll even join us if ya like."

"I'd like that very much, Mrs Faust," he says. "But I didn't know there'd be another here to make a deal."

"Oh? Oh, no. She don't want nothin' from ya. She just wants to hang out. Watch. Maybe play. We never done a three-ways before."

He turned to Lilith. "You don't wish to try for vast riches," and Lilith shakes her head, "world domination," she shakes it some more, "immortality?"

"It's overrated," she says.

"Oh, the high and mighty Christian, are we?"

"Yeah, right," I laugh. "She just wants to have sex with the Devil."

He stared at her. "What an odd woman. But what Devil would I be if I denied any of God's children a moment of ecstasy with me? Just remember the deal's between me and your girlfriend."

"No problem."

"OK, then. Shall we begin?"

"Sure," I says. I start takin' off my clothes. I catch the Devil eyein' my breasts as I pull off my bra.

"Y'know," I says. "I was wonderin' if I could work up to you plowin' my ass.

"Work up? My dear Mrs Faust, didn't my underling inform you? I don't do foreplay. No fondling of the breasts, no matter how impressive they might be, no cunnilingus, no anal-oral contact. Why, I don't even use lube."

"Oh, I didn't know."

"Would you like to cancel the wager?"

"Na, na. I'm just curious why no foreplay."

"I'm not a big fan of traditional sex."

"Bubeleh, where have *you* been? No foreplay is about as traditional as sex gets."

I don't think he likes me. He gives me this really lame-ass smile.

"If you must know, Mrs Faust, I'm an aficionado of the asshole."

"Oh," I says, havin' no idea what he's talkin' about.

"I find it a painful challenge for the contestant."

"No lube, I bet."

"Yes, Mrs Faust, you have made a bet," he says all impatient like. "So, if you don't mind, I have a very busy schedule. Please, just pull down your panties and bend over. This won't take long but it will hurt very much." He starts laughin' like some little boy who's had way too much sugar.

"Sure, sure." An' I'm standin' there slippin' my underwear off an' I stop. "You like challenges, right?"

"Obviously, Mrs Faust."

"An' you think the asshole's the hardest."

"Look at my devilhood," he says pointin' to his *schmuck*. It grows anotha foot right then an' there. "Now compare that with the average asshole and I call that a challenge."

"I guess."

"What, Mrs Faust? You had something else in mind?"

"Well, in my experience," an' I goes an' nods my head towards Lilith, "nothin's more of a challenge than eatin' a woman out. 'Specially a real butch one like my girlfriend."

The Devil looks back at Lilith like he'd forgotten she was in the room. "I wouldn't know," he says.

"Whaddya mean ya don't know? Yer the friggin' Devil. Y'know as much as Gawd."

"More," he adds, all bitter soundin'.

"More. Sure, more. But then ya musta eaten out a woman some time."

"Never."

"What? That's crazy. Was it 'cause you didn't enjoy it when you was a woman?"

"I've never been a woman, Mrs Faust. I'm the Devil."

"Oh, yeah, yeah. Right. I know ya ain't a woman. No more than yer the hung-like-a-fuckin'-horse *ganef* standin' before me. But ya musta taken the shape of one before?"

"No. I never have."

All I could think was "Don't that explain everythin'." But I goes an' says, "*Feh!*", an' pull up my panties.

"'Feh,' Mrs Faust?"

"That's right. Feh! Yer not the Devil. Yer just one of his little guys pretendin' t'be. I'm not gonna do anotha gawd-damned thing till ya get me the Devil."

"What? Don't be an idiot, Mrs Faust. Everyone knows I'm the Devil. I often take a pleasing appearance. Look at me! I know you're pleased. And my penis! Everyone knows it's colder than ice. Please, touch it."

"Ice, schmice. I bet every demon in Hell has a fuckin' icicle for a dick. I want the Devil. The big-D Devil. Lucifuh."

"I *am* Lucifer. The Bright Star. Look at me! Don't I look like a fallen angel to you?"

"Maybe. But I need more proof."

"I don't give 'more proof', Mrs Faust!"

"Fine, ya *shaygets,* then the deal's off."

Next thing I know I'm coughin' my lungs up. There's smoke everywheres. I'm screamin' to Lilith again to open a winduh. Then, it's gone an' there's the Devil doin' his imper-sonation of a woman. He's – she's – I'm no fuckin' good with these pronouns here – the Devil's turned himself into one of those scrawny supermodels that looks like they got a teenage boy's body with little round breasts glued on. Jeez, I'm thinkin', I'm learnin' way more t'night than I ever wanted to about who the Devil thinks is really hot. No wonder he came to Kurt first.

"Is that the best ya can do?" I laugh.

Oh, is *he* pissed. There's this big puff of red smoke an' then it's gone an' I'm starin' at Betty Bazoombas.

We're talkin' the American Porno Queen Dream. Trust me, I know. I've watched hundreds over the years. She's aroun'

5′10″ an' weighs no more than 135 pounds. That's 5 pounds
for her bleached hair an' 15 pounds for each boob. 40 Double
D. A course they're implants. Jeez, it's the Devil for
Chrissakes! Only he could have tits that huge an' a waist as big
aroun' as one of those starvin' Hollywood actress's arms an'
not fall flat on his face.

Did I mention, he's wearin' 6″ stilletos an' still not fallin'
over? I can't even stand in freakin' 1″ heels. While he coulda
probably danced a jig in those shoes on wet grass if I'd asked.
An' get this, 'cept for the heels, all he's got on is a little gold
ankle bracelet with a pentagram. I swear, nothin' else. That's
right. The Devil's butt nekked in my bedroom. Oh, oh, an'
he's gone an' shaved his twat. Yeah, all that's left of whatevuh
bush he had is this teeny, tiny Hitla moustache. What's that?
Y'know it. The perfect porno pussy.

"Can I call you Lucy?" is all I can think to say.

"No, Mrs Faust, you cannot," he says.

"And don't even think of calling me Lyle," says this man's
voice behind me.

I look to see what new demon's snuck into the house now
an' there's Lilith. She's gone an' turned herself into a guy.
Same feachuhs. A little talluh. A little thinnuh. Same killuh
schnoz an' a *schmuck* to match. That's right, people. A big
flesh-an'-blood dick.

"Whoa," I says. Lucy looks back an' I hear him sigh. I know
he's drippin' too. I can smell it. It's like this strong spice,
y'know. Turmeric. Yeah, that's it.

"What?" Lilith says. Her voice is real sexy an' suave
soundin'. Like Frank's. Sinatra, ya dope!

"Oh, this," she says. "Just a little shape-shifting I do for
parties." We're both starin' open mouth 'cause Lilith is one
hot guy. "Hey," she says, tryin' t'get our eyes outta her crotch,
"up here."

"Huh?" Lucy an' I says at the same time.

"Let's party, girls."

Lilith goes an' walks into the middle of the room, her dick
bobbin' along up in front, until she's standin' before Lucy.

"Go ahead. Touch it," she says. "You know you want to."

I nod my head without thinkin'.

"Whatever do you mean, boy?" says Lucy.

Gawd, the Devil's got the right-soundin' voice – all high an' breathy. But he sure as shit don't talk like no porn star. Sounds more like one of the Three Fuckin' Musketeers.

"It's colder than yours ever was," says Lilith.

"Impossible."

Lilith takes Lucy's hand an' wraps it aroun' her *schmuck*. The Devil makes a hissin' sound. Like some angry snake.

"Ow. It's too cold. It's too cold," Lucy says, tossin' his hair an' makin' all these whimperin' noises. What a whiny fuckin' girl! "It's burning me."

"I bet." Lilith thrusts her hips a few times so her dick's pumpin' away in Lucy's hand.

Lucy shrieks as he tears his hand away. He's cryin' an' jumpin' from one foot to the other an' wavin' his hands in the air an' blowin' on them like he just got done playin' Twistuh on top of a electric stove.

I can see his hands. They look fine t'me. Didn't even muss up his French manicure nails. The bitch. Guess it's not quite like bein' human an' stickin' yer fuckin' tongue to a frozen pipe.

"How did you do that?" he asks my man Lilith.

"It's just a matter of practice," she says, playin' with her balls – we're talkin' real low hanguhs here. "I've had more time than you."

"That's impossible. Only God Himself is older than I!"

"Oh, Lucy, do ya have a lot to learn t'night!" I says.

"Mrs Faust, *what* did I tell you about calling me Lucy?"

"Sorry, Yer Devilness." I turn my back for a second an' roll my eyes, hard, an' mutter a curse or two. Gawd, I wanna tear that bitch a new one.

"Not only," Lilith goes on, "is my dick colder, it's also harder and longer than yours."

"Oh, please, man!" Lucy says as he puts his hands on his hips an' tosses that hair of his. Gawd, it looks so South Shore.

"There's only one way to find out."

"Never," he says. He goes an' throws his big hair about some more. Y'know he's secretly wishin' I'd go find a fan from the attic an' bring it back to the bedroom an' spend the rest of the night aimin' it at him so he wouldn't have to keep that wind-swept look goin' by himself. I swear to ya. I can hear him whisperin' the fuckin' suggestion in my head. But I don't.

"C'mon," Lilith says. "You know you've always wanted to experience what it feels like for those wretched sinners impaled on your icy spear." Lucy starts to giggle like she's some nine-year-ol' girl at a slumber party.

"For once, you have the chance to experience that torment yourself." And Lilith's now yankin' on her *schmuck* as she talks. "You've seen them writhe and you've heard them shriek for centuries, but you have no idea why. In your head, you think you do. But in your body, you feel nothing. You're empty."

"What nonsense. Why, it's pure projection." Lucy's talkin' all quiet like now 'cause all she can do is stare at my girlfriend's king-size dick.

"Perhaps. Maybe more than you know. It's possible I was once good at giving torment myself. But that doesn't change the fact that you're still curious." And Lilith swaggers over to the bed an' lays herself spread eagle on it. Her long dick's pointin' to the ceilin'.

"C'mon, Lucifer. You know you want to sit on it."

So guess what, the Devil does just that. But not without makin' a total fuckin' production of it. He can't just walk over to the bed – who could in those heels? An' he can't just take 'em off neither. Na, he has to lift off the ground about four feet an' then hover over to the bed. Ya can tell he's havin' a hard time with the new body 'cause he's floatin' back an' forth over Lilith's dick, tryin' t'get his favourite hole lined up with it.

He's just about got it when Lilith goes an' says, "I need you to be facing away from me."

"Why" he says, soundin' real hurt. "Do I not please you?"

"You look great," Lilith says. She better be lyin' is all I have to say. "It's just that I have something special planned for you and it only works if you're straddling me the other way."

"Special?" Lucy says, all curious.

"Very," she says.

"For me?"

"Yes, for you."

That does it. Alla the sudden, Lucy's turned around an' squattin' on Lilith's *schmuck*. No foreplay. No lube. Just the way he likes it. He must, 'cause he's makin' these really scary cooin' sounds for every little bit of dick he takes up his ass.

"You don't mind if my girlfriend helps out," Lilith says, givin' her dick anotha thrust. "This is *her* deal with the Devil after all. She really wants to lick your clit while I savage your asshole. I promise you, it's right up your alley. You've got extreme pleasure and pain fighting it out throughout your body. A very delightful experience. But it might be too much for you. Being a virgin and all."

That does it. Lucy turns his head aroun'. Just his head – hey, y'knew he would – an' says, "Call me a virgin again and your girlfriend loses her bet."

"OK, Lucifer, calm down." An' Lilith goes an' lifts her hips an' the dick slides in deeper. Lucy makes this happy-soundin' grunt an' turns his head back. Lilith ignores him an' just keeps on talkin'. "I'm just saying you're good at what you know and after you experience this you may want to add it to your repertoire."

"A clever save, young man. Oh. Oh, oh! Oh, yes. Your penis is growing *colder* and *colder*!" An' the Devil squats down further on Lilith with a few more happy, piggy grunts. "But I must concur. I have been growing fatigued with the old routines. Well," he says, glarin' at me, "are you going to minister to my vagina or not?"

"Ya mean eat your pussy, right?" I says.

"I assume so. That is what the rustics are calling it nowadays?"

"Who ya callin' 'rustic', *Teifel*?"

"Girls, girls," says Lilith, laughin'. Yeah, sure, *she's* havin' a good time all right. All *she's* gotta do is sit there with her dick hard. *I* gotta eat out the Devil.

"My apologies, Mrs Faust," says Lucy. "Would you please eat my pussy?"

"Eat it?" I says, psychin' myself up. "I'm gonna devour it. Yuh're gonna come so hard . . ."

"How would I know in *this* body?" he says all snippy.

Lilith an' me, we just laugh. "You'll know. Trust me," I says.

I look over at the clock again. 12:27. It's time t'get this show on the road. So, I take my panties off an' put 'em on Lilith's face. She likes that. Musta made her dick harder or somethin' 'cause Lucy's gaspin' an' "ooohin'" big time now. I crawl up onto the bed where Lucy's squattin' on Lilith's flesh-coloured popsicle. He don't even wobble on his heels. We're talkin' fuckin' amazin' calf muscles an' lots a black magic here. Just keeps pushin' his ass lower an' lower an' spreadin' his legs wider an' wider so his pussy-lips are open an' waitin' for my killuh tongue.

By some miracle, I get my body into this *cockamamy* position where I can get my face into her twat without knockin' everybody off the bed. It looks like a real twat up close. Smells a helluva lot better than that cloud did too. But there's somethin' odd about it. Maybe the lips are too perfect, too perky. But then this is a pussy, not a twat, I reminds myself. They're supposed t'be perky. Maybe it's the clit. It kinda glows. Not like Rudolph or nothin'. It's real faint like. But it definitely glows. Then it hits me. If somethin' glows, it should be hot. But all that's comin' outta this pussy is a chill little wind.

Shit, I thinks. How'm I gonna get warm fluids outta this ice box. I tries to calm myself down. The cold could be comin' from Lilith's *schmuck*. A big part of me's afraid my tongue's gonna freeze to Lucy's cunt but the rest of me says I gotta play this out to the end. I've come too far to quit. Even my twat's givin' me her two cents an' tellin' me t'get in there already. I put my lips to his lips an' start lickin' my way aroun'.

"Oooh," says Lucy with this throaty little growl. "That's new. I want more. What else can you do? Well? Do it!"

The fuckin' cunt tries to grab me by my hair an' mash my face in his pussy but I bat his hands away. Then I goes an' blows on his clit. Real light. He likes that 'cause it shuts him up. I touch it with the tip of my tongue. It ain't ice, thank Gawd. It's cool, but it ain't ice. I got a shot here after all.

So I start takin' turns between my fingers an' my tongue with the Devil's clit. I'm suckin' here an' rubbin' there like my life depends on it. An' it does. But it's gettin' harder an' harder cause Lilith's got a really good fuck goin'. Lilith's slammin' her dick into Lucy an' Lucy's nearly jumpin' up an' down on

Lilith. Which means his pussy's bouncin' all around an' I'm gettin' a friggin' crick in my neck.

I pull my head out for some air while I give the Devil the finger, an' hard too. The clock says 12:37. Ten minutes. Only five more an' we're home free.

My finger musta done somethin' right 'cause we're getting some juices flowin' finally. I lick my finger. Not cold. Not warm. Somewheres in between. Like a really hot bath an hour later. What's that word that sounds just like this water feels? Huh? Tepid. Yeah, that it. His juices was tepid. If I wanted warm, I was gonna have to pick up the pace. Fast.

Lilith musta knew I was flaggin' 'cause she goes an' gives me a boost. She puts her hand between my legs an' starts playin' with my twat. Strokin' it. Rubbin' the juicy edges. Draggin' her fingers teasin'ly between my lips. Givin' little flicks of encouragement to my clit. An' boy'd that make a born-again pussy-eater outta me. I wa tonguin' like a mad woman. Then Lilith goes an' slaps my ass hard, an' again. Now, I'm tonguin' like a very mad woman.

"Why does *she* get her ass slapped?" says Lucy. "I want *my* ass slapped."

Jeez, I thinks, whadda whiner. Just shut up an' come already.

Lilith's hand disappears. I hear her tryin' to slap Lucy the same time as she's fuckin' him. Must be like battin' away two tetherballs. Y'know. Whatevuh. All that matters is that Lucy likes it an' he does. He starts doin' really impressive deep-knee bends. Gawd, don't that kill my neck. But I keep on bouncin' along an' eatin' the Devil's pussy. Even when he stops alla the sudden, mid-jump.

There's several things that tip me off to Lucy havin' his biggest O. I mean, I'm busy in his twat so I can't be lookin' aroun'. His juice is still lukewarm. So I gotta push my face in deeper an' lick harder. But I'm close enough to hear it all. Like Lucy's hole squeezin' Lilith's dick. Yer asshole don't do that unless y'got a majuh case of the shits or yer gettin' the fuckin' of yer life. It's makin' this awful crunchin' sound. Like yer walkin' on ice an' it starts to crack. Pretty gross, huh? I thought so too. But whatevuh gets the Devil off, y'know.

Then there's all this wailin' an' cryin' an' shit – from Lucy. He's in heaven – so to speak. Gawd Almighty, is he loud. C'mon, y'knew the Devil was gonna be a screamer. He's yellin', "Yes! Yes! Yes! I AM THE ANTI-CHRIST!" Honest. Whadda freak! An' it ain't hurtin' Lilith neither. She's just moanin' all happy soundin' while she's shootin' all these ice pellets – how else does a fuckin' icicle come? – inside of the Devil.

Then, I dunno why, I goes an' does somethin' completely *meshugge*. I bites into Lucy's clit. Boy, does he scream now. A course the *putz* likes it rough. What was I thinkin' before? Forget the tongue. Go for the teeth. An' I do. An' how.

It'd'a been easier to pull a bone from a Rottweila's mouth than get me to let go of Lucy. An' while I'm chewin' his clit, I'm lickin' the tip from inside with my tongue. A modified "Fat Ruth's Special." An' that's when I feel the temperature risin'. My face is gettin' wetter an' warmer.

Then he goes an' has anotha Big O. Fuckin' A! Am I lovin' Lucy now.

When the Devil's done shakin' an' shriekin', I stop bitin' his clit an' pull my face outta his still-throbbin' lips an' lick my own. "Well," I says, "whadda we have here? Tastes like warm fluids."

"What? That cannot be," Lucy moans.

"Lilith, whadda ya think?" She pulls her big icicle outta Lucy's ass – Jesus Christ, whadda sad sound he makes when that happens – an' leaves the Devil squattin' over nothin'. Then she slides out from between his legs an' rolls over t'me an' starts lappin' at my face.

"Tastes like warm fluids to me. Here, taste this, girlfriend."

An' Lilith puts her fingers into Lucy's twat an' then goes an' rubs the sticky juice all over his face.

"No, no, no," Lucy shouts, makin' a big to-do about it an' tossin' his bimbo hair aroun' again. "This is *not* what we agreed to."

"Hold the phone, *Teifel*, this is just what ya agreed to. I make ya come after yer longest go-round ever. Which I did. With the help of my girlfriend. An' it was all totally legal as ya would know, bein' the fathuh of all lawyers."

"What?" the Devil says. He sounds all tired an' dizzy. He's wobblin' a bit as he stands up on the bed.

"That's right. There was nothin' in yer contract that said I couldn't have help or that ya had t'be a man. I said 'the Devil'. There was no mention ever about 'he' or 'she'. Just 'the Devil' comes. That's it."

I hear this weird noise. Like snifflin'. It looks like Lucy ain't far off with anotha round of waterworks. Time to close the deal.

"An' I also said specifically, an' I quote, 'there'll be warm fluids'. End quote. I didn't say you'll come warm fluids. I said you'll come an' there'll be warm fluids. You did. There were. The end. I win. Now fork it over."

Next thing I know, the walls are runnin' with tears. Lilith an' me are on the floor. Lucy's hair is touchin' the freakin' ceilin' an' he ain't far below it, arms spread wide like he's You-Know-Who on the cross, his heels just danglin' in the air. What's this nut's obsession with Jesus? The bed's hoverin' next to us an' spinnin'. I'm waitin' for some hurricane wind t'kick in. That an' some loud organ music.

Instead, Lucy's face turns redduh an' redduh. An' he makes the fuckin' awful high screechin' sound without openin' his mouth. Then he belches out in this terrifyin' monster voice, "Oh, Christ!" an' disappears in a little cloud of the same ol' *farshtinkener* smoke.

Next thing I know, there's this light tippy-tap goin' on at the door. "Come in," I shout. An' Mr Mephistopheles pops that big white collar of his aroun' the door an' then I see his head. He's givin' me this fuckin' sly smile an' smoke's all curlin' out, as usual, from the end of his long cigarette holduh. He pulls it outta his mouth an' purrs somethin' like, "Congratulations, ladies. You've won."

So I'm all screamin' an' shit an' bouncin' on the no-longer-hoverin' bed an' Lilith's laughin' her ass off an' Mr Mephistopheles asks, "Mistress?" Lilith has to slap me on the *tuchis* t'get my attention, "Hey, what's that for?" She tells me he's talkin' t'me. To *me*. Mistress. Well, all right. I can do "mistress". So I says, "Yes?"

"Mistress, if you'll be needing anything in particular tonight, do let me know."

"Well, y'know, Mephi – can I call ya 'Mephi'?" I says, climbin' down off the bed.

"I would be honoured, Mistress."

"Great. You know what I could go for right now?"

"No, Mistress."

"Rick at Burguh Haven. Y'know, aroun' 1981."

"An excellent choice, Mistress."

"An' make sure he brings enough double cheeseburguhs an' fries for both me an' Lilith. Ya okay with eatin' meat t'night, *bubeleh*?"

She starts laughin' her ass off again. "It's been a while," she says, "but why the hell not."

"That's what I'm thinkin'. Why the hell not!" An' I goes an' grabs her by the dick. It ain't no icicle now.

"Y'don't mind keepin' this a little longer?" I says.

"Longer?" she says.

"Y'know what I mean." She gives me this nasty grin an' pulls me in to slip me some tongue. Did I mention I love tongue?

Eventually, I tear myself away. I gotta breathe sometime, an' I can feel Mephi watchin' us. Not that I mind bein' watched. But in Mephi's case, I know it ain't doin' a thing for him. I remind myself to order him to have a go with Rick when Lilith an' I are done with the Burguh Gawd. Hell, I bet he's gone without it longer than I have.

"Hey, Mephi," I says, turnin' to him. "Y'got all that?"

"Oh, yes, Mistress." An' he closes the door an' then opens it an' there's Rick, naked except for this big bag of burguhs an' fries. Boy did we *all* pig out that night.

By the next afternoon, I've divorced Kurt. Mephi an' Rick had to go to Florence t'get him to sign. Good riddance was all I could think. He an' that Gretchen bitch an' the Devil deserve each other.

By sunset, I had a new house in Sag Harbour an' I got one for Lilith next door. We spent all night testin' out the beds in both houses. In fact, for the rest of that year I was testin' beds an' bodies all aroun' the world.

This year I've been fuckin' *an'* readin'. Yeah, William Shakespeare. That's right. Him an' every other bastard that still got somethin' in print.

A course, now that y'know I got all these super*mensch* powers I bet ya wanna know what I'm gonna do with 'em next. A fair question. I don't know. But I've been thinkin'. An' it's gonna be big. It's gonna be very big.

Peace in the Middle East? Ya had to ask? A woman in the White House? A course. But it won't be me. I've got bigger matzo balls to boil.

Y'know, come to think of it, I might as well put one in the Vatican too. Just to shake things up a bit. Maybe a Madame President in Bejing an' Moscow. It's the second Madame Prime Ministuh for Israel that's gonna be the real trick. Y'think I'm kiddin'. I should know. I worked on a kibbutz one summuh. Some of those *sabra* boys are to die for, trust me. But ever try talkin' to a *muy macho* Jew. *Oy, vay iz mir.* All I can say is this shrew's gotta helluva lot a tamin' t'do.

But I said really big. End world hunguh? Such a question. A course. What am I, a monster? Somethin' much *bigger*.

Like, for example, turnin' all those fat farms in the strip malls into pleasure palaces for us plus size women. Gawd, how I've hated that name "plus size". Like we're one plus anotha woman. Talk about yer Addition Doublin' Disorduh. Na, I wanna turn that plus into somethin' good. That's right, people. I don't want my weight watched. I want it worshipped. An' that goes double for my twat!

But that's only the beginnin'.

For now, just remember my name. Ruth Vitale. Yer gonna be hearin' it any day now.

Hey, ya want anotha slice of the pecan ring? Good. Then we'll take a ride on my broomstick like I promised ya.

Melinda

Mitzi Szereto

It hurt at first. But then it got better. Just like they told her it would.

Melinda had never considered allowing anyone to tie her up. The idea of handing her body over to another person – of relinquishing her control and her womanhood to people she barely knew – had no place on her list of *Things To Do Before I Die*. Of course there were a lot of things Melinda would never have considered doing before the night she went to the annual company Christmas party, unescorted and conspicuously alone.

The event started off like all the Christmas parties that had gone before, with nearly everyone in attendance parading their dates before their colleagues, their overly-loud laughter and too-bright smiles making Melinda feel more out of the social fray than usual. Not fond of large gatherings, she immediately regretted her mistake in not having coerced her gay friend Joel into coming along with her. He was always a handy escort when she found herself in a pinch, particularly since he knew just when to fade into the background. But tonight Melinda didn't want to be bogged down with a date, bogus or otherwise. She wanted to be available, just in case. She'd even brought along her credit card to splurge on a room in the swanky hotel where the party was being held. Why, she could see the misty green landscape of Hyde Park from the window already!

As it happened, the only view of Hyde Park Melinda ended up being treated to on this wet December evening was the one from the hotel lobby. Evidently the creative head of corporate advertising had far more interesting things to do with his Saturday night than spend it with the office gadabouts, unlike Melinda, who really didn't have anything else to do on this rainy Saturday night. It was either the company Christmas party or cuddling up with the cat to watch yet another television documentary featuring a rhapsodic David Attenborough narrative on the sex lives of creepy-crawly things that live under rocks. At the moment Melinda was more concerned about her own sex life, which had definitely hit the skids.

This recent downward sexual spiral had gained some unwanted momentum thanks to Melinda's involvement with a man from her gym. In retrospect, she probably should have realized that anyone with that many muscles spent most of his time lifting weights and none on building up a career. Therefore it didn't take long for Melinda to decide she could easily forfeit all that hard defined male flesh in return for a steady bed partner with a steady salary and something to talk about beside abs and pecs. For after only a couple of steamy sessions, Blake and his weightlifting paraphernalia had virtually moved into her tiny flat. Granted, they were pretty good steamy sessions as steamy sessions tend to go, though certainly by no means fulfilling enough to warrant her financial support of the man – not even if his tongue claimed the distinction of being as muscular and rippling as the rest of him! Whether at her most exhausted or sexually apathetic, one dose of Blake's hard-working tongue between her thighs would be enough to make Melinda forget the pile of paperwork waiting for her at the office. It was only too bad the rest of Blake wasn't quite as industrious as his tongue.

As she stood by the bar sipping spicy Christmas punch from a plastic cup and nodding the occasional hello to a familiar face, Melinda's glittery evening bag burned an embarrassing reminder against her hip. The unused Visa card that had been placed inside it with such careful premeditation before she left home for the party now made her feel like a fool. At the time it had seemed like a terribly sophisticated thing to do. But as her meticulously made-up eyes swept across the crowd of revellers searching for the one face she most wanted to see, Melinda realized that the expensive French perfume lavished behind her ears and on the insides of her thighs had been wasted, along with the outrageous sum of money that had gone towards the purchase of her new black dress, which had looked *so-o-o* sexy when she'd tried it on in the shop. So profound was her disappointment on what should have been a festive occasion that she considered leaving. However, all this changed when her crestfallen gaze met that of a dark-featured young man who looked as out of place as she felt.

Perhaps it was the expression of contemplative amusement in his smoky Eastern eyes that set him so apart from the others in the noisy hotel banquet room. This, and the fact that he appeared to be the only male in attendance not drinking himself into a state of obnoxiousness or risking his teeth on the dried-out chicken wings, made his presence all the more noticeable. Or at least it did to Melinda, who found his aloofness strangely appealing. This was not a man who needed to call attention to himself. And neither, for that matter, was his fair-skinned female companion. For he stood in a gaudily decorated corner elbow-to-elbow and thigh-to-thigh with the most stunning woman Melinda had ever seen: an ephemeral white-blonde with eyes as amber as a cat's and the stealthy mouse-baiting movements to go along with them. How was Melinda to know that she would be that mouse?

Although not the sort to be physically attracted to her own gender, Melinda could not keep from staring at the feline young woman whose skin looked like it had been made from finely crushed pearls, just as she found it equally difficult to keep from staring at the *café au lait* young man whose conflicting features were every bit as striking as those of his companion. Melinda knew she was being fairly obvious about it, but she didn't mind if the couple noticed her interest. In fact, she secretly wanted them to. The contrast the pair made against the raucous backdrop of braying corporate types populating the area gave Melinda the impression they had wandered into the party by mistake or else out of boredom and the desire for a free drink. Either that or the Christmas punch had been more punched-up than usual and she had begun to hallucinate. Nevertheless, there was nothing at all hallucinatory about the sudden rush of moisture soaking the gusset of the black silk panties Melinda wore beneath her dress.

No one had spoken in the taxi. The only sounds were those of the London rain pattering teasingly against the vehicle's rolled-up windows and the ever-present *chig-chig-chig* of the diesel engine as this silent threesome made their way north towards Mill Hill. By now the drunken hilarity of the holiday celebrants had faded to a distant memory in Melinda's ears. Her breath grew heavy and increasingly ragged as she found herself being pleasantly squeezed between the two party crashers in the taxi's generous back seat, the sexually charged warmth of their bodies hinting at the delightful things to come, as did the flirtatious dance of their fingertips upon her widening thighs. Melinda had not said goodbye to her co-workers or informed them of her impetuous decision to accompany the mysterious couple to wherever they happened to be taking her on this soggy December evening. Unwise perhaps on her part, but tonight Melinda did not want to be her practical and reliable old self. Tonight she wanted to be someone else: the kind of someone who didn't care about things like caution.

For the man and woman pressing themselves so provocatively against Melinda's hips and thighs had shown no sign of knowing their fellow partygoers, which confirmed her suspicion that they had not been invited. Although why anyone would have wanted to crash a boring company Christmas do was a mystery. Much as it was a mystery why from out of a roomful of stunning females Melinda should be the one singled out as she stood about drinking punch in her brand-new black cocktail dress – one that looked indistinguishable from all the other black cocktail dresses being worn. Melinda, who did not classify herself as being in the drop-dead gorgeous league, nevertheless grew hotter and wetter by the minute at the thought of what would be done to her after the taxi had dropped them at their destination.

Indeed, Melinda would be made to feel anything but

average tonight, despite the fact that every part of her average self would be exposed to these two very un-average strangers. Her arms would be drawn back and bound with deftly executed expertise in a complex macramé of silken cord that even she would have agreed was a work of art in itself, had she been able to see behind her. Although perhaps it was just as well Melinda could not, since she would have shrieked with embarrassment at the sight of her unfolded buttocks and the lubricated pink plug of latex being inserted between them.

Masculine fingers formed dark fans across Melinda's fleshy rear cheeks as their smoky-eyed owner's female companion dropped onto her haunches to place the intrusive object inside the wriggling backside before her. In her present state of restraint, Melinda's hips would pretty much be about the only thing she could move. Had she tried to kick out with her feet, it would have been impossible. The braided length of cord looping around her ankles had been woven into the elaborate network of knots trapping her arms behind her, forcing Melinda into a pose of helpless subservience. Considering the circumstances, she found it curious not to be feeling any fear when she could do nothing to act in her own defence.

"Relax, Melinda," the man advised matter-of-factly as he checked her bonds. "Allow yourself to get used to the pain. Your reward will be so much greater."

"Don't fight it," concurred his female partner, placing a not-too-gentle cat's bite upon Melinda's flinching right buttock as emphasis. "You'll only make it harder for yourself."

Despite the reassurances of this appealing couple in whose hands she had perhaps foolishly placed herself, Melinda's instincts took over and she tried to eject the foreign presence from her rectum. Her efforts proved futile, however, for the object refused to budge thanks to a unique design that thwarted even the most determined attempts to expel it. The more force she used, the more the latex filled her, expanding like a dry sponge in liquid until Melinda would finally come to accept the fact that she had lost all ability to control what was being done to her body. There could be no going back for her now.

During all this time, not a word of protest would be put forth by the couple's helpless captive. For Melinda's mouth had already been fitted with a gag of sorts: a blue silk kerchief that would have looked more appropriate fluted to a crisp point in a gentleman's coat pocket than in the lipstick-smeared mouth of a bound and naked female at the complete sexual mercy of two individuals whose names she neither knew nor had bothered to ask. Speaking of which, how did the man know her name? Melinda was certain she had not told him or the woman. Actually, she had made a point not to tell them much of anything.

"Everyone has to have a first time."

The soft feminine purr of a voice startled Melinda, whose recent acceptance of her circumstances had not as yet extended to her latex intruder. So involved had she become in the act of ridding herself of its offending presence that her muscles were as tightly knotted as her bonds. Suddenly she realized how absurdly self-defeating it was to be struggling like this. Deciding to defer to the couple's advice, Melinda tried to relax. She closed her eyes and began to breathe deeply through her nostrils, willing the tension to leave her body until all that remained was a tension in her chest from her wildly thudding heart and an increasingly wild thudding from her vulva.

Melinda felt the amber-eyed woman's breath blowing a hot caress against her buttocks and she sighed into her silken gag. Having managed to calm down a bit, she would be surprised to discover that what was being done to her did not feel at all unpleasant. On the contrary, the cleverly designed series of ridges she'd observed on the surface of the plug before it had gone disappearing in a pink blur behind her gave rise to thoughts and desires she would never have admitted to aloud. For in the privacy of her mind Melinda caught herself wishing that the object penetrating her was not made of bloodless latex, but of hard male flesh – the engorged heated flesh she had been made to taste before her lips were fitted with the blue kerchief. She could still taste the dark-featured young man's slippery fluids in her mouth, along with the sweeter tang of his partner, whose moist female folds Melinda's tongue had likewise been called upon to please before its capacity to do so had been temporarily stifled.

While pondering what it might be like to be used this way by the nameless man whose hands held her open to the latex, Melinda's thoughts drifted towards such a seduction being undertaken by someone she actually knew, or at least saw nearly every day. Although she'd never confided her feelings to even her closest friends, Melinda had been suffering from a year-long infatuation with a work-mate – in fact, the very same work-mate who had been absent from the Christmas party and for whom Melinda would have gladly forfeited a week's salary in exchange for a hotel room, Hyde Park view or not! Unfortunately Caleb worked in a different department in what seemed to be a world away from her own, which only made it harder for Melinda to come up with a legitimate-sounding excuse to seek him out during office hours. She was a number cruncher and he a creative genius, two factors that didn't do much to bring them together.

Getting a man into her bed had never been a difficult task for Melinda. However, all that changed thanks to Caleb, whose oblivious demeanour shook her self-confidence. Perhaps she wasn't his type. Maybe he wanted a woman who looked like a celebrity or something. Maybe if genetics had blessed her with a few more credits on the impossibly gorgeous side of the ledger, she might have made an effort to strike up a conversation in the canteen or in the courtyard when Caleb drifted outside for a smoke. The problem was, every time Melinda got ready to initiate a casual confrontation, someone else would beat her to it: that someone generally being another female whose physical attributes and in-your-face sexuality far outweighed Melinda's own. Well, Caleb was probably too young for her anyway. For all she knew, he might even be gay. At least this would be what Melinda kept telling herself whenever Caleb turned in her direction, only to look straight through her as his lips sucked the smoke through the filtered tip of his cigarette. Oh, how Melinda wanted her clitoris to be that filter tip!

Caleb's impervious features shattered into red-hot fragments of pain as the young woman with the latex plug turned her attentions elsewhere by attaching a pair of small metal clips onto Melinda's upstanding nipples. The effect was like tiny teeth biting into the rubbery points and their startled recipient shuddered violently, prompting a disapproving *tsk-tsk* from her female tormentor, who readjusted the clips so they nipped more cruelly into the sensitive flesh. Melinda resumed the deep nasal breathing that had worked so well to calm her before and the pain in her nipples began to recede, giving way to a vexing heat. It was a heat that gravitated lower and lower and whose capacity to ignite a conflagration made itself apparent when another pair of metal clips were clamped onto Melinda's hairless vaginal lips.

Like the silent young woman wielding these bizarre tools of pleasure, Melinda had also been shaved to a virginal plain, leaving nothing secret and no sensation muted. Granted, she had received quite a shock when she found herself being confronted by a safety razor the moment she had stepped across the threshold of this innocuous-looking Mill Hill house, only to be twisted and contorted until every hair both topside and rear had been hunted down and excised out of existence. Had it been the man wielding the blade rather than his pearly-skinned collaborator, Melinda would have been too mortified to go through with the evening. But as the metal teeth of the clips sank provocatively into her intimate flesh and pain and pleasure blended into one, she knew she was ready for anything.

Melinda giggled into her gag at the thought of her tipsy colleagues at the party, the highlight of their evening the free-flowing liquor and the equally free-flowing office gossip, none of which was likely to include her. Good old reliable Melinda, every corporation's wet dream. You could always count on her to stay late and finish the job. After all, she had nowhere important to run off to. There were no Calebs waiting for her at the pub or at that romantic new Italian restaurant with candles and Chianti on the tables; nor were there any bottles of California Chardonnay chilling in the fridge for later when they went back to her place. Indeed, never would these party-goers have imagined the sexy scenario taking place a few miles to the north – a scenario featuring a pair of expertly twittering tongues acting in symphonic harmony upon the innermost contours of Melinda's clipped-open labia. Of course this wouldn't be the first time she'd been underestimated!

Glancing down at the heads of dark and light paying homage to her shaved sex, Melinda shook with the desire to touch this anonymous man and woman who had entered her life only hours ago. She wanted to feel their beautiful faces with her fingertips as their tongues worked with such artistry on her clitoris and its moist surroundings. But part of the bargain of her pleasure had been the inability to exert any control over what was being done to her. The gym-toned muscles in Melinda's arms and shoulders ached with frustration, much as they had ached earlier when going to her knees before the bared and expectant genitals of her hosts, who orchestrated the movements of their guest's mouth to their exclusive benefit, inspiring from Melinda's tongue a boldness she never knew it possessed. Yes, perhaps she even underestimated herself.

It had been easier with the man, who thrust his penis to and fro in her mouth like one might a vagina. Keeping hold of Melinda's chin-length chestnut hair, he pumped her open mouth to the point at which she thought her jaw would break, exacting punitive glances against her throat before finally emptying himself with a sharp cry on her tongue. For the first time in her life Melinda did not experience the urge to spit out a man's pleasure. Instead she wondered if the aloof Caleb would taste as sweet as this dark stranger who had forced himself upon her surprisingly eager mouth. "How lovely you are," he replied afterwards in a husky whisper, leaning down to kiss Melinda's sticky lips before surrendering her to the amber-eyed female waiting with impatience at his side. Melinda had nearly forgotten about the other woman, so mesmerized had she been by her unquestioning submission to the man towering above her humbly posed form. However, she would promptly learn that his delicately featured sidekick was not the sort to let herself be forgotten.

Performing orally on another woman would be far more complicated than the straightforward techniques needed with a man, particularly when the recipient happened to be no shrinking violet when it came to making her desires known. Melinda found her hair being grasped in the same manner as before, albeit with substantially more ruthlessness as the expensively cropped chestnut strands were almost ripped from the root. "Get to it, Melinda!" the woman ordered with a cavalier toss of her white-blonde head, her characteristic kittenish purr now a caustic bark.

Melinda felt a forbidden tingle between her thighs at hearing her name being uttered in conjunction with such a demand. The tingle gained in intensity, reaching near-orgasmic proportions when the young woman proceeded to rub her shaved and fragrant mound against Melinda's lips until arching her cat's spine in orgasm. Although she had never been involved sexually with her own gender, Melinda was not shy to thrust her tongue inside her partner's cream-filled vagina at the moment of her own climax, which had been achieved without any physical means other than the ghostly sensations of the pair of tongues that had gone before. It reminded her of the stealthy orgasms she experienced while asleep and which, upon awakening, would be followed by the discovery of her hands situated in innocent repose at her sides.

Melinda reflected often on that night of self-discovery in Mill Hill. Although she wouldn't have minded repeating the occasion, she hadn't been in contact with the man and woman responsible for giving her so much pleasure. The temptation to flag down a taxi and pay them a visit was one that became harder and harder to resist, especially since she had jotted down the street number of their house upon arriving back at her flat. But Melinda didn't believe they would be there when she arrived. The house had had a temporary feel to it, as if the occupants were just using the place for a quick layover on their way to other adventures, which probably included other Melindas. From what she could recall from the dizzying erotic haze she'd been in, the house had offered little in the way of furnishings– not that Melinda had been particularly interested in interior design that evening! Well, perhaps such things were best left as treasured memories, since it seemed doubtful that the overwhelming intensity of sensation she had been subjected to at the controlling hands of these two nameless and exotic strangers would ever be repeated. Even so, Melinda did not feel at all regretful. The dark young man and his amber-eyed companion had jolted her out of the humdrum dregs of daily life and taught her about her body's ability to achieve pleasure – a pleasure gained through restraint and pain. She had heard about people who got off on such sexual kinks, but had never bought into the pleasure-pain myth. Until now.

By the time she returned to the office after the Christmas break, Melinda had convinced herself that the couple had never existed. What had happened could only have taken place in her mind – a vivid erotic fantasy no doubt inspired by her year-long infatuation with Caleb. As she settled in for the first work week of the new year, she was surprised to find among all the pre-holiday clutter on her desk a tiny box covered in expensive wrapping paper. A late Christmas gift, was her first thought as she searched for an accompanying card. "Do you happen to know who left this on my desk?" Melinda called out to her assistant when her efforts to locate a card identifying the gift-bearer proved futile. A highly detail-oriented person, it annoyed Melinda when holiday gifts were not given on time.

"It was there when I came in this morning," came the assistant's unhelpful answer.

Melinda turned the little package every which way, puzzling over its contents. The box looked like the kind that contained earrings or a pendant. Not in the habit of wearing much in the way of jewellery, Melinda relied on her trusty pearl earrings for most situations, especially since joining the conservative ranks of corporate management. She had never been what anyone would have called a flashy person; therefore she hoped this mysterious gift would be something she could use, because if the giver hadn't bothered to leave a card, it was also unlikely a sales receipt had been enclosed in the event it became necessary to return the item.

Melinda waited for her assistant to leave before taking a letter opener to the attractive wrapping paper. She could not understand why her hands were trembling over something so ridiculously mundane as a pair of earrings; she could barely manage the elementary task of prying off the little lid. All at once Melinda cried out with remembered pain, for lying incongruously upon a dainty square of cotton was a pair of metal clips. They looked identical to the metal clips that had been clamped to her nipples and vulva not even three weeks ago. But surely that was impossible!

Melinda felt herself growing wet from the phantom sensations inspired by the unexpected reappearance of the clips and she squeezed her thighs together to calm the chaos taking place between them. Her face burned with embarrassment as she wondered who in the office might have been privy to the lascivious events of several nights ago. A folded square of paper had been tucked halfway beneath the bed of cotton and she plucked it out. To her frustration, it provided no clue as to the identity of her bondage-minded gift giver. All it offered by way of explanation was the word *Tonight,* along with a Maida Vale address. The note had been penned in a meticulous hand, the execution of the letters so tightly controlled and precise that Melinda could feel the intricate weave of silken cording which for one night had placed her in bondage. It would be all she could do to fight the impulse to relieve herself with her fingers right there at her desk.

With a similar sense of destiny to that which she'd experienced on her way to Mill Hill the rainy evening of the company Christmas party, Melinda took a taxi to the address on the note, the distinctive *chig-chig-chig* of the diesel engine adding an erotic sense of déjà vu to the occasion. The driver deposited her at the wrought-iron gate of a charming ivy-covered mews house, where from behind lace curtains a gentle light illuminated the mullioned windows. Melinda thought she saw a tall shadow move past the one nearest the door, although she could not tell whether the shadow belonged to a man or a woman.

Ever so slowly Melinda made her way up the cobbled walk, taking a perverse pleasure in prolonging the moment before she would at last come face-to-face with the person or persons who had summoned her. For it had, indeed, been a summons she'd received. The handsomely painted front door opened before she would even be given a chance to ring the bell.

"Hello, Melinda."

Melinda gasped aloud as the wetness that had been plaguing her ever since unwrapping her Christmas gift that morning soaked the gusset of her blue silk panties. She had specifically chosen to wear them this evening because they were the same shade of blue as the silk kerchief the couple from Mill Hill had used to bind her mouth with.

For standing before Melinda was the impervious young man who for the past year had occupied her thoughts and been the inspiration for her orgasms, the man she assumed never noticed her, who looked right through her as if she were invisible. But he was not doing so now. Instead the lips she had so often observed sucking the smoke through the filter tip of his cigarette formed a sardonic smile.

Caleb stepped forwards, a safety razor held ready in his right hand. "You can't imagine how long I've been waiting for this," he replied softly.

"And she's definitely worth the wait, darling," came a familiar female voice. Melinda felt a sudden shift in the air as the feline presence of the young woman who had seduced her bound figure came into focus, followed by her smoky-eyed male conspirator.

"I understand you have already met my good friends Stephanie and Naveen?" Caleb looked deliberately into Melinda's astonished eyes, as if the question needed no answer.

Naveen's *café au lait* fingertips reached forward to stroke Melinda's cheek. "Wasn't it thoughtful of Caleb to have invited us to the company Christmas party?"

Caleb's smile widened. "Oh, but the party is only just beginning."

The Lindy Shark

Alison Tyler

With a blare from the slide trombone, Lilly Faye and her Fire-Spittin' Fellas lit into the first number of the evening. Clara rushed to find her place, her polka-dotted dress swirling about her. Within moments she was grabbed around the waist, pulled into a tight embrace, twirled fiercely and without finesse, and then passed to the next man in line. This one had thick, meaty fingers that held her too tightly, creasing the fabric of her carefully ironed dress. She was relieved to be released to the next partner. Her ruffled red panties briefly showed as the third man spun her, dipped her, and passed her on again.

Aside from the briefest of observations, she hardly had time to notice what her partners looked like. Her appraisals were cut short with every turn, only to start fresh with the next. Even when a man did please her, there was no way to act on the attraction. The leader would call out to switch, and she'd be passed onto the next dancer. Still, she couldn't help but feel a wash of anticipation at the dim prospect that she would be matched with someone who not only suited her moves but also passed her stringent critique system. Although it hadn't happened lately, that didn't mean it couldn't. Maybe *he* would be here again. Perhaps he would notice her this time.

To the sounds of "Jump, Jive, and Wail", Clara found herself with five different men in a row who failed to please her. Handsome, but a poor dancer. Fine looking, but much too short. Sweaty. A groper. Bad, bad hair. Then, finally, as the leader called out for only the experienced lindy-hoppers to take the floor, she saw *him*. She watched him move through the crowd with that insolent look on his face. He had heavy-lidded eyes, a tall, sleek body. Like a shark on the prowl, he cut cleanly through the waves of dancers.

"Fine threads," a woman next to Clara said, staring at the man. "Racket jacket, pulleys, and a dicer," she added.

A little too "in the lingo", thought Clara as she refocused on her dream man – but the woman was right. His vintage zoot suit looked as if it had been tailor-made for him, the braces flashed when his coat opened, and the fedora added to his high-class appearance. He had an unreadable expression on his face, a steady gaze that almost seemed to look through her. Then he lifted his chin in her direction, letting her know that he had seen her and approved.

Of course he approved, thought Clara. Her sunset-coloured hair, dark red streaked with gold and bronze, was done in pin curls that had taken hours to achieve. She'd applied make-up in the fashion of the era – bright matte lips and plenty of mascara. Her vintage dress was navy with white polka dots, and it cinched tightly around her tiny waist. A pair of stacked heels sturdy enough to dance in, but high enough to make her moves look even more complicated than they were, completed her outfit. She waited for him to come to her side. The girls nearby twittered in hopes that he was coming for one of them.

"I'd let him into my nodbox," one murmured.

Clara agreed. She'd definitely let this man crease her sheets. She felt like telling the giggling women to give up – the man didn't have eyes for any of them. He was on his way to Clara.

A rush of nervous excitement pulsed between her legs and flooded outwards. Rarely did she feel this self-conscious – normally her moves expressed a quality that came from within, a radiance on the dance floor that couldn't be taught. This man possessed it too – that's what attracted her. Dancing could be a form of foreplay; she'd always known that. But at most of these swing sessions, there simply wasn't anyone she wanted to take to bed. Sure, she was picky when it came to men – both as dance partners and bed partners. That wasn't a crime, was it? If you chose the right person, for either activity, the results were much more satisfying.

The man reached her side just as a new song began. He didn't say a word, simply put one hand on her waist and steered her onto the floor.

She took her time checking him out. Up close, he was even more attractive. Those dark liquid eyes, like a silent film star's, were infinitely expressive. A deep inky blue, they shone beneath the crystal chandelier. His hands were large and firm, and they manoeuvred her with expertise, without roaming where they didn't belong. That was a surprise. Men often took the opportunity to fondle a partner, something Clara generally found distasteful. Now she wouldn't have minded if his hands wandered down a bit, if he tried a little stroking as they glided together on the dance floor.

Clara usually didn't have to think while she danced – her feet easily followed her partner's lead. But this man was making her work, executing several difficult steps from the very beginning, forcing her to concentrate. She forgot about what she hoped he might do to her and focused on keeping up with him.

Other dancers spread out to give them room, as if they sensed something big about to happen. And it did. As the first song blended into a second, and then a third, the duo found their zone. When her partner flipped her into the air, Clara let out a happy little squeal, something totally out of character for her. For the first time, the man smiled. It was as if a marble sculpture had cracked. For the rest of the dance, the moves came naturally. Clara no longer had to second-guess him, to think about where he was going. Instinctively, she followed.

When the music stopped so that Lilly Faye and her Fellas could take a breather, Clara kept following him – down the hallway from the main ballroom and into a small, unisex bathroom. This wasn't something she would normally do, but if he could dance like that, she thought, just imagine how he might make love. He locked the door behind them.

They could hear music drifting in from the ballroom – someone had put on a CD by Big Bad Voodoo Daddy, and it was loud. People headed out to the bar, and voices lifted as spirits flowed. Alcohol mixed with dancing could make people rowdy. Clara was relieved not to be out there with the throng making small talk.

The man lifted her up; she kicked out her heels automatically, as if he was still dancing with her. He wasn't. He set her down on the edge of the blue-and-white tiled sink and cradled her chin in one hand. His full mouth, almost indecently full for a man, came closer. Kissed her. Shivers ran through her body; she closed her eyes and floated on his kiss, not noticing when his fingers moved to the front of her dress and undid the tiny pearl buttons, buttons it had taken her ten minutes to fasten. She remembered standing in her bedroom, looking at her reflection, wondering if this man would be present tonight, if he would like what she was wearing.

Beneath the vintage dress she wore a modern, underwire lace bra and matching panties in crimson silk. The man stroked her breasts through the bra before unfastening the clasp and letting the racy lingerie fall to the floor. When she opened her eyes, she saw their reflection in the mirror across the room. They appeared dream-like, a perfect match. The way it was meant to be.

The man took off his hat and set it on the counter. Then he tilted his head and watched her as she slid out of her dress to stand before him in her ruffled panties, garters, hose and shoes. Though he didn't speak, he seemed to want her to leave the stockings on. Quickly he turned her so that they faced the mirror above the sink. He lowered her underpants and waited for her to step out of them. She watched in the mirror as he undid his slacks and opened them. She caught a flash of polka dot boxer shorts that matched her dress – another indication of how perfect they were together.

He leaned against her, the length of his cock pressed to the skin of her heart-shaped ass. The silk of his boxers brushed the backs of her thighs, and she sighed. He gripped her waist, letting her feel just how ready he was. His cock was big and hard, and it moved forward, seeking its destination. Without a word, he slipped it between her thighs, probing her wetness. She'd gotten excited during their dancing; her slick pussy lips easily parted and he slipped inside. Just the head. Just a taste.

The band started up in the other room, and, to the lindy beat, he began to fuck her. Clara felt as if they were still dancing. Making love to him was as natural as having him flip her in the air and twirl her around. She opened to his throbbing sex, and to the insistent beat of the music.

The bathroom's art deco style created a fantasy-like atmosphere, with its blue-toned mirror and tiled walls that echoed her sighs. Though he remained silent, the man seemed pleased by the way she moved, rocking her body back and forth, urging him to deeper penetration. He locked eyes with her in the mirror and, for the second time that evening, smiled. It began at the corners of his mouth and moved up to sparkle in his eyes. An intense connection flowed hot between them; she had been right to wait for him. She felt a sense of destiny as he slid his hands up her bare arms, stroking her skin, sending tremors through her body.

She liked the silence, their lack of words. Some boys talked through the whole thing, ruining it. Lovemaking, Clara felt, shouldn't be full of chitchat. She craved mystery, magic – and with him she had it. She felt the same way dancing. Some men talked when they danced, but if you danced well together, you could have an entire conversation without once opening your mouth.

This man seemed to know that. He understood. Not saying a word as he filled her with his cock, he held her gaze, trailing his fingers across her breasts, pinching her nipples between his thumb and forefinger, making her moan and arch her body.

Oh, yes, this was the way to do it, to the sounds of music, in dim twinkling light. She strove to reach climax in synchronicity with him. She squeezed him tightly with her inner muscles, watching his face for a reaction.

His eyes closed, long lashes dark against pale skin, strong jaw set as he held her tight. Yes, it was going to happen. Now. She closed her eyes, as pulses of pleasure flooded through her, gripping on to the edge of the sink to hold herself steady.

After he came he didn't withdraw, but remained inside her, growing hard again almost instantaneously. She sighed with pleasure as he extended the ride, this time taking her harder, faster. She felt as if she might literally dissolve with pleasure. Her senses were heightened, and when he brought one hand between her legs, plucking her clit with knowledgeable fingers, she came, biting her bottom lip hard to keep from screaming. She felt weightless, as she had when he'd tossed her into the air. When she looked in the mirror, she seemed transformed, a flush in her cheeks, a glow in her eyes.

She expected him to be transformed as well. After something so spectacular, shouldn't he be? But when he got dressed he hardly looked rumpled at all, his shirt still cleanly pressed, the fine crease on his pants in place. She felt suddenly exposed, with her bra and panties on the floor, her dress a puddle of polka dots. It would take a bit of work for her to sort herself out. He seemed to understand this, and gave her a final kiss and a wink, and then nodded with his head for her to put on her clothes.

He would meet her outside, she guessed, as she watched him leave, and then hurried to lock the door behind him, her heart pounding like the drum section of Lilly Faye's band. Her fingers trembled as she rebuttoned her dress, taking longer than it had earlier in the evening. She kept mis-buttoning and starting again, desperate to finish so that she could get back out on the floor and dance with him again.

Back in the ballroom, she was certain he would hurry to her side, would lift her up in the air again so that her dress would twirl the way it was meant to. Her crimson ruffled panties would show, and the scent of sex would waft around her like perfume. From now on, they would be partnered, showing off for the rest of the crowd. They would go back to her place that night, and in the morning she would take him to her favourite vintage store on Third Avenue. Would try on clothes for him. Would let him dress her. There were so many things they could do together.

But when she exited the rest room and saw him standing by the wall, he didn't seem to notice her. His eyes roamed over the crowd. She was about to wave her hand, to call out that she was right here, ready to dance. Then she noticed that the two women who'd stood next to her earlier were now at the bar across the way, and the man was heading in their direction.

One of the girls let out a high, flirtatious laugh. The man adjusted his braces in a practised, casual manner and tilted his hat forwards rakishly.

The room blurred before Clara. She saw the truth. Like a shark, he was moving again through the water of the dancers. After another kill.

Rayban

M. Nason

Rayban wouldn't take off her shades even when she fucked.
That was her pronouncement, not mine. She said it each time
I tried to remove her sunglasses, first when I undressed her,
then later as she leaned over me and all I saw was my own
reflection spread naked across her face. She had a solid body,
more sturdy than thin, broad-shouldered, olive-skinned, with
wide breasts and thighs. She dragged me down like she was
pulling prey into her den, and all the while my own image
stared back at me, filling her eyes.

"Let me look at you," I said.

"Oh, just fuck me," she hissed. "There's no time to look at
me."

On first laying eyes on her I had not foreseen such things. We
met in a coffee shop prone to tourists, a few blocks from the
river. I had suggested it, in my 17th e-mail. Her response had
been, Why not? Online, she was direct and glib, careless about
punctuation, somewhat rambling in her sentences though I
could never shake the feeling she laboured over each message.
That was my dark suspicion of her, something I hadn't shared
by the time we'd scattered our clothes across my living room
floor. She was backing towards the bedroom, nothing on but
unbuttoned jeans, tiger-striped panties and Raybans. I grinned
at her, but her expression didn't change. She backed into my
bedroom without showing the slightest curiosity about what

she might find there, just glanced once over her shoulder so she could steer herself towards the bed. By the time she pressed her legs against the mattress she had pushed off her jeans. She lay on her back, reaching for me in the same movement. I fell towards her, praying I would never be heard from again.

"Why 'Rayban'?" I had asked her early on. I liked the name. It struck me as creative, and certainly more creative than mine – NJMAN571.

"Because Raybans are cool," she answered. "Silly."

"Do you mean Raybans or just shades in general?"

"I mean Raybans," she typed. "Anyone can wear sunglasses. Girls wear sunglasses."

"Oh, so you're not a girl," I said. "Then what are you?"

"Isn't that what you're trying to find out?"

I knew so little about her. That struck me as she pulled me into a kiss, there on the bed, such a close kiss my eyelashes fluttered against the silver of my own reflection. Her hair was brown and shoulder-length, straight and full. I pressed against her with such force I felt her heat flooding through my skin. I had this impulse I didn't understand, to stop and breathe, pull away, but my desire was as absolute as gravity. "We're a long way from coffee," I whispered, but she didn't smile. She just rolled me onto my back.

I don't know what it is about type on a computer screen that one can find attractive, but even before I saw her that first afternoon I was concocting scenarios. She slipped into the coffee shop with no eyes and no expression, and all through our conversation she never allowed her features to grow more animated than a vague upturn of her mouth. We talked about art, we talked about the deer population in New Jersey, we talked about George Bush. To every point I made she responded with a nod. I remember sitting there, wondering what this woman was hiding. Then she looked away from me and towards the window, watched people stroll by on the street. The corner of her lips curled upwards. "You chose a nice place," she said.

"I like it around here. But I like anything to do with the water. Put anything within a quarter-mile of a river or the coast and it seems to take on a whole new personality."

For a moment she considered that. "You like the definition," she decided. "You like the boundary. Water gives everything a defined beginning and end. You like that."

"I don't know if that's true," I answered in an even voice. In the pit of my stomach I was vaguely offended. "I think I like the rhythm of the water, more than anything else – the way you can just sit and watch it move. It makes me think of exploring, of going to new places."

"Oh," said Rayban. "Do you travel a lot? Do you go to many new places?"

"Not as many as I'd like."

"Where do you go, when you travel?"

"I go to Massachusetts," I told her. "I was born there."

"So you go home," she said, nodding. "That's your adventure. You go home."

She pulled away my clothes with force enough to hurt, put her hand between my legs and squeezed. "Does this scare you?" she whispered. "Do I scare you?"

"No," I breathed. "Just a little."

"You shouldn't be afraid of people you fuck."

"I'm not afraid of you."

"I might be a crazy woman," she hissed, sing-song. "I might be a cra-zy girl."

I laughed but she ignored it. "Later you'll lick me," she said. "But first you have to fuck me, so you won't be afraid any more."

"You don't believe in taking time, do you?"

She stroked me, her rough gestures easing to a feather touch. "When we're out of time, I'll tell you," she said. "When we're out of time, you'll know it."

"You're married," I had observed in the coffee shop. "What do you want a boyfriend for?"

She shrugged. "How do you know I'm married?"

"Your profile says you are."

"And you believe it. Just because I typed it, you assume it's true."

"Are you really like that? Would you really type something like that just to see what happens?"

"No," she said. "I'd type something like that to throw the losers off the scent So I could watch their eyes when I told them I'm single, no attachments, maybe crazy. You wouldn't believe how scared guys get when they think you're going to rock their world."

She wouldn't take me to bed the first time we met. She took me the second time, after our second meeting for coffee. She drained her cup and pointed her Raybans at me. "What's my name?" she asked.

"All I know is Rayban."

"Would you fuck me if that's all you knew?"

"Well, it would be nice to know your name," I told her. "It would be nice to know what people call you."

"You didn't answer my question."

I frowned at the table. "Yes," I said, after what I thought was a suitable pause. "Yes, I would."

She nodded. "I figured you would," she said. "That's no surprise at all."

The whole time she kept her eyes towards me, but for one moment. When finally we were both naked and she had swung her leg over to straddle me, she took my cock in her hand and glanced down as she guided it inside her. I watched the way she wrapped her fingers around me, held my breath as she hesitated above me. As she lowered herself, she looked down at me again, her eyes still hidden, her face still set, and when I reached for her glasses she pushed my hand away. "You have to let me see your eyes," I breathed.

"I'm fucking you," she said. "I don't have to do anything else."

"Let me look at you."

"Oh, just fuck me," she hissed. "There's no time to look at me."

All of a sudden I had this thought that I shouldn't have even been there. By then it was too late. Rayban was all around me, and if I tried to look anywhere all I saw were her silver eyes and my own self underneath her. I am not a handsome man and the agitations of sex aren't anything like a dance with me. They aren't possessed of anything like grace or rhythm, they are simply manoeuvres of my body, dictated by the mechanics of my spine and my nerves and my desire. Until that moment I had thought otherwise but there on Rayban's face was sheer reality, tinted in silver. I watched horrified as I thrust beneath her. I reached again for her shades. Behind them her eyes would be glittering, amused.

The Mermaid's Sacrifice

Christopher Hart

We were in the garden behind the villa when he came to call.

Kit was hunched up on a sun lounger in the shade, reading a book. He wore a distant frown. I was wandering around on my own, in my usual daydream, skimming my palms ticklishly over the heads of the bougainvillea flowers, the oleander and hibiscus and the green tracery of the jasmine. It was very hot. There was a light wind but it was humid, the *libeccio*, blowing in from the southwest across the Mediterranean from North Africa and picking up all the summer mist of the sea as it came. It muffled everything, made everything, even the lizards on the crumbling villa walls, dreamy and slow. My thin cotton dress clung to me with light perspiration. I thought of nothing. Except maybe Kit.

A man was standing just the other side of the gate when I looked up and saw him, gasped, almost swallowed my tongue. I held my hand up to my mouth, schoolgirlish, infuriated by my own timid reaction. He smiled. He had a wolfish smile.

In fact, all his features had the properties of beasts of prey: the wolfish smile, the aquiline nose, the leonine mane (albeit greying at the temples), the deep-set eyes of some other unnameable hunter species glaring out of the dark night. "Signorina?" he said. His voice was a low growl, of course.

"Signora," I corrected him, lowering my eyes briefly to check for the shirt unbuttoned to the navel, the extravagantly hairy chest, the gold medallion. But he wasn't like that: navy blue shirt, only top button undone. No jewellery that I could see except a fine gold wedding ring. I opened the gate to him.

He was lean and rangy, with a high sunburned forehead and a wide sensuous mouth that looked good when he smiled, which was rarely. His hands were large, with strong, prominent veins; his stare piercing but not hostile – well, not quite. I guessed his age to be about mid-fifties, maybe older.

He held his hand out to me. "Leopoldo," he said, in a cultivated Italian accent. "My wife and I live next door."

I shook his hand. "Nancy," I said. "My husband and I . . ." I paused, bent my head, smiled self-consciously. I was beginning to sound like the Queen. I looked up again. "Kit – my husband – we're just staying here for a couple of weeks. It's lovely here."

He nodded gravely, said nothing, He stared at me for fractionally too long for comfort, and then said, "We would like to invite you over to dinner tonight. Just a simple dinner – the four of us."

I babbled that it was very kind of them to invite us, and what time should we be over, and we'd be delighted. He told me, nodded again, and turned and strode away. When he was gone I felt my shoulders relax.

Kit, of course, doesn't want to go.

He lays his book down on his chest and looks up at me and holds his hand up to his forehead to shield his eyes from the setting sun. A hank of hair flops over his hand. So young. I love him so much. "Do we have to?" he says.

"I've already accepted."

"You could have consulted with me first."

"I thought you'd . . ."

"I came here to get away from all that, and now you've gone and fixed up some tedious dinner party with a couple of old farts who'll have nothing to talk about and expect us to entertain them all evening, Thanks a lot."

"He didn't *look* like an old fart."

"Who didn't?"

"Leopoldo."

Kit mouths *Leopoldo* back at me in a sarcastic fashion, and then slams his book down and struts off into the villa to get ready for dinner.

I love him even when he's petulant.

Kit wears his ivory linen suit that he knows I like him in. So that's OK. I'm not so sure about the tie – too hot, surely? But I don't say anything.

I wear my long emerald-green dress with the narrow shoulder straps, and some bright red lipstick. Really bright. Kit looks quite startled when he sees me, and then smiles. "Hi, beautiful," he says, kissing me delicately on the forehead.

We walk next door arm in arm.

Leopoldo's wife is called Teresa, and she is extremely beautiful. She is perhaps ten years younger than he, very elegant and self-possessed, with eyebrows permanently arched high over her big eyes. Not plucked, just arched: sceptical, amused, worldly, permanently set for flirtation. Her skin appears finely stretched over high cheekbones – but not, please God, face-lifted – and her lips are quite thin. She compliments me immediately on my dress *and* on my lipstick, and she kisses me warmly on both cheeks. She herself is wearing a long black evening dress, and a gorgeous hematite choker, and, would you believe it, long black gloves up and over her elbows. Like some fifties film star: subtler than Sophia Loren, more voluptuous than Audrey Hepburn . . . a darker, more Mediterranean Grace Kelly?

Teresa obviously likes dressing up for even the smallest occasions. She must notice me eyeing her gloves because she looks down and caresses them lightly, each one, and gives me her most charming smile, and says, "Oh, any excuse to dress up these days, my darling!" in her charmingly accented English. Leopoldo takes my right hand and kisses it, his eyes fixed on my face from under his heavy brows as he does so.

Dinner is taken out in the garden. And what a garden.

We couldn't see it from our side because of the dense row of cypresses that they have growing around their private patch. Leopoldo leads us immediately round the side of the villa – I can tell it is large, and in rather better condition than the one we're renting – but other than that we don't get to see inside it. Behind, a wonderfully elegant, classical-style lawn stretches down to a grove of almond trees at the end, and down the centre of the lawn runs a very ancient-looking, stone-clad, long and narrow pool. Walking beside it I see that the pool is lined randomly with coloured tiles that reflect through the water and give it a strange metallic sheen. Leopoldo to my right, taking my elbow in his large hand, says, "Perhaps a swim later on, if we have not eaten and drunk too much?"

I nearly blurt out that I haven't brought a swimsuit, but I stop myself just in time, realizing that it would only justify his making some lecherous remark about skinny-dipping. I bite my tongue. Something lurches, deep inside me. I feel a slick of sweat over my upper lip.

It is all impossibly beautiful. The night is warm, and we dine outside, among the grove of almond trees that thickens into an orchard beyond. To either side are citrus orchards too, their tangy fumes filling the night air. The *libeccio* has dropped off, leaving the air still and sultry. An oval pine table and four chairs stand in the grass, surrounded by flambeaux on chains and poles dug into the ground. When we sit down, the orange light from the naked flames leaps and dances over our faces, emphasizing the brightness of our skin and our eyes, and (I imagine with a thrill) the sluttish scarlet of my lips.

Teresa and Leopoldo – "Call me Leo, *please*" – have a cook, of course: Tancredi. (No one could afford so palatial a villa along this bit of coastline and not afford a cook as well.) Tancredi mixes us our drinks – Kir Royales all round to start with – and then brings us our meal: *zuppe di cozze,* mussels in a hot-pepper sauce. Leopoldo tells me they were fresh this morning, relishing their taste, his wide lips glistening in the torchlight. Kit by my side starts to relax, I can feel it, and with the second glass of wine – some unidentifiable but perfect floral white – he begins to talk. And when Kit actually chooses to talk, he is wonderful. Soon he is deep in passionate argument about the real significance of the bull-run in Pamplona, and then the bull-leapers of Knossos, and then he even engages Teresa in conversation about the sad decline of haute couture. Teresa used to be a model – naturally. She often stays with Yves St Laurent in his pad in Morocco, it appears, and she tells an amusing story about Yves and the time he unwittingly ate a raw potato.

Leopoldo doesn't laugh, I notice. He watches her from the other end of the table, taking a steaming mouthful of sea bass – our main course – his dark eyes fixed on her, weirdly adoring. Teresa, it seems, rather ignores Leo. Clearly she knows him well. I feel I do too, already: and his name may be Leo, but if he's not a Scorpio – I'll swim naked in that pool, indigestion or not.

There's cheese, and fresh grapes and almonds, and peaches baked and drizzled with sweet almond wine, and we are all a little drunk, I think, but not so drunk that we will feel ill tomorrow morning. Drunk only on conversation and good food and fine wine and flirtation and the strange and unexpected beauty of this hidden garden and these two enigmatic people – as old as our parents but, I have to admit it, far, far cooler.

I need the loo. Teresa gives me directions – "Go in through the sitting-room doors and turn left and then right down the corridor and . . ." Something like that. But by the time I've got there I've completely forgotten, so I stumble around the darkened villa, giggling softly to myself, wondering at how huge it is, and badly needing a pee.

Somewhere down one of the hallways I find myself in a smaller room, with bare terracotta walls and a small, circular fountain in the middle, of grey-green stone, maybe marble, and looking very ancient. The fountain is running softly, trickling down over the stone into the basin, and above it is the figure of a naked girl. But not the kind you'd see in a civic fountain – not doing what she's doing. Not with that brazen abandon, her eyes stone-blank and closed, entirely absorbed in her own erotic oblivion.

And then I am abruptly aware of Leo beside me. He doesn't look at me, only at the naked figure there over the fountain. "Isn't she beautiful?" he says.

"I . . . yes, I suppose . . ." I stammer, wishing I could think of something wittier to say.

Then, only then, he turns to me and says, "I will tell you all about her. But later. First you need a bathroom, I think?"

At last! He shows some sign of chivalry!

But it doesn't last. The "bathroom" he leads me to doesn't have a lock on it. In fact, it doesn't even have a door. It is a beautiful little room at the back of the villa, tiled in sand and terracotta with marine motifs in the walls and floor – but no door. Quite open. Leo sees me hesitate and shrugs. "Go ahead," he says. "I won't watch."

I could have been offended. But suddenly I think, *Fuck it*, and do as he says. And what does he do?

He lights a cigarette. And watches.

Afterwards we walk back to dinner arm in arm as if it is all quite normal.

Maybe it is, round here.

Kit by now is gently, sweetly drunk. He gets drunk quite easily and becomes even more boyish than ever.

Teresa looks up and smiles at me. "Your husband is a university *professor*," she says to me. "So clever – and so young!"

"You wouldn't think it to look at him, would you?" I say dryly. Kit grins at me.

"Ah, poor darling," says Teresa, reaching out and squeezing his thigh. "I think he is – *delicious*."

Delicious, but drunk. Which is, no doubt, why he has completely forgotten, by the following morning, about their second invitation: to the island.

Instead, after final *grappe e caffè corretto,* and kisses and *arrivederla*'s and *domani*'s all round, we stumble back to our villa and fall into bed. And I want to make love to him then, across our bed, or rather for him to make love to me, pulling my dress up, not even taking it off. I so want him to make love to me. But he is too drunk. And even if he wasn't, I know too well that he would probably just turn away from me and murmur that he was tired, another night, and then fall asleep.

I do not sleep. I feel the blood coursing through my body and it is full of wine and a certain anticipation or even fear, as if I know something is going to happen, something beautiful and terrible, before this holiday is over. And my blood is awake, wide awake. Some time later, lying there, ears straining to hear the waves breaking on the shore below, I hear louder sounds: splashing, and screams. They are coming from next door. I get up and go to the window but I can see nothing beyond the cypress trees. As if in a dream I go down into our garden and across the cool grass barefoot to the trees, and the cypress branches brush against my skin and I press in close and look through.

Leopoldo and Teresa are making love. Still clothed, or at least half-clothed, they are wrestling with each other, standing waist deep in the shallow end of the pool, Leo grimly silent, Teresa bucking away from him, screaming and laughing as he holds her tight. Then they fall silent, first as he closes her mouth with a long and ardent kiss, then as he flings her back across the side of the pool and falls on top of her. She is wearing only stockings now, and her black choker, and the long black gloves. She wears them for him, I realize. She still knows how to make herself desirable to him. Hungrily he trails kisses down her belly and between her thighs. I see her move her thighs wider apart, raise a hand to her mouth. They make love then in silence.

I return to bed and lie on my back and my hand creeps between my thighs and I come, weeping, eyes closed, mouth clamped shut in silence.

The sky is still grey with the very earliest dawn light when I hear through my sleep the front doorbell ringing, It rings a second and a third time before I get to it, eyes half-shut, in a tatty white bathrobe that I know is far too short for decency.

When I open the door, Leo and Teresa are standing there, Teresa with a slightly enquiring smile, her eyebrows arched.

"Ah," she says. "You're not quite ready yet"

"Ready for what?"

"The trip to the island."

"Hmm?"

It seems that last night when I was indoors, Teresa asked Kit if he and I would like to join them for a boat-trip out to the island in the bay tomorrow morning, and maybe a picnic. They would pick us up early. Kit had accepted with alacrity – and then forgot all about it.

I wake him up with a vigorous thump on his head with a pillow. He's grumpy at first, and then hungover, and then gradually, as he showers and shaves and rehydrates with tea, he begins to whistle and hum and I know that he is suddenly rather looking forward to the idea of a day on the island.

He wears jeans and deck shoes and a T-shirt and his linen jacket, and, just to cap the Italian playboy image, his shades. I'll wear deck shoes too, and my short white cotton dress, and will sling my red jumper over my shoulders. Carry my straw hat.

"Swimming trunks, do you think?" he asks me.

"Shouldn't bother," I say, feeling mischievous. "We can always skinny-dip."

He reaches out and pinches my bum. "I'll see you downstairs when you've showered."

Head back, eyes closed, face and breasts and belly and thighs streaming with hot water, when I hear the bathroom door open and then the shower curtain part. I'm thrilled. It's been ages, too long, since Kit and I showered together. His gentle hands start to soap my back, massage my shoulders, plant tiny kisses in the dips and hollows, and I arch my back as his hand reaches down between my thighs and I twist my head to see him.

It's Teresa. She has undressed, I can see her clothes on the bed in the room beyond, and her hand is between my thighs, caressing softly, her eyes steady on mine, knowing I am transfixed, helpless. I cannot move. She puts her other hand around the back of my neck as if to hold me still. But she needn't bother. I am helpless and still, a willing victim, burning, immobile. I even slide my feet a little farther apart over the slick tiles to encourage her to touch me. I want to feel her fingers inside me. I have never done that before, with a woman, and never thought I would. It cannot be real. She moves her head slowly and sensuously under the falling water, as if feeling it thrumming on the top of her head like a hundred tiny fingertips, then she raises her face up to it, her mouth a little open, catching the warm water and letting it trickle out again over her face and throat. Then she presses herself hard against me, our naked flanks slippery against each other, and turns my head and devours my lips with hers. The water pours down over us, plastering our hair to our cheeks, mingled maybe with my tears, and I cannot move or speak and I do not stir. The kissing is slow and deep. I pull back a little so as to trail my tongue over her lips more lightly, but she does not let me, pulls me closer in again, our breasts sliding against each other, our nipples hard and tingling. She turns me half-sideways so that she can skim her flattened palm over my nipples, murmurs endearments in my ear, punctuated with flickers of her tongue against my earlobe, in the shell of my ear, gently probing – endearments in a language I do not understand, but that I understand perfectly. Then her hand moves down over my arched belly and between my legs again, and she reaches her other arm around my waist and holds me tight against her, curved into each other like spoons, and I stretch my legs apart even wider and feel weak and I have to turn and hold myself steady against her and bury my face against her, my mouth closing on her breasts and sucking them in deep, greedily. She rests her head on top of mine now, almost motherly, whispering what a beautiful girl I am, what a beautiful young girl, what a greedy girl, how hungry! Her fingers slick between my swollen lips and ease back and forth over the head of my clitoris, too slowly. I want to beg her to press harder, to reach down and press her hand harder into me with my own hand, but she will not let me, I know. I rest against her, utterly passive and obedient, knowing she knows best, and as I come, richly and shudderingly against her warm, moving hand ticklish with foam, I raise my face up to her again and want her, need her to kiss me again. She kisses me and then murmurs what a good, sweet, beautiful young girl I am, she kisses me on the top of my head, she nuzzles her mouth into my wet hair, she covers my face and neck with quick little kisses, she croons softly like a mother to her baby. I fall against her then as I might have done against my mother years ago, and she raises my face gently with a forefinger nestling under my chin and kisses me on the lips and parts my lips with the tip of her tongue and we stay like that for hours, it seems, just kissing, and the water cascades down around us and over us and through us, melting us, it seems. Melting the very heart of us.

And none of it matters. Afterwards we kiss and laugh and dress and return to normal. As if it is all normal.

Leo and Teresa are highly organized. I knew they would be, somehow. It's bliss.

The car is a huge silver Merc. When Leo opens the boot for me to put my bag in, I see there's this vast, old-fashioned hamper filled with bottles of wine and bread and cheese and olives and oil and . . . the Full Mediterranean Diet Plan.

Kit and I sit in the back and keep smiling conspiratorially at each other on that long drive down to the coast. The black leather of the seat is warm under me and I feel wet again already. I cannot stop thinking about it, and more of it, please, more. Down and down we go, round the hairpin bends, down from the hills to the sun-scorched coast, through olive orchards and lemon orchards, among cork oaks and sweet chestnuts, and towards the sea, ancient plane trees and stone-pines with the heat shimmering on their evergreen-grey canopies, and the odour of pine in the air so rich and intoxicating that I feel almost like bursting into tears, like a little girl. I squeeze Kit's hand.

The harbourside is chaos, as usual, especially as the local fishermen are landing a huge catch of pilchards that they have just ring-netted out in the bay. It's a cliché, I know, but these young Italian fishermen, these gods – glossy black hair, lean-muscled shoulders tanned dark and slick with sweat, their tight, white sleeveless T-shirts stretched across their chests, flecked brilliant red with fish blood, shouting and laughing and swaggering at each other – Teresa knows I'm admiring them because she is too, and a knowing girls' grin flickers between us. I can't believe it, but that brief exchange of looks makes me feel breathless, wetter still between my legs. What on earth is going to happen? I wonder. *Everything*, murmurs an inner voice. *Everything is going to happen.*

Leo gets a local boatman to motor us out to the island: hard-faced, bearded, scarily competent, navigating out past the rocks in the bay with one casual, strong hand on the wheel. Cigarette dangling from his grim mouth.

On the way out, I ask Teresa if anyone actually lives on the island.

"Not without our permission," she says mildly.

I gawp at her. "You don't mean . . ?"

She smiles, lays her hand on my arm, a tiny caress. "I'm sorry, I thought you realized. It is *our* island. Leo's, officially." She looks away towards her husband and back to me again, her eyebrows arched even more ironically than ever. "My *marito* is, *officially*, you know, the Count of the Island of San Michele."

I swallow. OK: I'm impressed.

"There will only be the four of us on the island," says Teresa, raising her arms above her head and turning her face into the sun and stretching languidly. "Free as birds."

The journey out to the island takes almost an hour, and the middle passage gets pretty bumpy, but as we draw near to the island both Kit's and my nerves are calmed by the awesome view, and the thought that it is the private property of one man. On the south side, intimidating sandstone cliffs rise sheer from the sea, deeply ribbed and eroded like the sculpted relief of an ancient forest or the bones of a whale. Inland I can see further sheer cliffs of brilliant white – marble, surely. And directly ahead, where the boat is taking us, a deep gully between high cliffs, with a small jetty at the back, in cold shade.

We disembark, Leo extending a chivalrous hand to me, and then ordering the boatman to carry our hamper up the treacherous stone steps to the cliff top. We follow him up.

The island is a dream. It cannot be real. I know Kit is thinking the same, because we have both fallen silent in wonder.

We walk for ten minutes along the cliff top, and then strike inland a little way, down a slope to a kind of sunken plateau. And there, in the middle, surrounded by more trees, is an immaculate, tiny marble temple.

Leo gives one of his rare smiles. "Not an original, of course," he says. "Built by one of my more eccentric ancestors, in the eighteenth century. You would call it a folly, I believe."

The temple has a narrow, shady portico, and two cedar-wood doors that swing open on massive hinges. Inside is just one small, stone-floored room, with a couch on either side, a small, low table in the middle, which looks incongruously Indian if anything, and a heavy oak dresser along the back. Leo orders the boatman to deposit the hamper on the dresser, and tips him generously for his pains. The boatman nods curtly and leaves.

Immediately Leo starts pulling the couches out onto the portico– Kit helps him – and then the low table, and finds plates and glasses in the dresser and brings them out too. Then he unloads the hamper and soon the table is covered in food and the glasses are filled with wine. In no time at all we are reclining on the couches, twirling glasses of iced champagne between our fingers while Leo, more relaxed than I have seen him so far, extols the beauty of his island, and its ancientness.

He tells us that holidays were invented here, in this great bay sweeping south of Rome, overlooking the sparkling Tyrrhenian Sea. He says that Rome was the first city in history that people felt a need to escape from, on occasion. "We all need a break from the usual, the habitual," he says. "From custom. Something different, to reawaken us."

"*Cum dignitate otium*," he murmurs, conjuring brilliantly with faulty but vivid English, the poet Cicero on his farm in his peaceful Sabine valley, and other wealthy Romans here, Emperors even, in their great villas, enjoying their rest and recreation.

"And what recreations!" he says, eyes half-closed. "You know about the Emperor Tiberius, I suppose? The notorious passage in Suetonius, where he describes how the aged emperor built an entire palace to lustful pleasures hereabouts, with grottoes where groups of two or three young people would perform sexual acts for him. And where little boys were trained to swim underneath him when he was swimming and nibble at him. He called them his little minnows." Both Leo and Teresa are smiling at this. "Do I shock you?"

Kit says nothing. I say, too firmly, "No." My mind is filled and distracted by weirdly vivid images of those groups of two or three young people, acrobatically entwined, murmurous and ecstatic, in grottoes and shady groves, on an island just such as this . . .

"Oh, and he kept a pet mullet, encrusted with jewels," he added. "Or was that Claudius? I forget now."

Later, we go for a walk. Just Kit and I, hand in hand, still dreaming, saying little, dozy with wine but excited too. It is all too marvellous.

We walk up a narrow valley thick with grasses and scrub: scrub oak, yellow broom and purple sage, thyme, lavender, all headily aromatic, broken here and there by the red bark of arbutus. And such wild flowers: cyclamen, and tall asphodel, and white star of Bethlehem, and higher up between the granite outcrops, brilliant purple and yellow rock-roses. There is terebinth and carob, and down below in yet another secluded valley we can see tamarisk and oleander growing and swaying gently in the breeze beside a trickling streambed. We see swallowtail butterflies, and a hoopoe, and way overhead a big bird of prey: a buzzard, probably.

"Can't we live here?" I say suddenly to Kit. I always say this when we go somewhere beautiful. "Rent the temple off them. I'm sure they wouldn't mind."

Kit smiles and says nothing. He knows it's all a dream.

That long summer day passed so slowly – that last day, as I think of it now, that last day of the old life. We returned to the folly and dozed along with Leo and Teresa, they in each other's arms on one couch, Kit and I on the other. Stirring and waking at one point, I saw that Leo's hand was between Teresa's thighs, and they saw me watching them and smiled back at me. I smiled, and closed my eyes, and tried to sleep again.

And when I awoke, much later, it was with a shock that I realized that the sun was setting over the mountains to the west and coming down over the bay to drown in the water before us, and it was rapidly getting dark. I asked when we were heading back, at which Leo stood abruptly.

"Soon," he said. "But first, I promised to show you something, to explain the statue that you saw at the villa- the girl in ecstasy, yes?" And he held out his hand to me.

I stood, and he led me away from the folly and down into the valley and we walked for a long time and it grew dark. I was afraid, but *more* than afraid – my palms damp with sweat, unable to speak. And then we came down from the valley to another cove, shut in on one side by fierce rocks that ran straight down into the sea. And from here we could see the sunset perfectly. Oh no, I thought – this is just too clumsy a seduction attempt. I'm going to giggle.

But rather than lay me down in the sand and tell me he needed me, he desired me, he had to have me, Leo retained a firm grip on my hand and led me instead into the shadows under the cliffs, to a small crevice in the black rock. He told me to go in ahead of him. And inside, everything changed.

Inside was a vast domed cavern with mineral walls that glittered as if studded with gems, traced with mica and quartz, encrusted like the skin of the emperor's pet mullet. Torches burned all around, set into the walls in iron bands; and illuminated most brightly, preternaturally illuminated, in the centre of the cavern, on a stone dais, stood a white marble altar, elaborately carved with figures, sea-creatures, mermaids, tritons, and nymphs entwined in foam. The torches also made the cavern hot, much hotter than one would have expected, like some primeval sauna, so that the air shimmered in the heat, and after the evening chill of the cove, I felt my body warming again and my skin suddenly breaking out in a slick of perspiration.

I could hear Leo talking to me now, explaining, but my head was humming so, I could barely take in his words. And the sea breeze was blowing in now from the mainland of Italy, soughing in the crevices of the rocks and sounding like a soft and far-off bugle call in the entrance to the cavern. Leo was talking about how water was the stuff of life, how some worshipped fire but really water was the heart of life, most passive and most powerful, seemingly shaped by everything and yet irresistibly shaping everything by its own primal force over all the aeons. The most ancient feminine principle, out of which everything is born. And any place dedicated to San Michele, he said, Saint Michael the Warrior-Archangel, was originally an ancient site of pagan worship, which is nature worship – such as this whole island, an island of unnumbered underground streams, and springs, and fountains, where people worshipped the principle of water centuries before Christ walked the dry and dusty roads of Palestine.

"And the mermaid, too," he was saying. "What is she? Half-woman, half-fish: fertility? Sexuality? The personification of our eternal mother, the sea?"

From a darkened corner of the cavern Leo turned and I saw he was holding a white robe. He told me to undress and lay my clothes away and put this on. Even while my mind still hesitated, I did as he said. Round the waist I knotted the belt of golden cord. And then he took my hand and led me out of the cavern and we waited there on the beach hand in hand, my bare feet in the still-warm sand, saying nothing, thinking nothing. I was utterly passive and yet I knew I was nothing like his slave-girl. Leo had led me here, and told me what to do, and yet I was not under his command. I was – how can I put this? – I was only the servant to *myself*, and to something greater than myself. Leo held my hand no longer like some domineering father figure, but as my servant, honouring me. And I remembered the look of adoration I had seen him give to Teresa, so many times.

And then I could hear a distant drumming, hypnotic, antique, an inexorable, almost militaristic rhythm, getting closer all the time. I glanced at Leo, and he looked curiously serene, uncharacteristically dreamy, rapt. Content.

Then round the corner of the far rocks came those who were beating the drums. Some were naked, some were half-clad in white; some were walking slowly and stately, holding torches aloft, others were dancing and cavorting around them, dressed in grotesque satyr masks and goatskin cloaks. Those who were walking slowly were all by contrast beautiful, male and female alike. The torchlight burned on their faces and their bare shoulders, and their skins were golden in the glow. As they came nearer their faces shone with sweat and their other-worldly rapt attention to the delirium of the music. They banged drums and cymbals and moved along the beach towards was if themselves spellbound and bewitched.

"Who are these, coming to the sacrifice?" murmured Leo, and turned and smiled at me, reverential, a little sad.

Then he took my hand and led me back into the cave. There he took a black strip of silk and turned me round so that I faced away from him, and he tied it around my head and over my eyes and secured it firmly behind so that I was in utter darkness. Blinded. And immediately all my other senses came to life.

I heard a noise like someone shaking out a heavy tablecloth and I knew that he was spreading something over the altar, and then he laid me down on it and I felt it was a thick velvet and I pictured it as a deep golden colour, almost inlaid, cloth-of-gold, and I could smell incense and woodsmoke and also human sweat and sex. And then I felt the presence of many more people as they filed into that cavern, and the air was warm and thick with the smell of pinewood and smoke rising up to the opening in the roof of the cavern, and they drummed softly now and hummed or chanted a low song that was in no language I recognized.

I felt human bodies pressing all around me, and hands running over me, lips and tongues running over my lips and over my neck and throat, and one who kissed me I knew was Teresa from her perfume and I turned my head a little towards her and smiled at her though blindfolded and she touched a fingertip to my lips and I sucked it softly. Unseen hands loosened my white robe from around my shoulders and drew it down to my waist. Other hands loosened the knot of my belt and pulled it free – I raised my hips slightly to help them do so – and more hands raised the hem of the robe and pushed it up so that it formed a crested white wave around my waist and the rest of me lay naked.

Then there was a pause, and I heard a noise I couldn't identify, and then the sound of hands being rubbed together, and when they returned to me I knew that they had been rubbing their hands to warm the oil they held cupped. Now they spread what smelled like olive oil over my skin, from my toes upwards, trickling it even between my toes, applying it with both fingers and tongues, warming it on my skin as they went. They held my hands outstretched and poured oil into my palms and massaged my fingers. They spread the grass-sweet olive oil up my legs and over my thighs, and I couldn't hold back a sigh and a gasp as they slicked it between my thighs, so gently, lingeringly, and I parted my thighs and wished those unseen fingers would stay there longer. Then strong hands lifted my legs behind my knees and bent them right up, and they poured more oil over me so that it trickled down between my rear cheeks, and further hands held my cheeks apart, and then a slim, delicate hand reached down and a small, subtle finger – a woman's finger, her little finger, surely – insinuated itself between my cheeks and inserted itself, just the tip, inside me, and caressed me there in a circling of oil and I begged silently for more, never to stop, oh more and forever.

They oiled my breasts and my neck and they covered me with kisses as they did so, so that I was exposed and caressed and fed on by countless mouths, tongues circling in dance-like movements over my breasts and around my nipples and then down over me until I bucked and writhed and wanted to hold my arms out to touch their hair and to embrace these unknown lovers, these worshippers. At last I could remain the passive body no longer, and I reached my hands out and caressed the naked flanks of those who stood around me, and a low murmur of delight went up from the throng and I guessed from the voices that the cavern held a hundred people or more and that every eye was on me. I felt two boys, young and firmly muscled, quite naked, standing to left and to right of me, and I ran my hand down over their lean bellies, my mind lascivious, whore-like, and found them rigid, standing out, and my fingers curled around them, each boy my slave in each oiled palm, and began to squeeze and caress them, and I heard their little gasps and felt their whole bodies tauten at my touch.

More mouths tried to kiss me, and I turned sideways to each

in turn and felt tongue after tongue – some gentle, some feminine, some hard and probing, some hesitant, some greedy – entwining with my tongue, and then one brought a mouthful of wine and we drank it between us from each other's ruby, wine-stained lips. Then one of the naked boys beside me pulled free from my hand and turned my head towards him and slid into my mouth and I closed my mouth tight about him and he tasted beautiful. I felt another naked form brush against me, and cool soft hands took my free hand and placed it between smooth thighs and it was a girl now and she pressed my hand flat into her curls and then, using my middle finger almost as she pleased, she used it to caress her lips and clitoris. Soon I was flicking my finger rapidly over her swollen bud, and she leaned forwards and her mouth closed on my breasts and she moaned softly and lay half across me while I brought her into raptures.

Between my legs, I felt tongues taking turns, and even competing to squeeze into me together, one on my clitoris, long feminine hair tickling over my belly, while another, perhaps a man, buried his face between my cheeks and ran his tensed tongue back and forth, slipping a rigid forefinger in and out of me.

My mouth filled with hot sperm, and then wine again, and then more tongues and another man pushed into me, and a woman must have straddled me and I felt her lower her salty lips onto my mouth. Then I felt a blind, probing head between my thighs, rubbing up and down and over the head of my clitoris and then back, teasing me cruelly, entering me just a half-inch and then easing back, and I arched towards him. I longed to reach down and grab the naked buttocks of that unknown lover and pull him deep into me, but my hands were filled with greedy men who would not let me go. Finally the stranger eased into me, strong and wide, stretching me, and beginning to pump faster and faster, fingers buried in the flesh of my buttocks. Others slipped their arms beneath the small of my back and lifted me up, exposing me more, so that a tongue, a woman's again I guessed, could skim over my clitoris, circle it, her hair draped over my belly, while the man fucked me so hard. I forgot how many times I came, it was impossible to count. It was continuous, without respite, I knew no tiredness. I filled with sperm, the man still throbbing pulled out of me, sperm flowed free and mingled with oil. They turned me on my side and raised one leg and another man quickly slipped into me, while yet another nuzzled between my buttocks and, very gently, oiled and slow, eased into my behind. The unseen, naked orgiasts around me must have watched in delight, and held my cheeks apart for the men to ease in better, and I felt them stroke my skin and heard them murmur soft endearments in my ears as I took them in, took both men in, and lapped greedily on fresh, lemon lips that she, another lover, another worshipper, touched softly to my mouth.

And I thought how they say that the taste of a woman is supposed to be like the saltwater taste of the sea, and then I understood everything, not with my mind but with my body, and my understanding deepened, wordlessly, all that enchanted night as I lay there and was worshipped and adored and made love to by my lovers as numberless as the stars in the sky or the grains of sand by the sea.

When I awoke I was lying under a soft woollen blanket on the sand, and Kit lay beside me. He was awake, propped up on one elbow, looking over me as I slept. Normally he was always asleep until long after me. But he was awake, and his face was alight. We looked at each other for a long time, and I didn't have a word to say. I knew everything was real. But where had Kit been? Did he know?

Then he leaned over and kissed me. "You were beautiful," he said, "last night." He smiled. "The Goddess."

Then I remembered. "The last one, my last lover – that was you?"

He kissed me in answer.

As the sun came up – and exhausted though I was, though we both were, so tired that we laughed out of tiredness like unruly children – we made love in the surf where the sea broke on the beach of the Island of San Michele. There was no boat, nor another soul around. We might be stranded on the island forever, and we laughed, and didn't care, and all we could think of doing was making love in the foam, fucking, laughing, he harder, harder, always harder, like a rock, a stone statue like that little smiling ithyphallic god that they worship in some places, and I melting before him and flowing around him like water like a mermaid like the spirit of the water that they worship here . . .

Gators

Vicki Hendricks

It was a goddamned one-armed alligator put me over the line.
After that I was looking for trouble. Carl and me had been
married for two years, second marriage for both, and the situation was drastic – hateful most times – but I could tell he
didn't realize there was anything better in the world. It made
me feel bad that he never learned how to love – grew up with
nothing but cruelty. I kept trying way too long to show him
there was something else.

I was on my last straw when I suggested a road trip for Labor
Day weekend – stupidly thinking that I could amuse him and
wouldn't have to listen to his bitching about me and the vile
universe on all my days off work. I figured at a motel he'd get
that vacation feeling, lighten up, and stick me good, and I
could get by for the few waking hours I had to see him the rest
of the week.

We headed out to the Everglades for our little trip. Being
recent transplants from Texas, we hadn't seen the natural
wonders in Florida. Carl started griping by mid-afternoon
about how I told him there were so many alligators and we
couldn't find a fucking one. I didn't dare say that there
would've been plenty if he hadn't taken two hours to read the
paper and sit on the john. We could've made it before the
usual thunderstorms and had time to take a tour. As it was, he
didn't want to pay the bucks to ride the tram in the rain – even
though the cars were covered. We were pretty much stuck

with what we could see driving, billboards for Seminole gambling and airboats, and lots of soggy grassland under heavy black-and-blue-layered skies. True, it had a bleak, haunting kind of beauty.

Carl refused to put on the air conditioner because he said it sapped the power of the engine, so all day we suffocated. We could only crack the truck windows because of the rain. By late afternoon my back was soaked with sweat and I could smell my armpits. And, get this – he was smoking cigarettes. Like I said, I was plain stupid coming up with the idea – or maybe blinded by the fact that he had a nice piece of well-working equipment that seemed worth saving.

At that point, I started to wonder if I could make us swerve into a canal and end the suffering. I was studying the landscape, looking ahead for deep water, when I spotted a couple of vehicles pulled off the road.

"Carl, look. I bet you they see gators."

"Fuckin' *A*," he bellowed.

He was driving twenty over the limit, as always – in a hurry to get to hell – but he nailed the brakes and managed to turn onto a gravel road that ran a few hundred yards off the side of a small lake. One car pulled out past us, but a couple and a little girl were still standing near the edge of the water.

It was only drizzling by then, and Carl pulled next to their pickup and shut off the ignition. My side of the truck was over a puddle about four inches deep. I opened the door and plodded through in my sandals, while Carl stood grimacing at the horizon, rubbing his dark unshaven chin.

We walked towards the people. The woman was brown-haired, wearing a loose print dress – the kind my grandma would've called a housedress – and I felt how sweet and old-fashioned she was next to me in short-shorts and a halter top, with my white-blonde hair and black roots haystack style. The man was a wiry, muscular type in tight jeans and a white T-shirt – tattoos on both biceps, like Carl, but arms half the size. He was bending down by some rocks a little farther along. The little girl, maybe four years old, and her mother were holding hands by the edge.

"That guy reminds me of my asshole brother-in-law," Carl

said in a low tone, as we got closer. I nodded, thinking how true it was – the guy reminded me of Carl too, all the same kind of assholes. Carl boomed out "Hey, there," in his usual mega-phone, overly friendly voice. The mother and child glanced up with a kind of mousy suspiciousness I sometimes felt in my own face. It was almost like they had him pegged instantly.

We stopped near them. The guy came walking over. He had his hands cupped together in front of him and motioned with his arms towards the water. I looked into the short water weeds and sticks and saw two small eyes and nose holes rising above the ripples a few yards out. It was a baby gator, maybe four feet long, judging by the closeness of his parts.

"There he is!" Carl yelled.

"Just you watch this," the guy said. He tossed something into the water in front of the nose and I caught the scrambling of tiny legs just before the gator lurched and snapped it up. "They just love them lizards," the man said.

Carl started laughing "Ho, ho, ho," like it was the funniest thing he'd ever seen, and the guy joined in because he'd made a big hit.

Us women looked at each other and kind of smiled with our lips tight. The mother had her arm around the little girl's shoulder holding her against her hip. The girl squirmed away. "Daddy, can I help you catch another one?"

"Sure, darlin' come right over here." He led her towards the rocks and I saw the mother cast him a look as he went by. He laughed and took his daughter's hand.

The whole thing was plenty creepy, but Carl was still chuck-ling. It seemed like maybe he was having a good time for a change.

"Reptiles eating reptiles," he said. "Yup." He did that eh-eh-eh laugh in the back of his throat. It made me wince. He took my hand and leered towards my face. "It's a scrawny one, Virginia – not like a Texas gator – but I guess I have to say you weren't lyin'. Florida has one." He put his arm across my shoulder and leaned on me, still laughing at his own sense of humour. I widened my legs, to keep from falling over, and chuckled so he wouldn't demand to know what was the matter, then insist I spoiled the day by telling him.

We stood there watching the gator float in place hoping for another snack, and in a few minutes, the squeals of the little girl told us that it wouldn't be long. They came shuffling over slowly, the father bent, cupping his hands over the girl's.

"This is the last one now, OK, sweetheart?" the mother said as they stopped beside her. She was talking to the little girl. "We need to get home in time to make supper." From her voice it sounded like they'd been sacrificing lizards for a while.

The two flung the prey into the water. It fell short, but there was no place for the lizard to go. It floundered in the direction it was pointed, the only high ground, the gator's waiting snout. He snapped it up. This time he'd pushed farther out of the water and I saw that he was missing one of his limbs.

"Look, Carl, the gator only has one arm. I wonder what got him?"

"Probably a Texas gator," he said. "It figures, the one gator you find me is a cripple."

Carl had an answer for everything. "No," I said. "Why would one gator tear off another one's arm?"

"Leg. One big chomp without thinkin'. Probably got his leg in between his mother and some tasty tidbit – small dog or kid. Life is cruel, babycakes – survival of the fittest." He stopped talking to light a cigarette. He waved it near my face to make his point. "You gotta protect yourself – be cruel first. That's why you got me – to do it for you." He gave me one of his grins with all the teeth showing.

"Oh, is *that* why?" I laughed, like it was a joke. Yeah, Carl would take care of his own, all right – it was like having a mad dog at my side, never knowing when he might turn. He wouldn't hesitate to rip anybody's arm off, mine included, if it got in his way.

The mother called to her husband, "Can we get going, honey? I have fish to clean."

The guy didn't look up. "Good job," he said to his daughter. He reached down and gave her a pat on the butt. "Let's get another one."

It started to rain a little harder, thank God, and Carl motioned with his head towards the truck and started walking. I looked at the woman still standing there. "Bye," I called.

She nodded at me, her face empty of life. "Goodbye, honey." It was then she turned enough for me to see that the sleeve on the far side of the dress was empty, pinned up – her arm was gone. Jesus. I felt my eyes bulge. She couldn't have missed what I said. I burned through ten shades of red in a split second. I turned and sprinted to catch up with Carl.

He glanced at me. "What's your hurry, sugar? You ain't gonna melt. Think I'd leave without ya?"

"Nope," I said. I swallowed and tried to lighten up. I didn't want to share with him what I saw.

He looked at me odd and I knew he wasn't fooled. "What's with you?"

"Hungry," I said.

"I told you you should've had a ham sandwich before we left. You never listen to me. I won't be ready to eat for a couple more hours."

"I have to pee too. We passed a restaurant a quarter mile back."

He pointed across the road. "There's the bushes. I'm not stopping anywhere else till the motel."

We crossed the state and got a cheap room in Naples for the night. Carl ordered a pepperoni pizza from Domino's, no mushrooms for me. The room was clean and the air and remote worked, but it was far from the beach. We sat in bed and ate the pizza. I was trying to stick with the plan for having fun and I suggested we could get up early and drive to the beach to find shells.

"To look for fucking seashells? No."

His volume warned me. I decided to drop it. I gave him all my pepperonis and finished up my piece. I had a murder book to curl up with. He found a football game on TV.

I was in the grip of a juicy scene when Carl started working his hands under the covers. It was halftime. He found my thigh and stroked inwards. I read fast to get to the end of the chapter. He grabbed the book and flung it across the room onto the other bed.

"I'm tryin to make love to you, and you have your nose stuck in a book. What's the problem? You gettin' it somewhere else and don't need it from me? Huh?"

I shook my head violently. His tone and volume had me scared. "No, for Chrissakes." His face was an inch from mine. Rather than say anything else, I took his shoulders and pulled myself to him for a kiss. He was stiff, so I started sucking his lower lip and moving my tongue around. His shoulders relaxed.

Pretty soon he yanked down the covers, pulled up my nightie, and climbed on top. I couldn't feel him inside me – I was numb. Nothing new. I smelled his breath.

I moaned like he expected, and after a few long minutes of pumping and grabbing at my tits, he got that strained look on his face. "I love you to death," he rasped. "Love you to death." I felt him get rigid and come hard inside me, and a chill ran all the way from his cock to my head. He groaned deep and let himself down on my chest. "It's supernatural what you do to me, dollface, supernatural."

"Mmm."

He lit up a cigarette and puffed a few breaths in my face. "I couldn't live without you. Know that? You know that, don't you? You ever left me, I'd have to kill myself."

"No. Don't say that."

"Why? You thinkin of leaving? I *would* kill myself. I would. And knowin' me, I'd take you along." He rolled on his side, laughing "eh-eh-eh" to himself. My arm was pinned, and for a second I panicked. I yanked it out from under him. He shifted and in seconds started snoring. Son of a bitch. He had me afraid to speak.

The woman and the gator came into my head, and I knew her life without having to live it, the casual cruelty and a sudden swift slice that changed her whole future. I could land in her place easy, trapped with a kid, no job, and a bastard of a husband that thought he was God. Carl said he was God at least three times a week. I shuddered – more like he was the devil. First he'd take an arm, then go for my soul, just a matter of time. He'd rather see me dead than gone.

There was no thought of a road trip the next weekend, so we both slept late that Saturday. By then, the fear and hatred in my heart had taken over my brain. I was frying eggs, the bathroom door was open, and Carl was on the toilet – his place of serious thinking – when he used the words that struck me with the juicy, seedy, sweet fantasy of getting rid of him.

"I ought to kill my asshole brother-in-law," he yelled. The words were followed by grunts of pleasure and plunking noises I could hear from the kitchen.

"Uh-huh," I said to myself. I pretended to be half-hearing – as if that were possible – and splashed the eggs with bacon grease like he wanted them. I didn't say anything. He was building up rage on the sound of his own voice.

"The fucker went out on Labor Day and left Penny and the kids home. She didn't say anything about him drinkin, but I could hear it in her voice when I called last night. I can't keep ignoring this. I oughta get a flight over there and take ol' Raymond out."

"How's he doing from his knife wound?"

"Son of a bitch is finally back to work. I should just take him out. Penny and the kids would be fine with the insurance she'd get from G.M."

"Oh?"

"Those slimy titty bars he hangs out in – like Babydoe's – I could just fly into Dallas, do him, and fly back. Nobody would think a thing unusual."

I heard the flush and then his continued pulling of toilet paper. He always flushed before he wiped. I knew if I went in there after him I would see streaky wads of paper still floating. He came striding into the kitchen with a towel wrapped around him, his gut hanging over. He seemed to rock back as he walked to keep from falling forward. He turned and poured his eighth cup of coffee, added milk, held it over the sink, and stirred wildly. Half of it slopped over the sides of the cup. His face was mottled with red and he growled to himself.

I looked away. I remembered that at 17 he had thrown his father out of the house – for beating his mother. He found out later they snuck around for years to see each other behind his back – they were that scared of him.

I knew going opposite whatever he said would push him. I could barely hold myself back. I pointed to the phone. "Calm down and call your sister. Her and the kids might want to keep Ray around."

"Yeah? Uh-uh. She's too nice. She'll give that son of a bitch chance after chance while he spends all their money on ass and booze. If anybody's gonna take advantage of somebody, it's gonna be me."

I handed him his plate of eggs and went to take my shower and let him spew. I heard him pick up the paper again and start with how all the "assholes in the news" should be killed.

Before this, it didn't occur to me as an asset that he was always a hair's breadth from violence. I'd tried for peace. I didn't want to know about the trouble he'd been in before we met, his being in jail for violating a restraining order. He'd broken down a door – I heard that from his sister because she thought I should know. I figured he deserved another chance in life. He had a lousy childhood with the drunk old man and all. But now I realized how foolish I was to think that if I treated him nice enough – turned the other cheek – he would be nice back. Thought that was human nature. Wrong. I was a goddamned angelic saviour for over a year and not a speck of it rubbed off. He took me for a sucker to use and abuse. It was a lesson I'd never forget, learned too late.

This sounds crazy – but something about the alligator incident made me know Carl's true capabilities, and I was fucking scared. That alligator told me that a ticket for Carl to Dallas was my only ticket out. It was a harsh thought, but Penny's husband wasn't God's gift either, and if Carl didn't get him, it was just a matter of time till some other motherfucker did.

At first, I felt scared of the wicked thoughts in my heart. But after a few days, each time Carl hawked up a big gob and spit it out the car window or screamed at me because the elevator at the apartment complex was too slow, the idea became less sinful. He was always saying how he used to break guys' legs for a living, collecting, and he might decide to find some employment of that kind in Florida since the pay was so lousy for construction. Besides, that, there was his drunk driving – if I could get him behind bars it would be an asset to the whole state. Or maybe I'd only have to threaten.

One morning he woke up and bit my nipple hard before I was even awake. "Ouch," I yelled. It drew blood and made my eyes fill up.

"The world's a hard place," he told me.

"You make it that way."

He laughed. "You lived your little pussy life long enough. It's time you find out what it's all about." He covered my mouth with his booze and cigarette breath, and I knew that was the. day I'd make a call to his sister. He wasn't going to go away on his own.

Penny did mail-outs in the morning, so I called her from work. I could hear her stuffing envelopes while we talked. I asked about the kids and things. "So how's your husband?" I added. "Carl said he went back to work."

"Yeah. We're getting along much better. He's cut back on the drinking and brings home his paycheque. Doesn't go to the bar half as much."

"He's still going to that bar where he got hurt?"

"Oh, no, a new one, Cactus Jack's, a nicer place – no nude dancers, and it's only a couple of miles from here, so he can take a cab if he needs to. He promised he wouldn't go back over to Babydoe's."

Done. It was smooth. I didn't even have to ask where he hung out. "Yeah," I said. "He gets to the job in the morning. That's what I keep telling Carl."

"He goes out Fridays and maybe one or two other days. I can handle that. I'm not complaining."

She was a good woman. I felt tears well in my eyes. "You're a saint, honey. I have to get back to work now – the truckers are coming in for their cheques. Carl would like to hear from you one night soon. He worries."

I had all I needed to know – likely she'd wanted to tell somebody and didn't care to stir Carl up and listen to all his godly orders. She wasn't complaining – goddamn. It was amazing that her and my husband were of the same blood. And, yeah, she was being taken advantage of – I could hear it. Now I had to tell Carl when and where to go without him realizing it was my plan.

That night I started to move him along. "I talked to your sister Penny this morning," I told him at the dinner table.

"Oh, yeah?" He was shovelling in chicken, fried steak, mashed potatoes with sawmill gravy, and corn, one of his favourite meals.

I ate with one hand behind my back, protecting my arm from any quick snaps. "She's a trouper," I said. "Wow."

"Huh?"

"I never heard of anybody with such a big heart. You told me she adopted Ray's son, right?"

"Yeah. Unbelievable." He chewed a mouthful. "Him and Penny already had one kid, and he was fuckin around on her. I'd've killed the motherfucker, if I'd known at the time. I was in Alaska – workin the pipeline. Penny kept it all from me till after the adoption." He shook his head and wiped the last gravy from his plate with a roll. "Lumps in the mashed potatoes, hon."

"She works hard too – all those jobs – and doesn't say a thing about him having boys' nights out at some new bar whenever he wants. I couldn't handle it." I paused and took a drink of my beer to let the thought sink in. "He's a damn good-looking guy. Bet he has no trouble screwing around on her."

Carl looked up and wiped his mouth on his hand. "You mean now? Where'd you get that idea?"

I shrugged. "Just her tone. Shit. If anybody's going to heaven, she will."

"You think he's hot, don't ya? I'll kill the son of a bitch. What new bar?"

"Cactus Jack's. I bet you he's doing it. She'd be the last to say anything. Why else would he stay out half the night?"

Carl threw his silverware on the plate. "I ought to kill the son of a bitch."

"I don't like to hear that stuff."

"It's the real world, and he's a fuckin asshole. He needs to be fucked."

"I hate to hear a woman being beat down, thinking she's doing the right thing for the kids. Course, you never know what's the glue between two people."

"My sister's done the right thing all her life, and it's never gotten her anywhere." He was seething.

"She's one of a kind, a saint really." I tucked my hand under my leg – feeling protective of my arm – took a bite of fried steak, and chewed.

Carl rocked back on the legs of the chair. His eyes were focused up near the ceiling. "Hmm," he said. "Hmm."

"Don't think about getting involved. We have enough problems."

"You don't have a thing to do with this. It's family."

I gathered up the dishes and went to the sink feeling smug, though I was a little freaked by the feeling that the plan might just work. I was wiping the stove when the phone rang.

"Got it," Carl yelled.

It was Penny. She'd followed my suggestion to call. I could hear him trying to draw her out. He went on and on, and it didn't sound like he made any progress. By the time he slammed down the receiver, he had himself more angry at her than he was at her husband. He went raging into the bathroom and slammed the door shut. It was so hard I was surprised the mirror didn't fall off.

I finished up in the kitchen and was watching *Wheel of Fortune* by the time he came out, their special Labour Week show.

He sat down on the couch next to me and put his hand on my thigh, squeezed it. "You got some room on your Visa, don't you? How 'bout makin me a reservation to Dallas? I'll pay you back. I need to talk to that asshole Raymond face to face."

I stared at the TV, trying to control my breathing. "He's not going to listen to you. He thinks you're a moron."

"A moron, huh? I think not. Make a reservation for me — "

I was shaking my head. "You can't go out there. What about work?"

"Do it – get me a flight after work on Friday, back home Saturday."

"Not much of a visit."

He squinted and ran his tongue from cheek to cheek inside his mouth. "I'm just gonna talk to the motherfucker."

I'd never seen murder in anybody's eyes, but it was hard to miss. I took a deep, rattling breath. It was too goddamned easy – bloodcurdling easy. I reminded myself it was for my own survival. I needed both goddamned arms.

That night I called for a reservation. I had to make it three weeks in advance to get a decent fare. I'd saved up some Christmas money, so that way I didn't have to put the ticket on my charge. I could only hope nobody ripped Raymond before Carl got his chance. The guy that stuck Ray the first time was out on probation. It would be just my luck.

The days dragged. The hope that I would soon be free made Carl's behaviour unbearable. I got myself a half-dozen detective novels and kept my nose stuck inside one when I could. I cooked the rest of the time, lots of his favourite foods, and pie, trying to keep his mouth full so I wouldn't have to listen to it – and throw him off if he was the least bit suspicious of what I had in mind. It was tough to put on the act in bed, but he was in a hurry most of the time, so he slathered on the aloe and poked me from behind. Tight and fast was fine with him. His ego made him blind – thinking he was smarter than everybody else, especially me, and that I could possibly still love him.

Thursday morning, the day before Carl was supposed to leave, he walked into the bedroom before work. I smelled his coffee breath and kept my eyes shut. A tap came on my shoulder. "I don't know where that new bar is," he said. "What was it? Cactus Bob's? Near their place?"

"Jack's. Cactus Jack's. I'll get directions at work – off the computer. No problem – Mapquest"

"Get the shortest route from the airport to Babydoe's, and from there to the cactus place. He's probably lying to Penny, still goin back to Doe's for the tits and ass."

I printed out the route during lunch. It was a little complicated. When I came in the door that evening, I handed Carl three pages of directions and maps. He flipped through them. "Write these on one sheet – bigger. I can't be shuffling this shit in the dark while I'm driving a rental around Arlington."

"Sure," I said. A pain in the ass to the end, I thought. I reminded myself it was almost over. I copied the directions on a legal sheet and added "Love ya, Your babycakes." Between his ego and my eagerness to please, I hoped he didn't suspect a thing. I couldn't wait to show him the real world when I gave him my ultimatum.

I got up in the morning and packed him a few clothes and set the bag by the door. I called to him in the bathroom. "Your ticket receipt is in the side pocket. Don't forget to give Penny my love." I knew he really hadn't told her a thing.

He came out and took a hard look down my body. His eyes glinted and I could see satisfaction in the upturn of his lips, despite their being pressed together hard. I knew there was some macho thing mixed in with the caretaking for his sister. In a twisted way, he was doing this for me too, proving how he could protect a poor, weak woman from men like himself.

I thought he was going to kiss me, so I brought on a coughing fit and waved him away. He thumped me on the back a few times, gave up, and went on out. He paused a second at the bottom of the steps, turned back, and grinned, showing all those white teeth. For a second, I thought he was reading my mind. Instead he said softly, "You're my right arm, dollface." He went out.

I shivered. I watched his car all the way down the street. I was scared, even though I was sure he had every intention of doing the deed, and I was betting on success. He was smarter and stronger than Ray, and had surprise on his side. Then I would hold the cards – with his record, a simple tip to the cops could put his ass in a sling.

I was tense all day at the office, wondering what he was thinking with that grin. Too, I hoped he'd remembered his knife. I went straight to his bureau when I got home and took everything out of the sock drawer. The boot knife was gone. I pictured him splashed with blood, standing over Ray's body in a dark alley. I felt relieved. He was set up good.

I went to the grocery and got myself a six-pack, a bag of mesquite-grilled potato chips, and a pint of fudge royale ice cream. I rented three videos so I wouldn't have to think. I started to crack up laughing in the car. I was between joy and hysteria. I couldn't stop worrying, but the thought of peace to come was delicious.

Carl was due home around noon on Saturday, and I realized I didn't want to be there. I got a few hours sleep and woke up early. I did his dirty laundry and packed all his clothes and personal stuff into garbage bags and set them by the door. I put his bicycle and tools there. I wrote a note on the legal pad and propped it against one of the bags. Basically it said to leave

Fort Lauderdale that afternoon and never come back – if he did, I'd turn him in. I wrote that I didn't care if we ever got a divorce or not, and he could take the stereo and TV – everything. I just wanted to be left alone.

I packed a bathing suit, a book, and my overnight stuff and drove down to Key Largo. Carl was obsessed with me in his lurid, controlling way. The farther away I was when he read the note, the safer I'd feel.

I stayed at a little motel and read and swam most of Saturday, got a pizza with mushrooms, like Carl hated. On Sunday morning I went out by the pool and caught a few more rays before heading home. I stopped for a grouper sandwich on the drive back, to congratulate myself on how well I was doing, but I could barely eat it. Jesus, was I nervous. I got home around four, pulled into the parking lot, and saw Carl's empty space. I sighed with relief. I looked up at the apartment window. I'd move out when the lease was up. I unlocked the door and stepped inside. The clothes and tools were gone. I shut the door behind me, locked it, and set down my bag.

The toilet flushed. "Eh-eh-eh-eh."

I jumped. My chest turned to water.

The toilet paper rolled. Carl came swaggering out of the bathroom. "Eh-eh-eh-eh," he laughed. The sound was deafening.

"Where's your car?" I asked him. "What are you doing here?"

"Car's around back. I wanted to surprise my babycakes."

I looked around wildly. "Didn't you get my note? You're supposed to be gone – I'm calling – " I moved towards the phone.

He stepped in front of me. "No. You don't wanna make any calls – and I'm not going anywhere. I love you. We're a team. Two of a kind."

"You didn't do it." I spat the words in his face. "You chickened out."

He came closer, a cloud of alcohol seeping from his skin and breath, a sick, fermented odour mixed with the bite of cigarettes. "Oh, I did it, babe, right behind Doe's. Stuck that seven-inch blade below his rib cage and gave it a mighty twist.

I left that bastard in a puddle of blood the size Texas could be proud of." He winked. "I let Ol' Ray know why he was getting it too."

He took my hair and yanked me close against him. He stuck his tongue in my mouth. I gagged but he kept forcing it down my throat. Finally, he drew back and stared into my eyes. "I did some thinkin on the flight over," he said, "about you and me, and how your attitude isn't always the best. I figured I could use some insurance on our marriage. You know? Penny'll remember you askin' her about the bars if she's questioned, and she wouldn't lie to the cops. Also, the directions are in your handwriting, hon. I rubbed the prints off against my stomach, balled up the sheet, and dropped it right between his legs. Cool, huh?" He licked his lower lip from one side to the other. "Oh, yeah, I found one of your hairs on my T-shirt and put that in for extra measure."

My skin went to ice and I froze clear through.

"A nice little threat in the works, if I needed it to keep you around. Guess I saved myself a lot of trouble at the same time." His eyebrows went up. "Where I go, you go, baby girl. Together forever, sweetheart"

He grabbed my T-shirt and twisted it tight around the chest. All the air wheezed out of my lungs, and he rubbed his palm across my nipples till they burned. He lifted my hand to his mouth, kissed it, and grinned with all his teeth showing. He slobbered kisses along my arm, while I stood limp. "Eh-eh."

Like the snap of a bone, his laugh shot chills up my spine and the sorry truth to my brain. I was the same as Carl, only he'd been desperate all his life. My damned arm would be second to go – I'd already handed Satan my soul.